"Fans of historical fantasy and Norse mythology should appreciate this well-crafted tale."   —*Library Journal*

"With *Mother of Kings*, Poul Anderson reminds us of the indissoluble links between history and mythology. The background details are perfectly realized, the plot is compelling, and the style is as crisp as the whir of a Viking ax. Read this, savor this—you'll be glad you did."
                    —Morgan Llywelyn, bestselling author of *1916*

"Anderson's swan song is *Mother of Kings*, a superb blend of history, detail, myth and fantasy."
                    —*Charleston Post & Courier*

"Meticulously researched . . . for fans of historical fiction and devotees of Norse legend it's a fine diversion."
                    —*Harrisburg Patriot News*

"*Mother of Kings* is Poul Anderson at the top of his game. As enthralling as *The Mists of Avalon*, Poul Anderson shows himself to be the true modern heir of those who wrote the sagas that inspired Tolkien and laid down the foundations of modern fantasy."   —Greg Bear, author of *Darwin's Radio*

"*Mother of Kings* is not to be missed. As the pages turn, be it times it seems as if one reads the old sagas hidden until now, set down centuries ago and only now just revealed, like a new Edda. Time and again one hears the ring of truth, but this tome is no dusty scroll: warriors and witches, lusty men, and the fires and the clangor of war come alive. Gunnhild, the *Mother of Kings*, stands like the hub of a great wheel of folk whirling around her in her intrigues and her strivings. Hers is a great tale—and we can never have too many great tales."
                    —Ed Greenwood, author of *The Kingless Land*

"*Mother of Kings* is a terrific read! Poul Anderson's new epic is a convincing glimpse into the past filled with the authentic sights and sounds of the Viking Age, and told in the language that echoes the genius of the Icelandic bards."
                    —Walter Jon Williams, author of *The Rift*

MOTHER OF KINGS

POUL ANDERSON

A TOM DOHERTY ASSOCIATES BOOK
NEW YORK

This is a work of fiction. All the characters and events portrayed in this book are either products of the author's imagination or are used fictitiously.

MOTHER OF KINGS

Copyright © 2001 by Trigonier Trust

A Tor Book
Published by Tom Doherty Associates, LLC
175 Fifth Avenue
New York, NY 10010

www.tor.com

Tor® is a registered trademark of Tom Doherty Associates, LLC.

ISBN 0-765-34502-1

First edition: September 2001
First mass market edition: January 2003

Printed in the United States of America

0 9 8 7 6 5 4 3 2 1

To
Astrid Hertz Anderson (in memoriam)
Karen Kruse Anderson
and
Astrid Anderson Bear

mothers and queens

CONTENTS

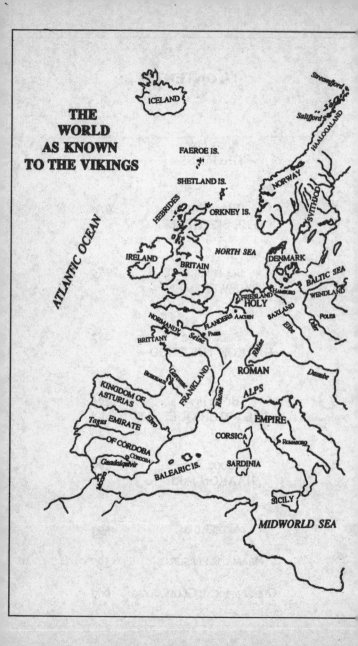

THE
WORLD
AS KNOWN
TO THE VIKINGS

ICELAND

FAEROE IS.

SHETLAND IS.

ORKNEY IS.

HEBRIDES

IRELAND

BRITAIN

NORTH SEA

ATLANTIC OCEAN

NORWAY

Streamsfjord

Saltfjord

HAALOGALAND

SVITHJOD

DENMARK

BALTIC SEA

WENDLAND

FRIESLAND

HAMBURG

HOLY

SAXLAND

Poles

NORMANDY

FLANDERS

Aachen

Paris

Elbe

Oder

BRITTANY

Seine

Rhine

ROMAN

Danube

KINGDOM OF
ASTURIAS

Bordeaux

Garonne

FRANKLAND

Rhone

ALPS

EMPIRE

EMIRATE

Tagus

Ebro

CORSICA

Romaborg

OF CORDOBA

CORDOBA

SARDINIA

Guadalquivir

BALEARIC IS.

SICILY

MIDWORLD SEA

NORTH CAPE

FINNMORK

KOLA PENINSULA

KARELIA

Dvina

BJARMALAND

LAKE LADOGA

ALDEIGJUBORG

ESTONIA

HOLMGARD

Volga

GARDARIKI

KURLAND

Dnepr

EAST BULGARS

DREVLYANS

BULGAR

Don

ITIL

KIEV

PECHENEGS

KHAZARS

CASPIAN SEA

BEREZANY

MAGYARS

BLACK SEA

WEST BULGARS

BYZANTINE EMPIRE

ARMENIA

MIKLAGARD

GREECE

Tigris

BAGHDAD

CRETE

CYPRUS

Euphrates

PERSIAN GULF

Nile

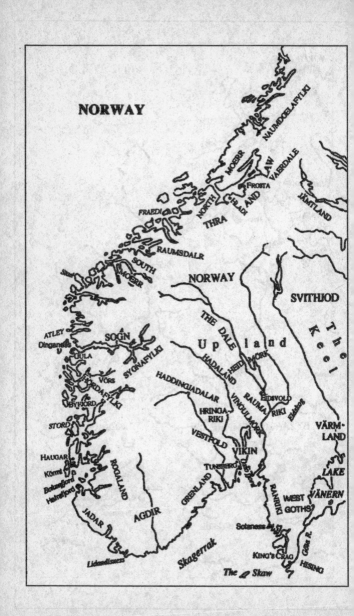

WESTERN ICELAND

BROADFIRTH

HJADARHOLY

White River

BORG
Digra Ness

Borga Fiord

THINGVELLIR

REYKJAVIK

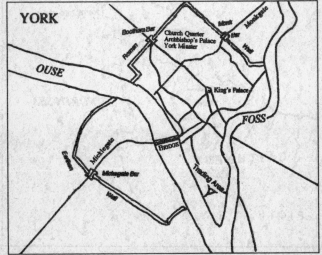

YORK

Bootham Bar

Monk Bar
Monkgate

Church Quarter
Archbishop's Palace
York Minster

Wall

OUSE

King's Palace

FOSS

Micklegate

BRIDGE

Easegate

Micklegate Bar

Wall

Trading Area

Index to Maps

Each place name is listed for the map on which it first appears.

BOOK ONE

THE FINNS

Wind snarled and skirled. Smoke from the longfire eddied bitter on its way upward, hazing lamps throughout the hall. Shadows flickered. They seemed to bring the carvings on pillars and wainscots to uneasy life. Nightfall came fast at the end of these shortening days. Soon there would be nothing but night.

"Go find the knife before high tide bears it off," Father told Seija. "It's a good blade. I'd hate to lose it."

"I—maybe no can," she said in her broken Norse.

Father grinned. "You can try. Don't you Finns have witch-sight?"

Already his mood was better. He had cuffed the thrall who forgetfully left the tool behind at sunset after having cleaned some fish down by the water. With kicks he had sent the wretch stumbling toward the byre, where bondsmen slept among cows. That cooled his wrath.

"I try," Seija muttered. She could ill say no, a mere woods-runner lately brought to Ulfgard for Father to bed.

Nonetheless, new and strange, she had caught Gunnhild's eager heed. "I'll go too!" the girl cried.

Mother half rose from the high seat she shared with Father. "You will not," she answered. "A child of seven winters? A granddaughter of Rögnvald Jarl, trotting after a Finn? Hush your witlessness."

"I would know better," said brother Eyvind loftily. "Unless, of course, a foe was upon us."

Gunnhild stamped her foot on the clay floor. "I will; I will."

Özur grinned anew, wryly now. "It's not worth a fight, as headstrong as you are," he deemed. "Take a warm cloak and keep dry, or I shall be angry. Yngvar, watch her."

The man nodded and went for his own cloak and a spear. Kraka leaned back with a sigh. She was a haughty one, whose husband mostly let her do what she wanted to, but she had learned not to gainsay him.

The three passed through entryroom and door. Gunnhild stopped on the flagstones. Wind yelled. Astounded, she let go of her woolen mantle. It flapped back like wings. "O-o-oh," she breathed.

The sky was a storm of northlights. They shuddered and billowed, huge frost-cold banners and sails, whiteness streaked with ice blue, flame red, cat's-eye green. Their silence scorned every noise of earth. A few stars glimmered low and lonely southward.

Seija stretched forth an arm from her wrap. Her fingers writhed. Through the wind Gunnhild heard her sing, a high wailing in her unknown tongue.

"What's that?" asked the girl. Chill bit. She gathered her garb close.

"I make safe. Ghosts dance. Many strong ghosts."

Gunnhild had seen northlights before, though none like these. "I heard—Father told us—it's the watchfires of the gods."

"Troll-fires, *I* think," growled Yngvar. He drew the sign of the Hammer.

Seija stilled her spellcraft and led the way down the path from the hall and its outbuildings. While no moon was aloft, one could see almost clearly. They reached the strand. The woman walked to and fro, hunched, head bent so that the cowl made her faceless, casting about. Maybe she whispered. Tide had washed away the fish guts and scales that would have helped. Only a narrow stretch of cobbles was left, sheening wet. Kelp sprawled in swart heaps and ropes. The wind scattered its sharp smell.

Gunnhild stayed beside Yngvar. Awe rolled over her.

Behind, the bank lifted steeply to where the roof of the hall loomed black, with ridges and crests hoar beyond. On her right the wharf jutted alongside the ship-house, two darknesses. Nighted likewise were the heights across the inlet. Even here, waves ran wild, spume blowing off their manes, stones grinding underneath. They broke a ways off. The water then rushed at the land, poured back with a hollow roar, and came again, farther each time. Peering past this as the wind lashed tears from her eyes, she saw the open fjord gone berserk, outward to the sea. Northlight shimmered and flashed over it.

A thrilling passed through Gunnhild. The mightiness!

Seija halted. She took off her cloak, weighted it with her shoes, raised her skirt, and waded out. The flow dashed halfway to her knees. Spindrift flew, a salt rain. She bent down to grope. After a little, she straightened. Something gleamed in her hand. She went ashore. Drenched, her gown clung to a short, sturdy frame. Running to meet her, Gunnhild saw that she held a bone-hafted knife, surely *the* knife. "We go home," she said.

Gunnhild stood wondersmitten. Witch-sight indeed? Yet the woman shivered with cold and the night dwarfed her.

A fire-streak lanced into the sea. Gunnhild gasped. She had never beheld a falling star so lightninglike ablaze.

"There Odin cast his spear." Yngvar's voice was not altogether steady. Did he believe what he said? At the end of the world, all the stars will fall from heaven.

Seija sang a stave. What did she think? She made for the path. At the top waited warm earthly fire. Gunnhild lingered till Yngvar urged her along. She wanted to show the Beings who raved abroad that she was not afraid. She would not let herself be afraid.

11

Spring had come, sunshine that melted snow till streams brawled down mountainsides, hasty rains, skies full of homebound wanderbirds, suddenly greenness everywhere, blossoms, sweet breezes, the promise of long days, light nights, and midsummer, when for a while there would be no night at all. In clear weather the fjord glittered as if Ran's daughters had strewn silver dust.

Over the rim of sight hove three ships. Folk shouted and milled about. Gunnhild sped to an outlook near the garth, half hidden by two pine trees. It was atop the grass-grown barrow of the Forefather, and forbidden, but she didn't think Ulf the Old would be angered. He got his offerings, he had never walked, and thus far he had kept other bogles away from the steading.

What she saw stabbed her with loveliness. Those were nothing like Father's broad-beamed, tarry knarr. Lean hulls flew through the waves, twenty or more pairs of oars driving each. Stems and sterns swept upward like swans' necks or snakes about to strike. The hues of the paint might have been stolen from the rainbow, but gleamed more bright. Sunbeams flared off helmets and spearheads. She thought giddily that they beckoned to her.

Two masts lay in their brackets, for the wind was low. The one on the leader was standing, though sailless, to bear a white shield. As the craft drew closer Gunnhild spied a dragon head on the little foredeck, dismounted. She had heard that these were tokens of peace.

Even so, Father called on his men to take arms and follow him to the strand. They were the half score who had work around here today. Others who would have rallied were elsewhere, fishing, sealing, or readying their farms for the season. Tough warriors at need, they could not hold off the strangers; but while they died, the women, children, and lesser housefolk could flee into the woods.

The first crew neared the wharf, backed water, and lay still. Hails passed between ship and shore. The Ulfgard men lowered their spears. The sailors hung their shields on the bulwarks, another heartcatching sight.

Gunnhild should have been in the hall. She scampered to the path and down with the fleetness that ten winters had given her.

The ship was pulled alongside the wharf and made fast, taking up nearly all the room. The rest grounded. From the first sprang a man, to clasp hands with Father. Gunnhild gasped. Never had she seen his like.

He was young, tall, broad-shouldered, lithe. His face was sharply cut on a long, narrow head, eyes a bleached and whetted blue, hair and close-cropped beard golden against fair skin that sea-light had washed with bronze. He must have changed clothes aboard, for his tunic was richly embroidered and trimmed with marten, the breeks green wor-

sted, the shoes white kid. A sword hung at his left shoulder.
He would have no use of it today, Gunnhild thought, but
his weapons would always be near him.

"Greetings, Özur Thorsteinsson." His voice rang. "I've
often heard of you, and looked forward to this day."

"And I know of you, Eirik Haraldsson," said Father.
"Welcome. I've hoped you'd call on us." To his men
crowding around: "Here we have a son of King Harald
Fairhair."

They gaped and mumbled. Gunnhild wondered how
much of Father's speech was shrewd guesswork. Trading
afar, he must have heard many things and learned how to
put them together.

One would not think him wily, from his looks. He was
big, burly, beginning to grow a potbelly. His face was blunt
and red, the full black beard oddly spotted with ruddiness.
Under his hastily donned coat of mail and its padding were
the soiled garments of work. But he dealt ably in his cargoes of pelts, walrus and narwhal tusk, walrus-hide rope;
his coin-hoard swelled further each time he came back from
the southern markets. Although at home he went whaling
or hunting across the highlands both summer and winter,
he also oversaw the farm, gave judgments between men
that they agreed were good law, and sometimes cast runes.

"No other lord would likely guest in the high North," he
went on, "but now that your father's set you over Haalogaland, you'd want to see more of it. Had you sent word
ahead, a feast would be waiting."

Eirik grinned. "As was, you busked yourself for an onslaught?"

"Well, one is never quite sure."

"You need not have feared. It's been years since my
father quelled the last Norse who raided in Norway, together with those dwelling in the Western Islands."

Özur bristled the least bit. "I was not afraid."

"No, no," Eirik said quickly. "I did not mean that. All
know you're a bold man."

"Belike you know as well that I often went in viking
myself when I was younger." Each slow word fell like a

hammer driving a nail. "These years I mostly sail in trade down to the Thraandlaw, but now and then farther."

Eirik nodded. "Yes, I said I've heard much about you, a great seafarer, landholder, and hersir." Thus he acknowledged Özur as a chieftain born to the rank.

"You understand, then, that your father's grip on these parts is as yet loose. I speak not to dishonor, only frankly. We must look to ourselves. That's why we took a stand, till we were sure of who you were."

Eirik eased. Nothing untoward had been uttered on either side. However, he still talked as warily as a man walks on thin ice. "We're bound past North Cape to the White Sea. There we'll raid the Bjarmalanders or maybe trade with them now and then. But I wanted to meet with you, ask about things, and of course show you friendship, my own and the king's."

Özur laughed. "Good! But I'm a shabby host, to keep you at the dock. Come." He took Eirik's arm. "We'll do what we can for you today. By tomorrow there should be quarters ashore for all your crews, and a feast that goes on for as many days as you wish to stay."

Gunnhild could almost hear his whirring thoughts. His workers would furnish booths, clear outbuildings, and spread clean straw, for the sleeping of those men who overflowed from the hall. Besides slaughtering beasts and breaking out dried and salted food, he'd send to farms around the neighborhood for swine and kine. Enough ale should be on hand. Harvests were skimpy, some barley and oats but mostly hay for the livestock. Folk lived off their herds, the woods, and the sea. However, Özur always kept full casks.

The Ulfgard men mingled with the newcomers, who had now swarmed off their ships. Talk buzzed. They spoke their words more softly in the South, Gunnhild heard while her heart pounded. And so many of them, bursting in on the same old faces as sunlight bursts through a leaden overcast!

Father and Eirik Kingsson started up the path. The rest straggled behind, busily chattering. She went along offside, over rocks and tussocks. It was seemly for a goat, not for a wellborn girl. Father frowned at her, then shrugged. His mouth bent a bit upward. Of his children by Mother, those who had lived, he was sterner with her brothers than with her. It was Mother who kept telling Gunnhild what she must and must not do.

About his by-blows she knew little, nor cared. Most had belike died small, as most small children did. The others had gone into the household or Finn-tribe of whoever wed their mothers: each of them a pair of hands for the work of staying alive.

The path opened onto the garth, which filled its patch of level ground. Earth lay muddy, churned, puddles ruffled by the slight wind, but flagstones made walkways. Near the byre, a dungheap steamed into air that woodsmoke likewise touched. The buildings formed a square, linked by wattle fencing: barn, stalls, sheds, workshop, bathhouse, made of turf with a few timbers. Two wagons waited, one for muck, one for everything else. Winter had dwindled the stacks of firewood and hay. Behind were pens for cattle, sheep, pigs, and reindeer, when they were not out foraging. Ducks, geese, and chickens strayed free.

The hall lay on the south side. Its walls were of upright split logs, rounded outward, painted black under red runes and beasts that warded off night-gangers. A few windows, covered with thin-scraped gut, let in some daylight when their shutters, on the inside, stood open. The hogbacked roof was sod, newly green with moss and sprouting grass, bolstered by slanting baulks. Smoke blew tattered from holes at the ridge.

Women, children, hirelings, thralls bustled about, in upheaval at this guesting. Hounds barked and bayed. A flight of crows took to their swart wings, harshly jeering. Behind rose birchwood, and the hillsides, where scrub and dwarf willow struggled amidst lichenous boulders, and the mountains. Cloud-fluff drifted white through a boundless blue. Down below sheened the fjord.

Gunnhild wriggled through the crowd, close behind Father and Eirik. Mother met them at the front door. Seeing that there was no threat, she had donned good clothes, if not her best—pleated linen gown; panels fore and aft, caught by a silver brooch at either shoulder; amber beads between them; a headcloth over the heavy coils of her hair, which had been the hue of the amber until gray crept in. The keys of the household clinked at her belt. She was a comely woman, tall and well shaped, with a straightforward blue gaze. Lately, though, she was losing weight, and a flush mottled the jutting cheekbones.

"Greeting, Eirik Haraldsson," she said aloofly. Word had sped beforehand on the feet of a boy. "I hight Kraka, wife to Özur, and make you welcome of our house." She beckoned. "These be our sons." Yellow-haired Aalf and red-haired, freckled Eyvind trod gawkily forth, said what they could, and withdrew to stare.

Kraka barely glanced at Gunnhild. Wrath rushed hot and cold through the girl. Yes, she had been unladylike, but was she to be nameless before the king's shining son?

She swallowed it. One way or another, she would make herself known to him.

"I have heard of you, lady," Eirik was saying. "You are a daughter of Rögnvald Eysteinsson, who was the jarl of North Moerr and headman over Raumsdalr, are you not?"

"I am." Her answer sounded stiff. Her mother had been a leman her father had for a while—of good yeoman stock, but when Özur Dapplebeard came and asked for the maiden's hand, the jarl must have reckoned that this was as well as he could do. Not that it was a bad thought, making ties with a hersir in the North.

She coughed. Gunnhild heard how she gulped rather than spat.

Eirik gave her his steely smile. "Ever was your father a staunch friend of mine," he said, "and for this he had honor and gain."

Kraka nodded grudgingly. "Yes, that is true."

Eirik went straight ahead. "It's also true that my father outlawed Rögnvald's son Walking Hrolf for a strand-hewing in Norway. But everybody has heard how well Hrolf did for himself in the West.

"And it's true that two of my half-brothers burned your

father. But one is since dead, and my father King Harald sent the other away. He made your brother Thorir jarl of Moerr and gave him his own daughter Aalof to wife."

Then Kraka smiled too. She knew this well, but for Eirik to set it forth before her household was to offer goodwill and respect. It meant still more coming from one with a name for being grim and toplofty. Of course, he'd have it in mind that a jarl ranked second only to a king. "Let me bring you your first horn of mead, before I try to make your first meal among us worthy of you," she said.

Gunnhild did not slip free of helping with that. But throughout the work she looked, listened, and thought. The thinking went on that night and the next day and afterward.

Eirik's crews were a lusty, noisy lot. She heard many boasts from them, not only about themselves but him. He was twelve winters old when his father let him go in viking. He, the king's most beloved son, had ranged over the Baltic, the North, the Irish, and the White Seas, to Wendland, Denmark, Friesland, Saxland, Scotland, England, Wales, Ireland, France, Finnmörk, Bjarmaland—sometimes trading, oftener fighting, looting, burning, bringing home rich booty of goods, with captives for sale. Gunnhild recalled tales her own father had told of his own raidings. They paled beside these. Her heart beat high.

Meanwhile thralls shambled past on their lowly tasks, broken men, unkempt women soon used up. Özur was no more harsh with them than needful, but they got somewhat less kindness from him than his horses did. A few times at the midwinter offerings, when the year had been bad, he had given Odin one that was no longer strong, hanged on a tree at the halidom. Free workers, taken in from poor homes that could not keep them, were a little better off. And Özur did rather well by his foremen, and in a gruff way by those he called his tame Finns, whose skills furthered his hunting, whaling, and sealing. But their lives were so meager, as were the lives of all crofters, smallholders, and fishers—huddled in sod huts, breaking their hands in toil on gaunt fields or on the oars of boats that often never came back. Always they went in dread of hun-

ger, storm, sickness; and Father himself had wondered today if vikings were upon him.

How handsome Eirik was, how splendid his garb and
gear, how lordly his ways! *He* had nothing to fear; let the
world fear him. What wealth must fill his houses—besides
gold and other fine things, warriors, skalds, traders, outlanders, newness from everywhere! What was Ulfgard but
a forgotten beggarly outpost?

Come the feast, host and guest would vie in giving gifts.
She knew Father's could not match Eirik's.

Maybe Eirik had a skald with him, who would make a
poem in Father's honor. How empty it would sound.

Gunnhild straightened. She nearly spilled the laden tray
she was carrying. No, she thought, she would not become
anyone's underling, nor would she forever be a nobody.

III

Seija bore Özur no children. Whether this was by happenstance or her wish and lore went unasked. Folk
looked on her as a spooky sort, best left alone. Kraka had
soon said she would no longer have this witch in the hall.
Özur yielded and ordered a dwelling made for her, well
away from the garth. He set her to watch over the swine
when these roamed fending for themselves in the warm half
of the year. She was eerily good at that, seeming to know
when and where anything went amiss. Meanwhile she grew
leeks and herbs for herself and gathered roots, sedges, berries, and suchlike wild food. Bread, milk, and stockfish she
got at the steading, where she did not otherwise come. Özur
might bring a crock of ale along when he sought her,
though after a while this was rather seldom. Gunnhild was
there often.

Mother did not like that. Father allowed it when his
daughter had no work on hand. At first he had asked what
they two did. Gunnhild answered truthfully that Seija told
tales from her homeland and taught her things about the
use of herbs in cooking and healing. She did not speak of

what else went on. It was nothing of weight, but he might have forbidden it as beneath her rank.

And now even a girl of thirteen should have been asleep. But this was high summer, when the sun slipped barely and briefly under the waters. Soon, for a short span, it would not set at all—midsummer, when everybody from everywhere came here. Then Özur's land was a sprawling, brawling camp; the freemen met to settle things among each other, to swap yarns and wares, to handsel deals; at the halidom the balefire burned and blood flowed, whereafter the offerings were roasted and feasting began. Few slept much in the season of the light nights. Time enough for that when winter laid blackness upon them.

This evening Gunnhild could not, however hard she tried. At last she rose from her heap of sheepskins. The room was gloomy; she must fumble with clothes. The girls and unwed women who shared it—those who were not already outdoors—stirred in their dreams; straw ticks rustled dryly. In the long room, men snored on the benches. Father and Mother had a shut-bed past which she stole very softly. The doors were not latched, for anybody might have to go to the stoolhouse and a boy kept lookout above the fjord. As she left the garth for the woods, Gunnhild heard thumping, grunting, and panting in the bushes offside. She had done so before, and sometimes happened on the sight itself. This time the noise quickened her heart and heated her cheeks. She hastened onward.

A trail wound amidst birch and pine. Few of the trees were close together, though underbrush grew thickly. Sky reached well-nigh cloudless behind darkling needles and leaves that long, low-slanting sunbeams turned green-gold. Deeper in, the light was lost among shadows, through which the birches showed ghostly white. Moss on fallen trunks glistened wet and rich. The air lay cool but still full of noontide smells, flowers, earth, pine gum. Birds called. Squirrels darted fiery up the trees and chittered. Once, far off, something bellowed thunder-deeply—a bull aurochs?

The trail gave on a small clearing. A spring bubbled near a turf hut, hardly more than a den. Smoke sifted through the thatch roof, off a hearthstone whereon a fire smoldered banked. The door stood open on Seija's belongings. They were poor and scant. She stood at an upright warp-weighted loom, for she wove wool given her and traded the cloth for a tool or a haunch of meat.

As swiftly aware as a cat, she sprang forth. The two halted, gazing, in search of words. Seija was short, full-formed, with a wide face, nose curving to a point, brown eyes, brown hair in braids. She could have covered her head like a wedded woman, but seldom did. Today her feet were bare, her garb a shift of faded blue wadmal.

"Greeting, child," she said. Her Norse had become fairly good. "I'm always glad to see you." She looked closely. "But you are troubled."

Gunnhild gulped and nodded. "Mother—" She could not go on.

Seija waited.

"She's worsening fast," Gunnhild said in a rush. "Thin, hardly any strength, and she coughs up slime with blood in it. Father's cast runes." It being no holy thing, she had watched while he cut them on sticks, which he tossed so he could read how they fell. She had tried it herself when nobody was watching. "He says it bodes ill."

Seija nodded. "I have heard. Once in a while I have seen. I'm sorry." She did not say, "She has no love for me." Kraka's feeling was not hatred but scorn, with maybe the least unspoken and disowned touch of fear.

"Nothing has helped that we and two different wise-women did. Can't you?"

"She would not let me."

"Oh, but if you could—"

The Finn-woman sighed. "I have no strong spellcraft. Only a few tricks. As often as not, they fail me."

"You told me your brother was teaching you more."

"Yes, we have women—" Seija searched for a word. "—somewhat like your spaewives that I've heard tell of. But I was taken too early from my Saami."

"I have been thinking." Gunnhild strove not to shiver.

"That brother of yours off in Finnmörk, is he a great wizard?"

"If anyone is, Vuokko—"

Gunnhild broke in. "Why has Father never spoken of him?"

"Have you forgotten? Vuokko was not there. Your father sailed north—"

"Yes." Gunnhild said it aloud, working to straighten out the jumble in her head. "I remember. The walrus and narwhal were few that year. He went after more. I, I've wondered if what he really wanted was the faring, after so long a while since he was last abroad." She had come to know him.

And Özur had found some Finns, down from the woods to make a catch on behalf of their tribe. A maiden among them caught his eye.

A fresh chill went through Gunnhild. "Would your brother have stricken Father dead?"

"I think not. The vengeance afterward would have been frightful."

Gunnhild twisted her mouth into a smile. "Anyhow, my father paid for you. Didn't he?"

"Whether or not this was my father's wish," Seija said flatly.

"Was it yours?" Gunnhild had not asked such a question before. New tides and bewilderments had begun to rise in her.

"I have made the best of it."

Seija looked off into the sun-flecks and shadows. Gunnhild could barely hear her. "But I dream of wandering free through the wide lakelands, with kin and friends and our own, olden ways. Sometimes I find mushrooms that help me dream. Of late, it has even seemed to me that—" Her words dwindled away.

"If we sent for your brother—" Gunnhild faltered.

Seija shook her head. "I don't think they could find him and bring him here in time. And your mother might be unwilling to see him." After a span, in which Gunnhild heard only the honeyed call of a cuckoo—what ri it to be so happy?—the Finn-woman said: "And she may well be beyond all help."

The will of the norns stood not to be altered, Gunnhild thought. But that Mother, strong, beautiful Mother, should be hollowed out like this—It was horrible being helpless. "Tell me about him," she well-nigh begged. "Tell me about your home." Anything to make her forget.

Belike, in the mood that was upon her, that would be hurtful for Seija. Well, only Gunnhild ever sought her out for more than a swiving. Let her repay.

Seija smiled sadly. "As you wish. As you have need of." She waved at a log. "Be seated. Would you like some bread or a bowl of curds?"

In a while they were side by side. Seija soon fell into her own tongue. Gunnhild did likewise. Over the years she had picked up knowledge of it. Father said it might come in handy. He did not have much of it himself, mainly from his dealings, though his mother's mother had been a Finn-woman. Neither Aalf nor Eyvind could be bothered to learn.

What Father had not heard about was the bits of witch-craft his daughter also gained.

IV

Summer waned; days shortened; the first sallowness stole over birch leaves; often at sunrise hoarfrost glimmered on the ground. Fields lay harvested, and on every threshing floor a young woman had held the Old Woman, the last sheaf, in her arms while the workers danced and shouted in a ring around her. Slaughter-time was not yet, but nuts and berries were thickly ripe in the woods, where stags bawled and clashed. When the moon rose full it lingered late, beckoning hunters.

This year, for some days, a hunt more earnest went out from Ulfgard. A crofter of Özur's had been found slain with his two children, the house robbed of such of its could easily be carried away, together with foodstock, fowl, and flesh off the one cow. When Özur heard, from another tenant who happened by soon afterward, he went straight to the lonely little steading, looked it narrowly over with a tracker's eye, and cast runes. He himself was among the men who sought forth with hounds, scouring after the ill-doers.

"I have a good guess who they are," he said. "It began three years ago and well inland from here, but word passed widely around. The brothers Kol and Mörd dwelt by themselves, because they were surly and threatful and nobody could get along with them. When they slew a neighbor for no rightful cause and would not pay for him, they were outlawed. Every man's hand being against them, they must needs flee into the wilderness. Since then they've skulked about, stealing or worse at outlying garths, too woodscrafty to chase down. I didn't think they'd ever come this far. Belike the folk yonder have, at last, been closing in on them, and they're trying elsewhere." He laughed. "Let's hope that was unwise of them."

To Gunnhild it was at first thrilling. But when again and again the search bands trudged home with naught to say, she cared less and less. As a girl, she knew hardly more than what she overheard, or what Aalf and Eyvind flauntingly told her. This soon ran to "Yes, we must have frightened them off." Then her father ended the hunt. There was, after all, much else to do. She barely marked it when he swore that poor Gisli would nonetheless not lie unavenged, and gave no heed when he spoke aside, quietly, with men of his whom he trusted. Cloverbee, the cat she thought of as hers, had had kittens. Two were let live, and they were weanling. That was something near to her, unlike the dull round of her duties.

So on a brisk morning she left the hall with one in her arms and started across the yard. It nestled close, a fuzzy brindled ball that sometimes ticklingly licked her wrist. As she passed the fence gate, her father's man Yngvar strode to her side. "Where are you bound, young lady?" he asked.

"To see my friend Seija," Gunnhild answered. "It's been a long while."

"We'd not have allowed you to, with those cutthroats in the neighborhood."

She had not thought about that. The knowledge shocked into her. She gasped. "Then why was she left there all alone?"

Yngvar shrugged. "It wasn't likely they'd come so near us while we were after them. And having her in sight would do your sick mother no good." His look went stern. "Our hunt did find signs that they haven't yet gone far. Keep away from the woods."

Seething, Gunnhild stiffened. "Can *you* forbid me?" Özur was fishing on the fjord and Kraka slept heavily after a bad night.

"I'll take that on myself, yes."

"Send a man along with me, if you're afraid."

Yngvar stood for a bit unspeaking before he shook his head. "No. We—we can't spare any."

"That's silly, this time of year. And don't think I haven't seen how somebody, man or boy, is always elsewhere." Coming home closemouthed too. She'd not asked about it, for such things were not women's business unless they were told. Now she wished she had made it hers.

"Keeping his eyes open. If you go, you'll be turned back." Yngvar smiled. "Wouldn't you liefer I did that, between the two of us, than a lowly lout?"

Gunnhild sniffed and stalked from him.

Sheer foolishness, she thought in wrath. And cowardly. How had this been for Seija, with news of what was going on and only the herd of swine on hand? Gunnhild would not yield to it. But she must be cunning. A woman always must, if she wanted to keep any will of her own.

She walked three times around the garth as though working off her anger and then to Ulf's barrow as though to sit at its foot and sulk. Nobody seemed to be watching. On the far side of the mound, the two pine trees hid her. The ground beyond was only grass-grown, and beyond it was a stubblefield. But everything stretched empty. She reached a neck of the woods and slipped into its shelter. Thence she made her way through undergrowth, at which she had won skill, until she found the path she wanted.

The hut lay peaceful amidst wind and restless light, door open. "Hallo," Gunnhild called. She jumped down over the threshold into its half-underground room. The fire glowed dull red, banked, beneath sudden duskiness. Seija stood at her loom. She started, with a thrall's wariness, before she saw who was here and said, "You! Welcome!"

"How have you been?" blurted Gunnhild.

"I've missed you, dear. Come, sit. Will you eat, will you drink?"

"I should have—Well, they wouldn't have let me. Haven't you been afraid?"

"Not greatly. I can't fear much anymore." Seija brightened. "And now I have a guard."

"What? Where?"

"When they gave up the hunt for the outlaws, your father had a blind made in a thicket nearby. A lad stays in it, turn by turn. If he sees them, he'll run and bring help. You haven't heard?"

"No, nothing was said about it." Gunnhild's wonderment at that gave way to another question. "But he'd have seen me come too, and, and Yngvar said I'd be sent back."

"You got by him, then." Seija snickered. "I daresay he went aside to squat." Misgiving stirred. "He will see you come out."

Gunnhild tossed her head. "I'll tell him that if he tells anybody, I'll make him rue it." Her father might learn anyhow, but if so, she'd cope with him.

"Well, done is done. We'll stay inside and talk softly. I am so happy you are here. Why are you carrying that kitten?"

The small one had not liked the scramble through brush. Gunnhild had had a struggle and taken a few scratches. It calmed down after she was on the path. She handed it over. "For you. A friend to have. I'm keeping her sister. We'll give them names that are alike."

A tear or two shone. "Oh, Gunnhild, you are—kind." Seija cuddled it to her breast and cheek.

Having set it on the floor, she hastened to fill bowls with

water, curds, and scraps of meat. "Hark, she's purring!" she laughed. Both sat on the floor to play with it.

Darkness blotted the doorway. Seija screamed.

A man sprang in, and a second. They were big men, but gaunt, ragged, filthy, faces nearly hidden by tangled, matted hair and beards. The stench of them hit Gunnhild in the belly. Each had a rolled-up bundle tied to his shoulders. One gripped an ax, the other a spear.

"Ho-haw!" roared he. "What have we found here, Kol, hey?"

"Something better to eat than we've got, I hope, and yonder's a jug," rasped the axman. Yellow snags of teeth glistened. "But first and later fun, yah, girls?"

The outlaws, Gunnhild knew. This could not be real. She must rouse herself from the nightmare. It querned in her skull. But everything around was as before, the loom, the kitten's bowls, the coals on the hearthstone, the hands she lifted. But the boy would have seen. He must be speeding on his way. How long to reach Ulfgard? How long for men to seize their weapons and dash back? It wasn't so far; it couldn't be far. Sweat burst cold over her skin. She shrank against the wall.

Seija snatched up a bowl and threw it. The clay shattered on Kol's nose. She cast herself at him and wrestled. "Gunnhild, get out!" she yelled.

The spearman was sidling toward the maiden. The doorway stood free. She hurtled forward. The spearshaft slanted between her ankles. She went over. He made a stride across her. She stared at him looming in the way. "I've got her," he said gleefully.

Seija writhed in Kol's hug. She clawed for his eyes. His free arm tore her loose. The hand cuffed her. She lurched back. "Keep watch at the door, Mörd," he panted, and to Seija, "Behave yourself, bitch, or it'll be the worse for you." He wiped the blood on his nose and some snot that fell from it while he shook the ax at her.

"I'll bar the door, and we'll have these chickens safe," said Mörd.

"No. Somebody could come by, and we'd be taken unawares. Be our lookout. I'll spell you in a while."

The kitten mewed afright and crept near Gunnhild. She clasped it against her breast as she stumbled to her feet. Was it a child, was it a luck-charm, was it only something to hold?

Kol lifted the ale jug and slurped greedily. "You always go first," Mörd grumbled. "I'm thirsty too."

"You'll have your time, I say." Kol guffawed. "For you, looking on can be the start of the fun."

"Well, then, I'll take first go in this pretty little heifer." Mörd glared at Gunnhild. "You'll be sweet to us, understand? Both of you. Otherwise—" He reached out and plucked the kitten from her arms. He dashed it to the floor and ground his heel down on its head. There was a tiny crunching sound. Brains and blood squirted from under the shoe.

Gunnhild backed away to the wall. Piss trickled along her thighs, warm and wet. She fought not to throw up. The world wavered around her.

"I won't keep you waiting long," Kol said. She heard it as a hollow ringing. "That farmwife wasn't much, was she? This ought to be better." He turned to Seija. "Down on the sheepskins, you."

The Finn-woman had regained her wits after the blow. She stood straight before him and answered almost steadily, "Why? You'll kill us anyway, won't you?"

"Not soon, if we can stay awhile. No, not soon. Be good, and we might even take you along when we go. Be bad, and I'll break a few bones before having you."

"I see. Yes, spare me and I'll be good." Seija drooped her eyelids. Her voice went throaty. "I can be very good. Don't hurry with me. I'll show you many things."

She was stalling for time, Gunnhild thought. Father's men must soon be here, any heartbeat now, it wasn't far, and they were stalwart men, swift on their feet, ready with their weapons. Soon, soon!

"But *I* won't stand waiting forever," growled Mörd.

"You'll like watching," Seija murmured at him. "Later we'll do still other things, you and I."

"Don't lose sight of the outside," snapped Kol. "Nor gripe about it, when you'll be first with the filly."

"Behold," Seija breathed. "We begin thus." She drew the shift over her head and let it drop. Gunnhild had never before seen those breasts, blue-veined under the snowy skin, nipples sunrise-pink, or the moist dark curls.

"Hoo," gusted from Kol, and "Yo-o-o" from Mörd.

Seija swung her hips. "What have you for me?"

"I'm a bull," Kol choked.

Mörd leered at Gunnhild. "I am too. You'll find out."

Kol let his ax fall to the floor. The wildness fleeted through Gunnhild that she could jump over there, grab it, and split his head. Then Mörd's. As he had her kitten's. No. It could not be. But Father's men were on their way. Why was it taking them so long?

Kol tugged at his belt and lowered his breeks. His prong strutted. Dizzily, Gunnhild recalled what she had a few times erstwhile glimpsed in the bushes, and thought that this was a stub. But enough, ghastly enough.

Seija trod over to take it in her hand and stroke it. "Oh, yes, yes, yes," she crooned.

Kol gripped her bruisingly by the forearms. "Down, quick!"

Seija sighed and, slowly, writhed her way onto the bedding. Kol knelt at her feet. He spread her legs. Mörd drooled. Where was Yngvar, where were the men?

"A-a-ah." Kol thrust in. He plumped his full weight on her. His buttocks began to move, faster and faster. She lay still, her fists clenched beside her.

Kol whooped, shivered, and stopped. "Well," Mörd barked, "are you done at last?"

"For now." Kol rose, pulled up his breeks, and belted them. "Your turn." His shoe nudged Seija. "Off the fleece, you. Make way for the next."

Father, Yngvar, Odin and his valkyries, where, when?

Kol took his stand in the doorway. Mörd went over to the jug and gulped from it. He set it back, belched, and crooked a finger at Gunnhild. "All right, you, let's go."

Fear and bewilderment blew out of her. Wrath and hatred

flared, swift as northlights, cold as wind off a winter sea.
She shrieked, or she howled. Blindly, she seized the other
bowl, broke it on the earth, and grasped a shard. It might
gouge out an eye, at least, if she had any luck. She'd make
him kill her. He'd have nothing but her lich to befoul. Afterward her ghost would give him no rest, grinning and
clacking, whirling down woe after woe upon his sleeplessness. As he moved in on her, she crouched to leap.

Kol reeled back from the doorway. An arrow quivered
below his chest. He fell, yammered, and flailed about. Mörd
yowled. He went after the spear he had leaned against the
wall. Her head gone altogether clear, Gunnhild kicked it
aside. As he stooped and groped for it, the doorway darkened once more. But it was Yngvar who sprang through,
sword in hand.

With a meaty *thwack,* he took Kol's head half off. Blood
spurted, then flowed in a tide. Men boiled behind him. Gunnhild could not see in the press of them what happened to
Mörd, but it was short and it spilled his guts. More blood
ran free, with the sharp reek of death.

Özur's men drew aside. Seija stepped forward. She had
taken Mörd's spear. She jabbed it into dead Kol, again and
again.

Yngvar caught Gunnhild to his breast. "We, we knew
not you were here," he stammered. "We knew not, I swear.
Oh, but Hrapp will answer heavily, that he left his post,
even for a little!"

At the same time she passed by, flitted in the back of
Gunnhild's awareness. Could there have been a norn at
work?

But she would not weep. She would not. "Why didn't
you come sooner?" she gulped.

"We never knew you were here, lady, lady. Else we'd
have outsped the wind. It was your father's bidding. If anything could draw the outlaws nigh, this shieling would, off
by itself. Warned, we'd creep through the woods with, with
stealth, till we had them ringed in, and so make sure of
them."

"I—I see." Gunnhild withdrew from him. She could understand, she thought dimly, she could forgive, and much of this had been her own doing. What Father and Mother would say—But later, later, she'd deal with everything later.

She found herself in Seija's arms. "Oh, my dear, how glad I am for you," she heard.

"D-didn't you foresee?"

"I never looked for this. And b-besides, my lore is scant."

"But you—for you—"

Gunnhild felt the shrug. "I'll put it behind me. No worse than—" Seija broke off. "But if you, Gunnhild, if you find you're dwelling on it and your dreams become bad, seek me. I do know a few healing spells. I can lift it off you. Wrong would it be, wrong, if you bore scars for life from a happenstance like this, or lost wish for the love of men."

"I'll bring you the other kitten" was all Gunnhild could think to say.

Her tongue shaped the words almost of itself. Inwardly the knowledge was swelling in her: Father had *used* Seija, not only for a bedmate but as bait in a trap. So did the strong ever make use of the weak.

She, Gunnhild, had today been among the weak. She would never again let that come about.

What further witchcraft she could learn ought to give strength—strength of her own, which she might or might not choose to add to the strength of some good man. Over and above that, though, she would seek strength wherever and however it was to be had, and weave her webs to bind it to her.

V

raka Rögnvaldsdottir died next year in the fall. Her oldest housewomen cleaned her and laid her out. Her husband closed the eyes. Their children stood beside him. How strange she had become, the pain gone but also the lordliness and laughter, willfulness and warmth, nothing left but a waxen mask drawn tight over her skull. No breath moved the shrunken breasts. Were the cloth that bound those jaws undone, she still would not speak.

She had better not. Gunnhild fought down a shudder. Bold Aalf and brash Eyvind seemed alike daunted. Father sat hunched throughout the night when they kept watch. In the guttering lamplight she marked with a slight astonishment how gray he had grown.

Kraka's death having been foreseen, the pyre was ready, the grave dug. Ulf had ordered himself buried whole in a ship with his weapons, the barrow raised where he could look seaward, and such was still usage in the South, but Northland folk oftenest burned their dead. Nevertheless she wore her best clothes, and behind the bier men carried things of gold, silver, and amber, together with everything from a distaff to a goblet of outland glass, which would go into the earth beside her bones. Boys hurried forth, bidding the whole neighborhood to a three days' grave-ale. At that time Özur would kill a horse. So highly had he thought of his Kraka.

Meanwhile Gunnhild stole away from Ulfgard and walked the mile or so back to its burial ground.

Clouds scudded beneath a wan sky, their shadows hounding the heatless sunlight. A hawk wheeled far overhead; a gang of rooks winged murky just above the trees. Wind blustered, sent fallen leaves a-whirl and a-rattle, swayed the upper boughs of the pines. Nearly bare, birches stood like skeletons in sere brush. Grass around the charred leavings of the fire had gone sallow.

Gunnhild stopped at the raw soil of the newest filled pit in the clearing. Her outer garment was only a woolen gown, but she was hardly aware of cold. The wind fluttered her skirt and the unbound hair of a maiden. For a span she stood dumb. Then she could whisper no more than "Mother."

She did not really know why she was here. To seek understanding? Even peace? In her last two years the illness made Kraka bitter. She would brook no rede or deed that was not her own will; she grasped after more than her share; she spat ill-wishings and bad names at the whole household. None but Özur could shout her into stillness, and he was more apt to storm out. His sons found things to do that kept them away. That was less easy for his daughter. She schooled herself to say nothing about it to anyone.

"I should not have hated you, Mother," she said at length, into the wind. "Often I did not; truly I did not. Had I known an herb or a spell to heal you, oh, I would swiftly have brought you back to what you once were. Did I know what witch or—or god wreaked this and had I the might, I would avenge you. Fearsomely would I avenge you."

Barren though the words were, they did not strike her as dangerous. Rather, they heartened. It was as if, through them, she called the woman's haughtiness up into herself.

Let her remember that Kraka was born to Rögnvald the Mighty, jarl, warrior, near friend of the great king. Remember what Mother had told of her half-brothers, Gunnhild's uncles—among them Einar, who took the jarldom in Orkney and cut the blood eagle on the back of his father's killer, though that man was a son of King Harald; and Hrolf, outlawed from Norway, who gathered a ship-host of Norse and Danes, roved and reaved widely, and won from the French king lordship over that land into which Northern settlers poured until now it was known as Normandy.

Baneful was the night long ago when King Harald took Snaefrid to his bed. Her Norse name notwithstanding, she was a Finnish witch. Yet he loved her—too dearly. She bore him four sons before she died. Afterward her lich stayed as fair and fresh as ever in life, and the king would not have her buried, but swore she must surely soon live anew. Well it was that at last a wise man told him he should have fresh clothes put upon her; for when she was lifted, foulness and stench broke loose, and Harald was healed of his sorrow. Her sons grew up to be troublemakers, who lusted for higher standing than the king would give them. Haalfdan Longleg and Gudröd Gleam got many men together, ringed in a house where Jarl Rögnvald was, and burned it. Harald's anger then made Haalfdan go in viking to Orkney, where Turf-Einar caught him. Feeling he must avenge this, King Harald fared overseas with a fleet, but in the end agreed to take sixty marks of gold as wergild.

Today Gudröd dwelt unscathed in Agdir, Sigurd the Giant in Hringariki, Rögnvald Highbone in Hadaland, where they called him a black warlock.

Gunnhild clenched her fists till the nails bit into the palms. Someday there would be a reckoning.

A gust slapped her with chill. That and the stinging in her hands drew her thoughts back whence they had strayed. She had not come here to brood on things about which she could do nothing—yet.

Nor should she be angry with King Harald. Father and Mother both had told of his many women, some wellborn, some lowly, some whom he wedded and some who were only lemans for years, months, days, a night or two. They had borne him no few sons and daughters. It behooved him to do well by these. Indeed, did he not, the sons, at least, would become wolves, preying on the kingdom. His masterful blood ran in them all.

Year after year had he wrought and fought, beginning far south in Vikin, to which he was born, overcoming kings and jarls and chiefs, overawing yeomen, until at Hafrsfjord he smote the last great gathering of his foes and was king of all Norway.

Along with much else, he took away freehold; henceforward, men had their land not of olden right but through him. Those who could not abide his harshness took ship. Many went to Orkney, Shetland, Ireland, or Normandy. Others sought to newly found Iceland.

Most folk stayed home and were not unhappy with Harald Fairhair. When he was not crossed, he was openhanded to those who served him well, raising the foremost to high rank, giving handsome gifts to the rest, always setting an overflowing board. When he made the name of king mean little more than lordship over a shire, beneath his sway, he ended the endless wars between them. Though they might still fall out with each other, it was now their own followers who fought, not levies of yeomen who would rather tend their fields. He went after the vikings who harried the shores, scoured their strongholds, caught and killed them at sea, set ship-guards and coast-watch, until the land was free of them. Thereafter trade grew and grew; Norway opened fully to the outside world.

True, Harald was not almighty. The jarl of Hladi, who headed the Thraandlaw, was well-nigh on a footing with him. Beyond it and Naumdoelafylki stretched Haalogaland, where the king merely sent men each year to fetch the scot paid him by the Finns.

Well, Gunnhild thought, that could be bettered.

Not that she wanted Father made an underling. "No, no," she cried to her whose ashes lay here and who maybe listened. But had not Grandfather Rögnvald been Harald Fairhair's staunchest waymate? Should not a worthier son carry the work onward?

They said that Harald set nine wives aside when he wedded Ragnhild the Mighty. She was daughter to Eirik, a king in Jutland. Soon afterward, Gorm made himself king of all Denmark; but Ragnhild was kin to him also. The child she bore got the name of her father, Eirik. Later she died. This Eirik was the son whom Harald Fairhair loved the most and made his heir—Eirik, who once for a few wonderful days called at Ulfgard.

"I will never yield," Gunnhild said into the wind. "Through me, Mother, if none else, our blood shall flow greatly."

VI

Özur was not long widowed. Ulfgard needed a lady. Geirmund Arnason was the man second most well-off in these parts. The oldest of his daughters not yet wedded was Helga. During the winter Özur asked for and got her.

Thereafter he almost never came to Seija. But Gunnhild went there still more often than before.

Helga was only three years her elder. They did not get along. If he heard a quarrel break out, Özur would roar it to sullen silence, but he was not always on hand. And straightway after the midsummer offerings, he sailed on his trading. Aalf had fared with him for some years, and latterly Eyvind too. Those three being gone, hard feelings came forth unhindered, thereby growing harder.

Gunnhild sat brooding in the hall. Earlier Helga had ordered her out of the high seat, as was the right of the lord's wife. Now Gunnhild slumped in the seat for an honored guest, across from it. Sunlight and mild air streamed through open doors. She paid them no heed. She wished she could do likewise with the two serving women who were scrubbing dirt and soot off the wainscots. They chattered all the while, the same witless everydayness month after month, year after year, in the same few clacking words, broken by the same hen-cackles of laughter. She knew not why she lingered here, unless that it was like scratching a sore.

Helga came in from outside. She halted, peered, then strode to the honor seat. There she stood, arms akimbo. Gunnhild glowered at her. It did not help things that Helga was two inches the taller. Yellow braids showed themselves from under her headcloth. Her belly bulged with child. Sourness pinched her mouth.

"Idle again, Gunnhild?" she snapped. "Are you sick?"

The girl straightened and stiffened. "No," she answered. "I was thinking."

"Well, we've a bundle of carded wool in store. You can think while you spin thread."

"I will when I'm ready," Gunnhild mumbled.

"You are ready now. Go fetch the stuff."

Gunnhild jumped to her feet. "Do not talk so to me!" she flared. "Am I a thrall?"

"No. Thralls work. You sit like a sow in her pen, or drift about like—like the stink off a dungheap."

"Y-y-you dare speak thus—to Özur Dapplebeard's daughter?"

Helga fell still, a little shaken. She had let ill will run away with her. After a bit she said less strongly, "Oh, yes, you'll whine to him when he comes home. But he shall have the truth from me."

Gunnhild felt she had gotten the upper hand. Lest she lose it, she flung back, "Let him deem who's right. I will take no more shame from you."

She stalked out. Helga glared after her.

Yngvar and some other men were in the yard, hitching two horses to the clean wagon. Rakes and forks stood aslant in it. They were about to bring in the cut hay. How she yearned to ride with them!

"Good evening, Gunnhild Özurardottir," Yngvar hailed in his grave way. He was headman at Ulfgard when its owner was elsewhere.

"Good evening to you, Yngvar Hallfredarson," she said thickly.

"Where are you bound, if I may ask?"

"To walk awhile."

Yngvar glanced at the open door. "I heard ugly words." Gunnhild felt her face whiten with rage.

"It is not well when women fight like that," Yngvar went on. "It can lead to men killing."

"Are you against me too?" Gunnhild cried.

Yngvar lifted a hand. "No, no. I am only grieved. Do take your walk; cool yourself off." He knew there were no outlaws left alive in the neighborhood, or anyone else who would dare harm her. "I'll try to say something to—the lady of the house. When you get back, best will be if you both let this lie dropped."

Gunnhild nodded, once, and left him.

It seethed in her. How much longer could the wretchedness go on? Should she ask Father to find her a husband, young though she was?

No! Bound to a yeoman whose hands forever smelled of the barn or to a fisherman and his reeking catches, bound inside the rim of this land, never to see what reached beyond, never to rule over more than a few grubby workers? No!

The woods softened her mood somewhat. Air lay laden with greenness, now and then a birdsong. Dusky blue rested behind the outburst of leaves overhead and pine boughs that had gone aglow. Red-gold light ran low past the boles;

shadows faded away in the haze of it. The midsummer sun did not yet sink below worldedge, but went around, rising and falling, eventide slipping eerily into daybreak and back again. Folk slept a few winks at a time, as if they would hoard up life against black winter.

Grass and blossoms—heart's-ease, little spotted orchis—blanketed the ground at Seija's hut. She stood at its door. A wreath of herbs ringed the haggled brown hair; a necklace of lemming skulls crossed the dingy wadmal gown. "Come in," she bade. "I awaited you."

Gunnhild stopped short. A wondering passed chill through her. Of late Seija had been more strange than ever, short-spoken, often falling into stillness while she stared at something unseeable. She had lost weight, though she did not seem ill. Rather, it was as if a fire that had smoldered in her was rising at last, fed by her flesh—and by what else?

"Indeed?" Gunnhild stammered. "I, I have not been here for a while."

"No one has," Seija said. "Not in the body."

"What mean you?" Gunnhild heard how thin her voice was. Anger at that swept misgivings aside. "I'd have liked to come, but I get scant freedom these days."

"I have had none till now. Come within. Let us talk."

The hut was half below ground. They hiked up their skirts and stepped down. Gunnhild took the stool. Seija hunkered on the clay. Though the door stood wide, dimness always dwelt around a hearthfire that barely smoked. The few pots, bowls, and kitchen tools seemed to crouch in the shadows beneath the loom. Witchy things that Seija had made over the years—roughly whittled sticks and bones, rocks and a reindeer skull daubed with blood long since dried black, a small earthen shape that might be a man's, a god's, or a troll's—seemed to watch and hearken.

Seija's hands drew signs while she sang a stave too low for Gunnhild to make out the Finnish words. They rose and fell like the midnight sun. Gunnhild's skin prickled.

Seija leaned forward on her haunches. She spoke softly

but keenly. Her eyes, agleam in the gloom, never let go of Gunnhild's. "You are my one friend."

Gunnhild held back from answering more than, "I wish you well." She and her dreams had been growing away from here, more and more into the Norse world. The childhood sharings, even the day of the outlaws, could almost have happened to somebody else. This sudden awakening of the memories was not wholly welcome.

"Do you wish me free?"

"What?"

The question shivered. "Would you help me go home, and so help yourself become great?"

"How can I?" Gunnhild blurted in bewilderment. "I will not betray my father."

"What cares he about me? Nothing. Yet he will not send me home. It's too much trouble, and what would he gain?"

"If he did let you go, you'd never get through the wilderness alone, on foot. Would you?"

"No. Nevertheless I have made the trek. Not on foot, no. My soul has gone."

Gunnhild caught her breath. "How?"

"Hark. You know—I've told you—during all these years I've striven, over and over, to dream myself home. I was torn too soon from my Saami and the noai'de—you would say wizards—who were teaching me. I must grope my own way forward, with shards of memory to go by. The songs I made up, the dances I trod, beating a stick on a log for want of a drum, the herbs and berries and mushrooms I tried—" Seija's voice broke. Her gaze went elsewhere. "Sickness—tears—"

Gunnhild's heartbeat shook her.

After a while Seija looked back at her anew, eyes dry, and said quite steadily: "In the end, I found pain. See." She drew back her left sleeve to show the swollen, oozing redness of a bad burn. "Pain, along with song, dance, drumming, witch-food, loosed my soul. I toppled into night. But a bird winged forth, a swallow, and that bird was I. Over the mountains it flew, over woodland, marshland, lakeland, swifter than the wind, till it found the dear ranges of Finn-

Her heart leaped to and fro. "Seija—" She snatched after breath.

Özur scowled. "You see too much of that little hag."

Bitterness gave boldness. "Who else have I? Time was when you saw her often enough."

Özur snorted. "What has she done?"

"Nothing wrongful. Were she to cast a spell against us, I'd forgive—"

"*I* would kill her."

"She hasn't!" Gunnhild said hastily into the wind. "She can't, she lacks the craft, nor does she want to. I swear she does not. But this year—" The tale spilled out of her.

Özur listened stock-still, his face wooden, the spear held straight skyward. At the end, he asked slowly, "Do you put faith in that?" Gunnhild nodded. "Or is it your wish that does?"

She fought down the feelings that stormed in her and gave him words she had picked beforehand. "You know Seija has some witch-sight. It doesn't always come to her, and never reaches far, but she hadn't learned much when you took her away. You know, too, Finns who have the gift and the schooling can send their souls abroad—women as well as men. Why should Seija strain after this for weary years, and at last torture herself, only to lie to me about it?"

"Folk can go mad and see things that are not there," Özur said starkly. "Or if they seek too recklessly, things can come to them, come upon them, that should have been left in the dark." His free hand drew the sign of the Hammer.

"Seija is not mad," Gunnhild avowed. "Nor has anything taken hold of her. I know."

They stood unspeaking. The wind keened, a cold stream over cheeks and brow. Three gulls rode it, watchful for any dead flesh the sea cast ashore.

"Father, I thought on this myself," Gunnhild went on. "I said she must show me. Let her send her soul forth again, this time to places I have seen but she not, that none would have told her about, farther off than her witch-sight ever went. I saw what she did, the song, the steps, the wild food, the firebrand, the sleep that was more like a swoon—I feared she was dying—What else could it be than true witchery at work?"

"What did you want to hear about?"

Gunnhild swept an arm around the arc of the water and the land beyond, westward a mile across this firth, southward a full seven miles, heights dimmed by wind-whipped mist. "Yonder." She smiled at him and made her voice warm. "Where you have taken me, Father."

He had now and then, sometimes without a brother along, when she, his one freeborn daughter, unmistakably yearned and cunningly asked. This was not in the knarr but in his boat of six oars, which he used when he went around the bays to talk business with men, or merely wanted an outing. How she loved the openness, freshness, newness! Even a squall that had threatened to capsize them was to her a wonder; never had her blood throbbed so high; she clung to a thwart and shouted for glee.

Özur tugged his beard. "Hm. And she did?"

"Yes. When she woke and—felt better—yes, she told me at length of the steeps above Whale Ness and the upright troll-stones there, and how the tide brawls over the rocks at Skerrystead, and the red-painted house on Elf Ness—oh, much, much, much, many of them things I'd forgotten, but when she began to speak of them I'd remember—" Gunnhild stopped, gasping.

Özur's eyes narrowed. "So you think she did earlier wing the whole way to Finnmörk."

Gunnhild clutched her cloak to her against the wind. "Yes."

"A hard faring."

Gunnhild nodded. "The fire. Oh, I gave her a stern trial. I don't believe she's done it anymore. She'd not scar herself worse. What woman would?"

"You tell me you're willing to."

Gunnhild shook her head till the hood fell back off it. "No, no, no. It was only that she could find no other way to unbind her soul. Her kinfolk know how."

"And you would learn."

"You've seen somewhat of it yourself, among them. You have! Why should *we* not wield it?"

Özur's look and voice went bleak. "Seid."

Gunnhild could not straightaway answer him.

"There are those among us who use that kind of witch-craft," Özur recalled to her. "Its right name is seid."

"I've heard mutterings about it," Gunnhild acknowl-edged. Her words rang: "Well, you cast runes!"

"That's different. Odin brought that lore back from the far side of death—runes for warding, helping, healing, fore-knowing. Not that I'm so skilled. But seid, howling songs, thudding drums, kettles aboil with deadly brews—it's un-manly. Unworthy. Unless for a Finn."

Gunnhild clenched her fists, letting her cloak flap as it would. "I am not a man. And I will not bring dishonor on our house. No, I'll raise us high."

Özur's mouth tightened, like his hand on the spearshaft. "You'd not lay a hex on—Helga?"

Scorn stiffened Gunnhild. "Never. That is indeed beneath me."

Özur scowled and stared past her. She saw unease upon him and went after it as a hound follows a deer.

"Would it be wrong to have your own witch, who fore-stalls storms, brings in fair winds, strikes down foes—Danes, vikings from the Westlands, robbers from inland—before they overrun us? We're so few here. Or—more than a spaewife—a seeress. One who can find what the will of the norns is. One such as Odin raised to tell the gods about the beginning and the end of the world."

What she thought of was strength, freedom, wealth, a name that would outlive her life.

Özur stood with his lips locked, a burliness looming like the barrow athwart the flying heavens, before he said, from deep in his chest: "I've thrice cast runes about you, daugh-ter mine. All I could read in them was that your weird is like none other. What it is, they did not spell."

"I'll take it on me!" Gunnhild cried headlong. She would ride it as a man rides an unbroken horse, steer it as he does a ship in a gale.

"I mislike this mightily."

She gathered her will and daring. "I shall have it, Father," she said. "If you naysay me, one night I'll take a firebrand of my own around the garth, and everything that is yours shall burn."

He did not curse or strike her. He watched her for a long while, where she stood unblinking before him as the wind tossed her long black tresses. Then he shook his head and rumbled, "I think you might. Yes, I think you might. You are a girl yet, but a she-wolf's heart is in you."

VIII

She talked him over enough that he gave thought to what terms he would set. Seija's tribe should first send him hostages. From his visits to the lands where they roamed, though the last had been years ago, he knew whom to name. He would take children of theirs. Finns were very tender of their offspring. These should be treated kindly and dwell with the settled Finns who herded his reindeer and helped in his fishing, sealing, and whaling. When Gunnhild came back to him they could go home, with gifts. If harm befell her, they would die.

When Gunnhild told Seija this, the woman's eyes widened. She sat for a while thinking. Then, most softly, she said, "No. I am only one. How many of ours does he want to keep? My tribe would disown me. I would disown myself."

"Father will be angry," Gunnhild warned.

"Let him do what he likes. He may find that some deeds bring bad luck. On the other hand, the friendship of the Saami may be worth something."

"Was yours and mine worth nothing?" Gunnhild shouted, and raged out of the hut.

Now she must wheedle Özur all over again. Further threats would be worse than useless. But surely he had not forgotten what she said that day at Ulf's barrow. He soon yielded. She guessed Helga had had a word or two about that. Her stepmother had become much less shrewish toward her of late. Belike Helga did not wish to make trouble that might get in the way of her going. Yet Gunnhild could almost hear for herself man and wife in the warm darkness of their shut-bed: "She's already sour at living here. If she does come back as a witch, what grief may we look for? Oh, she's your daughter, she'd not willingly harm *you*, but headstrong was she ever. Best you find her a husband—in the South. She hankers yonder anyway. Why not handsel it this summer, down in the Thraandlaw?" Something like that would get his back up, Gunnhild thought.

So she grinned to herself when Yngvar led a band of six off to dicker with those Finns. Her brother Eyvind went along. He was always eager for derring-do, the more so if he could brag about it afterward. They left on horseback, but homebound they mostly went on skis, leading their shaggy little long-maned horses, for snow fell early in the highlands they crossed. Meanwhile they had overnighted when they came on steadings, otherwise eaten their dried meat and hardtack and rolled up in their sleeping bags. They had had to ask where Seija's tribe was—one of Özur's Finns served as interpreter—but once they found it they were as well guested as such poor wanderers could do.

The word they brought back was that both wizards agreed to be Gunnhild's teachers for a year. If she then wished to go on with it, Özur must pay more than the handing over of a woman. They would meet Gunnhild right after the days began to wax longer than the nights, at a spot on the shore of the Streamfjord, well north of Ulfgard.

It was known to Özur and others, being indeed where he had gotten Seija. These were not Sea-Finns; they grazed their herds inland. However, their range was the nearest to that water. Some of them went there now and then to fish with hooks, stalk seal and walrus that hauled onto the strand, and trade with any outsiders who came by. They had built a house to keep folk and goods, weather being often foul and winter heaping high the snow.

Gunnhild would be with the tribe until late fall, learning

to ken the things she must use and give them names, as well as much else. Then as winter drew nigh, she and the two men would go back to the shore house. It was a wild and lonely stead, the more so when others would be forbidden to show themselves, but they must be untroubled while they schooled her in the spellcraft itself. To do it for a stranger like her was far harder than with someone who had grown up in Finnish ways. She would be safe. None of their own kind would dare come near, and Norse did not sail thereabouts in that season.

Özur grumbled that he had nothing but their word for this. Gunnhild blazed at him that they would gain nothing and lose everything by letting her suffer hurt, and if she was ready to fare, did he have less manhood than her?

It was a hard bargain for the tribe. They would be months without either of their shamans. Before then they must stock the house with all that was needful. As Seija had told Gunnhild, they gave this less for their kinswoman's sake, however sorely they missed her, than in the hope of more goodwill among the Norse than they had hitherto met with, and a friend in Gunnhild, who might sometimes speak on their behalf after she went home.

"I hate to think what goods they'll want of me to keep you beyond the first year," Özur growled. "Not that I believe you'll choose to stay. They live like dogs. But, true, they're a mare-hearted lot, who'd be afraid to lift hand against you." He brooded. "Yet—maybe—what that witchcraft of theirs could slyly do—"

"You had no fear of it when you were among them. Shall I, then?" Gunnhild answered.

And in truth the runes he cast seemed to bode well, though he could not read what it was that lay in store for her.

When she told Seija this, the Finn-woman was not overly glad. At last Seija said she too would seek knowledge. For her, that was through dreams. Long did she lie in that sleep. Afterward she would not tell Gunnhild what she learned, other than that Beings had spoken in riddles whose meanings were dark to her but that made her well-nigh wish undone the pact for her freedom.

Gunnhild first yelled that such unfaith was worthy of a cut throat, then quickly smiled, hugged the other, and murmured words of cheer. Seija owned up to having no real skill at spaedom, Gunnhild said. How did she know that her dreams were not misleading or misunderstood? Were there a risk, would not her brother have had warnings and steered clear of the whole thing?

"It is not myself I got forebodings about," Seija sighed. "Nor you, dear. Whatever doom is on Vuokko and Aimo may have blinded them; they are not almighty." Her head sank; she slumped and wiped her eyes.

"All men are born fey," Gunnhild said, "and all women too. But until the end—" She laughed. "—we can take whatever is within our grasp. This doing shall go well. Wait and see."

Seija did not try again. Whether or not it was another sign, she fell sick. At the worst, her brow was hot to the touch, her sweat rank, and she mumbled witlessly. She got over that but was long weak. At Gunnhild's behest, a trustworthy serving woman stayed in the hut to tend her. Gunnhild herself never went to sleep before she had made her way there through the murk and snow of winter, bearing good food and good words. "Ever have you been kind to me," Seija whispered more than once. Gunnhild smiled and stroked the damp hair. What a nasty trick of the gods or the trolls or whoever it was if this wretch died, she thought. An end to her soaring hopes!

The Yuletide feast kept her at work beside Helga. They hardly had time to snap at each other. Men came from widely around to be at the offering, which Özur led, and spend a merry while with him. The ladies of the house oversaw the lodging of them, the cooking and cleaning, serving and clearing; they themselves bore filled horns to those whom he would honor; for his sake Gunnhild must be blithe and well spoken to the young swains who had lately become aware of her. Surely the daughter of a great man—a jarl or a king—had less toil and more fun, she thought. Nevertheless she got her father to kill a ewe, besides the horse, for Seija's healing.

He reckoned that was worth an old one unlikely to bear more lambs. Still, the meat, stewed with leeks and thyme, was fit to set on his board. Maybe it won the help of the elves. However that was, in the month or so that followed Seija won back her strength.

But she stayed inwardly withdrawn, saying little and that only when spoken to. Her gaze seemed always to be elsewhere. After a while Gunnhild seldom called on her.

IX

The sun swung onward, higher and higher into the new year. Livestock began to bring forth young. Storm-winds hurled flights of chilly rain. Snow melted patch by patch; streamlets gurgled; mud squelped underfoot. Men spoke of plowing and seeding their meager croplands, of how much hay they might look for come summer, of harvesting the sea in earnest. Women longed to scrub the winter's grime and stenches out of their homes, dry their washing in open air, get around in the neighborhood and swap talk with wives of the same standing. Children rollicked wild whenever they had no work to do, or played the games children had played since time beyond memory. Youths and maidens turned moony. Oldsters sat outdoors on every warm day, letting it soak into their marrow.

Özur and Aalf saw to *Thorgunna*.

The older son of the house loved the sea above all else. Never did he miss a chance to go on the water, be it merely in one of the dugouts the steading kept for small tasks. As he grew up, he went with crews who cast nets beyond the fjords, then with sealers and whalers, then with his father a-trading. He quickly gained every skill there was. He hoarded whatever money he won, that he might buy a craft of his own. Already he bore the name Aalf the Shipman. Now Özur, who had too much else to do at this season, let him skipper the knarr to Streamfjord.

"Be heedful," Özur bade him. "Many of those straits are man-hungry. Listen to Skeggi." That grizzled sailor knew the way, mostly from chasing narwhal and walrus in earlier years. "But make what haste you wisely can and don't dawdle at the far end. We need the hands that go with you."

"I shall," Aalf promised. He was a big man of eighteen winters, rugged-faced, fair-haired, gray-eyed, not much like his noisy brother. As yet he was unwed, making do with thrall women and the humblest freeborn at home, whores down south; he hoped for a better match than any among his neighbors. He chuckled. "Oh, the lads are happy to have an outing like this, but if we're to miss the spring gathering, we'll lust the more to drink and swive back here."

Özur barked a laugh.

The knarr was a broad-beamed fifty-footer, painted black with red trim, gripping beasts chiseled into stemson and sternpost. Fore and aft were decks; otherwise the hull lay open. Toward each of these decks were two pairs of oar ports, eight altogether. A freighter was only rowed when needful, by men seated on their sea chests. Amidships reared the mast. Hauled aloft, its yard bore a great sail of homespun webbed with strengthening leather strips and dyed a now faded blue. This could be shortened if wind ran too high, or poled out for tacking; she answered her steering oar well. Faring in ballast as she was on this trip, she ought to make good speed for a merchantman. Homecoming would likely be slower, beating against the westerlies.

Aalf meant to stand well out to sea on that leg. Carrying his sister, he chose the sheltered waters inside the Lofoten Islands, even if that made him and his men do more rowing. For this—and their weapons—he took a bigger crew along than erstwhile, fifteen besides himself and Skeggi, tough young fishers and sea hunters. It was a boisterous gang who boarded.

The day sparkled when they caught an ebb tide and rode it from the Saltfjord. Gunnhild stood at the prow, clutching the forestay to steady herself. Gladness sang in her.

When they reached the sea and turned north, land, still

snow-speckled but brightening with growth, fell away on the left. Starboard it sheered against heaven. Sunlight shimmered and glittered on gray-green whitecaps. They leaped in foam where they struck the skerries and holms strewn widely about. They rushed and whooshed around the ship, which rocked, surged, plunged forward. Timbers creaked; wind whistled past rigging; Gunnhild felt a throb in the stay and beneath her feet. The air blew cold, with a little sting of salt. Clouds scudded. Cormorants bobbed on the waves or flapped blackly aloft. Gulls soared and dipped. When any swept near, she heard the mewing as if it cried to her in a tongue she might someday understand.

"Fair weather and a following wind," said Aalf, who had taken the lookout's post beside her. "We could ask for no better." He glanced down at Seija. "Are her witch-kin helping her come to them? Then she's paying."

The Finn-woman sat huddled below, knees drawn to chin. She shivered under a shaggy cloak Gunnhild had lent her. Already she had puked over the side. "I hope she'll soon get her sea legs," Gunnhild said, "or at least not reach Streamfjord too sallow and wasted."

"Whereas you're born to this, same as me." Aalf cupped his chin and thought. "But it would not be well for a woman to spend most of her life on ships."

Wontedly, the belowdecks were for gear and cargo best not stowed in the open. Now the forepeak had been left for Gunnhild and Seija, with a sailcloth strung across. Cramped though it was, it kept their things fairly dry and let them change clothes or use pot and hayballs unseen by the men. Seija cleaned the pot after each use. Once or twice a man started to mock at the sight, but a friend soon hushed him. Who knew what even a half-witch could lay on a fellow? However, it was Gunnhild from whose eyes they tried to shield their own overside doings.

Toward evening they drew near a big island, lowered sail, and rowed into a wick that Skeggi remembered. Here they could anchor close in, put out a gangplank, and go ashore. Some bore firewood, seeing none worth cutting, and an iron box in which coals were kept alive. They boiled salt meat and herbs in a kettle, to eat with flatbread taken from a chest. Others set up a knockdown bed brought along for Gunnhild and raised a leather tent over it. She would sleep on sheepskins and feather pillow, wool blankets above. Seija got a hide and a sack on the ground next to her. Two armed men were to keep watch during the night. The rest would lie aboard ship. A line strung from stem to stern gave backbone to awnings fore and aft of the mast.

Meanwhile they ate a meal scooped into wooden bowls. Aalf broached a firkin of ale; horns passed hand to hand. For Gunnhild he had a cup. She thought it wise to offer Seija a taste, where the Finn-woman crouched at the rim of firelight. Flames crackled, sparked, reddened the swirling, sweet-smelling smoke. Teeth, eyeballs, metal cast flickers back from shadow. Voices rolled slowly or burst into sudden laughter. It was man-talk, mostly everyday stuff and loutish banter, though when Aalf told something from his voyages his crew stilled and hearkened. Gunnhild choked down the wish to take part. What had she to say, a girl who had never before been this far from home? But when queens spoke, oh, then men gave heed!

The night was wondrously clear. As the crew yawned and trudged off, Gunnhild stepped aside from the dying fire and gazed upward. Stars and stars and stars crowded the dark, more than she knew of, so that Thor's Wain and Freyja's Spindle were almost lost among them. The Winterway stretched like a frosty river above shouldering heights and glimmering water. What might this hugeness know of gods, worlds, men, and their dooms?

The Lodestar gleamed and beckoned above a crest. Beyond waited Finnmörk. Gunnhild spent the night slipping in and out of eldritch dreams.

Men rose at dawn, chewed cold food, and were off. Skeggi had well reckoned the tides. *Thorgunna* walked on oars from the wick and caught the morning breeze outside. She heeled in waves that sunrise silvered and ran with a bone in her teeth.

Thus the days and nights passed. Aside from a few rainshowers, weather and wind stayed uncannily fair. Seija got over the worst of her sickness. Sometimes, when it was safe, Aalf let Gunnhild take the helm for a short spell. Meaningless though she knew this was, to have the steering in her grip made blood tingle.

Mountains loomed skyward, snow on their stony heads, flanks begrown with wilderness where a waterfall did not tumble down a cliff, islands matching mainland. *Thorgunna* threaded the waters between. Awe of the loftiness to starboard and larboard quieted men. When a cloud passed above, it seemed as if those heights were toppling on them. They spied teeming life, seafowl, seals a-bask on rocks, whales like reefs afloat, cod and halibut they took on lines they trailed aft, bears and even elk that had come down to shore. Cries reached them from above, sometimes a bellow or a howl from inland. Of man they saw little—campfire smoke, huts for fishers and hunters later in the year, the bleached wreckage of a ship. Few Norse made their homes so far north, and no Finns showed themselves. This was not the time or place either for trade or for paying scot, and who knew what a craftful of strangers wanted?

They did at Streamfjord.

Soon after the knarr turned in there, it was sail down, oars out, and Skeggi at the tiller. The span between Whale Island to larboard and a jut of mainland to starboard was broad enough, but now *Thorgunna* hugged the latter while her crew peered after the landmarks. Shoals were many and riptides tugged. The land grew flatter, thickly wooded. Then a lookout shouted, men hurrahed, Skeggi put the helm over, and the sweating rowers gusted their own thanks.

A stream flowed down to a strand against which fairly mild waves lapped. As the sailors dropped anchor, a half-score men ran from the woods. Seija reached forth her arms, called aloud, and burst into tears. Only Gunnhild, and maybe Özur, had ever before seen her weep.

The tide being high and Aalf not wholly trustful, he deemed it best not to ground but to lie where they were and wade ashore. He jumped out first, caught Gunnhild when she followed, and bore her to land. She thought this made her look helpless, but annoyance whirled away when she saw, close up, those who met her.

Like most of their kind, they were short and stocky, with wide faces, saddle noses, big eyes that slanted a little. Under the weathering and smoke-smudges their skins were light, and the hair and sparse whiskers of some were even yellow. Their clothes were leather and fur, cloth of Norse weave mingled in. Aside from long knives, which they kept sheathed, they were unarmed. The sailors lowered their spears and axes.

Two Finn-men trod ahead of the rest. Seija sped to one of them. He held her close and crooned. She laid her head at his breast and sobbed. He was of about thirty winters, strongly built, black-locked, his underslung jaw nearly beardless. The man beside him was the tallest of the band, somewhat older, lean, his eyes blue and bleak. He carried a wand made from a deer's legbone.

"Gunnhild," said Aalf, "you can talk with them, no? The thrall woman's blubbering too hard."

His sister swallowed. "Greeting," she began, hearing her awkwardness with the tongue. "I am she whom you awaited." Her heart thuttered.

Seija stepped aside. Her voice was uneven, her cheeks wet, but she spoke clearly, in Norse. "Here is my brother Vuokko," she said, and, waving at the other, "here my kinsman Aimo. They have come as plighted, and everything is ready."

"Tell them," Aalf ordered, "that we will go see the winter house. Tell them, too, that we will call for this maiden at this same spot a year hence. If she has suffered any harm whatsoever, woe betide your whole tribe."

It flitted through Gunnhild that King Harald might not like that. They paid him their share of hides, pelts, walrus ropes, and ivory.

"They, they cannot help it if—she falls sick or—or something," Seija stammered.

"They are wizards, are they not? Let them see to her well-being. And now you are home again," Aalf ended scornfully.

X

Long before this, one Ulf, son of Bjalfi, dwelt in Sygnafylki in Norway, not far from the Sognefjord. He was rich, owned broad acres, and claimed the rank of lendman, just below a jarl's. In his youth he had gone on viking raids with his friend Kaari, who was a berserker, and later he wed Kaari's daughter Salbjorg. On his mother's side he was kin to the famous warrior Ketil Salmon, son of Hallbjörn Half-troll. Ulf was a hard worker and a man of wise redes, but apt to grow sleepy in the evenings; many men believed that now and then his soul roamed after dark as a wolf. Hence he bore the nickname Kveldulf, Dusk-wolf. He and Salbjorg had two sons, Thorolf and Grim. There was strange blood in that family.

Yet Thorolf grew up handsome, cheerful, and open-handed. When he had reached twenty winters, his father gave him a longship. Thereafter he was often in viking, bringing home much wealth. Mostly this came from the sale of captives taken along the southern Baltic shores, but some was loot from across the North Sea.

Meanwhile King Harald of Vikin warred about until he had brought all Norway under himself. After Sogn and Sygnafylki fell to him, Thorolf entered his service and wrought mightily. Wounded in the last battle at Hafrsfjord, Kveldulf's son got well and made a marriage that brought him great holdings. High in the king's favor, he went yearly north to bring in the Finnish scot.

But he also gained foes. These slandered him to Harald Fairhair, over and over, until the king no longer trusted him. Things went swiftly from bad to worse. Men were slain. At last Harald took a host to ring in a farmhouse where Thorolf and his followers were, on the eve of going from Norway forever. When Thorolf would not yield, they set it afire. Those inside broke out, weapons in hand, to die fighting. Thorolf got as far as the shieldbearers around the king.

Harald Fairhair gave his hacked, pierced body the death-stroke.

Grim tried to get wergild for his brother. Nothing came of it. Instead, Harald laid hand on everything that had been Thorolf's. Now Grim and his father would no longer stay, but go to Iceland.

First they overran and killed a shipful of King Harald's men. In this battle Kveldulf went berserk. None could stand against him; he cut them down and raged onward. When such a fit had passed, the man was always weak for a while. Although he skippered skillfully the craft they had taken, old Kveldulf fell sick and died at sea. As he had wished, his crew made a coffin for him and set it adrift.

It washed ashore at Borgarfjord on the west side. Grim took land there, with meadows, marshes, and woods as well as plenty of fish and seal in the waters, plenty of seafowl's eggs on the rocks. He built a farm he called Borg and became one of the foremost men in Iceland.

He was big but otherwise unlike his fallen brother, being dark, ugly, and moody. Losing his hair early, he got the nickname Skallagrim, Bald Grim. His wife was Bera, daughter of a lendman in Sygnafylki. Most of their children died young. Four lived. The first son who did they named Thorolf. Then they had two girls, Saeunn and Thorunn, and last another son, Egil. Thorolf took after his namesake uncle, Egil after their father.

In Sogn in Norway was a young man, Björn, son of the hersir Brynjolf. Guesting in Sygnafylki, he met a maiden, Thora Orfrey-Sleeve, whom he wanted to wed. Her brother, the hersir Thorir Hroaldsson, who had the ward of her, said no. Björn came back by sea and stole her away. Though she was willing enough, this meant trouble. In spring he got a knarr from his father and set sail for Dublin, among whose Norse he ought to find haven. A storm drove him to Shetland. There he wedded Thora. Word came that King Harald had outlawed him, so next spring he and his bride left the broch that had sheltered them and steered for Iceland. Skallagrim took him in. He and Thorolf became fast friends.

Nonetheless he hoped for peace with Thora's kin. Word went back and forth over the sea. It helped that Skallagrim was Thorir's foster brother. Terms of settlement were reached. Björn and Thora returned to Norway. Thorolf, who felt restless at home, went along. Aasgerd, the little daughter of Björn and Thora, stayed behind at Borg, fostered by Skallagrim and Bera.

Having mended his fences, Björn settled down in his father's household. Thorolf stayed there too, and welcome he was. In spring he and Björn outfitted a ship, gathered a crew, and fared in viking to the Baltic. They brought back a good haul. Then they went off to call on Thorir Hroaldsson.

Eirik, King Harald's most beloved son, arrived soon after. Thorir had been his foster father, whom he saw whenever he could.

Thorolf and Björn had come there in a karfi belonging to the former. This was like a small longship, with thirteen oars to a side and bearing a crew of about thirty. She was a sweet and nimble craft, brightly painted. Björn marked how often Eirik stood looking at her where she lay docked. He advised Thorolf to give her to the atheling. Thorolf did, and Eirik rewarded him with friendship.

King Harald's anger at the house of Kveldulf had never lessened. He would not meet with Thorolf. However, for Eirik's sake Harald gave the man peace.

Thorolf stayed on in Norway for some years. At first he and Björn spent their summers in viking, their winters with either Brynjolf or Thorir.

But as Harald grew old and his strength waned, he turned the steering of the kingdom more and more over to Eirik, beginning with lordship over Haalogaland, North Moerr, and Raumsdalr. Eirik raised a strong household troop of his own. There had already been deadly fights between sons of Harald, and Eirik was thinking ahead. Thorolf Skallagrimsson joined this band and soon rose high in it. Now, while he was still mostly off in viking during the summer, he was otherwise with Eirik.

But one springtime Eirik deemed that Bjarmaland on the

White Sea must have healed enough to be worth a new faring. Besides, he had gotten wind of happenings there which he misliked. Thorolf kept the prow of the lead ship, and bore Eirik's banner when they fought—for fight they did, and hard it was.

XI

Endlessly wheeling through summer, the sun cast light that lost itself in boughs overhead and spattered on woodland mold. Leaves glowed golden with it. White birch and gray rowan lifted slim above thick undergrowth. Stands of pine and fir gloomed amidst the shades. Air lay cool and still, full of wet smells.

Vuokko halted on the game trail, raised a hand, and bent over. Gunnhild stopped behind him. She glanced back at Aimo. The other shaman's mouth drew tight.

They three had been long out, having left the camp shortly after it woke. Gunnhild felt how much she had walked, or scrambled through brush or squelped across bogs. True, this was better than the daily round of a Finn-woman, which she had to share. But she loathed her man-like breeks and coat even more than the garb given her for everyday use. Needful though they were right now, they smacked of the twistedness that the Norse muttered went with seid.

Mosquitoes whined in smoky clouds. At least the louse-hat she had rubbed on her skin kept them off. The trick had never worked as well at home as it did here. When he handed the leaves to her, Vuokko told her he had sung over them.

Louse-hat also yielded a poison, like wolfsbane. The thought flitted through her, how queer it was that the same thing could both help and harm, give health or death. She was learning uncanniness.

Vuokko pointed to the ground. "See," he bade her. "A fox has passed by." She easily understood him, having fast strengthened her grasp of the Finnish tongue. He showed her the dim spoor she would otherwise have overlooked. "You must become wise in the ways of beasts as well as plants—all the ways of earth, water, weather. That's how you gain power over them."

"But the girl will have no use for mere stalker's skills," said Aimo.

Vuokko straightened. "The world is one," he answered coldly.

"As we both well know, or you should know. Yet who shall ever understand the whole of it? And why should I call a prey to me when a trap or a weir can take it?"

"I was only showing—Let me do something stronger, then." Vuokko chopped an arm downward. "Hold still, you two. Watch yonder."

A squirrel was darting around the branches of a nearby fir, in and out of sight, a flickery red flame. Vuokko whistled. The squirrel stopped in surprise. The man stared straight at it. The squirrel stayed where it was, as if frozen. Gunnhild gasped.

"If you make the holy craft into a boast, I had better treat it more fittingly, lest it turn on us," said Aimo. "Loose that animal."

Vuokko scowled but drew a sign. The squirrel chirred and scampered wildly around. Vuokko looked at Gunnhild. "That was not for fun or brag," he said almost warmly. "I am aware of how you weary of your life in the tribe. You should see it's not for nothing."

Aimo unslung a short bow from his shoulder and took an arrow from his quiver. He whispered to it before he nocked it and drew the string. Vuokko's eyes stayed locked on Gunnhild. The mosquitoes shrilled. Somewhere a wild goose honked.

The bow twanged. The squirrel tumbled from mid-leap. A gout of blood followed like the tail of a shooting star.

Aimo trod over to pluck it from the bush into which it had fallen. Holding the torn little thing in his left hand, he freed the arrow with his right. "I never saw marksmanship like that!" Gunnhild cried in her amazement.

Aimo laughed. "It is the arrow. See." His reddened forefinger traced marks cut into the shaft. "I made it so, and sang over it. Now it will strike whatever I tell it to." He spoke to the carcass. "I am sorry, brother mine. This was done in aid of teaching the lore that holds the world together. May your wraith frolic gladly." He laid it down and made a sign over it.

"Yes, this too shall you learn, girl," said Vuokko, "though it's no great thing."

Gunnhild thought it would not be small if the mark were a man. Her flesh prickled as if with frost.

"Oh, I can catch prey by myself," said Aimo. "Come winter, on ski I overtake anything that runs."

"I think you will not overtake me," Vuokko growled.

This was not the first time a quarrel between them had threatened. "You are surely both mighty hunters," Gunnhild put hastily in. "But I am—a woman. I shall have to make my way with the Knowledge alone." She drew breath. The chill in her flared. "Such as sending my soul abroad?"

"That too you shall, if you are able," Vuokko promised.

"Not before you have the deep wisdom," Aimo warned. "And then we shall go forward very warily. It is a dangerous doing. I will not have you set at risk."

Gunnhild thought of wandering lost forever beyond the world of men. She kept the inward shudder hidden. Never would she seem unsure or afraid before these two.

"No, no, no," Vuokko agreed. "Now come; let us go on as we meant to."

The rest of that walk was given over to plants, mostly mushrooms and toadstools. The shamans wanted her to spy every kind they passed, however hidden it was in the brush, and tell them all its names and all its strengths and weaknesses. Whenever she went wrong, they made her say it over until she had it right. She was learning of deadly kinds, and kinds that brought about drunkenness, and kinds that raised dreams wherein one saw what no eye ever could, and kinds that were good to eat—but when those rotted, they too brewed poisons. Nearing the camp, she thanked both the wizards. They smiled. The anger in them had died down somewhat.

It would rise afresh, she feared.

Along the trail stood a tall, crooked boulder, overgrown with lichen. The bones of birds and lemmings lay scattered beneath it. The men stopped, bowed, fluttered their hands, and chanted words Gunnhild could not follow. She waited quietly aside, not knowing what, if anything, an outland woman ought to do.

Indeed, she knew little about the gods here. She had merely witnessed a few short rites, hardly more than luck-charms. Her father had said he believed the Finns acknowledged Thor under another name. If so, they did not give him the slaughterings of horse and kine that Norsemen did. Was this because they were too poor, or because they found their elves and whatnot were enough? They must feel no need of warlike help, for they seldom attacked each other.

Vuokko and Aimo had told her she would hear about the Beings during the winter. Within herself she wondered what that would be worth. The Finnish gods seemed as mild as the Finns themselves. Not even their wizards kept the tribes from being made booty of. Well, powers were of slight use to anyone who lacked the will to wield them against human foes, and warriors to back him up.

Or her, she thought.

She touched her breasts, as if to find the silver hammer that hung between them. In her quarters, among the few things she had been able to bring along from the ship, lay a small soapstone image of Frey; when she secretly took him forth and rubbed his upstanding yard, a thrill as of mightiness went through her. Thus did she call on sky and earth to be her warders, far though she had fared. Özur had also plighted a great thank-offering if she returned safely.

But otherwise she had only her own strength.

Having paid the rock its due, the men took her on into camp. There they said they would meet with her again in a few sleeps. Meanwhile, between worldly tasks she must go over everything she had learned until she had it by heart. She longed to throw a haughty answer into their teeth—she, daughter of a hersir, granddaughter of a jarl—but then they might ask someone to take her straight home. However, if they reckoned that tending fires, plucking feathers, gathering berries, and the dreary rest of it would meeken her, their witch-sight did not reach inside anybody's head!

She went on to her lodging. This camp was the biggest of those among which the tribe made their rounds, for here the reindeer were brought after midsummer from the woods and fens where they had ranged. Men and boys ran alongside a herd, steering it toward a pen of untrimmed posts. At this time of year, the beasts stayed close together for shielding against mosquitoes, and would follow any that was trained to lead them. Nevertheless they were half wild, apt to bolt. A few were kept to bear burdens and draw sleds in winter; the rest gave milk, meat, hide, gut, antler, bone.

Huts huddled around a clearing and off under the trees. Beside each was a njalla, a wooden shed atop a hewn-off trunk, which kept food and other goods beyond reach of thievish animals. A notched log leaned against it, a kind of ladder. Gunnhild had seen the like by Norse yeomen's houses, though there it oftenest rested on four stout tree boles, dug up and standing on their spread roots.

She also kenned the turf dwellings. Seija had had one at Ulfgard. Here, though, some were bigger and better, their walls and roofs made of logs chinked with clay and moss. Smoke curled out of them. Women and girls squatted in front, at toil that needed room and bright light. They chattered, shouted to and fro, broke into trills of laughter. The merriment baffled Gunnhild. Maybe their life was a bit less bad than the lot of the Norse lowly, a bit more free, but how hard and dull it was. How helpless.

She neared the house where she guested. Belonging to Seija's family, it was not quite such a hovel as most. The woman saw her, leaped up from the leather she was stitching to make a garment, and sped to meet her.

"Oh, Gunnhild!" she cried. Happiness shone through the soot and grease on her face. She caught the maiden's two hands in her own. "Wonderful tidings! I am to be wedded! Keino, son of—"

Gunnhild gave scant heed to the word-stream. It churned in her that she was about to lose the nearest thing to a friend that she had here. Not that Seija was like a sister—more like a dog or cat, whose nearness lent some cheer, some memory of home. Henceforth Gunnhild would have nothing to help her forget how the gaze of the wizards again and again slunk toward her.

"May all go well with you," she mumbled. And now Seija is out of the story.

XII

Where the River Dvina flowed broad and slow through a stretch of meadowland amidst marshy woods, men fought. Rygi Helm-Splitter had fewer well-armed and skillful warriors—Norse, Danes, Swedes, Russians—than did Eirik Haraldsson; but with him were a great band of Karelians, bowmen, spearmen, slingmen. The sheer weight of them should have overwhelmed the atheling.

When he saw them coming upon him, Eirik laughed. "Do they think we'll ship straightaway for home?" he said.

"Besides, *I* think if we did, they'd follow us along both shores, shooting us like swine driven down a dell," answered Thorolf Skallagrimsson. "Yon Rygi can't want us coming back with more strength to grub him out."

Eirik nodded. "A faithless man. He never told me outright to begone from his little jarldom. No, he stalled about till suddenly he could spring this on us. He may or may not live to be sorry. We'll take our stand on the riverside, where they can't get at us from behind, and see what happens."

Rygi's vikings shocked first against the shields. Behind him pressed and howled his wild, skin-clad allies. Shafts and stones sleeted from the flanks. Swords rang; axes thundered. Among the reeds, brown water began to redden.

High flew Eirik's banner in Thorolf's left hand. A friend warded him on that side. The blade in his right leaped. It caught a stroke. The foeman's weapon wobbled. Thorolf twisted slightly and hunched his shoulders. The next blow grated off his ring-mail. Lynx-fast, he struck beneath the other byrnie, into a leg. He felt bone give way. The stranger groaned, staggered, and sank to his good knee. Thorolf split his neck. He fell in a heap. Stench roiled. Gray though the sky was, blood shone fire-bright.

Nearby, Eirik warred as mightily. So did every man of his handpicked crews. The onslaught lurched back. Its forward rank stumbled against the Karelians behind and broke up in pushing and shoving. "Now, at them!" Eirik yelled. He put the horn slung at his side to his lips and blew. The call hooted over all battle noise. Thorolf forged ahead, step by thrusting step. The banner went above him, rippling from the cross-arm, an eagle black on amber.

Well-drilled, the crewmen formed a wedge that clove through the pack. Smiting right and left, they moved in on another standard. A huge man with a shaggy beard met them, bellowing like a bull elk. His ax crashed through a Norse shield, down to the wrist behind it. Then a sword slashed across his forearm. Blood spurted. He tried to hew again, but Eirik gave him his death-blow. Thorolf killed the man who bore his flag and cast it down.

When Rygi thus died, his host broke. Milling, wailing, they were sheep for the slaughter until they got loose and ran every which way over the meadow. Thereafter the Norse had room to throw spears and shoot arrows. The vikings who were left put up a harder fight, but they stood scattered in twos and threes. Knot by knot, as Eirik ordered, his men surrounded and made an end of them.

"No need to chase the rest," he said. "We'll find them later."

He grinned as he looked across the field. The dead sprawled, ugly as the newly slain always are; the badly wounded moaned, yammered, and threshed about, more and more weakly. His men searched among them for their hurt or fallen shipmates and took care of these. They seldom bothered to cut the throat of a foe, unless it seemed he might creep away. Some ravens already perched on lichs, picked eyes out, and tore at flesh. There would soon be many.

Beyond, Eirik's longships nestled against the shore. The

one that had belonged to Rygi lay farther on, moored with two sailless river freighters at a rough-built wharf. Above this loomed his stronghold. The hall roof showed over the stockade. Rygi and his gang had done well in the years since they took sword-land here. On horseback where they could not row, they raided, had scot from the tribes, got fighters to join with them. These bleak reaches held more wealth than one might think, hides, pelts, thralls, and also gold from Kola. Rygi sent his traders to the Swedish marts and even Aldeigjuborg on Lake Ladoga. It was small wonder that when Eirik Haraldsson, to whom word of this had drifted, came to learn what was going on, Rygi forbade him to roam freely about. That was Rygi's first mistake. Meanwhile he secretly sent for his Karelians, and with them attacked the Norse. That was his second and last mistake.

"We'll have work aplenty, bringing this country to heel," Eirik said.

"What?" Thorolf boggled. "We can hardly make your father or you king of it, as few as we are and as far off as it is."

"No, no. But we'll scour widely, avenging our losses and taking a rich booty. Yes, drive it well into the heads of these folk that never again shall they make trouble for ours. Traders will be thankful, and—they will pay the kingly house a share.".

Thorolf frowned. "That work would go too slowly. Well before it was done, we'd find ourselves frozen in."

Eirik nodded. "I know. We'll send the ships back to the seashore, with a guard, to wait for us—if we do decide to winter." He laughed. "First let's see if Rygi has left us enough horses, sleds, food, firewood, and ale. Come."

Thorolf nodded and went beside him toward the stockade.

Night in the late Bjarmaland summer was short and wan. Day still lighted the hall, however dimly, when Eirik and his men sat back fed, drank from horns filled by women who were now theirs, and hearkened to his skald Dag Audunarson. While this youth had been in the battle, at Eirik's behest he stayed somewhat back, that he might more likely

live to make a poem about it. Every man dies; fame does
not. Dag trod forth before the high seat and began:

> "Give to me your silence.
> Suttung's mead I'm pouring
> to tell how Eirik bloodied
> the banks of River Dvina.
> Hasty on the swan's road,
> sea horses bore him thither.
> Soon the moons of bulwarks
> beckoned to valkyries.—"

The staves were no more than middling good. Few of
their kennings were new or very striking. Nonetheless, Eirik
was in the best of moods. When Dag was through, he drew
a golden ring off his arm, broke it, and gave half to the
skald. A king should ever be openhanded.

XIII

Winter pressed inward, shadows leaping as light wavered, darknesses crouching at either end of the
house. Smoke off a peat fire glimmered ruddy, swirled
around a besooted kettle hung low above, and drifted toward the hole overhead. The room was not cold, but the
reek cut sharply at nose and eyes. Blubber in a few stone
lamps stank.

Aimo hunkered over a drum. The uneasy glow webbed
his face with murk. The drum thuttered to a small hammer
in his hand. His song rose and fell, eerie to hear. Charms
a-dangle round the drumhead—bones, claws, teeth, tufts of
wool—swayed with the shifting beat. Standing beside
Vuokko, Gunnhild could barely make out the signs painted
on the white reindeer skin. An arpa, a carved wooden rod,
skittered across them. Aimo was foreseeing.

The sounds ended. He leaned forward to peer at the rod,
how it lay, what this told. Gunnhild felt her heart slugging.

Aimo rose. "It bodes ill," he said starkly.

Vuokko glanced at Gunnhild, smiled, and answered, "Oh, now. Mishap need be no worse than something bothersome. Maybe we'll fail to hold off a storm, which keeps us indoors for a while." He smiled. "I would not call that so bad."

"I heed warnings when they come," Aimo said. "You are less wise, it seems."

"But this was no strong spell. We were only showing Gunnhild such use of the drum as anyone can make. And they often do," he added to her, "and sometimes get it wrong. I wonder whether you did," he went on to Aimo, "unless you are fearful. I do not think this is worth doing over with my full powers. The girl is not ready to understand what happens then."

She ran her tongue over lips gone dry. "Do you send your soul forth?" she whispered.

"You are truly eager to witness that, are you not?" Vuokko said, still cheerful.

Aimo shook his head. "My kinsman speaks like a fool," he snapped. "To go out among the Mighty Ones, unclad even in flesh, is a hard and dangerous thing."

"So I have told you already, as well you remember," Vuokko said to Gunnhild. "You'll learn somewhat of it later, but you would need years of work, forgoing, and, yes, suffering before you could do it more than fleetingly."

"Teach me what you can, then, in what time is left. I beg you," Gunnhild wrung from an unwilling throat.

Aimo's voice warmed. "That may be not so little. You have the gift inborn to become a great shaman. How I wish you would stay and learn onward."

Vuokko turned to her. It burst from him: "Yes, spend those years, Gunnhild! I feel how much lies sleeping in you. Let me waken it!"

More and more had she begun to await this. Nevertheless the words struck like a fist. Hers were the first that flew into her mouth. "No, I, I cannot forsake my kin—"

"Can you not? Wed me, and I'll make you a queen of the Otherworld."

"What?" shouted Aimo. "You would keep Gunnhild—

Gunnhild—in your wretched huts with you?" He curbed himself. "Some wild ghost has laid hold of my kinsman," he said to her. "I understand your needs, your wants. I can give you might in this world; kings shall heed you; wealth shall be yours beyond reckoning."

Anger sprang high in her. Too long had she been humble. "Then why do you live like this?"

At once she was sorry. Though they surely dared lay no hand on her, they could chop her schooling off, leave her emptily waiting for her ship. Or what bad luck could they brew, once out of her sight?

It was very welcome when Aimo said more calmly, "We have our own kin, who have their own ways. Never could we find a home among yours. But—take me, and I will give you—"

"Give you an oldster's pawings, and his brats," Vuokko fleered. "You shall have better from me, Gunnhild."

The wizards glared at one another.

"No, I will raise a hall for you, and fill it with fine things," Aimo said.

"With me," Vuokko said, "you shall have no more toil, but the elves at your beck."

Gunnhild wondered how much they lied. But she saw there was nothing to fear, not yet, if she handled this rightly; and she saw how, a knowledge she had not fully known was hers.

A few tears ran out when she bade them. She blinked, smiled, and told them softly, unsteadily, "You awe me. I am bewildered. You are both so dear to me. And what would my father think? What would he do? Oh, let us go on as before; strengthen me with your wisdom; lead me to insight that can help me. At the least, we must wait till my brother comes back and I can talk to him. Must we not?"

The wizards stood unspeaking. Flames flickered.

"Yes, that seems best," said Aimo at length.

"And don't quarrel," Gunnhild pleaded. "It tears my heart. I can't bear to see kinship broken because of me."

After more stillness, Vuokko said, "We should behave

as behooves men like us, Aimo. I never wanted to do otherwise."

"Nor I," said his copemate. "I have always held that a man must closely heed his words."

Gunnhild followed through, as a rower does his stroke. "And I, I'd not willingly weep or be weak in your nearness. I hope to stay worthy of you. But can I be by myself for a while? I'm shaken, I've need to gather my thoughts, and—oh—" Fresh tears glistened on her lashes.

"M-m, yes, we could go hunting," Vuokko said. "The weather's clear."

"We are short of fresh meat," agreed Aimo.

"And you are both such wonderful hunters," Gunnhild crooned.

Inwardly she shivered. She had uttered bald truth. Even when clouded, the dayless winter laid no blindness on these twain, and to them the stars were like sparks off the sun. Their skis bore them wind-swift over open snowfields, and like the wind did they weave their way among trees. They knew from afar where prey would be when they got there. Their arrows never missed.

Yes, they made their blunders, being men, but at the core they were terrible men. She had yet to find out the reach of their powers.

Having decided, they were quick to dress for outdoors, take their gear, and go. The entryway was three feet high and ten long, to keep heat inside. Gunnhild felt a short breath of chill and caught a glimpse of whiteness. For a heartbeat or two she wished she were going too. Whenever she was able to leave for more than a dash to the backhouse she felt unbound, the keen air a kiss all over her face.

Well, anyhow, for now she was alone. "Alone!" she rejoiced aloud.

Freed from the wizards, her look danced about. Not that there was much to see. The house was of the kind that Finns called a gamma, sod, thirty feet long and half as wide, the ends bowed. Elsewhere it would have sheltered a whole family and some livestock. Here it was meant for those bands who came down to the fjord. The outside walls rose barely five feet above ground, but inside it was dug out to make headroom for a tall Norseman. On an earthen bench lay the skins that were the men's bedding. A box held their garb, another box their witchy tools and stuffs. Wooden tubs stood by bowls, trenchers, drinking horns, bone spoons and cookware, three low stools.

The poorness of it all closed in on Gunnhild. She struck fist against palm. How slowly everything inched forward! Drumbeat, song, mushrooms, even painstaking work to cut signs in wood, those could send her beyond herself—but how seldom! When would she have gained more skills than any backwoods hexwife owned? Meanwhile, aside from what they told of spellcraft, the wizards' talk was as drab as their lives.

Gunnhild sighed. She had better use this little span of hers.

Reindeer skins, sewn together, hung at the north end of the gamma, closing off a room. She took a lamp and slipped around the curtain. Behind it were her bed, fetched from the ship, and two chests filled with her things. They took up most of the clay floor.

She undressed, found a clean rag, and went back to the kettle. With its warm water she washed herself. That was the best she could do. Would the steamful bathhouse at home ever get the last grime and stench off?

Sometime soon she must again scrub her cloths, if not her clothes, a thrall woman's task. It was bad enough, those men's eyes always seeking her, slyly ogling, without their noses snuffing her monthly blood. Or did they anyway?

This was how the lowly everywhere lived.

XIV

Spring came slowly and stormily to Bjarmaland. Folk were often weatherbound for days on end. When Thorolf Skallagrimsson left the stronghold after one such spell, he wanted to stir his legs and breathe clean air as much as to see how things looked by now. His leman went beside him.

Wind blustered cold and wet. It shook leafless birch boughs and rustled the junipers. Snow still decked the ground, but most had melted on top and then frozen, melted and frozen, till it lay in shapeless heaps gray with dust. It was melting anew, potholes and puddles everywhere, a few skulls and bones of Rygi's troop bared to sight. Boulders nearby outlined the shape of a ship, beneath which rested Eirik's fallen. Clouds scudded. A flock of crows passed by, harshly calling.

Man and woman halted at the riverbank. Ice stretched unbroken to the other side, north and south to the worldrim. Thorolf smiled. "Good," he said. "Nearly all the snow's off, but we keep a road for horses, wains—" He laughed. "—and skates."

Stricken, she stared up his great height to the strong, blunt face, neatly trimmed golden beard, blue eyes that years of sea-glare had edged with crinkles. "You go soon?" Her voice trembled. She was a Karelian, young, short, buxom, her hair more fair than his. He had not taken her from the stock of women kept here, but from a camp he found later while ranging around. Because she was comely and he hoped she'd warm to him, he forbade his followers to kill anybody or loot so much that her tribe would starve. During the months afterward she had picked up some Norse and he a useful bit of her speech.

He nodded. "In a few days. You've seen how my lord Eirik champs and stamps to be off."

"But your ships?"

"They're where the river meets the sea." His mood kindly, though he wasn't sure if she'd understand, he made it clear. "They've been drawn ashore, and the ice may well linger a ways beyond, but we can skid them to the water." They were warcraft, light and lithe, built for such handling. Rygi's freighters had long since become firewood.

She touched the arm beneath his cloak. "Ice—ice floes, you say?—grind, crush."

Thorolf shrugged. "Eirik's a breakneck fellow, true. But

thus far the gods have been with him, and we should have the wit to steer shy of things that merely float." He gazed westward before he murmured, "I'm eager too."

She swallowed. "You come back?"

"Maybe." He didn't think so. The yearning that waxed in him was for Borg, his father's Icelandic homestead.

Her hand fluttered over her swelling belly. "Your child."

"Belike." Thorolf squeezed her shoulder and smiled down at her. "Fear not. We won't torch the buildings when we leave. You and the others can stay. Men will quickly learn we've gone. They'll swarm here. I daresay one will take you to him. If you bear a boy, and he becomes a wander-minded youth and can speak Norse, send him to me. If I'm alive."

Her fists clenched. "How I know?"

"Word may find you. Wait."

Never before had he heard her ply his tongue so well. "Yes, a woman must needs be good at waiting." She clamped her lips together and looked away, across the dying snow.

XV

Sunlight from the east seeped through overcast and woods. Trees stood darkling, as if their shadows had drained upward into them. Old snow lay in patches on the sodden mold. Air hung still but raw.

Gunnhild had gone outside the gamma. Of course the Finns did also. Their faces were haggard and hollow-eyed within the unkempt, unwashed hair, for these nights they slept poorly. Better rested, she strove to keep her bowstring tautness hidden.

"We have no need to hunt," Aimo said. "And this is the lean season."

"But I would so like some fresh meat," she wheedled. "Or even a few fish?"

At once Vuokko laughed. "Then we will go!"

"Go by yourself," Aimo told him.

Vuokko lost his bit of mirth. "No," he rasped. "You shall come too, or I stay."

Both glowered. By now neither would leave the other alone with Gunnhild.

She was using that. Through the penned-in winter months, stiff words had often passed between the wizards, but none unforgivable. Outright wrath or hatred was not the Finnish way. Yet if these two waxed angry enough, what might they let loose?

"Oh, my teachers, my beloved masters," she begged. Bitterness that she must speak like this crowded out uneasiness.

Vuokko's glance sprang from Aimo to her. "Beloved?" His voice stumbled. "Then why will you forsake me?"

Aimo followed on his heels. "Abide, Gunnhild. You have hardly set foot on the path of knowledge."

"You know I cannot," she said haltingly. She did not say aloud that her flesh crawled at the thought. "My father would never understand, he'd think you'd bewitched me, and he could well come after you sword in hand. Only teach me what more you can in the time that's left us." All too much time, at least another month, maybe longer. "You and your Saami will forever have a friend in me."

"Never would we do you harm." Aimo shook his head. "But the forewarnings are bad."

Vuokko likewise went grim. "Here we can ward you. We cannot from afar."

Well did she remember their drummings, chants, and dream-seeking sleeps, day after day during dayless winter and onward while the sun returned. They told her that something boded ill, but what it was or whom it threatened stayed unknown. Sometimes they had to force themselves to go on with her schooling.

She had wondered if the doom was hers. Could the thwarted lust of the wizards bring it, though that was not their will? A sickness, a shipwreck—She had learned how untrustworthy spellcraft was, how easily it could miscarry or turn on the one who wielded it. Not for nothing did most Norsemen call rather on Thor than on uncanny Odin.

But she scorned such thoughts and thrust them off. They did not become a woman of her blood. Nor was it given that any mishap would fall on her.

"You'll surely soon quell whatever it is." She made a smile. "Let's not be woeful today. Let's bid the springtime welcome."

Vuokko snatched after cheer. "That's right. Yes, we'll seek for something tasty to roast."

Aimo frowned. "I wish you would not go a-walking meanwhile," he said. She went down to the fjord whenever she could—out of the stifling gamma, away from the shamans and their murky lore, to be with the water, the wildfowl, the steep island beyond, and the sea behind it.

"Why, you've cast spells against wolves and bears," she said.

"There are worse dangers. Do not give me need to avenge you."

"Men?" scoffed Vuokko. "Who'll come by this early in the year?"

"I'll not wander off today." Gunnhild yawned. "I'm weary. I may go back to bed."

"Then we'll leave you in peace," said Vuokko.

They busked themselves. Belike they were right about game being scant. Well, Gunnhild thought, when she next wanted to be rid of them, she could again talk them into a hunt; and every day gave them time to search longer.

After they were gone, she stood awhile, being starved for light. A raven's hoarse cry broke through. It was as if Odin's great black bird recalled to her that if she was to do what she had in mind, she had better not linger. She shivered, doffed the encumbering cloak, folded it under her arm, and opened the outer door. How she hated shuffling through the entry, crouched like a thrall about to be whipped. Once she had shut the inner door behind her and straightened, she must wait till her eyes widened to the banked, smoky fire and the dull glow through the hole in the roof. How she hated everything here.

Most of all being forever meek toward a brace of Finns. Yes, what they had taught her should be of help. But noth-

ing, not even her wish to know more, nothing would keep
her in this hovel once Aalf had landed. And that those two
dared dream of lying with her recalled that day of the outlaws and raised a killing rage in her throat.

She swallowed it. She had shuddered beneath her clothes
when owl hoot, cormorant flight, cloud shapes, or the scuttering arpa foreshadowed harm, which the wizards could
not read more deeply. But she would not quail. Maybe she,
however unskilled, had it in her to see what they were blind
to; they often spoke of her inborn witchiness, and she herself had always believed that the norn at her cradle sang
no everyday weird over her.

Quickly she lit two lamps with an ember, took them behind her curtain, and set them on a chest. Thereupon she
started soaking some dried mushrooms from the wizards'
box. They ought not to mark that any were missing. She
had already brought in a length of thin, hard hempen rope,
telling them she wanted to work on tying hex-knots in this
as well as in leather cords, and—she'd laughed—she would
rather not have them witness her awkwardness. She looped
it on the floor at her bedside, the knotted strands an inch
or so apart.

Opening her other chest, she reached under a layer of
garb to find a small bundle of feathers. She had gathered
them below a swallow's nest when she lately went by herself to the fjord and brought them back tucked between her
breasts.

Holding them, she felt a sudden rush of fear. Heart thudded; sweat trickled and stank. Was she indeed ready to send
forth her soul? Vuokko and Aimo said they would soon
lead her. Should aught go wrong—the World Beyond was
altogether strange, a haunt of flint-stern gods and prowling
fiends—they would be there to shield her.

Gunnhild stamped on the dread. That they should behold
her naked soul was fouler than if they looked on her unclad
body—which surely they often did in their minds, and grew
hard in their dirty breeks. Today she could try to wrap
herself in a seeming.

She might come to grief. More likely, at worst, she

would only fail. Seija had groped her way to doing it. True, in the end she had gotten the help of her brother. But Gunnhild now knew more than she did. Nor would Gunnhild go on such a quest as hers, merely a flit across the land nearby. She grinned. What would the wizards say when they found this maidenhead was no longer theirs to take?

Well, their hold on her would be much weakened, threats to cut her schooling short gone hollow. She'd calm them.

They had shown her how to make a shaping, though they had not let her keep any stuff for it. In this dim light, her fingers were wiser than her eyes. She sang the needful song as she tied the feathers into a rough bird form with a string also out of the chest. Gripping it in her left hand, she spread her arms and danced where she was, treading the earth, reaching for the sky. A second song-spell keened. She must keep her thoughts on it, wholly on it, following its rise and fall until she left herself behind.

When it told her to, she drew up her skirts, knelt on the rope, and ate the mushrooms. There she stayed, swaying and singing.

She was leery of striking the drum, as the noai'de did. She had not yet fathomed its full powers. But Seija had had no drum either. Instead, she used pain to break the grip of the world upon her. Gunnhild wanted no firebrand mark for them to wonder at, marring her skin for life. Though slower, this should hurt enough.

The strands bit into her weight. She attended to the pangs, let them grow and grow, joining the song and the movement and the troll-food until they were everything that really was, she and the house no more than the shadow of a dream.

The hum of untellably many huge bees filled her head. She whirled down a maelstrom.

She was in the wind and of the wind. It shrilled, driving her through heaven. Its iciness tore at her to rive her asunder like one of the clouds among which she blew. Far, far below, unseen in the hasty mists, resounded the grinding of a mighty quern and the song of the giantesses who turned it.

Not herself, but that which she had gotten into her bones,
took hold. She reached out, caught shreds of fog, hauled
them from the wind, wrapped them tightly around her. She
made them into wings, body, beak, feet. The swallow
sheered earthward.

Below the clouds, sight became almost unbearably keen.
It scanned woodlands, mountains, islands, a wrinkled gray
sea that ringed them all in. She rode the wind and searched
for she knew not what.

Something showed on the worldrim. She swooped toward it.

Four lean ships bore southward. The hindmost was battered and faded, maybe taken from a foe, the rest bright,
stems and sterns curving haughtily upward, a dragon head
at the prow of the leader. Sails strained; hulls plunged; rigging quivered. It was as if she could hear strakes creak and
taste the spindrift off white-maned billows.

Closer she drew. Men saw her. They stared, agape. One,
taller than most, stood by the mast of the dragon. He had
shoved back the hood of his cloak. Hair fluttered tawny
about a narrow head and cleanly carved face. He did not
shout and point like the rest; his look upon her was as
steady as a snake's.

Across a span of nine years she knew him.

And somehow, amidst the sprawl of land and sea, she
knew he was nearing the Streamfjord.

The swallow tilted on the wind and slanted south.
Streamfjord, she called in her dream, put in at Streamfjord;
your luck awaits you there.

The ships dropped from sight. Something screamed behind her. She fled from it.

She woke. Lamp flames guttered; darknesses shifted to
and fro. Nightmare clutched her.

She struggled free and rose painfully to her feet. Never
again would she do this skin-turning so lightly, nor often
at all.

Yet she had done it, and more too, more than she had

ever foreseen. Hopefulness flashed like unsheathed steel.

She laid it aside. Need was to think, now while she was yet alone, think hard on what to do if that should happen for which she yearned.

XVI

The ships entered the narrows at Whale Sound. Their crews struck sails, laid masts and spars in the brackets, and took to the oars. Winds had become too tricky. Moreover, few of them had ever been here, and none knew these waters at all well. Rocks and riptides might lurk anywhere. That night they dropped anchor in the lee of a small island at Sandness Sound and slept as best they could in the hulls, as if this were a deep-sea crossing.

In the morning they reached the east end of the Streamfjord and turned west. Tide raced between an islet ahead and Whale Island to starboard, so they hugged the mainland, which they had meant to anyway. Here also the going was rough. Whitecaps surged and hissed. Ships bucked; oars groaned in their ports; men swore. On either side the land was low, with leafless boughs stark against evergreens; ahead, it rose steeply to heights hooded in snow. Flaws of wind hit like clubs. Haze dulled the sun. Aft whence they had come, a wall of dark cloud was lifting over straits and peaks.

Thorolf squinted yonder. "I mislike that sky," he said. "It's wrong for this time of year."

He and Eirik stood on the foredeck of their ship. The dragon head rose as tall as them, snarling at whatever foes or fiends might lair hereabouts. The other craft trailed, well apart lest two of them run into the same sudden trouble. The men easily braced themselves against roll and pitch, but their eyes were never at rest.

"We'll halt well ahead of the weather," said Eirik.

"Where?"

"I know not quite, nor does anyone with us. But some

Norse sometimes trade with the Finns somewhere nearby.
Özur Dapplebeard and others have spoken of it." After telling them to make for the Streamfjord, Eirik had been asking
around among the sailors. Thorolf had mainly kept to himself, thinking his own thoughts.

The Icelander shrugged. "Well, if that's the most you
know." Given the friendship between them, he could talk
freely. "But I still say this is a risky thing you do."

"And I say that bird the other day was a sign."

"For good or ill? Who ever heard of a swallow on the
wing when the sun stands barely at equinox? As kittle as
this sky."

Eirik sighed. "And as for Streamfjord, I tell you once
more that the name flew into my head even as the bird
went past. Why else should I remember it, and feel glad
about it? Besides, the swallow was bound hitherward."

"It seemed to be," Thorolf said.

Eirik gave him a hard squint. "I can't believe you, of all
men, are afraid."

Thorolf flushed. "No. But if this is a snare, it's surely
set for you. I'd not see you go blindly forward."

"Then what would you do? For I'm bound I'll look into
this."

"I've been thinking on that. Let me take a few men and
scout." Eirik frowned. Thorolf raised a hand. "We need you
with the ships. If I wanted to strike at you, by spellcraft or
otherwise, I'd go after them. Stranded, we'd not likely ever
see home again. And too many in the crews are too uneasy
about these things."

Eirik nodded. He had seen enough faces sullen or tightly
locked, enough charms fingered; he had overheard mutterings. A glance down the hull showed him no better.

"I call none of them cowards," Thorolf went on. "But if
something worse than a mere onslaught should come
against us, they might break and scatter. You can hearten
them to stand fast."

Again Eirik nodded. He knew how fear could sweep
through a battle array and send warriors running like hares.
"A wise rede, yes."

"My band will return this evening, or tomorrow at latest, and tell you what we found. If we don't, you'll know that bird was no friend."

Eirik's laugh barked. "And if you find nothing, why, then maybe it did not have us in mind at all." He peered landward and pointed. "That looks like a good spot to begin."

"I see no mark of traders."

"Since you're being wary, wouldn't you rather camp elsewhere than they do?"

Thorolf's dourness cracked in a smile. Headlong Eirik was, but also shrewd. Shouted orders rang to and fro.

Tide was ebbing; the ships could safely ground. Keels grated on the bottom. Sailors jumped overside, made fast, and brought their stuff ashore. They were less noisy than was their wont. Eyes kept straying toward the shadowy depths beyond, or aloft to the mewing gulls. Yet when Thorolf called for followers, most of the men crowded around. Nobody wished to seem daunted. He chose three, Arni, Brand, and Halldor, whom he knew to be seasoned woodsmen. He himself was mainly a seafarer. They gulped some food, gathered their gear, and set off.

Long did they search, at first almost haphazardly. Though they never got more than a few miles inland, the wilderness reached huge. Brush crackled; rotted leaves, duff, moss squelched underfoot; snow slumped in the shade; the heavens hung leaden. That overall gloom deepened as the sun wheeled from east to west and behind the spreading storm clouds. They towered ever higher, the hue of bruises. Wind blew dank and chill. Otherwise silence brooded, seldom split by a caw or a croak. Arni said at length that, while he found spoor of small game, there was none of bear or wolf. "Strange," he mumbled. "The bears should be awake, and not all the wolves would follow the hoofed herds south for the winter. It's as if they were banned."

"We are in Finnmörk, and a ghost has led us," said Brand harshly.

Halldor made the sign of the Cross. He had been baptized in England, together with fellow vikings who, cut off by a shire-levy, had thus saved their lives. Arni lowered at him and said, "That god is a long way off."

"You know I offer to Thor," answered Halldor, "but in this witch-land, what harm in calling on Christ as well?"

Thorolf touched the sword hilt at his left shoulder. His voice clanged. "I trust this the most. Trollcraft and priest-craft alike have never helped much against it."

The rest plucked up boldness and kept on with their hunt. After a while more they began to find traces of man, which they read for their leader—a tuft of dyed wool snagged on a bush, bits of charcoal, a broken arrowshaft, bones scarred by knives, at last footprints not yet blurred away. The tracks brought them to a clearing. There stood a big gamma with its outhouse and three njalla sheds.

They stopped and stared around. Nothing stirred but evergreens soughing in the wind and thin rags from the smokehole. "Hoy, we must have come on the shelter for Finns when their fishers and traders seek salt water," breathed Arni.

Halldor chuckled without much mirth. "If so, we could have done it faster and easier. See, yonder's a path going northward. It must end at the fjord."

"We may have done well not to use it," said Thorolf. He drew blade, though he left his shield hung on his back. "We'll have a look within."

He went first. The outer door was unbarred. He squatted down and waddled through the entry passage. Light drained past him to pick out the inner latchstring. He pulled it, flung that door wide, and sprang to the floor. At once he bounded aside to let the next man by, then took his fighting stance.

The sword sank. He gasped.

A woman stood by the hearth. As the sight of her brightened in his eyes, he knew that never had he seen any this fair. Not Finnish garb nor grime nor youth—sixteen winters, he would learn—lessened the loveliness and the queenliness of her.

She was of middling height but seemed taller, as straight as she held herself. Slimness swelled in hips and high breasts. Her hair fell unbound to her waist in maiden wise, shining raven's-wing black against milk-white skin. Round head, strong cheekbones, and snub nose might tell of a little Finnish blood, but already he knew her for Norse. A full mouth curved above a firm small chin. Beneath arched brows her eyes were big, wide-set, thick-lashed, and—he found when he saw her in better light—a changeable gray-green.

She smiled at the four who had burst in on her; flawless teeth gleamed. Her voice was soft, somewhat husky. "Welcome," she said in their tongue, with the Northland burr. "I had hopes of your coming."

"Who, who are you?" stammered Thorolf.

"I hight Gunnhild, daughter to the hersir Özur Dapplebeard. And you, I think, are men of Eirik, son to King Harald."

Slowly, Thorolf sheathed his sword. His followers, still dumbstricken, lowered their own weapons. "That's right." He named himself. Halldor drew the Cross again. Thorolf thought they might not like a witch to hear their names, and did not utter them as yet. For his part he would not behave other than fearlessly. "How do you know this?"

"That's a long tale, which I must tell quickly." She moved forward, lynx-lithe, to lay a cool hand in his for a few heartbeats. Steadily holding his gaze, she said, "I wish I could give you drink and then a feast. I will, too, if we live. But today time is short. Will you hear me out, Thorolf Skallagrimsson, and believe me, and do as I ask?"

He thought of what had already happened. His heartbeat thundered. "We hearken."

She drew breath. Her words never faltered. "I am here to learn spellcraft from two Finns who're the greatest and most knowing warlocks in the whole of Finnmörk. They're now out hunting. They both want me. They're so cunning that they follow spoor like hounds, whether the ground be frozen or thawed, and on ski they're so swift that nothing can outrun them. Whatsoever they shoot at, they hit. They've made an end of everyone who's come near. When they're angry, the earth itself turns away from their eyes and everything alive falls dead before that look. You must not get in their way. But I will hide you here in the gamma."

Even Thorolf's henchmen bristled at this. He waited for her to go on.

"Then we'll see whether we can kill them," said Gunnhild.

XVII

She had told more of Vuokko and Aimo than she knew to be true, and a few things she knew were not. But she wanted these warriors eager to attack, yet not reckless. Given a chance, the shamans could indeed freeze them with a glare, then raise a sight from which the doughtiest of men would shrink. They might not kill, but if they spared Thorolf, he must withdraw and tell Eirik the booty here was not worth the cost. Sure it was that they would never willingly let him take her away. When Aalf came, they could say they had forbidden her leaving for her own sake, because they descried that bad luck sailed in those ships. And maybe it would. Maybe, horn-mad, they did have the might to call up a storm that wrecked him.

However it all was, she needed them dead.

In the days after her sending she had thought on what to do and made ready, little by little, whenever they were not on hand. Last night she woke from a dream in which she kissed Eirik. With a frost-cold thrill, she felt her seeking-spell had worked and he was nigh. This morning she spoke sweetly to the Finns. They were racking themselves apart, she said; they must get a good sleep. If they shot a fat quarry—some partridges, a stray deer, a young seal?—hunters like them could do it, no matter how sparse the takings—the food should ease them. Her look and voice hinted at more. Weary though they were, they trudged off.

They would be back anytime.

Gunnhild beckoned to Thorolf's gang. "Come." She went to her curtain of skins and folded it aside. "Stand behind this. Not a word, not a cough or sneeze, or you're done. Wait and listen."

Thorolf hung back. "You move overly fast."

She stamped her foot. "I must! You too. Wait, listen, and learn if I'm right or not."

One man swallowed. "I wonder if we hadn't best leave."

Gunnhild's eyes met Thorolf's. She smiled. His will stiffened. "No," he answered, "we'll see this through. The woman is not about to run. Shall we?" Shamed, the men followed him.

Nonetheless, he held the curtain open, to watch what she did. She took a leather bag outside.

The sky was nearly black. When a low sunbeam struck between clouds, it had the hue of brass. Wind moaned; the evergreens roared. Air flowed around her like a river off a glacier. She sang into it as she strewed ashes from the bag over the ground. Likewise did she as she backed through the entry and went around the floor.

Hardly had she ended when she said, "They come!" Thorolf let the curtain fall.

Aimo and Vuokko scrambled down from the inner door. Wrapped and lashed to their backs were the parts of a yearling deer. They had skinned, gutted, and cloven it on the spot. Blood smeared their hands.

Gunnhild laughed softly. "Welcome home. You are too soon; I was tidying for you."

They stood peering back and forth. "Who has been here?" asked Vuokko.

"Why, nobody."

"That is strange," said Aimo, "for we found man-tracks nearby and followed them here, but then they were gone."

Worn out, neither was thinking clearly. "Well," said Gunnhild, "maybe someone came by but dared go no farther and went back the same way, unbeknownst to me. Tomorrow you can seek him if you like."

Vuokko let the business drop. "See what we've brought. We cleaned it to spare you that toil."

This also made less weight for them to carry, thought Gunnhild. "Thank you; thank you. Masters, I know I've often been stubborn, and I'm sorry, but—oh, let there be no more ill will between us."

Aimo was also gladdened. "Your folk would drink to that till they were drunk and quarrelsome. We shall have better cheer."

He and his kinsman set down their burdens and stoked up the fire. Rusty light flickered on smoke, which swirled off into the hooting wind. Gunnhild swept the floor. The ashes were dust-fine. They blent with muddy soil to cover tracks from any but the closest search; and the wizards had been too worried about her for that. Indoors the ashes did the same, until the twigs of her besom scratched away every mark. The Finns sliced off what meat they wanted. The water in the kettle, already warm, boiled. They threw most in to stew, but the tenderest they spitted before they hunkered by the fire to roast it. The rich smell drowned whatever whiff of untowardness they might still have caught.

Gunnhild quietly spread the hides on the earthbench to make a bed for three.

"Let us eat," said Vuokko. "I'm wolf-hungry."

"That's a dangerous word," Aimo reminded him. "Wild spirits are abroad. They might hear."

Gunnhild joined them. "With you two on guard," she asked merrily, "what can they do but wail, poor things?"

They all sat down. None said much while they hacked chunks of meat into the bowls on their laps and picked them out with their fingers. The men were too tired; the woman had her own thoughts. But when they were through, she murmured, "I'll wash these tomorrow. It's far more needful that you be well rested. Our bellies are full; the house is warm; the weather outside might as well be night."

"We can try," croaked Aimo, "though for sleeplessness like mine there is no help." The mushrooms were for sendings, farseeings, and oneness with the Powers.

"I think there is," answered Gunnhild. "Come, we'll lie down together, and I'll soothe you."

Vuokko's jaw fell. "You—will lie—beside me?"

"Beside us both?" Aimo asked dazedly.

Two or three tears glimmered in the soot on Vuokko's

cheeks. "I had well-nigh lost hope," he whispered. "Gunnhild, why?"

She rose from her stool. "I have been less kind than you two," she said. "I want things to change."

"You'll keep your hands to yourself," Aimo told his kinsman.

"And you the same," snapped Vuokko.

"I only wish for you both to sleep," Gunnhild said. She walked to the bench. They stumbled after her.

She stretched out in the middle. "Lie down one on each side," she bade. They did so. She put an arm beneath either head. "Sleep. Sleep well; sleep long."

Like weary children, the wizards snuggled close and shut their eyes. The fire sputtered. Misshapen shadows slithered across the walls and hulked in the corners. Wind blustered around the gamma. It rushed among boughs with a noise as of surf. Gunnhild waited. Soon she felt the steady breathing.

Before the weight numbed her arms, she slipped them free. Aimo stirred. A sob rattled in Vuokko's throat. She kept very still. They sank back into their darknesses.

A while yet she waited. Time crawled. At last she sat up, grasped shoulders, and shook them. The Finns did not move. She rose to her knees between them. Singing a spell under her breath, she lifted first Vuokko's head, then Aimo's, and lowered them again. The men stayed deep in slumber. Maybe she had had no need of the spell.

Now. It shivered in her.

Two big sealskin bags with leather drawstrings hung from a peg. Folk packed things into them when faring by sled. She fetched them. For a span she stood looking down at the sleepers. This would be the deadly risk. She wished the Norsemen could help, but the touch of a stranger might well rouse the Finns at once, and when they opened their eyes, he would be prey to their trollcraft. She set her teeth, slung the sacks around her neck, crept onto the bench, and knelt behind Aimo's head.

Bracing herself against the wall, she raised him anew till he sagged half sitting, held thus by her knee. He jerked and gasped. Before the slumber-mists could clear, she slipped a bag over him, down to his elbows, drew the cord tight, and knotted it behind his back. He threshed, giving out a muffled, meaningless cry. Vuokko sat up of himself, stunned with sleep. She bagged him likewise. "Gunnhild!" she heard. "Gunnhild!"

She sprang to the floor. They blundered against one another, blinded and bewildered. But they'd quickly find their feet and work themselves loose. "Thorolf!" she called.

The seafarers bounded forth. Thorolf's sword whistled. With a hard thwack, it split Vuokko's neck. Two of his men thrust spears into Aimo. The third was a bit slow. Seeing the wizards go lifeless, he drew a cross over his brow and heart.

Blood ran down the bench and over the floor. Where it caught firelight, it shouted red. A sharp stench rolled after it. The newly dead befouled themselves. Well, she had often watched slaughterings, and had been saved when the outlaws were slain.

Lightness welled through her. It whirled. She almost fell. Thorolf took her arm. "Are you well, Gunnhild Özurardottir?" she heard as if from afar.

Victory sang. "Yes." She laughed aloud. "That was boldly done, Thorolf Skallagrimsson."

"It was easy for us. You were the daring one." He turned to the others. "Get those carcasses out of here."

They did, lugging the bodies in such a way that most blood drained into the sacks. Thorolf wiped his sword on a sheepskin and sheathed it. He looked straight at Gunnhild and asked, "What would you next?"

"If your lord Eirik Haraldsson will take me home, I'll be thankful," she said. "My father will too."

He grinned. "I think Eirik will soon have his own reasons for giving thanks."

She stepped close and took his hands. "But you are my true friend, Thorolf," she said low. "May no man ever break our friendship."

His followers had left both doors open. Suddenly

lightning-flare burst through and lit the room blue-white. Thunder crashed; they felt it in their bones. Rain slammed down like a waterfall. Huge hailstones skittered across the ground. Again and again lightning dazzled, thunder deafened. Between flashes, they were blind.

The men crawled back, drenched. With doors closed, the racket was lessened. He who had crossed himself shuddered. "This ought not to happen so early in the year," he said.

"We've wakened the Finn-trolls," said another.

"Now Thor is driving them off," said the third stoutly.

Thorolf stood tall. He laughed. "Whatever, we're unhurt, no? If we must spend the night here, I've known worse. Spread something over that blood—clothes from a box— and start more of yonder meat cooking. My belly's scraping my backbone. Aren't yours, lads?"

He was wonderful, Gunnhild thought. Were it not for Eirik, she could hardly find a better man.

Thus they passed the time until they lay down to sleep. Though mead and wine were lacking, they had no dearth of talk. Their fears gone, men offered tales and brags to the fair young woman. She told them as much as she deemed wise. "I am no witch, nor ever wanted to be," she said. "I came to learn what can help our folk, healing, warding, foreseeing. And we can deal more deftly with the Finns if we know what they know."

"That may well be less than many believe," said Thorolf. "Why else are they helpless before us? And you hoodwinked these two right handily, Gunnhild."

She nodded. "I did gain some useful skills. But not only was theirs a woebegone life; they lusted after me." She tossed her head. "That must I avenge." Then, hastily, "Not that they ever had their will."

Thorolf chuckled. "I've fought my share of battles, but never would I try forcing you, Gunnhild."

The storm ramped until midnight. Morning sparkled. Thorolf told a man to go bid Eirik bring his ships to this strand. He and the others packed what she wanted to take with her and bore it thither. While alone in the gamma, she cleansed herself and donned the best garments she had along. When the ships came, she was there for them, shining like the young sun.

XVIII

Sails poled out, the ships beat southwesterly across a sea gray, green, and foamful. It whooshed and rumbled. For the most part they ran steadily, aslant, in a long rise and fall. Strakes creaked; walrus-hide rigging thrummed. Sometimes a prow bit straight into a wave, foam spouted, water fell down into the hollow hull, men bailed. Otherwise they were at ease under the racked oars, aside from the helmsman and a few who kept watch. Some loafed on leather-covered piles of booty amidships, some sat on the lashed-down sea chests that rowers used for benches. There was no shelter below the small decks fore and aft; those rooms were crammed with food, water kegs, gear, and more plunder.

Gunnhild stood on the lee side of the lead ship, near the foredeck. The dragon head at the stem had come down, for they were passing friendly shores and it would not do to anger the land-wights; but the sail flaunted bright stripes behind the webbing that strengthened it. A hand reached from under her hooded cloak to steady her. Spindrift salted her lips. She gazed landward, eyes narrowed against the sea-glare.

Gulls soared white, cormorants flapped black, in a clear sky. The westering sun cast shadows to bring out the ruggedness of the great island a mile or so to larboard, one of the chain along their way. Snow dappled its heights, but the first faint green had touched their foothills. Surf wreathed the strand.

Her heart leaped. Eirik had come to stand beside her.

Looking up, she saw his hatchet face crease in a smile, which it did not do often. "Fair weather today," he said, "but we're bound to hit foul before we're home."

"I look forward, if that's not an unlucky thing to say," she told him. "It should be stirring."

He laughed. "You won't have to pull an oar or swing a bucket!" His voice mildened. "Still, it shows you're hardy. Few women like being at sea."

She was silent before she said, "Best if I do. I may well spend much of my life thus."

He raised his brows. They were bleached almost white. "What makes you think so?"

She glanced away. "A feeling. I know not whence. But such feelings have been right now and then."

He peered at her. "Maybe you've dwelt too long with witchery," he said slowly.

She looked back and gave him her best smile. "But you are bringing me home to my own folk. . . . No, already I am among them."

As if caught off guard, he wet a finger and lifted it into the wind. "We must soon come about if we're to make the campstead I have in mind for tonight."

"Isn't this rather early?"

"Safe landings and snug coves are few hereabouts."

"Would you put in every night if it weren't for me?" she asked.

"Belike not."

"You are very kind." In truth, he had been throughout. She slept in a tent on her knockdown bed. And—though when she needed to piss during the day, her skirts hid the pot given her—she would have loathed hanging her bare bottom over the side as the crew did, to wipe it. They weren't shy about that, and inwardly she enjoyed the sight when a man dropped his breeks. But she was a wellborn lady.

Eirik smiled again. "I'm in no hurry while you're aboard."

"You'll guest at Ulfgard, won't you?" she blurted.

"Hm." He stroked his short beard. "It would be hard for me to leave, unless you came along."

Happiness stood up in her and shouted. The whole world rocked. This was what she had set her heart on, that for which she had worked every wile she could think of.

She reined herself in. Now she must stake everything on a bid for all the gold in the Rhine.

"I mean that," she heard Eirik say earnestly.

She caught her breath. "You'd wed me?"

She saw him taken aback. "Well—"

"My father would gladly give his yea."

Eirik looked out to sea.

"He bears only the name of hersir," Gunnhild went on, "but he is the foremost man in northern Haalogaland. A good ally."

Eirik nodded, somewhat stiffly.

Gunnhild sighed. "Am I being too forward? Forgive me." She grew stern. "I'll say no more than this, that I'll be leman to no man. Not even you, Eirik Haraldsson."

He frowned at her. "You speak boldly for a woman alone among vikings."

She became tender. "I'd grieve if ever I offended you. But you might find my love worth having."

Eirik's grin flashed. "And surely your hate is worth not having. Worth a man's life, I think. I like the soul in you, Gunnhild. You are my kind." He leaned nearer. "And you're lovely to behold, witty to talk with—" As always, he sprang to a decision. "You'd make the best of wives for a king."

She pressed in, as wolves press in on an aurochs. "Amidst the rest of them?"

His laugh rang. "Unlike my father, I have none yet. You'll be the first."

And the last, if she could bring that about, she thought. Nor did she want any other woman he might bed henceforth to mean anything to him. Such a one could breed sons who would grow up as threats to hers.

XIX

He did not, after all, visit Ulfgard, but kept on to a holding he had in the south of Haalogaland, bearing her along. However, he sent one of the ships aside to tell Özur

Dapplebeard of this and bid him to the wedding feast. Having reached haven, he lodged Gunnhild with a wealthy yeoman nearby, though she was often at the hall. Then at once he put the household and herdsmen to work making ready. He was not a man to suffer much waiting for whatever he wanted.

Word ran to everybody of mark, far and wide around. Özur came down with a full crew. Among them were Gunnhild's brothers, Aalf the Shipman and Eyvind the Braggart. Özur brought not only rich gifts—knowing he would get better—but fine clothes and jewelry for her. His daughter must show that she came from a high house.

Feasting swelled as more and more guests arrived, until men filled the yard and spilled out over the land. They talked and talked, swapping news, sometimes making deals, sometimes falling into quarrels that they dared not let become deadly—not here. They sported, boating, swimming, wrestling, racing, spearcast, bowshot, ball, stallion fights. Some played board games, tossed knucklebones, or set each other riddles. Eirik's staff of women, led by the three with whom from time to time he had slept, got no rest when the trestle tables were set up, the bowls of water and the towels for hand washing carried around, and the food brought in—beef, pork, mutton, fowl, fish, cooked with garlic, leeks, peas, turnips, herbs; wheat and rye bread; butter, cheese, honey, berries dried and stewed. After the boards were cleared away the women still went along the benches, filling horns with ale or mead. A man of standing or a son of his might ask one whose looks he liked to sit at his side, and maybe she would leave for the night when he did. Even the hall had sleeping room for no more than Eirik's picked warriors and foremost guests; others used clean places in the outbuildings, or tents and booths beyond. The night was well on when the last of them lay down. It was not all drunken gab and laughter. Dag the skald chanted staves old and new, about gods and heroes. From the high seat Eirik spoke words of weight or acknowledgment; he gave gifts from his hoard as behooved a man with the name of king and the kingship over the whole of Norway ahead of him.

He told Gunnhild of halls bigger and more splendid farther south, but she had never yet seen the like of this. Painted timber, shake-roofed, it reached and reared huge, beam-ends carved into dragon heads, gables into vines and gripping beasts. Pillars, likewise carved, ran the length of the main room, upholding roof-beams, and flanked the high seat. Three fire-trenches went down the middle of the floor, which was hard-packed clay daily swept. Hides, renewed whenever they showed wear, blanketed the benches, under oaken wainscots and colorful tapestries. Lamps hung manifold from chains. A door off the entry gave on a row of lesser rooms along the north wall, but there were windows above its roof as well as in its own side, and more along the south, so that during the day the hall was never gloomy.

Behind it stood the farm buildings and pens. Children, dogs, and other creatures kept that ground lively. The hall itself lay beside a flagged yard, together with storehouses, workers' houses, cookhouse, bathhouse, and bower. In the last of these, women could spin, weave, and be by themselves. It had a loftroom. There slept those newly wedded.

That morning Gunnhild rode from the yeoman's garth in a wain whose panels were a welter of engraved entwinings, the hubs trollish faces. Two white horses drew it, their harness silver-studded, iron triangles jangling to frighten off evil Beings. She sat between two maids on a bench cushioned with outland silk. Silk too was her veil; her gown and undergarb were of the choicest linen, held together by heavy brooches. Heavy too were the necklace and rings from her old home. A wreath of windflowers circled her brows. On horseback before and after rode a score of Eirik's guards, helmets, byrnies, and high-held spears agleam, Thorolf at their head.

Leaves were unfolding on trees, still small, trembling in a breeze that bore smells of growth and song of birds lately come back. A few clouds drifted fleecy. At the hall, horns lowed to welcome her, and Eirik strode forth to help her down.

She thought how she didn't really need that, but today

had better be the shy young bride. Himself in embroidered, fur-trimmed tunic, worsted knee breeches and hose, gold on his own arms, silver and amber at his throat, how dazzling he stood there! His only weapon was a knife at his belt, and his wonted stark short-spokenness had thawed into friendliness toward all.

But then he left, the men trooping after him. Gunnhild knew where they were bound. A mighty boulder in a grove had long since been chiseled into a block. Two horses stood tethered. A man waited with a hammer to stun them as they were hauled struggling to the stone; another held an ax to kill them. Kettles and cutting tools lay where a needfire had been kindled. She had heard little about what else went on—not likely quite the same as at Ulfgard—but it would feed the gods.

She spent that while in the hall among the women. Mostly they made much of her, when they were not working. Eirik's lemans were slyly spiteful. She clawed straight back and they gave her a wide berth thereafter.

The day had worn on when the men brought in their kettles of horseflesh and set to drinking. Gunnhild shared Eirik's high seat. They themselves drank outland wine from glass goblets. She merely sipped, for she wanted to keep her wits and her witchcraft. When folk came to talk with the bridal twain, she spoke quietly, choosing each word beforehand.

The boards were set up and laden. The feast grew uproarious.

Yet after it was done, and eventide dusking the hall, a horn blew and a hush fell. Dag trod before the high seat. Quoth he the ballad of Skirnir, which told how Frey won Gerd for his wife; and a lay in praise of Eirik; and a third in praise of the house of Özur, likening Gunnhild to Freyja. For this he got a whole golden arm ring.

Özur himself followed, to give his daughter away where everyone could hear. Eirik made known that his morning gift to his bride would be a hall and broad acres down in Vikin, well-staffed, with a chestful of coins from as far away as Serkland. Gunnhild took the rings off her fingers and gave them to the wife of Thorir Hroaldsson, Eirik's foster father, as her bridal fee.

Aalf and Eyvind begged leave to speak. They asked if Eirik would take them as his men. He said yes, they looked to become stout warriors and this would forge another bond between the houses.

More gifts went to and fro. Horns were raised and drained to each of the highest gods.

Because Gunnhild had asked that it be he, Thorolf Skallagrimsson bore in the hammer of the offering, now washed and polished. He laid it on her knees, the sign of Thor, and called on Frigg to bless her and her husband. When he had taken it out again, she was wedded.

Men shouted, crowded around with good wishes, dipped horn after horn into a tub of ale that had been lugged in, drank their health, victory for him, well-being for her, strong sons for them both.

The fires could no longer stave off deepening shadows. Lengths of pine branch had been carried in. Each man or boy lighted one at the coals and took it outside. Lamps would shine for them when they returned to the hall and drank till dawn. First they had a gladsome task. Flames flared and snapped beneath the earliest stars.

Thorolf took the lead. After him walked Eirik and Gunnhild, arm in arm. The others swarmed behind, whooping the lewdest, coarsest redes they knew. Thus they shooed off night-gangers and furthered fruitfulness.

Their torches ringed the bower. Thorolf went inside with the newlyweds, up the stairs. Opening the loftroom door, he bade them a merry night and closed it behind them.

Wax candles from the South lighted it. Wreaths of juniper and of last harvest's grain hung on the walls. A table held wine, bread, and roast lamb. The floor was strewn with sweet herbs. The racket down below seemed a long ways away.

Slowly, Eirik took off Gunnhild's wreath and veil. He let them drop. They looked at one another by the candle-glow.

"I never thought I would wait this long to have a woman I wanted," he said from deep in his throat.

"May I be worthy of it," she answered, knowing full well she would.

He drew her to him and kissed her. It could have been hard and hasty, but she pressed her lips and herself against him, hungrily, leading him on and on.

He plucked at a brooch. She laughed and helped him undo it and more. When her last garment fell, she spread her arms a little and turned around thrice, her black hair swirling, before she drew the bedcovers aside and lay down.

"I'm told this is unseemly," she murmured, "but does either of us need a nightgown?"

"No, by Thor's own whacker!" He scrambled out of his clothes. She took him to her.

She did not yield to what pain there was—less than she had awaited—or set her teeth against it. She made it a part of what happened. Almost, her soul took wing. When his haste was behind him, her hands and mouth roved until his began to do likewise. They came together afresh. Already that time she foresaw what a bliss this would soon be to her.

As they lay back, he said, "Were it not for what I felt, and the blood spots, I'd hardly have believed you a maiden, Gunnhild."

"I've given thought to what might please you," she whispered into his ear. And over the years she had asked of Seija and other knowing women; but mostly it was her own daydreams and sleepless nightdreams.

He chuckled. "Well, you *are* a witch."

She knew not how much unspoken wisdom, older than mankind, her spells and seekings had awakened in her. It was well that she had gone to the Finns.

And it was well that in the end she had gotten them slain.

Memories and graspings alike lost themselves for this while in happiness, as salt does in sun-warmed water. "I'll become better," she said, "for you, beloved."

He kissed her with a softness none else had ever met

from him. "And you are wise beyond your years. I have been lucky. We'll make a pair the world will not forget."

They began to fondle anew. Before long she was crying out, "Fill me again! Stuff me full of our children!"

She was to bear him nine.

BOOK TWO

THE BROTHERS

1

In his later years King Harald dwelt on one or another of his holdings in southern Norway. After the last wedding guest had gone home, Eirik busked for a voyage to meet with his father and show him his new wife. "He'll surely like you," Eirik said to her, "but we'll speak as little as may be of your stay in Finnmörk, for he hates everything that smacks of seid."

"What if he mislikes me?" fretted Gunnhild. "I'm no king's daughter, such as you might have gotten."

Eirik shrugged and laughed. "I may do so later."

Gunnhild thought she would see to it, by whatever means, that that did not happen.

To them as they sat in the hall on a rainy day came Thorolf Skallagrimsson. The longfires did not much lessen a dank chill. They smoked badly, stinging eyes and nostrils. Thorolf's fair hair was the brightest sight in the gloom roundabout. "My lord," he said, "as you will soon be off, I now ask leave to go my own way."

He had spoken before of his wish to see his kinfolk again after all these years. Throughout them, sailors had brought news from Iceland, which he eagerly heard. The latest was that his sister Thorunn had wedded a well-off young man named Geir Ketilsson. He wanted to fill a knarr with trade goods, always welcome yonder. Eirik had not naysaid this. Gunnhild was sorry, for she and Thorolf had become great talk-friends; sometimes gaze lingered on gaze for more than one heartbeat. Still, Thorolf had promised he would return in the following summer.

Eirik answered loudly enough for everybody to hear: "You have served me faithfully. May you have the best of crossings. There's something I want you to take along." He beckoned to a footling, who knew what he meant and fetched an ax that he laid on the knees of the young king. It was a big and splendid weapon, its blade darkly shining, the steel chased with gold and the shaft with silver. Eirik took it up in both hands and reached it forward. "Here is a gift from me for your father, Skallagrim."

Murmurs of wonder went the length of the hall. Though not stingy, Eirik seldom showed any kindness or much friendliness; and many remembered the bad blood between those two houses. Thorolf's smile flashed white. His thanks were warm. The eventide drinking would be happy.

Gunnhild masked the unease she alone felt. Somehow, suddenly, all this goodwill boded ill. She had cast no foreseeing spell. It was something she knew, as if in a dream.

Like a hound casting about after a spoor, she searched within herself for any reason she might find. Sailing down from Finnmörk, and then here, she had talked with more Icelanders than Thorolf, and listened to talk between others when they did not think she was in earshot. The seed of Kveldulf that had taken root at Borg was a seed strange and wild. Already in his seventh year Thorolf's younger brother Egil slew a playmate with whom he had had a fight. This led to a clash between grown men in which seven died. When Egil was twelve, he and another lad named Thord found themselves matched in a ball game against Skallagrim. The old man was being beaten, but as dusk fell he grew so strong that he dashed Thord to the ground hard enough to kill the boy, then set at his own son.

A serving woman who had fostered Egil cried out for him to stop. She was called Thorgerd Brak, a big woman with a man's strength, somewhat of a witch. It was thought that Egil must have learned a few things at her house. But she could not stand when Skallagrim in his madness turned on her. He chased her out over the cliffs and there cast a stone that pitched her into the sea. Soon Egil avenged her by putting an ax through the head of a foreman of Skallagrim's. Neither father nor son spoke about these things, then or ever.

And yet Egil was already a skald, whose poems grew steadily better.

Gunnhild had not had the heart to bring such tales up

with Thorolf. Nor did she now. She merely huddled into herself and wished he were not going there.

Maybe, she tried to believe, her fears stemmed from nothing but a touch of sickness. It did seem that she was carrying her first child.

11

Next after the high king, the jarl of Hladi was the mightiest man in Norway. Under him were the rich shires of the Thraandlaw, with farms, woodlands, fisheries, and shipping in and out of the great fjord. The Thraands were many, a stiff-necked folk, quick to take arms for their rights. Close to them, headman at their Things when they met to try cases and make or unmake laws, leading them also in offering to the gods, the jarl could sway them far more readily than anyone else. It was lucky for Harald Fairhair that, when he was hammering the kingdom together, Haakon Grjotgardsson thought it best to fight at his side. Together they overcame eight lesser kings. Harald put Haakon over the lands these had ruled. The two men often met, and Haakon fostered Harald's sons Gudröd and Haalfdan the Black. When Haakon then died, his own son Sigurd took over the jarldom; the boys stayed with him till they were grown.

Sigurd Jarl was a wise man, who wanted to be friends with the yeomanry. He gave them justice, and help if they needed it, as well as good gifts whenever he guested their leaders. Thus he won their troth, which made him more powerful than even his father had been.

King Harald had many children by different women. Some of his sons died young, of sickness or mishap or in battle at home or abroad. Seeking to end quarrels among them, which had now and then become murderous, when he was fifty years old he called a Thing at Eidsvold. There he gave kingship over the most important parts of the land to the strongest fourteen of them—under himself. Each got

half the scot and other intake of his shire, with the right to
sit on a high seat a step above any jarl although a step
below Harald when he was there. Most of them hoped to
become the over-king after his death, but it was Eirik whom
he named his heir. This did not make them love their
brother, as Eirik well knew. Nor did he like having them
lie in wait.

Harald Fairhair was in his seventieth winter when he begot his last offspring. This was on a young woman whose
family stemmed from the island of Mostr and who therefore
came to be known as Thora Mostr-staff. She was of good
yeoman stock, tall and comely, but had gone into service
in one of the king's houses in Hördafylki. That was common enough, a way of earning favor for her kindred. When
he stayed there awhile and brought her to his bed, nobody
thought the worse of it.

Sigurd Jarl had business down that way. It happened he
was homebound when her time drew nigh. Word went out
that the king was at Saeheim, northward. Sigurd stopped
for the night at the house. Thora asked if he would bring
her along, for surely Harald would be glad to see and acknowledge the child. Sigurd was willing. In the morning
she boarded his ship.

The season was barely summer, the weather tricky. They
kept to sheltered waters between islands and mainland,
rowing oftener than sailing. When a storm blew up, they
put in early to wait it out under the hill called Hellunn.
That was when Thora's pangs came upon her.

Wind yowled, streamed and struck, laid cold claws under
garments that rainshowers and sea-spray had drenched.
Waves were not big here, but they chopped like axes, iron-
gray as the sky. No dwelling was in sight, only grass, bushes,
and trees that tossed boughs still thinly leaved. Rocks littered
the shore. The tide being high, Sigurd cast anchors fore and
aft, close in. From there a gangplank reached the shallows.

Thora knelt in the bilge. Sometimes she shuddered;
sometimes she moaned a little. Sigurd took her by the hand,
helped her rise, and led her over the plank. The pitching

ship might well throw her down and smash the bairn's head. The land was at least steady.

Thora splashed ashore, then went to her knees again. Among the rocks she brought forth a boy-child. No midwife was there, but men among the crew had knowledge from byres, while she was wide-hipped and sturdy. Sigurd himself cut the cord and tied the knot.

The newborn yelled lustily and soon suckled thirstily. Sigurd poured water over him and named him Haakon after his own father. The storm died down. The ship fared onward.

King Harald agreed this was a promising cub. For the next few years he let Thora live on a farm of his, well honored, and Haakon with her.

111

Gunnhild's first was born in a room where candlelight set tapestries aglow. Charms of the finest workmanship hung also on the walls. Three skilled women were there to help. She was down on the floor, but with straw thickly spread and clean towels over it. The women changed these and her shift often. Meanwhile they wiped the sweat off her with soft cloths that had been soaked in herb-steeping hot water and wrung out. When her strength flagged, they upheld her. From time to time the oldest donned catskin gloves, got onto a high three-legged stool, and called on Frigg the mother of Baldr, Jörd the mother of Thor, and Ingrun the mother of Frey and Freyja. The second, who had a lovely voice, sang songs of hope and cheer. The third tended a firepot from which wafted sweet smoke.

Nonetheless, Gunnhild was young and slender. The birthing grew long. Pain was a haze in which she toiled, lost from the world until a sound of wolf-wind and dashing rain came to her like a rallying horn-blast in battle. Each throe was a sword-slash.

She would not scream, she told herself again and again; she would not cramp over or fall and writhe; she would bear down as and when they bade her. And somehow she would find a way to use the spellcraft she knew of.

Pain could unbind the soul.

Bit by bit, chant by silent chant, while day waned and night flowed in, she withdrew—never altogether, for to sleep now would mean death, but at last she steered the thing on the straw as a helmsman steers a ship. What she heard and felt was like no more than sea and weather. Awareness flew aloft and swept northward.

The moon flew with her among ragged, fitfully lighted clouds. Mountains fell behind, huge darknesses broken by fjords, lakes, fosses, glaciers. The lowlands of the Thraandlaw—this must be the Thraandlaw—broadened from its bayshores, hoar beneath the moon. A hall and its outbuildings sprawled murky. Fire-glow glimmered through gutskins stretched across windows. The men who still sat at their ale got no sight of her when she passed through the roof—or did a few shiver in a gust of cold? She found a side room and hovered above the bed there. Here was no light at all, yet she saw the woman asleep and the bairn in a cradle beside.

She knew them. News had come south, of Thora Mostrstaff and her yeanling. Gunnhild had given it slight heed. She was nearing her own time, and Eirik's grown brothers were the threat on hand.

Now it stabbed her that the norn who sang over this Haakon had not laid any small doom on him, or on others whose lives he would touch. But she was helpless, not even the swallow she once had been; her soul flitted naked.

As if hauled on a tether, Gunnhild returned. The oldest of the midwives eased out her child; the other two lowered her onto her back.

"It is a boy," she heard dimly. Hearing and sight sharpened when she beheld the squalling red one, her son and Eirik's, the first of the kings she would bear. Her man had said that if it was a boy and healthy, he would name it Gamli.

The afterbirth followed. The women washed Gunnhild anew, gave her fresh clothing, helped her into bed, let her

drink water. Haakon faded in her mind, a dream half remembered.

What she thought when she could again think clearly was
scornful. Men boasted of the dangers they had met, the
sufferings they had overcome. What did they know?

IV

In the fall Skallagrim had kine driven from his meadows
down to Borg for slaughter. They milled about, lowing
and bawling. Horns tossed; smells rolled; hounds barked;
men and boys shouted, running around to keep the herd
together. Skallagrim ordered two led over to the house.
There he told the carls to hold them fast with their necks
crossed. He himself laid a broad flat stone underneath. Now
he took the ax Thorolf had brought him from King Eirik.
He had said nothing when he got it, only hung it over his
shut-bed. Today he swung it so that the air whistled. It
hewed both heads off in one stroke, they thumped on the
ground, blood spurted, but when it hit the stone the edge
crumpled and the blade cracked. Skallagrim looked at it
awhile, saying no word, before he took it back inside and
threw it onto the crossbeams over the fire. Nobody cared
to ask him what he meant.

Otherwise, in his gruff and moody way he gave good
guesting to Thorolf and eleven men from his son's crew.
The house could sleep more than that. It was turf-walled,
for trees were small and sparse on Iceland, swiftly being
used up. However, rich men like him could buy timber
from Norway. Also, driftwood came ashore where Kveldulf's coffin had grounded. When the early land-seekers
threw the pillars of their high seats overboard, they had
more in mind than a sign from the gods. Thus Borg roof
rested on stout posts and beams, above well-furnished
rooms whose number had grown over the years.

On the whole, Thorolf's time there was happy. He bick-
ered with Egil, who behaved more overbearingly than befitted a lout so young, flared into reckless-mouthed rages,

or brooded surlily for days on end. But oftener he hung on his brother's tales of far lands and daring deeds, with hunger in his dark eyes. Besides, Thorolf was not always at home; he rode widely about to visit elsewhere.

That lessened more and more as winter lengthened. More and more Thorolf was in speech with Aasgerd, daughter of his friend Björn Brynjolfsson, foster daughter of his parents, Skallagrim and Bera. They chatted; they laughed; they played games or shared what household tasks they could; she sat beside him spinning thread while he carved a spoon or a haft; they took walks with no other company than his spear. She was a well-skilled maiden, merry though firm when she needed to be, her face fair, blue eyes, soft lips, a few freckles across her nose, flaxen hair spilling down a slim back. The eerie beauty of Gunnhild stopped haunting him.

In spring he told his father he would fare east. Skallagrim spoke against it. "You've made enough famous voyages," the old man warned, "and the saying goes, luck is likelier with few than many. Take rather as much of the holdings here as you think will make you a great man."

"I must carry out this one journey," answered Thorolf. "I've given a promise. But when I come back I'll settle down for aye. Meanwhile, though, Aasgerd shall sail with me to her father in Norway. So he asked of me before I left."

"Well, do as you wish," Skallagrim sighed. "But I've a feeling that if we part now we'll never meet again."

Bera said little. She only let her gaze dwell on her son.

Egil wanted to go along. He made himself a pest about it. His beard was a black fuzz and he had not gotten his full growth, but he hulked as big as most men. "No," said Thorolf. "If our father can't curb you at home, I'll hardly take you abroad. It wouldn't do for you to show the same soul yonder."

Egil reddened and whitened. "Then it could be that neither of us goes," he snarled.

Thorolf's ship lay ready in Brakasound, the inlet where Egil's witchy foster mother, Thorgerd Brak, died. That night a gale blew up from the sea. Egil went out in the dark and cut the moorings. The ship drifted free. Thorolf and his men had tough work getting her back. When they upbraided Egil, he told them he would do more harm if they wouldn't take him. Peacemakers stepped between. The end was that Thorolf let his brother come aboard.

At their farewell, Skallagrim took down the ax. The shaft was smoke-blackened and the steel rusty. He handed it to Thorolf. Quoth he:

> "Flawed in the very forging,
> failed has the wolf of the wound.
> Soft and a coward, it slyly
> sought to bring me to trust it.
> Back let it go, this blade
> so bent, the charred wood-griever.
> Need for it was there never,
> not though it be a king's gift."

Once out at sea, Thorolf cast the misused ax over the side. Such a mark of his father's abiding hatred was unlucky at best, he thought. Then as he looked the length of the hull to where Aasgerd sat, he brightened.

Again he stood before Eirik and Gunnhild. Now, however, it was in Raumsdalr, one of the shires over which Harald had given Eirik kingship, this hall bigger and much finer than what Eirik kept in Haalogaland. Yet both came down from their seat onto the floor to greet the Icelander. Eirik clasped his hand and bade him welcome. Gunnhild laid her own hand in his—fleetingly, and he pressed hers not at all; nor was his glance on her quite the same as before. She drew back, closely watching and listening.

"Yes, we had fair winds almost throughout," Thorolf told her husband. "We made landfall at Hördafylki, steered north, and put in at Sogn, for we were taking the firstborn daughter of my friend Björn Brynjolfsson back to him."

Eirik nodded. "I've heard that Brynjolf died and his sons divided the inheritance between them."

"Björn is still a man of standing. He found out for me where you were, and of course I hastened onward to greet you." Thorolf smiled. "Likewise I bring greetings from my father, with his thanks for your gift." He turned and beckoned to the men at his back. "He sends this to you, King Eirik."

Gunnhild saw how stiff the smile and heard how flat the voice had gone. Nobody else seemed to. Instead, they crowded near while Thorolf's followers carried a long, thick roll forward, laid it down, and spread it out as much as room allowed. Sunlight through the open doors fell on a longship's sail of the best make, red and white stripes behind a flying raven. Murmurs of delight lifted. Gunnhild's look flickered across the sailors. They too were holding something back.

She could guess what it was. Thorolf had wealth of his own, and no wish for trouble in Norway. Well, she wished none on him, even if it stung a little that the tall, handsome man had cooled toward her. But she wanted to know more. A king, like a cat, lived longer the better his knowledge of what went on among both hawks and hares. There should be ways to find out. Eirik was inviting Thorolf to winter with him. That would give time enough to get somebody drunk or otherwise loose-tongued.

"I thank you, King," Thorolf answered. "First, though, I've errands elsewhere. As you see, we are but few. I left my ship and most of her crew with the yeoman Gudlaug Shark-slayer and borrowed horses from him to ride hither." His grin went grim. "And I left my brother Egil in charge— so I called it—for I'm not sure he'd be a seemly guest."

If he took after Skallagrim, Gunnhild thought, that was quite likely.

Eirik laughed his short, clashing laugh. "He might learn a few things here. But what is this business of yours?"

"It's with Thorir Hroaldsson, in Sygnafylki, whom you well know." Thorolf's uneasiness left him. Gladness shone in his eyes and throbbed in his words. "We may be there for some while. When I brought Björn his daughter Aasgerd, he said nothing against my wedding her. But it would be well to get her uncle Thorir's yea also."

Oh, yes, Gunnhild thought, that was wise. When strong families thus linked, first they had all kinds of understandings to reach, about holdings and everything else. Then one might hope they would stay banded together—unlike the sons of Harald Fairhair. What with the undying unforgivingness between the old king in Norway and the old chieftain in Iceland, Thorolf and his Aasgerd could well come to want powerful friends.

"May things go as you wish," said Eirik. "Before you leave, you'll spend two or three days with me." He did not ask. "We'll feast, go hunting and hawking, swap tales of what's happened to each of us since last time."

He would question Thorolf at length about Iceland, Gunnhild thought, but he would not hear anything Thorolf did not choose to tell. Maybe she could. She was still feeling her way into kingcraft. Already she had given soft words, silver, now and then some help with woes they were having, to men who struck her as trustworthy. Runners, spies, stealthy killers, who knew what else? Eirik was ruthless enough but too straightforward.

Not that she didn't find him the lordliest of men. He rose above others like an ash tree above thorns or a stag with antlers dew-glistening athwart heaven. It was only that she wanted to help him, and their son Gamli, and their next son who might now lie in her womb, and their every child after that. The blood, the house, the name.

VI

Some months passed quietly. Thorir the hersir made Thorolf, Egil, and their crew welcome on his great farm in Sygnafylki. Although he was King Harald's man and had fostered King Eirik, he himself had been a foster son of Skallagrim before Kveldulf moved away. The breach had grieved him; the likelihood of a healing gladdened. He said he would indeed help further the match with his niece Aasgerd.

Therefore after a short while Thorolf sailed back to Björn. They quickly handseled their bargain. The wedding called for a real feast, so it was set for fall after harvest, at Björn's home. Meanwhile Thorolf returned to Thorir.

Egil had stayed behind throughout. He was not getting on well with his brother. Moreover, having seen what was across the fjord in Sogn, he thought it would soon bore him. Thorolf agreed, and could all too readily foresee what that would lead to. On the other hand, Sygnafylki offered much in the way of sailing, fishing, hunting, wenching, and other sports. Besides, Egil was making a friend in Thorir's son Arinbjörn.

One would not have looked for that, as unlike as the two were. Arinbjörn was a few years the older, fairly tall, burly, though fast on his feet and nimble. Sandy hair and beard rimmed a broad, hook-nosed face with downward-slanting blue eyes. Mostly he was forethoughtful in his speech and slow to anger, but when he got stubborn about something it was wise to yield.

Nevertheless a fellowship grew between him and Egil, until it became a bond. They did things well together, whether it be a romp, a lark, their share of work at the steading, or whatever else. Both were good with their hands; Egil joined in the building of a boat. They had much to tell each other about their homelands and the folk therein. Arinbjörn enjoyed Egil's poems, both olden ones the younger fellow had learned from everybody he met who knew any, and new ones he made himself. Every well-brought-up man could do that, but Arinbjörn fell into awe of Egil's gift.

In those months Egil grew ever more swiftly to full manhood, taller, thicker, stronger, till he loomed above most others and overmatched them. Being happy here, and having Arinbjörn for an example, he somewhat curbed his hotheadedness and mildened his roughness. This made Thorolf look on him more kindly.

It turned out that the bettering did not go deep.

Summer drew to an end, the crops in, stubblefields and hay meadows brown, birch leaves yellowing, a nip in the winds, the sky full of southbound wings and wild cries. Men readied ships. Not only Thorolf, Egil, their followers, Thorir, Arinbjörn, and others of that household, but no few of the bigger men in the neighborhood, all were invited to the wedding in Sogn. The garth bustled and roared with them.

On the eve of their setting forth, Egil fell sick. Cough racked him; fever burned him. He lay abed loudly wishing he could find and kill whatever wicked Being had wrought this. He barely brought himself to wish Thorolf a good journey.

In a few days he got well, but that was too late. He yawned and rattled around through the dullness into which the steading had fallen.

Thorir's steward Ölvir had also stayed behind, to see to his master's business. This was a stocky man, grizzled, his pug face seamed, but still lively. Now he needed to go forth and gather in the rents on land that Thorir owned here and there. He would take a boat with twelve workmen for crew. Egil asked if he could go along. "Well, we've room enough aboard," said Ölvir, "and one more man might prove useful." So Egil took his sword, shield, spear, and a few spare clothes and joined him.

Ölvir was right. The weather turned bad as they came down the fjord. When they rounded the last ness and bore north, they met stiff, foul wind and heavy seas. They rowed on until evening. Then the island Atley stood before them. They landed, drew the boat above high-water mark, and made her fast. Not far inland, Ölvir knew, lay a big farm belonging to King Eirik. The men set off for it to get shelter overnight.

Thus Egil first met Eirik and Gunnhild.

VII

A king, with his household warriors and other needful folk, shifted from home to home every few months, if not oftener. He must show himself widely, speak with leading men everywhere, learn what was happening, quell unrest, give judgments, be headman at offerings, hand out gifts, and all else that went with being lord. Besides, so many followers ate a steading bare; and houses took a while to be rid of the dirt and stenches that had built up while they were there.

Eirik and Gunnhild were thus zigzagging a slow way south when they came to Atley. Word had gone ahead, as always. Their tenant and steward, one Bard, made things ready. Not only would there be unstinted food and drink; there would be seasonal rites in honor of the neighborhood goddesses. The work beforehand was somewhat overwhelming. Moreover, Bard was close-fisted. The visit would be costly for him. This may have thrown him into a bad mood, which of course he dared not show, and blunted his wits.

However, he set forth plenty. At the holy boulder in a shaw nearby, the king himself killed a fat cow, beheading it with one sweep of his ax; he joined Bard and an elder in dipping rune-marked twigs in the blood and sprinkling the worshippers; when he asked the goddesses for their help and blessing, his shout rang into the booming wind like a command. Thereafter men crowded into Bard's house, out of the weather. Women brought ale while the meat and other good food cooked; after the eating was done and the boards taken away, merriment grew uproarious.

By then eventide had set in. The drinking bade fair to go on half the night or longer. At Eirik's side in the high seat, Gunnhild looked up and down along the walls. Light of fires and lamps sprang ruddy across faces, flashed off teeth and metal, cast uneasy shadows over wainscots and among the roof-beams. Smoke drifted thin, still rich with food smells. Wind brawled and shrilled. She wondered why its cold seemed to reach in and touch her. The honey and herbs of the mead she sipped had somehow gone bitter.

Eirik too looked around. Men of the household stood nearby, their ale horns in their hands. His men filled most of the benches. He leaned forward and crooked a finger. When one who saw came before him, he asked, "Where's Bard? I don't see him anywhere." Those who needed to piss merely stepped out the door and came straight back.

"He's looking after his other guests, lord," answered the islander. "He should be done soon."

"Other guests? How's that?"

"About a dozen off the sea, King. Bard took them to an outbuilding where we keep fire," which was always troublesome to kindle afresh, "and had it stoked up for them to dry their clothes. Then he had a board brought in, with food and drink. I helped. He's gone back now with two thralls to see this is cleared away and the travelers have clean straw to sleep on."

"Who are they?"

"They serve the hersir Thorir Hroaldsson, lord. He's gone north for a wedding."

Eirik stiffened. "What, men of my foster father's, treated like that?" His voice lashed. "Bring them here. Now!"

The islander stared into the lean face and well-nigh quailed. "At once, King." He hurried off.

Gunnhild laid a hand on Eirik's. "Don't be too hard on those carls," she said beneath the hubbub. "Belike they didn't know who Thorir is." It was as if the wind and the shadows were warning her of something. She had a chill feeling that the Finnish wizards could have told her what it was; but she had sent them out of the world. Keep the peace, she thought; hold the wild night at bay. Keep safe the child that had lately quickened in her.

"Maybe not," Eirik snapped, "but if Bard doesn't either, he'll get his nose rubbed in it."

That unhappy man came straightaway back, the newcomers close behind. He was middle-aged, squat, squint-eyed, of lowly birth but a hard and able worker. "Lord," he stammered, "I, I thought—these wayfarers, wet and roughly clad—and no room for them, really, at your feast—"

He seemed all the smaller against the stranger who stood at his back. Gunnhild's gaze went to the latter. The sight of him was like the storm suddenly smiting her. He bore a doom, she knew, nightmarishly unsure how she knew. For a flash she wished she had never gone to Finnmörk. She stamped the fear underfoot and, holding on to a mask of calm, narrowed her stare.

He was young but huge, bull-necked, the mighty shoulders slightly hunched. Brow and chin were broad, jaw thick, under stiff black hair and beard; eyes smoldered dark beneath a bony shelf; the shaggy eyebrows met. His nose too, though short, was grossly wide, like the lips along his gash of a mouth. Easy it was to see what wrath burned red in him.

Eirik greeted the man at his side. "I know you, Ölvir," the king said. "Welcome, for my foster father's sake." The tight smile died; the bleak eyes swung back to Bard. "As for you, hitherto I've thought well of you, so I'll let this mistake of yours go by. But make it up tonight!"

"Yes, my lord," Bard mumbled. "I did wrong. I'm sorry."

"You did swinishly," snarled the big young man. "King, not only did he doss us in his firehut; he gave us nothing better to eat than bread and butter and curds, nothing to drink but whey." The eyebrows worked in his face, one up, one down.

"As hungry and thirsty as we were, it tasted well," said Ölvir. Clearly he too would rather keep the peace.

"Who are you?" Eirik asked the first speaker.

"Egil, son of Skallagrim in Iceland and brother of Thorolf, whom you well know," growled the answer. "Ill has this Bard dealt with me."

"He'll make it right, I said," Eirik told him curtly. To Ölvir: "Take the honor seat across from me, let your crew sit below, and we'll enjoy ourselves."

Those who must now stand said nothing against it, under the king's eye. Egil plumped himself down beside Ölvir.

Bard hustled about, seeing to it that the horns of the new guests were kept full.

This being a holy evening, to drink hail to someone or something was lucky. The king had begun it with the cup to Thor. Then the headman of his guards plighted the king. After a few more such olden usages, it became open to anybody. When the wish struck him, a man would rise, or lift his horn high if he was on the floor, and shout "Skaal!" loudly enough to be heard. The women scurried around with their buckets, bowls, and ladles, topping every vessel. The man named what he had in mind. It might be a friend, even a woman, or a kinsman, or a forebear; it might be a call for well-being, good harvests at home and good booty abroad; it might be a vow to do this or that. "Skaal!" howled the rest, and each of them drained his horn to the bottom.

As time went on, this happened ever oftener. The vows got reckless. "I'll raid in Scotland and bring home a shipful of girls!" "Nothing so easy or safe for me. Next year I'm off to Denmark!" The first blowhard glared at the second, but a third man caught his arm and whispered in his ear, with a nod toward the king and queen. Talk and whoops and snatches of song brawled on. Belike it would mostly be forgotten tomorrow.

Gunnhild was glad she need not join in. She could sit and, behind a locked face, scorn the foolishness. Eirik must show what they believed was manhood, but bousing never went to his head. He answered those who drunkenly spoke to him in such short wise that they did not linger.

A newcomer reeled to his feet and made for the door. He did not get there before he doubled over and yorked. Retching, he staggered on into the night, toward the firehut, where he would sleep it off. Another gagged and made better haste. Well, thought Gunnhild, they had had a hard day and scant food. Her look kept stealing across the room to Egil. She hated the sight, but it was as if her eyes had gotten a wariness and a will of their own. He said almost nothing, only sat sullen, gulping down hornful after hornful.

Still another of Ölvir's men sickened, and another and another. Bard himself helped bring drinks to that gang. Maybe he was trying to dampen what anger they still felt. More likely, Gunnhild thought, he hoped to be done with them soon; and their heads in the morning would avenge his shame. Through fire-flicker and smoke-haze she saw how he pinched his mouth together.

Now almost all of them were gone, leaving filth behind. A woman filled a horn for Bard. He bore it to Ölvir. Thorir's steward gulped, wet his lips, and did not reach for the peace offering. Egil snatched it instead.

Those who spied the rudeness fell silent. They stared toward the empty stretch of bench under that seat. None had yet cared to sit there again. Through the half-hush, Gunnhild heard Bard scoff, "You must be thirsty." He went off and fetched a fresh horn, which he brought to Egil. The big man took it. A verse rolled from his throat:

"You told the foeman of trolls—
    tricky, you robber of graves—
lacking was drink for your lodgers.
You lied, while you gave to the godlings.
Mean in your heart, you made mock
    of men who to you were unknown.
Badly you dealt with us, Bard.
Base do I therefore call you."

Bard quivered. "Drink up and stop sneering," he choked, turned on his heel, and walked stiffly away.

Egil snorted, tossed off his hornful, and bellowed for another.

Gunnhild leaned toward Eirik. "This is outrageous," she hissed. "Shall that ruffian treat your man thus?"

"Let it go," he said. "Everybody's drunk. He's a rowdy, yes, but his poem was skillfully made. And he's Thorolf's brother."

"He stinks of danger."

"No, it's merely puke and farts you smell. True, he's spoiling for a fight, but I'll not have that here."

The unborn stirred. What she would do burst upon Gunnhild like surf against a cliff. She did not stop to wonder about it. If she tarried, her will might falter. "I must go out," she said. The steadiness of her voice was faintly surprising to her.

Eirik nodded. She stepped down. The crowd parted for her. Passing near Bard, she caught his glance and tossed her head the least bit. Having been too busy to drink much, he understood. He waited a short while and came after her.

They met in the entry. Weapons stood stacked against the wall. Steel sheened with what light trickled through the inner doorway. Beyond the outer door, wind hooted.

"I'm sorry, my lady," groaned Bard. "It dishonors us, that boor hogging drink after drink and still claiming he's thirsty."

"He knows full well that it does," Gunnhild answered. "But he's worse than a bother. I think no few men will die if he leaves here alive."

Bard shivered. Though little was openly said about it, many had heard something of her background. "In—indeed?"

"Go find a good big horn," Gunnhild ordered. "Meet me in the bower."

She went forth into the night. The wind snatched at her. She must take hold of her headcloth lest it blow off. She paid that no heed, nor the chill or the shrieking. The same firmness was upon her that she had reached in the gamma of the Finns. Egil Skallagrimsson was one to get rid of.

The bower was small but snug, meant mostly for women and such things as their weaving. A bed had been set up for her and Eirik. Candles burned in quietness. "Go," she bade the maidservant who waited. "Help in the hall. When you see the king and me leaving it, come back here."

Alone, she first sought the pot. Squatting on the ground like a bondwoman would have been barely less nasty than fumbling in a strange, unlighted outhouse. Quickly, then, she bent and searched through her baggage. She found the small bottle she wanted before Bard knocked.

She wasted no time with him. "Hold the horn out," she

said. He caught a breath when she poured something dark into it. "Now take it back, carefully, get it filled with ale, and give it to that Egil. Mark it first, though, to make twice sure it goes to him and none other."

He whitened. "A deadly brew?" he whispered.

She laughed. "Unmanly? Well, I am a woman." Starkly: "And I am your queen."

"But—"

"Men die of many things. If he cramps and heaves and must be borne away, and tomorrow they find him cold, that's not unheard of." Bard shuddered. "Go, I told you. If you spill a drop of this, woe will truly be upon you."

He mustered boldness. "I won't fail. And I, I'll not be sad."

She stoppered the bottle and hid it again. Surefooted in the murk, she made her own way back. Windows glowed ahead like embers. She wanted to be there when the thing happened. Not erenow had she used this knowledge she won in the North. Did the same icy thrilling sing in a man bound for a death-fight?

She took her seat by Eirik and peered after Bard. Yes, yonder he stood by the ale tub. A maid ladled the horn full for him. In his other hand was a bit of charcoal. He scrawled on the horn and gave it to her. Gunnhild saw him point at Egil. The woman bore it to the Icelander. Gunnhild strove to keep her hands lying loose on her lap. From out of her mask she watched Egil.

Ölvir slumped beside him, half asleep. Egil must have been swilling everything brought for both of them. He took this. The woman went elsewhere, unwitting. A sideways glance showed Gunnhild how Bard turned his back.

Egil did not toss the horn off. He held it before him, looking closely all around it. The thought shocked through Gunnhild that he must all along have been more aware and wary than he seemed.

With his right hand, Egil drew his knife. He stabbed the ball of his left thumb. With the same point, he scratched on the horn.

Runes, Gunnhild knew sickly.

He sheathed the knife, took the horn in his right fist, and rubbed the bleeding onto the scratchings. His bear-growl rolled forth:

"I round the horn with runes,
    reddening then their spell.
Words I cut in the wood
    that wild on the oxhead grew.
Drink did we freely the draught
    drawn by the merry maidens.
This, signed by Bard himself—
    we'll see how it works on us."

The horn cracked asunder. The ale splashed on the bench.

He had learned that much wizardry, at least, Gunnhild knew. What witch in Iceland fostered him?

And night had long since fallen, and Egil was the grandson of Dusk-wolf.

Eirik tautened. Most men were too drunk to have seen what went on. A few nearby gaped without understanding. A woman or two stifled a scream. Egil's black eyes met Gunnhild's. He grinned.

Ölvir moaned, put elbows on knees, clutched head in hands. Egil bent toward him. Sheer luck, Gunnhild thought dizzily. Or else it meant that a different weird awaited the two of them.

The Icelander clapped the steward between the shoulder blades. "Hoy, now," he said, well-nigh cheerfully. "Time we put you to rest, eh?" He rose, offering an arm. Ölvir lurched up and clung to it. Asking no leave of the king, saying naught whatsoever, Egil led the tottering man away.

Bard trotted after them. Fear and shame ransacked his face. He gripped a horn. The ale slopped with his haste. "Wait," he called. "Wait, Ölvir. Have a last drink with me. A friendly drink."

Egil and Ölvir passed into the entry. Bard did too. Gunnhild heard him cry, "No—" and thought Egil must have grabbed the horn. Then the dreadful voice rolled again, with laughter behind it.

> "I am half drunk, and Ölvir
> is altogether done for.
> The rain from the oxhead's root
> is rushing down my throat.
> Unsteadily you stagger,
> good spearman, but for me
> the storm of Odin—skaldcraft—
> has started raining poems."

There followed a yell and a thud. Two thuds. Wind howled through an open door, sent sparks flying off the fires, snuffed some of the lamps.

Eirik leaped down from the high seat. "Bring lights!" he shouted. Gunnhild sat frozen.

On her way out soon afterward she saw what he had seen. Ölvir sprawled snoring in a pool of his own spew. Bard lay beside him. A sword, which must have been Egil's, taken off the stack and lightning-fast unsheathed, had thrust from belly to backbone. Guts sagged loose; blood muddied the floor; death-stench hung sharp.

Earlier, the king's men had sought the firehut. Roused, Ölvir's crew mumbled that Egil had dashed in, taken his other weapons, and sped off.

"Well," Eirik bade, "seize every ship and boat on this island. Quickly. Come daylight, we'll hunt him down and kill him."

He spoke no word to Gunnhild, then or ever, about the shattered horn. Belike he guessed at something but did not want to hear. No matter, Gunnhild thought at first. Egil would soon be dead.

But search though they might, they did not find him.

VIII

Almost two weeks had passed when Thorir Hroaldsson came before Eirik. The king and queen had gone on to another garth. Although the hersir left in search of them as soon as he could, that was a hard overland ride.

Gunnhild did not witness the meeting—men's business, and unhappy. But later her husband told her about it. She gathered more from guardsmen whom she had charmed with her beauty and soft words.

Eirik's warriors stood armed around the room. Thorolf's few had set their own weapons aside. They waited at his back while he trod before the high seat and greeted the king.

"You are less welcome than you might be, if you are sheltering Egil Skallagrimsson," Eirik told him. He never blustered; his angers were wintry.

"He is at my farm in Sygnafylki, yes," Thorir answered. "I hope to make peace."

"I would hear nothing of that from anyone but you, and unlikely you are to get your wish. Why do you fare on his behalf? I thought you an honorable man, Thorir."

The hersir flushed but stood rock-steady. "Troth belongs to honor, King. I am here for Egil's brother Thorolf, who fought at your side more than once, and for my son Arinbjörn, who is Egil's friend. Arinbjörn swore that in this matter they two shall suffer the same doom." Thorir was still for a bit. It was a cloudy day. Fitful sunlight flickered through the house. "Youthful rashness, you may well think, but my son stands by his oaths, and I will stand by my son. He has talked of becoming a man of yours, if you will have him."

The offer glanced off Eirik's ice. "Do you know what Egil did?"

"He has not hidden it. Rough he may be, but no nithing. And, King, it was not a small feat to swim from Atley to Saud island through those seas."

"Where he killed three more of my men, and left the rest stranded."

Here and there, a grin scuttled to hide itself beneath a mustache, a snicker stayed well down in a throat. The affray had had its funny side. Thorir's followers stayed grave. They might have to die this day, fighting as best they could.

Eirik went on: "Belike you know I set a guard on every ship and boat. When we could not find him anywhere on Atley, I sent parties out among the smaller islands around. Thereafter I must needs leave, but the news has been given me. Nine men landed on Saud. Three stayed by their boat; the rest went searching. Egil prowled out from where he was denned and fell upon those three. Their friends found them slain and the boat gone. They were there for days and nights before someone saw their fire and took them off. The grazing livestock they had to slaughter for food stands likewise against Egil."

"He rowed that long, heavy boat by himself, the whole way back and well into the Sognefjord," said Thorir. "A doughty man."

"Strong as a bear or a wild boar, though I call him a wolf's head." From beneath Eirik's weather-bleached brows, out of the hatchet face, his eyes stabbed. "What have you yourself seen?"

"We'd come home from Thorolf's wedding the day before. He and his bride were with us. Ölvir's crew had returned a little earlier. It was well done of you, King, to let them go in peace. They gave us the tidings. Thorolf and Arinbjörn were heavy-hearted. They feared they would never see Egil again. But next morning, there he was."

"Tell me how he boasted of his misdeeds."

"He told the truth." Thorir squared his shoulders. "I'll keep nothing from you." Afterward Gunnhild thought that the tale would get around anyway. Folk overheard things. Nor was Egil shy. "He made a verse about it. He's a skald, King, a skald in whom lies the seed of greatness."

Eirik leaned back and bridged his fingers. "Say me the verse."

Quoth the hersir, ungladly but stoutly:

"So have I freed
myself from the house
of the guardian of Norway,
and Gunnhild withal,
that three of the men
of that thane of Odin
are faring hence
to the halls of Hel."

Slowly, Eirik nodded. Poems did more to keep fame alive—like the wind that spreads dandelion seeds, year after year after year—than any runestone. And Egil's had at least been respectful of him.

Nonetheless talk went on for a long time. Eirik would not readily come to terms. "It's true what my father told me," he said, "that never is anyone safe with that family."

Yet Thorir was his foster father, and laid the case in his hands. Arinbjörn was his foster brother—a few years younger, and as boys they had sometimes quarreled, but by the time Eirik left they were good friends. It beseemed a great man to be great-hearted.

The upshot was that he said, "We may reach some kind of agreement. Part of it must be that Egil shall not long linger in my kingdom. Then for your sake, Thorir, I will take wergild for Bard and those others, and ransom for the kine."

He set it high. Thorir had brought marks of silver along and paid on the spot. They ate and drank together that evening and in the morning, though rather coolly. Then Thorir went home.

When Gunnhild first heard about the hersir's arrival, she had guessed what the errand was and urged Eirik to get Egil killed, along with anybody who took the Icelander's side. Now she did not nag him. That would only raise his hackles. Instead, he ought to remember, and later seek her redes beforehand. Also, their new son would help strengthen her hold on him. When alone one night, she had sung songs over something she bought from a hireling, unbeknownst to her husband, the stones of a gelded stallion colt. Thus she made sure that this second child he got on her would be another son.

IX

Eirik and Gunnhild spent Yuletide with King Harald Fairhair in Hadaland. There they heard the full tale of a thing that had happened during the summer.

Harald was in Vikin, on a holding of his at the Oslofjord, when a ship came in from England. The skipper gave out that he bore a gift from the English King Aethelstan. Their tongue yonder was enough like that spoken in the Northern lands that folk who took a little trouble about it could understand each other. When the news reached Harald, he bade the crew be brought to him at once, and received them well.

Aethelstan was called both the Pious and the Victorious. He had earned either nickname. His grandfather had been Aelfred the Great. His father Eadweard and Eadweard's sister Aethelflaed, widow of the earl of Mercia, had together led the warring that threw back the last Danish onslaught and went on to bring the Danes of East Anglia under English sway. On Aethelflaed's death, Eadweard got the kingship over Mercia as well as Wessex. The princes of Wales gave him allegiance and paid him tribute. After Eadweard died, Aethelstan took Northumbria, and made the kings of the Scots and of Strathclyde acknowledge him their overlord. Not lightly would he send messengers to Norway.

The headman of these held forth a sword. Its hilt shone gilded; the sheath was inlaid with gold and silver and set with gems. "This does King Aethelstan send you and asks you to accept," he said loudly. Delighted, Harald grasped it. "Now you have taken the king's sword according to his will," said the spokesman, "and so you are his vassal; for he who takes the king's sword becomes the king's man."

A priest had come along in the ship and the English were newly shriven. Still, they may have shivered inwardly as red and white went across King Harald Fairhair's face. But he only tossed the weapon aside and coldly ordered that they be lodged elsewhere than with him.

It was not his way to fly into rages. Rather, he held himself shut until his wrath had drained, and then thought about what to do. On the following day he talked with the wisest among his friends. They all counseled him to let the outlanders go home unharmed. He did, giving them no word to take back for Aethelstan.

Over the winter he often brooded upon the trick. It could not have been meant to lay any real claim. Nor could it have been a mere taunt. He decided it was a warning, that the Norse had better leave England in peace. Harald was old and sated, but his sons were not. He thought how he could reply in kind.

Meanwhile Gunnhild had brought forth her new son. This birth went easier than the first. Eirik gave her her wish and named him Rögnvald after her grandfather. Erelong she was again with child. Many offspring would make it likelier that her blood and Eirik's would rule. She handed them over to wet nurses so that her own breasts would not soon begin to sag. Keeping her youthful looks was one way of keeping Eirik her own. Finding fresh ways to rouse his lust was another. Sometimes, when nobody watched, she also tied cunning knots in a string braided from her hair and his—a lock quietly gathered up when he had it cut—while muttering a Finnish chant; or she rubbed her little Frey image with goat's fat; or other such spells.

Above all, she worked toward becoming his helpmeet in kingcraft. He was strong, fearless, hard-souled, shrewd, but not a deep thinker. She believed she could learn what redes to give him. If then he heeded her, let the world beware!

First she must know what went on. A few spies were in her pay. Mainly, though, men who had tidings gave them to her freely, whether or not they knew they were doing so. Her talk and smile dazzled them. That was an easy skill to gain, as dull-witted and full of themselves as most were.

In this wise, among other things she kept track of Egil. He and Thorolf spent the winter at Thorir's. By spring they had readied a longship and raised a crew. Off they sailed in viking, down past Norway and through the Danish straits into the Baltic.

Thorolf, she thought, Thorolf who freed her from the wizards, who spoke with her so flowingly and warmly, whose head shone bright beneath the sun, whose eyes had once seemed to hold a wordless yearning, Thorolf was now not only the brother—which was hardly his fault—but the brother-in-arms of hateful Egil. The oftener she remembered, the sharper grew her bitterness.

A while later she heard how King Harald had sent north for his son by Thora Mostr-staff, Haakon. Nobody knew whether the mother wept after saying farewell. She had wedded a yeoman in the neighborhood, but later took sick and died.

Harald sent Haakon to England in a ship skippered by one Hauk, called Highbreeks, a mighty warrior and close to him. The Norse found King Aethelstan in London, holding a grand feast. Hauk told those of the crew who followed him ashore how to behave. The man who went first into the hall should go out last. They should all stand in a row at the table, with the same distance between them. Each should have a sword at his left side, but hang his cloak to hide it. Thereupon they entered, thirty tall men.

The English waited in tight stillness. Hauk trod up before the king and gave seemly greeting. Aethelstan made him welcome.

Everybody had wondered at seeing a little boy with the Norse leader. Now Hauk lifted him and set him on the king's knee. Aethelstan asked what that meant. "Harald the king bids you foster this child of his by a serving woman," Hauk told him.

A gasp went around the room. Aethelstan snatched a sword that lay beside him and drew it. Said Hauk: "You have taken him upon your knee, and you can murder him if you like; but you will not have made an end of all King Harald's sons."

He turned and strode from the hall. His men fell in behind him. Aethelstan signed for peace and no one else stirred until they were gone. They went straight back to their ship, rowed down the river, and hoisted sail for Norway.

King Harald was much pleased. Well had he answered the English sending; for he who fosters another's child is reckoned the lowlier. The two kings were now even.

Aethelstan had not the heart to slay an innocent youngling, who sat there fearless. He took Haakon into his household, had him christened, and raised him as one of his own.

Unfriendliness heightened between Eirik and his brothers.

In fall Gunnhild learned that Egil and Thorolf had returned, and somewhat about their farings. They harried widely, as far as Kurland. There a band of men caught a smaller band led by Egil and took them captive after a stiff fight. They bound the vikings, whom they threw into an outbuilding on a farm. Night was falling. In the morning they would torture the prisoners to death.

Egil worked loose from his bonds and untied the others. With the help of a Dane called Aaki, who had also been held there, they broke out. The end of it was the Kurlanders slain, the farm sacked and burned.

Aaki and his sons joined the Norse. Late in the season, they guided a raid on the Danish trading town Lund, which left it likewise looted and ashen. On the island of Fyn they stopped at Aaki's great garth and, after a feast, bade him farewell.

Elsewhere the brothers landed as peaceful guests, until they came home to Thorir. Some of the poems Egil had made along the way got through to Gunnhild. They clanged and clashed; they would live for many lifetimes. Might *his* be short.

Further news: Thorir's son Arinbjörn invited Egil to stay with them a second winter. Thorir warned that that would not sit well with King Eirik. Arinbjörn said that that could be handled if Thorolf stayed there too—where, after all, his wife was. Gunnhild's lips writhed. She crooked her fingers.

Among the seafarers under the same roof were two kins-men of Thorir's, brothers named Thorvald the Hothead and Thorfinn the Stern. They had become as near friends of Thorolf Skallagrimsson as Arinbjörn was of Egil. The dark months saw much merriment.

First, however, Thorir sought out King Eirik. His foster son welcomed him more kindly than last time. "Blame me not if I house Egil this winter also," Thorir asked.

"You shall have your wish," Eirik answered, "though it would have gone otherwise if anybody else held a hand over him." He was in a mellow mood.

Gunnhild could not well speak up until she and her husband were alone. Then she rounded on him as she had never done before. "I see, Eirik, it's with you as aforetime. You let men talk you over, and forget the harms done you. You'll spare these Skallagrimssons till at last they're the death of your closest kin. If you make naught of Bard's killing, I don't."

Eirik's cheer left him. "Gunnhild, no one pushes me into ruthlessness more than you do. Time was when you were fonder of Thorolf. I'll not go back on my word about those brothers."

"Thorolf was a good man till Egil ruined him," she spat. "Now the two of them are the same."

Eirik's hand chopped downward. Enough, it said. Gunnhild wrangled no more. She must bide her time, she knew, and weave her web, as women always must.

X

Every year, late in spring there was a mighty offering at Gaula in Sygnafylki, for a good summer and harvest. Men flocked to it from widely about and stayed on for days, talking, drinking, sporting, dickering. Gunnhild thought something more might be done. The land and steading belonged to King Harald, but he was hardly ever there. Eirik would be this time, and she with him, now that she had lightened herself of the boy they named Guthorm.

The young king had come to think highly of her brothers
Aalf the Shipman and Eyvind the Braggart, skilled sailors
and hardy fighters; but their overbearing ways made them
disliked among yeomen. She met with them in a loftroom.
"It might well happen in that crowd that somebody or other
got killed," she said. "I'd like it if that was a son of Skallagrim, or better yet both of them."

"Not at the steading!" said Aalf. "That's hallowed
ground while the gathering lasts."

"I know," said Gunnhild, "but men will be camped
widely around and milling about."

Eyvind threw back his red head. "Then it'll be done," he
laughed. He was the reckless one.

"We'll try our best," Aalf promised, Neither son of Özur
Dapplebeard knew Thorolf more than slightly, nor Egil at
all, but their sister's hatred was enough for them. Also, she
would see to it that they were well rewarded; and surely
her husband would be far from displeased.

With guardsmen and servants, then, Eirik and his queen
took ship for Gaula. It was an easy faring, as if wind and
sea alike hastened her toward her revenge. Each eventide
they stopped where the leaders, at least, could sleep under
a roof. Into the Sognefjord they turned, and on and inward,
between ever higher shores, where waterfalls speared down
into woodland depths and farms clung to cliffs, until they
reached the wharves they were after. Ships and lesser craft
already lay manifold, but dockroom waited for the king's.
A footling ran ahead and soon men brought horses for the
lordly ones to ride up the road to the steading.

The hall stood bright with hangings, pillars carved to
show the twelve highest gods. The evening feast was worthy of it. Gunnhild hardly tasted the mead poured for her.
Man after man came before the king to hail him.

Her heart sprang. Now it was Thorir, and Thorolf at his
side, Thorolf who had no right to look so fair. If only he
were as ugly as Egil!

Eirik answered the hersir's greeting with a smile, the
Icelander's with a nod. Thorolf's face tightened. His gaze
barely flickered across Gunnhild's. Then the two went and

took their seats. What with those in between, she caught no more than glimpses of him thereafter. Was he less mirthful than most, or was that merely her wish? She slept ill that night.

Next noon Aalf visited her at the bower, as they had agreed. She had taken care to be alone. Her question pounced. "Is Egil here?"

"No," he told her. "I've mingled with folk from there and heard. When Thorir was making ready to go, he said to his son Arinbjörn that Egil must stay behind. What with Egil's temper, your wiles, and the might of the king—his words—it would be too hard to keep watch on things. But Egil would only stay if Arinbjörn stayed too. Which Arinbjörn did, for friendship's sake. They say he'd like sometime to join your husband's household warriors. I think a man so faithful would be worth having."

"Maybe, if ever he gets free of Egil," Gunnhild snapped. "Well, send Thorolf from here down to Helheim. That may bring the brother out of his snug safe shelter."

Aalf frowned. "It won't be easy. Thorir and Thorolf stick together all the time. Two other men are never far from them, big, tough bullyboys. I heard they're kinsmen of Thorir's, who went in viking with Egil and Thorolf." He shrugged. "We'll have to see how it goes."

Gunnhild bit her lip.

The days wore on. She could do nothing but be the queen, whether warm or aloof. Tents spread like mushrooms over the fields, among the plank booths. The throngs swirled and jostled, gabbed and gamed, sweated and stank. At length the great day dawned. It was gray and windy, with quick rain-showers, but a roof stood over the slaughterstone; never mind how wet wool on wet men smelled. Thereafter they choked the hall, where the tapestries had been taken down because the horse blood was to be sprinkled everywhere. They ate of the seethed flesh and drank of the broth.

Gunnhild kept offside, like the few other women who were not serving. Now and then she could even be by herself, to stride back and forth in a lesser room gnawing on her wrongs. Naught else. It would have been unwise to carry along any means of witchcraft—which, moreover, might well anger the gods. But then she must sit by Eirik in the high seat, amidst the gorging and guzzling, until she could plead weariness and withdraw to the bower where they slept, away from the sight of Thorolf.

Next morning, those who were farthest from home began to leave. In a few more days, everything would have ended. Crossing the yard, Gunnhild spied Eyvind and beckoned to him. They stood aside and spoke low. "Why have you done nothing yet?" she put to him. "Are you afraid?"

He flushed beneath the freckles. "I've told you before, there's been no opening. Thorir's too careful of Thorolf."

She sighed. "Well, maybe you can kill one of his men? That's better than letting them all get away." A little, little easing of the hurt and wrath in her.

"It could well be," he answered more happily. "Aalf and I have been behaving friendly, hoping we can get near enough. He's more or less given up, but I'm keeping a sharp eye out."

Eyvind believed himself crafty, Gunnhild thought. Almost, she wished she had not asked for this. But how could she take it back without seeming qualmish and thus weakening her hold on both her brothers?

He saw a fellow he knew, shouted to him, and went from her.

Two mornings later, she recalled her fleeting regret.

Eirik was tarrying only to lead the farewell offering that would give Gaula back to everyday life. Meanwhile he went hunting or hawking, or heard what such men of mark as also lingered had to say to him. He need no longer sit up late among drunks; nor did the lendmen, who were King Harald's reeves in their own shires, or the hersirs, who upheld the laws in their own neighborhoods, or the elder yeomen. Gunnhild was glad of at least this much. She didn't like his lovemaking much when his breath reeked of drink, though she gave him a show of eagerness.

He woke still earlier than wonted on that day. As he swung to the floor, she roused too. His face stood keen-edged, in the dimness of the room. "Something's astir," he said. When she listened closely, she too caught sounds of muffled unease. A lynx does best to sleep with ears cocked.

Eirik scrambled into breeks, shoes, and sark. He hung sword at shoulder and strode out. Gunnhild took longer, for the sake of a seemliness she inwardly cursed. Coming through the door, she found the eastern sky steel-gray. A belated star glimmered in a west still dusky. Thin mists smoked low above dew. Trees and buildings hulked shadowy. Air hung cold. Though nobody spoke loudly, words drummed through the hush.

She went to Eirik's side. He stood before a band of men. Apart from spears sheening wanly overhead, they had no weapons in hand, but some wore their own swords. Haggardness told of a sleepless night. Her brother Eyvind was at the forefront. His fists were knotted and his right cheek twitched. Aalf stood grim beside him. On the other flank were Thorir, Thorolf, and a bearlike, unkempt warrior who glared red-eyed. Thorfinn the Stern, she'd heard, a sea-mate of Egil's, another guest at the same house. A block of men kept these apart: yeomen who dwelt hereabouts, led by the lendman Skopti Sveinarson.

Skopti was saying: "—well that you're here ahead of the sun, lord. It was a long night, and tempers are frayed." Nobody wakened a king, unless in the direst need. He might be having a foresightful dream.

"We will hear this case at once, but in lawful wise," Eirik answered. "To the hall!" On the way he muttered to Gunnhild, "It seems Eyvind the Braggart has done a manslaying there."

"What?" The world rocked. She snatched a breath. It smoked back from her lips. "Yes, we'll hear this out."

Though it was not quite right for a woman, she took the high seat with him. "We'll have no squabbling to and fro," Eirik said. "Let the aggrieved speak first."

Thorir did. "Last night Eyvind killed a man of mine, and in the very halidom."

"My brother," snarled Thorfinn. "My brother Thorvald, who gave him no threat. King, I saw it."

"Say on, then," Eirik bade him.

"We were drinking in here." Distraught with rage and grief, Thorfinn talked wildly. Other witnesses offered words more helpful. Bit by bit, like sight of a headland through a storm, the tale came forth.

A number of men had stayed long at the ale horns. Thorir and Thorolf had gone to bed, but Thorfinn and Thorvald were awake. Eyvind and Aalf were too, and joined them. It seemed to be well meant. Indeed, Özur's sons had already tried for good cheer with these two. At first all went well. They drank in a foursome, passing a horn around from hand to hand till it was empty, then shouting for more. Aglow after a while, they decided to make this friendlier yet by drinking in pairs, Aalf with Thorfinn, Eyvind with Thorvald.

Gunnhild moaned within herself. How often had she heard what this could lead to. As the drinkers got drunker, they grew more and more boastful, they strutted their manhood, they would brook naught that might be the least demeaning. And sometimes at last one said the other was drinking more than a fair share before passing the horn over, and the other flared up at that, and the end was harsh words or worse.

"He called me a mare and asked if my witch-sister would bring in a troll to be my stallion," rasped Eyvind when Eirik told him to speak. "No man can sit still for that, can he?"

They had not nicknamed Thorvald the Hothead for nothing, Gunnhild thought. Yet Eyvind must have blared as loosely—or had he?

Eirik cut straight through to the truth. "If you'd kept your wits about you, you'd have kept the peace. If you woke angry today, you could have brought suit at the next Thing, or you could have challenged him to fight it out in a holmgang"—on an islet, the ground marked off by willow stakes, blows given turn by turn, and he who stepped out of the ground, or fell, was the loser. "You, though, had a sax with you," Eirik ended.

"How could I be sure of these ruffians' good faith?" Eyvind answered sullenly.

Even his brother Aalf gave him a hard look. Nobody else had borne weapons into the hallowed house. Knives were tools. Eyvind had kept the short sword hidden under his cloak, till suddenly he yanked it forth and stuck it into Thorvald. Not much blood gushed, though the man died after a few gasps. It had been a skilled, knowing thrust.

She had egged him on to this, Gunnhild knew. But how could she know he would be such an utter fool about it?

"Men of your household, King, and men of Thorir's well-nigh came to blows," said Skopti. "But others of good sense went in between. Now it lies with you."

"You did well," said Eirik grimly. "Eyvind, the law is the law. Because this manslaying happened where it did, at your hands, the law names you a wolf in the halidom, and outcast. I will hold my hand over you only as long as it takes for you to go from Norway." He turned to Thorir. "But for goodwill's sake, will you take wergild for your man, and Thorfinn for his brother? I leave it to you what the payment shall be."

"No," choked Thorfinn. "I'll kill that murderer wherever I find him."

Thorir shook his head. "I have never taken payment for a man," he said, almost sadly, "and I will not now."

So, after a time that dragged for Gunnhild, the meeting ended. The king, she, and her brothers walked out in the young sunlight, alone for this short span.

"I think something of yours went less well than it might have, Gunnhild," Eirik said.

She stiffened. "Would the outcome I wanted have been bad?"

"Leave that be. Done is done. Eyvind, you've been my sworn man, and Aalf is yet. I'll not forsake you. Go you must, but it'll be with a longship and crew, and a word from me to my Danish kinsman."

Eyvind gulped, wiped a hand over his eyes, and stammered, "Al—always will I be your man, lord, and, and your sons' after you."

May he do better by them in that morrow, Gunnhild thought.

Word reached her not too long afterward that King Harald Bluetooth had received Eyvind and his following well in Denmark. Eyvind was known to be among the best of fighters. Harald Bluetooth gave him some land and set him to standing offshore guard against vikings.

By then she had other things to deal with.

XI

King Harald Fairhair hated seid. Eirik felt less strongly, but did mistrust such doings. Gunnhild had known this was true of most highborn men. She never said more about her stay in Finnmörk than she had to. Rather, she led her listeners to think it had been a youthful mistake, which would have become a dreadful one if she had not been saved barely in time. Yes, she learned a few things yonder, mostly ways of healing and helping, but nothing great nor any threat to anybody.

When she met the old king, she had set herself to make him believe it too. Soft speech, warm smiles, worshipful glances, the least swing of her hips, quickly won him over. As for Eirik, he did not ask what uses she might now and then make of her skills, whatever they were.

In truth, there had been little thus far, forecastings and farseeings within narrow bounds, ill-wishings and well-wishings that she was never sure had wrought anything, the cantrips that kept his love from straying—although she knew her worldly ways had the most to do with that. Only during her first childbirth had she again flown free, maybe because the later ones were easier. When alone for a long enough span—which was seldom—she had cooked some brews and made some things that she kept hidden. Otherwise at such times she merely went through her knowledge lest she forget, dancing, singing, drawing signs; or she brooded upon it, tried to deepen her understanding of it. Naught more.

Now suddenly need came upon her.

Down in Vikin King Harald got news of a man in Hördafylki who was becoming well-known as a wizard. This Vitgeir foretold the morrow, turned maidens' hearts toward men, cast blights or blessings, for those who paid him. Harald deemed there would be too much anger in that neighborhood if he had Vitgeir killed out of hand. Instead, he sent a messenger with his order that the business stop at once. The messenger brought back an answer in verse.

> "Is it strange we do seid,
>   such as we are,
>   made to be born
>   of man and woman,
>   when Rögnvald the Highboned
>   readily does,
>   Harald's son
>   in Hadaland?"

The king went white. Verse had its own power, whether or not it be itself a spell. It reached for the soul.

When Gunnhild heard, she knew what it meant. Here Harald had had recalled to him that Rögnvald Highbone was among his sons by Snaefrid, who had been a witch or worse. In time he forgave them for that, and made those who still lived shire-kings. But Rögnvald had taken to spellcraft of his own, become mighty in it, and gathered others about him. Few men had told his father what went on—few were sure, and belike fewer yet dared—but folk in the Uplands where he had his seat went in awe of him, and dark tales drifted out. Hitherto Harald had given it a deaf ear and a blind eye. He must not have wanted even to think about it. Now the staves were flung before him, for everyone to hear that, set beside Rögnvald Highbone, the likes of Vitgeir were mosquitoes, hardly worth swatting.

King Harald kept silent. Soon, though, he and Eirik withdrew to a room where no one could overhear them.

Night had fallen when Eirik came back to the house he used at this holding of his father's. He found Gunnhild awake in their bedroom. Fully clad, she sat on a high, three-legged stool and stared into the flame of the one lamp that

was lighted. Sometimes her gaze followed the smoke upward. It curled and twisted oddly, for the night was hot,
altogether windless. The dull glow barely touched her face.
Beyond it dusk filled the room and blackness the uncovered
window.

Her skirts rustled in the thick stillness as she rose. Her
eyes seemed huge, seeking his, the pupils as wide as a
prowling cat's, the whites aglimmer. "I think you bear tidings," she said low.

Eirik's grin was no kind of smile. "You know I do."

"Can you share them?"

"Well, you'll hear soon enough. I'm to do something I've
been hankering for. King Harald has at last come to agree-
ing. Tomorrow I get men together and the stuff they'll need
for hard riding. The day after, we're off to make an end of
Rögnvald Highbone."

"I had a—foreboding of that."

Bleakness passed through Eirik's look at her; then he put
aside any questions and said flatly: "Too long has he
worked his trollcraft. It's sheer defiance of our father.
Whatever he has in mind, we'd better forestall it."

"I think it may well have to do with you."

Eirik nodded. "If he's alive when our father dies, he'll
likely grab for the kingship over all Norway that our father
wants to leave me."

And if he won it, what would become of their sons?
Gamli, bright, merry, flaxen-haired, running everywhere,
soon ready to be fostered out in a household that would be
kind to him; Rögnvald, namesake, but of the great jarl, not
the witch-king, stumping around earnestly trying to talk;
Guthorm, newly out of the cradle—and the next to come
and the next, blood of her and Eirik, life and the fame that
outlives life. An owl hooted beyond the walls, a voice of
darkness and forgottenness.

"More brothers of yours than him have the same
thought," Gunnhild said. Those who held shires egged their
folk on with promises. Others scoured about in viking or
in outland wars, not really working off their anger but gain-
ing followers. She and Eirik had talked about this erenow.

He shrugged. "Well, here's a beginning."

The owl hooted again and yet again. Its claws seemed to strike into her. She grabbed both Eirik's hands. "I know something of what Rögnvald Highbone knows. Do you think he won't be aware of you moving in on him? That he'll merely sit there?"

"He won't have time to raise a levy against us."

"But to bring down death on you—a landslide, a galloping sickness, grisly sights, blind fear—No, take a while to make better ready. Let me help."

"And let him get word of it. And smirch my name as one who used seid. No! Your cunning didn't work so well for you at Gaula, did it?"

Because Thorir Hersir had been shrewd and Eyvind the Braggart witless, she thought bitterly. Or maybe because the norns had woven together her weird and Egil Skallagrimsson's. She swallowed anything further. "You are the man," she sighed. "I can only send my hopes along with you."

He surprised her a bit by answering slowly, "Not that you're unwise, Gunnhild. Far from it." He threw his arms around her waist and pulled her to him. "How well I know!"

XII

On the third day after he left, Gunnhild told her wenches and carls that she wanted to spend that night alone. They should sleep elsewhere than in the house. "I have thinking to do, and maybe a helpful dream will come," she said. "If you happen to see or hear something, keep nonetheless away." She slitted her eyes. "And then best will be for you if you don't gossip about it."

As evening closed in, she shuttered windows and bolted doors. The weather had changed. Wind whined; rain whispered. Lampflames wavered; smoke and smell eddied. Dusk deepened and shadows stirred, misshapen as trolls. She unlocked a chest. From beneath costly silks she took what she wanted and carried it into the bedroom. That door she also made fast.

While dried mushrooms, of a kind that most folk shunned, soaked in a bowl of water, she laid everything else out and shed her clothes. Raw damp kissed her skin. She undid the knot of her hair and let the black locks tumble free over shoulders and back. A necklace of eagle feathers, wolf's teeth, and wildcat's claws became her garment. It had taken years, money, and wariness to get all this, little by little, mostly from hunters who were poor enough to search it out for pay, afraid enough to say nothing. With her own hands she had woven and carved.

She had not known until now when or if she was going to want it. She had merely vowed to herself that what she did and suffered in Finnmörk would not have been for naught, and never again would she be as helpless as that day in Seija's hut. Nor did she yet know how much use she could get from it. This was all untried, the outcome of thought, dreams, wordless feelings. So *should* it be, she half believed. If she was wrong, it could mean death or more than death.

She bared her teeth at the fear. For Eirik and their blood, she went into childbed over and over, as he went into battle. Tonight she set forth on a way that might go down hell-road. But without her he might well be bound yonder himself. Her sons were small. They still had need of their father.

Never would she forsake them or him.

A drum could have given her away. Having eaten of the mushrooms, she clapped her hands while she danced around and around the lamp she had set on her spaewife's stool. She kept her gaze on the flame. As the beat took hold of her, the tiny fire seemed to widen, a gate through which she began to see reaches that went on beyond sight. When she knew the time was right, she stopped, took two leg-bones of a deer carven with runes in her grip, and knelt on the knotted cord. She shook the bones, swayed on her knees, and sang, eyes steadfast on the flame.

The rain strengthened. Its rushing filled her skull. The

wind wailed. It lifted her on wings of pain and whirling-ness. But she must not leave herself. Not altogether. "Rögn-vald Snaefridarson," she wove into her chant, "I behold you, I hear you, I, the night wind, I, the new moon, I, the shadow forever at your heels. You know me not, you know me not for what I am, your bane, Rögnvald Snaefridarson. I seek you; I seek you; I seek you—"

The flame opened. Half of her flew into it, through it, skyward and northward. Half of her sang spells. Dizzily in the room and flesh, knife-keenly in the air and soul, each was with the other.

Clouds rolled gray-white below; stars glittered above. The moon had long since set, but it was the first new moon after Midsummer Eve, when balefires had burned high everywhere in every land, and it remembered them. Ahead of her Thor's Wain wheeled around the North Star, that some said was the eye Odin gave for wisdom. The moon belonged to older Powers, to earth and sea, begetting and bearing, wizards and witches. Norsemen offered to the gods in hopes of winning their goodwill. Shamans sought one-ness with the world in hopes that it would do their will. Eirik called on Odin, who bestowed victory or death as he saw fit. Tonight Gunnhild called on herself.

The rain fell behind. She swept over land that grew ever more high and steep. Hamlets, steadings, and their fields lay murkily edged by wilderness. Then red stars glowered on worldrim. She flew downward and nearer. Buildings squatted near a brook that gurgled over rocks and glim-mered dim silver. She knew Rögnvald was there, They sat up late inside. She passed through the roof and hovered in the smoke below the rafters.

Fire, tended by thralls who cringed more than most, leaped and crackled the length of the hall. Its light shud-dered over the men on the benches. Few looked like fight-ers. Some were old and gnarled, some grizzled, some young but their eyes not. They were well though plainly clad. Warlocks seldom showed off wealth. Here was a gathering of them from widely around.

The man in the high seat was tall, his face gaunt, with a

plowshare jaw under a swart beard. He was saying: "This will mean more than staving off a foe. Understand that. We cannot bring on an uprising against King Harald—not yet—but we can make the Uplands a stronghold against him." Rögnvald grinned. "It may be that he falls sick and dies, or comes otherwise to the end of a life that's already been long."

"First we must cope with the threat of him," said another.

Rögnvald jerked his head in a nod. "Have I not laid this out before you? A dead woman warned me—"

Gunnhild, in the flesh at the king's garth, shivered. Maybe Rögnvald spoke truth. Maybe it was even his mother whom he had troubled in her grave. However he did it, he had gotten forewarning that his father would disown him. Therefore he sent after lesser wizards. Humble and weak though many of them were, surely none as learned as he, together they could wreak untold harm. And Eirik's troop must be drawing nigh. He had guessed it would take him less than four days.

"Best not dawdle," said one.

"No," agreed Rögnvald. "Now that we're here, we'll find out what's afoot, and where, and make ready."

So, when by himself, he lacked the skill to spy afar. He was not so fearsome after all. However, an adder can bite while a man is crushing it underfoot.

Rögnvald pulled his tunic tighter about him. "Is something wrong, King?" asked a man nearby.

"No," Rögnvald muttered. "Only that it's gone cold, hasn't it?"

Gunnhild withdrew.

Now she must blind them. She was not a Gan-Finn such as could sell a bag of winds to a Norse skipper or raise a storm that wrecked him. But tonight she was halfway one with the world and its weather.

In the room at King Harald's garth she sang and beckoned. Above the hall in Hadaland she flowed herself into the air; she shaped herself into water. Mist began to blur the stars. After a while the steading lay wrapped in fog so thick that no man could have groped his way through the night outside. Witch-sight would find only shapelessness. A sending could flit above, but what could it see below? Most likely the warlocks would take this for happenstance and wait for it to clear. They did not know how short a time was left them.

Gunnhild dared not linger. They might somehow catch a whiff of her. And she was drained. Hardly aware any longer, she fell back down from the Uplands like a river falling to the sea.

A roof snapped shut on the sky. She was alone with a guttering lamp. Dazed, she barely stumbled through locking her things away before she toppled into bed. Next day she was dull and wrung-out.

Strength came back. And then Eirik did with his news. The fog had not hindered him and his men, once day broke. It lifted as they neared the steading. They ringed the hall in with spears and set fire to it. Women and housefolk they let out, but they killed such warriors as tried to follow. Rögnvald and his wizards burned.

Eirik won high renown for his deed. Gunnhild said nothing about her part. The kings would have looked too askance at it. Skalds did not make poems about birthing either.

Rögnvald's Snaefrid-brothers might want revenge. Gudröd Gleam in Agdir was the nearest. Throughout the months that followed, Gunnhild ill-wished him.

XIII

Gudröd spent that winter with his foster father, the skald Thjodolf of Hvini. Toward spring he grew so homesick that he ordered his ship made ready. Thjodolf warned him this was a bad time to sail. He even made a verse about it. But Gudröd would not listen. After he rounded the southern tip of Norway a great storm sprang up off Jadar. The ship went down with all aboard her.

That was one fewer to vex Eirik, Gunnhild thought when she heard. She could not tell how much she had had to do with it, but at least she had striven to help her man. Maybe next time she could find means not so thankless.

Somewhat later she got news that Egil and Thorolf were again off in viking toward the Baltic, with four ships. She could only hope they would come to grief. No spell of hers seemed to bite on the sons of Skallagrim Kveldulfsson. Someday, though, somehow, if the gods would not strike them down, she might wreak something herself.

Meanwhile there was enough else to do. Any lady of a big household must steer it day by day, keep track of everything that went in and out, hold the staff to their work, look to their needs, settle their squabbles, make sure that every guest was done by as befitted his rank and honor, be aware of all that happened which her husband might not know of and counsel him about it, take a lead in skilled womanly work such as weaving—it went on without end. If the lord was going away, he would leave a trusty man in charge; then the lady had better see to it that that man did what she felt was best. A queen was the lady of many households, and, above them, the whole kingdom.

Not that Harald Fairhair had ever put any real reins in the hands of a woman. But he had had scores. Whenever he wedded, it was mainly to forge ties with kinfolk. Eirik had only Gunnhild. The rest were fleeting sport, now and then, here and there. He took none openly and lastingly as a leman. Which was as well for them, Gunnhild thought. It was she with whom he truly lived. And, more and more, he told her what was on his mind and heard her redes.

This in turn, more and more, got other men to seek her help with this or that. What she did for them might anger still others, and the anger might fester into hatred. But so the world was; and from every happening, she learned.

Spring lost itself in summer, balefires blazed when the sun turned, the year waned toward fall, and again Gunnhild went heavy with child. Restless, Eirik had fared off to raid in Ireland. When he came home, he found her icily wrathful. She had lately gotten word from Denmark.

Much news flowed into a kingly house, not only from elsewhere in Norway. Ships plowed the seas throughout the

North, most of them in trade, though few chapmen hung
back from plundering when they could without risk. They
went as far west as Iceland, as far east as Aldeigjuborg on
Lake Ladoga, as far south as the lands of the Moors. Men
also trekked by horse and river, bearing such goods as furs
and amber into the Holy Roman Empire as well as the
vastnesses of Gardariki. Some even reached golden Miklagard, where the Emperor of the Greeks had his seat, or
Serkland beyond his realms. If afterward they called on a
Norse king, and they often did, they brought their tales and
tidings.

Thus, bit by bit over the months, Gunnhild had heard
what befell Egil and Thorolf. They veered from their first
aim and bore southwest for Jutland. After harrying there
they went on to Friesland, where they stayed for the rest
of the season. It was a land hitherto unknown to them, and
seemingly they got a wish for knowledge of it. At length
they headed back, belike meaning to put up at Thorir's for
another winter, heedless of Eirik. Egil's ship was the fas-
test. Given a fair wind, she ran ahead of the others. When
she reached the landmarks of the march between Friesland
and Jutland, he stopped to wait for his brother.

Several men had been camped thereabouts on the lookout. Two of them came from the marshy woods to Egil.
They were carls of Aaki, the Dane whom he had saved in
Kurland, with a warning from him. Eyvind Özurarson had
been able to keep track of the Icelanders. As the time when
they would likely return drew near, he took a strong fleet
around to the west coast. It lurked north of here, to catch
them when they passed by. Eyvind made no secret—far
from it—of his lust for revenge; and King Harald Bluetooth
had a reckoning of his own with them.

However, said the men, they themselves had been watchful, and knew that Eyvind had gone off for a little while,
being bored with sitting still. He lay not too far off with
only two ships, mere karfis, to set against Egil's dragon.

At once Egil bade his men take down the awnings and
row very quietly. They did so through the night. By dawn-
light they found the prey at anchor. Straightway they at-

tacked, hurling stones, spears, and arrows. No few of
Eyvind's men fell. Those who were left fought when Egil's
closed with them, but had no hope. Eyvind cast off his ring-
mail, jumped overboard, and swam ashore. Likewise did
those among his crews who could. Egil brought the two
ships back, together with all gear and weapons.

Thorolf had arrived. Aaki's messengers witnessed what
followed. When they got home, they told him and others.
Aaki had broad holdings and no few men at his beck. As
yet, the king held the outlying parts of Denmark too weakly
to quell the likes of him. From his hall on Fyn the word
went from mouth to mouth—little changed, if at all, for
honest men listened carefully to news that mattered and got
it well into memory—until it reached Gunnhild.

Egil told Thorolf how he won his booty, and added:

> "Hard and good we hit him,
> here alongside Jutland.
> Well did Denmark's warder
> wage the fight against us.
> At last, though, Eyvind Loudmouth
> left in search of shelter,
> wisely, through the water,
> and with his men swam eastward."

The mockery alone was a knife-thrust. "I think that after
what you've done, we can hardly go on to Norway," Thorolf said. Egil laughed and answered that there was no dearth
of places. He had no wife to leave behind.

King Eirik's mouth tightened when he heard. "Thorolf
was right," he said slowly. "Not even Thorir Hersir could
stay my hand now. We'll bide our time."

Gunnhild thought about that wife and her small daughter.
But no, to go after them would be unworthy, and useless.
Indeed, it would mean an unhealable break with Thorir,
Björn Brynjolfsson, and their kindred.

She felt her son kick in her womb.

He was born a little before Yule, when Eirik and she
were with Harald Fairhair in Haddingjadalar. The high king

had grown heavy, white of hair and beard; but he lumbered to the fiercely yelling bairn as a bear does to a beehive, himself poured the water, and bestowed his own name. A feeling rushed through Gunnhild that here the gift of mightiness passed straight from the old to the new.

XIV

Through the next two years and more, from time to time she heard about Egil.

From Denmark, the brothers sailed with their following south along Saxland and Flanders. Thereabouts they learned that King Aethelstan of England needed fighting men and great gain might be had in his service. They crossed the narrow sea through rough fall weather and rowed up the Thames to London, better than three hundred strong. When the king was told, he received them gladly. After talk about pay, honors, and other terms, they became his men. During that winter he got to be good friends with the Icelanders. Gunnhild could understand why. Thorolf was fair to behold, well-spoken, quick-witted, altogether winsome—were it not for his foul brother. Egil must be somewhat likable in his harsh way, when he chose, or he could not have gotten along with such folk as Thorir Hersir; and then there was his skaldcraft. Both bore tales of far lands and stirring deeds.

Aethelstan had set one condition. He would take no openly heathen men under his banner. Thorolf, Egil, and many others did not want baptism, but they agreed to be prime-signed. By this rite they showed Christ enough deference that Christians could freely deal with them, without forswearing their own gods.

So Egil still looked mainly to Odin, the lord of war, the father of wizardry, he who swung hanged on the world-tree Yggdrasil for nine nights to get the runes that meant power, but also he who had borne the mead of poetry forth into the world. Egil would, Gunnhild thought. When Thorolf named any god at all in her hearing, it had been Thor, red-

bearded slayer of trolls, bringer of lightning, thunder, and
the rain that quickens the earth.

She herself ought to feel somehow close to the one-eyed
Wanderer. He raised the dead to foretell the morrow for
him; he himself had gone beyond death and down into the
deeps of hell. Yet always he was in and of the sky. When
he swept through the world beneath, folk knew him oftenest
as the leader of the Aasgard's Ride, dead men on bone
horses with coldly fiery hounds, galloping along the night
wind in chase of a ghost quarry. When men fought, he
chose who should win and who die.

Frey, Freyja, Njörd, the Vanir of soil and sea, offered
more to women. But merely to worship them, though well
enough in childbirth or when hoping for a good harvest,
was likewise to give oneself over. Were we always helpless? In Finnmörk they believed that man, whether he or
she, was at the very core of the world, which was a huge
wholeness. Man, no less than gods, could steer it, was indeed needful for its life. And the spells had lifted her out
of herself.

Nevertheless, the shamans could not hold off the Norse
and Swedes, who laid burdensome scot on them when they
did not rob them outright. Nor was that which Gunnhild
learned from them anything overwhelming. It had its uses,
but in the end, what ruled was raw strength.

No, Gunnhild thought, that was not quite true. Cunning
showed where the sword ought to strike and how. This was
something a woman could give her man and her sons.

As for Thorolf, maybe after dwelling awhile in England
he would become Christian. Nearly all the Danes who
swarmed there and took land, these past hundred years or
so, had by now. Christendom was so vastly more wide and
rich than anything left in the North. Egil, though, would
always be too stubborn.

She herself wondered about it. She had met Christians,
both outlanders and Norsemen who had taken baptism
abroad, but they said little about their faith, at least to her.
They did not drink to the gods, and went aside to do whatever they did for worship. Thralls captured overseas had

even less to say, and nobody cared, unless maybe the children of the women among them. While priests had long been moving into Denmark, few, if any, had yet come farther north.

She had gathered that they believed there was only one god, who had gotten himself born as a man and walked on earth till he was killed and went back into Heaven. The death was not for knowledge or power like Odin's, but a kind of wergild for some wrongdoing long ago. Those who served this Christ faithfully went to him after they died and lived forever in happiness. However, they remembered the earth. Often they came back and helped folk who offered to them—much like elves or other Beings. Or so she understood the story to go.

What caught at her was that otherwise the Christians when at home seemed to do their worship not anywhere and anyhow they liked. Everything was ordered from faraway Romaborg: through men on the spot, called bishops, who thus held sway like lendmen or even jarls. Maybe, with them at his side, a king could bring his own headmen to heel.

It was only a thought in her.

She wondered whether Thorolf and Egil had met Haakon Haraldsson, Aethelstan's fosterling. Recalling her foresight, she shivered a bit.

Then fresh news came in.

The English king gathered warriors wherever and however he could, because the lands he had laid under him, Wales, Scotland, Danish Northumbria, were seething. Next summer the storm broke. Constantine, king of the Scots, came south, laying waste as he fared. Olaf, Norse king in Dublin, joined him with a host, as did the Welsh lords. The Northumbrians rose, men hastening to make war beside the strangers. Vikings from Norway and the Western Islands swarmed there too. Thousands together roared into Mercia, smashing all who tried to withstand them.

Aethelstan in Wessex rallied his troops and levies. As they moved north, he sent messengers ahead to his foes. He bade them meet him at a place he named, rather than ruining England. There they could fight, and whoever won would rule the kingdom. No man who cared about his name could well naysay that. And so the two hosts camped on the moor at Brunanburh.

For some days they sat while word went to and fro. Aethelstan offered the invaders a silver shilling for every plow in the land if they would go peacefully home. After talking it over, they said they wanted more. Aethelstan added money for each freeborn man of them. Constantine answered that he would take this, and also Northumbria. Then Aethelstan told them they could leave without battle only if they returned all their loot and Constantine became his vassal.

"The warriors must have grown restless meanwhile," said Eirik when he heard.

"I think both sides were playing for time till their whole strength could reach the field," answered Gunnhild.

He gave her a long look before he nodded. "Yes," he said. "Shrewdly thought."

The invaders attacked first. They worsted the English but did not break them. At the following sunrise the hosts strode back and forth, shields bright, spearheads and helmets shining, banners afloat on a brisk wind, horns and shouts riving it. Then they fell to.

The battle raged throughout that day. Foremost among the killers went Thorolf and Egil. At the end, the foe scattered and fled. Egil led the chase, his sword Adder hewing down man after fear-bewildered man. The dead lay in heaps and windrows across the moor. The cries and groans of the wounded met the shrieks of the birds wheeling earthward for their red food.

Egil found Thorolf slain.

No, thought Gunnhild, it should not have been Thorolf. She had not awaited such pain as now struck into her. The stark heart's-ease was that Egil suffered too.

An Icelander who had been on hand told about it. Egil bore the body off, washed it and arrayed it, while a grave was dug. He laid Thorolf therein with garb and weapons, and put a gold ring on each arm. His men heaped earth and rocks above. Egil spoke a verse:

> "Boldly into battle,
>   the bane of jarls, went
> Thorolf.
> First among the fearless,
>   he fell when Odin beckoned.
> Green upon his grave-mound,
>   grass will grow at streamside.
> His brother's grief is bitter.
>   Best that it stay hidden."

What else he thought, he kept to himself.

As nearly as Gunnhild could reckon out, the meeting at Brunanburh happened about the same time, maybe on the same day, as she gave birth to her son Ragnfröd. She could dream that some of Thorolf's warrior spirit passed into him.

Sorrow did not hold Egil back from looming and scowling at Aethelstan until the king bestowed rich reward on him for his deeds, together with payment that he should hand on to his father and kinsmen. This greatly cheered Egil. He made a poem that said so. Ever was he a greedy one, though not stingy. The last Gunnhild heard that year, he was spending the winter at Aethelstan's court, in high honor.

The next tidings came from Önund, son of Thorgeir Thornfoot, who had a farm on the island Askey by the Hördafylki shore. Önund was the biggest of three brothers, so much so that he got the nickname Berg-Önund. After the death of Thora Orfrey-sleeve, Björn Brynjolfsson had taken a new wife and gotten a daughter on her. When she was old enough, Berg-Önund wedded this half-sister of Aasgerd.

He became friendly with King Eirik; they called on one another whenever they could. He it was who first brought the news that Thorir Hroaldsson had died. Thorir's son Arinbjörn had taken over the holdings. Eirik gave him his father's rank of hersir. "I know you mislike his being a

friend of Egil Skallagrimsson," Eirik said to Gunnhild, "but
he's otherwise a good man, utterly true once he's given his
word. There are too few like him."

Now in summer Berg-Önund, having business southward, found Eirik and Gunnhild staying at a hall in Agdir.
After they went inside and ale was poured, Eirik asked what
was going on around the Sognefjord.

Berg-Önund's huge frame shifted uneasily on the honor
seat. His craggy face drew into a frown. "This will anger
you," he rumbled, "but Egil is back in Norway."

Gunnhild swallowed a gasp. The fingers on her lap
hooked like talons. She had better not say anything, though.
Not yet.

"Tell me what you know," bade Eirik in a steely voice.

"I've talked with men of his, and gone to Sygnafylki to
see for myself," Berg-Önund said. "After all, now Arinbjörn and I have the same ties with Björn Brynjolfsson."
Who would leave riches to his heirs, Gunnhild thought. "It
seems King Aethelstan wanted Egil to stay on for life. Egil
answered that first he must see to Thorolf's widow Aasgerd
and any children of theirs. They had one who has lived, a
girl named Thordis. Egil in England didn't know this. He
spoke of the inheritance that would be his if Thorolf had
died childless." Berg-Önund grated it forth. He had his own
eye on that wealth, Gunnhild saw.

"Many of Egil's men stayed behind, but about a hundred
followed him, crew for a big longship. Arinbjörn gave him
a good welcome and lodging for as long as he wished. I
heard that Aasgerd was deeply unhappy at learning about
her husband, but she's bearing up well."

"I daresay Egil will not be so unwise as to stray far from
Arinbjörn's," hissed Eirik. Gunnhild understood. Enough
men already felt vengeful toward this king. He would not
take a band to slay a strong one whom he trusted, whom
he even loved, which he must if he was to get at that man's
friend and guest. The sickness in her lightened a little when
he added, "But watch for it as best you can, Önund, and
tell me at once if it does happen."

She would keep closer track than he.

Thus during the months word often sped to her through her network of spies. But there was nothing on which she could grip. Egil dwelt quietly.

By fall, however, he was downcast. He would sit unspeaking, head lowered into his cloak. At last Arinbjörn asked him what the trouble was. Yes, the loss of a dear brother was a sharp and heavy thing, but a man should go on with life. Egil answered in verses of tightly knit kennings. They must have heartened him, for he then said straightforwardly that he yearned for Aasgerd.

Together they brought this before her. She was not unwilling, but would leave it to her father and her cousin. A while afterward, Arinbjörn and Egil went to Björn, who was agreeable. They returned from that ride too soon, Gunnhild thought.

In winter, therefore, the wedding was held at Arinbjörn's. He spared nothing on the feast. Thereafter Egil was blithe. It seemed he was kind to his wife, for she smiled afresh.

In spring, though, Arinbjörn warned them not to linger in Norway. "Gunnhild grows ever more powerful," he said. "She hates you, and it really worsened when you met with her brother Eyvind off Jutland." Egil got a knarr and crew, loaded her with trade goods, and waited for the right wind. When it came, he boarded with Aasgerd and little Thordis and stood out to sea.

That was toward fall again, few ships sailing. Hence a while went by before Gunnhild learned he had made a good, fast crossing to Iceland and settled down on his father's steading Borg.

By then it mattered less to her. She had borne a daughter, Ragnhild. This child she would keep at home, nurse her, sing to her, raise her to womanhood as her own. Too soon did her sons go off to fostering. She dreaded that they would grow apart from each other like most of Harald's. With Ragnhild she could weave bonds of love.

That much tenderness would be as welcome as a cool, bubbling spring to one who has long wandered thirstier than she knew. By now, Gunnhild foresaw fresh bloodshed in Norway.

XV

Homebound from a summer's raiding in the Baltic, Eirik took his ships up an inlet near the Oslofjord, to Tunsberg. The town drew traders not only from around Vikin but from northern Norway, Denmark, and Saxland. It lay in Vestfold, over which Harald Fairhair had set his son Björn as shire-king. That man seldom went to war; instead, he sent merchant ships far and wide, growing wealthy thereby. Thus he came to be called the Skipper or the Chapman.

One by one Eirik's craft rowed through the gateway of the palisade, which blocked off the waterfront and met the landward stockade at either end. He lay to at a jutting wharf and led his crew ashore. His other ships anchored farther out, for the docks were still busy even this late in the season. Planks thudded under the feet of men loading or unloading, the hoofs of packhorses, the creaky wheels of oxcarts. Gulls soared and mewed in their hundreds. A sharp wind wrinkled the bay. Cloud shadows harried wan sunlight. Eirik strode between thatch-roofed buildings of timber or wattle-and-daub, over ground that yesterday's rain had made muddy. Men and women looked uneasily, children stared and shouted, at his mail-clad troop. Smells eddied, woodsmoke, peatsmoke, cookery, dung, dyestuff. A smithy door stood open on white-ruddy coals and clashing hammer. Above everything else loomed the king's hall.

Told of Eirik's coming, Björn had taken his high seat there. His guards flanked him. Although the newcomers stacked spears, axes, and shields in the entry, swords still hung at shoulders and metal sheened on bodies. Björn did not rise for his half-brother, but greeted him rather coldly and offered him only the seat for an honored guest, across from his. Ale and mead were brought. They drank without much cheer.

After some words of news had dragged themselves to and fro, Björn asked, "Why did you stop here?"

"This is the time of year when you send his half of the Vestfold scot and rents to our father King Harald," said Eirik.

"Or else I bring them to him myself."

"I know. Well, give them over to me, and I'll spare you the trip."

Björn flushed. He sat unspeaking for a bit. One could hear men breathing throughout the hall. "No," he said then. "That's my work. I will always oversee it."

Eirik frowned. "Don't you trust me?" he asked slowly.

Björn did not answer straight out. "It is also my honor. Nobody shall take that from me."

"Are you so unsure of it?" fleered Eirik.

Björn reddened more deeply. "I am not, and I say nothing against others, but in some I have scant faith."

Maybe he had heard, maybe he now remembered, how Thorolf Kveldulfsson had been slandered about the gathering of the Finn-scot and ended by dying at King Harald's own hand. His arm chopped like an ax helve. "I will do as I've been wont to do, and will not talk further about it."

Eirik on his side had whitened beneath the weathered skin. "I have a greater errand anyway. We've had a long, hard faring and run short of everything but booty—and weapons. Some of the thralls we took, too, have gone sickly and might die on us if they don't soon get a rest and a good feed. We'll camp for a few days. Give us food, tents, and drink."

Again Björn sat for a span, thinking, before he shook his head. "No. I don't want a gang like that here, nor will the townsfolk. Brawls and killings would be too likely. Best you leave no later than tomorrow. You haven't far to go at all."

Eirik narrowed his eyes. "Do you withhold help from your brother?"

"If I believed you were in need, it would be unmanly of me," growled Björn, "but as is, it would be unmanly to yield."

"You kick me out, then, like a dog?"

"No. But this is my kingdom. You have your own."

They wrangled thus, barely keeping their seats, Björn's voice ever louder, often choking, Eirik's low and hard. At last Eirik got up. "I won't demean myself by staying any longer," he said. "Nor have I any thanks for so close-fisted and boorish a host." Men's gaze tracked him as he and his stalked from the hall.

He was silent on his way back through Tunsberg. No warrior cared to speak either. When townsfolk, drawing aside, beheld the faces, the same hush fell over them.

Aboard his ship, he ordered her out to anchor with the rest. There he sent for their skippers, who came to him by the boats that most of them towed. Talk was harsh. "If Björn were the peaceable man they call him," Eirik said, "he would not have given me such a slap. He must be plotting against me." Nobody wondered aloud what Eirik himself had had in mind.

Keen eyes saw a band of men ride through a gate, northward along the bay. "Yonder goes the king," said a household trooper who hailed from these parts. "Belike he's off to a house he owns in Saeheim, two or three miles hence."

"Withdrawing lest a fight begin?" asked another.

"Or to hatch an egg he's brooding on," clipped Eirik. "We could be waylaid and overwhelmed. Such things have happened often enough. At the very least, he hopes we'll skulk cowardly off. The name of weakling brings on weakness; men turn to leaders they think are strong. We'll forestall him."

His ships rowed from the haven, down the inlet and the fjord beyond sight of town. Where shoals met a wide strand, they grounded. A farmstead lay nearby. Warriors jumped ashore and ran to it. "We'll not hurt you if you keep inside till we're gone," the headman told the dwellers. "Otherwise, you're dead."

The sun set. Leaving a few behind on watch, Eirik took his vikings north. A half-moon fled among clouds. Wind shrilled and bit; dry leaves flew off darkling trees; stubble-fields reached gray and shadow-pitted; sometimes a dog howled. They bypassed the bulk that was Tunsberg, found the road beyond, and hurried over its ruts. Soon a few houses crouched before them, the hamlet Saeheim. Windows glowed in the biggest. Björn and his followers were at drink.

Eirik beckoned right and left. Well drilled, his men sped to ring the building in. The noise was nonetheless loud. Firelight flickered forth as the front door opened for those inside to peer out. Eirik trod into it. "Tell King Björn that King Eirik is here to go on with our business," he bade them.

A yell arose. Iron rattled. "He'll not burn us, that wolf's head!" Björn shouted.

He had never been a man of war, but he had had his battles, and kept ships alive in storms. He ordered his guards to press through the doorway heel and toe. The first died quickly; those behind broke free and laid about them. Swords clattered; axes thucked; cries flew up to the hasty moon. "Björn!" called some and "Eirik!" others. Else they could hardly have told friend from foe in the murk.

Yet Eirik's men were better clad for strife, and knew well what to do. Björn got no time to rally his. They died alone or in small bunches. Feet trampled the wounded where they writhed, bones crunched, or feet slipped on spilled guts, while the death-reek thickened.

When stillness had fallen, but for heavy panting and a few groans, Eirik sought Björn. Drops of blood fell off Eirik's shield, down onto the sprawled lich. Björn gaped hollowly back. "You fought well, brother mine," Eirik said. "May your grave-mound long stand untroubled." He grinned. "But you'll agree, won't you, now you're one fewer to fret about."

His followers looted the house, taking a goodly plunder, and went back to their ships. In the morning they sailed on homeward. Harald Fairhair sighed but said only that a fitting payment and peace should be made.

Folk throughout the shires of Vikin were in an uproar. They had liked King Björn. This work boded ill. Björn's half-brother and friend, King Olaf of neighboring Vingulmörk, vowed vengeance. He took Björn's widow and son into his care, and claimed lordship over the slain man's Vestfold. Thenceforward Eirik bore the nickname Blood-ax. Both he and Gunnhild rather liked it.

XVI

Weather or no, that winter he took ship north to Moerr to see to his holdings and power in those two shires. Landing near the mouth of the Thraandheimsfjord, he lodged with his men at Sölvi, where he had a garth. Thence he would make his rounds by land and water, and there he would make the Yule offering. Gunnhild stayed in the South, being again very near her time.

Word of this passed down the great bay to Thraandheim. The shires of that rich, rolling land stretched widely north and south along the sea, eastward into the mountains. Its folk were strong and stiff-necked, with ways and laws of their own. King Harald had bestowed lordship over it among his sons Haalfdan the White, Haalfdan the Black, and Sigröd. Haalfdan the White had since fallen in west-viking. The other two got along well, both having been foster sons of Haakon, the mighty jarl of Hladi. After Haa-kon's death they stayed on with his son Sigurd, who was about their own age. Sigröd, though, being the youngest of the three, kept somewhat in the background.

To Sigurd, then, came King Haalfdan the Black. The jarl made him fittingly welcome. Hladi overlooked the inner fjord. Its lands reached beyond sight, grainfields, meadows, woods, farmsteads, hamlets. Its ships filled many sheds, and in summer lined many wharfs. Hladi hall reared huge, with soaring roofs, high rooms, cunning carvings, and beautiful hangings, as grand as any king's. Its outbuildings well-nigh made a small town. Folk swarmed, workers, warriors, women, children, guests often in great numbers. Fine were the gifts to the foremost among them. Wealth stuffed cof-fers and strongrooms. Kings came and went, but the jarls of Hladi abided, lifetime after lifetime, they who owned the hearts of the Thraands.

"I must talk alone with you, as soon as may be," whispered Haalfdan after he and Sigurd had greeted one another.

The jarl nodded. "I thought so. I can guess what it's about, too. Well, let it be at once, while your men are settling in."

He gave a few orders and the two of them walked off, half a dozen guards at their back out of earshot. Taking a path above the water, they left the garth behind. The sky was low and leaden, glooming toward eventide. Air hung raw-cold. Patches from the last snowfall dappled sere grass. A shaw of birch stood barebones white, firs like harbingers of oncoming night. Crows cawed.

"Well?" asked Sigurd quietly.

Haalfdan rushed into it, as fiery as he always was. "You must have heard that Eirik Blood-ax is at Sölvi."

"Of course." Sigurd glanced a bit upward at the king, who topped him by half a head. Sigurd himself, though not tall, was as broad-shouldered and well knit; gray eyes looked out of a strong-boned, blunt-nosed face. The hair and beards of both men were swart. "Before you ask, no, he does not have a big following. You have more. But his are all picked and proven fighters."

"Still, they're not awaiting callers, are they?"

"I don't believe they are, nor do they mean to do any harm. Think, though. When we unleash that kind of hound, we can never foresee where he'll run or what he'll pull down."

"Eirik has already let slip the beast," rasped Haalfdan. "Rögnvald, Björn—who's next? Worse yet, our father backs him."

"I think King Harald mainly fears that when he's gone, his sons will rend asunder the kingdom he hammered together."

"But must the high king after him be Eirik? Belike few of his brothers would long outlive that. And the Thraands have been glad enough to have me steering them."

Sigurd did not remind Haalfdan that he and Sigröd had

ties to him, their jarl, who stood between them and over-weening Harald. "Folk elsewhere might feel otherwise," he said half under his breath. Then: "Are you here to ask my rede about falling on Eirik? It is; don't."

Haalfdan paced on, scowling. Sigurd Jarl was wise as well as wily. Also, he was an unstinting offerer to the gods, who therefore must look kindly on him. Nevertheless—A crow jeered. "What if I do anyhow?" he barked.

"I won't help," Sigurd answered. "It seems to me that things here in the North have not yet come to swords' point, and you're being rash. Nor will I hinder. Whatever this leads to, I and the Thraands will stand by our kings as long as they stand by us."

"Then why will you not now?"

"Because later on there may well be more need of my strength."

They walked and talked until the unseen sunset turned them back. That evening the feast ended early. Haalfdan was set on his course and would start off at dawn. In summer it was a long day's ride from here to Sölvi, but days were dwindling down to a glimmer. How fast anybody could go after dark hung on the weather.

Thus it came about that Eirik woke in the middle of Haalfdan's second night.

Maybe it was luck; maybe it was in the song the norn sang at his cradle; maybe it was Gunnhild's warding spell. The house at Sölvi had turned out to be foul-smelling, not yet sweetened as it should have been. His troopers didn't mind, but Eirik had straw heaped in a shed offside and slept there.

Racket of hoofs and halloos yanked him from dreams. He leaped to his feet. His hand knew its way through blackness to clasp the spear that rested beside him. Cat-wary, he opened the door a crack and peered. A nearly full moon shone aloft, a frost-ring around it. His breath smoked in its icy light. Helmets, byrnies, and blades sheened amidst shadow. Men had surrounded the house. They were springing off their horses, drawing swords, raising axes, slanting spears. Outrunners of theirs must stealthily have fallen on outposts of his, Eirik knew; then the lot of them galloped the last mile.

As he watched, warriors surged from the doors. Edged iron cut them down. More attackers made ranks to bar every way out. Kindled from tinder, a torch flared.

They were after him, Eirik knew. If they got him, his sons were foredoomed to wretchedness or early death.

Five of his guards had by turns spread their sleeping bags on the ground by the shed. Unheeded in the tricky light, they joined him. "We can dash forth and die with our fellows," Eirik said, "but better is to escape and avenge them." Fumbling in the gloom, he donned clothes, underpadding, and mail. They all wrapped cloaks around themselves before they stole off. His ships lay not far away, a few watchmen on the strand beside. He chose one and put everybody aboard. Undermanned, she rowed slowly seaward. Behind her, fire flickered against the stars like northlights and the roar of burning came faintly like surf.

On his way back, Eirik learned who had led the onslaught. When King Harald heard, he went as wrathful as ever he got. At once he and Eirik called up levies to go north. Haalfdan the Black heard, and raised his own; Thraandish men flocked to his banner.

However, others went between, hoping to make peace. Among these was a skald, Guthorm the Dwarf. He was with Haalfdan, but had formerly been with Harald, and was still a friend of both. Indeed, once he had made a poem in their praise. When they offered him a reward, he only wanted that at some later time they should give him what he asked for. This they plighted. Few gifts were greater than a well-wrought verse of honor, and a man of honor could not give less in return. Now Guthorm asked for peace. Because of him and the rest, maybe Sigurd Jarl above all, the kings came to terms. Having duly paid for the slain, Haalfdan should keep his lordship, while he and Eirik kept hands off one another.

Gunnhild clutched her new son Erling to her breast. Haalfdan the Black had tried to kill her man. He had come near doing it. Thereby he had earned death.

XVII

The host against his son was the last that Harald Fairhair raised. He did not go along, being too old for hard faring. When peace of a kind followed, it was as if something within him sighed and let go its hold on his strength. Thereafter, most of the time he sat thickly wrapped in furs against the winter cold, maybe inwardly speaking with friends, foes, and loves long dead, maybe fighting again his battles and hearing again the shouts of victory.

Eirik and Gunnhild were with him at his great steading on the island Körmt, hard by the Rogaland coast in the southwest, for the springtide offering. He stood in a bleak wind and spatters of rain, where flames hissed and smoke blew low: big, his white head high, but the shoulders slumped as if under the weight of a paunch the stiff legs could hardly upbear. When he walked back to the hall, it was slowly. Often Gunnhild saw his lips tighten within the beard, against pain.

That evening after meat he bade the headman of his guards call for silence. The fires themselves seemed to crackle softly. Eyes gleamed steel-white. His voice still rumbled, but the lack of many teeth slurred it. "Hark and hear well. I, Harald Haalfdansson, your king, speak, I who broke every king and chieftain that stood against me and laid all Norway under my hand. I quelled vikings and robbers; I gave good laws; I brought trade and wealth flowing in; I made us mighty in the world. But Elli, who wrestled Thor to his knee, has her grip on me. While I am yet above earth, I will see to it that my work does not fall to bits when I am gone, but passes into strong and able hands. Hear me. I now give to my son Eirik the full power that has been mine. I call on you to witness this, and call on the Things throughout the land to hail him when next they meet. Eirik, henceforward be at my side."

He sagged back, the breath quick and rough in his throat. Tall, straight, lithe, Gunnhild's man rose and went between the fires to sit by his father. Cheers roared like the sea storm-driven against a cliff.

Gunnhild smiled and was gracious throughout the rest of that guesting. But already she was thinking ahead. This bestowal was no surprise. Nor would it be to Eirik's brothers.

During the summer, word after word arrived about them. Olaf of Vingulmörk, who had gone into Vikin after the killing of Björn the Chapman, took the high seat there when the folk-meeting made him king by its own will. With him were his son Tryggvi and Björn's son Gudröd, both fast-growing youths who would soon be men to reckon with. Even worse was that matters went likewise in Thraandheim, where Haalfdan the Black was upheld as overlord.

Eirik kept rule in the South and West, as far north as Moerr. That was not so little, either in reach or in riches. However, his brothers held back all the scot and rents of their lands. Messengers he sent to them bore cold answers home. Harald Fairhair only muttered that any new wars were Eirik's to wage. Leave him with his dreams.

"Yes, burnt-out he is," said Gunnhild sadly, in a room where none could overhear.

"Yet never was there such a fire," said Eirik.

"Shall yours smolder out?" Gunnhild stroked his arm, sinewy beneath her fingers; the gold hairs tickled, the blood quickened in her. "No, you'll not let that happen."

"First I must needs make firm what I have. Too many yeomen chafe and grumble."

"I know. Nonetheless, something further might be done."

"What are you thinking of?"

"That can wait," she purred, and took his mind off it.

More was at stake than money. Whenever King Olaf in Vikin saw fit, his ships could beset the way to the Swedish marts, the Baltic, and maybe Denmark. Haalfdan held sway over Finnmörk and the best fishing grounds, as well as freedom to prey on shipping bound west overseas if he chose. Both had fighting men at their beck who ought to be Eirik's. Both had sons who would someday threaten hers if they lived.

The year wore on. Eirik was often away. Mostly she spent those times at a kingly hall on the head of the broad Byfjord in Hördafylki. Open to the sea but sheltered by outlying islands, this offered a good harbor and easy defense. Hence merchant craft went to and fro, a small but growing town clustered at the waterfront, and a well-kept road wound inland. There was, though, little farming and only some grazing hereabouts, for steep hills rose around the neighborhood, heavily wooded because of the mild, rainy air. Among the trees crowding behind the kingly garth, she had a bower built, where she could be by herself when she wished.

Her four older sons were now fostered out and she seldom saw them, while Erling was as yet babbling. Ragnhild ran swiftly, light-brown hair afloat. She was a willful child, heedless of how others felt, but learning from her mother that there were better ways than throwing a fit to get what she wanted.

She watched as Gunnhild steered the household and dealt with men, among them the traders from outside—elsewhere in Norway, the lands of the Goths and Swedes, Denmark, Wendland, Gardariki, the Westlands, Iceland, sometimes the Empire itself. All, visitors and dwellers alike, hearkened closely to the queen and did her bidding, not merely because her husband was the Blood-ax; her redes were shrewd and her knowledge of what went on in the world seemed wider than that of any among them.

They caught bare glimpses, or none, of others whom she met with for short whiles now and then, meanly clad and afoot. They did wonder what she wanted of such wayfarers, and what she was up to when alone in her bower or walking without a guard in the wood. However beautiful and winning, she was an uncanny one.

The housefolk knew it when Geira came from the eastward heights and Gunnhild received her well. They could only whisper their guesses about the why of it. Though Geira sat at the far end of the hall, among the lowly, who hardly dared say a word to her, she ate as well as any man, drank enough for two, and slept that night on a feather mattress in a shut-bed.

A few times before, she had been seen here, and a few tales of her had sifted down from the hills. Neither maiden, wife, nor widow, she dwelt in a lonely hut outside a tiny hamlet. An old man who twitched his face and mumbled to himself tended the bit of a farm. She also lived off what folk gave her. They were afraid not to. Besides, she had some skill at leechcraft, the healing of livestock or blighted crops, finding lost things, reading dreams, and the like. She claimed farsight and foresight. She went on the roads for weeks on end, striding with her staff and a pack on her back, a man-tall, rawboned woman in whose uncovered, uncombed, stiff gray hair hopped lice that no loving fingers ever picked out. After a look at that craggy, leathery face, the toughest ruffian let her be and the poorest crofter gave her shelter. The small goods she got for her witchwork along the way, she swapped for what she needed.

In the morning Gunnhild led her along the path to the bower. Wind shrilled. A wrack of clouds flew ragged beneath a gray sky. Evergreens soughed. Lately fallen birch leaves scrittled yellow. The building was less than warm, but at least held off the wind. Fire glowered on its hearth. Gunnhild sent away the girl who had tended it, showed Geira to a chair, and with her own hands poured drink, not ale but Southern wine.

They sat down, gaze to gaze. "What do you want?" asked Geira bluntly and hoarsely. "Your man did not say."

"I would like to give you silver," Gunnhild answered. "You could buy yourself ease for the rest of your days."

"I meant, what do you want of me?"

Gunnhild drooped her eyelids and dropped her voice. This surly, bearlike fearlessness was what she had heard of and hoped for. "I'll tell you straight out; then we'll talk about the whats and whethers. But if ever a word of it leaks from your lips, you'll be plying your trade on hell-road."

"I knew that as soon as your man said what he said. Go on." Geira tossed off a gulp of wine.

Gunnhild sipped hers. "Do you know of a man up north

who calls himself a king? Haalfdan the Black. I want him dead. I've brewed some stuff that can do it. I need someone who can slip it into him."

Geira was slightly taken aback. "I, I'm not one who'd ever come near a king—my lady."

"I've thought on it. Yes, you take a risk and you may die, but if all goes well you've much to gain." For a wretch like her, anyway, Gunnhild thought. Yet a wretch who had learned slyness from grim teachers. "See you, I'll shortly send a ship yonder, crewed by men I trust. They'll take gifts to King Haalfdan, and questions about coming to agreement with King Eirik. I know—I have ways of knowing—Haalfdan will be at the haven where the River Nid runs into the Thraandheimsfjord, for the offerings and feasting at summer's end. Of course he'll spurn the bid. However, he can't do less than guest the crew. You'll go along. As far as my men know, it'll be to bear a word from me to somebody unnamed yonder, who'll pass it on to my father in Haalogaland. To this day, he and I keep few secrets between us, he being a runemaster. That's what I'll tell my men."

"What's my real task?"

"You'll mingle in the throng of lesser folk in the hall, get to know women—thralls, it may be—and put one of them in awe of you. Who among the highborn will pay any heed? Give her a flask I'll give you. You must find your own way forward to how all this shall be done. But if you're anything of a witch, you can lay a wee spell on a weak-minded girl to make her believe that here is a wonderful drink for the king. Maybe she'll think it will make him love her—or whatever seems best to you. Thereafter go back to the ship, hide aboard her, and wait. She ought to leave on the morning tide, if that happens which I hope for."

"Hemlock's a bitter brew, if that's what you use. Honey won't hide it."

"I've made—I know how to make—a brew of toadstools that blends with ale."

Geira looked almost frightened. "Won't the king's men

grab that wench and wring the truth from her? Then your crew will never come home."

"You must weave your plan on the spot, with whatever threads you find. I think, though, you should have her bring Haalfdan the beakerful when it's late and he and everybody else are too drunk to mark or remember who she is. He won't feel the poison at once. She'll fear for her life and say nothing. Or if somehow she is found out, by then my ship should be well at sea."

The two sat still. The wind whistled around the little house. After a while Gunnhild added: "My own spells will fly with you."

They talked for a long time.

Meanwhile another business gnawed at her. Sooner or later it would reach Eirik and he would have to deal with it. The news had come to her that Egil Skallagrimsson was back in Norway.

XVIII

Noontide glimmered dully through the scraped gut across the windows. Otherwise light in the hall was from lamps, doors being shut against chills and fires not yet stoked up. Summer had bleakened as it waned, more than in most years. Nevertheless Arinbjörn had sailed down to Rogaland.

Not many, free or thrall, were here at this time of day. They stayed silent and aside, as if to cover themselves with the duskiness. Arinbjörn stood, not sat, before the high seat. Downward-slanting eyes in the hook-nosed face met squarely the eyes of King Eirik and Queen Gunnhild.

"Yes, I am here on behalf of my friend," he told them. "You must have gotten wind of him, but not, I think, the whole truth."

"Say what you will," bade Eirik. Gunnhild swallowed the seething within her. The hands in her lap felt cold.

"As you know, King," Arinbjörn began, "Björn Brynjolfsson, my uncle, died last year. Berg-Önund took everything that was his, treasure, house goods, kine; his underlings are on every farm that was Björn's; the rents go to him. Egil heard of this in Iceland. In spring he took ship for Norway to claim his share of the inheritance. He thinks that should be all of it, but surely at least half. His right is as good as Önund's, if not better. Both are wedded to daughters of Björn, and his wife, Aasgerd, is the older. She came with him. They sought to me. I made them welcome and have lodged them, as was fitting.

"I warned him that Önund is greedy, unrighteous, and overbearing. Moreover, he stands near to you, while your lady is Egil's greatest foe." Eirik frowned but did not cut Arinbjörn off. "However, Egil has never knuckled under. I got him to see Önund and talk it over." Arinbjörn grinned lopsidedly. "That wasn't easy. At last, though, he did. To show peaceableness, he even went there not in a ship but a skuta." Gunnhild knew well that that was a boat, in which each rower pulled two oars; it could carry a score or so of men.

"Berg-Önund received him surlily on Askey, and scorned his claims. When Egil said his wife was of higher birth than Önund's, Önund sneered that, no, she was thrallborn." Anger shook the hithero steady voice. "Aasgerd, my sister! Well you remember, King, her parents' wedding was made lawful."

Gunnhild could no longer hold back. "*I* remember that King Eirik made Egil outlaw in Norway," she spat.

"You have been helping him for years," Eirik said slowly, "you do so now, yet you call yourself true to me."

"I am, lord," answered Arinbjörn. "We are foster kin. It's only that I'm also true to my friends."

"Say on."

"Önund raved foully. It's astonishing that Egil didn't fell him then and there, with his fist since they were unarmed."

"His lust for gold overrode his honor," Gunnhild said.

Arinbjörn bit his lip. "Instead, there before witnesses he summoned Önund to the Gula Thing. He put the case under its law. Önund said he would come, hoping Egil would not go from it alive. Egil left. Then I thought I should seek you, King, as soon as I could find beforehand where you'd be. That took a while."

"Indeed Egil is brash, to come forth from under your wardership when he's an outlaw," said Gunnhild.

"That was years ago," Arinbjörn answered stoutly. "Through his wife he's kin to a family of high standing. He has a lawful suit to bring before his peers."

"Why are you so fond of him? What has he ever done for you?" She barely stopped herself from asking if he had played stallion to Arinbjörn's mare. That would be unforgivable. It would demean her worse than him. Eirik himself would be wroth.

The king's long head nodded. "I've sometimes wondered too," he said.

Arinbjörn flushed. "We took a liking to one another when first we met. I was young then, he younger. Once, hunting in the woods, we blundered on a she-bear with cubs. She came at us. We were after birds or hares, no hounds to help us, no weapons better than spears. Together we staved her off till she quit and went away. Thereon we swore friendship—blood brotherhood, for we were bleeding and let the blood drip into a print of both our feet. I have abided by this, and I know he won't fail me should need arise."

Yes, Gunnhild sighed to herself, men were like that.

Arinbjörn looked straight at Eirik. "I also know, King, that you will allow us law."

A crafty move, Gunnhild thought. It spoke to Eirik's honor. After what he had done in Vikin—needful though the work was, she thought—many looked askance at him, seeing him as utterly ruthless. He could use more goodwill.

"I must think on it," said Eirik warily.

Gunnhild foreknew he would give a yea. "If you agree," she told him, "best you be at that Thing yourself, with a strong following."

"Never would I threaten you, my foster brother and king," cried Arinbjörn.

"Well, I'll be gathering warriors anyway," said Eirik. "If

you truly are faithful to me, maybe next year you can show it."

He guested Arinbjörn that evening, though coolly. In the morning the hersir set off for home, where Egil waited.

The Gula Thing would meet in spring. While she did not make the mistake of nagging Eirik about it, from time to time Gunnhild slipped a word like a dagger into their talk.

Winter had whitened the land before she heard in full how Haalfdan the Black suddenly crumpled, heaved, and toppled. He went mad before he died.

But the Thraands boiled in, set his brother Sigröd on their Thingstone, and hailed him king. He was no more willing than Haalfdan to yield to Eirik. Quietly behind him stood Sigurd Jarl.

A new life quickened in Gunnhild's womb.

The tale seeped from garth to garth, from end to end of Norway, that she had sent a witchwife to poison King Haalfdan. Her friends and Eirik's hotly called this a lie. Whenever an outstanding man fell deathly ill, they said, tongues wagged the same foolishness; but who knew how many the ways were in which he could have come to grief? None but her spies and runners told her what was being muttered; nor did Eirik ever speak of it. He was busy among the chieftains of the shires that were his, making ready for war.

XIX

Their son Gudröd was born while King Harald Fairhair lay in sickbed at his steading on Körmt. For days and nights he waged his last battle, which was for the breath that shushed and rattled in him. Once he said this was not bad; when he closed his eyes, he could dream himself back to a seashore, listening to the surf, looking out to the ships beyond. But then he sank into dumb darkness, the flesh so wasted that the great bones seemed already to jut forth, and onward into death. They buried him nearby, heaping over him a huge mound, upon it a gravestone of two men's height.

Now Eirik alone was the high king, with half the kingdom to win back.

First he would deal with a lesser case, if only because he meant to begin in the North. The south, southwest, and middle of Norway were well in hand. He would make sure of Sogn and the shires around it, rallying their headmen to him and raising levies. They would be at their Gula Thing in springtime, at the mouth of the Sognefjord.

Thither he sailed in seven fully manned longships. Berg-Önund and his brothers joined them along the way, also with a big following. They found craft of several kinds beached or anchored. Among them he kenned a dragon belonging to Arinbjörn. About her lay a small fleet of karfis, skutas, and rowboats. Arinbjörn too had brought a strong band, yeomen over whom he was hersir. They looked up to him; if ever they had to choose, it would be he for whom they fought. Horses, still winter-shaggy, ridden here from far inland, grazed on the hills that rolled green from the water.

The Thingstead bustled and racketed. Smoke blew off untold campfires. Tents and booths stood everywhere outside the meeting ground. Eirik's booth had been readied beforehand, roomy and well furnished. His cloak fluttered red in the wind. Beside him walked Gunnhild. For a woman to be at a Thing was well-nigh unheard of, unless she had a suit of her own to bring. But she was the queen and this was her will.

For three days, though, she waited, trying not to stew. The men who came to greet her did not linger. Eirik was off at the gathering or out among those he needed to talk with, sometimes well into the night. Her two serving maids had early learned that she found their chatter wearisome. It would be unseemly for her to ride or stride away to the newly leafing trees, and unwise indeed to cast spells. She could only sing her songs of ill-wishing behind her lips.

So while her heart leaped high when the time came, as she went out with the king bitterness burned her throat. Yet she must stay calm and cold, her mind a whetted weapon.

The Thing had gone over its laws—long-windedly, no doubt—and settled on any changes that seemed meet. It had taken up the question of kingship. Some few had said these shires ought to hold aloof, but in the end they voted to stand by Eirik Haraldsson. Now they would hear lawsuits.

This was on a level field. Men walled it in, packed close, farmers and fishers in blue or gray wadmal, the more well-to-do in wool and linen, hats or stocking caps on most heads. A hill blocked sight of the water. Blue sky, wandering white cloudlets, sweet air felt strangely far off. Hazel stakes driven into the turf and linked by ropes—the ropes of halidom—marked a circle. Inside were benched six and thirty men of middle age and grave mien, the judges. Arinbjörn had picked twelve from Sygnafylki, Thord of Aurland twelve from Sogn; the ones from Hördafylki sat a little apart.

Facing them, outside the holy ring, were benches for those men who were bringing suits and those of high rank. Behind these clustered such henchmen and others as they had taken along out of their followings. Everybody was unarmed, unless one reckoned their knives, but often glares flew back and forth. When the lawman had called for silence, it fell thick. Gunnhild heard the breathing at her back, harsh and heavy.

Sheepskins covered the bench for Eirik and her. They were soon too warm beneath her gown. She could not shift about; she must sit haughtily straight and still. Her eyes could rove, she could turn her head slightly. Yonder—it leaped at her—were Arinbjörn, and Egil by him. The hersir had paid her a short visit. The Icelander had enough wit to keep himself well aside.

She would know those heavy, meeting brows, thick nose, gash of a mouth, headland of a jaw, bull neck, were the two of them in Helheim. The great frame had filled out even more, but the hair had gotten thin, the bushy beard flecked with white. His goodly clothes fitted him ill. Scarred hands clasped knees. She knew that his own eyes, black in their caves of bone, darted to and fro like a wild beast's.

Eirik hardly moved either, nor did anything show on his sharp features. Gunnhild was glad that her brother Aalf the Shipman, who had taken her to Finnmörk and gone with her to the South, stood at her back.

The lawman called the case. Egil and Arinbjörn rose. They walked to take a stand between the king and the judges. Berg-Önund lumbered from his seat to loom at the farther side, almost as ugly and angry as Egil. All gave Eirik a few words of due respect. Gunnhild could not tell whether Egil's were hollow or hopeful.

Stillness came down. Somewhere a horse neighed. A hawk swept high overhead. Then Egil trod forward. Having brought the suit, he would speak first.

The deep voice rolled across the field and over the wall of watchers. "I, Egil Skallagrimsson, take witness to this, that I bid Önund, son of Thorgeir Thornfoot, or any man who may undertake his defense, to hear my oath and my complaint and claim against him, with all the truths and the words of law that I will set out. I bid him in lawful wise before this gathering, so that the judges may hear me in full.

"I take witness to this, that I hereby swear a lawful oath before the gods of law and justice, Njörd, Frey, and almighty Thor, that I will plead my case truthfully, justly, and lawfully, to the best of my knowledge; and I will bring all my proofs and witnesses in seemly wise, and speak faithfully, for as long as I am in this suit."

It was wrong that he have so rich a voice, flowing and booming, singing and thundering, like wind and waves, Gunnhild thought. Likewise was it wrong that he knew his way through the tangles of the law. Well, but he must be holding his wolf-soul on a leash. It strained, plunged, and snarled in his breast. If someone—if she—somehow made him let go, it would raven forth and folk would remember why he had been outlawed in Norway.

Knowing the burden of his words, she only half listened to them. Her thoughts were on how to undo him. He gave

his grounds for claiming the inheritance of Björn Brynjolfsson, in that his wife Aasgerd, Björn's daughter, had the
right to it; that she was freeborn in every branch of her
forebears, among whom were hersirs and even kings;
therefore he asked the judges to award him half of what
Björn left, both lands and movables. It was a straightforward speech such as would go well with hardheaded, heedful men.

He ended and stepped back. Berg-Önund came to the
fore. "My wife Gunnhild," he said, with a glance at the
queen of the same name, "is the daughter of Björn and his
wife Aalof, whom Björn lawfully wedded. Gunnhild is
Björn's rightful heiress, and therefore I have taken everything he owned, because I knew that Björn's other daughter
had no claim to the inheritance. Her mother was stolen
away and made a leman, against the will of her kinfolk,
and dragged from one land to the next. But you, Egil, think
you can behave here as you have everywhere else, overweeningly and unrighteously. That will not help you here,
for King Eirik and Queen Gunnhild have promised I shall
have law and justice wherever they hold sway."

His speech became one long sneer. He had witnesses to
show that Thora Orfrey-sleeve had gone about with vikings
and Aasgerd was born outland in outlawry. Egil himself
was outlawed, yet he cared so little for the king's word that
he returned to lie about his thrall woman being an heiress.
The judges should award Önund the whole of the estate,
and Aasgerd to the king as forfeited property.

Egil's jaw muscles worked, his hands knotted, and sweat
studded the broad brow. Otherwise he stayed rock-still. Arinbjörn was white when Önund ended. As he took over, a
shiver went beneath his words.

"We will bring witnesses, King Eirik, and thereto lay
oaths, that it was clearly agreed when the quarrel was made
up between Thorir my father and Björn Brynjolfsson that
Thora's daughter Aasgerd would have rights of inheritance
from her father Björn. Moreover, we will bring witnesses
to what is widely known, lord, that you yourself lifted

Björn's outlawry, whereby the whole case that had hitherto
stood between the men became empty."

This was for the king at least as much as for the judges.
Gunnhild thrilled at what Eirik might say. But he sat unstirring, his face a mask. On the one hand, she knew, he
hated Egil and Önund was a friend. On the other hand,
Arinbjörn was his foster brother, and in spite of everything
seemed as dear to him yet as any man could be to that
steely heart. Also, there was the matter of law and of how
these hundreds of men would look upon whatever he did.
Gunnhild set her teeth.

Again Egil stepped ahead, to stand before her bench. His
gaze locked on Eirik's ice-blue eyes. Neither man winked.
The hush deepened. Quoth Egil:

> "The thievish son of Thornfoot
> thrallborn dares call my wife.
> Gross is Önund and greedy,
> grabbing what is not his.
> Warrior, hear my wish.
> My wife shall have her rights.
> Son of kings, we will speak
> and swear to naught but the truth."

Silence stretched. Gunnhild strangled a shriek. Here she
sat helpless, she who had brought down kings, while Egil
was free to wield the witchcraft of a skald. So skillfully
wrought a poem—kennings interwoven, "spearshaker" for
"warrior," "pourer of the ale" and "goddess of the needle"
for "wife"—so quickly made, on the spot, roused awe. A
poem brought a kind of deathlessness, the memory of a
man living on in fame or in scorn till the world ended.

From as far away as the hawk that hovered on the wind, she
watched Arinbjörn call his witnesses, twelve of them, men of
mark. Yes, she heard through the wind within her, they had
been there when Thorir and Björn came to terms. They offered to take oath that what Arinbjörn said was true.

The judges drew together and talked low among themselves. The wind blew stronger.

"Yes," she heard their spokesman say, "we are willing to take these oaths, if the king does not forbid it."

Surely the king wanted to. Surely he hungered to slay the evildoer who had killed men of his, brought shame and exile and defeat on his queen's brother Eyvind, spurned his orders, and by openly coming here mocked his might. Sleet lashed on the inner wind.

"I will say neither yea nor nay to that," answered Eirik, flat-voiced.

Egil must not go scatheless. It would be humbling. It would be dangerous. Suddenly calm, back to herself, fully and coldly aware, Gunnhild knew she could stir her husband's manhood to break through his carefulness.

She turned to him and spoke evenly, sharply. "Unbelievable, lord, how you suffer this big Egil's effrontery. Belike you wouldn't stop his mouth though he snatched after your kingdom. But if you won't do anything to help Önund, I'll not let Egil tread my friends underfoot and rob what belongs to Önund." She sprang up. "Aalf Shipman, where are you?" she cried. "Take your crew to the judges and see they don't render a judgment that's unrightful!"

She had talked beforehand with him. Not knowing what would happen, he nonetheless plighted his help in any need of hers. She had raised him to what he was, she his sister and queen.

He whistled to the men around him. They dashed at the ring. Knives flashed. Blades cut through the halidom. Hazel stakes went down. The six and thirty shouted, astounded, outraged. Warriors shoved them. They gave way. Aalf and his gang held the circle.

Uproar burst loose. Men roiled about, yelling. Many drew their own knives. But those were not real weapons. Bewildered, none attacked those who stood side by side at the middle.

Egil shouted above the ruckus: "Can Berg-Önund hear my words?"

"I hear," bawled the other.

"Then I call you to a duel. We'll fight it out here and now at the Thing. Let him who wins take all we've striven for. If you beg off, may you be every man's nithing."

Önund growled like a hound. Arinbjörn plucked at Egil's sleeve, aghast. Glee welled in Gunnhild. Her foe had lost hold of himself.

She well-nigh felt the same chill gladness shine from the king. Later he could settle with the law—Egil's challenge was as great a peace-breach as Aalf's onset, if not more— or, shaken as the folk were, he might override it. But when matters had come to a head like this, it was time for Eirik Blood-ax.

He stalked forward, light-hued, lithe, against the swart hulk, their heights and maybe their strengths alike. He grinned. "If you hanker to fight, Egil," he said, "we can grant you that."

The Icelander lowered his fists and hunched his shoulders. A vein throbbed in his temple. "I'll not fight you and a whole troop," he rasped, "but if they let me, I won't hang back from meeting them on the same footing, man to man. And for me that'll be regardless of whoever it is."

Eirik froze. For a heartbeat those in earshot also went stock-still. Egil had as good as challenged the king himself.

Arinbjörn understood. His followers had closed in from behind his bench. The rest of the men who heeded him were making their way to him through the milling crowd. He caught his friend's arm and pulled. His voice rang hard. "We'd better go, Egil. Here we can do no more for ourselves." With two others he half urged, half hustled the Icelander off.

When they had hastened a few yards, Egil wrested free. He whirled around, shook his fist, and roared across the field, "I call you to witness, Arinbjörn and Thord, and all those men who hear my words, headmen, lawmen, yeomen, that I lay a ban on all the lands that were Björn's. Nobody shall dwell there or build there or work there. I forbid them to you, Berg-Önund, as well as all other men, homelander or outlander, high or low. And any who do I name lawbreakers, peacebreakers, and offenders of the gods."

He turned back. The band passed over the hillcrest, out of sight.

The hubbub was dying down. Men stood in scattered clumps, stared, muttered. Their leaders went among them, getting them quieted. None drew near the judgment circle, where the followers of Eirik and Önund gathered. Aalf stood tall amidst them. He and Gunnhild swapped a smile.

Eirik beckoned his warriors to rank themselves before him. "Arinbjörn's gone to his ships," he said. "Go you to ours. Tell those there to strike the awnings and make ready to launch. I'll come as soon as may be."

Gunnhild cast a glance toward the sun. It had not moved through heaven that she could see. Had the time really been so short? As Eirik went from them, she hurried to meet him. "Where are you bound?" she asked.

Though she foreknew he would answer, "To find Arinbjörn and Egil, and get Egil killed if we can," it flamed in her. At last, she thought, at last.

XX

Only bit by bit, in jagged shards, through the months afterward, did she learn how the hunt went. Men who had seen this or heard that stopped by on their farings and told. Often what one said about a happening was not quite the same as another who was also there said. They had seen it differently, or remembered it differently, or forgotten some part of it. As pieces came into her hands, she fitted them together until she held the whole.

And that she would never forget. She could not.

The first reached her soon and unbroken. Eirik's warships had run swiftly through the straits between mainland and islands, into the Sognefjord. There he spied Arinbjörn's longship. She turned in to a sound. Eirik followed and lay alongside. He asked if Egil was aboard. Arinbjörn said no, as the king could see for himself. When further asked, the hersir could not but say that Egil and twenty-nine other men had taken a skuta and gone off to Steinsound, where he had left his knarr.

Oh, he looked for trouble at the Thing, Gunnhild thought; if nobody else made it, he would.

The king had already marked several craft bound that way. He ordered his own rowed there too. Night was falling as he drew near the inlet. He had anchors dropped. At daybreak they went on in. Through dawn-mists they made out the freighter.

Her crew saw six longships coming at them. Egil bade them get into the skuta. Eighteen did. The rest stayed, thinking the odds better where they were. All armed themselves fast. Egil had those who came with him row between the land and the dragon passing nearest the land, which was Eirik's. Then things went at breakneck speed.

In the dim light, none of the king's crew spied the skuta before it was going by. Egil rose and hurled a spear. It struck the steersman, who was close kin to Eirik, stabbed into his rib cage, and dropped him dying in a gout of blood.

The king's orders clanged across glimmery waters. Three of his ships turned about, threshing white foam, and gave chase to the skuta. The rest sought the knarr, hemmed her in, and sent their crews aboard with ax and sword. Some of Egil's men won free, made it to shore, and ran inland. Ten of them died. The attackers took everything off that was of any worth and set the knarr afire. Flames answered the new sun with roar and reek.

The three hunting Egil were two men to an oar, while the skuta was shorthanded. They began to overhaul. But between two islands went a narrow, shallow channel; and the tide was at ebb. The boat slipped through where the ships could not. By the time they had gone around, they had lost the quarry. Eirik returned grimly to the Thingstead.

There, before everyone, he made Egil fully an outlaw, whom any man might kill and owe no wergild.

Berg-Önund asked uneasily if he could stay home when the levies went to meet with the king. He thought it would be risky to leave his farm while Egil was loose. Eirik allowed it.

Thereafter they sailed south. When they overnighted at Aarstad, a holding of the king's near Askey, he told Frodi, who oversaw it, to stand by Önund if need be. This Frodi was a handsome young man, kin of his. With him dwelt Eirik and Gunnhild's son Rögnvald.

The boy was then eleven years old. His limbs had lengthened since last his mother saw him; he was shooting up toward man-height and manhood. Straight and strong he stood. Under the flaxen hair his face was much like his father's, but his laugh much more ready. It sounded spring-clear, for his voice had not yet broken. Already, though, he bore himself boldly, withal wisely for his age. Pride surged through Gunnhild in a warm wave. She longed to hug him. She wished she could have had him with her his whole life, to watch him grow and love him. But he was highborn.

In the morning the ships pushed onward.

Eirik brought his queen to the steading at Byfjord. They had a few wildcat nights together; then he was off to his war. Gunnhild settled down with Ragnhild, Erling, and Gudröd. There was enough to keep her busy. From time to time, news arrived from the North.

Egil had found Arinbjörn at home. "I awaited no better from your dealings with the king," said Arinbjörn when he had heard, "but you'll not lack for money. I'll pay you for your loss and get you another ship." Egil gave gruff thanks.

That ship was ready, with a cargo of lumber to boot, when the rest of Egil's men who lived reached the garth. Thus he had a crew of almost thirty. Everything was done in some haste, for one thing because Arinbjörn himself did not mean to stay here long.

So Aasgerd boarded while her husband and brother bade one another farewell. Egil knew his friend would join the king, and was not happy about that. He must have been brooding on the verse that now ripped through the wind:

> "All ye gods and Odin,
>   drive Eirik out of the land!
> Harm be his lot and hatred,
>   he who robbed me of wealth.
> Frey and Njörd, send fleeing
>   this foe of every freedom.

> Be wrathful, Thor, and bereave
> the wrecker of the halidom."

The housefolk and even the warriors shuddered. Such a curse was a fearsome thing. Arinbjörn frowned. "Mishap may fall on more men than it's meant to," he muttered. Nonetheless he clasped Egil's hand and wished him luck. He stood on the wharf watching the ship till she was gone from sight.

Egil did not at once steer for Iceland. He lay to at the skerry called Vitar, off the outlying island Alden. Little shipping passed this way, but fishermen went there often. From them he learned how Eirik had outlawed him altogether. Blackly wroth, he glowered over the sea until he stood up and cast another verse eastward.

> "Land-god, the road is long
> that the lawbreaker's set me on,
> Blood-ax, the bane of brothers,
> badly led by his wife.
> Gunnhild it is who gave me
> grounds for taking revenge.
> Once I was quick to work it.
> I wait now and bide my time."

The man who uttered this to the queen stood stiff-backed before her. Shocked stillness filled the hall. Her mouth drew taut. She stared ahead, as if beyond the walls. At length she smiled at him and said, "Tidings are tidings. You did well," and gave him half a gold arm-ring.

The weather at Vitar was calm, with land breezes from the hills at night and sea breezes by day. One evening Egil hoisted sail and tacked westward. The fishers had been asked to watch for him. Some rowed to the mainland and told how he had gone. The word soon reached Askey. Berg-Önund gloated. He sent home the men who had guarded him; they were costly to feed. He rowed to Aarstad and bade Frodi come help him make merry; he had lots of ale. Frodi took a few men of his own and returned with him.

Rögnvald stayed behind. He was reckoned too young. Restless, he led off a dozen men who kept with him, the king's son. They got in a six-oared karfi of his and went to the neighbor island Herdla. Afterward and always Gunnhild could well-nigh see the brightly painted hull, oars dancing on wave-sparkle, gulls white, Rögnvald's fair hair like a banner at the prow. Eirik owned a big farm on Herdla. Its steward was one Thorir, called the Bearded, who had fostered Rögnvald and now gave him a hearty welcome. Here too was no dearth of drink.

Meanwhile Egil had let his ship drift for a few nights. When a strong sea breeze sprang up, he told his crew they had better make landing before they found themselves clawing off a lee shore. Near Herdla they took haven in a bight. After dark Egil went with two men in a small boat to Herdla itself and sent one ashore as a spy. This man garnered the tale of the two feastings—a drunken housecarl spoke freely to him—and that Önund, Önund's brother Hadd, and Frodi were at Askey with no more fighting men than Frodi's handful.

Back at his ship, Egil anchored offshore and had the crew arm themselves. He put twelve on watch. Seventeen fared with him in a skuta she had towed, through the strait to Askey. At eventide, on muffled oars, they entered a creek and nosed in among the reeds. Egil left the others there and walked into the woods. He bore helmet, sword at shoulder, shield on arm, and bill in hand.

Meeting some herd-boys, he fooled them into believing he had found a bear that had lately been raiding the farm. Yonder it was, in that thicket, he said. A boy ran off to tell them in the house. As was their wont, only Önund, Hadd, and Frodi were awake this late. They grabbed their weapons and followed the boy. By starlight and half-moon he led them to the edge of the wood and pointed to the brush the stranger—who had said he was going home—had shown. Seeing branches and leaves stir in the gloom, Hadd and Frodi ran to get between this clump and the woods. Önund went straight forward.

He met Egil.

He cast his spear, Egil his bill. Egil had slanted his shield; the spear glanced off. The bill went into Önund's. The shaft dragged at it. Egil was first to unsheathe sword. He thrust into Önund's belly. As Önund staggered, Egil hewed at the neck, almost beheading the man.

Hadd and Frodi heard. They dashed to do battle. Egil yanked his bill free and cast it again. It went through Frodi's shield and breast till the point came out the back. Hadd's sword clashed against Egil's only a short while before Egil cut him down.

The fear-smitten boys crept nigh, ready to bolt across the field. Egil chopped a hand at the fallen. "Now be herders of your lord Önund and his fellows, so wildfowl and beasts don't tear at their lichs," he panted.

Back to the boat he went and fetched its crew. They broke into the farmhouse, surprising every suddenly awakened man, slaying any who did not flee. They looted it, and wrecked what they could not carry off. They drove the kine down to the creek, slaughtered all, and took as much meat as the boat would hold. Away they rowed, Egil at the steering oar. He was still in a killing rage. Nobody dared speak to him.

Daybreak shivered on the waters. Treetops stood wan above shadowy islands. A karfi rounded a headland, bound the other way. "That belongs to Rögnvald Eiriksson," the spy said.

It came out later that someone had seen Egil's ship and borne the word to Herdla. The king's son had started at once to warn Önund.

Eirik half rose. "Row!" he bellowed. "Give it your backs, you scuts! Row!"

The skuta leaped. Her bow wave hissed. Men on the karfi gaped. Their oars faltered. This was happening too fast for them. Egil rammed her amidships. Though she was bigger, she heeled over. Sea poured across the bulwark. She righted herself but wallowed. Egil's rowers upped starboard oars. Shafts snapped on the stricken craft as the larboard rowers swung the skuta alongside. Egil sprang. His men swarmed after. They were more, fully weaponed. Wading in water that soon splashed red, they slew everyone in that hull.

After they left the karfi and she drifted off, the gulls came wheeling downward.

When Gunnhild heard, the world went black in her sight.

She swam back from the whirling depths and looked forth into a day heartlessly bright. Rögnvald, cried her thought. Oh, Rögnvald, men died and too often it was the mothers that bore them who laid them out and closed their eyes. But so soon, Rögnvald, so soon? And she afar, he given to the seafowl.

More news followed.

When Egil landed on Herdla, he and his men headed straight for the farm. Thorir the Bearded saw them coming. He pelted elsewhere with the household. The wayfarers plundered, returned to their ship, and made her ready.

While they waited for a fair wind, Egil busied himself.

When the wind came, he went onto a rock that jutted toward the mainland. In one hand he bore a tall, stout hazel staff he had cut. In the other was the head of a horse. Standing on the rock while the sea moaned below and a wrack of clouds blew out of a nearing rainstorm, he set the horsehead on the staff and lifted it upright. "Here I raise a nithing-staff, and I turn its curse against King Eirik and Queen Gunnhild," he called. He aimed the head at the hills that rose hazed across the strait. "And I turn this curse against all the land-wights who watch over this land, that they wander bewildered and cannot find their way home until they have harried King Eirik and Queen Gunnhild from the land."

He wedged the staff into a cleft, the head still staring yonder. With his knife he carved runes on it. Thereupon he went down to his ship and his wife. Storm or no, his crew set sail for Iceland.

That was a dark and mighty spell he cast, Gunnhild knew. Next after a man, a horse was the foremost of offerings; and many were the men whose blood was on Egil's hands. She thought belike those runes held the two poems in which he had asked for the wrath of the gods. Each half-verse would take thrice the number of all the runes, which

Odin had hung for nine nights from the world-tree to win.

But she knew other powers, powers of drum, song, dance, food gathered in wilderness and drink brewed in loneliness, powers growing from the wet black earth and falling from the moon, to loose the soul and steer the weapon that does not miss. She had six sons left her, and a seventh in her womb. Her man had the kingdom.

Someday they would get their revenge.

XXI

Ships thronged the Boknafjord and its strands. Men arrived afoot and on horseback, day after day, to fill those hulls that had not come here already laden—carls, hinds, yeomen, led by their greatest landholders, few of them warded by more than a helmet, a shield, and a coat of leather, if that, but bearing spears, axes, swords, bows, slings. It was as big a levy, from as widely around in the shires that Eirik held, as he could lawfully raise or that could feed itself for as long as he could lawfully keep it.

Jarls, lendmen, hersirs, and their guards were fully, gleamingly outfitted. Packhorses trudged; wagons creaked. Tents bloomed on the shore, among the bags and blankets of the many who had none. Fires crackled and smoked; meat sizzled on spits or boiled in kettles; sausage and dried fish fried. Day by long day the noise and unrestfulness swelled, until the hills themselves seemed overwhelmed.

Then horns blew, ships slid into water, men scrambled aboard, masts and their rigging were raised on high. Well out to sea, sails went aloft, splashes of color strewn across the waves. A fair wind for the southeast had come up. It stiffened and shrilled. Waves brawled before it, spindrift flying off their white manes. Sails strained; rigging thrummed; strakes groaned; keels plunged. Yet clouds were scattered and hasty. The nights stayed light. Through their short silvery dusk one could still easily make out land, islands, reefs. By the second morning, land's end was in sight and they put the helms over.

The wind lowered but also swung westerly, driving them up the Skagerrak in long, foaming tacks, sails poled out but no need to shorten. If anything, the worst trouble in the whole voyage had been to hold the swifter craft back from outrunning the slower. Dragon-prowed, wisent-prowed, stallion-prowed, swan-prowed, they swept toward the Oslofjord.

"I wonder if Queen Gunnhild didn't witch us this weather," muttered a man in his beard.

"Would you call that bad?" asked another. His laugh sounded uneasy.

When they reached the inlet that led to Tunsberg, the wind slackened off and died out. "We'll stop here," said Eirik, "get a little sleep, and walk on to our war."

None cared for the work of making camp. They rested aboard under awnings or ashore under sky. But fires burned high and widely about, in fields and on hilltops, for this was Midsummer Eve.

Eirik found Arinbjörn a ways down the strand by his ships. Figureheads and masts stood tall athwart the wan gloaming, where few stars glimmered. Water sheened behind the shadowy hulls. It chuckled against them, very softly in the hush. The ness on its farther side was an eastward darkness above whose treetops stole already a faint brightening. Balefires made tiny candleflames or flickering red specks. Dew spangled nearby turf. The mild air smelled of it and of leaves. A stand of birch was as white as a maiden's skin, their crowns as fair as her hair. An owl hooted from them, over and over.

"Greeting, King," said Arinbjörn low. "A good faring, no?"

Eirik nodded. "I think we've come well ahead of the news of us."

"Dwellers hereabouts have fled, some surely to the town."

"What of it? Our foes have scant time left to busk themselves. Belike not all their levies have gotten here yet."

King Olaf in Vikin and King Sigröd in Thraandheim had well understood what their brother was about. Sigröd came down with what men he could muster. That was merely some hundreds. It was a long haul from his kingdom; he could not promise they would be home for harvest; the law said that no man had to be gone when his land needed him. Although Olaf's kingdom was smaller, its full strength would be too many to feed for weeks on end, so he had put off sending the war-arrows around until lately. He and Sigröd stayed together in Tunsberg. The town must now be coming alive with shouts and torches, while horsemen galloped everywhere to bring in those who were out at the fires, helping bless the kine and dance the summer in.

"Glad I am to have you again at my side, foster brother," Eirik said.

"I was never away from it," Arinbjörn answered.

Eirik's voice harshened. "Stoutly enough did you stand by Egil Skallagrimsson against me."

"I told you, King, he's my sworn friend. I'm grieved at the split between you. He's not an evil man. Headstrong, a bad one to cross, yes." Arinbjörn smiled. "There are those who say much the same of you, King." He added nothing about Gunnhild. "But in his rough way Egil's true to his own friends and honest with them. He may well be the best skald who ever lived. His wife, my kinswoman, is happy."

"You know I want him killed."

Arinbjörn sighed. "That must lie between you twain, unless I can somehow make peace."

"Never can you or anyone else do that."

"Then let's set the whole thing aside, King. Egil is gone from Norway—forever, we may hope, though I'll miss him. You've other, bigger foes closer to hand. I thought we might talk about how to meet them."

Eirik eased a little. "Yes, that's why I came looking for you. In spite of everything, your arm is mighty and I know you'll keep faith whatever befalls."

"Bare is brotherless back." Arinbjörn did not tell the king that he had that saying from Egil. They went into the warlike business ahead of them.

Day broke. The host grumbled to its feet and, leaving a watch on the ships, rumbled up the road to Tunsberg. Dust puffed. Crops went flat where fighters spilled into fields. Farmhouses lay smokeless, stockpens empty. Birds and butterflies scattered, bright scraps of fear.

Erelong the stockade hove in sight, gates barred, the wharves and ships in front forsaken. Riding a horse that had been taken along, Eirik led the way around to the east side. Gilt helmet blazed, red cloak flamed in the young sunlight. A ridge lifted on his right. Ranked men roofed it. Spearheads flashed. A breeze rippled banners.

Eirik laughed, drew rein, and beckoned to his headmen. Shouting, stamping, his host gathered itself in three wedge-shaped arrays. He had the middle, gray Hauk Highbreeks the left flank, Arinbjörn the right. He gave the reins to a boy and swung down from the saddle. Horns dunted. War-cries howled. Eirik unlimbered an ax. Household troopers made a shield-wall around him, but he himself would also smite. His wedges moved forward. While Olaf and Sigröd held the high ground, Eirik's following was much the greater.

Nearer he drew and nearer. Arrows began to whirr. Stones began to rain. Onward he came. Spears flew. Wounded men wailed, too hurt to remember manliness. Crows wheeled above, and the earliest of the ravens.

The armed throngs shocked together. Steel clashed on steel, thudded on shield, bit into flesh, broke bone. Men pushed, staggered, went forward, fell back, fell down, and then feet trampled over them and ribs crunched. Inward the wedges clove. It blunted them; their sides buckled toward each other; the strife churned around them. But a seasoned warrior kept an eye on his leader's banner, swaying above the fray. He knew where he was and worked to stay there. Raw youths and unskilled hinds saw him and were not lost in the ruck. Thus they knew which of the bodies crowding in on them to beware of and strike at.

By King Eirik's order, his skald Dag kept aside on horse-back, trotting to and fro, overseeing the battle as best he was able. If he lived through it, his poems would tell the world how it went. Those inside saw only what was upon them. Otherwise it was shapelessness, wrath, and death.

So Dag beheld King Olaf's standard go down, the bearer slain. A new man took it. But Arinbjörn's had lurched close. When Olaf's fell the second time, it did not rise anew. Arinbjörn thrust on ahead. The ranks before him splintered. Some men dropped their weapons and fled. Others stood alone or in forlorn small bands. Arinbjörn's ringed them in.

Eirik burst through to the rear of the foe. He swung around and attacked from behind. Hauk's flank closed in on Sigröd's. He held it there while Eirik hewed into it.

Suddenly the fight was over. Men of the two lesser kings were running every which way, down the hill and across the grass, blind with dread. Men of Eirik's hounded them. The badly wounded crawled or sat bewildered watching the life drain out of them or lay gasping or screaming or in jaw-clenched stillness. The dead sprawled everywhere, ungainly, faces ashen and agape. Blood smeared them. It puddled and steamed on the torn earth. The air stank. The fowl circled low. The boldest of them landed, to start picking and tearing.

In Eirik's now ragged ranks men whooped, laughed madly, pounded each other on the back, jigged, skipped, alive, alive. A strengthening breeze unfurled his banners, many-hued, stitched with ravens, eagles, wolves, grinning and gripping little trolls, high against heaven.

Soon weariness brought quietness and slumped shoulders. "We'll see if the town will open itself to us," said Erik to Arinbjörn, Hauk, and others of his foremost. "If not, we'll pitch camp and wait a day or two in hopes. We can set it afire if we must, but I'd rather take it unscathed."

"We should first send searchers after Olaf and Sigröd, King," said Arinbjörn. "I think they fell."

"Yes," agreed Erik. "We'll give them honorable gravemounds. They too were sons of Harald Fairhair."

"And afterward?" asked Hauk.

"We'll send the levies home," Eirik said. "Our household troops will be enough to do what's left to do. Against my father's and my will, these Vikin folk hailed Olaf their king. We'll go through their lands and bring them to heel."

"I think we'll often have a fight," warned Arinbjörn.

Eirik laughed. "Of course. They'll learn better from that, and from fire and plunder where needful." He went stern. "Norway shall be whole again."

The summer was old when he came back to Gunnhild bearing his victory.

XXII

A north wind roared down the throat of the Thraand-heimsfjord and over its wide inner waters. They ran iron-gray, in heaving whitecaps and flying scud, to spout where they struck rocks and burst on the strands. Rain slanted river-thick, arrow-sharp, often mixed with hail that skittered across the streaming ground. Lightning forked through. Thunder rolled down and down an unseen sky.

In the high hall at Hladi, flames beat back shadows. Smoke drifted bitter. Figures carven in wood and woven in hangings seemed to stir amidst the dimness.

Sigurd Jarl sat with his guests. They drank not from horns but from glass and silver goblets. Yet this was no feast. They were few. Nobody else was there but his trustiest guardsmen. A pitcher stood on the board before each man so that he could pour for himself. If it went empty, a trooper would fill it afresh. The hall reached hollow around them.

No dishonor was meant. Later many more would come, food and drink overflow, a skald chant his lays, Sigurd give goodly gifts. These few were of high standing, lendmen, hersirs, wealthy yeomen, such as Narfi of Staf and Blotolf of Ölvishaug from the inner Thraandlaw, Kaari of Gryting and Aasbjörn of Medalhus from the outer. What they spoke of should not go beyond these walls—not yet.

They already knew their King Sigröd lay dead in the South beside his brother King Olaf. Sigurd had further news for the latecomers. "Faithful men got away to the Uplands with Olaf's son Tryggvi and with Gudröd, son of Björn the Chapman, whom Olaf fostered," he said. "I hear they're promising lads, but only lads. And who knows how long they'll be safe in the mountains? Eirik Blood-ax goes around Vikin, laying waste wherever they do not at once call him lord."

"It might have gone likewise in the Southwest, had Eirik fallen," said Blotolf dryly.

"It will go like that with us next year, if we don't yield," answered Sigurd.

"If he dares try," snapped Narfi.

The chieftains sat straighter. Great and rich was the Thraandlaw, a home for heroes. Hither had come Hadding from the South, long ago, to fell a giant and win a king's daughter. Hence had gone Bjarki to the South, he who became the right hand of Hrolf Kraki.

"He will," the jarl foretold, "and he will win, unless we can raise the whole land against him. Neither Sigröd nor his brother Haalfdan the Black left us anyone around whom we can rally. Sigurd the Huge, last living son of Harald Fairhair and Snaefrid, is content to sit quietly as shire-king in Hringariki, paying scot to whoever is in power. Anyhow, folk would belike be too leery of him because of his mother. Eirik will have all of Norway at his beck aside from what's ours. I wouldn't even hope for Haalogaland. Özur Dapplebeard is still a mighty man yonder—Queen Gunnhild's father."

"Maybe Eirik will deal lightly with us for your sake," said Aasbjörn. "Your father stood high with Harald Fairhair. After him, you did."

"That helped us. Nevertheless, here also he took away olden rights. You're as aware as I, or better, how the Thraands growl and seethe. Eirik Blood-ax will be worse, hard, harsh, grasping. I know him; I know him. We need a better king."

Wind yelled. Rain dashed against walls and roof. Lightning flared; thunder boomed.

"What are you thinking of?" asked Kaari of Gryting.

Sigurd Jarl leaned forward. "Not every other son of Harald Fairhair is dead or tamed," he told them. "One lives free. I saw him born, poured water over him, and gave him my own father's name. I say we should send to England."

BOOK THREE

THE WESTMEN

1

Bound back to Winchester from his triumph in Cumbria, King Eadmund halted wherever he deemed it well to speak with noblemen, give audience to commoners, and render judgment when asked to. Along the way, men of his court who had not gone to the war but home, or the families of some who had, joined the progress. Many of these had waited in London. His first stop after the great town was also along the River Thames, at Reading. Fewer than two score houses clustered there, but it was an important meeting place and strongpoint in a rich, well-peopled shire, the seat of an earl whose estate could guest such a following. That was where the messengers from Norway found him.

Early the next morning, two youths came out of the earl's chapel. Hardly anyone else had heard that mass; the highborn were barely stirring after a late eventide, the lowly had to be at their work. These two had lingered afterward for more prayer. They blinked when they passed from candlelit dimness into sudden blue, and stood for a while just beyond the door of the little building.

With the Danes no longer a threat thereabouts, the town was spreading from cramped earthworks and stockade, and the estate lay open to the river. Behind the chapel rose walls, roofs, smoke, muffled sounds of man and beast, now and then a busybody cockcrow. Before it, dew glistened on a grassy slope crossed by well-rutted paths, down to the water, where tatters of mist still swirled and eddied. The sun was newly clear of trees far off to the right. It cast long shadows across land dappled with the aftermath of harvest, whose green was ever so slightly dimming as summer waned. Air lay cool, still, altogether clear overhead.

"Did a sign come to you?" Brihtnoth nearly whispered.

"No," Haakon answered. "To you?"

"Why should it? You're the one called—" Brihtnoth gulped. "Called to your kingdom."

Haakon stared past him. "I wondered," he said as awkwardly, "if—through you—a saint might, might speak."

"But who am I?"

"My nearest friend."

Both fell silent, the fair skin flushed. There was no reason for that that either could think of, however their thoughts might grope and stumble. Yes, Haakon was a royal fosterling, but Brihtnoth's father had risen to chief of the royal guard. At fifteen years of age, Haakon was a few months the older; his strong-boned face and long yellow locks lifted a good two inches over Brihtnoth's brown curls and eyes, short nose, cheeks as yet almost girlish. Nonetheless they had romped together, played together, sported together, struggled together toward manhood, and seldom had either kept anything hidden from the other.

"You—you have many friends," Brihtnoth tried at last. "Everybody likes you. The king himself—"

Haakon drew a breath and steadied. His blue look went straight to meet the brown. "The king has been kind to me, yes," he said.

Eadmund was not such a close father to the Norse boy as Aethelstan had been, Aethelstan who died so unawaitedly these five years agone. For one thing, Aethelstan had never married and had no known children of his own, whereas his half-brother had outlived a first wife and taken a second. For another, it happened that Eadmund had been much away from home. Still, he saw to the foreign prince's upbringing.

Haakon sighed. "I hoped I'd soon be a fighting man of his," he said.

"We both would!" Brihtnoth cried into the new sunlight. "But now—"

Earnestness came upon Brihtnoth. He had always been more devout than most. It was he who murmured yestereven, aside, after the bearers of the stunning tidings settled down to feast, that Haakon should rise betimes and go pray for guidance. All at once his speech flowed more readily. "You are called. Is that not sign enough? Did God tell you otherwise? A holy work, to free your fatherland from a tyrant and bring it to the Faith."

Haakon nodded stiffly. "So the king said."

"And he thinks you can do it, too. He promised to send men along with you. Why do you hang back? *Can* you?"

"Am I worthy?" Haakon faltered.

"The blood of kings is in you. The hand of God is on you. Your name will live forever."

Haakon looked away again, to the river where the three ships that had brought the messengers lay moored. The long curves of their hulls seemed to blend with the last mists. "How beautiful they are," he whispered. "Yes, I'd be less than a man if I shrank from this." His look went back to Brihtnoth. "But I'll miss England. I'll miss you."

"And, and I you."

On Haakon's right ring finger shone a silver band, bearing small, knobbed crosses between beaded edges. He snatched it off and thrust it at his friend. "Here," he blurted. "Take this of me."

The other gasped. "What? You—The king gave you it."

"Yes. So it's mine to give onward, isn't it? But I don't want to make a show. Not of this. Not out in front of everybody. Don't you either. If someone asks, yes, you can say it's from me. But don't make a fuss."

"I—I wouldn't."

Brihtnoth took the ring and, unsteadily, slipped it onto his own left hand, where it would less likely be noticed. "But I've nothing to give you. Only my thanks."

"Oh, it's small, not worth much, aside from the workmanship. Something to remember me by, that's all." Haakon made a smile. "If I'm to be a king, I'll need to pass out costlier goods."

"I know you'll be generous. You've always been."

Again they were silent for a while, unsure what to say. A cow lowed; a carl shouted.

"What will *you* do?" Haakon asked.

Brihtnoth stared at the ground. "I don't know. Not yet. Maybe—maybe I'll take vows."

"We were going to be warriors together."

"I don't think I'd like that so much. Now."

Out of nowhere he could tell, heartiness burst over Haakon. He clasped Brihtnoth's shoulder. "Why, if you become a priest, I can send for you!" rang forth. "Can't I? I'll need churchmen for the holy work."

11

The fall of the year was well along, nights swiftly lengthening, winds chill, grass wan, most broadleaf trees gone bare, when Haakon mounted the stone at Frosta Thingstead. But on this day the Thraandheimsfjord, lapping around the jut of land, shimmered and glistened with sunlight. The same brightness goldened the wings of an eagle at hover far overhead. The air was nearly warm, as if it remembered the last spring or looked forward to the next.

Sigurd Jarl had spoken at length, telling why he had called a folkmoot. He was skilled in the use of words and at sending them forth so that the farthest-off listener clearly heard. Growls, now and then angry shouts had answered his tale of outrages and the threat of worse to come. But when he stepped down and Haakon stepped up, for a span there followed a stillness.

They knew not quite what to make of it all, these lendmen, hersirs, yeomen, chapmen, craftsmen, seamen, woodsmen. Warily they peered at the tall young buck. He did not seem to have his full growth, though he was already powerful, the shoulders wide, the arms and hands sinewy. His clothes were of the same stuff and cut as those of the Englishmen who had come with him and now stood rather stiffly aside. He had, though, stopped shaving, and while the hair on his face was soft and thin, it matched the fair locks that he had had shortened like a Norseman's. While he was unarmed, as befitted the Thing, those who met him earlier at Hladi hall had seen the gilt-hafted sword he bore, King Eadmund's gift, the lovely ripple-sheen of the steel, and heard how with it Haakon had cloven a quernstone from rim to hole. No better blade was known in the North.

Nor would a weakling have brought it overseas to unsheathe against Eirik Blood-ax.

Standing before them, he looked across their packed throng. Bright hues, fur trim, and polished metal garbed some, but mostly it was wadmal, blue or gray or dun, as strong and lasting as the wearers. Aside from the well-to-do, they were shaggier than the English, but not unkempt or dirty. A kind of haughtiness, a feeling of inborn freedom, stiffened the backs of the least among them. Tents, booths, and horses ashore, ships and boats at the water's edge, told of hard faring and a harder will. Weapons lay yonder.

Haakon lifted his right arm. A sigh like a turning tide went through the crowd.

His voice rolled from full lungs. He and Sigurd had had days to talk, both alone and with wise men. The jarl understood not only his Thraands but everything that went on in Norway. "Yes," Sigurd had murmured after many searching questions, "we did well—more than well—in bringing you here;" and he gave the newcomer deep-reaching redes and schooled him in how best to bear himself.

"Men of this land, which is also my land, you have heard the words of your mighty jarl and weighed them. Now hear mine. I know I still shape them like an Englander, but the tongue that does so is altogether Norse." In truth, Haakon was easily understandable, sounding no stranger in his way that someone from Vikin or Svithjod, Denmark or Iceland. "Likewise is the heart behind it. And the blood is the blood of your kingly house, I the brother of your own kings Haalfdan and Sigröd. My right is the same as theirs, which Eirik reaved from them together with their lives. It stands above his, for he is lawless and ruthless, while I will uphold olden law and rights. I will be just in my judgments, sparing in what I ask of you, and open-handed in what I give. To this, here upon your Thingstone, as I shall at every Thing throughout Norway, I plight my honor and my life."

Older men in the throng began to say wonderingly, "Why, this is Harald Fairhair, come back to us and young again." They recalled the good they had had from the great king as well as the ill.

"Hail me your lord. Lend me your help and strength to take and hold what is mine. For only under their rightful king may land and folk thrive."

And then soon—for he spoke straightforwardly, as Sigurd Jarl had told him was best—Haakon said, "It's true that my father took away your right of freehold. Today you are only tenants of the king. But when the kingdom is mine, I will give back that right. Every man in all Norway shall fully and freely own the land he lives on, as his fathers did before him, and so shall his sons and grandsons after him."

They gasped; then they roared. They surged about, wildly shouting, waving their hands aloft as if they held drawn swords, stamping, hugging each other, drumming their feet on the earth. Haakon stood and smiled. The sunlight spilled down over him.

It was a while before men of weight could quiet the meeting. Thereafter things moved fast. Haakon said a few words more, mostly about the need to pass the news along and make ready to fight. Sigurd took over and got business onto a lawful track. As one, the gathering chose Haakon their king.

"Now," said Sigurd to him when at last they had a little span by themselves, "we've work ahead of us. Your Englishmen are few, and won't stay. We have to get trustworthy warriors for your household troops. I've found some, but you'll need more. Likewise you'll need carls and maids and all else. And gifts to hand out—well, my hoard is yours till we've clapped hold of Eirik's. Already this winter we should move south and east, winning the chiefs and dwellers over to us. Give him no time to forestall us. Nor—even more, I think—that witch-queen of his, Gunnhild."

Haakon gazed at the jarl. Lamplight in the loftroom where they sat flickered across dark hair and beard, shadowed the furrows of his face. Elsewhere hulked darkness. A newly risen wind whined outside the shutters. Cold was creeping inward.

"You, you are so helpful to me," Haakon stammered. "I can't think how ever to reward you."

Sigurd grinned crookedly. "Oh, I'm seeing to the morrow of my house. Eirik and Gunnhild are no friends of it." The wryness that he often put on left him. He leaned forward, reached across the board between, past the crock and drinking horns, and laid his hand across Haakon's. "May you and I always be friends, King. May our houses always be." He let go, sat back, and looked into the shadows. "Well," he said low, "that lies with the gods, doesn't it? Or with the norns, but no use in offering to them."

111

Yuletide was not merry that year at Arinbjörn's holding in Sygnafylki. And winter wore on, day dim and hasty between two huge nights, the air raw when it did not rage, earth white where the snow had not been scuffed to mud that soon froze. Gulls swung mewing above lead-gray waters; crows cawed harshly from the woods; the peep of a wren sounded like a frightened wish that maybe someday, somehow summer would return.

Eirik had left Gunnhild here in fall. After he got the news from Thraandheim, he and his troopers had hard riding to do around the land, while she was again growing big with child. Arinbjörn had the strength on hand to keep her safe. The hersir and his wife did their best for her. But she seldom smiled and often withdrew from them.

She was in the bower one day when he sought her out. Two maids were there also, spinning and weaving. Feeling her mood, they held themselves as still as her. The sun was sinking low behind a sullen sky. Scant light seeped through the gut over the windows. Lampflames glowed dull yellow. It had gotten so cold and dank that better might have been to close the shutters and make for the hearthfires of the hall. The queen had said nothing about that, so neither maid did. She sat in the chair the room had, together with a few stools, a fur coat over her gown, and brooded.

The door creaked open, giving a glimpse of dreariness. Arinbjörn's bulk filled it. He trod through and glanced at the lowborn women. "Out," he said. They made haste to put their work aside. He waited in his own hairy coat till they were gone, shut the door, and turned to Gunnhild.

"Why?" she asked. "They're only wenches."

"Nonetheless, Queen, I thought you'd rather speak under four eyes."

Her voice stayed flat. "What have you to say?"

"This latest word—" Earlier some men on weary horses had come to the garth. "You share none of your thoughts, my lady, but you always seem to be listening. How well have you followed what's been going on these past months?"

She raised her face straight toward his. Her words sharpened. "As well as a woman can."

He gave back her look. A little of her hair showed from under the embroidered headcloth. He knew how all of it sheened black. The skin lay milk-white and firm over high cheekbones and down the slim throat. Eyes shone gray-green beneath arching brows, lips sunrise-red over flawless teeth. She sat as if ready to spring up unheeding of the weight that swelled her belly. Yet this child would be her ninth. He had overheard whispers about her—uncanny, that she was neither worn out nor in her grave.

"With you, that's closer than with most men," he said—not praise, a blunt utterance. "However—"

Gunnhild understood that the riders would not have spilled their message to everybody. It was for the hersir, to pass on as he saw fit. "The tidings are worse than ever," she broke in.

Arinbjörn nodded heavily. "Yes."

Bad enough erenow. The tale of Haakon Aethelstan's-foster and his promises had spread like fire in dry grass. When he led his Thraandish warriors to the Uplands, many yeomen there left their homes to join him, others sent their plightings and tokens, all of which he took with a way of thanking that by itself was said to endear him to them. They streamed to Thing after Thing as he went forward, and at each one they hailed him their king. Thence he had moved into the shires of Vikin. There too he met nothing but welcome.

"And now?" Gunnhild's question fell stone-hard.

Arinbjörn clenched a fist. "Haakon's nephews Tryggvi Olafsson and Gudröd Bjarnarson have met him. He's made them shire-kings of the lands their grandfather Harald Fairhair bestowed on their fathers—Ranriki and Vingulmörk to Tryggvi, Vestfold to Gudröd—on the same terms, that they acknowledge him their lord, send him half the scot and rents they gather, and help him as needed. This they swore to do."

Gunnhild fleered. Her speech stayed even. "There was another King Gudröd once that we were at odds with, and more than him. They were grown men. They are now dead. Yonder two are striplings."

"Not easily overcome, though," Arinbjörn warned. "King Haakon set able men to run things for them till they reach manhood. The messenger gave me the names of those men, and I know somewhat about them. Also, their folk—" His gaze searched the queen again. "The upshot is, King Eirik holds only the middle half of Norway."

She met the look. "He'll strike back in spring," she said.

"So will Haakon," Arinbjörn answered. "And the land everywhere is seething."

He stood for a while, shoulders hunched. Darkness waxed in the windows. Then he sighed. "Well, Queen, I've been weighing this, and I believe I should leave soon, with what following I can muster, and go to King Eirik. You know, don't you, he's down in Rogaland," at the hall where Harald Fairhair died. "Such a showing ought to hearten others, make them likelier to stay true to him. And he'll be that much further ahead in busking for war."

Gunnhild rose. A bleak eagerness shivered. "I've been hoping for this."

"I awaited you'd say so," he told her in his steady way. "He'd be glad of your skills—of your knowledge and wisdom, I mean. But for the sake of your unborn and yourself, you'd best go by sea. A slow, rough, cold faring this time of year, not overly safe."

"Shall I fear to do what Haakon's slut-mother did?" Gunnhild flung back.

"Think on it, my lady. To deem by what I've heard about him, King Haakon would not willingly let you suffer harm. We have days yet. Think on it."

"Do you believe I haven't already?"

"No," said Arinbjörn softly. "You would have."

"I felt a doom in Haakon from the first," Gunnhild nearly snarled. "We should have gotten him slain in his crib."

Arinbjörn scowled at that, but said merely, "King Harald would never have allowed it."

"Oh, yes, Harald Fairhair begot many a wolf."

The hersir held back from putting Eirik among them.

"Also—" Gunnhild drew breath. "You've been good to me, Arinbjörn, you've kept your word, but how I've longed to get away from here. I could never be happy under a roof that's sheltered Egil Skallagrimsson."

He stood stubborn, neither defending the friendship nor asking forgiveness for it.

Spite spat. "Egil! He who murdered my son and cast a black spell against my men and me. What else has brought this woe on us?"

She did not tell what she had tried against Haakon, if anything. Had his White Christ fended her off? Who knew?

"There are those who might say that King Eirik's overbearingness had something to do with it," Arinbjörn answered slowly. He did not add, "And you yourself."

She gasped. "You dare—"

Looming over her, he smiled grimly as he raised a hand for peace. "Oh, I'd never say that to anyone else, Queen, nor ever let him say it to me." He lowered the hand. "But here, we two alone—My lady, you are a wisewoman. You can think. Not many folk can. We sorely need thinking now, open speech and cool thought."

Her stance eased a bit. "Yes. You are right about that."

She had better not get angry with him. The abidingly faithful could become few. It was not enough to hope for victory. She must learn beforehand how to deal with the worst of outcomes, for her sons, her daughter, the blood that ran in them.

IV

In spring the kings called up their hosts, Haakon in Thraandheim, Eirik in the midlands and Southwest. But Haakon's was much the bigger; and the Vikin men, up in arms, were set to fight for him, as were the Uplanders; and no few leading men in Eirik's shires brought their followings not to meet him but to meet Haakon. He had misliked it when Gunnhild pressed him to send spokesmen abroad who would ask about help were it needed, but in the end he yielded. Ships with bold crews crossed the winter sea more than once. Now he must agree that she had been right. Thorfinn Jarl of Orkney would take him in. There was no other hope.

Those willing to go along gathered at the Byfjord. The ships that would bear them and, for some, their families, made a fleet. Day after day passed in waiting for more to arrive. To Gunnhild it felt like a mockery by the gods that it was here. In this town, beside these strands, among these hills and woods, she had dwelt, seen her son Erling begin to walk, felt herself growing close to her daughter Ragnhild, wrought the death of King Haalfdan the Black, and welcomed Eirik home from the war that gave him the whole of Norway—for how short a span!

"We have not yet been overcome," she said to the stars. "We shall never be."

But scouts told how Haakon was moving south, his strength swelling along the way. The time they could linger shortened as fast. The day soon came when Eirik, with his wonted battle-ax quickness, ordered they go.

That was on a chilly morning, after a rainfall that left grass soaked underfoot and made treetops shine on the heights. A few clouds scudded white. Untellably many gulls wheeled and shrieked. Ships rocked in the chop. But the tide had turned outward and the wind stood fair for Orkney.

Eirik bade her farewell at the wharf. He would sail in a

dragon, she in a big knarr better fitted to her needs. "We'll meet again yonder" was all he said. "Your ship's not so swift, you know, but you should pass no more than two or three nights at sea, four at most. I'll have good lodging ready for you and the young ones."

Nor could she, amidst eyes and ears, say much else to him than, "You will have begun work on our vengeance too. We have your kingdom to win back for them."

He gave her the least grin. The wind ruffled hair whose gold was fading toward steel-gray. The years had plowed the lean face and cut creases at eyes whose blue, always pale, seemed bleached by weather and the sharp glints off waves. Yet he stood as straight and moved almost as limberly as when first she saw him, while his sternness had become flinty. "That's my Gunnhild," he said.

After he went off to board his craft, Arinbjörn came to her. He took her hand. "Fare luckily, my lady," he said. "You have our tomorrows with you." Then he too was gone.

A bit later her brother Aalf reached her. Time had somewhat stoutened his big frame and worn down his handsomeness, but his mane was still yellow under a hat and his breast broad enough to strain his shirt and give a glimpse of pelt. "Our ship lies ready now," he told her. "Come." Warriors made way and fell quiet as their band passed. The townsfolk crowded nearby, gaping.

Aalf went down the gangplank first. Once in the hull, he lifted a hand to help Gunnhild board. She gave it no heed, caught her skirts, and took the steep slant by herself. He half smiled. "You've not lost your sea legs, sister," he said. The smile died. "I said to you, though, when I was taking you to Finnmörk, it would not be well for a woman to spend much of her life in ships."

She remembered. How long ago that was. "We don't know what our weird will be till it's done with us," she answered. An unspoken uprising stirred within her. Was everything indeed foredoomed? The shamans had taught otherwise—that man can lay his will upon the world, if he knows how, if he dares, and if he never falters.

She turned about to greet her children.

The sons embarked according to their ages. Gamli came alone. He had a few carls with him, but they would go in another craft, and his foster father was among those who had chosen to stay in Norway. Gunnhild's heart sprang. Too seldom since he was taken from her had she seen her firstborn. With fifteen winters behind him, he had shot up tall, slender but already strong, more growth ahead of him. Flaxen hair blew around a face becoming quite like his father's. The young beard was well along. He said merely half a score words to her, though seemly, before he moved off to join the seamen who stood in the bows. The sword at his shoulder swayed to the springiness of his walk.

Guthorm, at fourteen, had begun to remind her of his grandfather Özur. She could see that, as yet lanky and awkward, he would be thickset, with arms like a blacksmith's. Only a black fuzz grew on cheeks still soft, but she thought that already a shrewdness lurked behind the small eyes.

Harald, eleven, foreshadowed the swift-moving bulk, the rugged good looks and spear-sharp blue gaze that had been Harald Fairhair's, the king who named him after himself. His locks streamed as richly bright. He too was leaving a foster home. But whatever he believed, Gunnhild thought, he'd have want of a grown, sound man to take after, for the next few years; and Eirik was too little forbearing. Why not Arinbjörn?

Ragnfröd, at nine, was red-haired and freckled. He looked around him, spoke hastily to her, and dashed off with a brashness that was also like her brother Eyvind, away in Denmark.

Erling's five years had steadied the stumpy gait she fondly remembered. It seemed to her that he bore himself a bit too haughtily for a child. She set the uneasiness aside. Belike the man would be lordly.

A woman led Gudröd by the hand, for he was only three, chubby, dark-haired, his brown eyes darting right and left in amazement. She recalled King Gudröd the man, whom she had sought to make dead and who had drowned; she recalled King Gudröd the youth, who now sat in Vestfold as underling to Haakon Aethelstan's-foster—but the name was old in the kindred. Might her lad redeem it.

Sigurd suckled the wet nurse who carried him, unknowing of his namesake, the Thraandish jarl turned into her death-foe. A weariness flitted through Gunnhild. She was not old, she told herself, she had milk of her own for this ninth—oh, Rögnvald, Rögnvald, whom Egil killed and left for the gulls!—but that was to help keep this one her last. There were bounds to what inborn strength and earthborn spellcraft could do. She could ill afford, least of all right now, to become weak or a hag.

She tightened. These were enough, if she saw to it that they lived and got back their birthright.

Ragnhild came aboard and the grief fell away. Her seven-year-old daughter went straight to her and, fearless of stares everywhere around, hugged her. "Mother, Mother! We're b-bound for greatness. Aren't we?" Ruddy-brown hair tumbled down the slight shape, shining under the morning sun. Gray eyes lifted to her, the lashes blinking back tears. A smile quivered. But there was no dearth of heart behind it— yes, and self-will and trickiness, Gunnhild thought a little wryly. She gave the girl a few warm breaths in her arms before sending her aft.

Some other folk followed. Aalf shouted his bidding. The gangplank was withdrawn, the moorings slipped. Oarsmen at bow and stern thrust free; blades threshed to take the knarr from the shallows. Her yardarm rattled aloft. Her sail bellied. Town and hills dropped behind. She cleared the fjord, stood out to sea, and made for the Westlands.

V

Late in the year King Haakon trekked north overland. It went slowly, less because of shortening days and worsening weather than because he stopped as often as might be to talk with men, both high and low, hear them out, and judge between them if they asked. Yuletide was nigh when he reached Thraandheim.

Sigurd Jarl rode forth to bid him welcome. He would stay at Hladi rather than on the rebuilt kingly garth at Sölvi, which was far offside and much smaller. Here was where the meaningful gathering would be. Nonetheless, as messengers who went ahead had bidden, early next morning, when most of the guests were still asleep, Sigurd led Haakon to a house some ways beyond the hall. The falconer and his family who lived there had been lodged elsewhere and the inside fitted with tapestries, glass and silver beakers, and whatever else was fitting. It would readily hold Haakon, the half-dozen more he had picked, and servants to wait on them. The rest of his men were bedded around the garth as was wonted.

King and jarl walked across ground lately thawed and then overnight lightly frozen. It creaked underfoot. Cloud hung low and gloomy. Breath smoked into raw, windless air. The fjord was like tarnished silver. Hearthfires and candles made the house cheerier. Haakon told his chosen men to settle in. He and Sigurd hung up their coats and sat down in chairs with backs and cushions, brought from the hall. Baulks under the feet of the king's raised it a few inches above the other. A woman brought them mead. It was better than most, dry and cunningly herbed.

Haakon looked around, sniffed the sweetness of burning pine, and smiled. "This will do well," he said.

"It's not worthy of you," Sigurd answered rather flatly. "Nor of me, that I shall not guest the king under my own roof."

Haakon went earnest. He flushed. "Any other time, yes."

"Many are coming here. They'll wonder why the king takes no share in honoring the gods."

"They know why!"

"I think most do not, my lord. Not yet."

"Then I'll tell them myself, if you won't," snapped Haakon. "They'll be bloodstained from the offerings. The hall itself will be. They'll drink to heathendom and eat unclean food."

Sigurd sighed. "Well, King, you are a Christian. Let every man abide by his own gods." A skew smile stirred the grizzling darkness of his beard. "I've seen some strange ones here and there."

"Only one is the true God." Haakon leaned forward. His voice shook. "Oh, my friend, my friend, could I but bring you to him!"

"Best we leave that aside for now, King. We've other things to talk about." The jarl peered over the rim of his goblet, into the youthful face. "We'll be swamped with talkers."

Yuletide meant a great meeting at Hladi, the more so as Sigurd bore the whole cost himself. That lifted his standing in these shires even higher than his shrewd leadership did, and, he believed, kept him in the goodwill of the gods.

"After the three feast days are over, I think some leading men will stay for a while," he went on. "I hope you can then sit amidst them."

"Yes, of course." Haakon shivered with his wish for fellowship. "I, I'll move straight back—as soon as the hall's been cleansed—Mostly, though, always, I want to speak with you. I've so much to ask you about—you who called me to Norway, who showed me what to do and gave me every help—"

Sigurd's smile softened. "I'm glad I did, my lord. Whatever I can do for you, you've but to ask."

Haakon sat still for a while. The fire crackled; sparks danced, wisps of smoke drifted gray. He gulped deep, set the goblet on his knee, and let out: "I've been thinking—trying to think—while Eirik Blood-ax lives, can we look for any lasting peace?"

Sigurd was as suddenly stark. "I doubt it. And surely we'll have the Danes to cope with."

Haakon reined himself in. "Yes. You told me early on, I should mostly keep in the South and midlands to watch for them."

Sigurd nodded. "While I hold the North for you."

"I'll make this known while I'm here, give you full sway over these lands, Moerr, Thraandheim, and northward, as my sworn man. Will you tell me how to do it aright?"

Again Sigurd nodded, but with more eagerness than most

ever saw in him. Oftenest he kept his thoughts to himself till he was ready to move—though, quick-witted as he was, that might not be any long time. "So you want to learn our laws and abide by them," he said. "Yes, I am glad of what I did."

They spoke together.

At last the jarl said, "We've done good work, King." He stretched his back and arms. "Now let's go back to the hall to eat and drink while daylight lasts." Yuletide was a day hence.

Haakon rose, which allowed his host to rise too. He shook his head. "I thank you, but not this evening."

Sigurd showed no surprise. He hardly ever did. "Why, King?"

"If I've not lost track, today is Friday. Didn't you mark how I took only a piece of bread? These men and I will keep the fast as best we can," they from those of his band who were Christian.

During the past months, about three score Norsemen had taken baptism, together with their households. He had truly won some of them over. Others merely wanted to please him, feeling the new gods could well be strong. A priest from England who had stayed in Norway sprinkled them. Otherwise there had been scant time to tell anybody much about the Faith. Haakon must needs bear with the heathen, many of them in his own following. He tried to treat all with the same fairness. Sometimes, out of their hearing, he prayed that their eyes be opened before it was too late for them.

"Ah, yes, I'd forgotten," the jarl said. "Well, there's both salt and smoked fish in the larder as you wished, together with better stuff for the morning and afterward." His gaze was seldom as mild as now. "But I hate to think of you here alone while we make merry."

"I'll have cheer enough with my Christian men."

"Men." Sigurd grinned. "What about a wench or two or three to warm your bed? Easily done."

The blood left Haakon's cheeks. "No!" he cried.

"Hey? That's not forbidden you, is it? Have you tumbled none along the way?"

Haakon stood stiff.

Sigurd's look hooded itself. "I see. You've had a great deal to do. Though I never heard how any other son of Harald Fairhair let that hold him back. Anyway, things have gotten less hasty than hitherto."

Haakon shook his head so the honey-hued locks swung to and fro. "No. I—No. Forgive me, I thank you for your kindness, but—but she'd be heathen, wouldn't she, and—" His voice trailed off.

Sigurd shrugged the least bit. "As you will, King." He lowered his own voice, for the others were back in the room, although keeping away from the mighty ones who quite plainly did not want their nearness. "Of course, we do need sons of yours to uphold the right of your house after you're gone. The sooner the better, King."

"I—a queen—a Christian woman—Later, later. First, everything else there is—"

Sigurd put helm over and steered clear of the business. "No lack of it, my lord." He let the young man ease off. That took only a few heartbeats. Haakon had already shown himself to be nimble-minded. "But about such things, Lord, you've seen how my wife Bergljot walks big with child. Her time will come on her very soon, maybe even during Yule."

"May all go well," said Haakon in honest friendship. "I'll pray for her. And for the child."

"You can do more, King, if you will."

"What?"

"If the child be a boy, and lives, will you give him your name, as I gave you my father's on the strand-rocks at Stord?"

Haakon took a backward step. He lifted a hand as if fending off. "Pour, pour water over him?" he stammered. "But I'm not a priest and—the water's unholy—a heathen rite—" He came to himself and straightened. His breath had quickened.

"It would mean much, King, not to me alone but to all the Thraands."

Haakon understood. Being of the higher rank, he could hardly foster the boy, but this would make a tie nearly as strong. And it would be a greater gift of thanks than any golden ring or sword or ship, a gift to match an undying poem of praise from the best of skalds.

He smote fist in palm. His lips moved wordlessly. Sigurd waited.

Haakon swallowed. "Yes," he said. "I will."

He spent most of the night that followed on his knees in the thick darkness of his shut-bed, begging God's forgiveness. Or forbearance? This could be a sign, a harbinger of the winning of the Northland for Christ. Or could it be a snare of the Devil—of Odin, who brooded over the whole vast kingdom and would soon ride on its night winds to drink the blood of slaughter?

Where none but the saints could see him, Haakon wept. He knew so little. If only his priest were here to counsel him and shrive him. But Leofric lay left behind along the way, coughing, shaken with chill while his skin burned hot to the touch. Unless he was dead.

Brihtnoth would not have fallen sick. He was young and strong, yet already wise. He could read and write, arts about which Haakon had hardly troubled as he was supposed to, when horses and hounds, boats and bouts were calling. To Brihtnoth Christ's love was like the sun in summer. Nonetheless he was so gladsome, they two had been so happy together, rollicking as children, testing their thews as boys, talking the long, awkward talk of youths, that Haakon had never felt how winter-wan that sun fell upon him. Were Brihtnoth somehow to walk into this house, he would carry the springtime around his shoulders.

Step by stumbling step, Haakon made his pilgrimage back toward hope. He must stop forgetting that he was the king of Norway, the queller of Eirik Blood-ax and Witch-Gunnhild. Not only did it behoove him to be manly; it would be death if he were not. His gift to Sigurd would be small enough for his staunch friend, mere bestowal of a

name on an innocent babe. Though the deed would be heathen, why should good not come of it? It would strengthen
him in Thraandheim, and thus throughout Norway.

Yes, in this coming year he should be able to send for
more priests from the West, and more and more each year
after that. He would hold his hand over them, he would
build churches for them, as they went about their holy
work. And at last—maybe—if God so willed, not too long
from tonight—Brihtnoth could come too, whether as lay-
man or priest. And Haakon could open his heart to him.

Comforted, the king fell asleep.

VI

Light flew like laughter over small waves, aglint and a-
shimmer in a hundred shifting hues, blue, green, tawny,
foam-white. They murmured and chuckled as they played
tag with the shadows of hurrying snowy clouds. Birds
wheeled, soared, swooped, swam, swung again aloft, in
their thousands, gull, guillemot, cormorant, puffin, razor-
bill, curlew, kittiwake, skua, fulmar. Their cries brought
alive a breeze in which something of summer's warmth
lingered on into the fall.

Gunnhild had felt trapped indoors until she told her
maidservants to stay behind and went off by herself. Nor
did any man go along. They had gotten to know her moods.
While she stayed in sight, she would be safe—or even out
of their sight, for Thorfinn Jarl kept his Orkneys well
scoured of troublemakers, but they would not allow that.

His hall stood where the biggest island, Mainland,
pinched into narrowness before broadening again. It overlooked a sheltered bay, which opened on Wide Firth. Docks
and ship-houses sprawled into the water. Around the hall
and its outbuildings clustered lesser dwellings, storehouses,
workshops, stables, and the like: more than a thorp, less
than a town. At this time of day the fishers who lived here
were out in their boats, the waterfront almost empty.

Gunnhild strode north along the shore, over grass gone

sallow, the ground rising steeply beneath her feet. She had had enough of man-stench, smoke-stench, dung-stench, noise, crowding, and above all the chatter of women. She would be alone with the sky. Maybe its brightness could lessen the dark within her.

A year and a half, she thought, a year and a half in this land of heath, bog, rock, turf houses huddled on crofts where crops grew meagerly or sheep and kine grazed. True, it bred wonderful seafarers. Its vikings had raided Mother Norway herself till Harald Fairhair laid the Orkneys, Shetlands, Hebrides, and Isle of Man under himself. They still harried widely elsewhere. Traders also brought in wealth. The jarl, at least, lived well. But the sameness! When he moved from one of his holdings to another, it was from one treeless, windswept island to the next; and often blinding fog or crashing storm kept him penned in for endless days.

Oh, yes, Thorfinn Skull-splitter had made Eirik Blood-ax and Eirik's following welcome. He housed them, fed them, helped them in every way he was able. After all, he and Gunnhild were kin. His father Einar and her mother Kraka had both sprung from the loins of the great Rögnvald Jarl. Einar, having fought his way to the lordship of Orkney, caught Snaefrid's son Haalfdan Longleg and cut the blood eagle on his back, opening the rib cage and spreading the lungs. Thus he took revenge for Haalfdan's share in the burning of Rögnvald. Gunnhild herself had had somewhat to do with bringing down Haalfdan's warlock brother; she did not speak of this, but whispers about it had drifted even across the North Sea.

Thorfinn had not acknowledged Haakon Aethelstan's-foster his king. He still gave Eirik that name. His grip on Orkney was firm, he could call many fighting men to him, but he had no wish to swap blows with the newcome warriors. Rather, he stood to gain thankfulness, and belike riches. He and Eirik were soon friends. Already that first summer Thorfinn's brothers Arnkel and Erlend had sailed off with their guest to raid in Scotland and northern England.

Likewise had Gunnhild's son Gamli.

In this second year, her second son Guthorm also went along.

And she stayed behind. She, who was used to meeting with the highborn from all over Norway, with travelers from all over the known world, and, yes, with her spies and witches—she, who once sat with gold and silk and fine linen upon her, drinking wine, while skalds chanted, sagamen told of gods and heroes, chieftains weighed what deeds they should do—she abode in drafty rooms or turf-built bowers among louts, yokels, and women as witty as any other brood-mare. Were it not for her children, she thought she would have gone mad. But must her life shrink down to nothing else?

If she could fare like a man, herself leading men to war and fighting in their forefront, like Hervör of old—but that was a fireside tale. Could she send her soul forth to watch over Eirik, and in the body brew harm for his foes—but nowhere here was there any haven, any den, free for any length of time from eyes and ears and tongues. She had ridden out to brochs, cairns, cromlechs, menhirs, and barrows, such as stood manifold hereabouts. The awe of age and unknownness went cold through her blood. She longed as she longed for her lover to find if she could raise those ghosts, awaken those powers. But she was never left by herself with them.

Black and often gale-wild though the winter was, at least Eirik had been here. Then she had her stallion, and, more than that, a man who gave heed to her. His very nearness, as well as the news he brought—and the loot—struck a spark in Thorfinn Jarl. They talked eagerly. When she deemed it wise, Gunnhild asked questions. Having thought the answers over, she took them up with her man.

Thus she knew that young King Eadmund of England had died, murdered, about the same time as she and Eirik reached Orkney. Before then, he had driven out the two Norsemen from Ireland who had grabbed lordship of southern Northumbria, formerly the Danish kingdom of York. Now it fell into bloody disorder. Eadmund's brother Eadred took over and got it back under his sway. But it stayed restless. Many of its folk stemmed from Norway as well as Denmark. None had ever really known the peace that Aelfred and Aethelstan laid on the Danelaw farther south.

Seek out chieftains of theirs, Gunnhild told Eirik. Make promises; make bargains. Get us a foothold of our own. And she gave him thoughts about how to do this.

But again he was gone, he and the Einarssons and their fleet, these weary months. And so was Gamli, and so Guthorm. She could merely wait.

No, today she would go to an outlook more broad than at the end of the bay. Open sea was nowhere nearby. Islands, holms, and skerries hemmed this water in. But at Crow Ness the shore bent westward. Seen from there, the eastern headland stretched on the right, with Shapinsay across a channel beyond, but most things northward lay under the rim of sight. Standing on Crow Ness she could gaze over the waves, sway too slightly within her cloak for any watcher to know, sing too low for any to hear, and let the light upon them dazzle her eyes and dance into her head until maybe, for a short span, she became one with them. Then she could cast her wishes forth, and maybe they would fly on the wind as a shadow-spell to find him and whisper him a word of luck.

As she neared the point, that thin hope shattered. A man had been sitting, hidden from her by a tall gorse bush. He climbed to his feet, a slender man who leaned on a staff to help his lame leg. Though he was not elderly, his face was haggard and his hair gray. She kenned Dag Audunarson, the skald of Eirik's who had fared with him for many years and had chosen to follow him into homelessness. Fighting at the king's side last year, he had taken a sword cut such that his left foot was of scant use.

"Greeting, Queen," he said in his grave way. "Is something wrong, that you gang alone? Can I somehow help?"

Gunnhild could not find it in her heart to tell this man that he could go away. She thrust bitterness down and answered, "I hankered for a fresh breath. What brings you here?"

"I needed peace and quiet. The poem I'm making goes harder than most, I know not why." From the way he bore himself and spoke, Gunnhild knew. His pain must be bad today. Nonetheless he smiled. "But, Queen, your nearness will unbind me. Not that you must stay if you don't want to."

A faint thrill went through her. Sometimes a poem was more than words. "What is it to be?" she asked under the shrieking seabirds.

"In honor of my king when he comes back."

What else? If he came back. No, she would not think that ill-foreboding thought. Let her listen and will that the words call him. "Tell it to me."

"It's not done, my lady. It can't be, really, till I've learned what happened—" The voice cracked a bit. "—I who could not be there."

"Give me what you have."

"It's not ready, Queen. It's earned no reward."

"But I'll keep this day in mind, Dag Audunarson," remembering whether or not he had obeyed her.

"As the queen wishes. I do have a beginning, however rough."

He looked not at her but out over the firth to where it met the sky. Clouds were rising and spreading yonder, darker than overhead, belike forerunners of rain. At first the staves came wooden.

> "Hearken, you who hear me.
> He who feeds the wolf pack
> as freely as his followers
> get feasts and riches from him,
> and offers blood to Odin,
> Eirik, has come home now."

They caught at him and started to sing.

> "The fire of battle flickered
> forth against the ship-moons—"

Yes, Gunnhild thought, without the truth to fill it and give shape, this was merely a warp and weft of kennings. At best, it would never cry with the wind and crash with the sea. Dag was skillful enough, but he was no Egil Skal-lagrimsson.

Egil!

A black tide drowned the voice and the sun. Egil, who murdered her boy, called wreck down upon her house, scorned and scoffed at her, stole away faithfulnesses that had been hers, slew her man's men, made light of her man's law, had stood high with the Aethelstan who fostered Haa-kon Haraldsson, troll-ugly Egil, for whom fair and friendly Thorolf had in the end forsaken her, this death-foe walked free, beyond reach of the vengeance that alone could re-deem rightness in the world, slake her hatred, and soften her grief, Egil, Egil.

Dag broke off. The sound of a horn also drew Gunnhild back. Two miles away on the eastern headland, but blown from full lungs and borne on the wind, it was a deep haro through the bird-cries to say that the lookout posted there had spied a ship.

It did not become a queen to run. Gunnhild walked fast. She must hide the hammering in her breast, keep ready to take bad tidings tearlessly. Dag hobbled after her, falling farther and farther behind, often stopping to lean on his staff and gasp.

Thorfinn and his guards stood armed on the docks when she got there. They held back the lowly who milled half eager, half afraid, but they drew aside for her. The two older of their sons whom their father had told to stay here, flaxen-haired Harald and red-haired Ragnfröd, had pushed their own way to the forefront. And somehow her daughter Ragnhild had slipped past. She ran to join her mother. "Is this the king?" she asked. Gunnhild could not but throw an arm around the thin shoulders and hold the girl close to her. The light that so brightly and wildly hued the firth struck fire in those loose bronze tresses.

Gunnhild knew the longship that glided from the channel named the String and down the bay toward her, forty oars swinging to the same beat, the lovely sweep of her strakes, the shields hung along her bulwarks—ship-moons—and the red-black-and-gold paint no less high-flown for being weathered. The threatening figurehead had been lowered, not to anger the land-wights, but this was a craft of Eirik's.

Folk shouted. The ship moved swiftly, larboard oars withdrawn at the last eyeblink, to lay alongside the main wharf. Men there caught the lines tossed them and made fast. Men aboard shot out a gangplank.

It thundered in Gunnhild. Where among that crew was her husband?

Gamli, their first son Gamli, was first off. His beard had thickened. It shone, close-cropped, within the wings of his hair. How like his father he had become, Eirik when Gunnhild the girl beheld him. Though he had not taken time to don good clothes, but still wore sea-stained leather and wadmal, how like his father he walked.

He greeted Thorfinn in fitting wise. Through the buzz she heard that the jarl's brothers were also coming; he had outsailed them. Then, then he strode over to her.

"Hail, Mother and Queen," he said most weightily. Oh, underneath the manliness he was young yet. "I bear the best of news. Father has dealt with the Northumbrians of York. He showed them it was better that he guard than gut them. Now he sits in the town of York as their king. He sends for his household. I'll bring you to him within this month."

Ragnhild yelled her glee. She skipped about like a kid goat. All at once she remembered what beseemed a king's daughter and went stone-stiff.

Gamli's words grew a bit awkward. "They can't take anybody who's not Christian. Father has let the priests sprinkle him. So have I and Guthorm and most of the rest. So must you and my siblings. Christ is strong, Mother. In England I've seen what strength he gives them."

That was a little thing, Gunnhild thought amidst the whirling. Maybe later she would find it was a great thing. Well, she had long wondered about it. Here on the wharf she knew only that Eirik—heeding her winter redes, she thought, but she'd say nothing of that unless to him alone—

Eirik had won a lordship for himself and his brood. Striking from there, he should win back Norway. At least, once she'd learned more about England, she'd know better what to look for and what to do.

For now she could again have a shut-off room and open the locked box of herbs and bones and everything else.

Now, to begin with, she could throw her own curse over Egil Skallagrimsson.

VII

The church on the Sognefjord still smelled of fresh timber. It stood with the dwelling of its English priest, well apart from anything else, half hidden by a stand of fir. Thorleif the Wise had told King Haakon this would be best. It was unseemly that the houses of God and God's thane huddle, as small and stark as they were, by the great hall and the roomy homes of steward and foremen. Worse, some heathens would think the sight of them every day was unlucky. They could take it into their heads to rip the walls down, once the king and his troopers had left. If not, then still those who might otherwise be willing to hear the Good Tidings could feel shy of going in under the eyes of their friends and afterward being mocked.

Haakon and the Christians among his guards came out and started back toward the hall. Clouds lowered heavy. A bleak wind soughed through darkling boughs. It ruffled whitecaps on steely water. Beside the king walked the gray-beard, stoop-shouldered and squinting but a wealthy man whom everybody looked up to and called Thorleif the Wise.

Hearing mass again after so long had stirred Haakon's heart. "If only they all would!" broke from him.

"You've made a beginning, lord," said Thorleif.

Three ships from overseas this past summer, bearing half a dozen priests altogether. Three churches raised thus far. Here and there a handful of converts, not all of whom had stopped offering to the land-wights or even to the old gods.

Haakon himself had learned not to have a chaplain along as he fared around Norway. He would never let such a man eat at the far end of the hall and sleep in a byre like a wandering beggar. But neither would the chieftains at most steadings let such a man sit amidst them. The land would soon again have been in uproar.

"Too little," Haakon groaned. "Too slow."

"A hunter moves softly and unhastily, lord. Often he stands and waits for the quarry to draw nigh."

"This is no hunt; it's a rescue. How many will go to Hell who'd have been saved if they'd gotten the Word sooner?"

"By now no few have heard it," said Thorleif dryly.

"They have not understood it!"

"Something this new and strange is seldom easily grasped. You know how I myself thought about it for months before choosing it. And I don't make much of it in front of anybody, nor forbid anyone in my household to worship as he likes. That would merely earn me ill will and lessen my usefulness to you, King."

"But we can't leave everything to a few scattered holy men. We have our own share to take in their work."

"A king's work lies in this world. Men uphold you— and take your Faith—because you're doing it well."

"Oh, yes, peace at home, strength against outsiders, law—Law." Haakon's eyes widened until the wind whipped tears from them. His voice shivered. "I am the king. I can make new law."

"*Some* new law, my lord, for which folk find themselves ready. But for one thing, this business you've spoken of, that we must rest all day Sunday. Everybody will ask about work that needs doing every day, like feeding the livestock. And indeed, how can they make their livings if they're idle one whole day out of seven?"

Haakon sighed. He walked on for a while unspeaking. The hall and its outbuildings loomed ahead. A few fisher boats were coming up the fjord, homebound. Their catches gleamed silvery. It was stiff rowing, the crews chilled by the sweat and sea-spray that soaked their clothes.

"Even so," Haakon said, "I can make certain changes.

Can't I? I've been thinking. And Sira Eadwin, the priest
now down in Rogaland, he gave me a rede. Yuletide—"
As he recalled last year at Hladi, an inward shudder passed
through him. Thorleif saw it, and also saw him win back
at once to himself.

"You'll not get them to stop offering at that season,
King," warned the older man. "Too many would fear the
sun won't come back. Besides, in the bottom depths of the
gloom, who could do without this firelit cheer?"

Haakon nodded. "I know. It's as true in England. But—
but if we make the feast go on longer than three days, won't
they like that? And then they'll have time to do more than
slaughter, gorge, and swill. Time for—for peace and—ho-
liness—to find them."

"Hm." Thorleif stroked his fluttering beard. "Not a bad
thought, lord, no, not bad. If, say—hm—the law was that
every man must brew a barrel of ale and keep the Yuletide
hallowed while it lasts—There's not too much work to do
at midwinter. A law that they don't only give to the gods,
but make merry on their own, yes, I think most of them
would obey that."

"Then," Haakon said happily, "they ought to go along
with a bidding that Yule begin not at midwinter but on the
birthday of the Christ. Sira Eadwin thinks that'll plant a
seed in at least some breasts."

"Well—maybe, seeing how close those days are to each
other. The heathen will only keep a lengthened Yuletide.
Let's think on this, and get the thoughts of others." Thorleif
was silent for a few strides. "My lord, you're young.
You've many years ahead of you, m-m, God willing. The
stronger you become, the more you can do. But you've yet
to finish laying the groundworks of that strength, let alone
build it higher."

Haakon did not stiffen at such frankness, as Harald Fairhair or Eirik Blood-ax would likely have done. Here spoke
a friend. He had enough foes, and knew he would get more.
"I'm seeing to our defenses as best I can."

Thorleif nodded. "I know, lord. But the true strength of
a king lies in the love his folk bear for him. King Eirik

found that out. It wasn't weakness that brought him down; it was his high-handedness. Do not break law, lord. *Give* it. This Yuletide business may help, but it touches lives rather slightly."

Haakon flushed. Thorleif was talking almost as if he stood on the same footing as the king.

Well, but they were not out before any gathering; they were walking together, in a wind that blew their words away from the guardsmen at their backs. As he often did, Haakon felt how new he was in Norway, how far away England lay—two or three days' sail in a fast ship, nevertheless dream-far away. "What have you in mind?" he asked.

"A seed or two of another kind, King, for you to let sprout if you wish. These are not undertakings to go into lightly.

"Folk are growing in numbers. Their lives are changing in other ways too. Some old laws ought to be mended or ended. Some new ought to be made. Now, from the hunters and trappers of the North to the farmers and traders of the South, those lives are unlike. Each part of the land needs a Thing with laws fitted to its dwellers. Your grandfather King Haalfdan set forth his Eidsvold laws, which work well down there. Elsewhere, though—We here in Sogn could do with a renewal at our Gula Thing."

It blazed in Haakon. "Yes!" he cried.

"Slowly, carefully, lord," Thorleif said. "We can look further into it, you and I, while you're here. But you'll want the well-thought-out redes of many more. And then, north in Thraandheim, their Frosta Thing—For that you'd better work with Sigurd Jarl and other wise Thraands. This will take years."

"But at last—" Haakon gazed ahead, past the buildings, into the sky, beyond the clouds and wind to the sun. He laughed aloud, almost as a boy laughs in sheer gladness.

His feeling lasted through the day's big meal, when the leading men of the neighborhood ate and drank with him. The mead glowed in his blood.

Afterward Eyvind Finnsson rose to stand before him and

give a poem. This skald had been with Harald Fairhair, had kept aside while Eirik Blood-ax overshadowed the elder king, but come forward again; he was among those who saw in the newcomer a Harald reborn. He was tall and thin, his dark locks beginning to grizzle. But his voice rang.

"I have nothing new as yet, King, that would be worthy of you," he said. "However, lately a work from Iceland has reached me. Parts of it hark far back; parts are fresh. The whole is wonderful. I'm not sure who wove it together, but gifted he is."

Dusk was setting in. Lamps shone. Longfires leaped, crackled, and sparked. Their light wrestled with shadows stealing inward through the smoke. Warmth, chill, and smells of burning pinewood twisted among each other.

To Haakon, who had drunk a bit more than maybe he should, Eyvind seemed half in, half out of the world of men. "It deals with how everything came to be and how it shall end," said the skald. "The words are of a seeress whom Odin raised from the grave to soothsay for the gods."

No, thought Haakon through the buzzing in his head, he, the king, should not forbid this, wreck the mood, turn these men around him against him. Rather, let him listen and learn.

The hall grew very still. Only the sputtering fires and the wind outdoors sounded in their ears—they, and the chant.

> "A hearing I ask
> from the holy kindred
> and Heimdall's offspring,
> highborn or lowly."

Yes, Haakon recalled, didn't the tale go that Heimdall, the watchman of Aasgard, once went over the earth to beget the first thralls, yeomen, and jarls? He'd heard mere snatches of it. How little he knew, how strange it was to him, this land he had gained.

> "You want me, Warfather,
> well to say forth

>   all I can tell
>   of olden time."

Odin, Warfather, Father of the Slain, those whom the valkyries bore to his Valhall to feast and fight until Ragnarök
cast down all that was.

>   "So I remember
>   the mighty ones
>   of whom I was born
>   in bygone years.
>   Nine homes, nine worlds
>   I knew in the tree
>   whose roots run deeply
>   down in the mold."

The staves went on, full of strangeness, glimpses through
shadows.

>   "I know where Heimdall's
>   horn lies hidden
>   under the high
>   and holy tree.
>   Over it falls
>   a flowing stream
>   from Warfather's pledge.
>   Do you want to know more?"

Yes, Haakon had heard, Odin plighted an eye for a drink
from wisdom's well. And the Roaring Horn waited for the
day when it would call the gods to their last strife—those
gods who knew themselves foredoomed but stayed undaunted. How strong were they in this their homeland?

Harald Fairhair, greatest of kings in Norway, Haakon's
father, had given them their honor. He rested now in undying honor of his own.

VIII

A wind from the north went astray in the twisting lanes of York, milled about between walls and hissed under eaves. Most stenches scattered before its sharpness. Thatch, turf, and shakes blocked sight of the morning sun, but light spilled down from the wan blue. Wild geese were on the wing. Their honking blew faint through hoofbeat, footfall, creak, clang, mumble, all the manifold racket below.

The train that left the hall went on horseback, above the muck and mire of the streets. First rode a half score picked guardsmen, their chief Arinbjörn at their head. Helmets gleamed; cloaks rippled in rainbow hues back from rustling byrnies whose every ring had been shined. King Eirik and Queen Gunnhild followed, side by side. He wore a gold-embroidered black tunic trimmed with marten, blue breeks that flared over kidskin boots, a hat with a silken band above the wide brim, gold coiled at his throat and on his arms. The skirts draped past her leggings were of white wool. Leaves, vines, and beasts tumbled entwined through the weaving of the panels that hung from turtle-shaped brooches at her shoulders, under a heavy amber necklace. The cloth that covered her dark hair was red silk. After them came their sons and daughter, little Sigurd on the saddlebow of a warrior. Ragnhild's chestnut braids fell free beneath a silver headband set with garnets. A dozen more guards brought up the rear. None would need their weapons today, but never would their lord fare meekly.

It was no mean town through whose streets she passed. For all the war and woe that had gone by, it had grown strongly under the Danes. Even this late in the year ships crowded its wharfs, come up the River Ouse—on whose west side newer buildings now also clustered thick—from the Humber and the North Sea with goods to stuff the warehouses. Cargoes lay ready for them to take home. Beneath the crowding houses, many of them two or three stories high, often with overhanging galleries, some built wholly of wood and their posts bountifully carven, well-burdened wagons made a way through throngs—workmen, chapmen, sailors, fishers, farmers, herders, wives, children, hawkers, priests, thralls, beggar, now and then a whore or maybe a wandering ragged singer, surely thieves, and who could say what else? Doors stood open on workshops, everything from a stinking tanner's or dyer's or the noise and smoke of a smithy to a room where costly metals and stones were made into wonders. Inns brawled. The swine that went about rooting for scraps were seldom hungry.

And it was the heart of Yorkish Northumbria, whose broad plowlands, meadows, woods, and waters bred a stalwart folk, Danes, Norse, and English already melting together into one, a bedrock for the house of a king.

And Eirik had made himself that king. Yes, Eadred elsewhere in England called him an earl; but Eadred had not risked coming here. An ealdorman had taken Eirik's oath. Neither lord could look on it as binding. The one grip on southern Northumbria was that of the king from Norway.

The last street through which Gunnhild rode gave on a marketplace. Sellers and buyers alike drew back against the booths while the horses went past. Their bustle and chaffer died away. They stared as others had done, leery of the newcomers. Gunnhild saw no hatred, though, and a few raised an arm in bashful hailing. Arinbjörn had said it was understandable among the lowborn, after such strife as had gone to and fro, plunder and fire and death across the hinterland. They prayed to their God that this latest master would clamp down a peace that lasted awhile, and not be too overbearing. If that came about, said Arinbjörn, Eirik would begin to hear cheers.

On the far side of the market a low stone wall marked off a big close. There, behind the cathedral, stood most of the Roman works that were left. Though time had gnawed at their stone and brick, they were still in use by the Church and the city fathers. She had thought how they and the other remains must scorn the earthworks and palisades that today warded houses made of timber and clay. Would such might ever be seen again?

She lifted her head. The olden builders were dust. She had heard how their Romaborg was mostly wretchedness and wreckage. Their Miklagard still gleamed rich and strong at the eastern end of the Midworld Sea, but those folk did not even speak the same tongue. Here, today, were life and strength enough to raise a new greatness.

Her heed went to the cathedral before her. Hoofs rang on flagstones as the troop rode into the close. Stone too— the softly yellow limestone of York—was the church. Three goodly buildings flanked it, but seemed almost humble in its nearness. Nowhere in Norway, Denmark, or Svithjod rose anything as high or as cunningly made as this. The pillars of the porch were like menhirs set up by giants, but plank-smooth. The round-arched doors behind them stood open on hugeness. Yet Gunnhild had seen the leafy tendrils chiseled into their jambs; and the tower reached for Heaven.

Eirik drew rein and sprang from the saddle. He lifted a hand to help her down. When she leaned on its steadiness, a thrill shot through her, well-nigh lustful. He grinned. "You're not afraid, are you?" he whispered. "It doesn't hurt, and it's done me no harm."

She grinned back, she-wolf to he-wolf. "Nor has it mildened anybody I know of," she answered. "Do you really tell your sins to the priest? I should think you'd likelier boast of them."

"He shrives me. He'd better. Not that I've gone to him more than twice." The second time had been yesterday, because the archbishop held that God would be offended if the king did not when his queen and children were about to be christened. Eirik had thought that refusing would make more trouble than it was worth, and maybe bring bad luck.

Behind Gunnhild's face her soul thrummed. This was no small god to whom she went to give honor. His worshippers filled every land southward to the Midworld Sea and the Moors, eastward to the Wendish marches. More and more of them were to be met in the North. True, vikings looted his halidoms and cut down his holy men, without suffering more than everybody was sooner or later bound to suffer. But neither did those who forsook Odin. And Christians fought no less well; here in England, they had first halted the Danes, then battle by battle brought those former strangers under their king and into their Church. Their net of trade, and the wealth streaming along it, drew many to them. All the best swords were of their forging. The wise ones among them had lore going wider and deeper than she could fathom. Already in the short span since she came here she had seen and heard enough to know that.

She would not let awe daunt her. She would find her own way forward. Until she understood the White Christ better, she would not openly scoff, nor very openly break his laws. It might turn out that the best hope for her blood was indeed with him.

Yet she had known too much of the unknown, and felt it, not to walk wire-taut beside her man toward the house of the Christ.

Their brood came after, unwontedly quiet. The guards could not doff helms and byrnies without spoiling the show. Arinbjörn posted them along the wall. He put himself in the entryway, a spear upright in his hand. The rabble were not going to gape at this.

Three priests in white robes waited to welcome the kingly family. They smiled; they raised hands in blessing. Suddenly, as in nightmare, Gunnhild remembered how she had lured the Finns to their death. If only Thorolf—No, Thorolf was dead too, fallen in this same England, buried by his evil brother Egil. Aalf, then. At her back she had Gamli and Guthorm, her sons, blooded warriors by now, but how young they still were! If only her brother Aalf, the stout and steadfast Shipman, were here. But he had stayed behind in Orkney, saying that he was doing well enough. Besides, the king should have a man there to speak for him, with crews of his own on hand, lest Thorfinn Skull-splitter get above himself.

And, he had not said, should things go awry for his sister and her family, he would be able to take them in and help them.

Gunnhild sent that bat-thought off into the darkness whence it had fluttered. How had it found her? Why, unless Odin, the Father of Witchcraft, was spiteful?

What need had she today of any man other than the one at her side? Together they crossed the threshold.

In the vestibule Eirik and his sons unslung their swords and stood them in a rack. An angel painted on the plaster watched over it, his blade drawn, like a victor. As they entered the high-vaulted nave, a choir broke into song— song in the Latin tongue, rising and falling, as eerie to her as a Finnish spellcasting. The organ began to moan and thunder. It was as though sea and stone had become the skalds of Christ.

Light through window glass overwhelmed the candles on thirty altars. Saints stared stiffly from the walls. Though the wind blustered outside, baffled, the stones gave their hush and chill to the air. Incense sweetened it. Leading men of the city and hinterland watched their new king and his kin go slowly past. Some smiled. They had not been unwilling to help a fellow Northman take over, instead of a far-off Englishman to whom their own laws and rights meant little. Later today he would give these witnesses a feast, and gifts. Gunnhild looked forward to that. Thus far she, a woman, had barely met any of them.

Priests and monks, acolytes and novices were ranked on either side of the transept. Wulfstan's vestments glowed against their drabness. The archbishop of York stood before the high altar. His aged hand would take the holy water and sign the holy Cross on the brows of Gunnhild and her get.

He spoke solemn words, in which she did not find much meaning. Her boisterous sons had gone awkward. This grandeur and gravity came over their unhardened souls like a tide. Well, she thought, it would not wash Eirik Blood-ax's blood out of them. He and she would see to that.

Her gaze roved. Among those on her right she spied a young fellow she had met. Brihtnoth, his name was. Of middling height, sturdily built, he yet seemed boyish, with his round pink cheeks, curly brown hair, and shy way of speaking to her. Otherwise there was little to mark him out, unless one looked closely at a ring he wore, small but of lovely workmanship.

Archbishop Wulfstan had wanted Eirik's children to hear something about the Faith before he baptized them into it. These were not vikings yielding after an English victory, nor traders in search of deals. They were royal. In years to come, they might well set the courses of men's lives. He rejoiced when their mother told him she too was eager for the knowledge. She did not tell him that she once spent a year of hardship among the Finns to learn what they knew and win for herself whatever powers that might bestow.

The height of her short teaching had come with Brihtnoth. Being reckoned the brightest student in the cathedral school, who had entered it already able to read and write and with some mastery of Latin, he was chosen to show her the scriptorium and library when she asked about them.

The books, the books—They had laid hold of her; they drew her down into themselves like a maelstrom that was all the stronger for being so quiet—brilliant bewilderment of interlacings, pictures from a thousand tales out of two thousand years or more, and within those borders the close-ranked, tightly curved letters making words she could not read, an endlessness of words. Otherwise she had only seen one or two tattered leaves brought home as loot, something to show off and cast aside. Here was the living Tree.

Oh, she had cast runes like her father, and used them in spells; cut into a stone, they remembered dead men; but they were few and spare. What hoard of wisdom and witchcraft was this, before her eyes but beyond her reach?

It need not forever be.

Seeing how caught up she was, Brihtnoth had happily spent hours turning over pages and trying to answer her questions. Nothing but dusk stopped them. Now and then he asked questions of her, mostly about Norway. She liked him. Even though a hint of the child lingered, he was handsome.

She had found out that he was the son of a nobleman in the South. When she wondered why he had come this far to carry on his studies, he said, "The school here is famous," and then, reddening, glancing away, added low, "Also here I, I can better get to ken the, the Norse folk."

As they now stood in the great church, their eyes fleetingly made touch. She almost smiled. But no, that wouldn't do.

The rite began in earnest and she forgot about him.

Kneeling before the altar, feeling the sign laid upon her, she looked past the high priest to that which hung beyond and above, the image of the Man on the Cross. It was not as skillfully wrought as many carvings she had seen at home, be they figures or friezes or the fearsome head of a dragon ship. But something was in it that she had yet to understand, and must if she were not to fall into the helplessness of bewilderment. Not only song and drum, but pain could loose the shaman from the flesh. Odin hung, wounded with a spear, offered to himself, nine nights on windy Yggdrasil, to gain the runes; and he had since raised seeresses from their graves to foretell for him. What powers had his own sufferings, his own death won for the Christ? How could they strengthen her house?

She must gang warily, learning as she went. Meanwhile, whatever she said to the likes of Wulfstan, she would not utterly disown the old gods. Nor, she knew, would Eirik, though in his heart he did not care much either way. But she had also the Finn-way to think on, that man is not wholly under any gods or norns but helps uphold the world and, if he knows how, can take the reins of time in his hands.

After the baptisms the archbishop said mass. Gunnhild, offside with her daughter, had meant to follow it closely. Learn, always learn; knowledge is a weapon. But the words were outlandish, the music likewise. She would be hearing it again. Her thoughts went off to what needed doing in this world.

And outside it. She had vengeances to wreak. Haakon Aethelstan's-foster must wait awhile. But she once more had a big home. Now and then she could get away from all the eyes, ears, and tongues. She could have a room set aside where nobody came without her leave. She could gather together everything needful.

It would take months, in which she stole hours from her queenship, yes, from Eirik if she must. After all, it was for him. But she could hope to be ready by Yuletide.

Never yet had she sent a spell or her soul as far as she meant to. But lost Norway and her lost son cried out to her. Pain and death gave power. When the sun turned back, be it southward or northward, was when the doors between men and gods, world and underworld, opened the widest. In the dead of winter she would call Egil Skallagrimsson to come here.

IX

Soon after Egil returned to Borg, his father died in bed. He laid the body out himself and did all else that was right. Then he had a hole broken in the south wall, not to be mended until the lich had been borne through it. This was so that if Skallagrim walked he could not find his way back into the house. They buried him at the end of Digra Ness with his horse, weapons, and blacksmith's tools. The mound raised above him became a landmark for men at sea.

Taking over land, livestock, and movables, Egil settled down with his wife Aasgerd and stepdaughter Thordis. His fame and riches put him among the first men in Iceland. While King Eirik and King Haakon were at odds in Norway, no ship was allowed to leave it. Afterward, though, news enough came in, and Egil could feel that his curse had worked well.

Nonetheless, in the second winter after Skallagrim's death he grew moody. His unhappiness deepened as the dark season wore on. In spring he made known that he would be off to England. King Aethelstan was gone, but his successor ought to welcome one of whom the great man had thought highly, and maybe redeem some of those glow-ing promises. This hope lifted Egil's gloom. He readied a ship and a thirty-man crew. Besides trade goods such as sealskins and narwhal tusks, he laid treasures in the cargo, for bestowal whenever openhandedness was needful.

However, that was a year of foul weather. Not until summer was drawing toward fall could Egil hoist sail. Leaving Borg in Aasgerd's keeping, he beat across winds that grew ever more harsh. It took keen seamanship to hold a course when rainsqualls or hurtling clouds hid the skies more often than not.

Raising Orkney at last, Egil steered around those islands on the north. King Eirik's arm might reach that far. Southbound again, he and his men met a storm off the Scottish coast. Nowhere did they spy a shore not barred to them by breakers. If they passed any, it was at night and hidden from their eyes. The storm seemed to have no end. Rowing and bailing, rowing and bailing, they fought on along northeastern England.

Then as another twilight was falling, they half blinded by storm-flogged spray, half deafened by shriek of wind and roar of waves, all at once they found surf both forward and seaward. Now there was nothing to do but make for land. In Humber mouth the ship drove aground and broke up.

They saved themselves and most of the freight. Drenched, bone-chilled, worn out, they were no threat to some men living nearby who had seen and come down to them; but it would have been unwise for those men to attack for the sake of loot. Instead, they offered what shelter they could. From them Egil learned where he was, and that King Eirik and Queen Gunnhild sat in York, not far away.

Better were the tidings that Arinbjörn was with them, in high standing and close friendship. Egil made his decision. He had small likelihood of escape, even if he disguised himself, what with the many miles to go through Northumbria and the easiness of kenning him. He would not risk the shame of being caught in flight. Buying a horse on the spot, he was off before dawn to York.

He reached it next evening. Armed, but with a broad hat over his helmet and a cloak hiding his sword, he rode straight into the town and asked the way to Arinbjörn's house.

X

ing Eirik was at meat, Queen Gunnhild beside him. Here was not a Norse but an English hall. The high seat was at the far end of a long room. Table and benches had been set, with they two at the head, looking toward the entry. On the right they had their oldest son, Gamli, on the left Guthorm. Other places there would have been for honored guests, but none happened to be on hand. Guardsmen sat on either side of the board according to rank. It was not the English way to keep weaponed men along the walls, but so Eirik chose. A butler saw to it that goblets did not go dry.

Candles stood in their holders on the table. Their smell of burning tallow blent with the smell of roast pork in the trenchers. More light, as dusk deepened into dark, was given by lamps hung from the roofbeams. Behind them stretched richly woven tapestries. Instead of fire-pits, a stone hearth in the middle of the room was bulwarked to hold crackling logs. Hence the floor could safely be strewn with sweet juniper. Come winter, the hall would be more cold and dank than a yeoman's snug home, Gunnhild thought; but it was kingly, and she would wear the finest of furs.

The door opened. Likewise had the outer door swung wide; a chill draft made flames leap. A watchman stepped through. "Lord," he called, "the chief Arinbjörn is here to see you." He swallowed before he added, "It must be important. He has every man of his household with him, armed."

Gunnhild's heart sprang like the fire. Eirik's lean face showed nothing. "Let him in," he said evenly.

Seen from here, the other end of the room lay shadowful.

Gunnhild made out that Arinbjörn entered with eleven at his back. Helms and byrnies shimmered faintly. Arinbjörn trod ahead of them. He himself bore no mail, but a sword hung at his shoulder. He stopped near the king's right hand and stood rocklike.

Eirik smiled rather tightly. "Welcome," he said. "What do you want?"

The answer rolled steady as an incoming tide. "I have brought with me a man who has fared a long way to make peace with you. It does you honor, lord, when your foes come of their own free will from lands afar because they cannot bear your wrath. Deal by this man as behooves a noble. Grant him your forgiveness, since he has so much heightened your honor, he who crossed great seas and left house and home behind, with no other grounds for the voyage than that he yearns for your goodwill."

Eirik narrowed his eyes and waited. Glee blazed in Gunnhild.

Arinbjörn's followers had drawn nigh. Above them loomed one, unarmed, whom she knew, she knew. Bald and wolf-gray had Egil grown, but he hulked as huge, with face as rough-hewn ugly, as ever. For a heartbeat their glances crossed; then the black eyes sought the winter-blue gaze of the king.

Like a sword being drawn, Eirik hissed, "How have you dared show yourself before me? When last we parted, it was in such wise that there was no hope of your life from me."

Wordless at first, the Icelander walked forward and around the table. Gunnhild heard her sons gasp. They had not met him erenow, but well they knew of him. The men on the benches sat frozen while he lumbered by them. His bulk blocked off sight of the fire. Gunnhild half reached for the knife beside her trencher. Barely did she stay her hand. Useless to stick that puny thing into him. Eirik would take the revenge for which her spells had winged overseas to spook around Egil's head.

Candlelight sheened on the skull when Egil knelt. He laid his arms around Eirik's knees. The king sat stiff.

Quoth Egil in that unrightfully rich and supple voice of his:

> "Long I wended the wave-way,
>   though winds blew foul and wrathful,
>   spurring the horse of the sea-king
>   to seek this lord in England.
>   Now has the weapon-wielder,
>   well aware of his rashness,
>   fulfilled his goal by finding
>   the foremost in Harald's bloodline."

Arinbjörn had told him what to do, whirled Gunnhild's thought, Arinbjörn, who could not break faith with anybody once he had given it.

Egil let go, got to his feet, and stepped back to stand beside him.

Still Eirik spoke low but steel-hard. Otherwise Gunnhild heard never a breath, only the fire. "I need not count up your misdeeds against me. They are so many and so fell that any one of them is enough to cost you your life. Here you can look for nothing but death. You should have known beforehand that from me there is no forgiveness to be had."

She could not hold back; she must forestall whatever Arinbjörn had in mind. She twisted about and leaned toward her man. "Why not kill Egil at once?" she cried. "Or have you forgotten, King, what Egil has done, slain your friends and kinsmen, yes, your son, and raised a nithing-staff against you? Who's ever heard of the like done against a king?"

"If Egil has done harm to the king," said Arinbjörn, "he can pay for it with a poem of praise that will live forever."

"We'll not listen to his praise!" shrieked Gunnhild. "Lord, have Egil taken out and his head struck off. I'll hear no more word of him and have no more sight of him!"

Arinbjörn spoke to her, bleakly. "The king will not let himself be egged on to any nithing-work by you either. He won't let Egil be killed tonight, for a slaying after dark is murder."

Not mere manslaughter, Gunnhild knew. Gall seared her throat when Eirik said, "It shall be as you wish, Arinbjörn. Egil may live tonight. Take him home with you, and bring him back in the morning."

"Thanks be to the king for his greatheartedness." Arinbjörn waited a bit before he went on: "We hope, lord, that tomorrow Egil's cause will stand in a better light. For if Egil has done you much wrong, there were grounds for it, the ills he suffered from your house. Your father took the life of his uncle Thorolf, a good man, for no other cause than that some knaves slandered him. And you, King, withheld from Egil his lawful rights against Berg-Önund, sought his life, slew his men, reaved his property, even made him an outlaw and hounded him from the land. Egil is not a man who will meekly take goading. Whoever would judge a man should think on what he has undergone. Now I will take Egil with me to my house for the night."

"You may go," said Eirik almost in a whisper.

Arinbjörn, his guest, and his following left. They did it as was seemly when leaving a king, but firelight off ringmail rippled through shadows.

Eirik sat silent. Nobody else dared stir.

She would get him alone, Gunnhild thought wildly, she would upbraid him, urge him, use every wile she had on him.

No, she must be careful. His face was locked, but she knew how stirred up he was. If she tried too hard to steer him, that cold rage could turn on her and the time would be long before he again listened to her. Best if she planned what to do in the morning, and how.

Meanwhile, though, she need not toss seething. Arinbjörn had spoken of Egil ransoming his head with a mighty poem of praise. Yes, surely Egil would spend the night making it. And no skald was more gifted.

She turned back to Eirik. "My lord," she said softly, laying a shakiness into it, "this business has sickened me. May I go to the room that is mine?"

He nodded, maybe only half hearing. She rose and went out. Silence still brooded behind her.

There seemed to be bounds on what she could do with spells, here in a Christian land. Yet that little might be enough.

XI

About midnight, Arinbjörn's men left off their drinking, which had gone on unwontedly late, and went to their rest. He climbed the stairs to the loftroom where Egil was.

One lamp guttered. Chill stole in through a peephole. The big man sat hunched on a stool. It was as if he belonged to the unrestful gloom.

He looked up when floorboards creaked. "How goes the poem?" asked Arinbjörn. Egil had said he never believed he would praise King Eirik, but Arinbjörn told him he had no other way out.

"I've gotten nothing done," he answered dully. "A swallow's been perching at yon peephole all this while and twittering. It's not given me an eyeblink's rest."

Swallows are not night-birds.

Arinbjörn shivered but said, "I'll go have a look." He went away to another room with a door leading onto the gallery. Treading forth, he found stars and a nearly full moon. It threw ghost-light across roofs and silver onto the river. As he moved along the rail toward the peephole, the light caught wings. A bird, or something that bore the seeming of a bird, flitted off. He sat down, leaned against the wall, and waited for sunrise. The bird did not come back.

XII

That was a day of thin sunlight and a small, whittering wind. The king's household was astir betimes. A band of ready warriors gathered around the hall, but they said hardly a word. Eirik ate scantily, likewise unspeaking. Gunnhild took nothing. She could not have gotten it down.

The boards, trestles, and benches were borne out. The hall brightened a little as the sun wheeled higher. Every feeling whetted, Gunnhild heard the noise outside, tramp of feet, clink of iron. Arinbjörn was here, again with his full following.

A guard told this. "He may enter, and whomever else he wants," Eirik bade.

That was Egil and half the men of that house. The rest waited in the yard. The spears that some held must stand like slim trees with shining crowns, Gunnhild thought. Those who had come in took stance in a bunch near the door. Blackly among them towered loathsome Egil.

The weariness of the night gnawed and dragged at her. To send the soul abroad cost heavily. And then Arinbjörn had come out. She could do nothing but slip back into herself. After that she lay staring into the dark and hating.

She would not yield to any weakness. She would not. She thrust it down and tautened in the high seat beside her man. He sat still and watchful.

Arinbjörn trod slowly to stand before them. As yestereven, he was armed with merely a sword. His clothes were good but not showy—a sign of respect, Gunnhild deemed. He halted, raised a hand, and said, "Hail and greeting, King."

"Welcome, Arinbjörn. You always are," answered Eirik, less warmly than hitherto but, she knew, meaning it. "Say freely what you will."

The downward-slanting eyes in the blocky face met his. The words walked steadily. "Here I am with Egil. He has not tried to run away in the night. Now we wish to know what his lot shall be. I believe I've earned something from you, in that I've never spared any trouble in word or deed on your behalf. Everything I owned in Norway, and kinfolk and friends, I left to go with you when every lendman forsook you. That was no more than right, seeing what you had done for me."

Gunnhild leaped at the opening. "Stop that, Arinbjörn,"

she broke in, "and don't go on and on about this. You've done well by King Eirik, and well has he rewarded you. You owe far more to King Eirik than to Egil. You ought not ask that Egil slip unscathed from King Eirik, after all his ill-doing."

Her husband frowned. She closed her lips. But could she hope she had called the truth back to his mind?

"If you, lord, and you, Queen, have agreed that Egil shall not get peace," said Arinbjörn, "then it is the way of honor to give a foeman a week's grace wherein he may save himself. Egil came here of his own free will. He should have that much from you. Let him go. Thereafter let whatever befall that may."

No, that must not be. Gunnhild could not keep aside. She had the skill to sneer the least bit, not overdoing it, while ice flowed with her words. "It's easy to see, Arinbjörn, you're a better friend to Egil than to King Eirik. If Egil can ride away for a week, he'll reach King Eadred." She must touch her man in his manhood, without making him angry at her. "But King Eirik can't hide from himself that he's becoming less than other kings. Not long ago, nobody would have dreamed King Eirik lacked the will and might to take vengeance on the likes of Egil."

Did she feel him freeze at her side?

Grimness came over Arinbjörn. "Nobody will think the better of Eirik for killing the son of an outland farmer who has come to give himself to his judgment," he said stonily. "But if he wants to heighten his fame by that, then it will be known far and wide. For henceforward, what happens to Egil shall happen to me. Dearly will you buy Egil's life, King, before we have fallen, my sworn men and me. I had not awaited that you would rather see me lying dead on the ground than give one man his life as I ask."

Breath sucked in throughout the hall. Guards and the newcome warriors glared at each other. Hands stole toward weapons. Dismay struck into Gunnhild's breast. Would Egil end his troll-work by raising war under her roof?

The hands dropped when Eirik spoke. His hatchet face

was a mask, his voice iron. But she, who knew him, heard the pain beneath it.

"You're setting much at stake, Arinbjörn, to stand by Egil. It would grieve me to do you harm, if things go so far that you'll die before you see him killed." The voice flattened. "But guilty Egil is, whatever I may have done to him."

Silence laid grip, until Gunnhild faintly heard the wind around the walls. Eirik looked straight at Egil. His beckoning was like a sword-cut.

He made it, though. He would hear the poem. Gunnhild's nails bit into her palms. Her last hope was that it would be poorly done, worthless as wergild—and Arinbjörn agree, and withdraw from the man who failed his faithfulness. She had tried. The gods and all dark Beings knew how she had tried during the night, what she gave, that wrong be repaid and Rögnvald have blood for blood.

Egil came down the length of the hall, stride by stride, to halt a step farther on than Arinbjörn. He too was well clad, though the borrowed garments were tight on him. From under their shelf of bone, his eyes locked with Eirik's. The king sat spear-straight, the narrow head high, gaze unwavering as a snake's. The gray beard stirred; the gash of a mouth opened; the words rolled loud and deep.

> "Overseas I went,
> on westfall bent.
> When the last ice broke
> I launched the oak.
> The freight aboard
> was from the hoard
> of Odin, lays
> of honor and praise."

The knowledge shocked into Gunnhild. Here was a twenty-stave drapa, the utmost a skald could give to a king, and of a kind altogether new, the lines not only alliterating but end-rhyming, a thing never heard in the Norse world before today and never to be forgotten in it.

She wanted wildly to jeer that England lay east of Iceland. No, such a breach of seemliness would wreck her standing. And, well, she *had* seen to it that he was blown out of his way.

> "At the king's command
> I have come, and stand
> here as his guest
> to give him the best
> of all I bore
> to England's shore,
> words that shall name
> his worth and fame."

What a liar he was! But it was shrewdly done, to call himself Eirik's guest. To naysay that could look mean-souled. And the life of a guest was holy.

No, not always. Sometimes hospitality had been a trap. But then many would remember Eirik as less lofty than the drapa was lifting him.

> "Think, if you will,
> that thanes who keep still
> and pay heed as they ought
> shall hear how you fought.
> Men have fully known
> of your foes overthrown,
> but Odin can say
> where they afterward lay."

He had no need thus to call for silence. Every ear was his. She too felt the singing and thundering, as though the sea itself gave worship to Eirik.

> "Feeding ravens, the lord
> often reddened the sword.
> Spears flew to draw blood
> in the arrow-flood.
> Meat the wolf got

> from the woe of the Scot,
> Hel's feet on the dead
> where the eagles fed."

It caught the listener up, stave after surging stave. Yes, there was witchcraft in poetry. How well she knew. And Egil wielded it against her.

> "Valkyries woke
> when the warrior's stroke
> on shield-rims rattled
> as, ruthless, he battled.
> Steel snapped at a hit,
> or it hewed and bit.
> The string on the yew
> cast stings that slew."

Those cunning, weaving kennings underlay the whole spell. They made the world and time a background for the king's greatness. Egil had not said "shields," but "the ski-fence of Haaki's rock." Haaki was a sea-king of old; thus the sea was his rock. A ship was the ski of the sea; thus her fence was the row of shields hung along her sides. All this Egil brought together and linked with Eirik.

Yet was not the whole thing hollow, strength and stalwartness, blades and blood, with never the name of a field where Eirik fought or a foeman he had felled? Was it that Egil had scant knowledge of those deeds, or was there underneath the ringing chant a mockery too sly for any but her to hear? Could she bring them to believe that?

But he left war behind. His utterance slowed and mellowed. She thought of sunlight streaming through clouds when a storm dies away.

> "Yet I must make clear
> for all men to hear,
> on his land he keeps hold
> but is loose with his gold,
> freely gives treasure

>   in fullest of measure,
>   nor thinks to get praise
>   for his thriftless ways."

Oh, that was deftly done. Throughout, he told of what was best in Eirik, what nobody gainsaid, first the bravery, then the openhandedness. She had no way to call it untrue.

Amidst the hush, the drapa drew to its end.

>   "My lord, I have said
>   what lay in my head.
>   It is well that men heard
>   my every word.
>   Now Odin's mead
>   I have emptied indeed,
>   as had been my will,
>   to your warlike skill.

>   "The stillness I broke
>   by myself when I spoke.
>   Your warriors harked
>   to my words, and they marked
>   how I handled my praise
>   of your high-flying days,
>   and they'll not forget
>   what I've now forthset."

Silence reached over the hall like a sunset. Egil and Arinbjörn waited.

When Eirik answered, sternly though he did, Gunnhild knew she was beaten. "The poem could not have been better. And so, Arinbjörn, I've decided what to do about myself and Egil. You have borne his cause to the uttermost. So for your sake I'll give you your wish, that he leave here whole and unharmed. But you, Egil, take care never to come back into my sight, nor the sight of my sons, and never near me or my men. This once I give you your head, because you gave yourself into my power and I'd not do anything shameful to you. But know that you have no peace

with me or my sons or any of my kin who have right of
vengeance on you."

Egil was too wise to smile, thought Gunnhild amidst her
bitterness. Nonetheless his voice boomed unabashed.

> "Gladly I take
> this gift of yours,
> my helmet-crag,
> however ugly.
> Where is the man
> who's had any better,
> unstintingly
> bestowed by a king?"

Where, indeed? thought Gunnhild.

The blunt, blundering *honor* of men!

Arinbjörn made his thankful farewell. He, his followers,
and Egil went out unhindered into the day.

She could say nothing about it afterward to Eirik. That
would be worse than useless.

She would not weep, she thought, nor would she scream
aloud before she was alone.

XIII

Here she had no network of spies as in Norway. It would
take years to weave one in this land where she had
come as a stranger. But the king got news, and she was
there to listen as often as a woman could be. She must not
show her wrath. If she turned her back on him, she would
likewise on her sons and Ragnhild.

So she heard how Egil's crew, whom Arinbjörn had already sent for, reached York with their goods on the very
day of the head ransoming. He gave them lodging and his
protection. Thus, she thought bitterly, they became free to
stay unscathed and sell their wares. Meanwhile Arinbjörn
got together a hundred of his own, armed and on horseback.
The troop rode off to bring Egil to King Eadred. They did

not have too far to go. It was known that he had come north.

Gunnhild set herself to wait. She thought long and hard, she cast a healing spell, and slowly she quelled her anger at Eirik and quenched its venom. He had not really been an utter fool. He had been led into a trap such that what he saw as his uprightness and good name would not let him cut his way out.

Arinbjörn returned with his following after some days. He went straightaway to the king. This was on a gray day of bleak wind. Most trees outside the town stood leafless. Eirik was in the yard, at weapon practice. The man against him was young. Eirik had told him not to hold back, but strike with his best. It went unsaid how one of Eirik's years must work to keep up strength and skill. Most of the foes he met would be like this warrior. The swords were wooden, but weighted. They hit hard.

The king called halt when Arinbjörn trod in sight and led him into the hall. When he took off helmet and coif, the faded hair was damp with sweat that ran down his cheeks. He left the byrnie on. "Well, how did things go?" he snapped.

Gunnhild had seen and stolen in. She beckoned a servant to bring ale, then held back, though in earshot. The fires were banked; no lamps were lit; the dusk of the room half veiled her.

"We found King Eadred easily enough," answered Arinbjörn. "For his brother Aethelstan's sake he made us welcome. He was not so warm toward me, though. Lord, he's taken his household troop and many others up from Wessex, into Danish Mercia, gathering still more as he went. I didn't linger, for he was making ready to raise the levies thereabouts. He can mean nothing else but to bring South Northumbria back under him."

"I looked for this, though I hoped he'd wait a while longer," said Eirik. "Tell me everything you saw, everything you heard."

Rather than the high seat, he sat down on a bench, Arinbjörn beside him. They began to talk, their speech low and quick.

Gunnhild carried the filled horns to them with her own hands. Arinbjörn offered her a slight smile. "What of Egil?" broke from her.

"The king invited him to stay, but he chose to go south and winter there," Arinbjörn told her.

"That's as well for them both," said Eirik starkly. "Were he in that pack, Eadred would have had no peace with me till I'd gotten back the head I gave."

He did not want her to ask further, Gunnhild knew. Not today. He would not let himself get enraged when the business of war was at hand. Oh, but she could well think how Egil had spoken a stave of open mockery. And when he and Arinbjörn parted, what kind words and rich gifts passed between them.

Nevertheless, Arinbjörn had come back as fast as he could ride. Eirik would have sore need of him. She withdrew into the shadows.

From then on, scouts and messengers arrived daily. Yes, Eadred was in Yorkish Northumbria, killing, looting, and burning. He would not let up until these shires yielded to him.

Eirik sent the war-arrow forth. Men flocked to the town from widely around. They made no brave sight, camped with hardly a tent against the rainshowers that muddied the earth and doused their fires. Few among them owned better arms than a leather jacket, a kettle helmet, an ax or spear. They coughed and grumbled. Their wet wool garb stank. But they were Northmen, with homes to defend.

Food for them quickly ran short. However, the news soon arrived that Eadred's main force sat in Chesterford. It seemed likely they would stay there through the winter, a threat of what would happen in spring. The king himself was bound back south with a lesser host, still laying the land waste.

"We'll meet him," said Eirik. Horns brayed; the hoarse shouts rose; banners flapped aloft; the levy set off.

Gunnhild stood on a watchtower with her five younger

sons until the men were lost to sight. Harald glowered, his mood black. He was shooting up, down on his lip, keen at sports and battle-play. She thought him the brightest of the lot. He lusted to go. His father and his foster father Arinbjörn had said no, he must wait two or three years. Gunnhild knew a thin gladness. At least he would not suffer the doom that fell on the boy Rögnvald. Not yet. His brothers hallooed their farewells. The wind scattered the sound. Gunnhild saw two ravens on it, swartnesses under a sky where clouds flew ragged, above an earth gone dun and a river dully agleam. Did they foreknow? More would be gathering.

"We'll win; we'll win," crowed little Sigurd.

That might well be, Gunnhild thought. This was no mere gang of yokels. Eirik rode in front, Gamli on his right and Guthorm on his left. Arinbjörn came after, leading the guards and his own sworn men. They strode along in iron ranks. Behind them went the Yorkish nobles and their warriors, almost as well outfitted. Byrnies made a walking wall on either side of the farmers and herders. Come the clash, these seasoned fighters would stiffen them. Spears swayed as if wind-rippled. Their heads sheened around the bright, fluttering banners.

The victory would be Eirik's. She would not believe anything else.

Yet someday she must wait for him in vain.

Could she but help; could she but blast the English with lightning or wither Eadred with a curse. But she could not even try what spellcraft was hers. She must stay wakeful, wholly aware, a queen watching over her lord's stronghold. All she had had to offer him was a memory of last night, and that had been less than she longed for. He had needed his sleep.

Smoke began to rise over the northwest worldrim. Wind strewed it. Something was afire yonder. Yes, it had to be Ripon town, twenty or so miles upstream. Eadred was destroying it. Eirik would meet him nearby, late today or early tomorrow.

"Come," she bade her children. "We'll go back down."

They abided through that night and the day beyond. It was well that she was busy keeping things in hand.

He returned the evening after that. A messenger had galloped ahead with a blurry tale of a battle, great slaughter, the English driven off. She understood at once that it was not a true victory. Eirik told her the whole of it himself when he brought his host in. Their numbers were much lessened, and many who lived limped along badly hurt. She knew how often such wounds turned into deadly sickness.

Gamli and Guthorm had taken a few lesser cuts, which they showed while trying not to sound as if they bragged. Their father shrugged off his bruises. His face had gone gaunt. He spoke wearily. "We smote and shot, back and forth, till they withdrew. But they did it in good order, and our losses were as heavy as theirs. Nor can I feed the levy any longer. They'll have to go home." When Dag the skald said what a poem of praise this called for—jealousy of Egil dripped from his voice—Eirik gave him a crooked grin and answered, "Hold off with that for a while. I've too much else to think about."

To Gunnhild, when they were by themselves, he said, "One thing I'd better see to is quietly readying our ships."

Dreary Orkney stood forth for her in the half-darkness of the room. "Do you await we'll be driven out of here?"

Once more he spoke like a sword being drawn. "Who can yet say? But if we are, England will rue it."

The steel struck a spark. "And we may not be gone forever." The fire flared within her. She cast her arms about him.

The blow fell soon. To him, where he and she sat in their high seat, came in a body the leading men of Yorkish Northumbria. Some had fought with him; others were too old but still men of weight and mark. Their spokesman stepped forward. "Lord," he said slowly, "this is a hard thing, but needs must. You know by now that King Eadred turned back from the battle to his army and vows he'll savage this whole land till it's empty of dwellers unless it yields to him. He wrecked not only Ripon town but its minster and monastery, unchristian though that was, be-

cause Archbishop Wulfstan has the manor there. King Eadred feels Wulfstan betrayed him, working with you instead
of laying on you the ban of the Church. Lord, we must give
in or die with all our kindred."

Eirik nodded. "So be it," he said.

However long and deeply she had known him, Gunnhild
could not be sure what hurt lay behind the flat words. She
thought it was less than hers. *He* could still go roving and
fighting.

"Belike you'll see me again," Eirik said. The will hardened in her. Yes, the two of them had to draw back for a
while, but they would never quit. Besides, in her mind
Northumbria was hardly more than a means of regaining
Norway.

"You may go," said Eirik. They were plainly relieved to
get away with nothing worse than such a slap in the face.
Afterward he talked long with Arinbjörn and others.

And so at last they boarded their ships, to row down the
Ouse to the Humber and thence over winter seas to Orkney.
Ships again, Gunnhild thought. Had a flash of foresight
struck Aalf when he warned her about that, these many
years agone?

Arinbjörn stood at the gangplank as she stepped onto it
in the raw weather. "Be of good heart, my lady," he said
softly. "We have many tomorrows ahead of us."

Whatever he had done for Egil, she could not hate him.
She dared not.

XIV

As the next two years dragged on and ships called at
Orkney, each brought news along with the cargo,
mouth by mouth. Gunnhild fitted those shards into a wholeness.

Özur Dapplebeard was dead. King Haakon seized his
holdings. At least that meant his widow Helga and her brats
were no longer at Ulfgard, Gunnhild thought. As for her
father, he would have scorned to have her shed tears or,

worse, offer Christian prayers. Not that any church or priest was here. She did pry loose a little time by herself to cast a spell to help him on his way down hell-road.

Something like this had also happened to a man named Thorstein. Foster kin of Arinbjörn, he had come along west. Shortly before King Eadred invaded Yorkish Northumbria, he had learned that his own father in Norway had died and King Haakon had taken the property. Arinbjörn counseled him to go home and try getting it back. First he would do well to ask the help of the English king.

In the South he met Egil, whose crew had sold their goods and joined him. Egil also meant to fare east, and see about his wife's inheritance. As he put it, King Eirik and Berg-Önund stole this from him, and the last living son of Thornfoot, Atli the Short, still sat on it. Because they were both such near friends of Arinbjörn, and Egil stood well with King Eadred, he and Thorstein handseled help to one another.

In spring they found King Eadred in London, well pleased with the outcome in the North. He gave them letters to King Haakon, and to Egil a freighter laden with wheat, honey, and other wares. The two men made a swift crossing, sailed up the Oslofjord, and rode to a great garth of Thorstein's late father. There Thorstein set forth his claims before the king's men. The neighbors supported him. After several meetings, it was agreed that the matter would be brought to King Haakon himself. Until then, Thorstein kept the steading. He and Egil lived merrily together.

Meanwhile weightier tidings reached Orkney from England. To understand them, Gunnhild must hark back in her mind.

There was a man called Olaf, nicknamed Sandal, whose father Sigtrygg was overlord of Deira in the North. After Sigtrygg died, King Aethelstan had claimed that land. Olaf left for Scotland; he had wedded a daughter of its king. Later he went on to Ireland, being kin to the king of the Norse around Dublin. He returned to England as one of the leaders of the alliance that King Aethelstan defeated at

Brunanburh. Thence he must flee again to Ireland.

But when Aethelstan died, the South Northumbrians disowned the House of Wessex. Guided by Archbishop Wulfstan, who had Norse blood and always leaned toward them, they sent for another Olaf, son of King Gudfrid in Dublin. Olaf Sandal crossed over with him. After some fighting and some bargaining, Olaf Gudfridarson got a realm around Lincoln. From this base, he overran the land north of the River Tees. When he fell in battle, Olaf Sandal took the lordship.

But the Five Boroughs were Danish and Christian. They would not be ruled by a heathen Norseman, and overthrew him. His kinsman Rögnvald Gudfridarson made peace; both were baptized. Even so, within a year they had quarreled with King Eadmund, who led a host to York and forced them back once more to Ireland.

Still the South Northumbrians chafed. Their chieftains muttered about freedom and a Norse king, a man of their own kind. When Eadmund died, stabbed at Pucklechurch by an exiled robber who had returned unbeknownst, the restlessness in the North grew bad enough for the new King Eadred to go deal with. He wrung oaths of allegiance from the nobles and Archbishop Wulfstan.

They had broken these and taken Eirik Haraldsson.

All too quickly, Eadred came over them with fire and sword. Erelong they had to ask Eirik, with everyone else in his train, to leave.

But throughout that winter, the Yorkish Northumbrians brooded. They had much to avenge. As wasted as their land was, another English army could not well live off it. Nor did it lend itself anymore to the easy looting that heartened warriors. Through the Church, Archbishop Wulfstan was widely in touch elsewhere. After a while he told them they should call in Olaf Sandal from Ireland.

When Olaf arrived, they hailed him king. Now Eadred could only send a letter bidding Wulfstan to remember his earlier oaths. Otherwise Eadred must wait for York and its hinterland to regain health.

"We'll see about that," said Eirik when he came back in

fall from his viking cruise. He grinned his wolf-grin. "Be-like Olaf sits less firmly than he believes. He's not hitherto done so well in England."

"And there are bound to be those he's harmed, who want revenge," answered Gunnhild. "Nor can he be without foes in Ireland. If you can link with them—" Ever since she first heard, she had been thinking.

Eirik nodded. "We'll gather all the knowledge we can, and talk of it between us. I'll need wiliness like yours."

And maybe witchcraft, she thought with a cold thrill. Be that as it may, hope for their house soared anew. She narrowed her eyes and smiled at him through the lamplight. "Shall I show you some wiles tonight?" she purred.

In spring he was off again, but with fewer ships than before, and less with raiding in mind than learning and dickering. With him went Turf-Einar's sons Arnkel and Erlend, brothers to Thorfinn Jarl. They might in time gain much from standing now by their king. With him too went certain ones of sharp wit and smooth tongue whom Gunnhild had picked. They would win allies among the viking chiefs and sea-kings scattered around Scotland, the Western Islands, and Ireland itself.

At home, she kept on drawing in word from South Northumbria. No few yonder found themselves less than happy with King Olaf. He was greedy, often hasty in his judgments, while slothful about handling the lawlessness that ran wild after the war. Nor did he busk for the next English onslaught. Instead, he acknowledged King Eadred his overlord and paid scot, gold and goods that would have better uses at home.

Hope soared like a hawk in Gunnhild. With the help of a scribe and a trusty skipper she sent a letter in Eirik's name to Archbishop Wulfstan. It seemed unlikely, did it not— the letter said—that Olaf was merely biding his time till he could openly cast off the English yoke. Would it not be wiser to recall a king who had formerly done so, and would again, and now had powerful allies to set against the war-weary English?

Meanwhile she also heard of happenings in Norway.

During the winter Egil and Thorstein trekked overland to find King Haakon and lay their cases before him. By then Haakon was oftenest in Thraandheim. It was the strongest part of Norway and home of his greatest friend, Sigurd Jarl. The king granted Thorstein his rights. To Egil he said that, although things had not befallen luckily between his brother Eirik and himself, still he deemed it best to hold off from this matter.

Egil offered to go in his service, as he had done in King Aethelstan's. "I'd not be astonished if you and King Eirik soon clash again, and that you learn Gunnhild's given him many sons." Hearing this, away off in Orkney, she smiled.

Haakon would have none of it, after what Egil had done to his kin. Nor did he want him long in Norway. However, for the sake of King Aethelstan's memory, he gave the Icelander leave to follow up his cause in lawful wise.

On the way back south, Egil got hospitality from a hersir named Fridgeir, whose wife was a sister of Arinbjörn's. Their daughter was woeful. It turned out that a feared berserker, Ljot the Sallow, wanted her. She loathed him, as most folk did. He had challenged her father to fight about it. Egil went along, bade Ljot first do battle with him, and slew the man. He fared onward carrying boundless thanks.

Ljot had come from Svithjod. It was the law that if an outlander died in Norway without heirs, what he owned—which for Ljot was not little—would fall to the king. As Gunnhild learned afterward, though she was hardly surprised, Egil bore off some thoughts about that.

He found Atli the Short, who said that if anybody owed anything, it was Egil for the slaying of his two brothers. Egil laid suit against him. They took it before the Gula Thing. When Atli brought twelve witnesses to swear that the inheritance of Björn Brynjolfsson was rightfully his, Egil raised up an older law, that a fight between them should settle it. Atli cried that he should have called for this himself, to avenge those killings. He had won other holmgangs.

First, together, they bought a big old bull. It was usage that he who won would give such a beast to the gods. Then they armed themselves and went at it, while everybody else watched from outside the stakes. Both their spearcasts missed. They hewed with swords till both their shields were in splinters. Still they fought. Somehow Egil's iron would not bite.

There had been a spell cast here, Gunnhild thought. She wished it were hers. It might have worked better.

For at length Egil dropped his sword and rushed in barehanded. His weight threw Atli the Short to the ground. With his teeth he bit Atli's throat across. So died the last son of Thorgeir Thornfoot.

Still in his killing rage, Egil stormed over to the bull, grabbed its muzzle in his right hand and a horn in the left, and broke its neck.

Thus he got back his wife's inheritance. He spent a while in Sogn, seeing to the land and chattels, then sailed home to Borg.

In truth, Gunnhild gave the whole business less thought than she might otherwise have done. She had her own undertakings, weaving her web.

By then Eirik was back with her. His ships had docked on a clear day in fall, when sunlight flashed off waves and the wild calling of the wanderfowl went like far-off warhorns. The tidings he bore, joined with those that had come to her, were full of hope.

XV

A laden knarr sailed into the Thraandheimsfjord. She belonged to Ranulf Aasgeirsson, a man from thereabouts who often traded west overseas. Having wintered in England, he set homeward early in the season. Folk kenned his ship and sped word to Sigurd Jarl, who sent some in a boat bidding Ranulf dock at Hladi and lodge there as long as he wished.

Warriors beswarmed the huge garth, filled every building that could shelter them, pitched their tents across the fields. In the hall, servants were making ready to bring out the big meal of the day, for the sun was getting low. Wellborn men filled the benches. The jarl sat not in the high seat, which a fair-haired young man had, but in the seat of honor across from it. Ranulf led his crew thither and hailed him.

"Greeting and welcome, Ranulf," said Sigurd heartily. "You come at a good time. As you must have heard, the king is here. Lord," he added, "this is Ranulf Aasgeirsson, a worthy landholder and seafarer in the shire."

The chapman and sailors turned to pay their respects. Among them was a passenger, whose clothes and shaven chin showed him to be English, though a hooded cloak shadowed his face.

Haakon had an endearing smile. "I'm glad to meet you at last," he said. "I've heard of you, but you always seemed to be away when—" The stranger put back his hood. He too was young, his nose blunt and cheeks ruddy. Curly brown hair ringed a crown that had grown stubbly during the voyage. A number of the men on hand drew hissing breaths. They knew what that meant.

Haakon gasped. "Brihtnoth!" he cried. "Do I dream?"

The newcomer stepped forward. "No, King," he answered softly. His tongue handled the Norse with skill. "Though I have long dreamed of this day." He raised his left hand slightly. A thin silver band shone on the ring finger.

"Oh, welcome, a thousand welcomes!" Haakon leaped down to the floor and went over to seize the priest's hands in his own. A shocked stillness fell. The servants froze. Haakon looked around the hall. Light from outdoors flashed off his eyes. "Here is Brihtnoth, son of Gyric, who stood high with my foster father King Aethelstan and then King Aethelstan's brother King Eadmund. We two grew up together. We are like brothers."

"That is praise indeed," said Sigurd in a voice that carried from end to end of the long room. "Be as welcome among us, Brihtnoth, as you are with our king."

Brihtnoth flushed. "The, the king is too kind," he stammered.

"What blessed wind brought you here?" asked Haakon.

"You said—before we bade farewell, Haakon—" Briht-noth caught himself. "Before we bade farewell, lord, you said that if ever I was ordained a priest you would send for me. Well, I didn't want to wait."

Sigurd frowned. Others glared.

Haakon tossed his head and laughed. "We need not speak of faith today," rang from him. "We'll all be merry to-gether!"

Bit by bit, the tautness eased. It helped that Brihtnoth went quietly to stand with two or three youthful kinsmen of Ranulf's near where the end of the farthermost board would be. The rest of the crew must needs go outdoors, though Sigurd ordered they be well fed too. The jarl had Ranulf himself sit beside him. Women brought freshly filled ale horns.

"Had you an easy crossing?" asked Sigurd. "What news do you bear?" Again the noise in the hall died down, but now it was because everybody listened.

"Much has gone on," Ranulf said. "The greatest is this." He peered toward Haakon. "Shortly before we left England, after wintering there, we heard that King Eirik Haraldsson is back in York."

An outcry swelled toward uproar. Sigurd beckoned for quiet. Red and white chased each other across Haakon's face. He never could hide his feelings very well. During the meal, as question, answer, and talk boiled around him, he spoke curtly and ate fast.

It ended when he stood up, whether or not others had gotten their fill. He said that while daylight lasted he wanted to go outside with Brihtnoth and speak under four eyes. Nobody cared to say anything to that. The two left side by side. A score of guards fell in behind but kept well out of earshot.

They walked for a while wordless. The sun had gone under the seaward heights, but light still filled the sky and sheened on the fjord. Newly green grass and unfolded leaves tenderly brightened shadows. A mild breeze lulled, bringing smells of earth and a few chirps from the trees. Warmth rushed through Haakon. "Tell me everything about yourself, what's happened, everything," he said.

"Nothing much, lord—" began the Englander.

"Here we two are by ourselves. Let me be only Haakon."

Brihtnoth stared, dropped his eyes, and flushed.

"It's often been lonely for me," the king said. "I'm seldom away from others, but inwardly I'm alone. Share those years with me that we've spent apart."

"They were—nothing much—for me—Haakon—till today when I found you again."

The king shook his head wonderingly. "And you a priest, a man of God."

"My bishop agreed this is holy work and sent me off with his leave and prayers." Brihtnoth bit his lip. "But, God forgive me, I didn't come altogether for the sake of it."

"Enough that you came. You shall be my chaplain, and go everywhere with me. Nor shall you sit and sleep among the lowly. By now I'm too firmly in the saddle for anybody to want to cross me about any such small thing."

"I am not worthy."

"You are. I say so."

A flight of rooks winged darkly by, cawing. As if shying off from the matter, Brihtnoth asked, "How have you been doing? We've heard all too little about you overseas."

"Quite well in this world, God be thanked. In the soul— But there's so much to do, always so much to do." Haakon's face stiffened; his voice went harsh. "And now this about Eirik Blood-ax. Do you know anything that wasn't told in the hall?"

Brihtnoth drew breath. When he spoke it was crisply, as his father would have done. "Only this, that I studied in York while he was there, met him and his queen—she's a strange woman, Haakon, strange—and stayed on after they withdrew. Knowing what they're like, those two, and how closely it touches you, I kept my eyes and ears open as best I could. I saw how often ships plied between York and Orkney. I heard how men off them met with Northumbrian leaders behind closed doors, they tight-mouthed afterward. Also, while the commoners had reasons of their own to dislike Olaf Sandal, it seemed to me that most of the gossip that went around, about his wickedness, meanness, and vice, did him wrong. He wasn't truly that bad."

"I can think who made up those tales and got them seeded in the houses and inns," said Haakon grimly.

"It's not fitting for me to say who, but—Being in and of the Church, though rather newly ordained, I was also aware of how Archbishop Wulfstan received King Eirik's unacknowledged messengers, as well as the restless chieftains of Yorkish Northumbria. Word of it reached King Eadred too. As this past winter waned, he sent troops who seized Wulfstan and bore him away to imprisonment—in Jedburgh, we heard. That didn't sit well with the folk at home! But already then, word was drifting to me of men honing their weapons. And openly so in Orkney. I was not—Haakon, I wasn't a coward when I deemed it best I seek you. I think Queen Gunnhild even likes me. But I might have been trapped there."

Haakon nodded. "Of course. You took passage with Ranulf."

"First, you remember, he went south to pick up some of his trade goods. Not far south. The news got there before he started overseas," that Eirik and his allies brought such a fleet, and there was such an uprising when they landed, that Olaf Sandal and his own following fled back to Ireland.

"And that's what I know, my lord—my son—Haakon." Brihtnoth smiled a bit sadly. "How odd it feels that I should ever call you my son."

Haakon let that pass by. "Would you say Eirik had been a good king before, that they welcomed him back?"

"No worse than most, I gather," answered Brihtnoth carefully. "And unlike Olaf, he'd sent no scot to King Eadred, nor let Eadred's men in to do things like snatching off the archbishop. Neither will he now, I believe."

"Hm." Haakon rubbed his short, golden beard. "What do you think Eadred will try?"

"He'll not take it meekly, I'm sure. Otherwise, how can I tell, a simple priest?"

Haakon laughed, not quite mirthfully, and slapped his

friend's shoulder. "Priest, yes, but not simple. I know you better."

Brihtnoth smiled, shook his head, and kept silent. They walked on. Shadows and the eastern sky darkened.

Haakon hardened again. "Do you think Eirik will be content with what he now has?"

"I know not. But I doubt it. And his sons have no love of peace."

Haakon gazed ahead, as if through and beyond the stand of fir that gloomed near. "Therefore I must always be on guard against an attack from the west," he said low. "Meanwhile the land bleeds. King Tryggvi and King Gudröd down south are faithful to me, but too young to take warlike leadership, yet not young enough that older men can very well do it in their names. Oftener and oftener, viking fleets harry these shores. We Norse can only fight them on the spot, and if they lose a battle, they slip free. Because of Eirik, I can't spare the strength to go after the evil at its root. That's in Denmark. King Harald Bluetooth bears no kindness for us. Pray for me, Father."

"Always. I never stopped after you were gone. How I'd run whenever a ship came from Norway, to catch what word I could!"

In the grip of his thoughts, the king seemed hardly to hear. "On the whole, my folk like me. But this with the raiders—this, that I've waged no war, won no victory—it makes them wonder." He sighed. "Also, I'm told, that I've taken no queen to me, whose kindred might help us. And, maybe worst, that I'll have nothing to do with their heathen rites. By God's grace, hitherto the harvests and fishing have been good, even overflowing. But should they fail, the Norse will soon believe their gods are angry with me."

Brihtnoth crossed himself. "May the good years keep on—and you have your victory."

"Could I be free of the threat of Eirik—"

"God will help you to that also, in his chosen hour. For you are his apostle."

Haakon's mood turned rueful. "Not a very lucky one thus far."

"Why, even in England we hear of conversions."

"Oh, yes, here and there my few priests still give baptism. Mostly, I fear, it's taken for my sake, or in hopes of getting something from me. Not many have stopped sacrificing. I can't disown them for that, can I? And each year, the number of those who'll acknowledge Christ grows less. I think—I hope this isn't the sin of despair—" Haakon too drew the holy sign. "—I think few are left who'll forsake the old gods without stronger cause than I seem able to give them. A stubborn breed, the Norse." His shoulders straightened. He lifted his head higher. The evening star gleamed into his sight. "Brave, though, hardy, honest. I cannot but love them."

Brihtnoth held back from saying that not everybody in the Westlands would agree. "This Sigurd Jarl, our host, it's easy to see he's a mighty man. If he can be won over, Mother Church will gain a son almost as strong as you."

Haakon sighed more deeply than before. "Would that might happen. But he stands by his gods as steadfastly as by his friends. Nobody makes richer offerings to them than he does."

Dusk stole out of the woods and across Hladi. The breeze was going chill. Ever brighter shone the evenstar. More began to blink forth.

"And I can understand it," Haakon said, well-nigh under his breath. "I've heard the tales, the lays, from long and long ago. Greatness, heroic hearts—" He jerked to a halt. Again and again he crossed himself. "No! No!"

Brihtnoth stopped likewise, there in the gathering twilight. Soon they must start back. "Nonetheless you have to keep Sigurd's friendship," he said slowly.

"Without him, I think, the kingship would slip from my hands."

"That must not happen. You're the king who brings the Faith."

Haakon grasped Brihtnoth's shoulders. "I believed that when I came," he blurted. "It's weakened in me. To you, already, Father, I confess my zeal has flagged. But now that we're together—Help me; hearten me; be with me— I'll go onward. *We* will."

XVI

Eirik spent the first summer and winter of his return more on horseback than aboard ship. Riding around the whole of Yorkish Northumbria, he hunted down outlaws, often with hounds. He gave judgment to folk and gifts to their leaders. He readied them to fight if need be for a land that was now healing itself. His sternness and aloofness won him scant love but high standing in their eyes, together with some hope for a better day. That was all he wanted.

Likewise it went in York town. While cold toward those men who had sent him away, he did not penalize or openly sneer at them. For their part, they hastened to do whatever he called for. Even the priests and bishops said nothing to him about the heathen offerings he and many of his followers made. They did it well off in the hinterland, no more than twice or thrice a year. He heard mass a little oftener than that, though he never unbent enough to confess and take the Host. After all, the churchmen told each other, it was King Eadred who had clapped hands on their archbishop.

Mainly Eirik at home received outsiders: chapmen from abroad, hersirs and warriors from Orkney, vikings stopping to pay a friendly visit. Some of these last were sea-kings, men who claimed that name because a forebear or two had been of a kingly house, although their holdings were merely thorps or strongholds scattered around the Westlands— those, and their ships and wild crews. All such Eirik guested well. They broke the sameness here, gave his restless soul a look beyond these walls, brought news, bore off his messengers and spokesmen. Gunnhild welcomed them as eagerly.

Otherwise, aside from Eirik and her children, she was lonely. But then, she thought with a shrug, she always had been.

Through these men she followed, however brokenly, what was going on in the world. King Eadred, she learned, was not outright busking for a new war in the North. But during the year he invited Olaf Sandal back from Ireland and gave him the wardership of Cumbria, the earldom to the west and northwest of Yorkish Northumbria. When Eirik heard that, he barked a laugh. "Now we've less to worry about yonder," he said.

"Still," Gunnhild warned him when they were alone, "best will be to keep a sharp eye out. He's no weakling." She stood awhile in the guttering lamplight. "And yet," she murmured, "this might give us an opening."

Eirik tautened like a wolf catching a scent. He had come to know that mood of hers. "What do you mean?"

"Kings in Dublin have left other sons. With Olaf out of their way, those will be reaching for more than they now have. Might we show them it's worth their while to snatch not at York as aforetime, but at England?"

"Thor hammer me, what a thought," Eirik whispered. His eyes flamed. "What a queen I've got!" He seized her as he would seize a prey and bore her down onto the bed. His hands hauled on skirts and breeks.

He could be too quick and rough, like this. She was no cow in heat; she wanted to be kindled. As always, though, she bared her teeth in a grin and ground her hips against his. It was one of the tricks that kept him hers.

Let him tumble whomever he liked away from home, but let him never care for the wench or set her whelp on his knees. Let him never bring any in as his leman, giving her gold and a household of her own. Gunnhild understood that much of the awe she aroused, with the power that it led to, came from her being the one wife, the coequal in all but name, of Eirik Blood-ax.

Besides, she was greedy of him.

While he thrust and rammed, she counted back the days since last her blood ran. It should be safe enough tonight. She hated secretly killing with herbs a life that might have taken root in her womb. Nor was that very safe for her. Well, it happened seldom. Mostly the spells she cast, also in secret, seemed to shield her.

For she wanted no more children. She was still slim and

supple, her hair still raven black, her skin white and firm. She was not sure if other spells of hers were helping with that. But the breasts were hanging looser, the belly was no longer altogether flat. Nothing could overcome Elli, the hag who wrestled Thor himself to his knee. She could merely be staved off awhile. Thereafter most men would begin looking elsewhere.

Seven living sons must be enough to keep hold on a kingdom won back and keep the house standing through all the storms of time to come. In a way, it was good luck that Eirik lost Norway when he did. Those sons had left their foster homes early, or never been in any. Since then they had grown up under one roof; Arinbjörn was no more than a teacher and helper. Yes, they were haughty and touchy, as was right, but, with day-by-day knowledge of each other, they hunted together across the world. They were not going to fall into the murderous strife of Harald Fairhair's offspring. Together they would gain wealth, power, and fame.

Without ever telling them so, Gunnhild had raised them to that. She was doing it yet with the youngest, during these years when their mother meant more to them than they knew. Even the older ones, when they quarreled, settled it peacefully. If they could not by themselves, they asked her what she thought. Sometimes she wondered whether a lasting bond between them was her foremost, her only true dear wish.

Eirik shouted, shuddered, and got off her. She purred and stroked his beard while she hoped that now they could undress and blow out the lamp.

XVII

Word between York and Dublin traveled slowly, by fits and starts, and was never forthright. Eirik chafed because he could not go there himself and deal. Gunnhild was as glad of that, seeing that she could not well have come along to sit in. At least while this went on, which it likely would for a year or two, the Irish Norse stayed their hand.

There seemed to be peace with Northern Northumbria too, the English earldom east of Cumbria along the northern marches of the Yorkish lands, up to the Firth of Forth. It had helped Eadred in his war. After withdrawing to Orkney, Eirik had raided it more than once. But since his return here it lay as quietly as the English king himself. Spies found no busking for battle.

Winter closed in with gloom and snow and stormy seas. Fires burned high on hilltops and ale flowed freely in houses at Yuletide, everywhere around the land, whether or not the dwellers reckoned themselves Christian.

Easter was the time that well-nigh everyone kept holy. Any heathens would think it unlucky to offer to their gods while Christ went down into death and rose anew, victorious. Yet much of what folk did seemed to Gunnhild to hark far back. On Good Friday many of those out on the land and even some in town went around with blazing torches, crying on witches and evil spirits to begone. On Holy Saturday they brought in the Corn Mother. On the Sunday itself they kindled needfire near the churches. On the Monday they feasted, sang, and danced around a garlanded pole, praying to their saints for a good harvest.

At the Easter mass Gunnhild felt in her bones something of the power in the White Christ. She could only beg of it; and she would not. She, like Eirik, did take Holy Communion, for to keep from that at this highest point of the Church year would have upset too many in York. But their confessor was a mousy old man whom she had taken some pains to put in fear of her. If he had an inkling of how much she left untold, he said nothing about it and gave her only a few prayers to say when he shrove her.

She didn't believe it fooled Christ. Maybe he understood and forgave. If not, maybe she could make it up someday when her work was done. However that went, she would keep striving with every strength and skill that was hers, on behalf of the house of her children.

Besides, there were other powers. Who could tell which

of them had the roots running deepest down into the world and most widely below the earth?

Meanwhile spring stole back, shyly at first, then teasingly, brightness and bleakness, thawing and freezing, sunlight and squalls, until suddenly foals and calves tottered on greensward where earlier-born lambs skipped and the wanderbirds came home, kind by kind, from wherever they had been. Men pulled ships out of sheds to caulk and pitch and otherwise make seaworthy.

Eirik oversaw the work on his own. This summer he would fare again in viking.

He not only wanted to; he must. His men were beginning to grumble. His coffers were dangerously low. A king who was not openhanded with food, drink, goodly gifts above all, lost honor and risked losing kingship. Too many farms had not yet been built and sown anew; there was not enough scot to be had. Levies on trade helped. Now King Eadred had forbidden it with York. Any wares that came from there, his reeves seized wherever they could.

Moreover, the island chieftains, who were to rally to Eirik when he needed them, would lose faith and fall away if they gained nothing from the alliance. He felt that things were well enough in hand at his seat that he could go after booty.

Four of his sons were now of age to sail with him, and ragingly eager—Gamli and Guthorm as before, flaxenhaired Harald and red-haired Ragnfröd this time. Gunnhild stood among her women and guards on the wharf, watching the ships row down the river till they were lost to sight. Then she went back to steer the kingdom.

A while later came a letter from the north. The bearer was a close-mouthed Englishman. Brought before Gunnhild, he told her that he knew not what it said, but he was to warn that it should be unsealed with nobody to see who could not be trusted to keep silence. He was unhappy that he could not give it to King Eirik. Coldly, she bade him hand it over. Warriors stood by, armed. Eirik had ordered them to obey her as they would himself. The messenger heeded.

Alone, she turned it around and around. The parchment felt cold and dry under her fingers, like a snake's skin. What could lie here waiting to strike? If only she could read it! In the Christian letters lay a might and mystery beyond the reach of her runes. How much of its power did Christendom draw from them?

She sent for her tame priest.

What he read aloud to her was from one Oswulf, King Eadred's high reeve at Bamburh on the North Northumbrian coast. Newly given that rank, he wrote of his wish for peace and goodwill. He believed he could tell things King Eirik—yes, he or his scribe wrote "King"—would be glad to hear. He offered to come to York and talk about it.

Gunnhild frowned. This was strange. Did Eadred know? Maybe not. He must needs often let his men in these far parts do whatever they deemed best, without spilling time while words trudged to and from Wessex.

She sent the messenger home with her own word, that Eirik was abroad but should be back in late summer or early fall, and that he had said before he left that on this cruise he would not harry English soil. It was true. She had urged it on him. Witless, to stir the banked fires of wrath when he could as well go elsewhere.

This turned out to be a year of bad weather. Rain and hail lashed the earth; gales drove billows crashing and spouting ashore. Gunnhild yearned to loose her soul in search of her man. But no, that was always risky, belike the more so here where the Cross lifted high. Besides, whatever she found, she could do nothing. Let her set her teeth and keep in mind his doughtiness.

One day broke sultry and overcast. The wet heat thickened hour by hour until clothes hung heavy and reeking with sweat while throats felt choked. Nobody brooked much from anybody else if they could help it; hard words snapped. At last a breeze stirred. It strengthened swiftly to a west wind. A darkness lowering yonder drew eastward. Lightning flickered in it. Thunder muttered.

Gunnhild had been walking around the yard to think and breathe. Turning back to the hall, she passed near the women's bower. The door flew open. A serving maid stumbled forth. She held hand to cheek and sobbed.

"Hold!" Gunnhild cried. "What's wrong here?"

The wench shuddered to a stop. "N-nothing, Queen. I—I—"

"Lower that hand." Gunnhild saw a raw red mark that would become a great bruise. "Go where you will." She would not stoop to questioning a lowborn while others stared. But her daughter Ragnhild was in the bower. Gunnhild made her work there for a few hours almost daily. Fine weaving was a craft which it behooved every lady to know. The maid fled. Gunnhild stepped through the door. Lightning forked overhead; thunder crashed, Thor's wheels. The wind moaned.

The room inside was now dusky, but heat had called sweet smells from herbs mingled with the strewn rushes. The loom stood man-high, fathom-wide. Ragnhild whirled about from a tapestry taking shape on it. When she saw who entered, she seemed almost to crouch. Another maid cowered back into a corner.

"What's this?" Gunnhild asked. "Why did that girl run off?" However small the happenstance, it might besmirch the house.

Ragnhild straightened and glowered. "I told her she was a sloven, and slapped her," she answered sullenly. "She is."

"What did she do?"

"She was filling the next shuttle and dropped the ball of yarn." Ragnhild pointed. "See, it unrolled and got dirty."

"That was no ground for striking her. Nor did you hit with your hand. You used the sword beater, didn't you?"

"I was angry. This has been a nasty day. Everything's gone wrong."

"Get out," Gunnhild told the maid. She scuttled through the door. Gunnhild closed it behind her. The unshuttered window flashed and flashed; thunder rolled through the wind; there went a sough of oncoming rain. Gunnhild turned back to her daughter. "Only a witling flies into a rage over something so little." And seldom lives long. "Never give pain when it's useless to you. That's sheer wastefulness. Let me not hear of anything like this ever again."

"Yes. I'll go." Ragnhild took a stiff-legged step.

"Halt!" rang Gunnhild's command. The maiden jerked to a stop. "You won't sit and sulk and feel sorry for yourself. You'll learn from what's happened. I'll give you another task in the hall."

"Oh!" Ragnhild gasped.

For a span she stood with fists clenched at her sides and the lightning-light white on her eyeballs. How young she was yet, after all, Gunnhild thought. But taller day by day, it seemed, withy-slim but hips and breasts swelling under a gown maybe a bit closer-fitting than was quite seemly— she liked to flaunt herself; she joked and laughed with youths in the guard—and the chestnut hair flowing around a face eerily like Gunnhild's own.

She caught a shivering breath. "Oh, when I'm free, I'll— I'll—" She lost further words.

"No one is ever free," Gunnhild said. "No man may shun his weird. Nor may any woman. We'll be remembered for how we met it. Don't shame the blood you bear."

Tears burst loose. Gunnhild folded her arms, which she longed to lay around the lass, and watched.

Ragnhild fought down the sobs, wiped her eyes, and stood still beside the loom. After a while she gulped, "Oh, Mother, I do want to be like you."

Now Gunnhild could smile and offer a hand. "That's better. Welcome back."

Ragnhild caught it. How thin and soft hers was, Gunnhild thought.

"I, I want to be a queen too," Ragnhild stammered. "With a king like Father."

Yes, Gunnhild thought, given such a father as Eirik, how could any girl wish for less?

Ragnhild straightened in half-childish haughtiness. "And I will. Nothing shall stop me. Nothing."

Though today that high heart had made her blunder, time would teach it, Gunnhild thought. Then it would stand her in good stead. Christian women might creep from the world into nunneries, to live barren and helpless. But it was not right for any who bore the blood of Özur Dapplebeard, Rögnvald Jarl, and Harald Fairhair—Eirik Blood-ax.

"Good," said Gunnhild. "Let's get to the hall before the rain does."

XVIII

Sooner than awaited, a horseman galloped to York crying that the king's ships were rowing up the river.

Though glad to see his wife again, however many he might have bedded along the way, he was otherwise not happy. Over and over he had lain weatherbound for days on end. The Scottish, Irish, and Welsh shores he came to had already been picked gaunt. Even when he led his crews inland, they found less than he hoped for—barely enough to make his Orkneymen think it had been worthwhile and to keep his household until next year.

He brightened at Oswulf's message. Calling in the priest, he had a letter written to say he would indeed like meeting with the high reeve of Bamburh and plighted him safety whatever came of it.

Oswulf arrived on a day when a wind from the north rattled dead leaves across the yard. Eirik received him hospitably. Gifts passed between them. Eirik held a feast in his honor to which the chief men of York were invited.

Gunnhild misliked him from the first. She could not quite say why. He was a stout man with thinning reddish hair and watchful eyes. The teeth that had rotted from his jaws left him lisping. A shrewd and careful speaker, he drank sparingly. His words were of friendship.

Later he talked alone with Eirik. Later still, Eirik, alone with Gunnhild, told her what had gone on.

His grin shone through the cold, shifty shadows in their room. "Of course, he doesn't outright say anything against King Eadred. But he hints—hints stronger than I've yet gotten from Dublin—at alliance between us two, he to hold North Northumbria as I hold York, together casting back

any attack from the South. First—he's right about this—
I'll need more wealth to bind more warriors to me than I
now have. He's been sending spies around. He told me how
weak Olaf Sandal really is in Cumbria. And, beyond its
shores, it's hardly been looted at all."

Gunnhild's skin prickled. "Do you trust his bare word?"
she asked slowly.

"No, no. I trust in my strength. This was a poor year.
But during winter I'll look into things myself. If I find
Oswulf speaks truth, then come spring I'll gather a mighty
fleet—mine, and what the brothers of the Orkney jarl have,
and sea-kings everywhere. We'll ransack places seldom
touched erenow. We'll stuff our holds with booty. Then let
Eadred try whatever he likes."

"It's a great risk," said Gunnhild.

"For a great gain." Eirik tossed his head. "What else can
I do?"

She saw no hope of talking him over. The years with
him had taught her the signs. And this could work out well.
Already, though, she felt forebodings.

"I think all our sons had better stay behind," she told
him. "No knowing what King Eadred may do while you're
gone with so many of our spears, and openly defying him.
We may need such leaders here."

Belike it would take her the whole winter to get his
agreement. And then he must lay down the law to those
young wolves. But one way or another she would hold
them from this faring.

XIX

Again spring came back with the lapwing, to call fields,
woods, and wanderlust awake. On a day when haw-
thorn blooms scattered white across a land gone utterly
green, Gunnhild bade her man farewell.

The riverside surged with warriors, their kin, townsfolk,
farmfolk, and herders here to watch. Metal flashed; bright
dyes bragged amidst gray and brown. Noise rolled around

like surf and rose like the cries of sea-mews. As yet, walls and roofs to eastward blocked sight of the sun, but the sky overhead reached forget-me-not blue. A wind still cold from the night ruffled the water. Ships rocked a little at their moorings. Timber and tackle creaked.

Guardsmen had made a way through the crowd for the king and his household, and kept clear that wharf where his dragon waited. The crew were already aboard. He stopped at the gangplank. Maybe sleeplessness had slightly deepened the furrows in his lean face, but it left no mark in the springiness of his stride or straightness of his shoulders. His smile was almost wry. "May luck abide with you," he said. "But I think you'll see to that."

Gunnhild looked up into the frost-pale eyes and answered, "Our hopes and wishes will sail with you." What more could they say when their carls and wenches were listening?

"Our prayers," said Gudröd, and signed himself. No priest was there to bless those outbound. Though Eirik had heard mass yestermorn, ashes, bones, and bloodstains lay on a hilltop where he had made offering the day before.

Their other sons mumbled this or that, none of it mirthful. Three of the oldest four, who went with him last year, barely masked surliness. The rest had caught their mood, even nine-year-old Sigurd—all but Harald. He seemed willing to respect his father's judgment, however bleakly.

Eirik turned, nodded, bounded down the plank, and leaped into the hull. Seamen cast off and shoved free. Oars stretched forth. The dragon walked down the river. One by one, more followed, and more and more. Gamli stared after them, unstirring but for the fist he struck into his palm, over and over, a young Eirik Blood-ax chained.

Weariness weighted Gunnhild. Her loins, her whole body ached. She and her man had taken no rest this past night. Now she must bank the fire and wait.

She must be the queen. "Keep his kingdom for him," she said to her sons.

"Maybe we'll win fame thereby!" Erling's voice cracked and he reddened. Thirteen, he might have gone along.

"Since he doesn't let us do it otherwise," muttered dark, Özur-like Guthorm.

"This year," Harald told them. "This one year. There will be later years."

Gunnhild knew how hard-won that steadiness was. Yes, she thought, among them he took most after the grandfather whose name he bore.

They stayed until the last sternpost was lost to sight; then she led them home.

The weeks went slowly by. The weather was much better than before. Gunnhild could hope that that boded well for the vikings. She had enough to do that most of the time the work smothered her fears and let her sleep of nights; but her dreams were often bad. When her sons were not at weapon-drill, they hunted, wrestled, ran footraces, put on horse fights, and the first five lay with woman after woman. They were also apt to brood and pick quarrels with men. Their mother must sometimes step in to keep these from becoming deadly. They needed no ill will, here in York.

After about a month, a ship from the north brought news at last. Eirik's fleet had harried the eastern shores of Scotland, with some gain. Reaching Orkney, they lay to while the ships of Thorfinn Jarl's brothers Erlend and Arnkel gathered. At the Hebrides he met with no less than five sea-kings. Thence they all sailed onward. Soon thereafter a thick fog wrapped the islands for days on end. From them on it was as if the blind gray stillness swallowed every word about him.

Nor could Gunnhild get better than scraps of knowledge from the South. They betokened no threat. If anything, that made her sons even more restless and foul-tempered. Were it not that they stood in a good deal of awe of her and their father, the gods alone could say what recklessness they would have launched. She herself felt a waxing unease.

The springtime passed in sunshine and rainshower, birth and growth, trees full-crowned and full of birdsong. Each day was longer than the last.

Then tidings did come—from Wessex. A Danish chapman, Ivar Bentnose, had traded his wares there. Instead of sailing straight home, he went first to York, where he could sell dearly the English goods that King Eadred tried to keep out. Ivar cared not for royal wrath. His hair was white; after this voyage he meant to settle down quietly at home.

As they often did, three of the four elder Eirikssons had gone hunting. One always stayed behind, by turns. It happened to be Harald. He received Ivar well.

Next day he found Gunnhild and asked if they could speak alone. They went to a loftroom of the hall. Outside fell a drizzling rain. Lamps hardly brightened the room. Their smell of burning blubber was not unwelcome in this dank, chill air.

Two stools were the furnishing. Mother and son sat down. His gaze on her was troubled. "What do you know of goings-on southward?" he asked bluntly.

A foreknowledge of his aim crept upon her. Indeed he was the sharpest of her brood. How handsome he was too, shoulders broad within the fur-trimmed tunic, hair and young beard like the unseen sun. Were it not that his women meant less to him than his hounds and horses, she would envy them. "What do you ask of me?" she answered. "It was you who questioned Ivar at length. I only listened, as was seemly."

"You know we'd have heard you if you spoke, you, the queen. I wondered why you didn't."

She gave him a smile. "You were doing well." He was learning, she did not say aloud. "I'm sure you did this morning also, when you drew him aside."

"I got no more than yesterday. It doesn't seem King Eadred wants to fight this summer, but Ivar heard how he has men riding from end to end of Wessex. He must be telling his shire-lords to stand by for something. An ealdorman whom Ivar talked with thought he might move on the Welsh."

Gunnhild nodded. "He could let fall hints about that, while having something else in mind—if he's been shrewdly and secretly counseled."

"You grasp these things as well as Father does," said

Harald more grimly than gladly. "And you have ears every-where."

She sighed. "Would that were so. But this is not Norway. Here it's merely a few lowly ones, whom I get wind of mostly by happenstance and have brought to me. Packsack traders, tinkers, landloupers, witches—they get about, they hear things, but it's not from the seats of the high; it's only gossip. What I can gather seems to bear out that King Ead-red won't attack us this year. But give me time to weave a new net."

"If we have time. Still, this is useful, isn't it? And Father will be back, with his fleet and his warriors, by fall—and the Orkneymen not over-far away—won't he?"

"I know not," said Gunnhild into the dimness.

His voice hardened. "Have you cast runes?"

She sat silent. She had, and could read nothing. That in itself was disquieting, though, true, runes often failed.

Harald frowned. "A heathenish thing. Like your dealing with those witches."

"Ragged, houseless, hungry. Small strength in them for good or ill."

"As it ought to be, in a Christian land."

Gunnhild narrowed her eyes. "You went and offered with your father before he left."

"Because he wanted me to, and the others. We'd not anger him. Nor—maybe—the old gods too much. But worse, I think, would be to fall out with Christ." Harald grew earnest. "Mother, I wish you'd hear mass oftener. Re-member, the feast of St. John draws nigh."

Gunnhild's voice went flat. "As you like." She looked past him, toward a window, through the rain in it and be-yond.

He leaned forward. "What's wrong?"

She heard his fear for her, and his love, but as though across a rushing river. "Nothing," she said. "If we're done here, shall we go down to the hearth?"

It shivered within her: Soon now came Midsummer Eve, when gods, ghosts, elves, land-wights, all the unearthly walked abroad, while men and women went into the woods with songs and spells, to call blessing on the land and bane off it. Then if ever was witchcraft set free.

She had knelt before the Man on the Cross, given gifts to his Church, prayed for his redes and the help of his saints. Never so much as a dream had he sent. Maybe the fault was hers. She had not fully confessed, forsworn her sins, and humbled her heart as they told her she should. She could not.

Once, only once, an awe of him had taken her, when young Brihtnoth showed her the holy books. She had still felt a little of it when the holy water bedewed her brow. But it faded. Brihtnoth had left—to serve Haakon, she learned, Haakon in Norway. None since him had spoken with her that openly, been that ready to answer her questions, about the Faith. Priests might try it with Eirik, and seemed to be having some luck with his sons, but for them a woman need merely believe.

Yes, maybe she was in the wrong. Yet a great lord ought to reward his followers as befitted his greatness. Odin gave them victory or he gave them death, but he wanted no more from them than offerings and stalwartness, and he would guest them in his Valhall till doomsday. So many of them said. Whatever the truth was, men and women could leave undying names behind.

Through the loftroom shadows and the rain outside, it was as if she saw the Man on the Cross and the Man on the Gallows; but between those tall darknesses crouched the Man with the Drum. The thunder of it boomed; the song of him keened.

On Midsummer Eve she would again send forth her soul, to find Eirik, know how he fared, and bring him more than her wishes.

XX

A little house near the hall, formerly the home of the under-steward, had been turned over to her. It held the room that was hers alone. She sent off the staff, forbidding

anyone to come here until she said they might. It was not
the first time. They dared not talk much about it. And today
they were happy to be freed for joining in the celebrations.
Nonetheless she barred the door to the room before she
opened her locked chest.

Western England was not as far as Iceland, but tonight
she was sending not a witchy call but herself. She needed
a strong spell. Having put the dried mushrooms to soak,
she went about her other work while twilight slowly deepened into night. Shouts of merrymaking drifted in past half-
closed shutters, with warm, smoky smells from a balefire
at the hall. It was less to her, more sundered from her, than
a moth that fluttered through the window and around her
one lamp till it flew into the flame and burned.

She unclad herself. She donned the feathers, teeth, and
claws. She ate. As the feeling of otherness took more and
more hold of her, she danced, sang, shaking the bones
and a rattle, laid them aside at last to take a small drum
and beat it, everything whisper-softly, here in the shadow
of the Cross, but the tide of it rising ever higher, the wind
of it crying ever more shrilly. Air, at first cool, turned the
sweat over her nakedness to a cold whip. There was no
need of other pain. It was as if her will itself raised her.
Now blackness filled the window, barely hazed by moonlight. A single star glimmered there. It began to whirl in
her sight, around and around, a quernstone whose grinding
shivered the bones of the world. She put the drum aside,
snatched up the bird-shape of feathers, lay down on the bed,
folded hands over breasts with the bird-thing between them,
closed eyes, and went away.

The fire outside was sinking. She caught the heavy
smoke and wrapped it around her, breathed life into it. The
swallow winged aloft.

From on high, York was a huddle strewn with sparks,
the River Ouse a dull-silver snake, the stream Foss a thread,
winding over a huge, dappled murk. Fires still glowed
widely across it. This was not the summer night of Norway,
hardly more than dusk, nor eerily lighted by the midnight
sun of Finnmörk. Stars glittered, the Winterway glimmered,

in sable. A crooked moon, waning a little past the full, had climbed well up. Not far behind it gleamed the great wanderer that men gave many different names, Jupiter among the Christians. She turned her back on them. Eirik was somewhere in the west.

On she flew and on. In this shape she was tireless. She would pay for that when she returned to her body, pay more if she did not return. She gave it no thought. Her whole being had become a search.

However dark, the night was short. Dawn dimmed the morning star. Sunrise drowned it. Brightness shouted back off the Irish Sea. A thousand shades of green rolled inland.

North or south? Likelier north. She tilted on the wind and flew well above the shore, scanning and scanning. Neither hunger nor thirst did she know, and for that too her flesh would pay, or this soul if it lost its way home.

A hawk, early at hover, spied her and stooped. Air whistled with its speed. She flew on. It drew nigh and sheered off in a crackle of wings, affrighted. Otherwise she saw only seafowl and stray white clouds.

The sun went higher on her right, the moon lower on her left. Still she flew.

The land began bending west to make the head of a broad bay.

Ships and ships rested side by side on the strand at water's edge, like a row of swords. More rode at anchor nearby. Men walked about, raced or wrestled, squatted where their cookfires had scarred the earth. Sunlight blinked on steel. Gulls wheeled and piped, skulking for scraps. No gladness or fear could storm through her while she was wind, smoke, and ghost, but she knew what she had found. Single-minded as an arrow, she slanted downward.

Yes, these were men of Eirik's, yonder was his own ship, but they were few camped here, only watchmen. Some cast her a glance, a swallow at this time of day. The little knife-winged thing swept above them and lofted anew. There it seemed to look about before it left them, bearing east-northeast.

He had said he would strike afoot into Cumbria if he came on a spot that was weakly held. She made out no signs of any fight at all. The track of his troop was easy to follow, trampled grass and grainfields, a hamlet gutted and burned. She flew.

The land lifted in rolling hills and rounded bergs. Sheep grazed the heights; farms filled the dales. Winds flowed up from the warmth below. They tossed her till she learned how to ride them. The viking spoor led her onward. They had sacked steading after steading and three manors, slaughtered kine for food, taken horses to carry loot, hand-bound and neck-haltered young captives to sell. Now she saw smoke drifting from lately blackened wreckage. Nowhere did she come on token of any real battle.

From its uppermost ridges the land fell downward again toward a wide river. That and the valley stretched farther than she could see, even from the sky. The lowland glowed green with woods and meadows, amber with ripening crops. The smoke rising yonder was from the hearths of untold homes, the fires of smelters and many smithies. Thorps, villages, churches clustered everywhere; afar lay a small town or a big monastery. Here wealth unbounded waited for the taking.

In the hills above this side, near a hamlet not yet harmed, men fought.

Over brush-begrown swells flanking a rutted road came the English. Already their ranks crowded in on the Norse ahead and behind. Already the grass was reddened, dead men trampled to pulp and splinters. Swords clashed; axes thudded; horns brayed; throats howled. Spears, arrows, and stones hailed from the slopes.

The Norse held firm. Their banners waved steady-footed, markers for living bulwarks. She kenned Eirik's raven, oh, she kenned it, and there he himself was, tall, shining in helmet and byrnie, relentlessly hewing. She swung low, into the battle racket, among the hurtling shafts. She would fly above him, around and around and around, singing death away from the dear head, whatever it cost her, for as long as he needed to win his victory.

Something that was not wind seized and flung her. Something she could not hear shrieked. Something she could not feel struck ice through her. Helpless, she tumbled away. Almost, she crashed against a boulder. Barely did she slip free.

Again she tried, and again. The storms cast her back. The fight raged on unheeding.

She caught a clean updraft and let it bear her skyward. There she circled. There she watched what happened below her. She could only watch.

It was the slain, she knew, the wrathful new-made dead, rushing from the world. Nothing like her could cross their way to wherever they were bound, to Valhall with the valkyries or off onto hell-road or whatever it was. Men believed they knew, many and many a belief. She, the bare soul in the seeming of a bird, knew she did not.

To and fro the swallow went in heaven. The sun drew westward. It goldened an eagle that waited on high. Crows and ravens gathered lower down, black above the earth, ever oftener landing to pluck out an eye or tear off a strip of flesh. Eirik had always fed them well.

She watched the battle.

At first the Norse threw back each English onslaught. Eirik's banners crossed windrows of their fallen. He got his ranks arrayed so that every weapon was free to smite and every bowman, spearman, and slinger had room to work. They clove a path forward. Now and then, in spans of hoarse breathing, the foe regrouped their own shattered troops. The vikings whooped at them.

But more English were arriving, a swarm across the hills, fresh for the fight while the Norse wearied and grew fewer. It was as though for any man whom Eirik's cut down, three sprang up. They broke his right wing. He and his chieftains made the warriors left them into a shield-wall. Their shafts spent, they stood their ground, a rock amidst wild surf.

Bit by bit, the rock crumbled.

The sun cast level beams and long shadows from the west. The black flocks were now thick in the air and on the earth.

A horn call, a hundredfold shout, a crash of iron, and the English burst through. The battle became a maelstrom.

For a short while Eirik's banner swayed above it. Then it fell. She could find him no more in that surging of men, but a roar rose over the din and the mightiest of the slain went by.

She did not grieve; she could not until she was again human. Nonetheless she flitted awhile yet overhead. Maybe she would see him. Maybe she could keep the ravens off him.

Some Norse got free as the fighting turned into knots of men who hacked at each other with blunted blades held in shaky hands. Most fled by themselves, ran, stumbled, gasped, blindly bound anywhere. Surely they would be hunted down like wolves. Two bands of a score or less had leaders who kept them together. They beat off whoever attacked them. Otherwise the English were still too busy or too battle-worn. One band headed seaward, one inland. They soon passed from sight among the darkening hollows between the hills.

She dared stay no longer. Night would have fallen before she could land and walk around to search through the tumbled dead; and she was not an owl. Were she still in her room by morning, she thought her sons would be worried enough to break down the door. If they found her lying like a Finnish shaman, and naked, it would mean trouble with them as well as with the folk. She must not risk that. She was the queen.

She dipped as low as the waning death-winds let her, once, flew back aloft, and winged toward the gathering night.

XXI

After three days, Arinbjörn led his remnant into York town. They had gone slowly, as wounded and hungry as they were, drinking at whatever mudholes they happened on, hiding whenever somebody might spy them and tell the foe, until they were in lands they reckoned friendly. Four died along the way. The heat and pus in two more were going to kill them also.

Bathed, fed, his hurts freshly bound, he slumped in the honor seat and told his tale to Gunnhild and her sons.

"We saw beacon fires," he said dully, "but thought they were mere warnings, for nowhere was any host, or even any bunch of armed yeomen. We put into Morecambe Bay and grounded, ready for a fight. Nobody met us. King Eirik said this showed Olaf Sandal was still more redeless than he'd believed. Cumbria must lie open clear to the Vale of Eden, on into our Northumbria. So we set off thither, and at first everything went well. Too well, I began to think, but that was nothing a man could say, was it?

"At Stainmore they waylaid us."

Yes, Gunnhild thought as the words trudged on, Olaf had waited there. He must have had men out in swift boats, who brought him the news when they saw the viking fleet bound for his shore. Then did he gather his warriors and call for levies throughout the land.

He was not that cunning, and had he been, he could not have set this up by himself. Oswulf of Bamburh must have thought of it, been in touch with Eadred, guided Olaf, while he lied to Eirik and lured her man toward the trap. Oh, Eirik was not witless; he had sent his spies and scouts. But if Olaf and Eadred kept silence, it was not hard to mislead them.

She was still weary to the marrow. It was all she could do to sit straight. Inwardly she was too dulled to feel any depth of hatred for Oswulf. Later she would, a poisonous sea of it. Then she would have tried to throw a curse on him; but she'd lack the means, where she'd likeliest be. Later she would mourn for Eirik, weep for him when she was alone, see to the honoring of his memory and the morrows of his children. Today she could only hear:

"I saw my king fall. His mail hung in shreds. Bruises blackened him; his own blood reddened him. Yet he fought. The men around him died; the foe closed in on every side; an ax took him in the neck. Our ranks were shattered, our last hope gone. I rallied a handful and we cut our way out. We made for here rather than the ships, as others may have done, because it's a long haul around Scotland and I wanted to bring you tidings as speedily as might be."

"That was good of you," said Harald.

Yes, thought Gunnhild, ever was Arinbjörn faithful. Now she truly forgave him his friendship with Egil.

"You've given us warning," Harald went on. "As soon as King Eadred hears, what will he do but come north against us? This goes as hard to say as Father's death, but without him and his warriors we cannot stand. We shall have to withdraw."

Take ship again, Gunnhild knew. Back again to Orkney.

XXII

Shortly after they got there, three warcraft rowed into the haven at Wide Firth. Woefully undermanned, some aboard them weakened by wounds, they had nonetheless made a fair passage from Morecambe Bay—that much luck they kept. The skipper of Eirik's dragon was her brother Aalf the Shipman. Thorfinn's brothers Arnkel and Erlend lay dead at Stainmore, along with many another Orkney-man.

The jarl was guesting the queen and her sons here, and had found housing for the men, women, and children who came with them. Likewise he received Aalf well, if not cheerfully. Thereafter he said little as the newcomer told of the battle and escape, the burning of those hulls for which he had no crews, and the voyage home. Locked into himself, Thorfinn had been brooding on something. Gunnhild wished she knew what it was.

"Now that I'm back," sighed Aalf when the telling was done, "you, my sister and nephews, are of course welcome to stay with me, though my home is not as big and fine as this."

They thanked him and answered that they would pay calls. However, otherwise they would abide where they were. "It's a better spot for keeping track of things and a grip on them," said Gamli. "We'll soon have our own built—in time, more than one—fit for kings."

"Until we gain the true kingship that is ours," Guthorm laid to this.

Gunnhild saw Thorfinn's brows draw into a scowl. He quickly masked his face anew. She foresaw trouble. There was nothing to be done about that today.

"We waited with Eirik's grave-ale in hopes you would be on hand for it," she said to Aalf. "Now we shall hallow his memory."

She wondered if anything ever could. Surely the emptiness where he had been was unfillable. But his fame would live, and so, through his sons, would his mightiness. Henceforward, that was her life's task. In doing it, outthinking and outlasting whoever stood against it, she could maybe find some easing of the hurt in her, and in the end, maybe even a healing.

She had already set work afoot on the feast. It would last long, unstinted. Every man of standing left alive throughout Orkney was to come. Gifts to them would be kingly, gold, weapons, fine clothes, even some ships. Besides being right for Eirik, that would buy goodwill for his house and faith in its strength. Both were sorely wanted after what had befallen. Yes, then the treasure on hand would be scanty. But his viking sons could win more than they had spent, while taking blood revenge for him.

A storm blew in during the feast. Wind yelled; rain brawled; seas roared. Gunnhild thought that good. They too mourned him.

Smoke from the longfires drifted bitter through the hall, lamplight flickered over arm-rings and eyes, as the skald Dag Audunarson stood forth to say the poem he had made for his lord. The staves clanged amidst the wildness beyond the walls.

"In a dream I saw how Valhall
ere daybreak readied its welcome."

He shifted into the voice of Odin.

> "I had bidden my men to straw
> the benches and wash the ale horns.
> Worthy are those who will come
> of the wine the valkyries are fetching.
> With gladness I now await
> the warriors out of Manworld.

> "Bragi, I hear the thunder
> of a thousand fighters faring."

Dag gave words to the god of poetry:

> "The benches shiver as if
> Baldr were bound back hither."

> *Odin*: "Unwisely you spoke there, Bragi.
> Well do you know it is Eirik,
> the Blood-ax, who wakes these echoes
> as he enters into Valhall.

> "Sigmund and Sinfjötli,
> go swiftly to meet him in honor,
> the hero, if this be Eirik,
> he for whom I have waited."

> *Bragi*: "Why is it not another
> than Eirik, among all kings?"

> *Odin*: "His blade he has often bloodied
> in battles through many lands."

> *Bragi*: "Then why did you make him fall,
> as fearless as ever he was?"

> *Odin*: "Can you guess when the Wolf shall run loose?
> The gods have need of his kind.

"Hail, Eirik! Your strength and wisdom
are welcome here among us.
But who are those boars of war
you bring along behind you?"

Eirik's own haughtiness gave the last answer:
"Five are the kings that follow
their foremost, myself, the sixth."

Everybody praised the poem. The sons rewarded the
skald well.

It was not a bad one, Gunnhild thought. Yet—if only
Egil Skallagrimsson were not a foe!

XXIII

A man of Thorfinn's told Gunnhild that the jarl wished
to speak with her about a weighty matter. She said that
she would meet him in her room. It was upstairs in the hall,
and not big, but it was hers while she dwelt here. He should
come to the queen, not she to him.

The morning was bright, almost warm. She left the door
to the gallery open, for the fresh air and outlook over the
sparkling firth. Thorfinn entered by himself, better clad than
he was wont during the day. Gunnhild had donned a white
linen gown, embroidered panels, and silk headcloth from
abroad.

"Hail, my lady," he rumbled.

She gave him a cool look. He stood heavy and four-
square, grizzled, snout-nosed, squinting. "Greeting to you,
Jarl," she said, in a voice meant to recall his rank to him.
"Be seated." There were chairs. "Will you have a stoup of
ale?"

"That'd smack well." He did not thank her while he sat
down facing her, as if to make her remember that it was
his ale. But he did then add, "Queen."

Gunnhild signed to the wench she had kept on hand, who
bowed her head and went out. Something better than small
beer would indeed be good. Again her thought had touched

on the news lately arrived from England, that King Eadred had made Oswulf earl over York, over everything yonder that had been Eirik's. As before, a burning rose in her throat. Ale might quench it. "What have you in mind?" she asked.

"I'll speak of it with your—with King Eirik's sons, of course," Thorfinn began slowly. "But it seemed to me, Queen, you being their wise mother—if we two agree, they're bound to. Not that I believe they wouldn't. But I'm loth to have wrangling between us."

She nodded. "You have dealt with us as behooves an honest man of ours."

He reddened. His utterance harshened. "Well, I am the jarl of Orkney."

"And my sons are its kings."

"Haakon Haraldsson off in Norway says otherwise, I think. We've not forgotten how his father came over our fathers."

Gunnhild waited. Let him make his own opening.

"I stood by King Eirik. He was the rightful king. But he's gone, and most of his strength with him."

"His sons are rebuilding it."

Thorfinn raised bushy brows. "Enough? Can they? The Orkneymen too have lost much. They wonder how bare to King Haakon we lie."

"Thorfinn Skull-splitter does not fear Haakon Aethelstan's-foster, does he?"

The man bit his lip. "Queen, it's not that we haven't kept faith with you," he said, word by hammering word. "My two brothers laid down their lives for King Eirik." And the hope of booty, she withheld telling him. "Now his sons claim his rights over us and his scot from us."

"You'd like something in return," she murmured.

"Best for everyone will be that we bind our houses together, for the whole world to see."

Gunnhild foreknew what was coming. A breeze off the firth gusted suddenly chill.

"Otherwise, Queen—who can say?"

"What are you leading up to?"

"You know my son Arnfinn is widowed. He's my oldest; he'll have the jarlship after me. Were he to wed your daughter Ragnhild—You understand me."

"Say on."

"His wife bore him no sons that lived. His and Ragnhild's son will get the jarlship from him. Meanwhile I and all of us will do everything we can to help your sons back to the high seat in Norway."

That wouldn't be enough, she knew. It couldn't be. But if Thorfinn was refused this wish, any help he gave would be half-hearted at best, and belike if Haakon came he'd yield without a fight. Then Eirik's sons would be no more than sea-kings.

"It's worth talking further about," Gunnhild said.

The maid brought in two goblets.

XXIV

The afternoon turned cold and blustery. Sunlight speared between hurrying clouds. Whitecaps chopped. The seafowl still wheeled and screamed in their thousands. Gunnhild liked being out in such weather, her heart at one with the winds and wideness. It was Eirik's kind of weather.

Knowing her daughter, she led the maiden into it, ordering the guards to stay. They walked silent to Crow Ness, where they stopped and stood. Ragnhild gazed at her mother's hard-set face, shivered a bit, and wrapped her cloak tightly around her. "What's this about?" she asked, not quite steadily.

"Something I thought you'd rather hear first from me."

Ragnhild braced herself. "Say it, then."

"Thorfinn Jarl wants you to wed his son Arnfinn."

Ragnhild took a backward step. "No!" Her shriek mingled with the birds'.

"Yes. It's the best match you can make." Here where they were, Gunnhild did not say aloud. "Arnfinn will give you a rich morning gift. You'll be the lady of a great holding in Caithness, and in time the wife of the Orkney jarl."

Ragnhild's free hand clawed the wind. "Not him," she snarled. "That swine."

Gunnhild called him to mind, dark, hairy Arnfinn. Heavy drinking and a loud mouth had brought more than one duel upon him, but he won them. He had given out that he could not fare with his uncles and Eirik because he had to keep an eye on the Scots. It might be true. He did not lack boldness.

"A boar, if you will," Gunnhild said. "A boar of war, as your father was."

Ragnhild's cheekbones stood sharp under skin gone icewhite. "But I want a man like him, like Father!" she cried.

"And I wish we had him back. We bear what we must and take what we can get."

"Th-this—" Ragnhild laid both hands over her eyes. The wind caught her cloak, fluttered it back from her shoulders, streamed the dress tightly across her slenderness. Spray blew as salt as her tears.

Gunnhild mustered sternness. "Your brothers will agree. It's for the house. They fight for it, for your father's blood and its morrows. You can do this. You shall." She ached to draw the girl to her, hold her close, shield her, bear her away to somewhere happy.

Ragnhild lowered her hands, made fists of them, and let the wind dry her cheeks. "Or I can die," she said.

Gunnhild shook her head within the hood. "No. You wouldn't break faith with us."

Ragnhild stared for a while out over the sea. "Well," she said at last, "I—" She unclenched her hands and looked back at her mother. "Yes," she said flintily. "So be it. I'll live. And find my way—through everything. Yes."

XXV

They did not again speak alone together until after the wedding. Ragnhild would not. She talked no more with anybody than need be. Often she went walking, by herself aside from a guard or two.

She was wedded in mid-fall, soon after her older brothers got back. They had had only four ships and crews for a short voyage to Ireland, but the raiding was fairly good. Hence they came home blithe and were openhanded during the days of the feast.

It was a big one, chieftains among the guests. Ragnhild sat stiff, wreathed and bedecked, until time for her to go. Arnfinn's brother Haavard, who planted his seed so widely and so often that men called him the Fruitful, went ahead to open the bedroom door for the pair and shut it behind them. Torchbearers followed, flames flapping red and yellow in the dark, to keep evil Beings off. They shouted lewdnesses, to help bring children on. Arnfinn, thoroughly drunk, answered them in kind.

Groom and bride left when the last guest did, to cross tricky Pentland Firth while the weather held. That day was calm and leaden. A damp chill gnawed. As folk bustled about, Gunnhild saw her daughter standing by with nothing to do, nor, it seemed, any wish for it. She slipped over and plucked the young woman's sleeve. "Come," she said low. "I want to talk a little before we bid farewell."

Ragnhild obeyed, wordless and unsmiling. Gunnhild knew how to stride through a throng, staring down whoever tried to say anything. They could not go far, barely out of the garth, but she found a spot at the shore. Around them reached sallow turf, before them the gray water. Seafowl bobbed on it or swung beneath the low cloud deck, but not many today, nor crying much.

"I know not when or how we'll meet henceforth," Gunnhild said. Though Arnfinn would visit here now and then, his wife would stay behind. "Yet I've a feeling that we shall."

Ragnhild's gaze kept seaward. "Yes, maybe."

"I'll always hope for your well-being."

"And I for yours." Gunnhild heard no warmth.

"And your happiness," she brought herself to say.

"I'll have to make that for myself, if I can."

"You have none yet?" Gunnhild asked outright.

Ragnhild turned to stare straight at her as Eirik Blood-ax had stared at Egil Skallagrimsson. "I hate him," she hissed.

She had grown thinner, her face almost gaunt. That brought forth the great, shining eyes and the shapeliness of the bones underneath. Her words cut carefully, like a well-wielded knife. "The first night, he pushed me at once onto the bed, heaved up my skirts, gloated for a short while, slobbered, dropped his breeks, spread my legs, and fell on me. When he was done, he rolled over and snored. In the morning when he woke, he spewed into the pot before having at me. I breathed his breath. It's been the same since."

This was as bad as Gunnhild had feared. "He's seemly enough toward you in the sight of others, isn't he?" she asked slowly.

"Of course. I'm your daughter and Eirik's. As the lady at Caithness, I'd better not become a laughingstock. But I don't want his get. I'll have none, I swear."

Gunnhild had not taught her about herbs and spells. But there were other ways. If nothing else, newborns often died without anyone knowing why.

"You're on your own now, dear. And you've strong blood in you" was all Gunnhild could find to say. How could she whisper "I love you" to the steel before her?

Ruddy locks bound by the headcloth of a wife, Ragnhild's head lifted athwart the murk. "Oh, fret not for me. Nor for yourself or my brothers because of me. I'll take heed." The least of smiles bent her wan lips. "I begin to think of this as a dare."

A carl ran from the garth. "They're ready to board, my ladies," he hallooed. The women went down to the waiting ships.

BOOK FOUR

HAAKON THE GOOD

1

Word came to Norway that Eirik Blood-ax was fallen, his sons and their mother fled to Orkney with what was left of his following. When King Haakon heard, his eyes blazed. A fist clenched on his knee. "Now we're free to root out the evil," he said. Brihtnoth had never before heard such a voice from him, soft, cold, ashiver like a striking sword.

"What do you mean—my son?" the priest asked. Though the news had put the hall in an uproar, men nearby were listening.

"What else but the Danish vikings, who've grieved our southlands too long? Harald Bluetooth yonder must reckon me a weakling. He'll learn better. All Denmark will." And so would any Norse who thought his faith had sapped the son of Harald Fairhair.

Brihtnoth straightened where he sat, on the king's right hand one step below the high seat. "I'll be there!" he cried.

The fire in Haakon flickered. "You're no man of war," he said slowly. "I'll not have you cut down by some robber lout."

"Don't you remember, lord, when we were boys in England we hoped to become warriors together? I'll learn what I need to."

Haakon could only nod, and soon order that the best teachers in battle skills take his friend in hand. Throughout the winter months, Brihtnoth spent as many of his waking hours in dogged practice as his holy duties left him.

The king was also sharpening his weapon-craft whenever he could. There eagerness stormed up in him. He sprang like a wildcat. It was as if three blades whirred in his hand. He grinned for glee. Yet he used shield and feet so deftly that blows seldom landed on him, while his smote where they would have done harm were this a real fight. Soon he was beating most other men. This was not for want of their trying. They felt that here they had a leader born to reap victories.

However, he often sat down and talked quietly, at length, with any who were wise, such as Sigurd Jarl, or who knew the Danish lands and waters well. He did not mean to dash blindly off.

"After your folk have seen what you can do in the field, they should be readier to hear you speak of the true God," said Brihtnoth in one of the few short spans they ever got alone. "So this is his work we embark on."

"Because you bless it," whispered Haakon. Quickly he turned to everyday matters.

In spring he sent out the war-arrows. When seeds had been sown, he called up levies and ships. Mighty was the fleet he took south.

Scoutboats bore warning to the Danes. Haakon's own scouts told him how they scattered, some to Sjaelland, some to Halland on the Kattegat, some to Jutland. He steered for the latter. "It's the backbone of the kingdom," he said. "We'll see if we can break it."

Hearthsmoke hove in sight before the low green shore did. Shouts rang; oars whitened water; ships leaped ahead.

The little town they found fell with hardly a blow struck. The first Norse crews whose keels grounded swarmed forth, battered their way through a weakly built stockade, and were in among the houses, slaying, looting, taking captives, torching thatch roofs, before many others had made land. Haakon stood off till the work was done. When his crew grumbled, he told them they had small honor to win here. They would get battle enough soon enough. As for the booty, it was his, to share out later as he saw fit.

There was indeed not much worth taking, aside from some youths and maidens to sell for thralls. Having gone ashore with the king, Brihtnoth winced to see them stumble bruised and bound toward hulls where room had been left for the likes of them. Turf above the strand was crowded with men having older women by turns. The dead gaped glassily at heaven. Flies buzzed thick around spilled guts and clotting blood. When they saw an opening, gulls swooped down to snatch a bite. Behind everything else roared fire. Where a wattle-and-daub wall crashed, sparks rained upward through flames into the thick, stenchful smoke.

"Can this be right?" mumbled the priest. He crossed himself again and again.

Haakon shrugged. "They've done the same to our folk."

"These poor ones didn't!"

Haakon cast him a suddenly bleak look. "Are you sorry you came along?"

Brihtnoth swallowed. "No, no, of course not. You'll see how I, I carry myself in a real battle. But this—arses heaving like beasts in rut—is that manly?"

Haakon frowned the least bit. "I don't care for it either. Still, how can I forbid them the fun they've earned? You said we're in God's cause."

Brihtnoth had no answer.

As the fleet rowed on south, preying, sometimes sending bands inland to wreak more, he grew hardened to it. War was the way to punish Harald Bluetooth. Surely no few of the Danish vikings had made their homes hereabouts.

He took no part in it, and Haakon little, until one day when of a sudden they spied a great host of armed men waiting for them. The Jutes had gathered to defend their land. They had few ships or boats; the Norse could have passed them by. Haakon laughed. "This is what I hoped for!" he cried.

Brihtnoth's head swam. He clutched the wale and struggled for steadiness.

The Norse steered into the shallows, sprang out, and formed ranks behind the banners of their chieftains. Already stones and arrows fell among them. None but those who were hit gave it much heed. The weather was windless, heavy with heat. "I'll not stuff myself in a coat of mail," said Haakon cheerily. "I'd drown in my own sweat before any ax could fell me." Without even a helmet—his head shone golden—but only a shield and the sword Quernbiter, he strode among his picked guardsmen to the forefront of his array. Gasps of wonderment trailed him.

He had given Brihtnoth a full set of war-gear. The Englishman could hardly scorn that gift by leaving it off. Before long he thought maybe his king had chosen the better lot.

The hosts shocked together. That was a great battle. Afterward men told how Haakon went ahead so swiftly and strongly, hewing, hewing, that his standard bearers could not keep up with him. To Brihtnoth it was an unbounded, well-nigh shapeless tumbling and racket. He had no time for fear, prayer, anything but holding his place in line, warding, striking. His soul seemed to stand off, coolly aware, now and then telling him what he ought to do. The breath went in and out of him, hoarse and harsh. He did not feel the flesh wounds he took. It was a strange thing to look into the eyes of a man, an unknown man, who meant to kill him if he himself did not kill first—almost a weird kind of love. But he seldom knew what came of it. They swapped blows; then the strife bore them apart. Once he did see, hear, feel his blade go deep into a thigh. Blood spurted; the fellow crumpled; bones crunched underfoot.

The Jutes broke. They scattered and fled every which way. Norsemen hounded them well inland, cutting down any whom they overtook. Meanwhile Haakon saw to the binding of wounds—he said nothing about the cutting of hurt foemen's throats—and otherwise making ready anew. A few ships he sent home, bearing booty and men who lived but were no longer fit for battle.

Brihtnoth threw up, shivered as if naked in midwinter, sat, and hugged his knees to his chin. He was not quite alone in that. After a while they felt better.

When everyone was together again, Haakon set course east for Sjaelland. Now he was in search of vikings. Sometimes he left his fleet and went to look around with a few craft, smaller but nimbler than the rest. He was rowing down the Sound with two when he came upon eleven ships full of warriors. Straightaway he attacked them, and ended by clearing their decks.

Thereafter he could prowl widely over the big island,

plundering, burning, killing, taking captives. Those who paid him great ransoms, he let go. He did likewise on the Skaaney side of the strait. Whatever vikings he found, Danish or Wendish, he slew out of hand. If a neighborhood could not buy safety from him, he laid it waste. Thus he went on, as far as the rich island Gotland in the Baltic Sea. For the next few years its famous markets did lean business.

At summer's end he returned to Norway, hulls stuffed with plunder, crews wildly merry. Everywhere his folk cheered him. He stayed the winter in Vikin, though, lest Danes came seeking vengeance. None did.

King Tryggvi Olafsson, his young kinsman, had spent that season raiding Scotland and Ireland, showing himself to be a doughty warrior. Before Haakon traveled north in spring, he set Tryggvi over all the shires of Vikin, bidding him ward them and, insofar as he was able, keep footholds in those Danish lands on this side that Haakon had laid under scot.

Meanwhile, throughout the dark months, he had feasted widely around and basked in the praise of his deeds. A skald of his, Guthorm Sindri—the nickname was the name of a dwarf who wrought in gold for the gods—made a drapa in his honor.

> "Fearlessly wending his way
> over waves, the bold one fared.
> Woe he worked on the Jutes
> where awaited him the valkyries.—"

Haakon listened aglow, and rewarded it with a golden arm-ring. Brihtnoth sat glumly by. He understood that the king must bear with heathenness—as yet, as yet—but foreknew Haakon would not ask absolution for this. As for himself, while he was glad he had stood by his friend and proven his manhood, he did not willingly hark back to it. Instead, he prayed that Christ would lift the bad dreams from him.

Eastward over the North Sea drew what ships had once been those of Eirik Blood-ax and his men. Bright-hued at their head went the dragon of King Harald Gormsson's that had borne his word to Orkney.

This early in the season, weather was cold and windy. Seas rolled and chopped, spume flying off their manes. Oars groaned in ports, water sloshed from bailing buckets. However hard the crew tried to keep the queen snug, Gunnhild was never truly dry. Yet she strained forward like her sons in their own craft. Standing on the foredeck, cloak flapping in her grasp, she was first aboard hers to make out the low sand-cliffs of western Jutland.

Her work and wiles, her messages carried by daring sailors throughout the winter, had taken root. The nightshade was leafing.

She laughed a silent laugh. She had Haakon Aethelstan's-foster to thank for much of this. After his warfare last year, Harald of Denmark became very open to having new and angry allies.

Around the broad white strands of the Skaw swept the fleet, and down the eastern side of the peninsula. Wind turned fair, sails went up; the ships made good time. The wayfarers camped ashore that night. Eirik's sons fretted at this. They could well have sailed on by moonlight, they said. Gunnhild told them to calm down. Here they could ready themselves to come before their host like men of worth, not drenched water rats. As for herself, she thought, she had grown used to biding her time.

And so toward evening the next day they nosed into Vejlefjord and pulled alongside the docks at its end. Her brother Aalf the Shipman was among the first off. A man still lean, though his red hair was speckled with white and his beard like rusty snow, stood before the guards who had gathered. Aalf went at once to him. Hands clasped shoul-

ders. Across the yards and the years, Gunnhild kenned her
second brother, Eyvind the Braggart.

He greeted her honorably. Soon he was telling at length
of his great deeds and high standing. In that, he hadn't
changed. Still, it was clear that he had done well by his
lord King Harald, who had in turn done well by him. He
had sat here for a while with his men, waiting for her and
hers. Now he brought them to horses and led them a few
miles inland to Jelling, where the king was.

The land rose in long, rolling hills, a rich land, dark with
plowed fields over which breathed the first shy green of
their crops, meadows a deeper green studded with stands
of oak and beech, woods fencing the northwestern edge of
sight. Thorps rested peaceful along the well-kept road. Haakon of Norway had not ventured this far; here was the heart
of his foeman's might. The sun was near setting. It soaked
grass and young leaves with gold. Homebound rooks
cawed, black beneath big, woolly clouds. Air lay cool. It
smelled of sweet things and hearthsmoke.

Buildings sprawled around the hall at Jelling, well-nigh
a town. Above everything else loomed two huge mounds.
One, begrown with bushes and early blossoms, had been
raised over King Harald's father, King Gorm the Old. The
king's mother, Thyri, slept at his side. Widely beloved, she
had taken the lead in strengthening the Danework—earthen
walls, ditches, and palisades farther south, defense against
the Germans beyond. The second, its soil still raw, had
lately been made by their son King Harald in their honor.

Maybe he sought thus to win liking among his folk. His
older brother Knut had been fair to see, openhanded and
blithe, everybody's hope. An arrow killed him while the
two were raiding in Ireland. It was believed that Gorm, very
aged, died of grief at the news. So did Harald come to the
kingship a few years ago.

Between the barrows stood a shaw, a halidom, under
whose leaves blood offerings were made to the gods. Yet
Gunnhild had heard that the Christian faith was widespread
in Denmark, above all in southern Jutland. King Gorm, although himself heathen, had never forbidden missionaries.

Besides, no few Danes who went abroad came back converted; if nothing else, that made it easier to trade with outlanders. There were churches in the kingdom, priests, even three bishops.

King Harald's hall was as great as any in Norway. He himself trod forth to bid the sons of Eirik and their kin welcome, as heartily as lay in him to do. He was tall but rather potbellied, heavy-faced, dark-haired. His teeth were discolored; one fang hung out above the lower lip, hence his nickname. Gunnhild had heard him called cold, greedy, and grudging, although too cunning to be overly stingy. His wife, also named Gunnhild, was a quiet woman, born to one of the lesser kings whom Gorm brought under himself. To the queen from Norway, York, and Orkney she seemed somehow tamed.

Still, Harald gave the newcomers a feast and housing, with promises of better as soon as the news could get around that they had arrived. Already the next day he took Gunnhild Özurardottir aside to a loftroom and spoke earnestly with her.

"If you are too weary from your voyage, my lady, this can wait," he said. "But, between us, albeit your sons are kings in blood—and will be kings indeed, if I can help—they hearken to your wisdom; and in that, they are themselves wise."

He had been gathering knowledge of them, she saw. "I thank my lord. You are most kind."

"Our needs and wants run close together, I think. Here, under four eyes, shall we speak freely?"

A kindred soul, Gunnhild thought with a thrill. Nonetheless she must gang warily, watching every word. "As the king wishes. We bring you strong men, the rightful heirs of Harald Fairhair, and their warriors. They'll gladly avenge what Haakon Aethelstan's-foster has done to you, and more."

"Hm." Harald Bluetooth stroked his beard. "May I ask what you leave behind you?"

"I'm sure the king knows. We wedded ourselves into the family of the Orkney jarls. When we left, we gave Thorfinn

Skull-splitter full sway over the islands and all the scot they pay. So they are our friends. Belike crews of Orkneymen will join my sons in warfare. However that may be, you've nothing to fear from them."

"Good, good. Your sons—hm—fine young men, as fine as any I've ever met. Outstanding even among them—may I say it?—Harald, my namesake. Were he a child, I'd set him on my knee and foster him. As is, we'll see about giving land and other wealth to them all, enough to keep them and their households fittingly—and, hm, the means to wage war." Harald Bluetooth leaned forward. She caught a whiff of the breath from his mouth. "War on the foe we share, eh, my lady?"

She understood him full well. Should they, with help like this, overthrow Haakon and take Norway, they would do it as his vassals.

He might get a surprise about that, come the time, Gunnhild thought.

After a while the two of them went back down to the throng in the hall, clad in the best of linen and wool, furs, gold, silver, and amber, king beside queen. The other Gunnhild stood by like a shadow.

Three days afterward, Arinbjörn found Gunnhild the mother of kings standing aside from the roil in the yard, catching some fresh air. Wind murmured, driving away smells of offal, dung, and smoke. Clouds scudded across blue. "Queen," he told her, "I'll bring this forth openly later, in seemly wise, but may I first talk with you?"

He was well aware of whose hand was over her sons, she thought, and whom the king of Denmark would most readily listen to. She looked into the broad, slant-eyed, weathered face, ringed by grizzled hair and beard, and answered, "Yes, to me you may always speak freely."

"It's only this. Now that King Eirik's heirs have reached safe havens, I can go back and see to the lands and kindred I left behind in Norway to follow him. May I have leave?"

A qualm passed through her. She had grown wont to having this rock quietly at her side. Thought leaped. She had better put him on his honor. She froze her voice and bearing. "You know full well that here is no home for us, nor may we rest until his sons have won back the right that was his. But maybe this today should not astonish me, seeing how you set aside your oath to him and even were ready to fight him for the sake of his deadly foe."

He stood as if spearstruck. When he spoke, it was raggedly. "Queen, there was—there is blood brotherhood between Egil Skallagrimsson and me. And on that day he was no threat to my king. Rather, he'd given himself into the king's hands, and slaying him would have stained King Eirik's name. I, I do believe I did honestly by both of them. I followed my lord to his death, and so will I follow his sons and you, Queen—" He gulped. "—if you will have me."

Thereupon she gave him her warmest smile and her softest utterance. "Well said. Yes, you may go home for as long as you have need. I'll make sure of that. For I do have faith in you, old friend."

Did tears glimmer? He could barely mumble his thanks.

When, late that summer, she heard how Egil had also returned to Norway and Arinbjörn made him welcome, she only smiled again, though tightly. Might the Icelander fare ill on his errand, whatever it was. But it hardly mattered anymore. In the end, Arinbjörn was hers.

111

He knew better than to bring Egil before Haakon Aethelstan's-foster. But in spring he himself sought out the king, who was then in Rogaland. Their talk was friendly until Arinbjörn told why he had come. He had had forebodings about it, and Egil had grown so downcast during the winter because of it, that at last Arinbjörn offered to go plead his case. It was namely that the king had taken the rich goods of the Swede Ljot the Sallow, whom Egil slew. The Icelander thought they belonged to him by right. It was mostly on that account that he had sailed to Norway. Arinbjörn saw Haakon stiffen while he went on: "As far

as we can tell, King, Egil has the law on his side here; but
your reeves have laid hold of everything and called it yours.
What I ask of you, lord, is leave for Egil to follow up his
lawful case."

Haakon sat long before he answered: "I know not why
you undertake such business for Egil. He met me once, and
I told him then that I would not have him here in the land,
for reasons you know full well. Egil shall not lay the kind
of claims on me that he did on my brother Eirik. But to
you I say, Arinbjörn, you shall stay no longer in Norway
either if you care more for outlanders than for me and my
words. Well do I know how your thoughts bend toward
your foster son Harald Eiriksson. Best will you do to go
join the sons of Gunnhild now. I can hardly reckon on your
help if it comes to a war with them."

Arinbjörn reddened. He could only say hoarsely that he
was no man's betrayer. Nothing further was spoken. He
busked himself to return home as soon as might be. The
king kept cold and withdrawn even at their farewell.

Later, when they were alone together, Brihtnoth sighed,
"You may have done unwisely there. Steadfast men are all
too few."

"But his troth lies with heathen Egil and Gunnhild the
witch," Haakon snapped. He brooded. "Darkness everywhere, Hell's darkness."

"We will lift it," Brihtnoth vowed. Haakon did not smile.
The priest laid a hand on the king's shoulder. "Yes, it's
hard, loyalties and enmities so tangled, strife with your own
kin and your own folk. Your heart is torn."

"You understand," whispered Haakon, "you, the only
one in the world who's wholly at my side."

As for Arinbjörn, he went back to Sygnafylki with the
news. Egil took it badly.

Shortly afterward Arinbjörn had his guest called to a
room where a few witnesses were on hand. He opened a
chest and from it paid out forty marks in silver. "This
money shall you have, Egil, to make up for the goods of
Ljot the Sallow," he said. "It seems fair to me that you be
made whole by my kinsman Fridgeir and myself, because

you saved his life from Ljot. I know you did it for my sake. So it behooves me to see that you are not robbed of your rights."

Egil took the money with many thanks. Thereafter he and his friend were cheerful. They began to plan a viking cruise next year.

IV

Sundown smoldered red through a wrack of wolf-gray clouds. Thurso Bay surged and seethed with chop; the seas beyond roared wild, spouting where they broke over a rock or skerry. Murk stole from the east across the moors toward Arnfinn's hall and the buildings around it. Ragnhild Eiriksdottir stood outside, down by the wharf, where boats lay bottom up and ships were snugged into sheds.

The thrall Heth stood with her. Two of her husband's guardsmen leaned on their spears, inwardly growling and wondering when the lady would go to shelter. Everybody had grown used to her way of rambling out in the weather, but this was rather much. They could not hear what the two said, for the wind shredded it and flung it afar. Besides, half the words were Gaelic, which few Norse in Caithness had bothered to learn.

"So you understand, then, what you are to do and how, tomorrow night?" Ragnhild said.

Heth gulped. "I—I hope I do, my lady." She could barely hear him through the shrilling air.

She stared at him from under the hood of her cloak. It half darkened her face, but her eyes caught the dying light and gleamed big. "And you understand that if you fail—or, worse, if you betray me—how ill it will go, not only with you but with your sister?"

"I won't fail; I won't!" he cried. His own face, freckled and downy, seemed younger than the fifteen or sixteen winters behind it. Wrapped in patched and darned wadmal, his frame was thin but sinewy.

"Good." Ragnhild's sternness melted into a smile. She

brought a hand from beneath her cloak, almost touching his. "I've faith in you, Heth, oh, yes. And I'll keep faith myself. You and Gruach shall have your freedom, with horses to ride and food to carry, freedom to go home."

She had told him, won him over to it, in scraps and snatches, whenever they could have a few words not over- heard. As the lady of Arnfinn's land, she would steer it until a brother of his could come over from the islands. As a christened woman, she might well honor his memory not with a heathen offering but by releasing one whom he had used harshly but who had nevertheless given her good ser- vice.

Everybody knew Heth was her worshipful hound. After she got Arnfinn in a mood of drunken openhandedness, he had agreed that the thrall become her footling, to run her errands, groom her horse, and whatever else she wanted done. If she spent time drawing him out about his home- land, why, that kept her from sulking and spitting as often as formerly, and the knowledge might someday prove use- ful. There was no hint of anything untoward; they two were always in sight of somebody.

More and more, though, the somebodies were out of ear- shot. They thought nothing of that. What was Heth, any- way? A half-Pictish lad Arnfinn had caught a few years ago, along with his younger sister, when Arnfinn punished raids on his livestock by taking fire and sword far inland. The girl was set to housework and other drudgery. Of late, as she grew toward womanhood, Arnfinn had bedded her or lent her to a guest, but seldom, she being unwashed and not much to look at. Heth had been mostly a stablehand till Arnfinn's new wife first spoke a bit with him, then seem- ingly took a liking to him, as she had done to some of her husband's horses and hounds.

Heth swallowed again. "I—my lady, forgive me, but— Wonderful if you send Gruach home, but I—I'm not sure I want to leave you—"

Ragnhild's eyelashes fluttered. "We'll see about that, maybe," she answered tenderly. With a sigh: "Well, we'd better go indoors now."

A little kindness to a wretch went a long way, she thought. And after a while—Those who were around did not mark lingering glances, soft voice, fingertips that happened to brush him. They did not think what the sight of her, carelessly cloaked as she stepped out of the bathhouse, or other such glimpses, might do. Oafs, the lot of them.

She sighed again and trudged back to the hall. The guards followed. Heth trotted off toward the barn where he slept with his kind.

Firelight leaped. Arnfinn sat drinking in his high seat. "There you are!" he boomed. "What in hell were you doing out in thàt shit so late?"

"Breathing," she said wearily. "And then I remembered a few things I needed to tell my footling about making ready for tomorrow."

He leered. "I'll soon give you better things to think about." He belched.

In the blindness of the shut-bed, she not only suffered it; she stirred her loins and moaned. "There, now, d'you see, I knew I'd thaw you," he hiccoughed before he rolled off and fell asleep. He smelled of ale and stale sweat. He snored thunderously.

Next day the household set forth. It was Arnfinn's wont to shift to an inland holding of his at this time of year, leaving a small staff here in the winter sea-winds. No ship was likely to call before spring. Meanwhile the hall and its outbuildings sweetened.

What with goods and livestock to take along, he always made a late start. Moreover, days were short. Therefore he overnighted at a spot called Murkle, where he rented out a farm with a good-sized house. As erstwhile, he, his wife, and their guardsmen and servants took it over, leaving the tenants to shelter elsewhere. Ragnhild had been remembering the layout since last year.

A road of sorts twisted over the uneven ground along Thor's River, but the going was slow for such an awkward troop. Dusk fell as they reached the farm. A rider had been sent ahead with word. Arnfinn climbed off his horse and went straight inside to the lamps, roasting swine flesh, and ale. Ragnhild came more slowly. She caught Heth's eye through the gloom and nodded. He swallowed hard but nodded back.

Night closed in. A thrall banked the fire and went off to his own straw. Arnfinn's men stretched on benches or floor. He crawled into the one shut-bed. Drunk again, he had not troubled to change clothes, and there was no place free of eyes for Ragnhild to do so. She hated sleeping in the gown she had worn all day and must wear through tomorrow. She hung her cloak on a peg and got in with him. He fumbled at her, then went heavily to sleep. She lay in thick darkness and stench, waiting.

Christ—or Freyja, who was a goddess also of death—or someone or something else—give that this be the last time.

She had no way to count the hours other than whispering, over and over, the Ave and Paternoster they taught her in York. A long hundred of each should be enough. Having mouthed the last "Amen," she sat up on the rustling mattress and slid the panel aside. Breath and heartbeat quieted, fears and unsureness fell away. It became as if she stood aside and coolly watched herself move.

Smells and sounds of sleep mingled with a slight bitterness of smoke. After the lightless bed, she could find her way by the glower in the fire-pit. The clay floor was cold under her feet. She slipped her shoes on, put the cloak around her shoulders, and wove among the sprawled bodies to the door. Unbarring it, she stole through and closed it slowly, silently behind her.

Wind whined chill across shifty darknesses. A crooked moon flew amidst tatters of cloud. The nearby river sheened dimly. No one seemed astir; raiders could not take so many encamped by surprise. If anybody was awake, he would merely glimpse her on the short path to the backhouse. He wouldn't dare come nigh. After all, the lady must needs leave that door open to see what she was doing in there at night, and they had learned how dangerous it was to offend her.

The shack hunched black ahead. A shadow wrenched free of it. Heth crouched before Ragnhild. His upturned face was as wan and blurred to see as the glow on the clouds, but she heard how he gasped. "Is your heart strong?" she asked at once. "Have you the knife?"

"Yes—yes—" He half drew the blade from the sheath he clutched. Steel winked before he snapped it down.

"Then go," she told him. "The door doesn't creak if you're careful. They're hog-deep in slumber. Be soft-footed; be quick."

The blade was for a huntsman, heavy and keen. She had stolen it from Arnfinn's things weeks ago, hidden it, and told Heth where. Before they left yesterday, he had slipped it under his sark. It had taken a long while, bit by fleeting bit, to work him up to this.

He shuddered. "I've never—it's murder—God forgive—"

"*I* will not, unless you go. Tell a priest after you get home if you like. It's for your freedom—by now, your life—and Gruach's. Go."

He scuttled off, keeping low to the ground, as a weasel moves on its prey. She felt no need to enter the backhouse, but this must look right in every way. Without lifting her skirts, she sat down in the stink and inwardly counted more prayers. A part of her wondered how her mother would have handled it all.

Time. She trod forth, glad to be back in clean air, and returned to the house. Iciness thrilled in her. Here waited her hopes.

The door was shut. Either Heth had boggled and never gone in, or he had had the wit to close it again when he fled. She opened it and went forward.

As she reached the bed, she screamed.

Men bumbled awake. Peering through gloom, they saw the panel drawn aside. Blood, black in this light, soaked the mattress and spread across the floor. Arnfinn Thorfinns-son lay gaping and staring. A slash across his throat yawned like a second mouth.

Yes, Heth had done well indeed, Ragnhild thought. Following her rede, he must have put a hand down to pin her husband, muffled, for the little span of his death struggle.

Thereon he left as silently as he had come. Nonetheless she spied the wet tracks of his feet.

She screamed and screamed. They didn't know it was with overwhelming glee. In a rush she knew how taut she had been. To let go was like waking from a nightmare.

The guards crowded around her. The chief took her hand and croaked something meant to soothe. She clawed back to coolness and flared at him: "How could you let this happen? Nithings, every one of you!"

She had known that shame and shock would make them tools. To feel them thus in her fingers was giddying. Almost, she lost herself in it. But no, she was the child of Eirik Blood-ax and his Gunnhild. "Can't you at least catch the murderer?" she yelled. "Look; see his trail on the clay!"

"But, but the grass and, and muck outside must have wiped his feet," stammered a man.

"Fetch hounds! Kindle torches! Set both households searching!"

Now was when she could stamp into them, into all Orkney, that she was to be obeyed.

Men surged and shouted. Most ran about like beheaded chickens, of course, but she told some few—making her voice quaver—that the killer might well have gone to the river to drop his weapon and wash off the stains of his deed. So had she bidden Heth do.

They caught the boy headed back toward the camp, where he would be unmarked in the bewilderment. Torchlight shimmered off his dripping clothes. "That's the one!" Ragnhild shrieked. "Kill him!"

"But, my lady, we should ask—" began the chief.

"Your laziness let my lord die," she snarled. "Will you not so much as take revenge? Kill!"

"My lady, oh, my lady—" Heth wailed. A spear stabbed; a sword whirred. He crumpled to lie shapeless at her feet.

"He must have been brooding till he went mad," Ragnhild said into the sudden hush. Torch flames snapped and sparked. "Cunningly mad. I myself trusted him—" She made a sob, called up a few tears, stiffened, and ordered: "He has a sister. Find her and kill her too." Although

Gruach was to have been kept unknowing, she could well have felt something was in the wind. Besides, this was what a woman cruelly bereaved would want. "Then my Arnfinn will rest more easily."

There was other work to do, endless work, while the moon sank and day stole gray into heaven. With the help of her serving maids Ragnhild closed her man's eyes and got him fittingly laid out. The troop would bear him on to his inland garth, bury him with honors and treasure, hold as great a grave-ale as the place and season allowed. The news would not reach Thorfinn Jarl on Mainland soon. Meanwhile Ragnhild would have sway over the Caithness holdings. She had nursed thoughts about what could be done. Arnfinn never listened to them, but now she'd set things right and have something to show when the Orkneymen made it across the narrows.

She had understood from the first that her name was not going to go unsmirched. As they talked it over, folk would see odd gaps in this business. They would recall how she and he had never gotten along. Well, let them mutter. She meant to have too firm a grip for anyone to dare wonder aloud, not even his close kin.

Thorfinn was old and ailing. With Arnfinn dead, his likeliest heir was the next son, Haavard the Fruitful. She had felt how lustfully he looked on her. The last she heard, he, like his brother before him, was newly widowed and not yet rewedded. Let him see how well she ran things; let her get him alone for a while.

V

To Harald Bluetooth at Jelling came a man named Poppo with a goodly following. He was a bishop, but not one of the three in Jutland. Rather, he came straight from the South at the behest of the Emperor Otto, his mission to win all Denmark over to the Faith.

The king received him well. He could hardly do otherwise, as powerful as the German overlord was, to say noth-

ing of the trade with yonder realms. Harald lodged Poppo
and his confessor in a house near the hall, the rest of the
men beneath roofs humbler but not leaky. He feasted them
while he sent for his jarls and hersirs and others whose
counsel was worth hearing. These arrived speedily.

Gunnhild's five oldest sons were not among them,
though the king had bestowed broad lands on them, telling
the dwellers to heed these newcomers. They were off at sea
to harry the shores of Vikin. It was Erling's first such time;
she heard later that he showed himself the most ruthless of
all. Gudröd and Sigurd stayed behind with her.

Bishop Poppo was a stout, square-jawed man who spoke
flowing, if somewhat heavy, Danish. While he waited for
the meeting, he preached only to the Christians on hand,
though he eagerly answered men's questions about belief.
His own questions were searching; he soon knew well how
matters stood throughout this kingdom. Gunnhild would
gladly have talked with him at length. There was much she
wanted—needed—to learn. However, he said no more to
women than he must. Therefore she in her turn scorned the
priests he had brought along.

Nonetheless, she was a queen, kin to the king here, her
sons his allies. She was not kept out on the day when men
gathered to speak of gods.

This was in the great hall. She got a seat of honor, not
far down from the king's and the high guest's, a little below
his but a step above the benches which the leaders of
Denmark filled. On her left sat her namesake, Harald's
wife, very straight so that everyone could see she was the
taller. On the right of Gunnhild Özurardottir was her son
Gudröd. At fourteen he could be on hand, although she had
warned him to stay quiet. Brown eyes beneath unruly
brown locks were hawk-watchful.

Sigurd, twelve, was still too young. Besides, he was so
brash and boastful that folk were calling him Sigurd Loudmouth. She had sent him on a week's outing, lest he fall
into a fit of rage and make a ruckus that would shame her.

He was not unlike her brother Eyvind the Braggart, she
thought. That man was not here. Someone must keep ship-

watch, for Haakon's under-king Tryggvi of Vikin was as much a threat to Denmark as the sons of Gunnhild were to Norway.

But the time would come, she thought, when they were more than vikings—oh, far more. Then would Tryggvi rue his own raids.

Her brother Aalf sat nearer King Harald than she did, a grave and weighty man. Having abided in Orkney while she and Eirik were in England, he was as yet unchristened. But he seldom made offerings anymore, unless at the start of a voyage, and then mostly to keep his crews happy.

It was otherwise with some among the Danes. They listened grimly to their king say aloud the reason they were met, which they knew already, and ask Bishop Poppo to take the first word. Knuckles whitened as if around the drinking horns that had not yet been brought in.

Outside, wind gusted. Sun and cloud shadows sickled through open doors.

Poppo trod forth. His voice rolled deep. "Greeting and blessing. I am come at my Emperor's bidding—but more at the bidding of my master Christ, the lord of all men—to bring the truth into your land and you into salvation. Let me at the beginning tell you that I say naught against your fathers. They did wonderful deeds; but they were benighted, as everyone was before the Saviour came to earth and as too many of Adam's children still are. Only in Christ, the son of Maria, is bliss everlasting—"

He did not go on overly long. And soon he was speaking of the worldwide fellowship that was Christendom, the Emperor's goodwill, the widening of trade—the yearly herring run through the Sound would find huge new markets—and, to be sure, everything that Christian warriors stood to gain in the course of overcoming the heathen—the Moors in the far South sat on wealth untold—

Shrewd, Gunnhild thought. But she wished he would unloose more of the fire behind his eyes. Where indeed was the truth? Where was Eirik? In Valhall, burning in Hell, in the grave—his sleep would be restless—but no, he was never buried; the wind blew through his white bones and maybe he himself was in and of it.

Could she but know!

When Poppo was done, Harald called on Sveinn the Well-spoken from Fyn, as had been agreed beforehand. The old man rose. "We have heard our guest," he said. "We'll allow the White Christ is a god. His followers are many and strong; his works are seen everywhere. But how great a god is he? Has he the wisdom of Odin, is it he who lifts us out of ourselves in battle, did he beget the first of our kings? When storms bring the rain that quickens the earth, is it not Thor's hammer we see flying, his wheels we hear rumbling; and who but he holds off the trolls at the rim of the world? Aegir gives seafaring luck and sea harvests; when sailors do go down, Aegir's wife Ran makes them welcome. Frey the begetter, Freyja the lover, Frigg the mother are life itself—"

And naught from either side about what man might do, Gunnhild thought. Man, and woman, must meet whatever had been foredoomed elsewhere. Yes, a heathen could earn a seat in Valhall—or, at least, an unforgotten name— through dauntlessness. A Christian could go to a Heaven she ill understood by fighting for Christ; or by sheer meekness, which she understood even less. Never did she hear a word about the wholeness of man with the world, how they together drummed out the flow of time—not that she fully understood that either, but she had known a little of it, and it would not go away from her.

Nor would she let it. She would not slip hold on what power she had to upbear the house of Eirik Blood-ax.

Talk went back and forth, heartfelt, calm, stutteringly wrathful, sternly hard-minded. Harald Bluetooth said little while listening closely. The sunbeams lengthened.

At last Poppo stood among rising shadows and told them: "Enough of this. We'll never settle it so. By the king's leave, tomorrow I'll bear witness and show you beyond doubt the almightiness of Christ. Heat a bar of iron as hot as you wish, my lord. I will take it in my bare hand and be unharmed. Then will everyone believe?"

In his face and voice Gunnhild kenned utter surety. Through the sudden uproar she heard Gudröd draw a sharp breath. Well, she thought, belike a strong shaman could do the same. But best not to say that aloud, now or ever. After all, she had taken the holy water upon her own brow.

A feast followed, rather quiet and not lasting late. Men were thinking hard. Gunnhild slept fitfully during that short, light night. Memories, sorrows, hopes tore through her: Eirik, their children when small, her father and Ulfgard, Eirik, the Finns, Thorolf, Stainmore and the ravens, ghastly Egil, the quelling of Rögnvald Highbone and Haalfdan the Black, Eirik, Thorolf—Her loins burned. But she ought to put that aside and look to the morrow of her sons and Eirik's. Oughtn't she?

Next day she heard chanting from the house that Poppo had. They were holding a mass, she knew; he had confessed, been forgiven, was taking the flesh and blood of his Christ.

He came out clad in rich and orfreyed vestments, in his grasp the crooked staff of a bishop. The Danes stood taut and hushed around an open yard where the coals of a fire glowed white-hot. Blue flames flicked above, while heaven overhead reached cloudless and windless. Upon the fire lay the iron bar, itself nearly as white. Having crossed himself and said a prayer in Latin, Poppo offered his free hand, palm up. A smith lifted the bar in his tongs and laid it there. To and fro before the gazing and gasping walked Poppo. The bar slowly dulled in his grip. Gunnhild could not help marking how the men packed about her stank, as overwrought as they were.

Poppo tossed the now merely warm iron to earth. It thudded. He held his palm and fingers under King Harald's nose. Neither they nor the sleeve behind showed any scorch. "Do you see?" asked the bishop.

The king fell on his knees. One by one, others in the throng did too. Gunnhild kept her feet.

"You are right," the king said fast and loudly. "Christ is right; Christ is lord." He rose and glared around. "Everybody here shall be baptized, acknowledge Christ, and forswear heathenness. I will make all the Danes Christian."

He might well have done this anyway, sooner or later, Gunnhild thought. Her look went to the holy shaw nearby. A breeze had begun to flow, like a blessing. Sunlight trembled and leaves whispered on the trees. Now they would be cut down. Maybe their timber would go to make a church where they had stood. Strange to think so. Everything today was strange. She must wrestle with it, but in her heart, alone, for there was nobody to help her.

VI

Brihtnoth felt the news from Denmark was a sign from Heaven. "The time is overpast for leading your own folk to the Faith," he said.

Haakon nodded. "Else what strength will be given Harald Bluetooth against me?"

"You should not think thus," Brihtnoth reproved him.

"A king must needs," said Haakon softly. Hurt, Brihtnoth left.

Later, though, the priest helped the king put together a speech to give at the Frosta Thing. If the stalwart, stubborn Thraands could be won over, the rest ought to follow before long. And their leader, Sigurd Jarl the kingmaker, had been Haakon's friend from birth.

Thus Haakon fared thither with household and troops. Sigurd was not happy when he learned what the aim was. "You risk everything," he warned. Haakon would not hear otherwise. The jarl scowled and said flatly, "Well, then, I'll stand by you as best I can, but if you don't listen to my redes, the business may go even worse than I fear."

Undaunted, when the time came the son of Harald Fairhair mounted the stone and sent his words ringing over the crowd who were met.

He began by telling them that it was his wish and command to yeomen and crofters, rich and poor, young and old, free and thrall, men and women, that they all should let themselves be baptized and believe in one God, whose

son and self was Christ; give up offerings and heathen
gods; keep the holy days; rest every seventh day; and fast
on Fridays. As he spoke, the unrest grew. Growls went ever
deeper, cries ever more loud.

Yeomen held that the king sought to encumber their
work, and that in this wise they could never take care of
their farms. Workmen and thralls alike groaned that the
king wanted to take their food from them, and without food
they could do nothing. But, said many, it was like King
Haakon and his father and all that breed, to be free enough
with their gold but stingy with food.

Haakon reddened. He was indeed sparing at his board,
only because he hated the gluttony and drunkenness he saw
too often elsewhere. Sigurd plucked at his coat from below.
He bit his lip and stood still. Meanwhile the jarl called for
others to be quiet too. Slowly, uproar became hushed wariness.

A man of mark, Aasbjörn of Medalhus in Gauldal, came
forth. He spoke as weightily as the tide through the fjord.

"It seemed to us yeomen, King, when you'd held your
first Thing with us here in the Thraandlaw, and we'd chosen
you to be our king and you gave us back our freeholds,
that we'd touched heaven with our hands. But now we
know not where we stand—whether we still have our freedom, or whether you'd have us bound anew, in a way unheard of, that we must forsake that faith our fathers and
forefathers had before us, first in the age when they burned
their dead and now when we bury them. They were better
men than we are, and yet their faith has abided with us.

"We've had so much love for you that we've let you lay
down together with us what shall be lawful and right. We
freemen are still ready to uphold those laws you gave us
here at the Frosta Thing, which we agreed to. We'll follow
you and help you keep your lordship, as long as there's life
in any last one of us who're here today at the Thing—if
only you, King, will hold back from wanting more than we
can or will give you.

"If on the other hand you mean to drive this undertaking
of yours through with might and threat, then we yeomen

have agreed we'll be done with you, and find another lord, who'll allow us freedom to keep whatever faith we ourselves want.

"Now, King, you must pick one of these outcomes; and the Thing shall not end before you have chosen."

He stood back. The gathered men roared their yea. Haakon's guards gripped weapons; but the Thraands, though unarmed, outnumbered them and could quickly fetch iron of their own.

Sigurd Jarl hissed at Haakon to step down. Shaken, the king did. Sigurd got onto the stone and raised his arms. Again the unrest sank.

"It is King Haakon's wish, yeomen, never to fight with you," he called. "Not for anything would he lose your goodwill."

He being who he was, the Thraands heeded. After a while, two or three spokesmen said they would go along with that, if the king on his side would offer together with them for peace and well-being, as his father had done. Sigurd plighted this. Thereupon the throng shouted, more or less happily, and the lawman ended the Thing. As always, days went by before the last man had gone home.

Haakon, however, got Sigurd alone and hurled at him: "I said nothing while you, shamefully, sinfully, gave in on my behalf. For I've trusted you, heathen though you are—" He gagged on his wrath.

"I dare hope you were right in this," answered the jarl very mildly. "Believe me, you're dear to my heart, who gave your own name—which was my father's—to my son."

"But you planned this beforehand—with Aasbjörn and the rest—you did, didn't you?"

"Yes, insofar as a man can plan ahead, which isn't much. You see, King, you were set on telling them what you did. I foreknew that someday you would. But I also foresaw an uprising—you, maybe, slain—and we left leaderless, given over to Harald Bluetooth and the sons of Gunnhild. I thought best we set it up to forestall this, smooth it as well as might be, speech rather than spears."

"You told them I'd be there at a heathen feast!"

"As you'd better, King, if you want to keep the kingdom. By then I saw no other way. But surely we can work something out."

Sigurd waited a little span, in the flickering lamplight of the loftroom where they two sat, before he asked, low-voiced: "Is it indeed so dreadful? I think I've done well by you, and yet I also abide by the old gods. It seems to me they're worthy of it. Should I not try to be worthy of them? This Christ of yours is a stranger. Besides, remember your men, King; those in your guard and those throughout the land, who stand ready to die for you. Is troth ever wrongful? Then what about troth to their gods?"

After another while he went on, almost in a whisper: "And is not the world of the gods a wonderful world? Green Yggdrasil, wherein grows and shines everything that is—but also the tree from which Odin hung hanged to win the wisdom that lies beyond death—Thor, holding the trolls and their darkness away from us till the last winter falls—And they're ours, King, not something out of Romaborg and the Empire, but ours. Without them, how long can we stay ourselves?"

He shivered a bit and held his hands toward the lamp-flame, for the evening grew cold. "Enough. But think, I ask of you, King; think."

Haakon had no ready answer. His head whirled and querned. It struck him how Brihtnoth would mislike all this, and then that he really need not tell Brihtnoth. How much could a priest understand of what it took to be a king?

VII

Afterward Haakon often wondered whether that Yuletide forebode his downfall or foretold his upsoaring. Or both? He could not even ask his confessor. He knew what he would hear—useless to him unless he left Norway behind, everyone who trusted him and all his hopes for all of them. Here was naught of the straightforwardness of either the soul or the sword.

He went to Hladi as promised, with no priest in his train. The Thraands were still too touchy about that. This time he stayed at Hladi hall. Sigurd Jarl made him overwhelmingly welcome, but he said little and laughed never. Too much churned around within him—what would happen, what to do?—and a king should not show himself unsure.

He was not at the slaughtering itself, nor did most of the heathen think he ought to be. The gods might take that ill. Besides, men did not want their mood broken by glum outsiders.

Haakon knew what went on. Folk came here from far and wide, bringing with them whatever they would need, and every kind of livestock for offering. Foremost among the beasts were horses. Wildly went the surging, shouting, screams. Axes thudded; knives flared; blood spouted and gushed, the holy blood called hlaut. Most was caught in the hlaut-kettles. Into these were dipped the hlaut-staves, carved with runes and frayed at the ends, to sprinkle the halidom and the gathering with red. Fires roared; flesh cut from the bones seethed. Ale casks were trundled forth, to fill horns. Sigurd led in blessing. First they drained Odin's beaker, for victory and might to the king; then Njörd's and Frey's for peace and good harvests. Then many would drink to Bragi and make boastful vows, for which they were sometimes sorry later on. Last was a drink to the memory of friends and loved ones who were gone.

The early dusk drew in; a chill wind rattled leafless boughs; lesser folk went to whatever shelter was theirs; the great flocked to the hall. The king was already in its high seat. They hailed him, with watchfulness behind their eyes, and settled down along the walls. Flamelight wavered red, filled folds of clothes with darknesses, turned bloodstains black, gleamed off metal.

Sigurd Jarl took the first vessel, a goblet of shining Southland glass brimful of Southland wine. He rose from his seat beside the king's, a little lower, and said into a hush where only the fires gave tongue: "Blessed be this, a draught of life, luck, and faith. In Odin All-Father's name, let us drink to our king."

He brought it to his lips, took a mouthful, and handed it over to Haakon. That they so shared was a sign of friendship, well-nigh brotherhood. If Haakon did not, he might as well dash it in the jarl's face, or spit on every man there.

The king gripped it left-handed. With his right he drew the Cross above, before he drank.

Breath hissed; voices rumbled. A man sprang to his feet. Haakon knew him, Kaari of Gryting, rich and strong, a man whose word was heeded everywhere in the Thraandlaw. Gray hair and beard seemed to bristle as he cried, "What's the king up to now? Will he still not make offering?"

Sigurd answered at once: "The king does what every man does who trusts in his own might and strength. He hallowed the drink to Thor. He made the sign of the Hammer over it."

Haakon could say naught. That might well become deadly. Nor should he be unthankful to the jarl, whose quick wit had saved him from what Sigurd must have seen as sheer rashness. Sour fire seared his gullet. He quenched it somewhat with ale, set his teeth, and stayed where he was, even speaking when spoken to, until time for sleep.

Next day, when they were to feast, men of standing bore in a hlaut-kettle full of cooked horseflesh: for the heathen holy days were not yet ended. They set it down near the high seat, went before the king, and asked him to eat.

During the night, alone in his shut-bed, he had groped his way toward what he must and must not do. "No," he said. "Not for anything would I. This is forbidden food."

The guards of his who were among the guests tautened. Others were not far off. If it came to a fight, belike he'd fall, but not before sending many down to Hell.

The Thraands looked at his face. "Well," said their spokesman at last, "will you drink of the broth, King?"

"No."

Men rose and pressed in close. They reeked of wrath.

"Always erenow have our kings given the gods their honor. At least take a bite of the fat, lord."

"No."

Everyone was unarmed within the hall, but the Thraands stirred and snarled as someone called, "Lay hands on him!" A clatter sounded from the foreroom where weapons had been stacked. The guardsmen swapped glances and braced themselves.

Sigurd's voice stabbed through the racket. "Peace! Peace, I tell you, I, your jarl! You gave your oaths to the king. No grass will grow on the grave of an oath-breaker. Peace!"

Into Haakon's ear he muttered hurriedly, "And you yourself told them you'd offer. You came here to do it. Doesn't your own God want men to keep their promises? Let me settle this, lord. I don't want to lose you."

Both were now on their feet. Haakon stood wordless. The noise died away like an outgoing tide that will in its time come back. "King," said Sigurd aloud, "let us indeed make peace. We know how you were raised abroad, where they worship only Christ. We can bear with that, for you are a good king, who gave us our freeholds back, and wise laws, and avenged us on the Danes. But do you in turn bear with your folk and their ways, King, while we work things out between us. Come, breathe of the holy food, only breathe. That will be enough to keep peace and goodwill among us." He stared around at the gathering. "I myself, with my men, will strike against whomever breaks this peace."

Something gave way in Haakon. What would the Faith gain if he died in strife with his naming-father, his staunchest friend after Brihtnoth? "Yes," he said around a lump.

They stepped aside for him as he walked to the kettle. He snatched a linen cloth off one of the boards set for the feast. This he wrapped around the greasy handle before he lifted it, bent over, and quickly gaped. Stiff-gaited, he returned to the high seat.

Thereafter they could eat and drink in the hall, though not merrily as of yore. Next day the king made ready to go back south. Nobody was happy with the outcome.

VIII

Harald Bluetooth had given Harald Eiriksson a great holding in the north of Jutland, near Aalborg. That town, on the south shore of the Limfjord, was a busy market, the seat of a bishop. Westward the waters broadened from a strait to a salty tidal lake edged with marsh; at length they wound their way around many islands and through more straits to open on the North Sea. The hall bestowed by the Dane-king lay beyond sight of the town, other than its smoke, but word ran swiftly between them.

Gunnhild had spent the summer after Poppo's miracle guesting with this son of hers. His brothers had their own new homes scattered elsewhere. When he went off in viking with them, he left her to run things. She was still doing so as fall came. Her heart leaped when a boy sped in to cry that two longships had rowed in from the east, crowded with men and seemingly stuffed with booty. "Are they King Harald's?" she asked, unmistakably meaning her King Harald. He had left with three, but maybe he'd sent one aside to leave men off nearer their dwellings, or maybe there had been a wreck, or—

"No, my lady," the lad told her. "I wriggled through the crowd at the wharf and heard. Then I thought best I get back to tell you."

She gave him a close look from her seat in the bower. She had been overseeing the weaving of a tapestry. Along with beasts and intertwined boughs, some signs were in it that none but she understood. They had been on the drum in the Finn-hut.

He met her gaze half cockily, half slyly. Kisping was his name, son of a poor fen-dweller. He had come here on his own a few months ago to see if he, aged maybe thirteen, could better his lot. Something about him spoke to her and she said that he could try. Nimble, quick to learn, ready with chatter and small mischiefs but close-mouthed beyond his years when need was, he had gone from sleeping in the stalls and eating with the lowliest to being a footling of hers, who sat at the end of the hall and got what the household servants did. Thus far she had only trusted him with lesser errands, such as going to town today and dickering for fine wool; but she believed he could soon cope with more. Though he would never be tall, his scrawniness had become a wiriness that filled the clothes she gave him, his black shock of hair was trimmed and the sharp-nosed, narrow-chinned face washed clean.

"Who, then, is it?" she asked.

"Arinbjörn Thorisson, Queen, from Norway. I think he's got better than two hundred men with him."

How did the stripling know—yes, clearly he knew—what this was to her? She had not spoken of it while here. But of course folk who had been with her before would talk, bits and snatches which a shrewd, unheeded listener could fit together.

She kept her breath steady as she nodded. "He must want to meet with King Harald. We shall make ready to receive them."

They arrived toward evening, the long light burning on their mail and red on the dust that hoofs and feet raised off the road. Gunnhild went inside and took the high seat. The hubbub in the yard died down. Arinbjörn strode in alone. He did not seem to have changed, the blocky, slow-spoken man. "Greeting, Queen," he rumbled when he halted before her. "May all be well with you and with your son, my foster son, King Harald."

"In his name, welcome." She kept her voice cold. "Lodge here till he comes back. That should be soon. What brings you?"

"Queen, you gave me leave to go order my household and other business in Norway. That's done. I spent this summer raiding in Saxland and Friesland. When we reached Haals at the east end of the Limfjord, I made known that I'd seek the sons of King Eirik and hereafter fare with them. Whoever wanted to go on to Norway was free to do so. They did, in one of our three ships; but she was rather thinly manned, for most chose to follow me. They're good warriors."

A sudden waxing of strength, she thought. However, she held her gladness hidden and waited. Newly stoked fires crackled in the gathering dimness; smoke drifted sharp.

"Yes," said Arinbjörn doggedly, "Egil Skallagrimsson was with me. He skippered the third ship after we bade farewell."

"I want to talk further with you, under four eyes," she told him. "But now take the honor seat and drink, while the housefolk see to the lodging of you and yours."

The hall brawled with cheer and brags until late that night. Gunnhild caught tales of wild sailing and fighting. Over and over they were about Egil, his boldness almost berserk, leaping across a ditch that nobody else could and cutting down a swarm of yokels, hewing his way back to the ships through another pack and thus turning the battle for the Norsemen, the staves that rolled and rang from his lips, he, first of every skald who ever lived. She spoke, in few words, merely when spoken to.

Often her eyes rested on Arinbjörn. Across from her, he glowed as if with the fire itself; his laugh boomed; he was sheer manhood. Lust seethed up in her. So many years of nights alone. She held it leashed within her loins. Otherwise gossip and snickers would whittle away at the awe she needed.

In the morning she asked him to walk with her, rather than that they go into a loftroom. Let folk think this was for seemliness' sake. It would in truth keep her safe from him—or him from her, she thought wryly.

Besides, it was better for her thinking. She was much outdoors, afoot or on horseback; the few guards who trailed had learned not to break the silence.

The sky was an unbounded blue overhead, full of wings beneath strewn clouds, the calls of wanderbirds blowing down like dead leaves off branches. A breeze drifted to and fro, a touch chilly, smelling of wet earth. From the east the sun wanly lighted a land wide and low. A glimpse of the fjord shimmered on the edge of sight. Elsewhere lay shorn fields and sallow meadows, hayricks, woodlots gone brown and yellow. Among them hulked three dolmens. Folk feared those giant-works from an age forgotten and left offerings to slake whatever drows haunted them. Feared too was a mire some ways off. Reeds and willows ringed sullen water and unkempt hummocks, over which still sneaked strands of night-fog. Many beasts and a few humans had blundered in there and never been seen again. Sometimes on hot summer days weirdnesses wavered above it, like twisted glimpses of things elsewhere or things altogether unknown. Afar to the southwest gloomed wilderness.

Hope rose in Gunnhild from the day she first beheld it all. Here might be a land where she could again make herself more than a woman, more than a queen—a witch, to work upon the world for the furthering of her blood.

She and Arinbjörn had walked awhile along a path, four guardsmen well behind them, before she said, "Now tell me how it really is with you and Norway."

"My lady—" He broke off.

Her gray-green eyes, which in this light seemed cat-golden, caught his. She warmed her voice. "Tell me fully and frankly, old friend. I shan't be angered. You've shown how true you are."

"Well—" He cleared his throat and looked straight ahead. "Well, I tried to help Egil in his case, but King Haakon would not be moved. So I paid Egil. It was right, after what he did for my kindred. This summer, as you heard, we went together in viking. Now he's turned back to Norway. He'll winter with my kinsman Thorstein, whom he met in England, and then, he says, go home to Iceland. I don't think we'll see each other again."

She heard the sadness and thought what a kindly farewell that must have been, and what words—yes, from Egil's side, poems—would cross the seas between these two. If Egil ever did get home. Maybe she could yet do something about that. She thrust the whole question aside and pounced on what overshadowed it.

"Drop such bygones. What of yourself?"

He shrugged his thick shoulders. "It's not good between

King Haakon and me. I'm not outlawed, but because of Egil he no longer trusts me." With a sigh: "I'm afraid Thorstein too stands low in King Haakon's mind."

Later, slowly, little by little, she could show him what reason this gave, besides bonds of troth, to help her sons win their birthright. Today she only asked, "What of Haakon himself? We get news here now and then, but you must be much better aware."

"He's been having his own woes, Queen. Maybe that's partly why he's so harsh about Egil. Be that as it may, his—um—apostleship?—making his folk Christian, as I've heard King Harald Bluetooth is making his—it's not been going well. Above all, in Thraandheim this last winter."

The tale of that had flowed from end to end of Norway. As she listened, as she asked Arinbjörn more and more about what had happened and who the men against Haakon were and what they might do, her mind went winging.

Those heathen hersirs and rich yeomen would hardly want to bring in her sons—the sons of Eirik Blood-ax, and Christians to boot. But they seemed very close to striking a blow for what they looked on as their rights. It would not take much to push them to it. A sign or two, as if from their gods—

When her son Harald came home victorious—he must soon; he must be alive and victorious—she'd get him to give her a small house of her own. Meanwhile she could secretly be making ready. Her gaze roved from dolmens to mire. Yes, in this ghost-ridden land she could well do her Finn-weavings.

IX

They were chieftains, the eight who met late in fall— Kaari of Gryting, Aasbjörn of Medalhus, Thorberg of Varness, Orm of Ljoxu from the outlying shires; Blotolf of Ölvishaug, Narfi of Staf in the Vaerdale, Thraand Hook of Eggju, Thorir Beard of Husabo from the inner Thraandlaw. The day was dark outside the house; rain dashed on

hollow-voiced gusts. Fire flapped inside; lampflames guttered; light brought stern faces flickeringly forth amidst
shadow and smoke-haze. The men sat benched around a
board on which stood some jugs of ale. They filled their
own horns when they wanted, for nobody else was in that
room.

Blotolf took the first word. He had called this meeting,
he whose name meant Wolf of the Blood Offering.
"Enough with greetings and everything else. Let's go
straight for the throat. I couldn't give my messengers much
to tell when I sent them around to you, but you know what
it's about. You've all brooded on it."

"Yes," said Aasbjörn in his slow way, he who had spoken for the yeomen at the Frosta Thing a year ago. "The
king threatens our freedom. And yet—yet he's a good king,
mostly."

"You may not have heard of how he's behaving toward
the kinfolk of Thorir of Sygnafylki," growled namesake
Thorir Beard.

Orm shrugged. "That's down there."

"But it bodes what we may await unless we stand up,"
Blotolf said. "Dreams have come to me, nightmares. The
same, over and over. I stumble lost through a land gray,
cold, bare. Everywhere lie dead bones, gnawed by trolls.
In an endless wind I hear a mockery, 'You have forsaken
the gods. So the gods have forsaken you.'" He shivered,
which none had seen him do erenow. "What can it be but
a sign?"

Kaari, who had cried out against Haakon in Sigurd's hall,
clutched his horn till knuckles whitened. "Are we, then,
doomed?"

"No," growled Thorberg. "We're being warned. I've had
that dream myself, Blotolf. This can't be happenstance."

"Whatever our doom may be, we can meet it like men,"
said Narfi.

"But—but I've had a sign too—I think," said Thraand.
"Shortly before your man reached me, Blotolf, I slaughtered
a ewe to Frey. No big giving, but a daughter of mine was
going to be wedded, and I thought—Well, it was a clear,
crisp day. All of a sudden, a swallow darted overhead.

Thrice it winged around me, then flew southward. A swallow, at this time of year?"

"Why, nearly the same happened to me!" blurted Orm. "It seemed—I knew not—strange, and yet—But then your bidding came, Blotolf."

They stared at each other, eyeballs white.

"A sign of hope," whispered Aasbjörn. "But, but who else have we beside Haakon Aethelstan's-foster? The sons of Eirik Blood-ax would lay a heavier yoke on us."

"And Christian laws as well, no?" asked Orm.

"A land without a rightful king—a king of the god-blood—will be as unlucky as a land without its gods," Aasbjörn held.

Blotolf took over. "This is what I wanted us to meet about. I believe everybody knows the king's at Hladi again, with Sigurd Jarl. They'll go south to Moerr and hold the Yule feast there. He thinks it won't be so troublesome as last time. Well, *I* think we can make it be, and more. And that we must."

They sat silent. The fire sputtered. Aasbjörn gazed into it awhile before he half whispered, "Not to overthrow our king—no, no—but show him we mean to stay free."

"He may take it worse," said Narfi uneasily. "Harald Fairhair's brood has never brooked defiance."

"Are we men or are we not?" shouted Blotolf.

"And those dreams, those birds—" Thraand drew the Hammer across his breast.

They drank deep and put their heads together.

In the end they bound themselves. The first four would work to uproot Christianity throughout Norway; they would start by rousing the yeomen of Moerr. The rest would take ships down there soon after Yuletide to burn the three churches Haakon had had built and kill their priests, then return here to help make the whole Thraandlaw ready for whatever followed. They drank to this and swore to this by Odin of the fire, Thor of the storm, Frey of the earth, and Njörd of the sea. In the morning they would slay a horse for the gods.

X

To Thorstein in Vikin, while Egil was staying with him, came word from King Haakon. He heard it grimly.

On the rugged heights eastward grew Eidskog wildwood, almost empty of man. Beyond lay Värmland. Nonetheless, and although the dwellers there were more Swedish than Norse, King Harald Fairhair had brought it under himself, and took scot from it every year. When Harald grew old, he made one Arnvid the jarl in Värmland. Payment dwindled. It stopped altogether during the unrest after Harald's death. None of his sons found time to see about it. However, once Haakon Aethelstan's-foster sat firmly in Norway, he sent men to Värmland to bring him it. On their way home through Eidskog, they were set on by footpads and slain. The same happened to the next band. Tales went around that Arnvid Jarl was behind this, with the treasure taken back to him.

Now Haakon sent a third lot of messengers. They were to seek out Thorstein and order him to go gather the scot. If he would not, he must leave Norway; for the king had learned that Thorstein's uncle Arinbjörn had taken no few followers to join the Eirikssons in Denmark. Haakon was dealing sternly with all Arinbjörn's kindred and friends.

The news was borne by a man who rode ahead of the rest. When Egil heard, he said, "Easy is to see, the king wants you too out of the land. But this is no worthy task for a highborn man like you. I rede you that you call the messengers here, and when you speak with them, I want to be on hand."

Thorstein agreed. The messengers set forth the king's bidding. Either Thorstein went to Värmland or, outlaw, he went to the outlands.

"If he won't," said Egil, "then you'll have to fetch the scot."

They agreed unhappily. "Well, he won't, for it's so lowly a business. He does stand by his oaths, and will go with the king anywhere. As for this faring, he'll give you men and horses and whatever else you need."

The messengers huddled with each other. Then their leader said this would do, if Egil would come too.

Their thought was not hard to make out. The king would be glad if Egil was killed on the quest. Afterward he could handle Thorstein as he chose. "Well and good," Egil told them.

Thorstein felt it wrong that the burden should fall on his guest, but Egil would not hear otherwise. Soon he left with the eight messengers and three of his own crew. Thorstein gave them both horses and sledges, for snow had fallen early this year. The band started off toward the wilderness.

XI

An iron-gray sky hung low above still, cold air, winter-clad earth, and the fir-darkened heights flanking a narrow fjord. The hall that hosted King Haakon bustled with readymaking for Yuletide. Meanwhile he sat blithe, drinking with the two men dearest to him. Sigurd Jarl had guested him at Hladi before they went down to North Moerr. This time he had brought Brihtnoth along, to help him and his few faithful keep holy the mass of Christ. This year it should go otherwise than last.

A noise outside swelled, drawing nigh. A guardsman hastened from the door and told the lords: "It's the yeomen arriving for the feast days. All of them together, it seems like. They must have met somewhere first."

Sigurd stiffened. "What?"

"Armed, Jarl, King. Every man with spear, ax, sword, or bow. Shields, helmets, byrnies on those who own any."

"This does not look good." Sigurd turned to Haakon. "Let me speak with them, if you will. They know me better." And he them, was left unsaid.

Haakon sprang up. "I'll call my troop." They were lodged roundabout, none far off.

Sigurd rose too. "Better wait with that, King, till we see

what this means. If they try to push through such a throng—Those voices have an ugly sound."

Haakon followed a step after him. His head reared above the jarl's lesser height, shining golden, even in this dull light, against the older man's grizzled black hair and white beard. Brihtnoth trailed them, crossing himself.

Scores upon scores had stopped at the gate, a great block of men. Those who had mail stood at the corners to take the brunt of any attack. Mud splashed the rough garb of the rest. They had left a broad, dark trail of it. Their spears were like a shaw with leaves of steel.

Mumbles and growls died away. For a few harsh breaths everybody stood. Then a middle-aged man, whose bearing, byrnie, and furs showed he was rich, stalked forward. Sigurd went to meet him. Their voices crackled in the hush. Now and then a raven croaked.

"Greeting, Sigurd Jarl," said the man gruffly. "Welcome to Moerr, as we hope you and the king will make yourselves."

"Greeting, Bui Styrkaarsson" was the cool answer. "Odd, the way you've fared. Who put you up to this?"

"That recks little, Jarl. Let's only say that we in Moerr have had a year to mull over what happened at your garth last Yuletide. We'll not abide the king flouting the gods like that again, right in our homeland."

"The king worships his own God, who's a mighty one."

"And an outland one, Jarl. Nor does the king want us to stay friends with our gods, who watched over our fathers and their fathers for as long as men have lived in Norway. Shall Thor bring hail and lightning down on us, Frey blight our fields, Njörd sweep the fish from our seas, Frigg let our wives go barren? No, now the king shall make offering, as a king should and must."

Haakon gasped. "Never!" he shouted. "I'll die first!"

Bui glowered at him. "That you will, King, unless you do what's right and fitting."

A snarling rumble rolled after his words. Such few guardsmen as were on hand gripped their weapons tightly and shifted closer to their lords.

"This is too sudden, hersirs and yeomen," said Sigurd. "You understand. We'll withdraw and talk about it between ourselves."

Bui had surely given thought to that beforehand. "You may," he said, "but keep us not waiting till nightfall."

These winter days were very short.

"We shan't. My lord, if you will?"

The door shut behind the king and his men. Household folk cowered back into the deepening dimness of the long room. What firelight there was threw red across the gods, beasts, and snakishly twining vines carved into the pillars. The air felt as frosty as it did outside.

Haakon and Sigurd gazed at one another. Brihtnoth clung to his cross.

"They mean it, King," said Sigurd quietly. "And they outnumber both our troops. Not that we could pull those together before the wave broke over us."

Dusk or no, Haakon could be seen to whiten. His nostrils flared. He gripped the hilt of the knife at his belt as if it were his sword. "Have you gone coward?"

Sigurd shook his head. "I'll die at your side, King, if it comes to that," he answered low. "And we'll take many down hell-road with us. But none of us will outlive the day. The Thraandlaw and all Norway will lie leaderless, open to your foes."

Haakon's hand dropped. "It's mortal sin," he groaned.

Brihtnoth stepped over to him, took him by the shoulder, and looked into his eyes. "Needs must." His own voice shook. "You'll be forgiven. I'll absolve you, my son. Christ will, that—that you may go on as his apostle."

"No." It grated like a keel over a reef. "I'd feel forever—soiled—"

"Because you did what will save you to carry on the holy work, yes, to guard the Church herself?" Sharply: "Or because of your pride?"

Haakon's mouth twisted. "You're as hard toward me as those heathen are."

Brihtnoth let go. Tears on his lashes glinted in the fitful

light, through the bitter haze of smoke. "Oh, my brother, my bond-brother, I don't want you dead!"

He gathered himself and turned to Sigurd. "Jarl," he stammered, "would they, they think it enough if, if I gave myself to them for, for their butchery and their devils?"

Sigurd whistled. "They might well," he breathed. "A man, not a horse but a man, hanged up and speared—Yes, I believe they might well."

"No!" Haakon roared. "Yield a priest to them? What do you think I am?"

Brihtnoth had taken more and more heart. "You'll be saved from sin," he said. "And I'll gain the crown of martyrdom."

"And I'd be the worst of nithings," Haakon spat. "What could I do but fall on my sword?" He gasped and shuddered. "No, Sigurd, I'll give in."

The jarl almost smiled. "Do, I pray you. It's the only wise thing. First let me talk with them. I think they'll go along with your merely showing you don't scorn the gods." He picked his words. "You'd not scorn a brave foeman, would you? You might give ground before him without loss of honor, to fight again later. Shall I try to strike such a deal?"

Haakon jerked his head in a nod.

Sigurd left. Haakon and Brihtnoth stood frozenly. Nobody else dared stir. Only the fire danced and sang its dry song.

A slightly brighter gray and a gust of freshness streamed in as Sigurd opened the door anew. "Yes, King," he said, "it's handseled. If you'll eat a few bites, but drink all the holy draughts at the feast, they'll keep peace."

"So be it." Haakon spoke like stones falling, one by one. "For now."

"I—I'm glad," whispered Brihtnoth.

Sigurd cocked a brow. "Although you won't fly straight to your Heaven?"

"I'd liefer go there with Haakon—with my king—if God allows—But—" Suddenly Brihtnoth wept. "Forgive me. I can't bear to watch it happen. Let me be alone—The lesser house lent us—Let me pray for mercy."

"That's the safest course anyway," said Sigurd.

Thus it came about that the king whom Aethelstan had fostered took into his mouth some cuts from the liver of an offered horse and choked them down. He drained each beaker raised to a god without signing the Cross above. Nobody had the rashness to say more to him than beseemed them. Nor was there the wonted racket and cheer. Yet the fires leaped laughing.

Here in the high North, men had less knowledge than the Southerners did of the blood of Harald Fairhair.

XII

The buildings of Hladi hove in sight. The day was cloudless. Sunlight slanted from the west to blaze off water. The air was so cold that a man felt it flow through his nose. Shadows stretched blue across the snow on either side of a road that had been cleared of it. The sledges that were no longer needed had been left behind, with the heathen carvings on them and the iron jangles meant to frighten off evil Beings. Hoofs rang. Warriors afoot tramped after riding King Haakon, Jarl Sigurd, their own headmen, and Brihtnoth.

"There we are," said Sigurd, as merrily as he was able. "Now we'll have a happier time than hitherto."

"Not long." Haakon's voice fell dully. "I want to be with folk who are mine."

He had said little, none of it glad, as they fared back northward. Sigurd frowned the least bit before he looked across to Brihtnoth on the king's left—the road was barely wide enough—and asked forthrightly what he had not earlier: "Priest, didn't you get your God to forgive him what he must willy-nilly do?"

"I shrove him as best I could, Jarl," answered Brihtnoth, who had himself been short-spoken and troubled on the trek. Then, mostly toward the king: "When we're back in

the South I'll write to the bishops in Denmark and find out
if more penance is required."

He had not uttered this before. He had been turning it
over and over in his mind. Haakon rose in the stirrups.
Breath-smoke burst from him like shots. "In Denmark?" he
yelled. The headmen stiffened their faces.

"None are nearer—my son. And across winter seas—"
Within the hood of his cloak, Brihtnoth's round cheeks
flushed. "Fear not. A contrite heart is always the sacrifice
most acceptable to Christ."

"To beg of Danes—" Harald Bluetooth's bishops; the
friends of the Eirikssons.

From the hall a man came galloping. He drew rein before
them. They too halted. Sigurd kenned the guardsman of his
in whose keeping he had left Hladi while he was gone.
"What is it, Ketil?" he called.

"Bad news, King, Jarl," the man said. "When we spied
you coming, I deemed best I ride ahead and tell you at
once."

"Well?"

"The word came by ship." Even in winter, given fair
winds and weather, which one could not count on, it was
often faster than to go cumbersomely overland. "King, you
won't like it. Soon after you started hither, four shiploads
of men reached Moerr. They burned all three of your—
your halidoms there, and slew the offerers."

Brihtnoth crossed himself, again and again. "The
churches?" he cried. "Their priests? Oh, dear God—"

"Vikings in this season?" rapped Sigurd.

"No, Jarl. They didn't hide their names. Thraands, King,
led by the chieftains Kaari, Aasbjörn, Thorberg, and Orm.
Meanwhile, I gather, others have fared around kindling the
yeomen against your God."

"They're not about to rise, are they? Tell them the king
made offering."

Haakon sighed. "Yes, that can't be naysaid." His shoulders straightened. He spoke as coldly as the winter lay.
"But, Sigurd, I'll not bide in this nest of adders. I'm for
home tomorrow. And when next I come to the Thraandlaw,

it'll be with the might to pay them for their ill will and ill-doing."

Seldom had anybody seen the jarl shaken. "No, lord!"

"Forgive those who wrong you," Brihtnoth beseeched.

"It'd be madness to threaten them, King, let alone make war on your own Norsemen," Sigurd went on. "Here above all, in the Thraandlaw. Here lies the heart of Norway's strength."

"Hold your jaw," Haakon said. "I'll hear no more."

After a little they nudged their horses and rode on toward the hall.

XIII

Snow on the ground had grown old, but late flakes drifted thinly down. As murky as the day was, sight soon lost itself among them. The air was damp and raw beneath a brooding stillness. From Gunnhild's house, the hall of her son King Harald and the buildings around it were hardly more than a blot of darkness. It was a small house, log-built, moss-chinked, turf-roofed. A shed and three pens stood empty. He had lodged the crofter family who dwelt here elsewhere.

But for her he had richly outfitted it, and now in it she met with him and his brothers, seven kings together. Her houseman and maidservants had been told to betake themselves to the hall for this while. They were not surprised. She had sent them off before, whenever she wanted nobody watching. Young Kisping herded them along. Already he swaggered when he was not being sly, as useful as he was becoming to her.

There was only a peat fire, low and blue on the hearthstones, but giving warmth enough and its smoke sweeter than most wood. Light came not merely from stone lamps but from candles—wax candles—in brass holders. It fell over rushes on the floor, tapestries on the walls, chairs brought in and set in a ring around the hearth, furs and embroidery, amber and silver and gold.

The men held ale horns taken off aurochs, she a glass goblet. A cask stood nearby. They had not come to drink, though Ragnfröd had drained and refilled his already.

Gamli, as the eldest, took the word. "Well, Mother," he asked in his blunt way, "why are we here?"

Her gaze lingered a bit on him—how like Eirik he looked—before flitting across the rest. Guthorm, who recalled her father, without Özur's runecraft. Harald, nearly a rebirth of his namesake grandfather. Red-haired Ragnfröd. Flaxen-haired Erling, his sharp face tight, as it was most times. The brown locks and eyes, the sturdy bulk of Gudröd. Stocky, white-skinned Sigurd, his beard still a yellow fuzz but his first viking cruise behind him.

And she—she did not show her age yet. Not much.

Ragnfröd chuckled. "Because she wanted us to be. Why else?"

She smiled and answered them all: "You agreed with your brother Harald that it would be well to meet, and his home would be best for it."

"Not really," said Gamli, who had been settled in Fyn. "But since he wished it—" He shrugged.

"And since he feasts us full, and keeps lots of wenches," Sigurd leered.

"Let's get to business," said Harald. They heeded. He might be the thirdborn, but somehow, unspokenly, most often he took the lead.

"Yes, as you must have guessed, this was Mother's thought," he went on. "But, as always from her, wise."

Gudröd, maybe the one among them most in awe of her, asked low, "And now you'll tell us what you have in mind, Queen?"

"Harald knows, of course," she said. "We've kept it between us. Here in my house you can talk with nobody to pester, or hear and blabber."

Ragnfröd's mirth had fallen from him. He leaned forward, quivering. "Say on, we pray you."

Erling glared at him, as if he misliked having words put in his mouth. Belike he did. She knew that, aside from her, he yielded nothing to any woman but his seed, and little to any man.

"No, first you should speak, Harald," she said.

"Oh, it's straightforward," the host told them. "Think how we and King Tryggvi in Vikin have been raiding back and forth with no gain but booty—and ever less of that as the shorelands are wasted. If King Harald Bluetooth weren't so busy helping spread the Faith through Denmark, we'd hear questions from him about why this is, after all he's given us. He can't suffer it much longer."

"Well do I know," Erling clipped. He among them had seen the Dane-king most lately. "His folk chafe." An icy rage: "Those louts dare make trouble for God's anointed!"

"Louts to reckon with, however, if they're driven past what they can bear," said Harald dryly.

"Cut them down."

"No need," Sigurd put in. "King Tryggvi's been doing that for us." He guffawed. Nobody else did.

"It does not give the sons of Eirik a good name, does it?" Gunnhild murmured.

Silence took hold of the big men. Hands clenched on horns.

Gunnhild kept after them. "Not one of you is wedded yet."

No dearth of brats by lowborn women, some of them not badly fostered out. But highborn men hung back from making ties as risky as these. Thus far she had talked three of her brood out of pressing a suit beyond the earliest feeler. They could afford neither the shame of being outright turned down nor the feuds that would come from their avenging it.

Before they had time for anger she said: "That's as well, or better than well, I think. When you're kings in more than name, you can pick and choose, kings' daughters from Denmark, Svithjod, Gardariki, maybe the Empire itself."

She gave them a small span to think on that. Flames trembled. Shadows stirred.

She had said "you." "We" or "I" would have been a

mistake. Maybe none of them would catch the underlying truth.

While she lived, she would see to the well-being of Eirik Blood-ax's house. His sons, and their sons afterward, yes, their daughters—by women who stood high in the world— would be wolves, not sheep. A memory flicked through her, Seija's hut and the robbers, utter helplessness. The men didn't hear her gasp. She willed the memory back down into the dark.

"I think you can soon reach that," she told them.

"Say on, Mother." Harald's voice throbbed.

As she spoke, new strength and hope took shape in her, like a sword beneath the smith's hammer. "Haakon Aethelstan's-foster sits in the Norway that was your father's. But he sits less firmly than erstwhile. You've heard about unrest yonder."

Gudröd nodded eagerly. "How he buckled under to the heathen Thraands."

"That was the Yule before last. I've later tidings for you."

"How?" blurted Gamli.

"Tales drift in," Harald said. Gunnhild knew he did not want to know more than that. "Boats do cross the Sound, the Danish straits, the Kattegat itself, throughout the year. Our mother has ways of weaving bits and snatches together."

"Is that all, Queen?" Ragnfröd asked hushedly. "How much else could you learn in winter?"

"Harald told you I have ways," Gunnhild answered. She saw Erling and Gudröd cross themselves. But like the others, they stayed rapt, eyes never leaving her.

"You'll hear in full when sea trade starts afresh, and understand I'm right," she gave them. "Meanwhile, though, we should make ready." Now she had knowingly used "we."

"The truth is, at the past Yuletide the Northern yeomen put Haakon Aethelstan's-foster at spearpoint and made him take part in their rites. They burned three of his churches and killed the priests."

Harald sat quiet. Elsewhere she heard the indrawn breaths.

"He's beside himself with wrath." A smile went over her lips. "Wouldn't you be? He's gone south, where they're not so unruly. But after sowing, he means to return with a full levy as well as his household troop and pay this back."

Then she could let Harald take over, hawklike: "When better to strike? If Haakon's at war with his Northerners, he'll have stripped the South of many of its men. We've been raiding Norway here and there, off and on, two or three of us together, those who weren't away in Wendland or wherever. What we can do now is go as one, with every ship we have, every man, and anything Bluetooth will lay to that." Gunnhild thought of her brothers Aalf and Eyvind. Surely they too would be on hand. "We'll overthrow Tryggvi, take Vikin—and there's our foothold for winning back our whole kingdom!"

Although they were not in a hall full of warriors, and had drunk sparingly, the brothers rose and roared.

Gunnhild leaned back into the shadows. Let her sons carry it onward by themselves. Soon they'd believe everything had been their own thought.

XIV

Toward spring a band of men found King Haakon in South Moerr. He had stayed there since leaving Thraandheim, to keep the wildfire of heathen willfulness from spreading farther out of the North. The men had been sent by Thorstein down in Vikin. When he heard that they brought the scot from Värmland, he made them welcome.

Their tale was a long one. Egil and his following had had hard going through woodland and over mountains. Along the way they were set on by a gang at the behest of a farmer to whom he had given deadly grievance—because he felt the man had tried to poison him—but Egil killed two and the rest fled. When they reached Arnvid, the jarl told them he had indeed paid what he owed, and knew not

what had become of it. Still, Egil bore the king's tokens.
At the end of a short stay he was given a treasure of furs
and silver to take back. Egil grumbled that it was less than
what was due, nor did he see any wergild for the messengers slain earlier. The jarl said he had had nothing to do
with that.

Homebound, though, Egil and his men twice met Värm-
landers lying in wait, who fell on them. Egil took the lead
in hitting back. Their dead lay strewn in the wilderness. He
and his had merely a few wounds, none too bad for them
to go on.

He had done this not only by his own strength, but because he had gotten warnings and other help from farmers
in those parts, whom he had befriended. One man's daughter had for some while lain sick. Egil looked into the matter
and found a rune-carved piece of whalebone in her bed. He
read it, scraped the signs off into the fire, burned the whole
bone, and carved runes of his own, which he laid beneath
her. In the morning she was well. It turned out that a love-
sick swain had made the first set, hoping thus to win her,
but lacked skill.

King Haakon's priest Brihtnoth frowned. "Heathen
witchcraft," he said.

"And yet Egil used it kindly," murmured Haakon. "What
a strange mix of good and wickedness he is."

"All men are, my son."

It seemed clear that Arnvid Jarl was behind the whole
bad business yonder. And Egil had been right; the scot
borne to Thorstein was far from enough. Haakon vowed he
would take care of this as soon as might be.

Meanwhile, Thorstein and Egil had done well. The king
sent the band back with word that Thorstein could stay in
Norway, at peace with him. About Egil Haakon said nothing for or against. After all, the Icelander had made known
he would go home when sailing season opened.

And so he did, his knarr well laden. He settled down at
Borg, wealthy and mighty, with no wish to fare abroad ever
again.

Haakon had more reason to forgive those of Arinbjörn's

kin who were in Norway than Thorstein's sending him his scot. He could ill afford foes, or even disgruntled chieftains, in the South: for he meant to muster levies from those shires to chasten the Thraands with fire and sword.

He seldom smiled anymore. When he did, it was a twisting of a tightly drawn mouth. He spoke only in a few sharp words. No longer was merriment seen around him. He did whatever was called for but never asked others for their redes. If skalds of his, Guthorm Sindri or Eyvind Finnsson or anyone, made poems for him, he rewarded them as was seemly, but in such wise that everybody wondered how closely he had been listening. Brihtnoth himself felt the cold withdrawal.

However, the king could not well say no when at last this priest who was his soul-brother plucked up the will to tell him they must go aside and talk. They sought the chapel Haakon had ordered built a while ago. Above the altar, Christ on his cross looked down through the dimness of the stark and tiny room. Wind blustered around the walls, casting spatters of rain.

"This is for your sake, Haakon," Brihtnoth well-nigh pleaded. "Weeks of Sundays slip by between the masses you hear."

The king did not meet his eyes, less from shame than because his own gaze was too bleak. "I've scant time to spare," he snapped. "I'm in a bigger undertaking than you understand."

"You never lack time for the hersirs and other heathen men who come to hear what you want of them—" Brihtnoth's voice dropped. "Haakon, when did you last receive the Blood and the Body?"

The king made his grim grin. "No use my confessing till the business is done with. Heathen men? Yes, and much else, day by day. Needful."

"Your salvation is needful above all—"

"Enough! Have you anything further to say?"

Brihtnoth bit his lip and bowed his head. A spurt of hail rattled on the roofshakes. "My son," he asked after a while, during which the king restlessly shifted his feet, "you're hardening your heart against sorrow, aren't you?"

For a flash as of lightning, a shield-wall broke. "I have to make war on Sigurd!" Haakon screamed.

Iron clamped back down. "There is no other way. Not if I'm to keep my kingdom and my honor."

Brihtnoth signed himself. "Well, yes, you're doing God's work—"

Haakon whirled about and went out into the rain.

Brihtnoth held back thereafter. He tried not to show the hurt within him.

He did not go along in the mustering as he had gone along to Denmark. Too much then had sickened him. And now he recalled everything he had heard about Eirik Blood-ax, Haakon's brother.

Snow melted in gurgling freshets under the rain. Earth greened; leaves unfolded; wanderfowl came home; soil newly plowed and seeded warmed beneath a summer-bound sun. The war-arrow went from house to house in shire after shire. Men kissed their wives or sweethearts, took what weapons they owned, rode or trudged to South Moerr. Ships, freshly scraped and caulked and rigged, slithered thither. The neighborhood roared.

Then as Haakon was embarking, another ship steered into the fjord. Her crew had rowed their hearts out to get here before too late. The skipper bore tokens and tidings. The Eirikssons were come from Denmark with a big fleet. In a battle at Sotaness they had driven King Tryggvi Olafsson from his own ships. Vikin lay open to their plundering. They told the world that this was the least of what they had in mind. Whether from fear or hitherto hidden wish, no few Vikiners had already gone over to them.

When the king heard, he sat still for barely a breath. Then when he spoke, it was as if a sudden thawing went through him too. "Send straightaway to Sigurd Jarl and headmen everywhere who are not here today. We must all meet at once—meanwhile I'll wait—meet against these foes we share."

XV

Within five days, hulls cramful of men were striding over the water toward Haakon's. At first he was astonished. True, his messengers north had gone in a light karfi, rowing by turns without stop, far enough offshore not to blunder onto a rock in the dark. But few of these new-comers were lean longships. Most were of every kind from knarr to fisher boat. Not only must the crews of the slowest have worked themselves like oxen; they must have gathered before his word got there.

Spears and helmets flashed brighter than the sea-blink. Haakon tautened. Of course Sigurd Jarl had had spies and scouts out. He knew the king was coming, and about what time to await him. He had sent his own war-arrows well beforehand.

Haakon could feel the wariness at his back. Iron clinked; feet shuffled; voices mumbled. Was this to be an onslaught?

The Northerners hove to beyond the fjord mouth. One dragon moved landward. The figurehead was down and the mast stepped, a white shield hanging from the peak. Gladness rushed up in Haakon. He masked it as well as might be and stood, arms folded, on the wharf in front of his guards. His banner fluttered above.

The ship docked. A gangplank thumped. Sigurd Jarl walked to meet the king.

"Greeting, lord," he said steadily. "We are here to give you the help you want, if you will have it."

"Greeting," Haakon answered. "What does that mean?"

"I think you understand, King. These are the fighting men of the Thraandlaw, North Moerr, and as far up into Haalogaland as any were able to reach us from. They'd much liefer make war at your side than against you. But first there must be peace between all of us. Else—I hope I can make them turn home rather than attack."

Haakon nodded. "I looked for that."

Sigurd's eyes searched his face. "King, here are Aasbjörn

of Medalhus, Kaari of Gryting, and others who swore to uphold the gods by any means needful. Here are the yeomen who would hear of nothing but that you, King, honor the gods yourself. Yes, here are some who burned churches and slew priests. They ask for an end to the fears that drove them to this. I told them I did not know what you, King, would be willing to give."

Haakon's words came steady as surf-beat. "I have had these past days to think it over. They shall not believe that I yield anything out of weakness. They shall say this forth for all men to hear, and they shall swear to follow me faithfully and obey my laws, now and for as long as any of us may live. Then I on my side will give them peace and forgiveness. Every man in Norway shall have the right to worship as he sees fit, if he does not offer humans to the gods and does not raise his hand against Christians who have not harmed him, or against their halidoms."

"King," said Sigurd aloud and slowly, "that offer is high-hearted and openhanded, everything any among us hoped for and more than most did. I take it with deepest thanks, and I know that the men with me—your men, lord, now and henceforward—will do likewise, and thereafter gladly lay down their lives for you. Norway never had a luckier day than when we chose Haakon the son of Harald Fairhair to be our king." It seemed almost that tears glimmered in his eyes. "But this is so altogether like you, whom I named and who named my son. Well-nigh could I bless the foe that's brought us back together."

They clasped one another's arms and stood thus for a little span. Those ashore saw them athwart the sunlit water. A breeze stirred Haakon's banner and a lock of the hair that shone on his bare head.

Then they let go and Sigurd laughed low, a laugh that crackled like fire. "But the task on hand is to drive them out, killing as many as will glut the ravens. We'll talk about that, King, you and I, if you wish, as soon as the oaths have been given."

That took a while. The newly come ships must let off their crews, to make camp, roast meat, eat and drink, and often reawaken friendships with Haakon's, as the long summer day drew into twilight. While that went on, leaders kept aside to share knowledge and thoughts. The news had very lately reached the king that the Eirikssons had left the Oslofjord and crossed to Agdir at the southwest corner of Norway. Tryggvi Olafsson had, earlier, withdrawn before their overwhelming might. Maybe he was now trying to regain something in Vikin; but aside from that, he could not help.

In the morning Sigurd hallowed a stone with the blood of a black cock he had brought along. Thereafter he laid on it a heavy golden arm-ring. Yes, he was a foresightful one. Upon that ring, the chieftains plighted themselves to Haakon by Njörd, Frey, and great Thor. He in turn swore by his own honor to forgive them and free them. They could hardly ask more than that from him, not yet.

King and jarl had both seen to it that ships were well stocked with food, water, ale, and other needs. They set forth that afternoon. It was slower going than hitherto, rowing the whole way because none must outrun the rest, going ashore to sleep whenever that could be done because warriors must be kept fit for war. Still, they went on south, past the many islands and high mainland. Beyond Stad, a scout karfi met them to tell that the Eirikssons had heard about them and were bound north. Not far beyond Stord, on whose wave-washed rocks Haakon was born, the fleets met at the island Körmt.

There did both hosts make landing and draw up their arrays on Ögvaldsnes, across a strait from Haugar, where Harald Fairhair lay buried. Both were big. Both lost heavily in the battle. King Haakon kept at the forefront, shouting, reaping, every unsureness and dread forgotten while he fought. A kingly standard strove toward him. The two bands clashed. It became a wildness of smiting, striving, shoving onward across the fallen with breath harsh in the throat and head full of noise. Haakon spied a burly, rugged, black-bearded man who wore a gilt helmet and hewed from behind a shield-wall of guards. But it was not—barely not—Haakon who dealt the death-blow. Axmen of his bat-

tered the shields aside. One blade bit into the man's neck.
Blood spouted. He sagged onto the earth. His standard fell
over him.

At that, his followers broke. As always, once dismay
began, it went through ranks like a scythe. Chunk by chunk
of men, the troops of the Eirikssons gave way and fled,
some fighting rearguard as best they could in their weariness, back to their ships.

Men heaved at grounded hulls and scrambled aboard.
Oars clattered forth. Scattered, but raggedly regathering as
it went, the fleet of the Eirikssons stood out to sea.

Sigurd Jarl looked across the stricken field. "That was
skillfully done, truly, King. When the rest of your nephews
knew they had lost, they kept fear from running wild, and
got most of the folk who were left to them away alive."
His smile flickered wry. "Well, they're grandsons of your
father. We've not seen the last of them."

"Would we had felled more," answered Haakon. His
cheeks and brow were still white with battle rage. "Do you
know which one of them we got?"

"I think it was Guthorm, lord."

Haakon recalled in passing what was right and honorable. "He was a king. We'll leave some men here to bury
him. Yes, one or two should be Christian. But otherwise
we'll go after that wolf pack and bring them to bay."

It did not fall out thus. Every man on every ship rowed
his best, but all were tired and many were wounded. Haakon's could only hound the wakes of the foe. Off East
Agdir these caught a fair wind, hoisted sail, and set across
the Skagerrak for Denmark. There was no use in the Norse
chasing them farther.

Nevertheless Haakon had won a ringing victory. When
again his men were ashore, they surged around him; shouts
echoed off hills and over the waters; fires leaped; horns,
hands, and weapons lifted to hail him; reckless oaths were
sworn to him; love thundered around him. He felt it deep
in his bones, more than he felt the sun.

Sigurd Jarl found a short spell in which to ask, "What
have you now in mind, King?"

"Well," said Haakon through the racketing, flame-harried dusk, "most men had better go home, hadn't they? This land can't feed them for long, and they have their work to do."

"Of course, King. Still, I've heard as how there's some trouble off in Värmland."

"Yes." Quick eagerness sparkled. "Get Vikin back under Tryggvi as it should be, and then move eastward. That won't call for over-many men, will it?"

"I don't believe so, King. But let's think and talk about this tomorrow, we two."

XVI

At the mouth of a bay on the Jutland coast, looking east across the Skagerrak and southeast toward Fyn and Sjaelland, Aarhus had become a town of wharfs, warehouses, markets, workshops, biggest and richest anywhere in Danish lands north of Hedeby. The king kept it well guarded and visited it often. Even before his own conversion it was the seat of one of the three bishops thus far in Denmark.

To that man's house came Gunnhild. She went on horseback, for a queen ought not to walk through streetfilth. Some of her attendants had come with her from Aalborg and others from the kingly hall where she had now been given lodging. But after she dismounted she walked unfollowed to the door.

The house lay with two lesser buildings and the cathedral in a cobbled close. That church was of wood, small when one remembered the great stone work in York; but its threeroofed stave walls reared high enough into heaven. Rooks fluttered black around the spire. Clouds drifted fleecy beneath the cool blue sky of late summer. A breeze scattered somewhat the racket and smells of the town.

A priest and two acolytes waited for Gunnhild. They led her to a room where she could speak with the bishop apart from everyone else. She had asked for that, rather than

calling him to her. That any queen would do so, let alone
this queen, must mean something momentous.

The room was handsomely wainscoted and well lighted
by wax tapers. Two chairs stood with a little table between
them. A white robe around his gauntness, Bishop Reginhard sat beneath a finely wrought gilt-and-silver crucifix
from the Empire. He lifted his hand as Gunnhild neared.
The rushes on the floor whispered under her feet.

"Greeting, Queen." His voice, strong for an old man's,
had over many years lost most traces of his German motherland. His hair was a thin snowdrift, his face was creased,
but head rested upright on neck and some teeth were left
to keep the lips firm. "Be welcome in God's name and with
God's blessing."

She halted, lowered her lashes, and murmured, "Humbly
do I thank the reverend father." At that, his dim eyesight
sharpened upon her. "You are very kind to receive me. Ever
shall you be in my prayers."

"The queen is gracious," he said. "Do be seated and take
refreshment."

The acolytes brought wine in cunningly wrought glass
goblets, honeycakes on a platter, and napkins. They left the
door ajar for seemliness' sake—inwardly, fleetingly, Gunnhild grinned—but nobody would stay in earshot of anything less than a shout. She partook as sparingly as
Reginhard did. He asked how her journey had gone. She
told him it had not been bad. She held back from saying
that, had she had her wish, she would have been mounted,
working the unrest out of herself and faring twice or thrice
as fast as in the wagon that her rank and errand called for.
It had also been a bother to smile and make talk with the
well-off men who guested her along the way. But at least
yestereven in the kingly hall there had only been underlings, who left her free to think.

"Eighty miles, was it, ninety, a hundred?" said Reginhard. "A wearisome journey. If you had sent for me, I
would have come as soon as I could."

"You have too much else on your hands, lord, the work
of the Church and the furthering of the Faith. I really dared

not wait." He might meanwhile have heard news and had thoughts that set his mind, like bronze hardening in a mold, in another shape than what she hoped to cast.

Reginhard nodded. "You did bravely, then, Queen, all the more when you are mourning your valiant son."

Suddenly, unawaitedly, that called Guthorm back, the bairn in her arms, the youth growing into a manhood so much like her father in looks, gruff stubbornness, rough mirth, and, yes, now and then, kindliness, blood of her blood, child of her Eirik. She caught a breath. Her eyes stung. She blinked them while she uttered the words she had laid out for herself. "I, his brothers and I, we buy masses for his soul's repose."

Mostly, they planned his avenging.

Newer memories stabbed her afresh. As in Norway, as in England and Orkney, here she had woven a web for the catching of knowledge. Merchant ships went to and fro whenever they could bypass any fighting. Sailors talked with sailors, or with whores or anybody. Someone lowly, unheeded, maybe in a corner of an inn, listened on her behalf and brought the tale to her. Sometimes, also, she met a man who had arrived on business and sounded him out. Folk had gotten used to her piercing questions. They did not always hear those she asked elsewhere than at the garth or, lately, had Kisping ask. And there were still other means of learning, although she could not yet safely use them more than a little.

Thus already she had heard verses of a poem that the skald Guthorm Sindri—Guthorm!—made for King Haakon Aethelstan's-foster after the victory at Körmt.

> "Meeting, then,—how I remember!—
> the might of the lord of bowstrings
> soon made the sons of Eirik
> see that they could not match him.
> Beaten, they reckoned it better,
> those brothers, to hasten elsewhere.
> He followed them as they were fleeing
> to find for themselves a haven."

Wrath cold as a winter sea bore grief away on its tide. Through it she heard the bishop say shrewdly, "But I hear they have not given up their wants in this world. Nor, I think, have you, their mother."

Gunnhild got back her steeliness. "No, they shall have their birthrights. I'm here to speak with you about that, Reverend Father, forasmuch as my son King Harald and I dwell in your see."

She marked the slight uneasiness: "I cannot take sides in such a quarrel, my lady."

She pounced. "Not even in Christ's cause?"

He steadied, he whose flock were no less warlike than their unchristened neighbors. "The archbishop in Hamburg has issued no judgment. Mother Church can only pray that her children make peace with each other."

"But with heathens?" she snapped. "Or with one who's forsaken her?"

He started. "What mean you? King Haakon—" For the first time in their few meetings, she heard a quaver of age. "—he strives to bring his—bring the Norse into the fold."

"Maybe at first he did, lord Bishop, though with only half a heart. King Harald Gormsson lets nothing stand in the way of winning the Danes over." Well, many had already been Christian, and few of them seemed ever to have been idolaters as earnest as most Norse. Maybe it had to do with Denmark being a lowland, always more open to the outside. She swatted the useless thought off. "But you know how Haakon twice yielded to the heathen and shared in their sacrifices."

Reginhard's nod was stiff. "Yes," he said as if unwillingly. "It was that or die, or at least lose the kingdom. A hard choice. He could have gone straight to Heaven, a martyr. But—I and my colleagues in Ribe and Hedeby—we decided that to drink this bitter brew was in its way an offering to Christ. We did set him penances, through his chaplain."

"Not overly strict, I heard."

"No. Prayers, and land-gifts to the Church. His burden in itself is heavy." The blood of warrior forebears stirred.

"Moreover, this year he set out to break the will of the heathen against the Faith."

"Or against him, my lord?"

Reginhard sighed. "Yes, I fear that house has always been overweeningly proud. Nevertheless, he does God's work, as I trust your sons will."

"Dare I wonder if my lord bishop has as yet heard the evil tidings?"

He stared, swallowed, and said, "Speak, Queen."

"When my sons—King Eirik's sons went lately to overthrow him, Haakon did worse than make peace with his rebellious subjects to get their help for his unrighteous rule. He promised them they may henceforward carry on their devil worship unhindered."

"I—Rumors have reached me, Queen. Only rumors. They may be false."

"Forgive me if I say otherwise. My lord bishop will hear the truth as the weeks go by. I thought best you learn it sooner."

"This is—a grave matter indeed."

"My lord, if you would not lose Norway altogether for the Faith—until such time as her rightful kings reclaim her—you, all the bishops, had better make Haakon know how deeply he has sinned."

"If that's true, Queen. And any terms of absolution are for the Church to set."

"Of course, Reverend Father. But while you wait to find out more, would it not be wise for you bishops to get in touch and decide what to do if Haakon is guilty? I swear he is. Be ready to show at once that the Church is not weak and will not let God be mocked."

Gunnhild's voice flowed softly. "Let me beg forgiveness if I, a woman, a laywoman, am too forward. Nevertheless, lord Bishop, I must say for my own soul's sake that I know the Norse well. And year by year I've gathered knowledge of Haakon, and thought on him." How she had thought on him! "Is my counsel unworthy of a hearing? Only a hearing, Reverend Father, words that I humbly lay at your feet."

He could hardly answer other than: "Say on, Queen. Your wisdom is famous."

She would need several days, she thought, and charm as well as talk, before he agreed to do what she wanted and started winning his fellow bishops over to the same.

XVII

Birches were yellow when King Haakon came back. Wind soughed cold through all trees and clouds flew swifter than the uneasy birds, their shadows scything over faded meadows and dark stubblefields. Ahead loomed a hall, the dragons carved from the beam-ends seeming to threaten heaven as well as trolls and night-gangers. This was the house in Rogaland where Harald Fairhair died. Not far off, his howe and the tall runestone on it looked over a strait to the ness where his last son smote his grandsons.

Haakon's men rode into the yard with a shout. Horns dunted; spearheads flashed; a banner snapped in the wind. More than booty, they brought victory home with them. Now they looked for feasting, sport, women, and many gifts from the king.

Folk churned about to welcome him. What months he had been away! How wonderful to see him again, and so gladsome! Word had of course sped before him, and things were ready. The news was of his faring to reclaim Vikin, then on into Värmland, putting Arnvid Jarl to flight and setting another man in the post, taking heavy gild from those farmers who, witnesses told him, had hindered or slain his messengers, and sending off hostages before he went farther. That was into Västergötland, whose dwellers he scattered in battle and likewise laid under scot. Thus did he make a bulwark for Vikin against the Danish shires on the peninsula; or at least this was the groundwork of it.

Only then did he turn back. At the Oslofjord he and Sigurd Jarl bade farewell. The Thraands went home. Haakon disbanded the rest of his Norsemen, aside from the household troop, and rode to the holding at which he meant to winter.

When he saw Brihtnoth in the crowd, he called out cheerfully. When he saw the starkness upon the priest, much of his glee ebbed.

After the feast had gotten noisy, they two could swap a few quick words. "You are troubled," said Haakon.

Brihtnoth nodded. "Well might I be, King, like any Christian man."

Haakon braced himself. "Yes, we'd better talk alone tomorrow."

They met in a loftroom next morning. It was gloomy and chill. A storm had swept in. Wind roared and shrilled. Rain hammered the roof and dashed against the walls. Now and then came a burst of hail like knucklebones knocking.

Neither man sat down. They stood stiffly before one another, the king in fur-lined tunic and thick woolen breeks, gold coils enwrapping his wrists, the priest in a coarse brown robe and sandals on stockingless feet, a cross hanging on his breast. With none to overhear, they spoke as plainly as two yeomen.

Haakon took the lead, his voice calm but with iron underneath: "Best we go straight at things."

"For your sake above all," answered Brihtnoth. His own speech was firm, yet somehow tender. His face seemed doubly pale in the murk; he had mostly been indoors. "I know you've countless calls on your time, but this comes first."

Haakon tried to smile. "I've always time for you. What are you thinking of?"

"Surely you know. Your salvation."

Haakon's lips clenched. "I'll confess to you as soon as I can."

"You've seldom felt hurried about that. But it's not what I have to say to you today."

Haakon nodded. "I can guess. I knew you'd mislike my swearing oaths with the Thraands. Hark. Had they and I fought, the winners would have been the sons of Eirik

Blood-ax and Witch-Gunnhild. As it was, Christ gave us victory over every foe."

The question thrust: "Christ, or Odin? Often has Satan helped men to worldly gains, luring them on to damnation."

"Yes, I've let them worship as they wish. I'd scant choice. But they'll leave Christians in peace, free to preach."

"Preach at stopped-up ears and barred doors. Haakon, men who came home before you did bore ghastly tidings. They said that whenever your warfaring heathen offered to the demons, you were on hand."

"They told it happily! What else would you have had me do? The bond between us was still weak. I must needs strengthen it."

Lightning flashed, late for this time of year. Its glare passed blue-white through the gut stretched across the window. Thunder boomed like huge wheels rolling down the sky.

Brihtnoth bit his lip. "I understand. The news burned and froze me, but, yes, I understood how you might feel a need."

Haakon's voice shook a little. "Old friend—"

Brihtnoth raised a palm as if to fend him off. The ring glinted that had been his gift. "I'm not speaking for myself. Nor for—us. I bear the word of Holy Church."

"What is it?" asked Haakon flatly.

"I've kept it quiet, but now—" In a rush: "As your chaplain, I did what I'd done before and wrote to the bishops in Denmark to beg forgiveness for you. I tried to show what a cleft stick you were in. This year I must do it twice. Not long ago, the answer to my second letter reached me, signed and sealed by all three of the bishops."

"In Denmark."

"They're the nearest, as well you know. Although I've no doubt their archbishop will agree." Lightning and thunder broke in. "Haakon, this time they are stern. They say you have transgressed greatly—and it's true, Haakon—so greatly that only a saint can give absolution. You must go on pilgrimage."

The king took a backward step. "No!" he yelled amidst the wolf-howl of the wind.

"Yes. I told you there were two letters. The first would have sent you all the way to Rome. I wrote back, pleading that that's impossible unless you leave Norway forever. I strove to make clear how with time and patience you can evangelize this land through the love your folk bear for you, while—others—could not."

Haakon waited. Flashes and thunderclaps followed each the last in less time than a man might say a hasty Paternoster.

He could not hear, but he saw Brihtnoth sigh. "Well, I have the second reply, and it allows no further appeal. However, you may go to the shrine of St. Eadmund in England."

When Haakon kept still, the priest half smiled. "That's fitting, really. I believe it's a sign of God's own mercy."

He need not tell what they both had known from childhood. A hundred years ago, the Danes under Ivar the Boneless took King Eadmund of East Anglia captive. When he would neither renounce Christ nor become the vassal of a heathen, they bound him to a tree and made him a mark for their bowmen. These days, no few of those who sought to his tomb at Bury St. Eadmunds came from the Danelaw.

A dream flitted across Haakon's eyes. "England—"

"We'll go together." Brihtnoth's eagerness yielded to earnestness. "You must also swear that when you return you'll never again attend or take part in an unholy rite, and you'll work more strongly than hitherto in bringing the Norse to the Faith."

Likewise did Haakon harden. "No. It cannot be."

Thunder crashed. It was as if a hammer had hit Brihtnoth in the belly. "Haakon," he cried, "not even this?"

Strangely, now it almost seemed to be the king who beseeched. "Can't you see? Have you forgotten the world? If I left, at any season, for any span of time—while I was gone, Norway would lie bare to the sons of Gunnhild. Oh, surely she's had a hand in this. Yes, and Harald Bluetooth also. Can the smith leave the sword half forged? Norway's no more welded together than iron bars on the anvil. Sigurd Jarl and I, we talked about the new laws we need for defense. That work comes first."

Brihtnoth reached out toward him. "Haakon, Haakon, your soul comes first. Till you've made your peace with Mother Church, you're excommunicate. I *cannot* shrive you."

"I could be murdered in England," said Haakon shakenly. "The saint's namesake, my foster father Aethelstan's brother, was. Gunnhild has her ways."

Brihtnoth tightened. He used scorn like a whip-touch on a horse. "Do you fear her more than you fear Hell?"

Haakon chilled. "Were you any other man at all, I'd draw sword on you for that."

They stood awhile. The lightning flashes grew fewer and fainter. The thunder-wheels growled farther off. The wind slackened somewhat, the rain fell less thickly.

"We share so much," said Brihtnoth at last. "Don't take it away from me."

"I can't break my promises to the men who went into battle under my banner," said Haakon as low.

"You'd set your—your honor in their eyes above God's judgment on you?"

"I dare hope God will understand faithfulness." The fading lightning flickered; the thunder muttered. "Arinbjörn Thorisson does." Hakon squared his shoulders. "Be that as it may, I am the king here."

Sudden bitterness lashed. "And you're bent you'll stay king to the end of your days? You, a man without a son?"

Haakon stood.

Brihtnoth's anger melted. Tears gleamed. "If, if you do, I can't stay and, and watch you damn yourself," he stammered. "God forgive me, I've not the strength to, to suffer that. I'll have to flee."

Haakon's look through the dusk of the room was hawk-bleak.

"I'll always pray for you. Always." The priest fell on his knees. He clutched the cross in both hands and lifted it, trembling, toward the king. "But I beg of you, today—"

"It does not become a wellborn man to beg," said Haakon.

He strode off. Brihtnoth hunched on the floor.

The storm mildened as fast as it had risen. Rainfall went on. The king donned a hooded cloak and walked forth into it. For a while he wandered along drenched woodland paths, then out to Harald Fairhair's barrow by the sea, where he stood speechless and unstirring. The guardsmen who came behind could only shiver, snuffle, and sneeze. They did not risk asking why; they had learned something about his moods.

XVIII

When Thorfinn Skull-splitter died, his oldest living son, Haavard the Fruitful, became the jarl of Orkney. Under him the islands lay in peace and well-being.

A sister of his had a son called Einar, whose fondness for eating got him the nickname Bread-and-Butter. He was nonetheless a chieftain with a goodly following, and a doughty warrior who went in viking most summers. When, this fall, he steered into Wide Firth, his uncle happened to be at the hall on the neck of Mainland, and gave a feast that lasted for days.

Nobody listened more keenly to Einar's tales of his doings or asked livelier questions than Haavard's wife, Ragnhild Eiriksdottir. She sparkled, her smile flashed, her laugh sang, long lashes fluttered over bright eyes, and beneath the gown of fine linen her hips swayed when she walked. Men said aside to each other that they hadn't seen a woman so bewitching since she herself came here to wed the brother of her late husband Arnfinn.

Afterward a coldness fell between her and the jarl. Among other things, she bore him no child. As if to keep up his own nickname, he now oftenest bedded lowborn wenches or thralls. She stayed sharp of wit, but also sharp of tongue and inwardly withdrawn. In the days and evenings of this merrymaking, she bloomed anew.

From the start, she and Einar talked much together. Soon it was apart from others. A maidservant or two would be at hand, or at least in sight, but these had been picked by her, young girls taken in raids and brought along from Caithness. She had seen to it that they learned little Norse, and had made them as fearful of her anger and fawningly thankful for a small kindness or soft word as any bitch hound.

She told Einar over and over how braw a leader he was. He grinned and strutted. When one day she added that he would make a far better jarl than Haavard, and that whoever wedded him would be a lucky woman, he was shocked. "Don't say such things," he chided her, awkwardly rather than strictly, "you, a lady of worth, wife of the greatest man in Orkney."

Her look searched him. He was big-bellied for his age, but big too in shoulders and thews. "I think my life with Haavard won't last much longer," she answered. "And to be frank, if you don't want the power and fame for yourself, many others wouldn't be so honest."

He stuttered but did not scold further or stalk away. Her smile sent warmth aflow around him. "That same high-mindedness would soon make all of us in Orkney glad to be—under you," she purred.

She kept after him throughout his stay, not pushing over-ly hard but not letting up either. Sometimes she told him somewhat of how wretched she was with a swine like Haavard. Other times she spoke at more length of how, behind the spendthrift show, Haavard was a dolt and a coward, bound to bring woe unless he was gotten from underfoot. At last she murmured of what help she could give toward that end.

So did she kindle greed and lust in Einar and blow them into flame. Before he went home, they had made the deal that he would kill his uncle and she would wed him.

XIX

A lean, pinch-faced young fellow came to the bishop's house in Aarhus and asked to see the reverend father. When he made known to the acolytes that he was from King Harald Eiriksson and Harald's mother Queen Gunnhild, they led him straightaway to Reginhard. Duly humble, he gave his name, Kisping, and his errand. His lord and lady had heard that lately there arrived here an English priest from Norway, one Brihtnoth. With winter drawing near, any ship from abroad raised talk; and the knarr that brought this man belonged to King Haakon Haraldsson yonder, crewed by the king's own troopers. They let the priest off and stood again out to sea, northbound, the very next day.

The bishop nodded. "Yes," he said low, "Queen Gunnhild would soon hear." Louder: "How does it concern them at Aalborg?"

"They're bound to wonder, Reverend Father," answered Kisping, smoothly and smiling. "Furthermore, Queen Gunnhild well remembers Brihtnoth from York. He did more than he may know to open her eyes to the Faith. If he's broken with the foe of her sons, she'd be most happy to see him again."

"And question him endlessly, hunting his knowledge as a ferret hunts mice." Reginhard sighed. "I know her."

"Forgive me, lord, if I get above myself. But is not King Haakon under the ban of the Church? Is that why Brihtnoth left him?" When the bishop stayed silent, Kisping smiled anew. "My queen—it's not in my message, lord, but she has remarked that maybe a peace between everybody can somehow be worked out. For this, of course, the sons of King Eirik will first need to understand fully how things are in Norway."

"Pious words." The old man's voice was parched. "Well, despair is a sin. And certainly their wishes must be considered. Come back tomorrow, messenger, and we'll talk with Brihtnoth."

On that day Kisping saw the priest haggard, eyes dark-rimmed for lack of sleep. Wearily he told how King Haakon had offered him passage to England but had not forbidden his choice of Denmark. There he would try his poor best to make the bishops relent.

"That cannot be," said Reginhard as he had already done, sadly, unshakably. "I will ask on your behalf—"

"The reverend father is merciful," whispered Brihtnoth.

"But you should know as well as I that Mother Church has yielded the utmost she can, and found it too little for Haakon's pride."

"Haakon's need, my lord. If Solomon could offer on hill-tops—" Beneath the gaze from the chair, half blind though it was, Brihtnoth shrank. "No, I'm sorry, the Saviour forever changed that."

"The prophets had already done so." Reginhard sat awhile. Stillness thickened. "Well," he said into it, "however much in vain, my correspondence will take time. Meanwhile sailing season ends and you, Brihtnoth, must winter here in Denmark. King Harald Eiriksson has kindly invited you to spend the time with him. Yes, I know you still wish King Haakon well. But I think you should go. There's talk of peace, which would call for an intermediary. Whether or not anything comes of that, you will be serving the cause of Christ."

"The king's mother, Queen Gunnhild, will be delighted," added Kisping. "She hopes you've not forgotten her. She told me—" He lowered his voice. "—that year by year she's thought of ever more things you can likelier make clear to her than anybody else could."

Brihtnoth brightened slightly.

XX

During the summer King Haakon and Sigurd Jarl had spoken together about the need for better defense. No longer should foes come as if out of nowhere and widely lay waste before men could gather to meet them. The king would make a new law. All shoreland as far up the rivers as the salmon swam would be divided into ship-raths according to how many dwellers there were in the shire. Every such district must keep ships ready to go whenever levies were called out; and the size of these craft as well as their numbers were set forth. Moreover, great stacks of firewood were to be piled on the hills, near enough to one another that folk could see from one burning to the next. In this wise, Sigurd reckoned, the war-beckoning would run from the southern end of Norway to the northernmost Thingstead of Haalogaland in seven days or less.

Before winter storms and snows could hinder travel, the king sent messengers everywhere. When next the Things met, their chieftains and lawmen were to tell of his bidding and start the work. He did not look for anybody to balk. It was another of his laws that folk agreed were wise. Besides, thus far in his kingship Norway had mostly had peace, and always good weather, harvests, and fishing. No one wanted to rise against him or even gainsay him, now that he was also friendly with the gods.

Yet he was not unaware of mutterings about his lack of sons. Indeed, it seemed strange how he left women alone. A Christian priest might or might not. In lands where the Church held sway, he often was married. One heard tell that this could hinder his rising higher; but there wasn't room for very many bishops anyway. Surely, though, all kings had their queens, or at least their lemans. Any house in Norway would be more than happy to make such a tie. What ailed this otherwise outstanding man? What would become of the land after his death?

Having sown his word, King Haakon himself went around Rogaland. Thus he honored leading men thereabouts; he heard what they had to say; meanwhile the hall at Haugar was cleaned and aired. Among those who guested him was a hersir, Aaslaug Thorkelsson. He had a daughter, Gyda, a well-built and well-spoken maiden who caught the king's eye. Not many words went between them. However, those were cheerful. Soon afterward, he astonished many by sending spokesmen to ask for her hand. For her morning gift he promised not only gold and silver but a big farm he owned.

The wedding was at Yuletide, when folk flocked to Haugar, offered to the gods and at King Harald Fairhair's barrow, and made merry. It was hallowed in the best olden way. The feast was bountiful and went on for a week.

In bed with Gyda, Haakon did what was rightful and fitting. He liked seeing her curly brown locks and round, blunt-nosed face.

XXI

The days had shortened and bleakened, tumbling down toward winter. Life bustled throughout the year in and around Harald Eiriksson's hall; but Brihtnoth stood apart from it, like a dead tree on a riverbank. The young king had received him as well as he would any smallholder who came to call, then lashed him with questions about Haakon Aethelstan's-foster's strengths and weaknesses. Brihtnoth pleaded that he, a priest, knew naught of such things. Harald scowled and thereafter gave him scant heed. Nor was his ministry needed. When the king's household went to church, which was not often, it was in Aalborg town.

However, for his mother's sake he had given the Englishman food and lodging. Gunnhild had set up the latter, an offside hut not far from the house she used, scrubbed, newly chinked, and furnished sparely but with enough. There he could shelter from uncouthness, think his thoughts, and pray his prayers.

More and more of the time, though, he was with her. They did not hide that she wished for ghostly counsel. It struck folk as odd, but nobody wondered aloud in her hearing. Nor did anyone listen closely, after an icy look from her. Yet it was clear that they talked about faith. Norse and Danes alike grew used to seeing them a little withdrawn at mealtimes and other gatherings, or walking miles through fields gone dreary. So they did not take it amiss when sometimes those two closed a door behind themselves. If Brihtnoth was not really her confessor, still, there were things one said to nobody but a priest. Besides, when would Queen Gunnhild ever bare her soul out in the open?

Nor did she now. She told him in a few mild words that she did not hold his closeness to Haakon against him. It stemmed from their childhood, and a man who turned his back on a friend was hardly a man at all. Yes, he did well still to wear the ring he'd said, when she asked, that Haakon gave him.

But she hoped to make him see that she and her sons were not fiends. He might even come to see that they were in the right. Be that as it may, she harked back to York. She thought that he, in kindness and forbearance, might enlighten her. There was so much she wondered about. Even when she was queen in that stronghold of learning, no churchmen heard her out. At best, they mumbled something and said they must be begone.

Brihtnoth smiled a bit. "I fear you may have overawed them, my lady."

She sighed. "I didn't mean to. They told me it was enough to believe, pray, and do good works. Enough for a woman. You, though, you can unbend, can't you?"

As grieved and lonely as he was—yes, and at loose ends, he acknowledged to himself—he was shortly doing his eager best. He also acknowledged that she was fair to behold, showing her years very little, and a mind-catching talker.

Thus, early on: "That God is one and three—it's a truth I've struggled to grasp. For if he as the Father was in Heaven while he as the Son walked on earth, why then the Holy Ghost? Was that a sending of himself, like a Finnish wizard's?"

"My lady!" Brihtnoth gasped. "Never dream such a thing!"

"Forgive me. I'm blind. I grope. Guide me."

Trying to answer her further questions, he found he knew less than he had thought. She didn't pursue him about it as a pagan Roman philospher might have. "Why should we, small and death-doomed, be able to understand everything?" she said. "God is one with us and the world, which lies mostly beyond our ken."

"No, Queen, again you go wrong. God and his creation are not the same."

"I see. What I was taught in Finnmörk seems to linger in me. Help me get rid of it."

From this, in days that followed, their talk often went to the beliefs in yonder wilderness. "You must have heard many an ugly tale about me and what I brought back," she said. "Most is untrue. All is unfair."

He was caught up by what she told of it. "Heathendom, yes," he murmured, "but a—almost a sweet heathendom, isn't it? The love of God's creation can be a beginning for the love of God." Gunnhild, who had given long and hard thought to her words, smiled. Inwardly she grinned.

Thus did she foster his trust in her, and on her side be less and less a queen when they were together. It was as if she reached shyly forth out of her own loneliness.

At length they could speak frankly.

Rain rushed chill, blurring sight, gouging streams through mud. They were in her house. A maidservant was too, a girl who had learned better than to gossip about her mistress—not that anything untoward happened. Gunnhild and Brihtnoth sat in facing chairs. The fire glowed low, its smoke smelling of summery heath; lampflames flickered, shadows stirred. She had led the talk homeward to themselves.

"I can well think what wound you bear," she said softly. "Haakon was your friend."

His fist clenched on his knee. "He *is*."

"But Christ is more dear to you."

He crossed himself. "Of course. Yet I pray for Haakon."

She nodded. "As a true friend should. However, I don't believe you want him praying for you—not now—do you?"

He shuddered and shook his head.

"Brihtnoth," she went on gravely, "you've heard, but maybe you've not fully understood, how bitterly Haakon has wronged me and mine. He cast my lord and love Eirik from the kingdom that was Eirik's by right, by the will of their father, to wander among outlanders and suffer their hatefulness. It brought about Eirik's death afar, unshriven. His bones lie unburied on unhallowed ground. Now Haakon has brought a like death on a beloved son of ours."

"But, but he buried him. He told me he did."

"With never a priest there to sing a mass. Above and beyond his wickedness in this world, Haakon wrongs Christ."

"No—He means well. Always. In his soul he still loves—" Brihtnoth swallowed. His gaze dropped. "Loves righteousness," he said.

"You give him too much. But then, you are a wellspring of Christian charity. Would that a little might trickle from me."

"Oh, Queen, that wish by itself is, is God's grace upon you."

"I fear not; I fear not. I only wish I could feel the wish." Gunnhild leaned forward. Light raised, shadow deepened the roundedness of her bosom. "You've heard, you've seen, how benighted I am, how much heathendom clings to me yet."

"M-my lady, here in the North—most who're christened—they're hardly more than that, Christians in name. But you, you want to know; you seek the truth."

"Help me, Brihtnoth, wise man, holy man."

"No, no, I'm not."

"Let's stumble ahead side by side, then. You do know the way far better than I. Maybe—at its end—maybe you can bring me to where—I too can pray for Haakon's soul."

"Oh, my lady!"

She let a holy stillness fall, then calmed the talk until it was of everyday things. Henceforward, she knew, he was in her hands.

Yuletide came. Folk flocked to the hall from widely around, to meet, feast, and be glad. Only Brihtnoth shared none of the mirth. Rather, it was as if the darkness of the season seeped through his skin and filled him, with not a glimmer of what fleeting daylight the land saw. As lady of the king's household, Gunnhild had no time free for cheering him. He sat by her in the hall, but even then she could spare him few words. Otherwise he said well-nigh nothing, and drank unwontedly hard.

The second day after the mass of Christ's birth yielded to early night. Food had been eaten and boards cleared away. Good smells still twined through the smoke. Pinecones tossed into the fires added more and crackled happily. Lamplight enriched the hues of tapestries, shone off gold and silver and amber, stroked the women who went to and fro keeping ale horns full. Laughter burst here and there in the surf of men's voices.

Gunnhild called across the floor to her son: "It grows late for your mother, Harald."

The big young man who looked like his grandfather raised brows. "Why, we've hardly begun to drink."

She threw him a rueful smile. "I'm not what I once was."

"Well, then, a good night to you, Mother." Harald sounded a bit eased. The same uplift of mood showed on nearby faces. Men who were in awe of her, or slightly afraid, could now be as boisterous as they liked.

"Poor Brihtnoth." Gunnhild turned to the priest. He sat slumped, staring into his horn. He started and straightened at her touch. "Come, best that you too seek your bed." He blinked and slowly nodded. "It's dark out. I'll lend you a guide." She raised her arm. Kisping sped from the end of the room where he was benched among the lowly. She had told him to be ready for this, and what to do.

He took Brihtnoth's elbow as the priest stepped down to the floor. "I'm not drunk," Brihtnoth said. "That's a, a swinish thing to be." Those who overheard glared at him, but none would show anger at the queen's chosen talkmate.

"Of course not, Sira," Kisping answered with his easy smile. "However, you should not have to be your own torchbearer."

They stayed until the queen had left. The night was cold, stars thronging overhead, hoarfrost gray on the ground. Footfalls thudded stonily. Two guardsmen saw Gunnhild to her door. A maidservant let her in. "Go back with them," Gunnhild told her. That was no surprise. More often than not she sent her attendants away at eventide. She never said why; it was her will. Some folk thought she did not want any blunderer breaking in on her dreams. They might well be more meaningful than even a king's. Others whispered that maybe she didn't always go at once to her rest.

Alone, she waited. After a while she heard a knock and swung the door halfway open. Brihtnoth stared bewildered. Behind him sputtered and flared Kisping's torch. "Good. Now snuff that and stand watch till I send you off," she bade her footling. "Let nobody by." He nodded beneath the hood of his cloak. Gunnhild gently drew Brihtnoth inside. She shut and barred the door.

"What is this, Queen?" he mumbled. "He was taking me to my hut, then suddenly—Why?"

Her smile flowed as warm as the low blue fire. "Fear not," she said huskily. "It's but a thought of mine. I've seen the sorrow waxing in you. Yes, this is a bad season to be among strangers. Could a quiet talk with a friend help? And then maybe a shared prayer for your soul's peace?"

"Friend?" He raised a shaky hand. "Queen—"

"No, tonight your friend. Surely you had many aforetime."

"None like—They were men. I'd known most from childhood. And it was long ago—" He squared his shoulders. "I'm sorry, my lady. I babble. Unmanly of me."

"Not so. Brave you were to come here, when you could have gone to your England. But I think our feast has awakened memories that overwhelm your heart. Your Yules weren't like this in Norway, were they?"

"No. We few Christians kept the holy days by ourselves. But—" A dam broke. "But it's not that, that I miss the old cheer and larking at home—It's that I think—"

She stroked fingers across his hand. "Speak freely. You'll not be the less dear to me."

"Now Haakon stands at a heathen sacrifice!" he cried. Tears ran forth. "He eats horseflesh, he drinks to demons—"

"Take heart, Brihtnoth. He's not lost yet, is he? Not while he lives and can repent."

"No, but—"

"We may bring him to repentance," said Gunnhild aside. It went past Brihtnoth. "Stained with the blood of slain beasts—You, who've been so kind to me, your sons—if they cast him down in his sins, down into Hell—"

"Brihtnoth, you've known this from the first." Her voice did not reprove; it laved him. "What's made it such a knife twisting in you? I think our Danish Yule is indeed calling up too many memories."

"Ghosts, God help me," he groaned. "Christmases in England, joyous, innocent, Haakon and I and all our friends— Everybody loved him."

"As they loved you." She took his hands in hers.

He looked down at them. His gaze fled from the ring he wore. He looked back up at her, blindly. "No, no— Queen—"

"Brihtnoth," she breathed, "you've given me more counsel and comfort than ever you knew. Tonight let me help and comfort you."

She laid her arms about him. He shied. She smiled and did not let go. "Don't be afraid," she whispered. "We're alone. You have leave to weep."

His head sank onto her shoulder. The sobs shook him. She held him close and murmured.

From there, one thing led to another. Priest, sometime warrior, redesman to a king, he was else a boy.

At first, down on the bed, he hardly knew what was happening or how it had begun. She bestrode him. Afterward he wept again. She consoled and, in a while, taught him. At last he slept.

She lay beside him, thinking. He'd better go before dawn. She could trust Kisping. That lad understood well what his own welfare sprang from and how easily he could get his throat cut. Brihtnoth would keep silence too, even to his confessor, until he could take ship for England. She would make sure of that, and of whatever more she wanted of him. It wouldn't do to have folk snicker about her. She and her sons were not strong enough to shrug it off.

He was no Eirik—oh, Eirik! But he was sturdy, and she rather liked him, and the years had grown long in which she had nothing but her fingers and make-believe.

Also, she thought in the dying firelight, while he would never knowingly betray Haakon, she could now tease many small truths about her foe out of him, which taken together might show her where next to strike. She had turned his heathen against Haakon, then his Church, and still he was unbowed. There must be some way to bring him down.

XXII

Haavard Jarl had another sister with a son called Einar. This was a gaunt man, harsh and grasping, wherefore he was known as Einar Hardmouth; but like his cousin, he was a chieftain with warriors and ships at his beck. While he was a Yuletide guest Ragnhild made herself agreeable to him and they talked more than once at some length. That was less than it had been with Einar Bread-and-Butter, as stiff and short-spoken as this Einar was; nor were they ever alone, and to him she spoke well of her husband. Nevertheless he went home very aware of her, though not of how deeply she had sounded him.

In spring Haavard shifted to a holding of his at Stenness on Mainland. Ragnhild had slipped him the thought. True, the stead was somewhat lonely, but there he could hear what was on the minds of men who otherwise could not readily see him. And there—for of course everybody knew of the move well beforehand—arrived Einar Bread-and-Butter with a pack of men outnumbering the guards.

Haavard went to meet them. The fight was short. Haavard fell, what was left of his following scattered, and Einar held the ground that ever afterward was known as Haavard's Field.

Before he could go on to the hall, Ragnhild had gathered her servants and a handful of men-at-arms and fled back to the bay on Wide Firth. At once she sent after Einar Hard-mouth.

The Orkneymen seethed. They had on the whole liked their jarl, and he had done no harm they knew of to his nephew. The deed of Einar Bread-and-Butter seemed foul, the more so as gossip went that he had hatched it with Haavard's wife. When Ragnhild heard, she said hotly that this was a lie. She wanted nothing to do with the killer. Instead, she stoked higher the feelings against him.

Einar Hardmouth came as she had asked. She told him in the hearing of others how shameful it was that Haavard lay unavenged, and she would do whatever was needed to set things right. "The man who carries out the work will win honor from all goodfolk," she said, "and the jarlship as well."

Einar narrowed his eyes. "They say, my lady, you don't always utter everything that's in your head. Whoever takes this up may want more than the jarlship. He may look for you to give what is not less."

She sent him a slow smile. "He will be worthy of it," she answered.

He soon went back to make ready. Ragnhild sent to Arn-finn's and Haavard's brother Ljot Thorfinnsson, begging his help in staving off Einar Bread-and-Butter. He was a tall, handsome man, well thought of everywhere in Orkney. Ragnhild set herself to getting to know him.

XXIII

Early in spring Harald sent to his brothers around Den-mark, asking that they meet again. His uncles Aalf the Shipman and Eyvind the Braggart came too. When all were on hand and had feasted, they gathered next morning in Gunnhild's house, where nobody else listened.

She told them at length what she had learned about Haa-kon Aethelstan's-foster. That he was fearless in battle they knew already. That he was bound to keep his kingship was only to be awaited in a son of Harald Fairhair. For this he had even set aside the Faith and joined in heathen rites. He had also taken a queen. Having given his folk that much, he brooked no further stubbornness. There was little or none anyway. The Norse deemed his laws wise, his judgments righteous. Their land lay at peace; trade throve. That the years went on yielding good harvests ashore and at sea made them believe the gods loved him as they themselves did.

Yet there were hidden weaknesses. He leaned heavily on Sigurd Jarl of Hladi for counsel and backing, and Sigurd was growing old. Beneath the boldness and cheerfulness beat a heart sorely troubled—about the God he had forsaken if not quite forsworn; about Christian priests who shunned him and laymen gone cool toward him; about his wife. After all, he had wed the first and best he happened upon; they were not much together, and only newly was she with child; he showed no thought of adding any women who would bind him to houses more powerful than a hersir's. He was ever more headlong in what he said and did. Unless warnings were from Sigurd, he was apt to shut them off with a harsh word. So far these things did not matter much; but they could be played upon.

"These are deep insights, Mother," said Gudröd low.

"They are true," she answered.

"How did you get them, sister?" asked Eyvind sharply. "They smack of witchcraft."

"Be still, brother," growled Aalf. "You always rush ahead like a blind boar."

"You know how the Queen Mother gathers bits of truth from everywhere and weaves them into a whole," Harald told him mildeningly.

"I've not spent hours, day after day, with that former chaplain of his for nothing," said Gunnhild. "And, yes, whoever else had anything to tell. I've thought long and hard about all I heard." And had raised dreams by means she did not speak of.

"What is your rede, then, Mother?" asked Gamli, as eagerly as Eirik once did.

"Do not try again soon to overthrow him," she said.

Harald nodded. "No, hardly this year. We need to build back our strength."

"Nor next year—"

"Hold!" Sigurd broke in. "How long to wait?"

His disrespect drew frowns. Before a squabble could waste time, she said, "Don't sit idle either. Make a few small raids, two or three ships at a time, striking fast and straightaway leaving. Mostly, though, let them merely see the dragons pass by. They'll light their beacon fires; the kingdom will rise to arms, and find it was for naught, over and over. Lesser vikings will pluck up heart to try raiding on their own, making the burden on the defenses heavier yet. But the Norse cannot know beforehand how much lesser those are, not worth turning out whole shires for. After a while Haakon will grow weary of bootlessly hastening off. I told you he's not as long-suffering as he was. Besides, he thinks he has better things to do."

"Such as what?" sneered Ragnfröd the Red.

"Giving law and justice; binding Norway together into one true kingdom."

"And leaving it in Satan's hands," snarled Erling.

"Set that aside," Harald bade. "First we must overcome him."

"And avenge our brother Guthorm," said Ragnfröd.

"How long to wait?" Sigurd cried anew.

"Until the time is ripe," Gunnhild told them. "We'll see when that is."

Harald shook his head. "No, Mother. You are wise, and we'll do as you want this year, and maybe a ways into next. But we can't well dawdle beyond that."

"We *will* not," said Gamli, his face more than ever like Eirik's.

"If nothing else," Harald went on, "our men would get too restless. Oh, we'll go harry Wendland, and maybe Ireland or wherever, such of us as aren't pestering Haakon. That'll help. But too many of them have homes back there, and hopes of return and reward. Then there's my namesake Harald Bluetooth. We'd better not let him give up on us."

Yes, Gunnhild thought, the Dane-king had taken the setback at Agdir much amiss. "Let me seek him out," she said. "I think I can make him willing to bide as long as need be."

Ragnfröd's voice fell surprisingly soft. "Can you make us willing, Mother?"

"He who runs too fast will be winded before the end of the race, if he hasn't stumbled and fallen."

"A rede for lynxes, sister mine," answered Aalf. "Wolves don't stalk their prey or lie long in wait for it."

Gunnhild knew starkly that he spoke out of the years he had known her sons and many more of their kind. It had not been the way of Eirik Blood-ax either.

"Well," she said, "at least we'll have a year to see how things go." Rising, with a wry smile: "Now I'll leave you to wrangle till we meet at mealtide. I ought to oversee that, Harald."

The young king grinned back at her. "As you wish, Mother." Gunnhild had never wanted whatever leman he was keeping at the hall to get above herself. "Thank you for all you've given us." The same rumbled around the room. Before she crossed the threshold, they were at their wolves' business.

She did not go straight between buildings, but took a path offside. There was no need for guards when men were widespread, working the fields, every free one with his spear in reach. They often saw her stride this way, thinking thoughts they were shy of wondering about. Once the trail had passed through a meadow where livestock grazed, it was used by few but hunters who went after hare or grouse on the heath: for it wound by a dolmen and on along the haunted mire.

This day was utter springtime. Sunlight poured around tall white clouds, down among untold wings, through air soft and sweet-smelling and full of birdsong. A mist of green over land and trees had thickened to a foam, fast becoming a sea. Raindrops glinted on shrubs. That weather had not muddied the little-trodden path, though puddles gleamed. A man stood under a leafing oak. Nearing, Gunnhild saw anemones clustered at its roots.

Most folk would have hastened onward. The dolmen brooded nearby atop its hillock, great rough stones spotted with lichen, walls and roofs of a den for uncanniness. Whoever dared meet here would stand in sight of everybody and yet be alone. Now and then, walking, talking, Gunnhild and Brihtnoth had done so.

When he spied her he quivered, made no unseemly dash but called, "My lady!," half in gladness, half like a beggar for alms.

She halted before him and smiled. "Greeting. How good to find you."

"I waited—remembering—I hoped—"

A song she sang in her house shortly before her sons arrived might have had something to do with that. But she also knew he would indeed hope.

"Speak freely, my dear," she offered him.

"W-with you—Is this the last time?" he stammered.

She nodded and made her voice wistful. "Yes. I told you before, it would seem queer if we both dropped from ken tonight of all nights."

"Yes. Of course—Your honor in their eyes—"

Tomorrow he left with a band of Aalborg men going to Aarhus. A chapman's knarr lay there, loading for England, the first of the season. She had had Kisping get him a berth aboard.

"And yours." She sighed. "We've stolen some lovely hours, haven't we, you and I."

His look said: You did. How could I have? What could I ever do but your will, my lady, my lady, with my soul in my thanks?

"Well, we're at the end of them," she said. "I never found a believable way for you to stay here."

He steadied. "Nor could I," he sighed. "No, I must back to England, and make my peace with God." He had sworn to her that his confessor there would keep the secret. Among other things, Brihtnoth belonged to a high-standing family. "And you, Gunnhild, you too—"

"But it wasn't a very dreadful sin, was it? Common enough, Christ in his mercy knows. We were happy, and harmed nobody else." When she saw him begin to stiffen, she said quickly, "Oh, I'll do what's right." She would judge for herself what that was. "May everything be well for you always, Brihtnoth," she breathed.

After a while in which birdcalls rang and lilted, she asked, "Why did you want to meet me today?"

His shield dropped. "I—to say farewell and, and thanks. Did we really do wrong? At first I believed—but I no longer know what to believe, God help me." He crossed himself as if unaware that he did. "It feels somehow—that you've healed me—But what was the wound?"

She thought she knew. However, to say it would be unwise. She was not quite done with him yet. "Maybe I helped you begin looking forward to the rest of your life on earth. Go, Brihtnoth; go with my blessing. Rise to heights worthy of you, churchly or worldly or both, as you choose. Find a good English girl; wed her; have children; be happy. Let any memory of me only be a small glow in your breast."

"Oh, my queen—" His voice failed.

"Be sure I'll never forget you. It will be lonely without you." She had thought about luring another man. But no, not soon. However careful she and Brihtnoth had been, tongues must be wagging a bit. Best let them fall to rest. She had taken him because she could get more out of him than pleasure, welcome though that was. She could bide her time again.

Cat-deftly, she struck. "If only I had something to remember you by, something to take out of hiding, hold, look at, yes, and pray over, pray for your well-being."

"I've nothing to give," he mourned. "Would God I did."

A breeze wandered by.

"Oh, but you do," she cried. "See, that ring you wear."

He stared down at the silver band. "This? But, but Haakon gave me it, these years agone, before he left England—"

She pressed inward. "I know. You've told me. I understand how much it means to you, whatever has happened since. But can't you then understand how much it will mean to me, such a sign of your love?" She caught and held his gaze. Her words went steely. "Also a sign of how you've at last put Haakon the apostate behind you."

He had fared in war; he had naysaid his king; she saw him quail. "No, I, I'll always pray for him."

"As a Christian should," she said; then, once more warm: "But you're bound afar. The ring will have a home in my heart."

He fumbled numbly to pull it off. "Be it yours, Gunnhild—my lady—"

She took it from him. "My everlasting thanks, dear one."

"M-maybe somehow it'll—will help bring peace between you—and him—"

"Maybe," she said. "Who knows? I think, though, Brihtnoth, this is a shackle off your soul."

"I know not," he said in his bewilderment. "You're so strange, so wonderful—"

"Enough," she told him gently. "Look ahead, I say; look ahead to your new life. Now we'd better not linger, nor sit together at eventide." They had stopped doing it weeks ago. He could never keep his glance from sliding to her. "I'll see you off in the morning; we'll steal a last look and smile. Fare you ever well."

She turned and went back to the hall. Her left hand closed around the ring. She'd slip it to Kisping, with a whisper that he bring it to her tomorrow.

One of the dreams she raised had told her to lay hold of it. She was not sure why, other than that it stood for a small, secret victory over Haakon. But she had a feeling it might be worth more.

XXIV

Although they were Norse who had taken over the Western Islands, ships plied between them and Denmark. Gunnhild need cast no spells to follow what went on in Orkney.

Thus during the summer she learned how Einar Hardmouth led men against Einar Bread-and-Butter, who was sulking at home, and slew him. Thereafter Einar Hardmouth looked to become jarl; but his uncle Ljot had meanwhile called a Thing and gotten himself hailed. It helped that Ljot had somewhat hastily wed Ragnhild Eiriksdottir, which gave him a claim on the holdings and troops of his late brothers, her former husbands. Gunnhild grinned at the news. She could guess who had steered these happenings.

Einar Hardmouth returned to his own island and tried to gather warriors. He said he had been cheated out of the jarlship he earned, and now would take it. However, he could not muster nearly enough. No promise of rewards drew Orkneymen who would rather have a son of Thorfinn Skull-splitter over them. Besides, they thought Ljot was a good leader. It was said that he and Ragnhild got along well, and soon in his eyes she stood far above his other wives, for he found her counsel worth hearing.

That word reached Gunnhild together with the tale of how Ljot Jarl at length got Einar Hardmouth seized and brought before him, and soon afterward ordered Einar beheaded.

Two more Thorfinnssons were left. Skuli, not liking the outcome, crossed over to Scotland. Gunnhild thought of the years-long strife between the sons of Harald Fairhair. Well, Ragnhild must deal with this as best she could. While Gunnhild lived, her sons, Eirik's, would not fall on each other's throats.

In the meantime, not very gladly, she had sought out Harald Bluetooth. That was late in the summer, for he had been away making the rounds of his kingdom, Fyn, Sjaelland, and other islands as well as Jutland and Skaaney. This did not take him as far north as Aalborg, those parts being well in hand. It was elsewhere that he needed to meet with high-ranking men, hear them out, give them gifts, and make sure they understood how strong he was.

Back in Jelling, he found much waiting for him to deal with. Yet he could hardly do otherwise than receive Gunnhild and talk with her as she asked.

Only guards and servants were there, and only for the

sake of fittingness, when they met in an upper room of the
hall. They wore furs, for rain hammered on the roof and
air was raw.

"I could well have made use of your wisdom, Queen,"
he said. His lip lifted over his bad teeth, an uneasy smirk.
"Things were sometimes a little touchy, eh, eh. Above all,
with the new-made bishops thereabouts."

"I can see how, King," she answered. Here they two
could speak more or less forthrightly. "You've gotten them
named from among Danes rather than being Germans, so
they're not beholden in any way to the Emperor. But that
means they're of the great Danish houses, which remember
the days before they came under your father King Gorm."

The Church was a weapon, she thought, or a tool, for a
king to quell an unruly folk; but like the dwarf-forged
sword Tyrfing, it could become its owner's bane. Then the
next king would be the underling of the bishops' rich kindred.

Yet without the Church, she thought bitterly, a king must
always fear the ill will of the yeomen.

Harald slapped his knee. "Ho, ho, I was right! You're as
shrewd as they say. I'll drink to that."

His try for cheeriness went nowhere. Gunnhild smiled,
purred, "My thanks, lord. Maybe my thoughts can help you
ever so slightly toward the ends you have in mind," and
pressed in on him about her sons.

After the losses they and the men he sent with them had
taken in Norway, he did not want to risk more. "Let's see,
Queen; let's wait and see." But Gunnhild gave him no plea
he could straightforwardly turn down. She spoke of his
honor, of how she could not believe he'd flag merely because one battle had gone wrong. That would hardly make
the Danes look on him as almighty, would it? He still had
Haakon's raids on their shores to avenge. Not that she
dreamed he would fail to do so, oh, no, never. Nonetheless,
the sooner the better, didn't he agree? His forebears were
no coalbiters; all the world knew their blood lived in Harald
Gormsson. She dangled before him the scot that Haakon
was now taking in, pelts, walrus and narwhal ivory, horn,

silver, gold; she told of many doughty warriors to call up
for his wars. Maybe foremost, she said, was that Haakon
had betrayed the Faith; Norway lay benighted, her folk
doomed to Hellfire. Bringing them into the fold meant the
salvation of those who did the holy work. Mother Church
and her bishops must uphold a king who lent his strength
to it.

"But—well, what if we fail again, Queen? It could happen. Odin—Christ gives victory as he chooses."

"Then, of course, my lord, you and the sons of Eirik must
withdraw and hold back for a longer span. Yes, it may
happen." Inwardly, grimly, Gunnhild knew how rash they
were. "On the other hand, things may go well. And Christ
never gives up, does he?"

Thus, bit by bit, day by day, she brought Harald Bluetooth around.

In fall, one by one or two by two, her sons came home
from their viking cruises. The winter wore on.

XXV

Late next summer, they sailed from Denmark with crews
from earlier farings as well as their troops, and a still
greater number of Danes lent by King Harald Bluetooth.
The wind fair for Norway, they swiftly crossed to Agdir;
thence they went north along the coast, resting neither day
nor night. No fires were lighted to warn. For one thing,
usage was that this go from east to west, but now the attack
had taken a new course. For another, after too many rous-
ings of the whole war-host for naught, folk grumbled aloud
and King Haakon had set heavy fines for whoever started
the beacons without strong cause. Therefore the ships
reached Wolf Sound ahead of the news and lay becalmed
for seven days. Men who spied them sped to bring him
word. They found him on the island Fraedi off North
Moerr, staying at the garth Birchstrand. The only men with
him were his guards and such yeomen of the neighborhood
as he was guesting.

He brought together those reckoned wisest and asked whether they thought he should hie to battle with the Eirikssons in spite of their badly outnumbering him, or pull back northward to gather more fighters. Thereupon rose an aged yeoman called Egil Woolsark. Aside from the name and the huge body, he was nothing like Egil Skallagrimsson, but had in his youth been a mighty warrior who often bore the banner of Harald Fairhair. His face was furrowed, his hair and beard white. Yet he gave answer: "I was now and then in battle with your father, King Harald, and sometimes he had more, sometimes fewer men than his foe. But he always won, and I never heard as how he asked his friends to tell him to flee. Nor 'ud we like to teach you that trick, King; for it seems to us it's a bold chieftain we have, and every last one of us will faithfully follow you."

Deep voices rolled and crashed around Haakon; this was what they all felt. His cheeks flamed. He lifted his golden head on high and said his own wish was to fight with what strength came to hand.

At once he had war-arrows cut and sent widely around. From as far as these were borne, men took their weapons and hastened to his side. Then said Egil Woolsark: "For a while I was afraid this long peace would never end, and I'd die indoors on a straw-bed. Much liefer 'ud I follow my chieftain and fall in fighting. Maybe it'll happen."

As soon as the Eirikssons caught the right wind, they set sail and steered on north to Stad. There they learned where King Haakon was, and went to meet him. He had nine ships. With these he lay to in Feeyjar Isle Sound under Fraedarberg. The Eirikssons drew up a little southward with their more than twenty ships. King Haakon sent a messenger to them, bidding them go ashore on the mainland to Rastarkaalf, where he had marked off a battlefield with hazel wands. It was broad and flat, at the foot of a long and rather narrow ridge. The Eirikssons agreed, led their host afoot across the neck of land in Fraedarberg, and took stance on the chosen ground.

Before the fighting began, Egil Woolsark asked King Haakon for ten banners and ten men to bear them. These he got. He took them behind the ridge and waited. Haakon brought his troop out onto Rastarkaalf, raised his own banner, and strode about arraying them. "We'll make our line long," said he, "so they can't outflank us, though they're more than we are."

The clash became hard-fought. Though Haakon's folk stood stoutly, they were being whittled down. Wounded groaned and dead sprawled on earth sodden with blood.

Meanwhile Egil made his ten standard bearers go well apart from each other, up the slope until the banners showed above the ridge.

Suddenly men in the uppermost ranks of the Eirikssons saw those flags flying among the ravens, moving onward against them. Few think coolly in the midst of battle. It seemed this was a company much bigger than theirs, about to fall on their rear and cut them off from their ships. They shouted it forth above the clatter and cries. Fear kindled. It spread like wildfire before the wind. Some turned and fled. At that, all but the guards did. When the young kings saw their host break, they too gave way. King Haakon's men yelled. He at their head, they pushed briskly after. His sword Quernbiter flashed and reaped.

Once Gamli Eiriksson had gotten higher onto the neck of land, he looked back and saw that those giving chase were no more than he had been fighting. He roared an order to blow the war-horns, and mustered his ranks afresh. Likewise did his brothers and their Norsemen. The Danes kept on fleeing. This was not a war for which they had much heart.

King Haakon and his men reached the Eirikssons. Theirs were now the greater numbers. Again a sharp fight began. It ended with the invaders again taking flight. King Haakon stayed on their heels.

East of the ridge, a flat field ran along the range of hills, bounded on the west by steep heights. Most of Gamli's men went that way. King Haakon hounded them until the last one lay slain.

Gamli himself led those warriors who kept beside him

down south of the ridge. On the flatland he turned and made ready to fight anew. Others rallied. His brothers brought their own guards and vikings to stand with him.

Here Egil Woolsark went in the van of King Haakon's men, his ax hewing right and left, till at last he came face-to-face against Gamli. They swapped blows. Gamli took deep wounds. Egil fell, and many besides.

Then Haakon arrived from his slaughtering. Strife blazed afresh, Haakon in the forefront. Man after man went down under his sword.

Erelong the Eirikssons knew it was hopeless for them. They withdrew as best they and their beaten followers could, to the sea. But those who had already fled had pushed most of the ships off the strand. The rest were still grounded, with the tide fast ebbing. There was no way to float the hulls before Haakon's howling troop overran them. The Eirikssons, with what was left of their band, sprang into the water and swam to the ships that were free. No few among them drowned, weighed down by their mail and their weariness. Bleeding, staggering, Gamli could not go even that far. The blunted sword dropped from his hand. He snarled and died in the shallows.

Oars rattled forth. His brothers stood out for Denmark.

A hoarse shout rang from the land. Weapons shook aloft, still dripping red. Otherwise Haakon's men wanted only to sit down and rest for a while.

Thereafter they went about doing what they could for their badly hurt, killing such of their foes as stirred, and dragging the grounded ships above high-water mark. They laid their dead in some. Egil Woolsark and those who had been at his side got one to themselves. Watchmen kept birds off during the night. Next day the grave-ships were hauled to the battlefield, to be covered with earth and rocks. High stood the memorial stones raised on Egil Woolsark's mound.

May he have gone home to his Odin, Haakon thought: then shuddered, for he no longer knew what his own doom would be, nor that of any man.

XXVI

Wind and rain mourned around the house of Gunnhild. Candles and the peat fire barely held darkness at bay. Shadow lay thick in the corner where Kisping squatted. His eyes glistened out of it like bits of ice. He was the only servant there when she greeted Arinbjörn Thorisson; she knew he could hold his tongue.

Woman and warrior sat in facing chairs, he stiffly, feeling awkward, she easeful and watchful as a cat. "I wanted to speak alone with you because you're the most trustworthy man I know," she said.

He gripped his ale horn hard. "The queen is too kind," he muttered.

She raised her brows. "This queen?" After a sip of the wine she held in a cup, she said from low in her throat, "You were at Rastarkaalf. You must have kept your head while well-nigh everybody else lost his. Tell me what happened."

"About King Gamli I can say very little, Queen," he rumbled softly. "I was off on the right with King Harald and his other guardsmen. It was all a welter anyway."

"No," she said, "Gamli's death is not what I have in mind," Gamli, Gamli, so like his father, even unto leaving his bones among strangers, Gamli gone forever. Well, five sons lived, to take revenge and the rights that had been his and Eirik's. "Tell me about the whole faring, what you saw along the way, what you learned from the battle, what you think about it."

"King Harald asked me somewhat the same, as he did my fellows. For now he's the first of the brothers and—" Arinbjörn stopped to pick his words. "—if I may say so, he was always the most thoughtful."

Gunnhild harked back to the likes of Brihtnoth, Bishop Reginhard, even Vuokko and Aimo long ago in the Finnhut. "I'd not call any of them a deep thinker," she said wryly, "though Harald is quick of understanding and can look beyond the end of his nose."

Arinbjörn spoke with care. "He did say to me, Queen, the two of us aside from the rest—he said you'd been right, we struck too soon, and now we'd better go with your rede for as long as needful."

"How long will my sons deem that to be?"

"Doesn't that lie mostly with King Harald Gormsson? I don't know him myself, but I'd guess it'll take a while to get his help again."

"Of course," Gunnhild snapped. Bluetooth must be wondering whether this whole undertaking was unlucky. She would have to win him over as she did before, in more than one meeting.

She curbed her anger and softened her voice as she leaned forward in the firelight. "Arinbjörn, you gave up much to come back and stand by the sons of him who had your oath. Do you never long homeward?"

He cracked for the span of a flame-flicker. "Oh, my lady—" Draining his horn restored steadiness. "We'll get there yet."

"And then you'll not find the house of Eirik Haraldsson unthankful. But first we must *do* it." She sighed. "Well, the warfaring's not for me, a woman. Nor, they say, is the planning of it. But a woman does look at the world otherwise than a man. She may sometimes see what he does not."

Unwonted wariness showed on Arinbjörn's blocky face. "And you are the wisest of women, Queen. You ken far more than most of us."

He was thinking of spellcraft, she knew. Best lead him from that at once. "What I hope to get from you today is not what my son King Harald doubtless did, thoughts about troop arrays and outfitting and suchlike. Nor do I want a tale of blows and brags. Leave that to the skalds. I'm after the feel of things, what it was like to go there and be there."

"I, I'm not sure what you mean."

She smiled. "Take your ease, Arinbjörn. You've earned it." She signed Kisping to refill his horn. "Remember aloud.

Let your words wander. It may bring back something—"
She dropped her voice to a murmur. "—something unheeded by others, maybe by anyone wakeful, something
such as comes to us in dreams."

"Well, I—" Arinbjörn grabbed the horn from the footling
and gulped. "The gods, uh, the saints know I'm no sooth-
sayer, not any kind of wizard, only a man."

"That's enough." A man who had been close to Egil
Skallagrimsson. He was bound to have felt, however un-
wittingly, a breath from out of this world—elven or hellish
or whatever it was—and it would have left a mark on his
heavy soul, like a frostbite scar that ever afterward twinges
at touches too light for hale flesh to be aware of. "What I
seek is nothing witchy, nothing forbidden, only a fuller understanding of how things are." What she might later do
with it was not his business. "If nothing else, those were
my sons who fared thither, a son of mine who fell. Share
it with me."

"How, my lady?" he asked, bewildered.

"Sit back, old friend of ours. Drink. Talk."

Thus did she draw him out, unsure herself of what she
was searching for: the landward steeps and fjords, the waiting for a wind, the challenges back and forth, the fighting
back and forth—

Slowly she began to see, to take in, the truth of what she
had gropingly guessed, how Haakon breathed his own battle gladness into his men and how much they loved him. It
would not do merely to drive him out of the land as Eirik
was driven out. While he lived, the Norse would not yield
to any other king. So his death would be shattering to them,
if his death could be wrought.

Curses, poison—no, not from afar, not when Norse
witches and maybe even Norse gods must be watching over
him, whether or not he wanted it or knew it. Besides, the
folk would disown her sons, who would themselves disown
her, if ever she got their names linked to seid.

She hid her thoughts and led Arinbjörn onward. It was
close to mealtide at the hall when she let him go. "You've

been more than helpful," she said. "You've soothed my grief a little."

"I'm glad if I have, Queen," he mumbled.

He donned his cloak and walked off into the rain.

She sat down again and brooded. It was as if the darkness closed in on her. Haakon must fall in battle, as Guthorm and Gamli did. But how, when he seemed, like his father, to bear victory in his blood?

The wind keened outside. Where beyond it were they who once lay as bairns at her breast? They died in their sins, which were not small, as lustily as they had lived. Odin would have made them welcome. Dag's last poem for Eirik smote through her. But these had been Christian men. Had they not? If only a song and a drum could make them one with earth and heaven—but she had put that behind her. Had she not?

She'd better be off to the hall herself. They'd soon dine there, and she must be its lady. At least she could return here when the unseen sun was setting.

From the night on the other side of it drifted a fog-wisp of thought. She snatched. Her fingers closed on nothing they could grasp. Yet—

She straightened in her chair. "Kisping," she said.

His lean frame leaped to stand before her. "Yes, my queen?"

"I want you to start learning the use of bow and arrow."

She had seldom seen him gape. "What? But, Queen, I'm no warrior."

"There's no haste. I'll keep you busy, never fear. However, in between, you'll work on marksmanship. I may someday find it called for."

He hooded his eyes. "As the queen wishes."

It was not at all clear to her what she wished. She had only a sudden, shapeless foreknowledge, which might or might not be meaningful. But she felt somehow that when her sons again went after Haakon's life they would have her spellcraft secretly behind them.

XXVII

Time passed. The sons of Gunnhild went raiding. By turns, they harassed Norway. Otherwise they saw to their Danish holdings and households, horses, hawks, hounds, their ships above all. They visited, guested, feasted, sported, made merry, and begot brats whom, heeding her warning, they did not set on their knees.

Nor did she find the wheeling seasons dreary, however much she yearned ahead. She fared often across Denmark by wain or by water, to call on her sons, King Harald Bluetooth, and other men great in the land. Some she could charm; some were a little afraid of her, hiding it as well as they could; all would uphold her and the Eirikssons or, at worst, not speak against them in council and at the Things.

At the hall near Aalborg she spread her ever-growing net to catch tidings from far and wide, but she got them straightforwardly too. News throbbed along trade routes running west to Iceland; north to Finnmörk and Bjarmaland; east through Svithjod to Aldeigjuborg and Holmgard; south to the Midworld Sea and Serkland; southeasterly to Kiev, Miklagard on the Golden Horn and its empire, the depths of Asia. She drank of the knowledge—the whole wonderful world—as thirstily as heroes in Valhall drank the ale of the Aesir. It was not to gain power; it was for its own sake, her mind flying free.

Off in Orkney, Ragnhild still seemed glad of her new husband, Ljot Jarl, though she had not borne him a child. However, he must needs be much away from home. His brother Skuli had gone to Scotland, whose king gave him the rank of earl. Thence Skuli returned to Caithness, where he gathered a host and led it over the straits to overthrow Ljot. That became a stiff battle. Ljot had the victory and Skuli fled back to Scotland. Ljot came after him, stopping in Caithness to add to his own strength.

Skuli rode north again with an army lent him by the king of Scotland, an earl at his side. The brothers met anew in the Dales of Caithness. Ljot went in the forefront of his men, smiting till the Scots broke and scattered. Skuli stood his ground with a handful. They were hewn down.

Ljot brought Caithness wholly under himself. This sat ill with the Scots. He must look for a troublous morrow.

King Eadgar ruled an England peaceful from the North Sea to the Welsh marches. Few vikings had the recklessness to harry it any longer. Pickings stayed better in Ireland, where the olden kingdoms were more at war with each other than with the Norse, who gained by making shifty alliances among them. Meanwhile the shores and rivers were apt to lie unguarded.

Gunnhild's kinsman Walking Hrolf had cloven a way for settlers in what was now called Normandy. His grandson, young Duke Richard, married a daughter of the French Duke Hugh. While the Norman lords were vassals of the king of France, they ran their domain as they chose. Nothing was left of Northern law and right; farmfolk were beginning to seethe.

Though his overbearingness made him foes, Egil Skallagrimsson stood high in Iceland. He had had children by his wife Aasgerd, two sons and two daughters who lived; lately she had borne him a third son, but then the second-oldest took sick and died. Good, thought Gunnhild. Let him know what such a loss felt like.

On the plains sweeping south from Wendland, Mieszkoi, of the ancient house of Piast, conquered everything between the Oder and the Warthe rivers. So did he become the first king of Poland. He was receiving Christian missionaries.

North of Danish Skaaney, Bleking, and Halland, the king of the Swedes ruled strongly and quietly. Each spring a hallowed woman drove a wain bearing an image of Frey in a closed shrine around the land to bless it. Twice yearly, at the turnings of the sun, folk flocked to the huge halidom at Uppsala, where fires smoked high and men as well as beasts were hanged on trees, pierced by spears, offerings to the gods. Riches flowed through such marts as Birka and Helgö. In Gardariki, across the Baltic, traders went down the rivers to Kiev, or even onward to Miklagard.

Kiev was the strong heart of a commonwealth that grew and grew. Svyatoslav was its new king. He was mostly off fighting the wealthy Khazars, the wild Pechenegs, and other tribes. The real ruler was his widowed mother Queen Olga. She bloodily avenged her husband Igor on the Drevlyans who killed him. She changed the slow and risky gathering of scot to a tax. She stretched Kievan sway north to Holmgard, which she called Novgorod, and south to the borders of the Greek Empire. She visited Miklagard herself, became a Christian, and tried to convert her folk—though she would not acknowledge the Eastern Emperor her overlord, but rather sent west to Germany for missionaries. This was her only failure. Hardly anybody took the Faith. When Bishop Adalbert arrived, Svyatoslav booted him out. Several of the bishop's following got slain on the way home.

Gunnhild had had worse defeats. She wished she could meet Queen Olga.

The Saxonian King Otto was crowned Holy Roman Emperor and set about enlarging his realm. His dealings with King Harald Bluetooth were uneasy.

Down in Spain, the kingdom of Castile was growing apace, while a new Caliph of Córdoba was bulwarking his Moors. The Greeks wrested Crete back from the Arabs. Near their frontier, the Magyars raided into Bulgaria, leaving a broad wasteland behind them. Then worthless Emperor Romanus died and, after some trouble, Nikephorus Phokas mounted the throne. He was a man of war and of iron will. Soon he regained Cyprus.

Meanwhile the English bridged the Thames at London. Monks in the Alps founded a hospice to help travelers across those mountains. Often something else that somebody had heard and happened to remember flitted by Gunnhild, a few words to tell of Arabs who were writing about the stars and Jews who were writing about speech itself— Her lust to know more must go unslaked.

As for Norway, traders spoke of peace and good years. Sometimes, though, a swallow winged yonder.

XXVIII

King Haakon and Sigurd Jarl had always kept in close touch. The last Yuletide they would ever share, Haakon spent at Hladi. Later he rode around the Thraandlaw, showing off his might but mainly giving gifts, righting wrongs, and whatever else he could do to keep the folk and their chieftains his friends. Returning to Hladi, he stayed there in the best of fellowship till spring. When at last he went back south, the jarl's oldest living son sailed with him—he who, newborn, had been given the king's name and sprinkled with water by the king's own hand.

He was now a young man, wide-awake and witty, who had already traveled peacefully about in Norway and in viking abroad. Nevertheless Sigurd asked if this Haakon could now come along. "You can still use a little polishing," said the father with a smile, "and it will be helpful for you to see something of kingcraft at first hand." He turned grave. "You two need to know and understand one another, so when I'm gone you can trustfully work and war together."

Already Haakon the king and Haakon the jarl's son felt a liking. Their voyage down the coast went blithely.

When the crews saw Harald Fairhair's barrow loom against heaven, they stood in from the sea and lay to at Körmt. A hard-rowed karfi had gone ahead with a message; everything was ready for them. Guards who had waited by turns at the landing raised spears and a shout before they warped the king's ship against the wharf. Though the hall was not far off, other men came at a gallop, leading horses for the foremost of the newcomers to ride.

This was a day cool and sweet. Grass glowed newly green. A wind laden with earth-smells as well as sea-tang soughed through pine boughs. Birds filled the blue with wings and cries. Before debarking, the Haakons had donned good clothes from their chests; but for the king the horse herders brought a gold-embroidered tunic, and for his guest a red mantle trimmed with marten.

"That was well done, lord," said the latter as the saddle leather creaked beneath them. "You must have an able steward."

"It was my queen, surely," answered the former with a slight shrug. "She knew I'd return here, and told me she'd arrive well ahead of time."

"A thoughtful, lady, then, worthy of her lord."

Although merely courteous, the words jarred King Haakon a little. Was he being unfair to his Gyda? Harking back, he remembered how seldom she was with him. He fared too much, too hard, from end to end of his kingdom.

Men swarmed in the yard to roar their greetings. She had invited everyone of mark from far and wide to feast with him. Springing to earth and striding forward, he saw her at the front door between two roofposts carven with twining vines and gripping beasts. Her gown was of the finest white linen under richly hued woolen panels, her headcloth embroidered. Gold rings coiled on her bare arms. But at her belt hung the bunched keys of a housewife. As Haakon neared, the round face lighted up.

On either side of her stood the highest-ranking guests. Closest on the right was a lean gray man whose voice pierced the hubbub: "Hail and welcome, King!"

"Oh, ever welcome," said Gyda, almost too low to be heard.

"I bring an outstanding man with me," said the king, "my namesake Haakon, son of the great Sigurd Jarl."

They looked at the stranger. Like his father, he was of middling height, but more powerfully built, wide shoulders and thick arms. His face was handsome, broad, high in the cheekbones, hawklike of nose, the neatly cut hair and beard midnight black. Above a ready smile, the greenish-gray eyes were always watchful.

"So this is our queen." His speech flowed as smoothly as his gait. "Glad I am to meet you, my lady—queenly indeed."

Gyda flushed. "In, in my lord's honor," she faltered.

Mostly she dressed like what she had been, a woman of the well-off yeomanry.

"I can hardly give you everybody's name at once," said the king. "However, here—" He went through them, they answered in seemly wise, till he came to the gray-haired man. "This is Eyvind Finnsson."

"Of course!" cried young Haakon. "The famous skald. I was only a boy, off in the corners, when I saw you at Hladi, but never have I forgotten. Later I was unlucky enough to be elsewhere each time you came, but how I do know your poems. All men do."

"I couldn't go with the king on this journey, being ill when he left," Eyvind sighed.

"You're well now, I hope, as I hope to hear the staves you must have been making."

"What else should I do than praise my king?"

Guthorm Sindri, another skald, who had gone along, bristled and snapped, "First *I* will tell of how he traveled in splendor."

Eyvind stiffened. "King," he said, "you know I was with your father King Harald Fairhair while Guthorm was still a younker on a farm."

The older Haakon chuckled. "Two skalds are like two cats in the same house." Then, earnestly: "You are both good men. How can I set one above the other?"

Haakon Sigurdarson took the word. "If I may, my lord, let me offer a way out. Since they can't both speak their verses at once, why not let sheer happenstance choose? That can't shame either of them." Everyone stared. A hush spread slowly across the yard. He put his right hand behind his back. "Watch, whoever stands at my rear. I've spread either two or three fingers. Eyvind, as the elder, will you guess which? If you're right, you shall go first, otherwise Guthorm; but both shall have the same honor, and skald-gifts of the same worth; and he who is second today shall be first tomorrow. King, is this your will?"

"It is," said Haakon Aethelstan's-foster.

Cheers rang. Even the skalds nodded and smiled. Eyvind lost the guess but took it well: "It may be that tomorrow

I'll have something to say forth about you too, Haakon Sigurdarson, if it please the king."

"I also, ere you leave us," said Guthorm hastily.

Guests then streamed into the hall, where the ale casks waited. They would drink before the dining boards were set up, and drink onward after these had been taken away. King Haakon got Haakon Sigurdarson aside as they went in. Queen Gyda stayed close to them.

"That was cunningly done," said the king. "I must remember the trick."

The young man grinned. "Well, my lord, I've gathered that it doesn't pay to affront a skald. King Eirik and Queen Gunnhild made a bad mistake when they did it to Egil Skallagrimsson, no?"

"You shall have a reward of me—not big, for this had better stay between us, but what would you like?"

Tongue licked lips. "Frankly, lord, a woman for my bed while I'm here. It's been the only lack, sailing south."

Yes, he was a lustful one, thought the older Haakon, however wise beyond his years he might be. The king turned to his wife. "Gyda, can you see to that?" he asked. "A maidservant, but not a thrall—freeborn and willing."

"I'll deal kindly with her, my lord and lady," young Haakon promised.

"She'll have my thanks too," said the king, "and something more besides," for pleasuring the son of the man who made him what he was, counseled him and helped him and stood by him through everything.

Gyda reddened, bit her lip, but nodded. Too late, her husband thought this was a lowly thing to make her do.

Nevertheless she soon joined him in the high seat. Haakon Sigurdarson sat across from them in the honor seat. The benches were full. Talk livened as the women went to and fro bringing drink.

"What's gone on lately in the South?" asked the king.

The lawman of the shire, sitting nearby, told him: "Some days ago, three warships went by Lidandisness—only three, but dragons and fully manned. This early in the year, they must have come from Denmark. Likeliest Jutland, for if they were out of Skaaney or Sjaelland, they'd have been seen passing Vikin. The ship-levy turned out, but by then they were gone."

Haakon Sigurdarson, who had been following keenly, leaned forward. "Could those have been Eirikssons?" he wondered aloud.

Anger surged hot in Haakon the king. This was not what he had wanted to come home to. "Why, if they did nothing?" he growled.

"To lull the Norsemen, maybe," said his namesake carefully. "Your Kings Tryggvi and Gudröd have had oddly little trouble for quite a span now, haven't they?"

"I've gotten a bellyful of folk taking fright like chickens. No more of it."

Gyda touched her husband's arm. "Everthing's gone well, really," she told him, "other than that I've missed you." She brightened. "Wait till you see our daughter. Little Thora—how she's growing! Cheery and dear—" But this was not man-talk. "Whenever you wish. She'll be so happy."

Mirth waxed in the hall. A plump young woman brought Haakon Sigurdarson a filled horn. Leaning over to let him see the cleft between her breasts, she spoke to him softly but boldly.

He laughed. "You, then? What did you call yourself? Thorgerd? Why, what a lucky name."

"How?"

"Thorgerd Shrine-bride watches over me."

King Haakon overheard. Up north he'd caught a few remarks about Thorgerd Shrine-bride. Lesser goddess, valkyrie, fetch, whatever she was—yes, through a sign or a dream, a Thraandish lad might well come to believe that such a Being was his heavenly helper, even as a Christian might call on some one saint.

"Sit down," said young Haakon. "Share my seat; let's drink together." He laid an arm around her waist and drew her to his side. "Later we'll do more." She giggled.

He was wholly a heathen, thought the king. Well, then he had never forsaken Christ.

"You're suddenly sad, my lord," murmured at his ear.

He roused. "No, no. Only a memory flitting past." He mustered a smile, lifting his goblet and voice. "This is a day for making merry!"

"Oh, it is," whispered Gyda.

All at once he felt the warmth from her, like the glow from a banked but living hearthfire. His gaze swept over rounded bosom and hips, back to the eyes with their fluttering lashes and the half-open lips. Yes, he knew, almost astonished, it would be good when tonight they were alone.

Not since his mother had a woman truly loved him.

XXIX

Now at last the will of King Harald Bluetooth hardened anew. Many and much had worked on him—Gunnhild, her sons, her brothers, Danes who hoped for fame and loot; priests urging that while Haakon the Apostate lived, the Faith could make no further headway yonder; his wish for revenge and for showing the world how mighty he was; the riches of scot to be had; Norse allies to help keep the German Emperor south of the Danework wall. And so he agreed to a third onslaught, with ships and levies of his to make it overwhelmingly huge. Aalf the Shipman and Eyvind the Braggart would lead these, while their nephew Harald led his own brothers and the men who had for so long followed them.

As Gunnhild counseled, nothing of this went abroad beforehand. Each chief must quietly see to it that his own folk were ready to go whenever bidden. If they got a feeling that he had in mind a viking cruise more high-reaching than most, it would seem believable. Danish yeomen need only be called up and brought to the ships that would be waiting for them. As that time neared, no traders, whether Danes or outlanders, would be let go from Denmark until the fleet had gathered at the island Hlesey in the Kattegat and set sail for Norway.

Thus Harald Eiriksson's steading was not yet abustle

when Gunnhild went to Bersi, its smith. She had sounded him out over the years. Lowborn, unwedded, ugly and surly as a troll, he knew not what to do or even how to feel when she now and then tossed a smile and a mild word into his loneliness. Other words of hers, spoken as if by-the-by, blew a cold wind over that thawing and froze it in the shape she wanted. For not only had he heard the whispers about her witch-skills; his baptism had hardly touched him. On certain nights he went out on the heath by himself to kindle a fire that glimmered small and red. He kept a thunderstone beside his straw pallet. It was also whispered that he had taken it from one of the dolmens and now, when alone in the dark, unwrapped it and worshipped it.

His hammer was banging when she trod into the smithy. Though the door stood open, he worked in gloom and smoke. His sooty face lifted and gaped. "Lady," he mumbled. "Uh, uh, lady."

"I want to talk with you and nobody else," said Gunnhild.

"Uh, yes. Right. Get out!" Bersi grunted to the boy puffing the bellows. "Well away. But not too far for me to shout you back when I want you." Pop-eyed, the lad scuttled off. The coal-glow began to fade as the hammer fell still. However, the smith was merely making a horseshoe. He peered at her from his thicket of hair and beard—upward, for broad and thick though he was, his bandy legs made him shorter. "What's the lady want o' me?"

"We must be quick today." Her voice thrust. "You shall forge me an arrowhead."

"Uh—*uh?*"

"For a fleinn."

"The lady knows o' such?" asked amazement.

"I do. It's the deadliest kind, with sharpened barbs on the head. And this shall be of your best workmanship, the skill and care you'd give to a sword. Moreover—and let nobody see—something besides iron shall go into it." She opened a hand to show him a silver finger ring. "Beat this into the metal."

"A—an arrow for a king?" he wondered.

Her smile flickered tight-lipped. "Yes, for a king. But be sure the silver does not show. And when you get it shafted and fletched, do not let that man put on any banding or other mark. I'll handle such things myself."

He gulped and shivered. "Quickly, now, I said, before somebody pays heed to this," she bade. "Take the ring." He held out an unsteady arm. She laid it in his paw, to shine on blackness till his fingers jerked shut around it.

"They'll know you come in here. C-can't help that."

"Yes, tell them the same as I will if they ask, that you're to make a lock-box for me." He hunched, belike afraid to guess what she'd keep in that box. "It's merely a tale, understand. We'll say I've allowed you to let the work wait for a while, you having other things you must do first."

"The arrow—"

"That as fast as ever you can, without giving away what's in it or who it's for. The sooner I have it, the better the reward I'll slip you." She smiled again, grimly. "I hope you never will find time for that lock, but will shortly be overwhelmed with work on war-gear.

"Meanwhile can you do what I ask as I ask, and hold all others from knowing?" He nodded dumbly. "Woe betide you if you fail in either. Keep faith, and I'll make you glad you did."

She left in a swirl of blue cloak and snowy gown. He stared into the day before he made signs and muttered words against bad luck and wicked Beings. Then he took out his thunderstone, rubbed it between his hands and over breast and loins, wrapped the ring up with it, and laid them aside. Stepping to the doorway, he bellowed for the thrall boy, "Hoy, stir your filthy feet; we've got that shoe to do over!"

Tomorrow he'd send his helper off on some errand. Beaten flat, smeared with grease and charcoal dust, the ring could go unmarked in among the short lengths of iron rod he'd cut for welding into the shape the witch-lady wanted. He had never told the boy what he was going to do next— nor much of anything else—so this shouldn't give rise to chatter.

It was indeed not long till a servant knocked on Gunnhild's door. He said Bersi had stopped him and asked him
to beg the lady's forgiveness for having a question about
her lock-box. "I'll see him," she said calmly, and walked
across the yard to the smithy.

Again Bersi had sent the boy elsewhere. Folk spied her
go inside, as they had done before, though again it was
only for a little while. It was not what another woman
would do, but she was unlike other women, and they remembered things much less easy to unravel. Maybe she
wanted some runes chiseled into the case. Two or three who
were devout crossed themselves.

"Here 'tis," said Bersi, holding up the arrow. "Is it to the
lady's liking?" He came near cringing, he who went away
alone for night offerings to land-wights or whatever they
were.

She took it and looked. The shaft lay snake-slender and
snake-smooth in her hands. She turned it over and over,
stroking it from gray goose feathers to narrow, bluish-
brown head. When she thumbed the point and barbs, she
found them keen.

"You have done well, Bersi." Her full smile washed over
him like sunshine through clouds. He dropped his gaze but
straightened as much as his stooped back was able.

"In reward," Gunnhild murmured, "I could give you
gold, but it's hard to see how you'd make use of it. Instead,
would you like a thrall—not that boy told off to help you,
but a woman of your own?" Into his hoarse gasp: "Oh,
Drumba's no beauty." She was in truth about as squat and
homely as he was. "But that would seem odd, and you'd
also have trouble with other men. She's strong, a more or
less willing worker, meek enough if she's beaten a little
once in a while, and—she knows many things to do with
a man." Gunnhild had seen to that, in ways which never
showed her part. It took hardly more than learning what
each of her underlings was like, then from time to time
nudging the right ones together. "Nobody will wonder. I've
already said aloud that it's wrong a man as useful as you
has no better a life."

Bersi could only swallow and stammer. "Give thought and let me know," said Gunnhild. She went from him with the arrow under her cloak.

This summer had thus far been warmer than most. The next day was as hot and still as ever anybody had heard of. Gunnhild bade her women and the guards stay behind when she walked forth, telling them sternly that she meant to think and would take it ill if some fool broke in on her. They obeyed, as much listless as awed. Of course, men would keep an eye out, but if she happened to go back of something for a while not too long, they wouldn't fret; there were no outlaws afoot.

Stark though her will was, she strode with this freedom singing in her. Heaven stood hard and cloudless, the sun a forge-fire. Few birds were aloft; few insects creaked in grass gone dry. The air smelled scorched. Rightward at the rim of sight shimmered a steely light cast off the fjord. She passed the lone oak where she and Brihtnoth had met. Beyond hulked the nearest of the dolmens. She went behind the mound and its huge stones. From there she saw—half saw—things shine and waver above the haunted mire, glimpses of trees and water and hills nowhere hereabouts, the Otherworld abroad at midday.

She took the arrow and a knife from hiding and laid them aside while she uncovered and unbound her hair. It tumbled downward. Gray was streaking its black. To take more clothing off out in the open would be too risky. Nor did she want to bare herself to the sun. Not any longer. Mirrors had shown her the crow's-feet at her eyes. Breasts had begun to sag, belly to hang. Though not too much yet, surely not too much. She was not ready to give in to being old.

She danced and sang beneath the blank sky, upon the dry earth. She cut her marks in the arrowshaft while telling it what to do and why. In the end she knotted her hair as best she could, fastened her headcloth, and gave a short prayer to Christ before she started back. Did he not want his Faith brought to Norway?

Kisping would sail with her son Harald against Haakon, as a bowman. She knew neither of them would like that, but she'd bring it about. First, however, she and Kisping must talk alone, maybe more than once.

He might not be needed. If he was, maybe nothing would come of it. But at least she'd have done what she could for her sons and Eirik's.

XXX

Going about through southern Norway, King Haakon passed into Hördaland. A hall and farmstead called Fitjar stood on the big offshore island Stord. Here he settled in with his following and sent for the yeomen from widely around to come feast and talk with him. Their boats and small ships crowded his warcraft, which bore him by water when he chose. Yard and buildings swarmed noisily with men.

It was soon after midsummer, nights hardly more than a twilight between two long, long days. About noon, the king and his guests went indoors to meat, for they would be at it quite a while.

Sunlight flooded around a few white clouds and hundreds of winging, crying seafowl. A strong breeze cooled and salted its warmth. Although a lesser island blocked sight westward from Fitjar, watchmen at the northern tip of Stord had a wide outlook over fjord and sea. Whitecaps glittered green. Now and then a whale breached mightily afar. Southward, along the edge of the farm, wildwood stood tall and murmurous. Grain rippled. Horses, kine, and sheep grazed their paddocks; swine, geese, and chickens wandered among the buildings. Ripening, the land dreamed. The watchmen grumbled a bit at missing out on food and drink, but not too unhappily. Their turn would come. Yes, they had much to look forward to. All Norway did.

Then over the worldrim hove a sail, and another, another, another. Ships were bound fast from the South, heeled over in the wind. Sometimes a spark of brightness flared—gilt on a figurehead? The men could not yet tell.

The king ought to hear about this, they said. But none

of them wanted to bear the news, so heavily did he penalize everyone who raised mistaken tidings of danger. While they dithered, more ships appeared. Indeed the king must know. A man quicker-witted than the rest dashed off. When he reached the hall, guests and guards were milling about, chatting, quaffing, finding their seats on the benches. Servants jostled by, setting up food-boards. The watchman found Eyvind Finnsson in the crowd, plucked the skald's sleeve, and panted that he had better come and look at something; there was no time to lose. Eyvind went straightaway out with his guide to the point. By then many craft were in sight.

Eyvind hurried back to the hall. Men had seated themselves as befitted their ranks. Eyvind trod in to stand before the king. He spoke through the hubbub: "Short is the time for doing, but long is the time for dining."

The cheer in Haakon froze. "What's afoot?" he snapped. Silence clapped down on the room. Eyvind answered:

> "The sons of Blood-ax are bidding us
> to the byrnie-Thing to meet them.
> Our need is not to sit idle
> but now and swiftly bestir us.
> To warn you of war is risky;
> this word must I nonetheless utter.
> Lord, we should linger no more,
> but leap to take up our weapons."

"You are too wise, Eyvind, to bring us any tale of war unless it be true," said the king. He rose to tower at the high seat. "Take down those boards!" he cried. "We'll go see."

Men flocked to the point and beheld what bore their way. Huge was that fleet. From each hull flashed mail and spearheads.

Haakon gathered his household troopers in council. Should they meet this onset with what help was on hand or scramble aboard their own ships and flee? "It's easy to see," he told them, "that we have a much greater strength against us today than ever before, even though it's seemed likewise when earlier we met the sons of Gunnhild."

They hung back, none willing to speak first. Wind sighed; waves rustled. At length quoth Eyvind:

> "Njörd among men, to steer northward
> now would be unwise of us,
> seeing as how from the South
> comes sailing the fleet of King Harald.
> Better it is to go boldly
> to battle at once, great sea-lord,
> holding our shields in our hands,
> hastening toward the foeman."

"That was a manly rede, and after my own heart," said Haakon. "Still, I'll hear what others think."

There being no more doubt as to what the king wished, most then said they would rather fall like men than fly before the Danes. This would not be the first time, they said, that they had been few against many and yet had overcome.

The king thanked them for their faithfulness and bade them go arm themselves. So did the yeomen when they heard. Otherwise, they knew, their homes would soon be in ashes, their kine slaughtered, any of their womenfolk and children who were worth having led off in bonds.

Haakon himself donned his mail, girded on his sword Quernbiter, put a gilt helmet on his head, took spear and shield. Thereupon he led the fighters to a meadow near the shore, got guardsmen and yeomen together into one array, and set up his banners. At his right hand loomed Thoraalf Skaalmsson, known as the Mighty although he was only eighteen; it was said that he and King Haakon were of the same strength. Eyvind the skald kept nearby.

Meanwhile the invaders had reached the strait between islands, grounded their ships in shallows or on strand, mustered themselves, and raised the standards of their leaders. Armor gleamed; painted shields glowered; spears stood against the sky like a woodland: for their host spread from water to pines in its deep wedge-shaped ranks, outnumbering the Norse maybe six to one.

King Haakon had Thoraalf hold his weapons while he pulled his byrnie off and cast it from him. A ragged hurrah lifted at his back. Men saw this less as recklessness than fearlessness; it kindled hope.

War-horns brayed; war-cries rang; seafowl took screaming flight. Earth thundered dully as the newcomers moved forward. Spears, arrows, slingstones flew thick. The first men fell; the first blood ran. The Norse stood their ground. Soon sword and ax clattered, hewing, cleaving.

To and fro swayed the struggle, wild and red. However fewer they were, the Norse gave as good as they got. Danes lay at their feet in windrows. Haakon shouted and thrust ahead. The line before him buckled. Grass began to show between clumps of foemen.

Thoraalf beside him, he went in front of his banner, smiting right and left. He had always been easy to ken among others, and today the gold on his helmet shone sunlike. More and more weapons turned toward him.

Forethoughtful, Eyvind the skald had tucked a hat under his belt as he left the hall for the battle. He pushed close and dropped the hat over the helmet. Busy with slaying, Haakon barely heeded.

Gunnhild's brother Eyvind the Braggart yelled through the din: "Has the king of the Norse gone into hiding, or has he fled? Where now is the golden helmet?" He laughed and sprang forward. Aalf the Shipman went with him. Like fools or madmen they cut blindly around them.

"Keep coming as you are coming," shouted Haakon, "and you'll find the king of the Norse!"

Nor was it long before Eyvind the Braggart got there. He swung his sword at Haakon, but Thoraalf rammed his shield against him so hard that he staggered. At once Haakon let go of his own shield, gripped the hilt of Quernbiter with both hands, and in one blow split Eyvind's helm and head down to the shoulders. In the same breath of time, Thoraalf killed Aalf the Shipman.

Onward over their bodies went Haakon and Thoraalf.

Close on either side and at their heels pressed the Norse. They had held their ranks more firmly than the Danes. So strong was their onset that they scattered the foe as a hard-driven prow scatters the water and makes foam of it. Fear came over the host of the Eirikssons. As often in a fray, it rushed through them like a tide-race. Suddenly they were all in flight, away toward their ships.

Haakon led his men after them, unstoppably and unstoppingly cutting them down. Their dead, their dying lay strewn, heaped, everywhere on the battlefield.

A few took heart, cornered wolves. They halted to make a stand. Again spears and arrows hailed.

From such a band stepped a skinny young bowman. "Make way for the king's bane!" he shrilled, and loosed a fleinn.

It struck Haakon at the left arm, deeply into the muscles under the shoulder. He dropped to one knee. Those of his followers who saw crowded around him. At this, the whole Norse onslaught wavered.

That gave the defeated a span in which to get away. The bowman scuttled along. Theirs was no ordered withdrawal. Many, cut off from their ships, threw themselves into the strait. Many others, however, were able to launch hulls and climb in. Among them were the sons of Eirik. Oars clawed water.

Haakon lurched to his feet. Leaning on Thoraalf's arm, he cried, "Onward!" The Norse rallied. He in their van, they sought their ships to give chase.

XXXI

Haakon bled heavily. When he had been helped aboard his warcraft, he lay down in the forepeak while a man skilled in such work tended him. Cruelly barbed, the arrowhead would not come loose, but must be cut free. Hard though he tried, the leech could not stanch the wound.

By now the crew had settled on their benches and were rowing forth. Haakon looked for a while at the wet and reddening cloth bound on him. "No," he said out of white lips. "Make an end of this strife. Let every man go home in peace."

His word flew from ship to ship. The Norse were not sorry to obey and turn back, as weary as they were, few of them without friends or kinsmen to grieve for. Yet neither were they very glad; nor could they be when they knew not what became of their king.

"As for me," he bade, "take me to Aalrekstad." This, not far north, was a house of his, where Queen Gyda waited.

Coming into the open fjord, his warriors saw the last of the Danes drop from sight. They snarled. Then they bent their backs anew to the oars, for they would be passing between islands, where the wind often got too tricky for sail.

The sun sank westward. Rays streamed long across the water, shadows across the hills. Haakon lay wordless, gazing into the sky, while the leech took cloth after blood-soaked cloth off him and put a fresh one on. Nobody else spoke either. The creaking of oars and gulls went lonely through stillness. Breezes chilled off.

Rocks made it too risky to go on after dark. Toward sundown they lay to under a knoll. Ashore, they made the best bed they could of hides and fleeces, and carried him to it. Those who were his nearest friends knelt beside him. They could barely hear his whisper. The lapping of water on stones was louder. The rest of the crew stood around, heads bowed, spears held point downward.

He looked up through dimming eyes to the bearded, weatherbeaten faces above. "This is my last bidding to you," he told them. "By the oaths you swore me, heed it well." He gasped for breath. "You know I have no child other than a little girl. Send word to the sons of Eirik, that they shall now be kings, but ask them to give my friends and kindred all honor and kindness."

"Lord," blurted Thoraalf, "we've got some of your house with us yet."

"The sons of Gunnhild—will never give up—and I

think—Gudröd and Tryggvi could not hold them off—
Spare Norway their wrath."

"But, King," said Eyvind the skald low, "you may live
on."

Haakon shook his head slightly. Sunset light gleamed off
the sweat on his skin. "If—I'm given—a longer life—I'll
go from you—to Christendom—and seek forgiveness—for
what I've done—against God." He smiled sadly into their
grief. "But if I die—in this heathen land—bury me however you will."

He closed his eyes. The breath rattled in his throat. Night
fell, wan and nearly starless, with nothing to hide the weak
death struggle.

His followers wept, the harsh, racking sobs of men who
had not since they were bairns.

As the tidings went everywhere, friend and unfriend alike
mourned. They said that never again would Norway see so
good a king. His body was brought to Saeheim in northern
Hördaland and laid to rest in full mail, the sword Quernbiter
at his side, a great mound over it. Men spoke at the gathering when the work was done, praising his deeds, wishing
him in Valhall.

Months afterward, Eyvind made a poem about how that
happened. It began with the names of two valkyries.

> "Göndul and Skögul
>   the Goth-god sent
>   to call from among all kings
>   an atheling born
>   with Odin to fare
>   and a home to have in Valhall."

It went on to tell of Haakon laughing as he reaped foes.
The staves clanged and crashed. When the valkyries came
for him, he wondered why. They told him Odin had indeed
given him victory. Now he would have honor among the
gods for as long as earth and heaven lasted. Bragi and Hermod welcomed him. At first wary, he said that Odin seemed
of ill will and he would keep his weapons handy. But when

they brought him in, he found gladness. Happy was the day of his birth; forever after his death would he be remembered.

It ended:

> "Free of his bonds,
> the Fenris wolf
> shall ravening rage through the world
> ere in Haakon's stead
> there sits a king
> who is match for a man like him.

> "Kine die,
> kinfolk die,
> the land lies lost to woe.
> Since Haakon went
> to the heathen gods
> many men have been thralls."

Although the poem was never forgotten, some said Eyvind took it from the one for Eirik Blood-ax. Henceforward the nickname Skaldaspillir, Skald-cribber, clung to him. But always everybody called King Haakon the Good.

BOOK FIVE

THE WITCH-QUEEN

1

For the last time before leaving Denmark, the sons of Gunnhild met in the house that was hers. Thence they would return to their homes, gather their men and ships, come back together at Hlesey, and set course anew for Norway.

Her gaze went across them. They sat in a half-ring, from Harald, almost thirty years of age, as strong-willed and sometimes thoughtful as the grandfather Fairhair whom he so much looked like, to stocky, yellow-haired Sigurd, maybe more haughty and loud-spoken than quite became his nineteen winters. Between them were the brash, freckled redhead Ragnfröd; fair-hued, sharp-faced, sharp-tongued Erling; bulky Gudröd of the brown locks and the brown eyes that to this day watched her with some awe.

These, at least, were left her.

They had rumbled their greetings and filled their horns. Now Harald said: "Mother, best if you take the first word."

"Yes, what can you tell us?" asked Gudröd eagerly.

"Little that you can't have foreseen," she answered. "However, you're here to make your plans. Rather than talking into each other's mouths, you may find I can more quickly set forth what's true and what's wise."

"What else than that we're the kings of Norway and had better not be slow to lay hold on it?" snapped Sigurd.

"Easy, brother," said Harald. "The question is: how. And—Mother, you have your ways of finding things out."

Erling scowled. "And ways of making them happen," he muttered.

"Silence!" bade Harald. "I'll hear no word of those foul lies about—what went on at Fitjar—not even from any of you."

"No, nor I," agreed Ragnfröd. "They slander all of us."

Gunnhild smiled. "Thank you, my good sons. Yes, we'll keep your names swordblade-bright." She stopped for a few heartbeats. The hearthfire flickered, shadows shifted. "But for the sake of that, as well as your lives," she told them, "I warn you not to rush ahead like wild boars, but to *think* ahead."

She had them caught, she knew, hearkening like the gods to that spaewife who foretold how the world shall end.

"First and always," she said, "hold together. The same father got you; the same mother bore you; you grew to manhood under the same roofs. Let nothing break the bonds between you, nothing ever, anger, greed, the wily words of ill-wishers, pride itself. Keep tight the shield-wall you share, for many are they who will want you dead.

"We're bound for a kingdom not glad of us, a kingdom that's yours only because the man you felled"—let them so deem it—"left it to you. Most of those who acknowledge you will do so only because that was his wish.

"And others will not.

"Steer for the middle of Norway, Hördaland, Sogn, the neighboring shires. Settle in there, for there's where most of the chieftains will stand by you and speak on your behalf, strong, well-liked men such as Arinbjörn Thorisson after he's come back into his own. Deal fairly with them; bear with them if they sometimes gainsay you; make them your friends.

"Elsewhere, hold off. The Thraandlaw must be in uproar. Sigurd Jarl can keep the folk from utter recklessness, but he'll nurse revenge in his heart. He'll bide his time, though, watchful. Let us use that time to search for ways of bringing"—she gave them a chill smile—"peace to the North.

"Likewise for the South. King Tryggvi and King Gudröd will be readying to call up their levies. Give them no reason to. Make no threats. Don't show yourselves in those parts."

Erling bristled. "What?" he cried. "Shall we sit idle in merely half of what's ours by right?"

Sigurd nodded. "Soon all men would take us for sluggish cowards."

"And soon, then, they'd strike at us." Ragnfröd's lips twisted. "Flight back to Orkney—No!"

"Of course not," Harald said. "Hear the wisewoman out."

"You shall have what is yours," Gunnhild promised

them. "Only go after it carefully, bit by bit. Harald Fairhair did not win the whole of Norway overnight, nor can you win it speedily back. But do so you shall."

Her look and voice went stern. "That's if you're steadfast. None of you can overcome by himself. That way lies death. You must have one who's your leader throughout, even as a ship can have only one skipper. That should be Harald, the oldest among you." And the brightest, the best fitted for the task, she did not say aloud.

Sigurd reddened. "I, a low, scot-paying shire-king?" he yelled.

Harald lifted a hand. "No. We've thought on this, our mother and I. Each of us shall bear the full name of king. Each shall have his own holdings and household troops. We can't dwell together; that many men would soon eat the land bare. Yet one of us must deal with the world, and the world must know who he is."

Gunnhild rose. She stood in the uneasy light at the middle of the half-ring, a small woman before these big men, lords of lands and ships, warriors who had often slain other men and bedded other women. Somehow she loomed over them.

"Here, among yourselves, with nobody else listening," she said, "here on your own honor give Harald your oath, not that you shall be reckoned his underlings or pay him scot, but that you will faithfully stand by him while he steers Norway for the good of us all and the abidingness of our house."

They were still for a while. This did not take them altogether by surprise. She had been talking with them and teaching them, year by year. After a little Erling said slowly, "I'll swear to it if Harald and the rest of us will swear not to buckle under to heathendom, but instead crush it underfoot."

"That can't be done overnight either," Harald answered. "However, yes, we'll go forward with it wherever we can. I've no wish to burn in Hell alongside Haakon Aethelstan's-foster."

Gunnhild sat down. She had won what she set out to

win. Hereafter she must seem to be counseling them what to do, not ordering them.

"Also," she said, "besides salvation, the Church opens a way to more power for kings than ever erenow in the Northlands. Look at England; look at the Empire. Harald Bluetooth did."

Harald Eiriksson bridled. "Harald Bluetooth shall have no sway over us." The others growled agreement.

"No, but you need not boast of that—beforehand," said Gunnhild. "I've spoken with him, you know. After what he's given you, he does think you should be his vassals. However, there's enough here in Denmark to keep him busy. For one thing, he seeks ties eastward. Now that his queen, my namesake, has died, he's dickering to get a daughter of the new Polish king to wife. He'll leave you a free hand for a while, a span for you to strengthen yourselves in. This will be the more so if you do try to make Norway Christian. He won't want the Emperor to see him as getting in the way of such a work."

"Now there's a good rede!" cried Erling. She knew that much of his glee sprang from the sudden hope that she, his mother, was not after all a heathen witch.

Harald laughed. "Later on—who knows?"

Gunnhild let their talk surge back and forth, until in the end they filled their horns afresh, drew the swords they had put aside, drank and clanged and roared their oath to Harald and each other.

Thereupon they started for the hall. The foremost among their men awaited them. Great would be the drinking, bold the boasts and vows, before dawn again whitened the sky.

She could linger here for a breath and a thought. Having followed her sons outside, she stayed near the door, which she left open to let the breeze wander in.

It kissed her. A sweet smell of haymaking flowed through it. The sun had gone low in the west. A few clouds began to glow, beyond reaches of heath already dusking. So did the mists that eddied ghostly above the mire. Closer to hand, the crowns of trees shone shadowful. Rooks, flocking black across heaven, cawed louder in her ears than the manifold noises of King Harald's steading.

Farewell, she thought. Might she never see this land again. Still, it had sheltered her and hers, and in its small way it was lovely. Maybe sometimes, she thought, a slight wistfulness would touch her rememberings of it. Who could foreknow?

"Queen—" broke in on her.

She turned. Her footling Kisping had stolen out of nowhere, as often aforetime. He was bathed, neatly clad, and lately shaven, for he had the wit to keep the scraggly black whiskers off his narrow, sallow face. As wontedly, his gaunt frame hunched the least bit beneath her eyes.

"Forgive me, Queen, but may I speak with you?" he asked.

She had always disliked his hint of a whine. But she had never had a tool better for the uses to which she put it. "You may," she said, "if it be short."

"Queen, you'll soon leave Denmark."

Shipboard again, stabbed through her: cramped, never alone, striving not to fall and become a laughingstock, eating food as salt as the waters, drinking from a horn unsteadily held, and—however much the men tried to help her stay queenly—humbled by tumbling seas and bitter winds. It was not well for a woman to spend much of her life in ships. So had her brother Aalf the Shipman said, long and long ago when he took her up to Finnmörk. Yet she had.

Aalf, sturdy and true; Eyvind, wild and laughterful: killed at Fitjar, their bones most likely unburied, picked clean by carrion birds as Eirik's had been.

She willed grief away. She had her sons to think of, those that were left to her. "Yes, everybody knows," she heard herself say. "I'll welcome your coming along if you like. You've served me well." Not least in being close-mouthed. That was something too seldom found.

"It's been my happiness, my lady." Did Kisping snicker, barely? "And my gain. Oh, yes. Nobody else could do by me as you've done, my lady, and thankful I am."

"Come, then," she said. "In Norway I can reward you more openly than here."

He looked down and wrung his hands. "I beg my lady's forgiveness, but that may not be the best for either of us. More openly, I mean."

"Say on."

"Well, Queen, there *are* those tales—about me in the battle—Oh, no man really knows. It was a storm, a mad muddle. Nobody knows for sure what was going on. All I know, all I've told anybody, is, yes, of course I did my best throughout, though I'm the first to agree I'm not a warrior of much worth. Still—those tales will drift to the Norsemen. Many among them must yearn—oh, how unrighteously—to get revenge for their King Haakon. Whether or not they believe the gossip, still one of them may well catch me alone and take his anger out on me."

He was right, Gunnhild thought. There had been no way to keep hints from leaking free and folk from wondering and muttering. Now, a waylaying, an ax or sword, and if the deed came to light, why, the wergild for a man this lowly was small. "Then what have you in mind, sly one?"

"Well, Queen, if, once we're ashore, I go by another name—those of King Harald's men who knew me will give it scant thought or none. A few may grin and sneer." Kisping shrugged. "Their scorn will soon pass. So, I beg you, my lady, call me something else, anything besides Kisping."

This came near being funny. Yet it was not witless. Gunnhild smiled. "To me you'll always be Kisping, my ferret," she said. "However, let me think—hm—Ögmund? That's a name oftener heard in Norway than in Denmark. It won't mark you out." Inwardly she thanked him, that he had, for this short spell, whimpered her mind off sorrow and back toward hope. "Yes, I'd liefer not lose you, Ögmund-to-be. I've use for you still."

11

Harald reckoned he would stay in the hall on the Byfjord oftener than anywhere else. There was the heart of the midlands, where he and his brothers were safest, in a busy and growing harbor through which flowed men and wealth, while the waters could shelter as many warships as he might want. There his mother would find a home. He ordered her old bower torn down, enough trees cleared away, and a house built. That work took some time, for, although not itself a hall, it was to be roomy, laid out according to her wishes, richly decorated and furnished, with a high seat for her.

Through fall and winter, well into spring, he was mostly gone. The Eirikssons must fare widely around, show themselves and their might, get to know the leading men, get hailed kings at Thing-meetings—which happened, though with scant cheer—and one by one settle in on the lands which each was to have.

Harald worked to make peace with the lords left by Haakon. Spokesmen went to and fro, month after month. His words were strict but not overly harsh. He and his brothers would swear no oaths by heathen gods, and any try to make them take part in any heathen rite would mean war. Otherwise they were willing to bargain. Slowly agreement was forged. Gudröd Bjarnarson in Vestfold and Tryggvi Olafsson in Vikin were to keep the names of king and everything else that was theirs, on the same footing as with King Haakon.

Gunnhild's thoughts were helpful. There were no grounds to harm the widow and daughter of Haakon Aethelstan's-foster, she said. Rather, kindness would be wise. With soft speech and gifts not too costly, she brought it about that Gyda wedded a longtime follower of her and her sons. They bestowed a goodly holding on him and made him a hersir. He treated the former queen quite well and fostered his stepchild with the richest yeoman in the neighborhood. That neighborhood was off in the Uplands and did not see many outsiders.

It went harder dealing with the Thraandlaw and took longer. Those shires now paid no scot whatsoever, nor did they acknowledge any new king. But at length an understanding was reached here too. Sigurd Jarl was likewise to keep the same power as before; the Thraands would live under their own laws; in return, they would do nothing to trouble the Eirikssons. They and Sigurd having sworn to this by the God or gods that were theirs, Gunnhild thought the bond could easily be broken, come the day.

Meanwhile she was the lady at the Byfjord. Folk looked to her and heeded her. She received visitors, feasted them, questioned them, charmed those she could and slipped a little fear into those who stayed cold. They remembered her hereabouts, after all the years.

For her also this land was haunted—waiting for Eirik, welcoming him back, her youngest sons and her blossoming daughter, wreaking the death of Haalfdan the Black; Eirik bringing victory home from the South, and at last ships gathering for the flight to Orkney and everything that waited there.

Well, then, she thought, let here be where a new beginning took root.

Late in spring Harald returned, which he had otherwise done only fleetingly. Now he meant to abide for a while and tighten his grip on these parts. His foremost skald, Glum Geirason, had made a poem in his praise which gloated over how he avenged Gamli and Guthorm in the blood of Haakon Aethelstan's-foster. It went from mouth to mouth until it got to Eyvind Finnsson at his house. Thereupon the old skald angrily made one about Haakon's overcoming of Gamli. By then he had likewise told of Haakon's going to Valhall.

Those who wanted to curry favor with King Harald were quick to bring him news of this. Wrathful, Harald outlawed Eyvind. Anyone might slay him without owing gild for it, but the king might well give such a killer a handsome gift.

Gunnhild hastened to draw her son aside. No luck could

come of putting skalds to death. Theirs was the witchcraft
of words, which lived on after them. She reminded him of
what evil had sprung from the hatred of Egil Skallagrimsson. Even the harm that fiend did with his hands was less
than the bad name he laid on her and her man, Harald's
father. Besides, here there was kinship; on the distaff side,
Eyvind was a great-grandson of Harald Fairhair. Now was
a very good time for Harald Eiriksson to behave openheart-
edly. Everybody would think the better of him for it.

So friends went between him and Eyvind, who came up
to the Byfjord on promise of safety. Harald lifted the ban
on condition that henceforward Eyvind should be his skald,
as he had been King Haakon's. Eyvind took this and, in
the hall, under the eyes of high and low alike, gave back:

> "Never wavered your will
>   for warfare, Hördaland's king,
> when arrows broke on byrnies
>   as bowstrings drew taut and sang,
> but, Harald, strongly you held
>   the hilt of the clanging sword.
> Often have you offered
>   much eating to the she-wolf."

Men called the poem well done, and Harald himself was
pleased. Gunnhild deemed it utterly hollow—and what did
the skald really mean when he bespoke "the she-wolf"?—
but said nothing aloud.

Eyvind went home and, although now King Harald's
man, was seldom with him.

Still, as Gunnhild foretold, the forgiveness bought some
goodwill, or at least some easing of wariness. The brothers
could move further on toward unhindered overlordship.

On a hill a few miles outside the town a halidom had
stood for ages beyond knowing. Trees grew tall around a
barrow which folk kept clear of brush; on top of it reared
a standing stone, lean and lichenous. A shelter below gave
roof to wooden images of Thor, Frey, and Njörd, likewise
kept washed and freshly painted. They looked over a patch

of ground blackened by fires and a rock blackened by the blood of slaughterings. Thither twice yearly went yeomen, fishermen, hirelings, their wives and older children, to bless the land at the turnings of the sun.

Formerly dwellers in the town came too, and a few did yet, but the inflow of outlanders and new thoughts had made many Christian and weakened the beliefs of the rest. The little church that King Haakon built in his early days had lasted on through the later years. Its priest was a man born in the neighborhood, with barely enough learning to hold mass and hear confessions, his living mainly from the farm he owned; but when he rang his bell, the song went over the town and far across the waters.

Thus Harald met no foes when, shortly before midsummer, he led his guards forth against Thor.

They cast down the standing stone; they cut down the shaw; they heaped firewood before the altar and there they burned the gods. All through the short, light night those flames blazed and crackled. Then they flickered low on charcoal and ashes until, next day, rain wept them out.

Harald's brothers did the same, where and when they handily could.

Most folk were shocked. These seemed to them to be dreadful deeds. However, they could do nothing more than light their own fires on the eve. Maybe later. One did best to wait and see.

In Vikin and the Thraandlaw they were openly wrathful.

That summer turned bleak. Hailstorms smote cropfields and the fishing was poor.

Gunnhild kept aware of what was happening, but her whole mind was no longer on it. To her had come Hrut Herjolfsson.

111

Although highborn and lowborn were everywhere around and heedful of her, although she had the ear of King Harald and of her other sons when they came visiting,

loneliness gnawed. She could lessen it somewhat by going
out to be with sky, water, earth, wildwood, seeking a oneness with them such as she had sought in Finnmörk, but
never winning to it. She could not do this often, nor walk
far, without men worrying and searching for her. Nor could
she often send her household staff off, lest there arise too
much wondering about what she did by herself. She had
not altogether quelled the priest; it would be troublesome
if he began to ask and nag.

One eventide she did empty the house for a night, saying
that once again she needed silence for prayers and medi-
tation. From her locked chest she took the drum, the herbs,
the runic bones, things secretly gotten in the course of the
years. She ate, sang, danced about a lampflame that her
gaze never left, until sleep came in a dark tide and she lay
down to dream.

A man walked through that dream, tall, strong, golden
of hair and beard, his face not unlike Eirik's although the
eyes were a deeper blue and the mouth lacked hardness.
Longing kindled lust, hot in heart and loins. A wind blew.
It gained a voice, which keened high-pitched in the Finnish
tongue; but it told her much.

She woke blinded by night, shuddering toward calm. As
the first white light stole into the east, she went out and
breathed chill freshness. Dew washed her feet. Now there
was a thrilling in her, a looking forward. This had been no
more than a spell of farseeing, of foresight. She must think
how to use the knowledge.

A while after, in late summer, a hint of yellow on the
birches, she heard—no news was slow to reach her—that
a big ship was heading in. Calls had already flown between
it and the land. Gunnhild's blood leaped. "Are Icelanders
aboard?" she asked. Yes, she was told, the ship hailed from
there. It belonged to a trader named Özur, who had with
him his nephew Hrut Herjolfsson. "Then I know his errand," she said. "Hrut has come to claim an inheritance
that's fallen to him. But a man named Soti has seized it."
The talebearer stared at her and shivered a bit.

She sent him away and had Kisping—Ögmund, here—

brought to her. "Go down to the harbor," she bade. "Find Özur and Hrut. Tell them I invite them to stay with me this winter. Say that I'll be their friend, and if Hrut follows my redes, I'll stand by him in his claims and anything else he means to take up, and I'll also further his cause with the king."

Ögmund sped off. The Icelanders greeted him well when they learned he came from the queen. He drew them aside from the bustling on the wharf and gave them his message. They went off by themselves and spoke low. Ögmund could easily guess that Özur warned against offending Gunnhild. He took their yea back to her. "This I've awaited," she said. "I've heard Hrut is a wise and well-bred man. Now keep a lookout, and let me know as soon as they enter the town."

Friends and kinsmen of Özur's had gone down to welcome him. He and Hrut lodged with one of them for the night. On the way to that house, they met Ögmund again. He brought them greeting from Gunnhild, and told them she could not receive them before they had met the king. "Otherwise gossip would have it that my lady makes too much of you," said the footling. "But leave everything to her. Hrut need only speak freely to the king and ask him for a post among his guards. Meanwhile, here's garb that Gunnhild sends you." He gave Hrut a package. "Wear this when you go before him."

Next day Hrut and Özur went to the hall, ten of their friends along. Hrut trod in first, splendidly clad. King Harald sat at the drinking board with some of his own friends. His mother sat across from him among a few women. Her heart stumbled at sight of the newcomer. How beautiful he was!

The king also looked closely, and asked who this might be. Hrut told what his name, his home, and his business were. "I seek your help, lord, in getting my rights."

"I have promised that every man in this land shall have his rights under the law," said the king. "Is there anything else you wish of me?"

"Yes, lord," answered Hrut. "I ask for a place in your

guard, and that you take me as a man of yours."

King Harald made his face a mask and sat silent.

Gunnhild took the word. "It seems to me this man is showing you great honor. If there were many like him in your guard, it would be well filled."

The king's gaze thawed. "Is he a sage man?"

"Both wise and able," she said.

The king turned to Hrut. "I think my mother would like you to have the rank you ask for," he said. "But for the sake of worthiness and usage, don't come back here for half a month. When that time is past, you shall become a trooper of mine. Meanwhile my mother will see to your needs. Then come before me again." In that span he could find out what men knew about Hrut and thought of him; but it was not likely he would slight Gunnhild.

She beckoned to Ögmund, who had been standing by as watchful as a squirrel. "Take these two to my house and treat them well," she ordered. He led Hrut and Özur off. Their followers paid the king their respects and went home.

Gunnhild's house stood by itself on stone groundworks, some three hundred yards from the hall and garth. Its timbers were painted dark red-brown, like the trunks of the pines in back of it and on either side. A gallery ran around the upper story, beneath a high-pitched roof of cedar shakes. The outthrusting ends of the ridgepole and main rafters were shaped into beast heads that threatened any trolls or ghosts or night-gangers, but the porch pillars and the doorposts bore carvings of twining, leafy vines. This was a cold day where smoky clouds hurried under a leaden overcast, as many days had been since midsummer. Wind tossed the murky boughs. Rushing between them, it sounded like surf.

Inside, however, were warmth, a hearthfire scented with herbs, lamplight and candlelight soft upon tapestries. Wonderfully woven, these seemed themselves to be a wildwood, teeming with creatures four-legged or winged among trees and flowers never seen on earth. Hounds and horsemen chased deer, Sigurd Faafnir's-bane slew the dragon, warriors rode with ravens overhead and wolves close behind;

but some of the signs here and there were unknown to Norsemen.

Juniper rustled underfoot as Ögmund took the Icelanders through the long room. "Now you shall see it's true what I told you from Gunnhild," he said. He looked more or less squarely at Hrut. "Here is her high seat. Take it and keep it, even when she herself comes in."

Özur and Hrut swapped a glance. The older man shrugged, twitched a grin, and chose the lower seat on the right. Hrut stood for a little, thinking, before he did as he was bidden. Ögmund had maids bring them food and drink.

They had not long to wait before the queen arrived. Hrut rose. "Keep your seat," she said merrily. "It shall be yours all the while you stay with me."

She mounted the dais and settled there beside him. More drink was borne in, both mead and wine. The vessels were silver, cast with figures like those on the hangings.

Özur kept as quiet as might be. Talk ran in spate between Gunnhild and Hrut. He had never been slow of speech or dull of wit. From him she heard of his background: his forebears—among them the hero-king Ragnar Hairybreeks and a famous woman, Aud the Deep-Thinking; his home westerly in the Broad Firth Dales; then this business of the inheritance, a hundred marks, which fell together with a hankering to go abroad and make a name for himself. What with foul winds, the crossing to Norway took three weeks. She saw in his eyes and heard in his voice how long that had felt.

For her part she had endlessly much to tell, carefully, about her life and what she knew of the world. It gripped him.

Özur said early in the evening that he was getting sleepy. Ögmund led him to a shut-bed elsewhere in the house. Gunnhild and Hrut talked on.

At length she said, wholly aware of what she did and what power was hers: "Tonight you shall go upstairs with me, we two together."

"It shall be as you wish," he answered, not quite steadily.

But when she smiled at him, he smiled back. In this light she did not look overly old.

They took a candlestick of three branches with them. At once when they were in her bedroom she barred the door and swung toward him. He set the candlestick down and took her in his arms. When her headcloth came off, the coils of hair shone night-black, with hoarfrosty glints of silver. Nor, when shamelessly unclad, was she a hag, not yet, not yet.

He was hot, bull-strong, and quick to learn what she liked. Soon she flew from herself almost as wildly as with Eirik. At last they slept.

When they woke they dressed and went downstairs for their morning bread and drink. Two watchmen were on hand, as was wonted. Gunnhild stopped, looked up into their eyes, and told them sweetly, "It shall cost you nothing but your lives if you say anything to anyone about Hrut and me."

Their nods were stiff. Of course, there was no way to keep maids, carls, thralls, and the like from babbling, but they always did. The wellborn gave such gossip a deaf ear, or made believe to.

Özur asked leave to go stay with his kin, whom he had missed. Gunnhild granted it. For the next half-month, she and Hrut were mostly by themselves.

He did have his trade goods unloaded from the ship. At the end of the time, he ordered his gift borne to her—a hundred ells of wadmal and twelve sheepskin cloaks, Icelandic wares—in return for her kindness, as he said while others were with them. She thanked him. They snatched a short span alone for him to kiss her and say his own thanks. That kiss burned long on her lips.

"This is not farewell," she whispered. They must now sleep apart, but for the time being she was slaked. Indeed, walking to the hall hurt somewhat. At her behest, thirty men followed him when he went there to stand before the king.

"Well, Hrut," said Harald, "belike you still wish me to keep my promise."

So Hrut became one of the guard. "Where shall I sit?" he asked.

The king sighed. "Let my mother settle that."

Thus Gunnhild got him a seat among the foremost. A man of such rank could very understandably call on her now and then, to ask her rede about this or that, under four eyes. If otherwise he tumbled a few wenches, it would look all the more believable.

Hrut proved to be as able as she had said, and got along well with everybody. He passed that winter in good cheer and high honor.

IV

Heavy snowfalls and wild storms blocked most faring. Not until spring did Hrut learn that Soti had lately sailed for Denmark, taking the money of the inheritance with him. He went at once to Gunnhild. It gladdened her to say, "I'll give you two longships with full crews, and moreover the boldest man we have, Ulf the Unwashed, guest foreman." Hrut knew what she meant, the headman of those guards whom the king sent to find and kill foemen of his and on other dangerous errands. "But go to the king first, of course."

Hrut did so as soon as he got leave to and told how things were. "Now I'm minded to go after him," he ended.

"What help has my mother given you?" asked Harald.

"Two longships, with Ulf the Unwashed to lead the warriors."

"That's well done. And now I'll give two ships more, likewise manned. Nonetheless, I think you'll not have any too much strength."

All busked themselves fast. King Harald himself went down to see Hrut off. Gunnhild stood on the wharf in the wind, looking after him, till the last hull was lost to sight. She returned to her house full of thought. She could do more yet for him, that which nobody else knew how or dared to. The swallow was going to fly again.

Less friendly was the king toward many others. After all, they bore scant love for any of the Eirikssons. As Gunnhild wove her web anew, tidings of trouble reached her ever oftener. The earliest this year came when the snows had melted and the kings could make their rounds. Harald and his men rode into the garth of the lendman Gisli Gunnarsson, eastward in Haddingjadalar shire. Rain had drenched them; sleet had bitten them; they were chilled through and through. Word had gone ahead: hall and outbuildings were ready for guests. However, Gisli received them surlily. The mood at meat and drink was not cheerful.

"What ails everyone?" asked Harald at last.

"This bids fair to be another bad year, lord," said Gisli. "I wonder how long they'll go on."

"That's as God wills."

"Some say it's that the gods are wroth at what's being done to their halidoms."

"Heathen rubbish!" flared the king. He curbed his anger. "When folk have let the light of Christ into their hearts, all will soon be well."

"All was well aforetime," answered the lendman. A fist lay knotted on his lap like stubbornness itself. "There are those who miss King Haakon. This is nothing but the truth, lord. I could lie about it, but that'd be unworthy of you, wouldn't it?"

Yes, Gunnhild thought, most Norsemen who took the new faith while Haakon reigned seemed to have done so for his sake, because he was what he was. They were few, though, and at last he gave up trying, because he was what he was.

Her sons would not yield as he did. But hardly anyone would go to baptism to please *them*, whether or not offerings still went on afterward behind their backs. To bring in new missionaries would be to endanger those priests. The slaying of even one might unloose war between kings and yeomen. No, for a long time to come, her sons had better not wreck many more heathen shrines, and must beyond question treat men of whatever belief the same way.

Which might well be for the best, thought Gunnhild. The

world was darker and stranger than humans knew—than humans could know. Nor would she let go of what power she drew from its shadows. Never had she forgotten those outlaws in Seija's hut.

She did not utter this. Enough that men felt a breath of it from her.

Giving way came harder to her sons. King Harald repaid sullenness with coldness. When he left, Gisli, sour-faced, gave him a good horse with a silver-inset saddle and headstall; but the king in return gave merely a finger ring. Gisli was not seen wearing it afterward.

In truth, all the Eirikssons were getting a name for greedily grasping but stingily giving. Gunnhild wondered how folk could be made to understand. Each king had his warriors and more than one household to keep, big and costly, although his holdings were not great and the bad year had shrunk the scot he could take in. Why should he enrich men who barely kept hidden their hatred of him?

It came to be said that the Gunnhildssons buried their hoards of gold and silver. Eyvind Skald-cribber made a poem about this, recalling how treasure flowed from the hand of King Haakon the Good but did no longer.

As he might have foreseen, and maybe did, the staves reached Harald's ears. The king sent for him and, when he arrived, brought lawsuit against him for betrayal. "It ill becomes you to be my foe," said Harald as Eyvind stood in front of his high seat, with guardsmen grimly listening, "after you've entered my service."

The graybeard looked straight into his eyes and answered through the hush:

> "Only one lord had my oath,
> almighty king, before you.
> Now, with old age drawing nigh,
> not do I wish for a third.
> Faithfully did I follow
> the first. Two shields bore I never.
> I yield me today to you.
> My years will soon overtake me."

Harald remembered what his mother had told him. Still, he could not let this go by. He claimed self-judgment in the case. Eyvind wore a big, finely wrought golden ring, called Moldi because, lifetimes ago, it had been found in the earth, lost or left by some chieftain long forgotten. Harald said it would be his gild for the wrongdoing. Eyvind had no choice. Quoth he when he handed it over:

"I hope that you, who halter
 the horse of the sea, and I
 henceforward shall be friends,
 having thus made our peace,
 even though now you own
 the arm-ring that once was mine,
 formerly borne by my father
 and forebears from of old."

He never came near the king again. But, as Gunnhild had warned, his poems winged from end to end of Norway, and would not die.

Yet Harald was no more harsh than he felt he must be. Rather, if men showed him goodwill, he gave it back, often quite freely.

Thus, one time during this bleak summer, he was at Hardanger when a merchant ship came from Iceland. The cargo was sheepskins. The skipper had heard that hereabouts were many dwellers. However, nobody seemed to want the fells he offered. Having met the king aforetime and learning he was on hand, the chapman sought him out and bewailed how badly his undertaking was going. Harald smiled and promised to come have a look. In a fully manned karfi, the king was rowed out to the ship, which lay at anchor in the fjord. Seeing that the wares had nothing wrong with them, he asked if the skipper would give him one. "Yes, lord, and more if you want."

Harald took a gray-fleeced hide, draped it over his shoulders, and went back aboard his own craft. Before it left, every man of the crew bought a skin. In the next few days, so many came to do likewise that not half of them got any.

Thenceforward and ever after, this king bore the nickname Harald Grayfell.

Meanwhile Gunnhild had, while alone, tracked what happened in the straits and on the sea. Hrut's ships met those of an outlaw called Atli. A sharp fight began. Though Atli killed Ulf, Hrut gave Atli his death-blow. The victors took a rich booty, along with the two best ships, and fared on over the Baltic in viking.

They did not find Soti. He had doubled back to Norway. The swallow saw.

Like any wellborn householder, Gunnhild must needs go elsewhere from time to time, while her home was cleaned and aired. Now she rode to the Limgard neighborhood, where her son Gudröd was staying.

Soti grounded at Limgardside. To him came Ögmund and struck up talk, without telling whose man he was. "Will you be here long?" asked Ögmund.

"Three days, I think, refitting," said Soti. "Then we're off to England, and will never come back while Gunnhild rules in Norway."

The footling spoke disarming words and scurried off to his queen. He told her what Soti had in mind. She asked Gudröd to catch Soti and kill him. He had grievously wronged a friend of hers, she said. Nothing loth, Gudröd led his warriors off, overcame Soti, took him inland, and hanged him.

Gunnhild sent all the goods to the Byfjord.

About harvest time—and again that was a lean harvest—Hrut returned, well laden with gains. King Harald received him gladly, and heard the tale of his doings. "Lord," ended Hrut, "have what you will of my winnings." The king happily took a third. Now Hrut stood high indeed in his household.

Gunnhild told Hrut how she had gotten Soti done away with and saved his inheritance for him. He thanked her much, and gave her half of what was left him. Later, when they were alone, they gave back and forth another kind of thanks.

So passed that winter.

V

But as the days lengthened, Hrut's mood darkened. Ever more did he sit unspeaking among his fellows; nor had he much to say even to Gunnhild.

Snow melted; brooks brawled; buds unfolded in a mist of pale green; sunlight sparkled on wet grass; homebound birds filled heaven with wings and cries. Hrut took to walking off whenever he had time free.

For weeks Gunnhild watched without saying anything about it. She had foreseen this from the beginning, she thought with a daily sharpening sadness, but hidden it away from herself. Another witchcraft than hers was at work.

If she held back much longer, that which was going to happen would happen without her. Such a loss and shame she would not suffer. A day came when she and Hrut shared her high seat, nobody else about other than servants. Those would hear, and spread what they heard, but now she would as soon have witnesses. Let nobody ever think she had wept or begged.

He sat staring into the fire, a cup of mead untasted in his hand. Outside, wind blustered and rain hissed. She gathered her will together. "Are you sick at heart?" she asked.

His gaze did not leave the restless flames. "As the saying runs, 'Ill does he fare who eats outland bread.' "

"Do you want to go back to Iceland?"

Now he looked at her. His face and voice came alive. "Yes!"

She drew a breath before she asked, "Have you a woman yonder?"

She saw him go taut. "No," he said stiffly. "Nothing like that."

For an eyeblink she felt as though he had slapped her. His crew had known, and therefore she knew almost from the first, that he was betrothed to a fair maiden, Unn Mördardottir, back there. The wedding had been put off three years while he went abroad. She kept her knowledge quiet.

It was understandable if he felt shy about telling her. But today, when less than half that span was spent, he lied. Did he mean not to irk her who had been useful to him? Or did he not want to utter his deepest hopes to the old bitch?

"I don't quite believe that," she said coldly. Thereafter they spoke little, he awkwardly, and soon he left. She slept hardly at all that night.

By morning she could show the world a mask. Hrut was bound to seek out the king. He must have been waiting for sailing season, and his talk with her yesterday had set his mind hard. Gunnhild made sure to be there.

The weather had brightened. Sunlight through open doors goldened his hair as he trod forth to greet: "Good morning, my lord."

"What do you want now, Hrut?" asked Harald with a smile.

"I have come to ask your leave, lord, to go to Iceland."

The king frowned. "Will you have more honor there than here?" he snapped.

"Not so," answered Hrut, undaunted, "but everyone must take the lot that is given him."

"It's like pulling a rope against a heavy man," said Gunnhild from her seat. "Let him do as he likes."

Harald could not but grant it. After all, he had known that Hrut never meant to settle in Norway. So had she, Gunnhild thought; so had she. It was only that she had not awaited the end as early as this, and had kept it out of her mind.

Hrut thanked the king and queen. He would always praise their kindness and openhandedness, he promised. "I will see to it that you get as much meal as you need for the voyage," Gunnhild said. Men looked at her in some astonishment. After two thin harvests in a row, grain bins were hardly overflowing. But none cared to gainsay her.

He would never forget, Gunnhild thought.

And, yes, she thought, with a cold seething behind her teeth, she would also give that girl he was so hot for something to remember her by.

Hrut and his uncle Özur busked themselves. Özur had likewise done well, but he too felt home calling him. In a few days ship and crew lay ready.

Hrut was on his way through the town to bid the king and his friends farewell when Ögmund wormed through the crowd, plucked his sleeve, and muttered that the queen wanted to see him at her house. It would not take long. She knew he had the ebb tide to catch. He nodded, not very surprised, and went with the footling.

She stood by herself in the long room, between the strangely woven hangings. They looked at each other for a breath or two. Thereupon she walked forward. Her skirts rustled faintly in the stillness. From a bench she took a thing that had been lying there and brought it to him. "Here is a gold ring I will give you," she said. It was thick and finely wrought. She lifted his hand and slipped it over his wrist.

"Many good gifts have I had of you," he said.

She reached up, put her arms around his neck, and drew his head down. He smelled of salt and sea-winds. His mustache salted the kiss. But his lips did not stir. She let go, stepped back, and said low: "If my power over you is as great as I believe, then I lay this spell on you, that you shall never be man to that woman in Iceland on whom your heart is set; but with other women you may get along well enough. And now it will go ill with both of us; for you have had no faith in me."

He made a kind of smile, shook his head, mumbled something well-bred, and left. When he had gotten outside, she heard him laugh. He was too glad of his freedom to heed any forebodings. She stayed there, alone.

Thence Hrut strode on to the hall, where he thanked King Harald again. The king wished him godspeed. Hrut went back to his ship.

She would follow what happened, snaring the news from Iceland as she snared the news from everywhere. Meanwhile she got her mind off it—mostly—in furthering the welfare of her sons.

VI

Bitterness had not yet died out when she met with them. They came to her house at the Byfjord as had been their wont in Denmark and as she hoped they would keep on doing in Norway. Another storm of another bad year howled around the walls, dashing rain and hail at the roof. Lightning flared; thunder wheeled rumbling down an unseen sky. The carven dragons could only snarl at it.

She rose to stand before them, firelit against gloom. Her words lashed: "What do you mean to do about your kingship in Thraandheim? You bear the name of kings, like your forefathers of old; but you have few men and not much land, and they are many who share its yields. Eastward in Vikin sit Tryggvi and Gudröd. They may have some right to that, being of the kindred. But Sigurd Jarl rules the whole Thraandlaw. I cannot see why you let so great a kingdom lie under anybody but yourselves. Strange does it seem to me, that you go abroad in viking in the summers, but here at home let a jarl rob you of your father's inheritance. Your grandfather, Harald"—she looked at her foremost son—"whom you are named after, would have reckoned it a small thing to take land and life from a mere jarl, he who brought all Norway under himself and kept it until his eld."

The younger men scowled. Harald Grayfell said weightily, "Mother, it's not as easy to cut off Sigurd Jarl as to slaughter a kid or a calf. He's of high birth, with many mighty kinsmen, well-liked, and wise. I think if he knew we threatened him, the Thraands would rally around as one. We'd get nothing but harm. I don't think any of us brothers could sit safely among them."

Gunnhild had planned for something like this. "Then we'll set to work otherwise, and put ourselves forward less boldly. Come fall, Harald and Erling shall go to stay in North Moerr. I'll fare along. There we'll see what can be done, and take counsel together."

After talking to and fro, they agreed to it.

VII

Sigurd Jarl had a brother called Grjotgard. He was much younger and much less well thought of; nor did he have any such standing. However, he kept a fair-sized band of warriors and went raiding every summer.

King Harald sent messengers to Sigurd Jarl with rich gifts and friendly words. He said it was his wish to knit the same bonds that there had been between the jarl and King Haakon. Therefore King Harald invited Sigurd to visit, so that they could make this fellowship firm.

The jarl received the messengers well, took the gifts gladly, and gave them gifts as goodly and words as mild to take back. However, he said, he could not himself come to the king because he had too much to do where he was.

The messengers went from there to Grjotgard, bearing the same kind of gifts and the same kind of bidding. Grjotgard answered that he would visit.

Yes, thought Gunnhild when she heard, Sigurd was as wily and wary as ever; but he grew old, while ruthless youth followed close on his heels.

On the day set, or near enough, Grjotgard arrived at the hall in North Moerr. King Harald, King Erling, and Queen Gunnhild took him in with a heartiness overwhelming to such a fameless man. They also took him into their councils about many big doings, as though they found him wiser than most.

Before long he was ripe for that which they had had in mind throughout. They told him over and over how unrightfully Sigurd kept him down; but if he would stand by them in this, he would become jarl in his brother's stead, and have everything that Sigurd now held.

The upshot was that Grjotgard went home, laden with gifts, to keep an eye on Sigurd and let the king know of any openings.

Again Gunnhild waited.

When she recalled how she had done so in the past, this

was nothing. Well before the first snowfall, they heard from him. Formerly Sigurd Jarl kept a big troop of guards, but that was costly, and after the Eirikssons offered friendship he went about with fewer. Now he was making the rounds of his holdings. Shortly he would be at Öglo in the nether Stjoradale. There could be no better time to fall upon him.

At once King Harald and King Erling set forth with four fully manned longships. They came to the Thraand-heimsfjord and went on by starlight. Grjotgard and his vikings met them where they landed and led them.

Late at night they reached the garth where the jarl slept. Dogs barked, men roused, but by then it was no use. The warriors ringed the house in with spears and torched it. They let women, children, and thralls out, but any free man who tried to pass through a door they killed.

High brawled the fire. Its light glowed uneasily on iron and billowing smoke, hid the fading stars, and lost itself in the darkness of pinewoods. When timbers crashed down, sparks rained upward. By midmorning the flames flickered low over ashes, charcoal, and some blackened bones. The air stank.

Harald and Erling returned to North Moerr. Grjotgard deemed it wise to come with them.

VIII

It took no witch-sight to foretell the wrath of the Thraands when they learned of Sigurd's death. What caught the Eirikssons off guard was that this became no mere uproar, but swiftly and fully a readymaking for war. Men swarmed together, bearing weapons and food, from all the shires. Every vessel that could float went into the water. Gathered, the men hailed Sigurd's son Haakon their jarl and leader. He bore straightaway south with host and fleet. There was nothing for Harald, Erling, and Grjotgard to do but withdraw to Raumsdal and South Moerr.

Harald and his mother agreed that this could not have happened were it not for Haakon himself. The new jarl seemed already to own his father's knowledge, shrewdness, skill, and winningness, while the fire of youth made him a still more dangerous foe. "A worthy one," said the king with a stiff smile.

Gunnhild allowed herself a faint sigh. "I could wish for an easier one." She lifted her head. "Well, he can't keep such a following afoot for very long. They must soon go home. We'll deal with him as we did with his namesake—harry the Thraandlaw, inland as well as from the sea, give it no peace till either he yields or he comes to the same end."

Harald did not think it strange that she said "we."

So the months went by, winter, spring again—a year since Hrut left—then summer, harvest and fishing lean again, fall storms that wrecked ships and drowned men, another winter that in its deeps got ringingly cold, a new year as bleak as the last. The clashes between the kings' men and the jarl's were not few, some small, some bigger, bloodshed, looting, burning, with no real gain.

One or another of the Eirikssons often led a raid, but not always. They had business to handle at home. Also, they were wont to go in viking during the summer. More than rage and restlessness sent them abroad. They needed the loot, the captives to sell, and any other wealth they could grab. None ruled over enough land to support his households, guards, and the showing a king must make, the more so in these bad years. The scot from King Gudröd and King Tryggvi helped, but did not stretch. Under Haakon Jarl, not only did the Thraandlaw pay nothing; it cut the Eirikssons off from Haalogaland, the Lofoten fisheries, and Finnmörk, with everything that these yielded.

True, they themselves sent nothing to Harald Bluetooth, nor acknowledged him their overlord. The Dane-king was put out, but stayed his hand. He had much else to think about: his own kingdom, its ongoing christening, its highborn and yeomen who were chafing at his grip; his ties and trade with Poland and Wendland, off whose shores he built a stronghold manned with picked warriors; the Goths along the marches of Halland, Skaaney, and Bleking; the mighty

Swede-king behind them; the Holy Roman Emperor Otto, who grew old but whose forceful son of the same name had lately been crowned co-Emperor and nursed wide-reaching ambitions. Bluetooth could well someday find himself in need of a Norse ally.

The house of Eirik Blood-ax had been worse off than now, Gunnhild thought. It would be better off.

She ran her household. When she was there and Harald Grayfell away, she steered Hördaland. She fared about. She gave her sons redes, careful not to overdo it. She wove her web of newsbringers, spies, and gangrels ever broader and more tightly meshed.

Not all those who gave her tidings were lowly or came secretly, nor even most. Seamen, yeomen, tradesmen, craftsmen, herders, hunters often did, because she had ways of rewarding them. Reeves, hersirs, lendmen, sometimes their women, did, whether they liked her or not, because she had ways to lead them on when talking, or to make them understand that her ill will could bring grief on them. And some folk of any kind or rank did because in spite of everything, they thought it was best for the land that she know.

Thus Arinbjörn Thorisson docked his ship at the Byfjord wharf late in the second summer and brought his crew to the hall. This was a chill, gray, windy day; pines soughed loudly, crows winged low and darkling. Runners had gone ahead, and Gunnhild was set to receive the guests. She sat in the high seat, bedecked with gold, silver, and amber, to smile at the weatherbeaten men who came before her.

"Welcome," she said in her warmest voice. "You must have heard by now that King Harald is not yet home from west-viking. Stay here till then, take your ease, rest, and fatten yourselves after what I can see was a hard faring. It was good of you to come," this far south of Sygnafylki. These days Arinbjörn dwelt on his holdings there. Coming from the North, he had passed them by when he could have sailed straight into that fjord.

The square face drew into lines of trouble. "I've bad news for the king, I fear. Thor—Christ give he's not met with woe." A finger made a sign across the broad breast, belike the Cross although it could have been the Hammer.

He meant it, Gunnhild knew. Arinbjörn stood by his oath and his lord. Yes, she also knew he had not forsworn his Icelandic friend, and how Egil Skallagrimsson sent him a long poem of praise and thanks. She had, indeed, heard it from a seafarer who had gotten it by heart, when she ordered him to speak the staves and promised him safety. It was the richest gift any man could ever have made another, for it would live, and Arinbjörn's name with it, while the world lasted. But she could put this aside. She must, if only for the sake of her sons. It was by her counsel that Harald let Arinbjörn stay mostly at home. Thereby the king got a strong chieftain in those parts, well thought of everywhere, to uphold him and speak on his behalf.

"He has not," Gunnhild told Arinbjörn. "He won booty, but then was weather-bound. He's now at sea and ought to arrive shortly."

Arinbjörn squinted at her. His bulk stiffened a bit. Plain to see, he wondered how she knew. "I'm glad to hear that, Queen," he said slowly.

She waved a hand. "Come, be seated, all of you. We'll feast." Gaunt though the year and the years before had been, she always made sure of enough in her larders.

Women brought ale and mead. She let talk run free along the benches, as king's men and newcomers asked each other how things had gone, until the horns were drained and refilled. Thereupon she said bluntly, "Give me your tale from first to last, Arinbjörn."

He shifted a little on the honor seat. Sailor, woodsman, farmer, warrior, leader of men and judge between them, he had scant word-skill. "Well, Queen," he said, "I got together a troop and ships, as the king bade me. I'd guess the queen knows we were to hit the Thraands hard by both land and sea. My folk are trustworthy, I swear. I thought it'd be a surprise. But Haakon Jarl must have had spies out."

Yes, he surely did, Gunnhild thought, though she had not been aware of how many or how shrewd. Here was a fox—no, a raven, Odin's black bird, uncannily cunning, keen of eye and quick to warn its flock.

"We were headed north through the Updale when a gang attacked us," Arinbjörn said. "It wasn't too big. Neighborhood yeomen, we took them for. We beat them off without loss to ourselves. But they withdrew fighting. So we followed. Suddenly we were in a steep-sided gorge. They kenned this land; we didn't. Down from the woods growing on the slopes, men swarmed. We barely hewed our way out, those of us who lived, and fled. I did hold the lads together, else they'd've bolted blind every which way and been hunted down like hares. We won to the shore, to where our ships were going to meet us when they'd done their share. Half of them were lost. Haakon's fleet had trapped them in a strait between two islands, same as his ax-wielders afoot caught my band."

A breath gusted from him, like wind outside. "I'm sorry to bring such tidings, my lady, but truth is truth."

"Good it is to have a man who sets it openly forth," Gunnhild answered. "Tomorrow, maybe we can talk alone for a while."

The weather had slackened but fog swirled and dripped when they met in her house. Flames struggled with dankness and darkness. She beckoned him to a chair and took one facing him. A table between them bore glass cups and a bottle of outland wine. She praised him, the doughty and steadfast, as she plied him, until he unlocked himself.

"Queen," he said heavily, "I don't know if we can overthrow Haakon Jarl. I don't know."

"We can wear him down," she said, drawing him on.

"But meanwhile we wear ourselves down too. Yes, the Thraands are suffering, but so's the rest of Norway."

"The yeomen grumble. They always did; they always will."

"It's more than that. I meant to tell the king—" Arinbjörn broke off.

"Do, but tell me first. Here we can be frank. I think I can help you work out how best to lay it before him when a hundred others are listening."

Arinbjörn nodded, braced his shoulders, and said in a stumbling rush: "This year at the Gula Thing—No, nothing spoken out in front of everybody. But talk *amongst* everybody. Stuff such as I'd caught snatches of here and there, now and then. But so widespread! About—maybe an uprising? And what more was there that I didn't hear? They know I'm King Harald's man."

Nonetheless they trusted him this much, Gunnhild thought. Therefore she had better. "Who then would they have for king? Haakon Sigurdarson?"

"No, of course not. God gave that right to Harald Fairhair's blood. But, well, the talk went as how two grandsons of his live on in the Southeast, or Sigurd the Giant more quietly in Hringariki—Queen, I say nothing against King Tryggvi or King Gudröd, nothing. It's only what I heard folk wondering about."

Gunnhild nodded. This was by no means astonishing to her. What made it grim was the man who uttered it. "A sign, yes," she said, "as a cough may foreshadow something worse."

Arinbjörn plucked up the will to speak further. "A wasting sickness, I think, Queen. Too much of Norway's weary, hungry, mourning, angry. I've even heard say that the sons of Eirik are unlucky, that the heathen gods are taking revenge on them."

She could not quite hold back the gall. "They dare!"

Arinbjörn plodded on. "Not only the lowborn, Queen. The highborn too. As you and your sons must know better than I." It burst from him: "Why has none of them yet gotten a queen of his own?"

"They have found none they care to so honor," Gunnhild must needs tell him.

"No house they care to so honor," answered he, who had risked death often enough erenow. "Isn't that true, Queen? How many great houses can they trust anymore? It'd be unwise to woo a girl whose father hates the wooer."

"I know," said Gunnhild evenly. She had given her sons the selfsame warning.

"Forgive me, Queen. I've overspoken myself."

She bestowed a rueful smile on him. "You have not. Rather, I thank you for your straightforwardness. What you've said won't go beyond these walls. But it will stay in me."

Thus emboldened, he went ahead in his dogged way. "Queen, I know of men on both sides who'd gladly be go-betweens for making peace."

"We shall see," Gunnhild answered.

She would brood on it.

Before Harald returned to her, a ship put in from Orkney, belike the last of the season. The skipper told her that Ljot Thorfinnsson, the jarl, was dead.

The Scots had never stopped wanting that. While he was making his rounds in Caithness, a host of them went north against him. Although outnumbered, Ljot gave battle and drove them to flight. But many of his men who lived were hurt, himself not least. He crossed back over to the islands, but his wounds festered, fever took hold of him, he lay raving in his bed and soon died.

Again Gunnhild's daughter was a widow. Nobody else sought her hand. Men muttered that doom went with her.

IX

Gunnhild wondered whether the gods were fighting for their hold on man or for their very lives.

Victorious everywhere this side of the Moors and Arabs, Christ had now driven them from Denmark, and still he pressed on eastward. Yes, at his back they lingered in the Western Isles and Iceland; but once the motherland fell, or even before, those outposts too would be lost. As yet, the Goths knew little of him and the Swedes less. But he could leave such folk in their hallowed shaws at their bloody altar stones while he outflanked them through Norway. Let him take that fastness, and the rest of the North would lie open. Already he had won footholds.

The gods fought back, with weather and worshippers for weapons. They had brought him to a standstill. How long could this last? If Christ was almighty, why did his warriors not sweep everything before them?

True, her sons were no saints. They had striven for the Church mainly because they saw—she taught them to see—how it could bring the stiff-necked freemen to their knees, heads bowed, at the feet of the king. Erling was the most God-fearing among them, but his zeal also flagged when he found what scant headway they made. Could it be that Christ withheld his help from such Christians as these? Then why did he give it to the likes of Harald Bluetooth? She knew the Dane-king too well to believe that the faith in his heart was any more pure than the faith of Harald Grayfell.

Could the heathen be right? They would have been willing enough to set Christ in Aasgard and offer to him as they did to the rest. Might he be akin to the gods but bent on their overthrow—another Loki?

Gunnhild had lived so long with strangeness that she knew she did not know. The thought was shuddery that no one did or ever would. Let her not weaken herself by it, but get on with her fight. She felt time at her back, breathing frost over her hair.

The sword and the psalm had both failed against Haakon Jarl. She had her own way, the Old Way.

So had she sought out Rögnvald Highbone, more years ago than she wanted to reckon up, and wrought his death. He was a warlock. Haakon was only a heathen. She would go to him as she went to Rögnvald, not swallow but shadow, herself meanwhile awake in the flesh and ready to work witchcraft.

The sun was about to turn downward into the shortening days of fall. On that night, ghosts and Beings went abroad. One heard them in the wind, glimpsed them in the glooms. Cold blue fires flitted, graves groaned; folk laid flint and steel at their thresholds and stayed behind barred doors.

Again Gunnhild emptied her house, saying that once more she would pray and meditate alone. If somebody caught a whisper of song or drumbeat anyway, why, of course uncanny noises went through this dark. Whoever might think a little further about that had better keep his or her lips clamped.

Again she soaked the dried mushrooms. Again she shed her clothes. The air felt colder than erstwhile. But then, she was no smooth-skinned, high-breasted, taut-bellied girl anymore. She let her grizzled locks fall loosely to cover what they could. She donned the eagle feathers, cat's claws, and wolf's teeth. She ate the holy food. She drummed and sang, dancing around and around a tall three-legged stool on which one lamp burned, her eyes never leaving its flame. As the Seeing began, she laid the drum aside, took the rune-carved legbones in her hands, sat down on the floor, swayed, and sang herself away from herself. "Haakon Sigurdarson, I behold you, I hear you, I the night wind, I the oncoming winter, I your death. You know me not, you know me not for what I am, your bane, Haakon Sigurdarson. I seek you; I seek you; I seek you—"

She slipped through the flame.

A thin scythe of moon was rising, near the white wanderstar of dawn or dusk. Elsewhere blew rags of cloud. Between them she spied a few more stars, unutterably far and icy. Land rolled beneath, a huge murk into which fjords cut like steel. Westward glimmered unrestful sea. She flew forever, and she flew no time at all, while back in the house she swayed and sang and suffered the pain of this.

A storm loomed black ahead. But yonder gleamed the great Thraandheimsfjord. She slanted down toward Hladi.

Out of the storm rode one to meet her. The stallion was black, his eyes fire-coals, his mane wild in the wind over which he galloped. The rider's cloak flapped like hawk wings. Helm and byrnie cast back the fleeting light. Blood ran from the spear she gripped. Her scream ripped the sky.

The shadow veered off and fled.

Afterward, huddled back inside her body, dawn graying away the worst horror, Gunnhild remembered that Haakon Jarl oftenest called on Thorgerd Shrine-bride. Had his witchy gods, whose last strong defender he was, set that Chooser of the Slain to watch over him?

She stiffened her will and rose off the floor. Chill

numbed somewhat the ache in every bone. Whatever truth lurked behind this world, the only thing to do in it now was make peace. So must she counsel her sons, then school them anew in waiting.

X

uring that winter and into the spring, men of rank, Arinbjörn among them, went to and fro between the North and the South. At last their bargaining reached agreement and put an end to strife. Haakon Jarl was to keep the same rights and might in the Thraandlaw as his father Sigurd had had, while the kings should have the same overlordship and scot as King Haakon did. This was sworn to on both sides with the strongest of oaths.

The thought followed that even more good ought to come of face-to-face meetings. One of the messengers from King Harald, a clever-tongued little fellow called Ögmund, got Haakon Jarl aside. Of course no Eiriksson was afraid to show himself here. However, feelings must still run high in many Thraands. Might it not help soothe them, and be best all around, if the great jarl came down instead, to be heaped with gifts and honors?

Haakon hung back awhile, but in the end gave his yea. From his scouts he knew Harald's brothers were making ready for their viking cruises, some eastward, some westward. Nor was the elder king keeping more men about him than he needed. Besides, any betrayal this soon would cost the Eirikssons everything they had newly gained. Working quickly, to give no time for whatever might nonetheless brew, he set forth with a score of swift, fully crewed longships.

At the Byfjord he found everything laid out for a welcome such as had been promised. But only Queen Gunnhild was in the high seat. She told him her son Harald had eagerly looked forward to this day, and how sorry the king was that business which could not wait had suddenly called him away. She would do all in her power, on his behalf, to make the highborn guest's journey worthwhile.

Recalling how much power that was, Haakon took her words as in no way demeaning. Rather, her house praised his trustworthiness, when it received him with fewer warriors on hand than he had brought along. The feast became one to remember.

Nobody was surprised when she said quietly that they could meet under four eyes tomorrow if he liked, and from time to time thereafter.

Though the sky was bright when he came to her house, wax tapers cast light to sheen off polished silver, glow on wainscots, and deepen the hues of tapestries. Not only pinecones in a small hearthfire but incense in a brazier sweetened the air. The maidservants who brought wine in glass goblets were young and comely. Haakon took his seat of honor with a smile.

"The queen is most kind," he said. "Her kingly sons could hardly guest me better."

"Nor would I, I think, as yet," she answered cat-softly.

For a little while they sat watchful, the woman who kept an ageless beauty in her upright bearing, big gray-green eyes, and the bones of her face, the hawk-nosed young man within whose short black beard played a lively mouth.

"Well, true," said Haakon then, as carefully as she, "the blood that's been shed—But, forgive me, they did the shedding."

"Brothers of theirs—brothers and sons of mine—have fallen too. But now I hope the peace between us will last." Gunnhild gave Haakon back his earlier smile. "And I hope you hope it."

He chuckled. "They were right who told me you've a ready wit, Queen." After a sip from his cup he went on, his voice friendly, "I've a thought that maybe you had something to do with King Harald happening not to be here."

"I told you yesterday, a business he felt he must settle at once, lest a family feud spring up and kill too many good men, came to his ears right at this time."

"Hm. Far be it from me to question your word or his,

Queen. Quarrels are always breaking out, and surely it's wise to keep them from getting as bloody as they're apt to in Iceland. How fast any one of them needs to be dealt with, that's of course a matter of judgment." Haakon met Gunnhild's gaze and raised his brows. "Even so, Queen, I can't help wondering whether you nudged the king's judgment a bit."

Gunnhild laughed. He did too.

"I believe we begin to understand each other," she said. "We can talk freely and unbindingly."

He nodded. "Instead of out in the open, where the king or I or both might find we'd worked ourselves into a spot we'd rather not be in but can't very well back away from."

He was as shrewd as they said, and belike deeper, Gunnhild thought. "I can't gainsay that my sons are hard men." Haughty, unbending. "I cannot speak for them. But I can listen to you, try to see things from your side, give way when that seems best—skills every woman must learn." Again his brows flickered upward, though he kept his lips straight. "Afterward I can tell them what passed between us, and offer my counsel, for whatever it may be worth."

"Let us hope they will listen to that," said Haakon.

They swapped a quick grin.

They did not turn at once to questions still outstanding, such as fishing and sealing around the Lofotens, the gathering and sharing of Finn-scot, or giving help and shelter to men whom either a king or the jarl but not both had outlawed. It was enough this day to touch on these, and otherwise let talk flow wherever it would, as friends do when they are together after being long sundered.

"Your years in England and Denmark taught you much, didn't they?" said Haakon during it. "I could almost wish something of the kind had fallen to my lot—for awhile!"

"You've often been abroad yourself, I hear," Gunnhild answered.

"Oh, yes, and met with every breed of folk from kings to fishwives." And their daughters, Gunnhild thought. Whenever a maid came to pour, Haakon's glance slid across her. "But I've never dwelt among well-off Christians like you. I've never spoken at length with any of their learned men. A book—" He sighed. Maybe it was honestly. "Such wonders are locked away from me. Lore that reaches over the whole world and back to the beginning of time— You, though, you've dealt with bishops." His voice smoothed. "You were close to that priest who'd been dear to my namesake King Haakon."

It stabbed through her: How much did he know, or guess? A wicked mirth seemed to dance behind those eyes that were of nearly the same changeable hue as hers. "Sira Brihtnoth left Norway because King Haakon turned from Christ," she said mildly. "Yet he always thought well of your father too. All men did, my sons and I not least. Ill-willed was the norn who came between us."

"Gunnhild," said Haakon, as if frankly, "let's not bring up old rights and wrongs, not yet, not ever if we're lucky. Can't we go on today as we were, at our ease?"

"Gladly." She meant it.

That evening she had Ögmund see to it that each night Haakon would have a bouncy new bedmate. She put down any wistfulness in herself.

As the days passed, their talk ranged widely onward. He wanted to know everything she could tell him about Christian lands and Christian knowledge. When she asked him why he was, then, so bitterly against Christ, he went grim: "I've seen what his Church brings about, my lady. You have too. But we don't look on it the same way."

She didn't think he cared much about the olden rights of freemen. It was merely that in them and in the old gods were the wellsprings of his might. But also, she thought, to him those gods were as meaningful as she could wish hers were to her—if only she knew what hers were.

"Angels or Aesir," she mumured. "I wonder if they don't wage their war, not in the sky, but in our souls."

Haakon shrugged. "It's useless for us on earth to ask, I'd say."

Harking back to a night last year, Gunnhild didn't think he was being wholly straightforward.

Whatever he felt in his heart, they sometimes spoke of

strangeness. She had hopes of sounding out what the Powers really were that seemed to stand behind him, and how they could maybe be overcome or outwitted. No doubt he bore the same hope about her. Neither of them learned anything helpful. Yet both had much to tell of.

He had met enough himself: Men who saw their own fetches, knew they were fey, and soon died. Songs wailing eerily across moonlit seas, no sight of the singers, merfolk? Horns blowing, hounds baying, horses a-gallop across the night wind—the Aasgard's Ride?

But they recalled little happenings as well. Some that Haakon shared were funny. His words brought up before her, as if she'd been there herself, how a drunken Irish bard fell into a tub of ale and, as he lurched to his feet, his singing frothed. Nor was Haakon pigheaded when it came to the business between their houses.

They parted cheerfully. "I trust I'll often see you, Gunnhild," he said.

"And I you," she answered.

Oh, yes, underneath the heartiness, each had been probing, peering, and plotting. But never before with any man had she found such a kind of pleasure. Clearly, he had enjoyed himself likewise.

XI

Not long after Haakon left and Harald returned, a ship from Iceland lay to at Byfjord haven. It belonged to one Arni, who was in the guard but often visited yonder. At the hall he made known that he had with him the son of a high chieftain, who wished to pay his respects. The king said to bring this man here straightaway. Having listened in a corner as he often did, Ögmund sped to Gunnhild and told her. Thus she was also in the high seat when the two entered.

For her Arni was altogether overshadowed by the tall, broad-shouldered youth in red kirtle, blue breeks, cloak trimmed with sable, who walked lithely forward with head high and amber-hued locks falling in waves around a face she half knew. She held herself to a smile, but the heart sprang within her.

"Olaf Höskuldarson," she heard. "His father is the son of Dale-Kol. His grandmother on that side was Thorgerd Thorsteinsdottir. After Dale-Kol's death she wedded Herjolf and became the mother of that Hrut whom the king and queen know and who asked me to bring you his greetings."

"As did many other men of worth, lord," added Olaf.

Hrut!

"Be welcome for the sake of your kinfolk as well as yourself," said King Harald. "Good has the friendship been between our houses." He could be as forthcoming and fairspoken as anybody when he chose.

"Oh, welcome indeed," breathed Gunnhild.

"You shall be our guest for as long as you wish," the king went on. "We'll be glad to hear about you, your errand, and how they're doing in Iceland."

Gunnhild harked back. She had drawn in news from there as she drew it in from everywhere. Hrut had taken Unn Mördardottir to wife in the fall of the year he came home. Though he treated her kindly and let her run the household however she saw fit, folk marked that she grew more and more unhappy. Among each other they wondered why. Gunnhild knew. But in spite of what he did to her at the end, she had not wished grief on him that would last through his whole life. Let him get another woman in time, and do better with her.

"Take the seat of honor," King Harald bade. It went without saying that he meant Olaf only. "We'll drink, then dine, and then—" He laughed. "—drink onward."

"My fullest thanks to the king and queen," said Olaf. His own smile flashed. "I've heard always heard how openhanded and openhearted you both are."

Gunnhild wasn't sure how far she believed that. He might be too young to know what name her sons bore in many Norse mouths. Whether or no, he did not seem one

who would fawn. He merely had a gifted tongue—maybe
from his mother, whoever she was.

"My crew—" began Arni.

"We'll house them well too, of course," said Gunnhild.
She beckoned to the steward, who went off to take care of
it.

While day slipped into evening, the household heard the
tale of Olaf.

Back in the time of King Haakon, Höskuld had come to
Norway to buy timber. The Icelandic woods, never thick,
were falling fast before the axes. Next spring he learned
that the king had gone with his guard out to the Brenn
Islands to make the land-peace firm: for by law, the chieftains in Norway met every third summer to order such matters as called for his judgment. Höskuld went too, as did
many others. It became a kind of fair, where trading was
brisk. Wanting a woman, Höskuld bought one from a Gar-
darikian dealer in thralls, who asked a high price because
of her beauty although warning that she was dumb, uttering
never a word.

Höskuld took her home with him. It grew clear that,
speechless or no, she was quite sharp-witted; and her bearing showed good birth. That winter she bore him a son,
whom he named Olaf after his lately dead grandfather. Otherwise he slept with his wife Jörun and had rather little to
do with this leman. He left the raising of the child to her.
Already at two years of age—Arni put in—Olaf talked and
ran around like a lad of four.

One day outdoors Höskuld heard somebody else talking
too. He found mother and child beside a brook. There was
now no hiding that she was not really dumb. They sat down
together and she told him she was Melkorka, a daughter of
King Myrkjartan in Ireland—or so these names came off
Norse tongues. When she was fifteen, a viking crew caught
her. Höskuld said she had kept still too long about her be-
ginnings.

Jörun and Melkorka did not get along. When at last it
came to blows, Höskuld had a small house built some ways

from his steading. There Melkorka lived with Olaf. Hös-kuld provided well for them.

When Olaf was seven, an old but high-standing man, Thord the Bull, took him in foster and grew fond of him. Already at age twelve Olaf rode to the Thing. He always wore such splendid garb and bore such fine weapons that everybody kenned him from afar. Thus—laughed Arni—he got the nickname Olaf the Peacock. For all that, he was liked and looked up to.

Then lately the news came that Arni, who had again been in Iceland, was loading for return. Melkorka told Olaf that he ought to go overseas and find his high kindred. Höskuld was not much for this; and the wealth of Olaf's foster father Thord lay mostly in land and livestock, not goods that could be taken abroad. Thereupon Melkorka told him he could get what he needed from one Thorbjörn, a rich neighbor who had been smitten by her. She would wed the man if he promised to share what he had with her son.

When next Höskuld rode off to the Thing-meeting, Olaf hung back, saying he had too much else on hand; and the wedding took place. Höskuld was not happy about it when he heard. But since it touched on those who were near to him and he did not want a fight, he swallowed it.

Before her son left, Melkorka gave him a golden ring she had from her father as a teething gift. The vikings and slavers had let her keep it, since it added something to what she was worth. "I think he will know this again," she said. She also gave him a belt and small knife she had from her foster mother in Ireland, which her owners had likewise let her keep when they saw how much it meant to her. They didn't want her pining away. The old woman ought to know these tokens. Thinking far ahead, she had taught Olaf the Irish tongue.

He took the things from his belt pouch and showed them around. Gunnhild turned them over in her hands, gave them back, and said, "We should talk together, you and I. Maybe I can give you a rede or two that will help you in your search."

"Belike so," said Harald Grayfell. "She knows much, and

is very wise." He had more than an inkling of what she had in mind, she thought wryly.

That was a blithe evening. Gunnhild set herself to charm everybody, not least this newcomer.

When he came to her house next day, it was arrayed as it had been for Hrut and Haakon. She might even have had a little something to do with the weather turning black, howling wind and lashing rain—not that any summer had been really good in Norway for too many years. The house felt twice snug, and flamelight was kind to her.

They talked long, alone together, he beside her in the high seat, while they drank wine until she saw the glow upon his skin. Then she asked softly, "What has your kinsman Hrut said about me, Olaf? Be honest, I pray you. Have no fear."

"I need have none, Queen. He's had nothing but praise for you and everything you did for him."

Gunnhild felt that that could not be quite true. However, Olaf could not have seen Hrut often, and Hrut would never own to the ill she worked on him. "I would like to do as much for you, Olaf," she murmured, "or more."

Although well-mannered, he was not shy. It was easy to awaken lust. He was a strong lover, and quick to learn.

A few weeks passed happily. Among men, Olaf sported, drank, talked, was merry, made friends right and left. He kept a bedmate at the hall, a girl good-looking, freeborn, and very willing. It helped quench gossip about how often he was at the queen's house.

But as time went by, Olaf grew somewhat heavyhearted. One day he and Arni were sitting outdoors on a bench, letting a sunshine too seldom seen pour over them. Others bustled or loafed around. Gunnhild saw, and walked over the flagstones to greet them. Nearing, she heard Arni ask what was wrong.

Olaf sighed. "I have to fare off to the Westlands. I need your help in getting me on my way as soon as may be."

"Not so hasty," said Arni. "I don't know of any ships bound yonder from here. Wait till next summer."

Gunnhild remembered Hrut. Here was a longing she

could slake without hurt. As the men saw her and got onto their feet, she said, "Now you speak otherwise than before. This is the first time I've seen you two at odds."

Arni kept still, abashed, but Olaf said outright how much he wanted to go onward, since he knew that King Myrk-jartan was his grandfather. Besides fulfilling his mother's wish, he could hope to win renown and riches. Gunnhild looked into the frank blue eyes, smiled, and told him, "I'll outfit you fully and worthily for this voyage."

Olaf thanked her over and over. Thereafter he was again cheerful. Whenever they could steal a while by themselves, he gave her the kind of thanks she most liked.

With King Harald's goodwill, things went fast. Olaf asked for, and got, a crew of sixty. Gunnhild set Arni among them, and saw to it that they had everything they might need for seafaring, warfaring, or lordliness.

On the day they sailed, she and Harald went down to see Olaf off. "We'll lay our luck to yours, besides the friend-ship we've already shown," said the king. "This will be easy, for no other man has come to us from Iceland in whom we could put more faith." He truly liked the youth, and had been happy to see his mother blossom anew. "By the way," he asked, "how old are you?"

"Eighteen, King," said Olaf.

Harald Grayfell laughed. "Amazing! Why, you're hardly past your childhood. Come see us again when you head back."

"And bear with us always our deepest, best wishes," Gunnhild said.

After more thanks, the wayfarers boarded. Moorings came loose; oars came out; the longship strode down the fjord toward the sea. Gunnhild and Harald stood watching till the hull was gone from sight.

Clouds lowered and water chopped, iron-gray. Wind blew sharp. Gunnhild meant to do what she could toward blessing the journey.

Aside from her fears for Olaf, and they were slight, she felt no sadness. Her thirst was slaked for this while. If anything, her flesh ached and needed a rest. Once she had been young.

Over and above that, she wanted to think and take a hand in things again. There would be no time for laziness.

The wind hounded her as she walked back. Though summer was not yet ended, winter streamed in its chill. It keened of more lean years to come. Harald Grayfell could still do well by such guests as Olaf the Peacock, upholding his honor in their eyes. But food for his household had grown costly, and hunger stalked his lands. Her other sons were worse off.

She would gather them together and show them what must be done. The grumbles of the yeomen held some truth. There were too many kings in Norway.

XII

It became all the more pressing when her spies and messengers brought their news that fall. Riding around the Uplands, Haakon Jarl had met with King Tryggvi Olafsson and King Gudröd Bjarnarson in Heidmörk. To that meeting came also Dale-Gudbrand, the mighty chieftain of the Dale east of Raumsdalr and South Moerr. They gave out that it was only for talk about everyday matters, such as hunting and herding rights; they brought no big followings; they went home from it, lived quietly, and kept on paying what scot they owed. But who knew what they had started brewing?

Hence the brothers of Harald Grayfell were at his Yuletide feast, and more than once with him and their mother in her house. They reached a stark agreement and laid their plans.

Things did not work out altogether as they had in mind, but then, things never did.

Spring and the wanderbirds came back; darkness dwindled; snow and ice thawed away into rushing streams; buds opened; grass sprouted; a tender green lay everywhere over the land. Gunnhild's sons King Harald and King Gudröd

made known that in early summer they would go abroad
in viking as they often had, whether to west or east. Ragnfröd, Erling, and Sigurd would stay behind, keeping Norway in hand, till these two returned. They mustered crews,
rolled ships down to the water, laid in supplies, and set
forth.

All met at Körmt, where they feasted before the warlike
faring began. Ale flowed unstinted. Men fell to boasting.
They spoke loudly about who of them was better than
whom. At last it went so far that some likened the kings to
each other. One guard blurted that King Harald outdid his
brothers in every way there was. At this Gudröd sprang to
his feet, afire with wrath. He shouted that nobody was going to tell him he stood in any way beneath Harald, and he
was ready to prove it.

Uproar burst loose. Followers of either lord went for their
weapons. But some who were less drunk shoved between
the maddened packs and got them quieted. Harald himself
called sharply for peace, on pain of death. Rather grudgingly, Gudröd did likewise.

In the morning, everybody boarded their ships and stood
out to sea. There was no more thought of sailing together.

Gudröd bore south and then east along the shore. Harald
turned west; but when he got beyond sight of land, he too
steered east, through the Skagerrak and into the bight of
Vikin, keeping outside the islands and skerries.

King Gudröd Eiriksson laid to at Folden and sent a
friendly message to King Tryggvi Olafsson. Why should
they not go shares in a viking cruise across the Baltic?
Tryggvi answered happily that they could well talk about
this. Let them meet at Veggin, east of Sotaness. Awaiting
no harm, he arrived with only twelve men. Gudröd made
him welcome. Hardly had they sat down when Gudröd's
troop ran forward against King Tryggvi and his little following. He was buried there.

Meanwhile King Harald reached Tunsberg about nightfall. Hearing that King Gudröd Bjarnarson was at a feast
not far inland, he led his crews to the house through the
dark. They ringed it in. King Gudröd went out at the head

of his guards, but the battle was short before he fell, and many with him. Harald Grayfell's father Eirik Blood-ax had slain Gudröd's father Björn the Chapman hereabouts in much the same wise, long years ago.

Now the hard feelings between Harald and his own brother Gudröd could die away. They met afresh, made their troops one, and in the course of the summer brought all Vikin under their sway.

When Gunnhild at Byfjord heard, she took the news with outward calm, merely asking what else she should have looked for. But it was a hearthfire in her heart. So near had they come to such a murderous quarrel as brought down son after son of Harald Fairhair; but the bonds of brotherhood that she laid on them while they were growing held fast.

At the same time, she stayed lynx-wary. Their task and hers was not done yet.

XIII

Gudröd Bjarnarson had a son, also named Harald, a promising youth. He had been fostered by the lendman Hroar the White in Grenland shire, wherefore he was called Harald Grenska. When he heard of his father's death, he knew his own would soon find him unless he fled. With his foster brother Hrani and a few men he denned among kinfolk high in the Uplands. Well, thought Gunnhild, her Harald could seek him out after Vikin was tamed and make an end of him.

King Tryggvi had to wife Aastrid Eiriksdottir, a fair young woman now heavy with child. When Harald Grayfell sent men to ransack his hall and holdings, they learned that she had left together with her old foster father Thorolf Louse-beard and what money they could carry. Nobody knew where she had gone. It seemed, though, that other men, whom she trusted, were keeping eyes open and had ways to let her know what her foes were up to—for Harald's failed utterly to track her down.

Gunnhild scowled. She had had uneasy dreams about that unborn child. As soon as might be, she had better see what she herself could do about Aastrid.

At least Haakon Jarl stayed peaceful. Indeed, he sailed down to call on King Ragnfröd, who kept the steading at the Byfjord while Harald was gone, and to deal with whatever business there was between them. So he said. Mostly he was in speech with Gunnhild. They sparred as merrily as before. Sometimes they shared thoughts about weighty matters or about the worlds beyond this world. One clear, moonless night they stepped outside for a while and stood silent, looking up with wonder at the thronged stars and frosty Winterway.

He told her how, the year before last, he had been guested at a hersir's home in the Uplands, and slept with a woman. Lately that chieftain had sent her to him at Hladi with the son she had borne. Haakon acknowledged the boy, named him Eirik, and got him fostered by a good friend of his, Thorleif the Wise. The jarl smiled at Gunnhild and said this name ought to be lucky, seeing how great a man formerly bore it. She smiled back. But was yonder Thorleif the same who upheld Haakon Aethelstan's-foster in Thraandheim and helped him work out the laws of the Gula Thing? She said nothing. The visit ended agreeably.

After Haakon Jarl set homeward, Gunnhild took another night alone. The shadow winged aloft. Becoming a swallow, it swooped low above the roof that sheltered Harald Grenska, and marked the way over the mountains to reach him. But when it searched for King Tryggvi's widow Aastrid, fog wrapped those parts, a white blindness under the moon. Dawn harried the seeker away. Gunnhild could not risk being found unclad amidst her witch-things.

An iciness that struck through her flying soul told her there was in truth a doom in Tryggvi's child. What it was, she knew not, nor what norn had sung it.

Maybe she could try again, later when the nights were longer.

Happier news broke in on her thoughts. Harald Grayfell had taken over a hall, with its town and holdings, in Ranriki. This shire ran along the eastern shore of the Skagerrak; the hall was at King's Crag, a little inland from the mouth of the Göta River. There the king had anchorage for a whole fleet, overlooking both the straits and the sea. His messengers or his warriors could swiftly make his will felt throughout newly won Vikin; and Vikin ranked with Thraandheim as the richest, strongest part of Norway. Nearby to the south, with only a thin slice of Hising shire in between, began Danish Halland. Thus he could readily be aware of what both the Danes and the West Goths were up to. King's Crag was open to the whole world in a way the Byfjord could never quite be.

Harald wished his mother to come live there. He offered her a much better house, and everything else she might want.

Gunnhild walked through the woods, alone with her memories. Then once again she boarded a ship.

Harald met her in fitting wise. Beneath the sternness underlying all his moods, she saw, she felt, love.

Her new home was to her liking. And then, as she was settling in, a band of men on horseback arrived. He at their head wore a richly embroidered kirtle. A red shield with a golden lion on it hung behind his knee. Sunlight flashed off the gold on sword hilt and helmet. Olaf the Peacock had returned from Ireland.

XIV

Of course he would not have walked from the docks, nor sent a runner to beg for horses. He bought them on the spot. King Harald welcomed him warmly, Queen Gunnhild more warmly still. With many good words they asked him to stay. He accepted thankfully. After he had unloaded his ship, fine gifts went both ways. Olaf was now wealthy.

His tale filled a week of evenings. The sailing westward had gone hard, with thick fog and low, foul winds, until his crew were lost. Only Arni's skill found them their way to Ireland. There, at first, men took them for raiders and wanted them to come ashore unarmed. When Olaf refused, the Irish waded out to attack; but Olaf mustered his crew along the side so threateningly that they scrambled back and sent for King Myrkjartan. Olaf told the king the truth, was allowed to land with his weapons, and showed his tokens from Melkorka. Then Myrkjartan flushed, and said Olaf bore her looks. He would acknowledge this grandson. Norse and Irish went off together in the best of fellowship.

"And did you find her foster mother?" asked Gunnhild softly when they were alone.

Candlelight glowed across the bed on which they lay resting, her head on his shoulder. It washed his skin with gold; it seemed almost to smooth away her wrinkles and saggings. A cedary smell of lovemaking mingled with the slight, sweet smell of strewn juniper. She felt as tender as a girl.

He nodded. "Yes. She was old and bedridden, but she got up when the king told her who I was. I hugged her, set her on my knee—she was so small, so shrunken, a wisp—and told her how well her foster daughter fared in Iceland. When I gave her back the knife and belt she'd given my mother, she broke into tears. She sobbed I was a wonderful man, as I was born and raised to be. Throughout the winter she was on her feet, brisk and cheerful."

Gunnhild stroked his cheek. The beard felt silky. "It was like you, Olaf."

"When I was about to leave," he said, "I offered to take her along. My mother would have been glad to see her. But the king counseled against it, as frail as she was. It hurt to bid her farewell."

Gunnhild winced. "Let's not speak of farewells yet." She rolled around to kiss him. Her unbound gray hair spilled across his breast.

Olaf had richly repaid his Irish grandfather. Vikings from the sea and robbers from the hills worked much woe on this little kingdom. When Olaf and his followers joined Myrkjartan against them, they got rid of no few forever. Those who lived did not soon come back. However, it was

Arni who told how the king began seeking the redes of his Norse friends in other matters too.

At last he called a folkmoot, where he offered Olaf the kingship after his own death. Olaf thanked him handsomely, but answered that he did not want to reave their rights from Myrkjartan's sons. Better was short-lasting honor than long-lasting shame.

"Besides, my mother would never be happy again if I didn't come home to her," he said to Gunnhild when they were once more by themselves.

"Yes, you shall go when you wish, with my blessing," she wrenched forth. "But stay here through the winter, at least. Will you?"

He smiled. "My wish is for nothing less, my lady." He drew her to him.

He did, again, openly keep a wench where he lodged. Gunnhild had nothing against that. It helped head off gossip—and, she thought ruefully, gave her a rest now and then. Rather, Gunnhild felt a bit sorry for the girl. She had clearly fallen in love, and was not hardened to the loneliness that awaited her.

Mostly Olaf was among men, as became a man. Everybody liked him. King Myrkjartan had heaped treasures on him. Here in Norway he was openhanded. King Harald took him into the guard with high rank.

This was no mere show. Harald Grayfell and his brother Gudröd were often riding around Vikin, quelling unrest, giving judgments, tightening their grip on these shires. Sometimes they chopped down an idol or burned a halidom. Olaf kept aside from that. He had undergone primesigning but not baptism. If nothing else, he said with his wonted frankness, it would not sit well in Iceland; and if he did take the Faith, he would scorn to keep it under his cloak. King Harald bore with him, as he must needs with many other heathen, and even said he could well understand Olaf's plight. The Icelander spoke no further about it.

On none of these ridings did they go after young Harald Grenska. Gunnhild's network had already quivered with the knowledge that it was too late. This Harald had taken shelter in Svithjod. There he got friendship from one Tosti, the mightiest Swedish lord not of the kingly house, so often on warlike farings that the name of a valkyrie was laid to his, Skögul-Tosti. Harald Grenska was beyond the reach of Harald Grayfell.

Gunnhild thought of Haakon Jarl and the Shrine-bride he worshipped.

She had a foreboding, less about Harald Grenska than about his seed, what might spring from his loins. But his years were few as yet. Whatever doom lay in him would not come out for another lifetime or more.

Nearer to hand were King Tryggvi's widow Aastrid and the child she must by now have borne. Were it a son, he could grow up to claim Norway from her sons or grandsons. The thought crawled in her that he might win.

However, she did not again fly searching. While Harald Grayfell and Olaf the Peacock were gone, she had much to keep her busy. No, she was not the king, but she was the mother of kings. Men who knew what was good for them heeded her.

When she could—seldom—be alone, she only wanted to let her mind wander free, through memories and dreams. Her father, her mother, Seija, the out- laws that ghastly day, the Finns, Eirik, Eirik, their children, oh, Rögnvald slain in his bright boyhood, strife, flight, grim regaining, over and over, until everything shattered as she saw Eirik fall, and she must pick up the shards—No, her soul did not want to fly. How cold the sky was.

Surely her spies on earth would find what had become of Aastrid. There was no real haste. Soon enough the happiness would slip from her hands. Then she could give herself wholly back to the house of Eirik Blood-ax.

Although she and her Harald must turn a blind eye to heathen offerings roundabout, and themselves hear mass from the one priest at the one tiny chapel, it became a merry Yuletide. Folk beswarmed the hall; food and drink overflowed; mirth rang. The king gave Olaf a set of scarlet clothes from the Southlands. Between times, Olaf and Gunnhild snatched their own delight.

Or, rather, she knew well, she snatched hers; but she said nothing about that to anyone else, and little to herself.

Northlights wavered above snow that crackled underfoot. Icicles glimmered, hanging from boughs like knives. Again the harvest had been meager, both on land and at sea.

Once upon a time Eyvind the Skald-cribber had given all the Icelanders a long poem of praise. They voted him three silver pennies from every free man. These were made into a row of clasps worth fifty marks. As the hard seasons in Norway wore on, he had had to sell them one by one for food. This past spring there had for a short while been a strong herring run. He went out in a boat with his household men and took such a catch that he made some gleeful staves about it. But they soon ate it up. Afterward he even traded his arrows to whoever had salt fish to spare.

He stood on a ness, the ground iron-hard beneath him, overlooking iron-gray waves and sky, while the chill gnawed through his coat. Quoth he:

> "I sold for food the silver
> sent me by the dwellers
> on the icy island
> off in western sea-lanes.
> I've shot my shafts away
> for shining darts in barter.
> Luckless has the land
> been lying year on year."

XV

Raw winds and sleety rain brought in the springtime. As soon as the ways were at all passable, Gunnhild had her men out anew scouring the land for Aastrid.

Some of them thought she might well have gone to her father, a great chieftain at Oprostad. Spying around, they learned what could not be altogether hidden anymore, that this was true. From gossipy neighbors they got a tale which they brought back to the queen.

Aastrid, Thorolf Louse-beard, and a faithful few others had fled into the woods. Coming to a lakeshore, they borrowed a boat from a fisherman, rowed out to a holm where nobody lived, and made rude shelters. There Aastrid brought forth a man-child. Thorolf sprinkled him with water and Aastrid named him Olaf, after Tryggvi's father. Helped by fishers and hunters, to whom they gave money, they stayed until fall began to bite. Then they trekked over byways, hiding every night, to Oprostad. Aastrid's father furnished an outbuilding for them. After a while she sent her following home, aside from two maidservants, Thorolf, and his little son.

At once Gunnhild got together thirty men, with horses and weapons. Led by one Haakon—a Haakon she could trust!—they went off with orders to fetch back the son of King Tryggvi.

Olaf the Peacock happened to be out for a few days' hawking with friends. Gunnhild was glad of that.

However, he was bound to mark that those men were gone. He would be outraged if she tried to mislead him about their errand. Instead, the first time they were alone, she told him. He scowled. "That seems wrong to me, my lady, hounding a widow to wrest her only child from her."

"Oh, no," said Gunnhild, as if shocked. "Did you think I'd murder a helpless bairn?" Even though she had given them over to wet nurses early on, memories of her own sucklings tugged at her. "No, Aastrid shall dwell in peace, while he gets a home more befitting his birth."

She hoped she meant it. Give Olaf Tryggvason a foster father close to her, such as her Haakon, and he could be raised to become a sworn man of her sons. If he nevertheless grew power-hungry—well, that would be later, when she was dead, and Harald Grayfell could then do whatever was needful. She would warn the king to keep watch on the lad.

"M-m, maybe," said Olaf the Peacock.

She caught his hands. "Let's not speak of trouble. Not now. We've so little time left us."

He nodded. "Yes, I'll soon be gone." She heard how he strove to sound merely down-to-earth, and how eagerness trembled in him like a newly leafed young birch in the spring wind. Reaching up to take him around the neck, his hair like thick silk, she drew his head downward for a kiss.

His was not the only gaze turned seaward. Every week there was more riding back and forth, caulking and pitching of ships, war-talk. With Vikin laid under the Gunnhilds-sons, Harald Grayfell wanted to make a faring north to Bjarmaland, as his father had done—and on the way back met his mother. Riches were to be gotten yonder, as well as renown. Although they now took the whole scot of Vi-kin, the brothers were still straitened for means.

Gunnhild's Haakon returned with his band, muddied and wearied. He brought no child along. They had ransacked the home of Aastrid's father but found nothing of her or those who had lodged with her. The chieftain told them bluntly how friends of his had spied them yesterday, guessed what they were after, and sped to warn him. That same night he sent her off with guides and the rede that she make for Svithjod, where another friend of his was a mighty man. But he had not wanted to know what way his daughter took.

Haakon's warriors cast about. The spoor was faint and unsure, soon washed out by rain. During the next few days they asked widely around. They learned how a yeoman opened his door to the wayfarers, but when he heard from a man they had met on the road who they were, he woke them and sent them away. However, he must have given them food and lent them a worker of his who knew the woods well, for they were once more lost to all ken. Haa-kon angrily bade the yeoman lead them. He did, but Haa-kon thought he knowingly took the wrong path, for their search left them empty-handed. At length Haakon rode back to King's Crag.

Gunnhild held down her wrath. Upbraiding him when he had tried his best could only embitter him, and she had few

enough who were true to her. "You did well, in such a mire
of betrayal," she said quietly. "We may have better luck
another time." She gave him a fine cloak, and money to his
followers.

Nor would she take revenge on Aastrid's father and his
neighbors. They had not outright broken any law or flouted
the king's will. Norway smoldered. Unwise would it be to
kick those coals without strong cause.

Aastrid could not hide forever, and Gunnhild knew
where she was bound. The queen sent word forth over her
web. Trappers, woodcutters, charcoal burners, homeless
wanderers could speedily pass news across the mountains
of the Keel.

Meanwhile, Olaf the Peacock was going home.

He had asked the king for leave, as he must. "I'd rather
you stayed here with us, and had whatever standing you
choose," answered Harald Grayfell.

Olaf thanked him for this, as well as for the honor already shown him, but said that nevertheless his wish was
for Iceland, if the king was willing. "That shall not touch
our friendship, Olaf," said Harald. "Yes, you may sail come
summer, for I see how you yearn. Nor shall you have any
trouble about making ready. I'll take care of everything."

And he had a knarr outfitted and loaded with timber.
"This ship is yours, Olaf," he said. "You shall not leave
Norway in a hired vessel."

Olaf gave many well-spoken thanks. Later, alone with
Gunnhild, he said low, "The king has been very kind to
me, but I think I owe still more to you, my lady."

"Whatever I may have done has gladdened me," she
whispered. "You came to me like a clean wind off the sea."

Eirik had been a storm, she thought. Brihtnoth was a
warm breeze that murmured of the Southlands. Hrut was a
gust that happened by. She did not then understand that,
and so she wronged him. Olaf should not suffer for having
known her.

As before, King Harald and Queen Gunnhild went down
to the docks with him. The king uttered hearty good wishes.

The queen could not say much other than "Fare you well. Fare you ever well."

How merrily he sprang aboard.

It was a day of blue sky and white clouds. Waves danced, glittered, chuckled. The bright-striped sail drew taut, the masthead pennon fluttered like a wing, and the ship stood out to sea, bearing away Gunnhild's last breath of youth.

She had not wept for the deaths of her lord, her brothers, or her sons. Not where anyone could see. She would not for this. There was work to do.

After Harald's fleet went off—a fierce, brave sight—she felt she had better shift her lodging. The hall here was in need of cleaning and airing. Aside from servants and a few guards, it would stand empty till he got back. Her house, smaller and never filled, stayed sweet; but few men of mark would come while the king was away.

True, any of his brothers would make her welcome. But they were seldom at one spot for long. Having to feed their troops and workers, and lacking the inflow of cargoes that reached Harald, they moved about the shires that were theirs, battening on lendmen and hersirs. She was too old for such a life. Besides, it would be hard to keep folk awed.

She sailed to Körmt. Ragnfröd was at the great hall there when she arrived, but soon left. Now she sat nearer the middle of the kingdom.

A fast boat bore word that Haakon Jarl was on his way down. She made the household ready to receive him—also her guards, however unlikely an attack was. What could he gain by that? A few days later he came with two ships. The crews were fully armed, but figureheads were lowered and white shields hung at the mastheads.

"When I heard you were here, Queen, I thought it would be well to speak with you," he said. Teeth glistened in the dark beard, a quick smile. "Not that I'd slight your sons. Never! But you will know I mean no harm, and can tell them."

Oh, he did mean harm if ever he saw an opening, she thought. Although he had gotten wergild and costly gifts, his father was unavenged. Nor could he believe that her sons did not lust for his Thraandlaw. And he was quite right.

She smiled back. "That you seek me out in itself shows your goodness of heart, Jarl," she purred.

"What I hope to do is this," he said. "You must know—surely the kings do—that I've told the Thraands to stand by their weapons, and my warcraft are clear to sail anytime I bid them. I want the kings and you, Queen Mother, to know that this is not in any way aimed at them. My dearest wish is to keep the peace unbroken between us."

"May I ask, Jarl, why you then have, shall we say, half mustered your strength?"

"Let me be frank, Queen. I know full well your sons are honest. But grudges linger in many of the Thraands. When King Harald gathers his might and sails north, they wonder. They stir and mutter. It wouldn't take much to touch off a clash. Bad could lead to worse. By keeping my folk wary, I lower their fears. And so the peace abides."

And so he warned her and hers, Gunnhild thought. Or was this the start of a busking for war?

"I see," she said. "We'll talk at length about it. But first we'll feast. Forgive an old woman if she goes to bed early. Let it not dampen the glee."

In the next few days they did get together now and then under four eyes. Their business did not go much further than ways to make either side feel safer. Thus, Gunnhild told Haakon how she had counseled Harald Grayfell not to put in anywhere at the Thraandlaw and the king agreed. Haakon undertook to allow no viking cruises of more than three ships before Harald came home. Back and forth they went, two wildcats each taking the measure of the other.

But they strayed elsewhere too. "Sometimes I wish we had some men who could write like the learned among the Christians," he said once. She forbore to recall aloud that she was baptized. "Runes aren't good for much but memorials and spells." He gave her a glance. "I've seen Westland books, taken by raiders. It's been gladsome meeting you again, my lady. But if we had the leaves, the letters, the ink, word could pass between us far faster, easier, and oftener." He sighed. "And then, all the tales, all the truths in those books."

She had felt the same. "First we'd have to gain the skill," she said wryly. "Or, at least, keep men on hand who have it. Priests? Some of them do." Brihtnoth passed through her mind, a wistful ghost.

He stiffened. "No more Christian priests in the Thraand-law while I'm jarl at Hlaði." Though he had not burned the church raised by King Haakon the Good, he was starving it. He eased. "But let's not speak of unlucky things. Let's take up what's happened to us, and what we've heard from the outside world."

Gunnhild was very willing, within bounds. She listened; she told; she bandied words and thoughts. For this while she half forgot to miss Olaf the Peacock.

But as she watched Haakon's ships slide away north-ward, she felt anew how thin the friendship was. Even so did the heroes in Valhall share mirth before they went out to fight each other.

What she had been told about the Christian afterlife flit-ted through her. She shuddered a little. Whatever might lie beyond the world, she and Haakon would never arise to feast afresh, nor stride out side by side to the last fight of all.

Beneath everything, Haakon Jarl, who stood for the old gods and the old laws, was her foe.

Shortly afterward, another ship docked, with wares and news from Iceland. Olaf the Peacock had landed safely and been made happily welcome. Hrut's wife Unn had left him. Helped by her father, she declared herself sundered from her husband; with Mörd she rode to the Althing and on the Hill of Laws made the divorce known. The shameful grounds for it did not long stay hidden. Gunnhild foresaw that wounded feelings would lead to strife and bloodshed. Well, she had not wished anything like that on Olaf. She had fully known beforehand that she could not keep him.

Her wedding was forever to the house of Eirik.

Word came from over the mountains. Aastrid had reached Svithjod, to find housing and kindness with her father's friend Haakon the Old. Gunnhild sent her own Haakon—too many Haakons, she thought with a stiff grin—at the head of a score. He was to bring her offer to foster Olaf Tryggvason before the Swede-king. What with the Danes and the Wends to watch out for, that overlord would be loth to offend his Norse kindred.

The sun wheeled downward. The birches turned yellow. Gunnhild shifted back to King's Crag. She was there when Harald Grayfell steered into the bay. He had fought mightily in Bjarmaland; dead lay heaped along the River Dvina; hulls were stuffed with booty. It would hold them for a while, she thought—gifts to friends and guests, furs and thralls to sell for food—but only a while.

Late in the year, her man Haakon returned to her. He had tried with the Swede-king, then with the chieftain Haakon the Old. His words were soft. He told how good it would be for the boy. Aastrid said no, and Haakon the Old stood by her. Haakon the messenger rode back to the Swede-king and borrowed some troopers. He led them to Aastrid and spoke more sternly. Again she said no. Before he could begin on threats, a thrall of Haakon the Old, a hulking doglike man, ran forward and growled at him to begone. The thrall waved a heavy staff that could strike swords aside and break necks. Other thralls and field hands, gathered in a herd, now likewise rumbled and crowded at his heels. It seemed Haakon the Old had always treated them well. Haakon the messenger saw nothing to do but withdraw before his band took a beating. Back in Uppsala, the Swede-king told him it wasn't worthwhile pushing this business further. Gunnhild's Haakon could only turn homeward.

So be it, she thought; for now, at least. But this was a bitter ending to a year that had begun so gladly.

Winter laid its darkness on the land. Gunnhild abided.

She and Harald often talked about things. Among them were Haakon Jarl and the Thraands.

The sun swung upward, days lengthened, ice melted, land greened, ships plowed the seas again. One Icelandic skipper told in the king's hall how Olaf Höskuldarson had wedded Thorgerd Egilsdottir. It was reckoned a fine match on both sides.

Olaf the Peacock had wedded a daughter of Egil Skallagrimsson.

Gunnhild said nothing aloud. She sat frozen.

BOOK SIX

HAAKON JARL

1

The wind that roared in the trees was too cold for this time in spring. It foreboded another bad harvest.

Sunlight between hasty clouds flickered dimly through the gut across two windows. A hearthfire crackled under the racket outside and spilled some warmth into the room. Whenever a bit of wood, burnt free of a log, fell into the coals, sparks showered upward.

The big men seated around a drinking-board did not give much heed to their ale horns. Mostly their eyes were on the woman at the right hand of her eldest son.

Harald Grayfell took the first word when they began to talk in earnest. "Here, where we're alone, I'll not hide that it's been our mother who had me bring us together again."

Ragnfröd tossed his red head. "That was never well hidden," he laughed.

Harald frowned. Gudröd hastened to put in, "Well do we know she's deep-minded. However, the will to call us was yours."

"And the will to come was ours," snapped Erling.

"As shall be the deeds we do," Sigurd blustered. He lifted his horn and gulped.

Harald had eased. "You've likely guessed what this is about."

"Though I hope you've kept it to yourselves," Gunnhild said.

Erling's sharp face tightened in a scowl. "How can it stay unknown to him?"

"Of course it can't for long, once you begin openly making ready," Gunnhild agreed. "But he's let down the watchfulness he kept up while Harald was in Bjarmaland. Now let's give him no more forewarning than we must."

Sigurd's thick body leaned forward. "Him—Haakon Jarl of Hladi—who else could it be?"

Gudröd cleared his throat. "I believed—Mother, I believed you were keeping him—well, not unfriendly to us."

Harald smiled. "So she did, with skills to match his, buying us time. Today she and I think she's bought enough."

Ragnfröd sounded unwontedly unsure. "We didn't get very far against him before."

Bitterness rose anew in Gunnhild, as it had more than once since that news came from Iceland. It tasted like blood in her mouth. Her words went as coldly as the wind. "Yes, him and his high-bellied Thraands. If ever a folk wanted taming, there they are. True, we underrated them last time. We were only lately back in Norway. Our knowledge was slight. But we've learned.

"And now you hold Vikin, all the southern shires. They're yours to take men from. Go north together, each bringing his own levies. Raise more along the way. Your strength should be overwhelming."

"He's kept the peace and paid his scot," mumbled Ragnfröd.

"Biding his own time. I did not meet with him so often, sparring with his wits and sly tongue, for nothing. I tell you, he'll break with us as soon as he can. Even meanwhile, by holding the great Thraandlaw like a king himself, he mocks your power and thereby undermines it."

Erling flushed. "Also, he keeps the stronghold of heathendom. We won't crush Thor till we've crushed Haakon."

"And the Thraands!" cried Sigurd.

The talk went back and forth. Eagerness sprang higher and higher, like flames of a balefire.

"There is one thing," said Harald at length, more calmly. "Mother, you want us five to fare north in the same fleet. But during those weeks, anything can happen at our backs."

"I will be here," Gunnhild answered.

Harald nodded. "None could be wiser or more knowing—or harder of heart when that's called for. Still, Mother, you are a woman. Some men might believe they can get away with this or that. It'd be troublesome to punish them when I—we return. It'd make ill will for us among their friends."

Gunnhild raised her brows. "I've thought on that."

"Of course. You've told me. We should lay it out for my brothers."

Yes, he had some wisdom of his own. If only the rest had as much. "Bid a strong, well-liked man come down here to stay. Make known that he'll speak for you and uphold you in every way."

Gudröd grinned. "And you will—counsel him, shall we say?"

It stung her before she saw that this son, least of any, meant no gibe, merely that if the man was to be hull and sail for the day-by-day doings of the kingdom, the hand on the helm would be hers.

"Who have you in mind?" asked Ragnfröd.

"Arinbjörn Thorisson of Sygnafylki," said Harald. "None is more steadfast." He smiled. "True, he'll be unhappy at first, left behind. We must make everybody understand we don't reckon him weak, now in his later years, but, rather, mighty enough to give us this help."

Gunnhild herself had named him. She and he could go on overlooking his friendship with Egil Skallagrimsson. Indeed, to work with him and through him would lift the mood that had fallen on her.

Let Egil—let Olaf the Peacock—sit yonder in their sour gray Iceland. It would be she who unloosed the spears.

11

A while after Arinbjörn arrived at King's Crag, Gunnhild told him of a worrisome hearsay that had lately reached her. Those who brought it here had not seen much, but they had caught hints and mutterings. Something was going on among the yeomen and fisherfolk around Sotaness, not far to the north along the shore but seldom visited from outside. Gunnhild said Arinbjörn should send men to look into it. He answered that he would undertake this himself, and set off with a few of the guardsmen who had stayed. Short though the way was, they were gone for more than a week. When he returned, it was soon before the main meal of the day. Gunnhild already sat in the high seat. Standing before her, he rumbled, "Greeting and honor to you, Queen."

She smiled at him. Hair and beard were quite gray, the square face furrowed, but the burly, roughly clad frame unbowed. "Welcome back," she said. "How went it with you?"

"We had no fights, Queen." His voice shivered a bit. "But down at the landing we found another karfi, and the watchmen there said it had brought news from the high North. The crew didn't tell them what it was, for the skipper thought you should have it first."

"Rightly so." Gunnhild waved a hand at the man benched next to her. "Here he is, Valgard Hjörvardarson."

Arinbjörn nodded. "We know each other from aforetime in the king's troop. Good day to you, Valgard. What is your tale?"

Gunnhild laughed. "Oh, sit down first. Here in the high seat beside me. Let your men bench themselves. Drink, every one of you, for thirsty must you be."

Arinbjörn obeyed. "It seems the news is good."

"Well, it could be worse. Much worse."

Valgard gave it afresh. Arinbjörn listened narrowly, sometimes cupping an ear because he had grown a little deaf.

Northbound, the Eirikssons learned from their scouts that Haakon Jarl had mustered the Thraands and gathered his warships. But upon finding out what their strength was, he did not go to meet them but steered along both the Moerrs and Raumsdalr, plundering, burning, killing. His foes would get few fighters or foodstocks in those parts. Thence he sent most of the Thraands home and sailed on with a smaller fleet full of warriors.

"That was the last we heard of him," said Valgard. "When I left, the kings were at Sygnafylki, waiting for the wind to shift. Though foul for them, it was fair for a messenger like me."

Arinbjörn gusted a sigh. "Sygnafylki. Is all well with it?"

"Yes. As I've told, Haakon never came near them, and

by then they didn't look for him to. He must have put far
out to sea."

"That's no easy fox to trap," said Gunnhild, "but we will.
His evildoing shouldn't hinder the kings too much. By now
they're likely on their way again, with Thraandheim lying
open to them."

She looked at Arinbjörn. "Tell us about your doings."

The tidings had not made him gleeful. "I think we'd better speak of it between ourselves, Queen," he answered
slowly. "No offense to anyone. However, my guess is
you'd rather the tale doesn't spread."

Wildfire in a dry woodland, she thought with sudden
starkness. "As you wish. Come to my house in the fore-
noon." She wrapped cheer around herself like a cloak. "Today we'll feast, and drink to victory for the sons of Eirik."

With him to be headman at the party, she could go to
bed early without dampening things. Though his years were
more, it seemed that hers weighed the heavier. Well, they
had been fuller, love, loss, gladness, grief, yearnings, seekings, strangeness past any ken of his. Nonetheless she lay
long awake.

Wind in the morning hurled rainshowers. It whistled over
sparsely begrown croplands and kine gaunt at their grazing.
She had had her dwelling made as snug and bright a nest
for him as it had been for her sons.

"My croft," she sometimes named it to herself, wryly
when she thought how in it or in the one at the Byfjord
she sowed what seed she could and how often she *was* the
Norse kingship.

Arinbjörn entered. She seated them at a drinking-board,
with goblets and mead before them, and sent the staff out.
"Speak freely," she bade.

The slanted blue eyes locked with hers. "You remember
how I went off on my own, Queen, with a handful of men
and them picked for having family hereabouts."

She nodded. "And you remember I didn't quite like that,
as restless as the lowborn are." She had not forbidden him,
though. He was closer to the yeomanry, knew them better
than she even wanted to.

"Browbeating them would make it worse, I thought."

"But if they'd taken to their weapons—" Gunnhild let her voice trail off.

"I reckoned that unlikely, Queen, the more so when I had men of their own shire, some of them kinfolk of theirs, with me. Besides, I can't have much of a span left me, whatever I do. My wife's dead and I'm not after getting another; my living children are wedded, my grandchildren grown or well along toward it. Not a bad age for a man to make his farewell."

"But it would be," said Gunnhild softly, "right now when we need you."

A corner of his mouth lifted slightly before he went on. "Anyhow, I got to Sotaness, asked around, and dug out what was behind those snatches your, um, your lookouts had caught. I quieted the business down."

Flames hissed. "Tell me all of it," Gunnhild ordered.

Arinbjörn straightened on his bench. "As the queen wants. It wasn't sweet. The farmers and fishers and suchlike had met from a wide neighborhood to offer at King Tryggvi's howe."

Gunnhild kept herself sitting still. Tryggvi Olafsson, whom her Gudröd had lured to his death there—and she had failed to lay hold of Olaf Tryggvason, who would have this to avenge if he lived to be a man. She waited.

Arinbjörn plodded ahead. "They say—I don't, Queen, but they do, or did—they say King Tryggvi didn't die in honest battle, he was foully murdered. They say it's doings like that, and the wrecking of halidoms, they say that's what's brought hunger on the land. They lived well under good King Haakon, they say. Also, they say the new kings are stripping them to the bone and scorning their rights as freemen. Those at the howe slaughtered livestock they could ill spare, hoping he inside might somehow better their lot for them. There, I've said it outright, Queen, not as it ought to've been but as it was."

"I'm not amazed, nor angry at you." Gunnhild meant it. "What did you do about this?"

"I sent word to their foremost men—men of mine knew

who they should be—to come talk with me."

"You quelled them?"

The blocky head shook. "No, Queen. My old lord and yours, King Eirik Blood-ax, would've, true. But aside from my having so few along, I reckoned that threats or slayings would only set others astir. Nor would it be right, Queen," he said stubbornly. "They're suffering. If my household got as poor as theirs, if I felt so trampled on, well—" He cleared his throat. "I warned them what'll happen if this kind of thing goes on. I said if they'd lay off it, I'd see whether something could be done to help them."

Now Gunnhild stiffened. "There you went beyond yourself, Arinbjörn. Far beyond."

"Queen," he said, his stolidness unshaken, "I was King Eirik's man while he lived. I am your son King Harald's man while he lives, may that be long. For his sake, I've told you the truth. My rede is that the king go easier on the folk. But that lies with him—" He stopped while a flame snapped. "—and you."

She made herself lean back and shape a smile, although she felt how tight it was. "I understand. I'll say forth in the hall that you did well, and reward you."

But not by letting a skald make him a poem. He had one already, from Egil Skallagrimsson.

She'd better forget that and be glad Arinbjörn stayed among the faithful. They were all too few.

Late in the summer, Harald Grayfell came again to King's Crag. He and his brothers had won Thraandheim with scant warfare. Thence they went around the shires of the whole Thraandlaw, taking scot and duties, and laying heavy fines on the yeomen who had defied them. At last Harald, Erling, and Ragnfröd returned with most of their men, leaving Gudröd and Sigurd behind to keep a grip.

High flew the happiness. Yet the feasting was less than it should have been. Here too, larders were getting low.

Then as fall gloomed away toward winter, a storm-beaten ship lurched over the water with a freight of tidings from the North. Haakon Jarl was back at Hladi.

While the dark months wore on, the tale of what happened reached Gunnhild word by word, wayfarer by wayfarer. Haakon had led his fleet south, well beyond any sight of land, till he could swing east and make for the Skagerrak. That was no small feat of seamanship, Harald said grudgingly. Passing into the Kattegat, they lay to in Denmark, refitting and restocking. Whether or not the Dane-king had met with the jarl, he let them rest until, soon, they went on through the strait and across the Baltic to cruise as vikings. When fall set in they sailed west to Svithjod, where they found haven at Helsingland. There Haakon left his ships in care of a chieftain he knew and took his crews on horseback and afoot onward through Jämtland, fields, meadows, trackless wildernesses, up into the mountains of the Keel and over to the Thraandlaw.

The news of his coming went before him as though on the wings of ravens. Every shire rose in arms. On every fjord and island, ships were unmoored or rolled out of their winter houses. Men flocked to him, bawling welcome, flashing steel aloft, thundering on shields.

Gudröd and Sigurd could only embark their followings and withdraw. They settled in Moerr, where life was lean but folk were at least on their side after what Haakon had done.

During the winter, bands of king's men and Thraands raided back and forth, off and on, but the harm wreaked was only in the marches. Haakon Jarl sat where he was, wielding his power, offering to his heathen gods, in peace. Though springtime awoke anew, last year the Gunnhilds-sons had drawn so deeply on the stocks of their own lands

and the willingness of the dwellers therein that there could
be no question of faring again against him.

Not yet. Once more she must wait, and watch, and weave
her webs.

IV

As gutted as they were, Moerr and Raumsdalr could not
feed a kingly household for long. Anything gained in
forays to Thraandheim was offset by what the Thraands
bore away when they raided. Already before the days grew
longer than the nights, Gudröd and Sigurd must needs pull
back to their holdings in the South.

Haakon Jarl kept ships and warriors standing by. Many
more could swiftly be rallied. The years had been much
less bad there for both farmers and fishers than elsewhere
in Norway, so men had no dearth of provisions for war.
The Eirikssons did not risk going any farther north than
Sogn. So firm was Haakon's hold that during the summer
he went off with a troop, back through Svithjod to his fleet
in Helsingland, and spent weeks in west-viking. Gunnhild
believed he meant this for a mockery of his foes, to lessen
the awe of them.

Heeding his mother as well as his own head, Harald
Grayfell worked to keep it high. Yes, he said, the kingship
had been wounded, but not to death. It would get back its
strength. He and his brothers must show they were undaunted, as able and stern as ever, with trusty warriors at
their beck. An uprising was most unlikely. After all, who
else was left in Norway of the kingly blood? Only those
sluggards in Hringariki, sprung from Harald Fairhair's unlucky match with Snaefrid, who had never wanted more
than to be scot-paying shire-kings and farmers. Gunnhild's
sons were otherwise. They would reap fresh wealth abroad
and, if need be, spend some of it on grain shipped in from
yonder. The time would come when they could raise the

same might against Haakon as before; and then they would make sure of him and his Thraands.

The rest said he was doubtless right; but they were seldom blithe anymore. Sigurd took the setback worst, drinking enough for three and earning the nickname Loudmouth anew.

One day, making his rounds in Hördaland, he came to the dwelling of the hersir Klypp Thordarson. For this while, the weather had turned lovely. Light flooded from an utterly blue sky. Breezes drifted warm, laden with smells of the greenwood that decked the hills around. Though grain stood sparse in the fields, a lark sang above them and everywhere else wildfowl flew by or called from among the trees. The steading spread big around its yard, the house reared handsome. Klypp was a man of mark.

Cobblestones rang underhoof as Sigurd and his warriors rode in. A messenger had gone ahead, and cookfires smoked for a feast to which no few of the neighborhood had come. They went out to meet and greet him. At their head was a young woman. "Be welcome, King," she hailed. "Unhappily, Klypp is away for a few days, but I, his wife Aalof Aasbjarnardottir, offer you all that is ours to give."

Although they had not hitherto met, Sigurd knew that she, like her husband, had high-standing kinfolk. His gaze swept over her, then clung and crept. She was tall, full-bosomed, fair to behold; the locks of hair that showed below her headcloth were like amber. "All?" he murmured. He made his leer into a smile and thanked her.

Once in the high seat, he began to swill well-nigh as fast as the maids could fill his horn. He did speak with men about what had been happening hereabouts, what was awry that they hoped he would set aright, what they meant to bring up at their next Thing—but more and more curtly, broken by hiccoughs and belches. Ever his eyes tracked Aalof. When the boards and food were set forth, he slapped the seat and shouted to her, "Come; you shall sit by me."

She flushed. "Is that fitting, lord? I'll sit across from you, of course."

"No, no, you'll be here with me and we'll drink together. I'll say what's fitting. Am I not the king?"

Men stared. Some whispered to each other. There was nothing they could do, however, with the guards amidst them and more posted outside. They did not eat as merrily as they had awaited.

Sigurd pressed Aalof to match him, horn for horn. She hung back, and had small answers for whatever else he said to her. Mainly, loudly, he boasted of his warlike deeds and those he was going to do; oh, Haakon Jarl and the Thraands would rue their own births! Nothing but heathen witchcraft and their troll-gods lent them strength. It would not last. Sigurd would cast Thor down too, and drink in Hladi. He would be glad to guest Aalof there. He wanted to repay her kindness today and show her he liked her as much as she did him.

When he got to telling what a great lover he was, she asked him low if he wanted a wench for the night. "What, a thrall?" he boomed. "Toad-ugly, stinking of the barnyard? No, no, a king should have better than that."

He groped at her. She stood up. "Forgive me, my lord," she said very steadily and clearly. "I am only a woman, only the wife of Klypp Hersir, and I grow weary. Best I go to my rest now, so I'll be fresh to see you off with all due honor in the morning." Before he could speak further, she had stepped from the dais and was striding away between the benches. Neighborhood men cast her stiff smiles as she passed.

Talk sputtered low. Sigurd chafed and drank. Night fell. When housemen brought more wood for the fires, he cried, "No, enough, we'll to bed." Everybody but his guards seemed happy with that. A few of those grinned.

Straw pallets were laid out for the higher-ranking to sleep on the benches, the lower on the floor. Meanwhile they went out and pissed. At the end of this main room was a smaller one, with a shut-bed on either side, the right for Klypp and his wife, its panel closed, the left for wellborn visitors.

The steward led King Sigurd thither, wished him goodnight, and closed the door. A lamp flickered dull yellow, to show where the pot was. Noises grumbled toward stillness.

Aalof woke from uneasy dreams when her panel slid aside. Black across the light, Sigurd hunched over her. The hairs on his unclad skin made a bristly fuzz around him. He reached down to cup a breast. "Be glad, my dear," he said hoarsely. His breath reeked. "Tonight you'll get a better gift of me than gold."

She shrank back against the wall. Her hands batted at him, unheeded. "No, lord, no," she gasped.

"Yes, lady, yes. You'll have more fun than ever you knew could be. Tomorrow you'll walk bowlegged."

"I'll send for a woman, a fair young woman—"

"Why, I have one here." He crawled into the bed. The mattress rustled beneath his weight. "What, would you spurn your king?"

"I'll scream—"

Fumbling, he slapped a hand over her mouth. "If you do, there'll be dead men in this house, and I'll have you anyway. Your darling Klypp may not live long either."

He rolled her over, hauled up her nightgown, and pushed a knee between her thighs. "Aargh," he growled, and thrust his way in.

She waited it out. When afterward he asked, "There, wasn't that like Frey himself?" she said nothing. When he took her the second time, she lay as if lifeless. "Cold bitch," he mumbled, got off her, sagged down, and snored.

The thing could not go unknown. Folk heard a little, they saw more by daylight, and they understood. Bread was broken in a thick stillness. Aalof was the bleakest of everyone, the most shut into herself. The king said little; he had a headache. When he thanked her for the guesting and gave her a gold ring, she took it stonily. Nor did she call farewell as he rode off with his guards. But once he was gone, she wept.

Gunnhild did not hear about this for some while. She had so much else to deal with.

V

The Swedes and Goths gave scant trouble. Besides having their wealthy market towns, they mostly busied themselves eastward, trading and settling across the Baltic and far down the rivers of Gardariki. Indeed, the kingly house of Kiev stemmed from them.

But in Vikin her sons were close to Denmark. Uneasiness waxed on both sides. The herring runs through the Sound were still rich. More and more, fisher crews from the two kingdoms had been clashing, sometimes bloodily. Now and then Danish vikings plundered Norse chapmen bound through those waters. King Harald Bluetooth did nothing about any of it. Word seldom came from him. When it did, it was short and frosty.

"We need his friendship," Gunnhild told Harald Grayfell. "Let's try to make him understand he needs ours. I hear that his ties with the German Emperor Otto are growing strained."

At her rede, Harald Grayfell sent three ships to the Dane-king, loaded with gifts. Highest of these would be a poem of praise from Harald's foremost skald, Glum Geirason, who went along as chief spokesman. He was also to raise afresh a thought that seemed to have withered, of a match made between the houses—maybe even with Bluetooth's daughter Thyra; surely some close lady-kin. "The time is overpast for you to take a true queen," Gunnhild said. "We want power enough behind her that a son by her can keep yours after you are gone. Otherwise your by-blows will once again tear Norway asunder, fighting over it. When we've done this, we'll see about your brothers."

Thus it was with eagerness that she and Grayfell received Glum when he got back. Straightaway they saw on his face that the faring had not gone well. Other sons of hers might have questioned him unseemly fast. Gunnhild felt a small glow beneath the sudden chill when her Harald made the travelers welcome, had them seated and drink brought for them, and gave gold arm-rings to the skald and the firstman of the guards that went yonder. Only then did he say, "Tell me the upshot, Glum. Waste no breath on honeying it. Later we'll hear the tale from beginning to end."

Glum knew his lord too well and honored him too much to shy off. "Be it as the king wants," he answered. "We found King Harald Gormsson at Aarhus. He guested us fittingly and spoke mildly enough, in that roundabout way of his, so that it took days to learn what he really meant. He thanks you for your gifts and has sent gifts of his own back with us, though frankly, lord, I'd call them less than yours. He said that the sons of King Eirik and Queen Gunnhild were dear to him in Denmark, as they surely remember. He still bears only the best of wishes for them. However, he cannot help but feel they've shown little zeal for the Faith, and have yet to acknowledge his rights in Norway."

Whispers hissed around the hall. "Go on," said Harald Grayfell.

Glum obeyed. "King Harald Gormsson says he understands that it hasn't been easy for you and your brothers, lord. The Norse are a headstrong breed, and these are years of hardship for them. You have your hands full, and may not yet be able to spare payments. He bears with that for now."

Those men who had gone to Denmark nodded stiffly. Those who had stayed here caught their breaths and stared. "Go on," said Harald again.

"King," Glum told him, "he never said it outright, but he knows how to slip something across, day by day, word by sly word." That he spoke so boldly about another king showed the depths of his love and trust, Gunnhild thought. If only there were more like him. "He believes you and King Gudröd dealt wrongly with King Tryggvi Olafsson and King Gudröd Bjarnarson." Yes, Gunnhild thought, Bluetooth would have looked upon those two as a counterweight. "It makes him wonder—I'll utter it flatly, lord—wonder about the worth or wisdom of a wedlock bond such as I laid before him." Quickly: "What he said to tell you, however, King, was that he thanks you for this thought, that does him honor, and he will give it thought of his own."

It was not an affront, Gunnhild knew. Not quite. Harald Bluetooth was too wily for that.

Harald Grayfell whitened. She leaned close to him in the high seat and murmured, "Go lightly. Make no fuss about this. Tell everyone you'll think in your turn. Then bring up cheerier things, as though it doesn't matter very much."

"It does," he said from the side of his mouth.

"Yes." Once Haakon Jarl returned from viking, would he send messengers to Harald Bluetooth? "But no ax will fall soon. Watch. Wait. Make ready. Let slip no warnings."

He sighed. "Always wise, Queen Mother." Thereupon he barked a laugh. "So be it!" he cried. "Well told, Glum. Now we'll see what our kinsman in Denmark has sent us, and make merry for half the night."

Gunnhild felt an easing sweep through the hall, like the swift slackening of a tide-race in the fjord of her childhood. Best she leave, not to start anybody wondering. Besides, she didn't care for slurred, drunken gabble. She made known that she was tired—feeling her years, she said with a smile—and left.

Outside, the low sun was lost to sight; the stones of the yard lay shadowless under gray overcast. Wind whistled. She drew her cloak tightly against it. How cold was the weather farther north? She had heard that there and in the Uplands farmers were keeping their kine in barns throughout the summer, feeding them on what hay could be gathered, like Finns. The fishing grew ever more lean. But farther yet, the Thraandlaw shires were not doing unbearably badly. The land and waters in Denmark still yielded well. Was God angry that her sons had more or less given up on bringing Norway to the Faith? Then why did heathen Svithjod thrive? Had something gone wrong with the world itself, with Norse man's oneness with the old Powers of earth, sea, and sky?

A voice called her back. "Queen," it whined, "may it please you, I have news."

Ögmund stood there, sallow, skinny, stoop-shouldered. Although she did not stint him, he was drably clad. So he often was, to be less showy as he went about her errands. He must have shivered here for some while, knowing better than to break in on Harald Grayfell. She tautened as she answered smoothly, "Yes?"

"One of your lookouts has come, Queen. Sveinn Fox-nose. He says he has tidings. I gave him leave to stable his horse—a walking rack of bones, the nag is—and wait beside it in the warmth. Does the queen wish to see him?"

Sveinn Fox-nose, she recalled. He had no other name, never having known who his father was and forgetting about his mother once he had left her behind with her younger whelps. A woods-runner, hunter, trapper, surely a thief, but a fellow who ranged widely and heard much, earning pay when he brought her any worthwhile news. It was as if the wind passed between her ribs. "Bring him to me at my house in a little while," she bade, and walked onward.

She was seated when they came. At her nod, Ögmund then left them alone. Sveinn louted awkwardly, a gaunt and grimy man in patched wadmal and greasy leather. Living mostly outdoors, though a smell hung about him, he did not really stink. She waved a hand at a goblet on a table nearby. "Be welcome, and drink," she said. "Tell me what you have to tell; then Ögmund shall lead you to food and better lodging than a stable."

"I, uh, I thank—" He picked up the earthen cup and gulped the hot mead. "Aaah!" He braced himself. "Queen, I have this from your watcher Visbur the Swart, who rode straight across Svithjod till he found somebody who'd take it to you. I was stopping by at the crofter Gellir's—"

Gunnhild coaxed the tale forth. It stabbed in her.

Aastrid, widow of King Tryggvi Olafsson, whom Gunnhild's son Gudröd got slain, Aastrid felt she had sheltered long enough with the chieftain Haakon the Old. She had meant from the first to seek out her brother Sigurd across the Baltic. Now she was getting set to go.

Gunnhild filled in with knowledge she had already garnered. Sigurd had done very well in Gardariki. Today, among other things, he was a high-ranking guardsman of Prince Vladimir Svyatoslavsson in Holmgard. Although Vladimir was only twelve or thirteen years old, already he had made his mark. Given time and luck, he might well follow—maybe overthrow—his brother Svyatopolk, the Grand Prince down in Kiev. Meanwhile he held the land up to Lake Ladoga, and drew scot from as far as Estonia; and Sigurd had his ear.

Gunnhild thought of Aastrid coming to her brother. She thought of what they might think of—maybe together with Harald Bluetooth, whose new queen was Polish, or even Haakon Jarl. Aastrid would take her child along.

No ship from here would be fast enough to waylay her. Nothing short of witchcraft could head off Aastrid and whatever doom it was that Gunnhild winded in Olaf Tryggvason.

That would not be easy or safe. Over the years she had used what she learned in Finnmörk to learn more. Hags and seidmen whom she met in Norway had little power, far less than hers, but from each of them she had won scraps of further knowledge. At last she could go forth not only as a bird, and not only to spy.

But then she must draw on that which lay beyond the world of man, at a full moon, the turning of the sun, or some other time when strangeness went unloosed by night. If now she waited for such an hour, she would be too late. She must have another thing of darkness instead.

And nevertheless—She remembered what her shadow met above Hladi, and fought down a shudder.

She steeled herself to hope that no such Being kept watch where she was bound.

As she sent Sveinn off with a few coins in his grubby fist, she bade, "After Ögmund has seen to your wants, tell him to come back here, but tell him when nobody else is listening, and say he's to keep his mouth shut."

Ögmund, who sneaked everywhere, could find the thing for her—Ögmund, Kisping, he who had shot Haakon Aethelstan's-foster's death-arrow.

VI

Already in the following twilight he brought her what she wanted. Because he had promised such speediness, she had sent her housefolk away. "And begone until I come for you," she ordered. "That may well be late in the day tomorrow, or even the day after."

Word of this had reached Harald. He sought her out himself and asked what it meant. "As before, I will be at prayer, fasting, and thinking," she answered.

He looked askance at her. "Wouldn't that be better done in the chapel, and first you confess to the priest?"

"When did you last confess?" she gibed. Then, softly, "I said I must also think. My prayer will be for insight, a path for my sons through the dangers that beset them."

He pursed his lips but said merely, "As you wish, Mother," and soon went from her.

He had more than an inkling of what she did when alone like this, she knew, and he misliked it. Still—she grinned coldly—he was willing enough to take her at her word when something helpful might come of it.

Thus she herself opened the door at Ögmund's knock. Trees and buildings hulked black against a sky the hue of a bruise. Workers yonder were through for the day and gone inside. A breeze whispered, unseasonably chill. Somewhere afar a wolf howled. At that, the king's hounds began to bay.

The footling slipped over the threshold. She shut the door behind him. From under his cloak he took a small leather bag. "Here it is, Queen," he told her.

"Put it on the table," she said. "Where's it from?"

"Off in the woods, Queen, near what's left of a shelter. Folk say two outlaws denned there long ago. One took sick and died. His friend buried him but then was caught and slain. It's still shunned."

For the span of a gasp she was in another woodland hut, small, altogether helpless, with two robbers.

She snarled at the fear, threatened it, made it slink back into the underworld. Those men were dead too, cut down before her suddenly shining eyes, and she was never going to be helpless again.

"My lady?" She had not often seen Ögmund taken off guard.

"Nothing," she said, flat-voiced. "A thought passed by that surprised me a little. You were bold to dig there."

"The queen sent me. I kept telling myself the queen's hand was over me."

"As it will be while you stay faithful to her. You shall let fall no breath of this to anyone whatsoever. I'll take it ill indeed if you do."

"The queen knows I can keep a secret." He smirked. "The queen and I already share many, don't we?"

She wondered sharply what he meant by that. He was a slippery one.

"My lady has always rewarded me well," he said. "When I came back from the war with King Haakon—I own that this time also I must flog myself onward. There wouldn't be any hoard for a drow to sit on, but one hears of how even the lowliest dead can get angry when they're stirred, and call down woe on him who does it. For my queen I took the risk."

Yes, he was pressing on her, ever so shiftily. However, she'd better not lose time now in chastening him. She could hardly blame him for greed, and he had done what most men would have balked at.

She had filled a purse with coins not only from England but from as far as Serkland, and among them minted Empire silver. She dropped it into his hands, not touching them. "Here," she said, with a nod toward the door that he understood. He gave his fulsome thanks while he went out.

She barred the door. For a short while he lingered in her mind, a nasty taste. What was he really like inside? He must have tucked away a good deal of wealth by now, but he still lived among the servants and did not seem to buy anything besides fine clothes to strut in when he went to town—and, she supposed, the hire of a whore from time

to time, though maybe his hankerings were otherwise. She
should have taken the trouble to find out more; it was well
to know one's tools. But no, that would be demeaning.

Enough.

Still she hung back. What she meant to do was the worst
kind of seid. Christ would cast her into the undying fire if
she did not atone—if Christ cared what happened to heathens. The gods in Aasgard would scowl if they marked it.
Seija would grieve if she knew, if Seija was yet alive.

It was for the house of Eirik.

She mustered herself, stepped stiffly over to the leather
bag, and undid the cord. Reaching in, a hasty snatch, she
pulled forth what was inside.

The skull felt heavier than it should be. Mold clung in
patches to the yellow-brown bone. It smelled damp. The
few teeth were black snags. She raised it and looked into
the emptinesses where eyes had been. What dreams might
the worms have shaped as they hollowed out this head?
Nightmares, belike, if anything.

She set it down, reached back into the bag, and closed
fingers on the lower jaw. Good. She had told Ögmund to
make sure of that also.

Somehow it heartened her, in a wintry way. And the
night would not be very long. She must get on with her
work.

She bore the two parts to her loftroom, fitted them together, and set the skull on the high, three-legged stool.
With the flame of her lamp she lighted a candle and used
its hot wax to fix it so that it stood on the head like a single
horn. She blew out the lamp. Everything else waited ready.
Again she stripped herself, shook her hair loose, donned
the feathers, claws, and fangs. Again she ate the holy food,
twice as much as ever before. Again she drummed, danced,
and sang. When at last she sat down cross-legged and
swayed, she gazed not into the candleflame but into the eye-
hollows.

"Dead man, you have walked down hell-road; you have
fared far; I call on you to lend me the strength of the dead.
If you will not, may voles gnaw your bones, may ants nest

among your ribs, may trolls dig you up and scatter you.
But if you will, then my man shall bring this your head
home and make a blood offering on your grave. By the
Powers of the night and the wind, by earth and fire and
the hidden waters beneath, I lay this on you, I, Gunnhild
the queen, I, mother of kings. Hear me and heed me, outward and onward even if to the ends of the world—"

She lay down. The shadow flew free.

A few stars glimmered past wind-riven, hurrying clouds.
The land stretched utterly black. Broad Lake Vänern sheened within it, and other waters, but they soon fell behind as
she bore northeasterly. Blindly aware, she found the sea, a
shining sheet under a sky that here was more open, starful,
the faintest whiteness in the east.

A ship lay hove to, waiting for daybreak. The shadow
swooped low above. Although she had never met Aastrid,
Gunnhild knew her and her bairn, knew how things now
stood with her.

Haakon the Old had gotten her passage on a well-found
knarr, bound for Holmgard with trade goods. Her foster
father Thorolf Louse-beard and his own youngest son went
along, to see her safely to her brother. She and the children
slept in a kind of tent rigged for them at the forepeak. The
shadow glided through the sailcloth, saw a slight smile on
her lips, and flew off.

It found the low Estonian shore. Folk on farms were
beginning to stir. Likewise were the crew of a longship
grounded where they had camped for the night. They themselves were Estonians, mostly short, stocky men with high
cheekbones and slanty eyes, though fair of skin and hair.
One man showed himself to be their skipper. The shadow
slipped into his head.

Gunnhild did not know the tongue he spoke. It was much
the same as that in southern Finland, where the same
breed—whom the Norse called Kvaens—were clearing and
plowing land, pushing the reindeer-herding Finns she knew
north into the wilderness. Estonia itself paid scot to Holmgard, but otherwise mostly went its own way. These men
were vikings aprowl.

The skipper, like some others in his gang, spoke Norse. His name was Klerkon. The shadow whispered in his thoughts. He grew restless, walked about, peered aloft at the earliest gulls and cormorants, held a wet finger up to the breeze, and at last said he had a feeling that it would be lucky to steer straight west although that meant beating against the wind. His men grumbled a bit, but nobody wanted to gainsay him. Having swallowed their hardtack, they floated the ship and rowed free of the rising tide before they hoisted sail.

The shadow lurked watchful. Daylight would dim Gunnhild's far-sight and hurt her, but she must see how this went.

And so the vikings found the knarr on its way and closed with it. They laid alongside, made fast while they swapped blows with the other crew, and swarmed aboard. None of them took worse than flesh wounds, but Swedes fell like slaughtered kine till those who were left dropped their weapons and gave in.

Gleefully, the vikings bound them and shared them out to sell for thralls. The young woman, standing white-faced among the wallowing dead, might well have gone to Klerkon, but he owed another man for past help and let him take her. For himself, she being clearly of wellborn stock, he took the boy who clutched her hand, grabbing him away. He also got the old fellow who had kept beside her and the youngster with him.

He looked Thorolf Louse-beard over and snorted. "You'll be of no use, gaffer," he said in Norse. His ax swung and thwacked. Thorolf crumpled. Brains spilled from the cloven skull into the blood awash in the bilge.

The lad Olaf had wept. Suddenly he stopped. Dry and bleak, his eyes raked Klerkon. Three years old, he did not want to forget.

Rain blew out of the west, cloaking the sun. It let the shadow fly. Gunnhild came back to herself.

Drained of strength, aching everywhere, she could not linger on her pallet. She must rise, hide her witchy things,

don clothes, go out, and be the queen till eventide let her
sleep.

She had done what she was able to, against a doom far
off in time and only half seen. Hard nigh her stood Haakon
Jarl.

VII

News reached Vikin from Hördaland. Its yeomen were
in an uproar because of what Sigurd Loudmouth had
done to the lady Aalof. "I'd better go there and see to this,"
said Harald Grayfell grimly. "We'll send for Gudröd to
hold the shires here. He has his wits about him, I believe."

He thought for a while, then went on in more thoughtful
wise: "It would be well anyway for me to show myself in
those parts—yes, and winter there. Not only bring unruly
men to heel, but make sure of our hold on the West. Also,
it's nearer Thraandheim. We can the more readily keep
watch on Haakon Jarl and begin on the task of killing him."
He turned to Gunnhild. "Mother, why don't you come too?
The steward's house at the great hall at Hardanger is bigger
and better than yours here. I'll shift him and his family and
you shall have it. Your redes are always welcome." He
smiled. "And don't you like seeing new things?"

Another sea voyage. Already her bones groaned. But this
would be fairly short. And where Harald went, there went
the heart of the kingship in Norway; and he might well
have need of her. "Gladly, my son, since you ask it," she
said.

In a few days they embarked. She had a ship for herself
and those of her staff she chose to take along. Ögmund got
wretchedly seasick. She laughed to herself when he yorked,
then lay shivering in a wet bedroll, trying not to roll back
and forth with the hull. It might do him good. Of late his
hints that he really ought to have more and bigger rewards
had come close to wheedling. She'd rather not lose him,
but worse would be to let him get above himself.

The hall stood at Leirvik on the southern end of Stord,

the big island at the mouth of the Hardangerfjord where Haakon Aethelstan's-foster fought his last battle. That had been in the north, however, where the ground rose higher, wooded, full of game for the king's sport. The Eirikssons had thought his lodgings there might be unlucky, maybe haunted, and burned them. Besides, Leirvik offered better anchorage, with a hinterland for farming and grazing. A hamlet had grown to a small town, which King Haakon was also wont to visit. King Harald wanted a stronghold. He had ordered a hall and its outbuildings put up. When he or a brother of his was not on hand, a jarl they trusted kept it for them, warding the whole fjordland.

This man was a Christian. So were quite a few dwellers here and in the nearby islands. The Faith King Haakon brought had stayed with most of those who were baptized, to pass on to their children. He had built a church and installed a priest from England, who still had it together with the farm from which he drew his living. The Eirikssons had reckoned it wise to leave him be, and make donations. Gunnhild paid scant heed at first. She was busy settling in, and also had much else to think about.

Harald Grayfell had sent ahead, bidding Sigurd Loudmouth meet him here. The latter was glowering and sulking in the hall when the former arrived. Harald took him and their mother to a loftroom as soon as might be.

"I'll have you done," snapped Harald. "What ever got into you, to wreak such harm on the wife of such a man?"

"She egged me on, her looks at me," answered Sigurd sullenly. "You should have seen how she swayed her hips."

"That's what *you* saw, being drunk," Gunnhild told him. "I know you, my son."

"Well, it was an honor for her, wasn't it? Sleeping with a king. For her husband too. He ought to've seen that, but no, he's a blind, overweening boor. When I left, I gave her a gold ring worthy of a skald."

"Have you not heard?" Harald flung back. "I have." He glanced at the queen, from whom he had gotten the tale. He did not ask how she learned it. "As soon as you were gone, she went off to a bog and cast the ring in, with her curse."

Sigurd bristled. "Should we fear a heathen witch?"

"No. Not that I think she is. What you've brought on us, my dear brother, is what may become an uprising. And wouldn't Haakon Jarl feed the fire!"

Sigurd growled. "Best you curb your mouths, both of you," said Gunnhild sharply. It brought them to a halt. "Together the wolf and the raven can hold the bear at bay; but if they fall out with each other, he'll pick their bones."

Sigurd sank back, though his lips twisted. Harald shook his head, clicked his tongue, and said slowly, "Yes, done is done. We have to meet with these folk and settle it, while driving into them that we don't do so out of weakness. We want our backs safe when next we go north against Haakon Jarl."

Sigurd jumped up. "Well spoken, brother!" he cried, holding out his hand. Gunnhild quickly got them talking about ways and means.

On the morrow they sent messengers around, summoning the yeomen to a Thing at Vörs on the mainland, a gathering place from of old. Although this was harvest season, green beginning to go wan, dusk falling earlier at the end of each day, they would come. Among other things, they had less reaping to do than they wished for.

The steading brawled as Harald and Sigurd made ready. Then they rowed off with their followings, across the straits to ride on inland. Suddenly the hall lay hushed.

VIII

But Gunnhild now had time to get to know the priest. That would be well, for he was highly thought of hereabouts. Even the unchristened looked at him with some awe.

Aelfgar of Wessex was a tall man, lean, the deepset eyes smoldering black beneath the white hair. He went willingly enough to her house when she asked. Only two maids were on hand. After barely sipping the mead poured for him, he began: "Queen, we hear of you everywhere. You have fully earned your fame. But—I mean no disrespect, Queen; I have prayed for the help of Heaven in finding what to say— Queen, may I counsel you as a priest of Our Lord and Saviour, Jesus Christ, may I counsel you for the sake of the kingdom and your soul, that you show more piety?"

She had half awaited this. "I've hardly ever had freedom from worldly cares, Sira Aelfgar," she answered, calmly though not meekly, her gaze never leaving his. "King Haakon Haraldsson, who set you here, did less for the Faith than my sons and I have, until he turned from it."

Aelfgar crossed himself. "God have mercy. I've heard that he died repentant. Daily I pray that this be so, and that he will not burn forever, but be purged of his sins and saved."

He leaned forward. Yes, he was fearless, Gunnhild thought. "Queen, I say nothing against the sons of King Eirik. They have not forsworn Christ. What they do in this world—it lies beyond my humble purview. At most, I can only crave kindness toward my flock." His voice thrust. "But, Queen, they attend mass when they can. If this is seldom, so be it; men have their work, kings too. You, though, Queen—I hear things about you that surely aren't true. They cannot be. Yet—how often is the queen at mass?"

"When I can go," said Gunnhild with the slightest shrug.

"I should hope—Queen, for your sake, may I ask when you last took the Host? There are, as I say, these ugly tales. The truth ought to stop them."

Well, it was bound to come to this, sooner or later. "The truth," Gunnhild said, still quietly, "is that a king must sometimes do things to save the life of the kingship that— forgive a laywoman—I think Christ would never have done. Likewise must a mother of kings."

"Your sons confess, Queen. They say their Aves and Paternosters and are absolved."

Mostly they did, Gunnhild thought. And how much did it mean? A killing in the course of business was lawful for them, and as for dealing with heathen the same as with Christians, what leeway did they really have?

"It may be that I, a weak woman, am too afraid," she said. "Yet how can I tell you I've put whatever sins I may have done behind me, when I know full well I shall have to do them again?"

"I cannot believe they are too grave, Queen." The priest winced. "They should not be."

"I did not say they are, Sira Aelfgar. I said merely that I'd better wait till these doings are through with. Then I can make my peace with God."

He caught his breath. "My lady, my lady, I beg of you, you run a fearsome risk. How many holy days of obligation have you already missed?"

She turned her voice cold. "Now you go too far, priest. I am the queen. We'll speak no further of this today."

He said little at mealtime, and left shortly after. But she knew she had not heard the last of him.

Almost at once she learned he was sending word around. On Sunday after next, the church was packed. Not only were folk here from all over Stord; some were from neighbor islands, having overnighted with friends or in their boats. She would be rash not to attend. A place had been kept for her—in rightful honor, but also in a reek of damp wool and damp man. The incense did not help.

Besides singing the mass, Sira Aelfgar preached a sermon. Tall he stood before them, his eyes hotter than the few candleflames. Not since York had she heard a voice like that, a roll and beat as of surf, a strength as of the undertow. None in Denmark had had it—Brihtnoth, poor Brihtnoth nearly crooned—and here in Norway—How did Haakon Aethelstan's-foster get such a priest for this one spot? She found herself wondering, with a prickling down her backbone, if a norn had been at work already then, these many years agone.

"—the sin against the Holy Ghost, which is not forgiven—sin barnacle-crusted on the soul, sin gnawing it like sea-worms, until weighted and riddled it sinks beyond saving—At the bottom of the maelstrom lies the Pit, and below it the fire that sears and burns forever—

"—repent while yet there is time; confess your sins and do penance; be cleansed and free to take the Body and Blood of Our Lord—You know not, no man may know, how long a span is left you before it is too late—"

Yeomen, fishermen, handworkers, houseworkers, the few thralls shuddered and crossed themselves. Also Gunnhild made the Sign, while her eyes sought to Christ crucified above the altar. She had seen better carvings on pillars and the prows of ships; but the maker had given what skill was his to this, and something of dread and the unknown passed through his fingers.

Christ lived. Wise men said so, and lands that bowed down to him grew richer than Norway. But was Odin indeed no more than a demon? Many a victory had he bestowed. He won the runes of foreknowledge and healing when he swung hanged nine nights on the world-tree, wounded with a spear even as Christ was, himself offered to himself. And in earth, sea, sky, wind and woods, rain and sun, the quickening of spring and the deeps of winter, she felt the Old Powers.

Her head lifted. Yes, she was a witch. Were she not, her sons, Eirik's, would likely now be mere vikings. How could she give up the strength she wielded for them? The daughter of Özur Dapplebeard, the woman of Eirik Blood-ax, would not yield. Not yet. Maybe when her work was done, if ever it was. Maybe. Or maybe she would be taken into the halls of the gods, or maybe become one with the living world, or maybe lie quiet in her grave. There was no knowing. Meanwhile, how could she be other than what she was?

Folk milled about after the service was over. Gunnhild went straight to her house.

A while later, a maid told her that her footling Ögmund was at the door and wished to see her alone, if she was willing. She guessed what it was about. "Send him to the northside loftroom," she said, and climbed the stair in a swish and rustle of skirts. There she took a chair.

He crept in, bent over, wringing his hands. "What is it?" she snapped. "Be quick."

"Queen," he whined, "great Queen, I owe you everything—"

"I bade you, keep this short."

"Queen, I can't help thinking. What I've done, at your behest—Oh, I'm your handfast man, Queen; be sure of that. But for the sake of both our souls—"

"You want to confess and be shriven."

He braced himself. "Yes, Queen. Everybody must, or burn—"

"I forbid you."

He rocked on his heels.

"When I give you leave, you may," she said. "Not before. Not a word, not a whisper, or you're dead. I have my ways of finding out, you know."

"But, Queen," he wailed, "a confession is—is between me and the priest—me and Christ. Nobody else."

"Kisping," she said, "you've done many foul deeds. Not all were for me. On your own, your wickedness would have been for no more gain than a dog's. Lucky you were that I picked you out of the ruck.

"Kisping," she drove home to him, "you are what you are, and changing your name has not changed that. Nor can you ever. Live with it. If you confess to the priest before I let you, I will know. And then you shall taste Hell, oh, yes."

She softened her voice. "Whereas if you stay faithful, you shall do well, as you always have with me. On earth and, in due course, Heaven."

She straightened where she sat. "Now go," she said.

He slouched out. Had she seen hatred in his look? She had better keep a closer eye on him than hitherto. But useful he was, not lightly to be thrown aside.

This business of confession, though—Sira Aelfgar would not send Kisping's tale further. Not he. But he would call her in about it. Unless she renounced her ways and did penance—a great penance, openly humbling herself, belike making pilgrimage to a shrine abroad—he might well write to the bishop that he had an unrepentant and terrible sinner on his hands. She might be laid under the ban of the Church.

She could not afford that. Her sons could not.

Soon afterward, Harald returned, winter-bleak with wrath. Hardly had he and Sigurd arrived at Vörs, the Thing had not yet been made peace-holy, when the gathered yeomen rushed howling and roaring at them, weapons aloft. Badly outnumbered, the kings and their guards barely cut their way out of the throng. They left a half-score behind hacked down by axes, pierced by spears, beaten to splintery red mush by clubs, flails, and stamping feet.

"That was no sudden pack-rage," Harald said. "Somebody planned the trap and roused the yokels. Klypp Hersir—"

"From what I've been able to ferret out about him, I think not he," answered Gunnhild. "He's not a crafty one. I'll learn who it was. Of course, Klypp's embittered. Else he'd have taken gild and swallowed the shame put on him. Where now is Sigurd?"

"We agreed to keep apart for a while, not to seem cowed. He's bound for Aalrekstad."

Memory drifted through Gunnhild. She had heard once that that holding, somewhat north of here, was where dying King Haakon asked to be taken. Did this forebode anything?

She pushed the thought from her. "You'd both best sit quietly till the uproar ebbs, as it will if the yeomen aren't stirred up anew," she said. "Then you can set about restoring lawfulness. In the meantime, we are not without friends in Hördaland. We should guest them here or visit them in their homes, give gifts, speak mildly—yes, merrily when we can—and all in all show that it pays to stand by the sons of Eirik. Indeed, an invitation to a feast came in two days ago."

"I can hardly bring merriment along like my clothes, Mother."

"Oh, come, now! Why not take what mirth we may? Word was that an Icelander of some standing is at yonder hall, with a wondrous tale to tell from his seafaring. He's in Norway to claim an inheritance. If you help him, Harald, that will help you in men's eyes."

A short-lived smile tugged one side of his mouth. "I can hear you'll be happy to meet this fellow."

Gunnhild tossed her head. "So should you be. Why dwell in this world blind and deaf to it?"

Thus it was that the king, his mother, and a following rode off. By then Harald himself was in a better mood.

What happened yonder hurt her more than she would have believed.

The tidings that reached them as they returned to Hardanger were much worse. When Klypp heard where Sigurd was, he egged his kinsmen on; and the leader of the other yeomen, one Vemund, raised them afresh. They went to the hall and attacked it. The king's guards beat them off, dealing heavy losses, until they withdrew. But Klypp had gone straight for Sigurd, unstoppable, to run his sword through the king. At once a guardsman slew the slayer, who fell beside Gunnhild's fallen son.

So much had Klypp loved his Aalof.

IX

At least, Gunnhild thought, the Icelanders had brought some news from their island that awoke a cold gladness in her and now gave a little comfort. Egil Skallagrimsson had suffered a like loss.

His wife Aasgerd had borne him three sons and two daughters. The daughters got good husbands. Of the sons, the second, Gunnar, died of sickness. Egil did not think much of the youngest, Thorstein. But the oldest, Bödvar, was a most promising youth, big, handsome, as strong as Egil or Thorolf had been at his age. Egil loved him greatly, and Bödvar in turn was very close to his father.

This summer a ship had come up the White River with a load of lumber. Egil bought some. His workers ferried it off to him in a boat of eight oars; that took a number of trips. One day Bödvar asked if he could come along, and they agreed. They were six men altogether. When they were ready to start homeward, the tide was belated. Rowing against it, they were still out on the fjord at evening. A sudden southwesterly gale sprang up. It whipped the tide wild. The craft capsized. All aboard drowned. Next day they washed ashore.

When Egil heard, he rode straightaway to find the bodies. The first he came on was Bödvar's. He held it on his knee while he brought it to Digra Ness where Skallagrim lay. There he had the barrow opened, laid his son down beside his father, and had it shut again. His work gang was not through till sunset. While this happened, he swelled so that kirtle and hose ripped.

Back at Borg, he strode to the room where he most often slept and latched the door. He stayed behind it through day and night, abed, taking neither food nor drink. Nobody dared speak to him. But on the third morning, at earliest light, Aasgerd bade a man take a horse and ride as hard as it could go, to Hjadarholt in the Broad Firth Dales, the home of their daughter Thorgerd and her husband Olaf the Peacock. He was to tell her how things were and ask her to come. He arrived in the afternoon. At once Thorgerd had a horse saddled. With two men for guards, she rode the rest of that day and on through the wan short night.

When she reached Borg and entered the house, her mother Aasgerd asked if she had had anything to eat. "No, I have not," answered Thorgerd, "nor will I take any before I'm with Freyja. I know nothing better to do than what my father does, and I don't want to outlive my father and my brother."

She went to Egil's bedroom. "Open the door, Father," she called. "Both of us shall go the same way." He did. She trod in, latched the door again, and lay down on the other bed.

"It's good of you, daughter, to follow your father," said Egil dully. "Great is the love you show. How could it be looked for that I live after such a grief?"

They lay in silence.

After a while Egil asked, "What, daughter, are you chewing on something?"

"I'm chewing seaweed," she told him, "for I've heard it makes you worse. Else, I fear, I'll be too long about dying."

"Is it harmful, then?"

"Very harmful. Would you like some?"

"Why not?" He took it from her hand and crunched it.

After another while she rose, opened the door a crack, and called for water. A maid brought her a filled horn. "That's what seaweed does," said Egil. "It makes you even thirstier."

"Do you wish a drink, then, Father?"

He sat up, took the horn, and drained it.

"They've tricked us, Father," said Thorgerd. "That was milk."

Egil bit a shard out of the horn, as deeply as his teeth went, and dashed it onto the floor.

"What now shall we do, Father?" said Thorgerd. "It seems to me our will has been thwarted." He sat as if stunned. She gathered her breath. "Well, Father," she said, "I think we ought to live long enough for you to make a poem in memory of Bödvar. Then we can die if we still want to. If your son Thorstein must make the poem, it won't happen soon. Bödvar should not lie unsung, the more so if we aren't here to help drink his grave-ale."

Egil shook his big bald head. "I couldn't," he mumbled, "not even if I tried." Her look did not let go of him. At length he said, "Well, I'd better see what I can do."

He lay back, stared beyond her ken, and shaped the staves.

At first they went slowly, like men who bear a coffin to burial, but little by little they took on life.

> "Toilsome it is
>   to move my tongue.
> A stone on the breast
>   will stop the breath.
> It's hard to wage
>   the witchcraft of words

when a storm overthrows
the house of thought.

"The skaldic gift,
worthy of gods,
above all others
since olden time,
is locked away;
it will not leave
the hoard of the soul
because of sorrow.

"Hastily, happily,
words long heeded me;
the weapon of wit
was kept well sharpened.
But the surf now surges
to smash my boatshed
and beats on the door
of my father's barrow.

"For now my family
nears its finish,
like a woodland
laid waste by wind.
That man has lost
his merriment
who's seen his dearest
borne dead indoors.

"First I mind me
my father's ending.
Soon my mother
was missing too.
In the inmost soul
a memory is
of those, the old ones,
endlessly.

"That hole the billow
  broke in the ancient
  fence of my father's
  family grieves me.
  But the wound of my son
  slain by the sea,
  I know it will always,
  always be open.

"Of much has Ran,
  the sea, bereaved me.
  Alone is the one
  whom no one loves.
  The sea has cut
  my cords of kinship
  and broken the thread
  of life in my breast.

"Could I but seize
  my rights with a spear,
  then the destroyer
  would soon be done for.
  Could a mark be made
  on that wet thief-murderer,
  gladly I'd fight
  against the sea.

"But I have found
  my powers too few
  to battle against
  the bane of my son.
  Open it is
  for all to see
  how the old
  sit helplessly.

"Of much has Ran,
  the sea, bereaved me.
  Woe at kin-death

is late overwon,
latest when he,
the hope of our blood,
is taken off hence
to a brighter home.

"I know myself
that in my son
no mark of meanness
was ever made.
Strength and soundness
would have been seen,
had not Odin
laid hand upon him.

"Always were he
and I as one,
whatever else
others might do.
My house
he upheld,
the prop
of its pillars.

"Often I felt
the lack of a fellow.
Bare is the back
of the brotherless.
This truth I recall
when trouble arises:
long are the eyes
of a man alone.

"Shake, if you will,
the shire in searching,
there lives not a one
on whom to rely.
Here they'll barter
a brother for wergild

and make revenge
a merchandise!

"They say, and it's so,
 if a son is lost,
 no regaining is given
 but begetting another,
 nor is there hope
 of filling the hole
 left by a brother
 with the first and broadest.

"I do not care
 for crowds of men.
 Peace brings nothing
 but priggishness.
 My boy who is dead,
 a bit of his mother,
 he has fared hence
 to the home of his fathers.

"The foe of the ships,
 the foaming one,
 the slayer of men,
 stands against me.
 Strengthlessly,
 when sorrow drives,
 blunders the heavy
 burden of thought.

"My other son,
 struck by sickness,
 wasted away
 and wended hence.
 He was a boy
 without a blemish,
 not by anyone
 ill bethought.

"With the lord of life
I lay at peace.
Most carefully
I kept the pact,
till Odin himself,
the owner of dooms,
freely and willingly
ended friendship.

"I readily offered
to All-Father Odin,
the first of the gods,
since folk are wont to.
Yet must I find
for the father of skalds
that which is more
than might, in mishap.

"From the bane of the wolf,
old shedder of blood,
I got some faultless
featlinesses,
therewith a soul
that soon turned some,
lurkingly envious,
to open foemen.

"Hard am I hit.
Now stands Hel,
the unforgiving,
out on the ness.
Yet I will gladly,
in goodness of heart,
abide the day
when I shall die."

After the poem was done, Egil said it forth for Aasgerd
and Thorgerd and the household. Then he left his bed and
took his high seat. Soon he ordered a grave-ale, which fol-

lowed all the best olden usages. He sent Thorgerd home
with gifts and got on with his life.

As Gunnhild thought further on this, the chilly feeling
of rightness left her. Yes, Egil too had lost sons. But his
memorial to them would outlast their bones. What was
there for hers?

Both she and Harald gave Sira Aelfgar as much money
as they could spare from their coffers here, buying
masses for the repose of Sigurd's soul. They meant to give
more elsewhere. The priest tendered words of comfort and
the hope that lived in Christ, but to Gunnhild they rang
rather hollow. He must feel that Sigurd brought the killing
on himself. She said nothing aloud about that. It was true,
after all. Ever had Sigurd been reckless, without thought or
feeling for anybody else.

No, twisted in her like a knife, that wasn't really so. Not
quite.

She went to the church at a time when it would be empty.
Rain wept softly. Mist smoked in the raw air, blurring walls
and roofs, hiding the land beyond, muffling sounds. She
left her guard in the porch to keep others out, hung her wet
cloak in the vestibule, and went on alone.

The nave was cold and dusky, almost nightful. Two candles burned at the altar. They barely picked out him on the
Cross, more shadow than shape. She took no cushion, but
knelt on the floor at the rail. It made her knees ache; it was
a sacrifice. She tried to drive out memories of herself kneeling on a cord, but they would not flee; they skulked around
the rim of her awareness while she strove to pray.

"Lord," she whispered into the hush, "I know not if you
know what is in my heart. You can if you want, of course,
and surely your Father does, for they tell me he knows
everything. But why should he tell you? There's so much
else that must mean a great deal more. And why should
you look? My heart may well be an ugly sight in your eyes,

hard and heathenish. I don't know myself all that's in it.

"For I have lived by another law than yours. And I will for as long as I must. Afterward, if I'm still on earth—I cannot foresee what then, for I cannot tell what is truth, what to believe, or even if there is only one truth.

"Thus you see, Lord, at least I do not mock you with lies or meaningless fulsomeness. I've hoodwinked many, but I come honestly before you. And I ask no more than this, a boon that a mighty king can grant out of his honor to a lesser queen.

"I ask that you let me speak for a while, a short while, to your mother. You can easily bid her listen, can't you, Lord? I think she'd be glad to. She was once a woman. I've never heard other than that she's a wellspring of mercy, who knows well what sorrow is. Will you give me this, Lord?"

Nothing sounded; nothing stirred. The candleflames flickered not in the least. Gunnhild murmured an Ave. She felt cold and weary. The pain in her knees and the memory of a candle burning on a skull nagged her. They neither frightened nor awakened remorse. It was merely that she could not get rid of them.

Well, she ought not keep the Queen of Heaven waiting.

"Holy Mary," she said low, "will you hear a few words from one who is also a mother? Oh, yes, your son is the Son of God, and you a stainless maiden. My children have been men, and a woman; I got them in lust; sin was inborn in them. They've done their share of ill deeds, or maybe somewhat more than their share. But often they were driven to it; need lashed them, and the blood that runs in them would not let them cringe under that whip. No, they fought back. And never was any as wicked as you may well think I am. Whatever else they do that may be bad, it is not calling on heathen gods or working black witchcraft." Her voice stumbled. She bit her lip. "Or if my daughter Ragnhild does, a wee bit, very seldom—I don't know that she does—don't forget how she's been left in an unchristian land with never a priest to guide her."

Gunnhild lifted her head. "Holy Mary," she said, "for

myself I ask naught of you. I'm here on behalf of my newly dead son Sigurd.

"Yes, he was the wildest of the brood. He broke God's law again and again, he trampled on the rights of those beneath him, he fell at last on his own misdeed, unshriven, and I fear he never was as worshipful as he might have been. See, holy Mary, how I lower myself for his sake. I will not forgive those who brought him down. But that is my sin. You must find it all the worse because I cannot bring myself to believe it's wrong. I tell you this, freely, so you can know I'm honest when I say it has nothing to do with Sigurd. Always he loved me and honored me, his mother. Should that not be reckoned to his good?

"You understand. You are a mother. Oh, your Son was holy." Gunnhild uttered a shy laugh. "Mine have hardly been that. But they were, they are, dear to me, like yours to you. And did yours never, never worry you? Was there no childish mischief, no boyish foolishness, nothing to make you fretful or even a touch angry? He was God, but he was flesh too, wasn't he?"

Gunnhild sighed. "At least, we're told how you grieved to watch him die on the Cross and be laid in his grave. Why, if you knew he would soon rise and live forever? Because he was suffering, wasn't that why? You must have stood there recalling how blithely he skipped about you in your home when he was small. I don't have the same fore-knowledge about my Sigurd—only fears about his doom. But I remember him, three years old, dauntlessly stumping down the gangplank when we took ship from our kingdom for Orkney.

"He used to bring me his happinesses and woes. For a while, now and then, I could hug him and cuddle him. Of course, erelong he deemed this unmanly. And what a cocky little man he was! How gladsome to see him shoot up, romp, sport, gain skill after skill, till he was indeed a young man, knowing himself born to be a king—Was it like that for you, holy Mary?

"Then I pray you to understand that my Sigurd was not evil. Not in his heart. He was brash, reckless, thoughtless.

He would not stop to think ahead; he went forward, straight as a flung spear, whatever might come of it. He drank too much, and this was what brought him to his death. He would have learned some wisdom in later years, but they were not given him. I loved him nonetheless. I always shall. Holy Mother Mary, my son needs a lesson, but his is not a bad soul. He has not earned unending fire. I ask you to think on this, and then, if you will, say a word in Heaven for my Sigurd.

"Now I've kept you long enough. I thank you for your kindness in hearing me out. Farewell, Mother of God."

Gunnhild bowed her head over folded hands and said another Ave.

After a while she said three Paternosters, whereupon she lifted her gaze to the Christ and spoke aloud.

"Lord, let me end by talking once more to you, not as a beggar but as your scot-queen. I'll make the words few, not to try your forbearingness.

"The kingship over Norway belongs to the house of Harald Fairhair. So you chose, when he brought the whole land under himself and made it strong. The sons of Eirik are his rightful heirs. Who else is left? Sigurd the Giant never bestirred himself beyond his Hringariki shire; his son Haalfdan grows old as slothfully; his grandson Sigurd bids fair to be no more, merely a landholder who farms his fields and troubles nobody. Even if they wanted it, could such as these hold the kingdom together? Would they do anything at all for the Faith?

"Yes, it became sadly needful to do away with some others." Gunnhild frowned, sought words, and turned wry. "Well, Lord, I said I won't lie to you. My man Eirik and my sons did the work with scant sorrow. But anyway, done is done. Harald Grenska fled for his life, he has no strength in Norway, and besides, he's hardly more than a boy." She was about to add that Olaf Tryggvason was a sprig, and a thrall abroad if he lived, but her tongue locked at the name. She hurried on:

"We've made our mistakes, Lord. My Sigurd's was the worst thus far. He's paid for it. Must the rest of us pay too? Must the kingdom, and the Faith my sons would plant firmly in it? Who would gain from that, other than the haughty Thraands and their fiend-worshipping jarl? Would it not be better that you help us, enlighten us, and bring us to full victory?

"Lord, here is my offer. If you think it unworthy, be angry with me, not my sons. They know nothing of this. But if they win through, break altogether all their foes, gain the peace that comes with unshakable might, and if—if we get good harvests and good fishing again—then I will know you are God, the only god. I'll forswear heathenness, cast my things of witchcraft into the sea or the fire, confess every sin I can remember, and do whatever penance is laid on me.

"Lord, I'm thinking less of my soul—truly I am—than of what use I could be to the Faith. I know many things, many folk, and many of the ways of darkness. I can put your hounds on the spoor. My worldly redes have often been shrewd too. Haven't they? What if I gave them to the priests and bishops of your Church? Poor Haakon Aethelstan's-foster could only fumble, until he crumbled. It would go otherwise with the sons of Eirik and their mother.

"There you have it, Lord. My help for yours. I think it's a fair offer. Anyhow, it's the best I can make. If what they say is true, you made me what I am and thus you can fathom me. Do as you see fit, Lord. Now your scot-queen will go."

She crossed herself, said a last Paternoster, and went out into the slow rain.

XI

Passing through the yard on the way back to her house, she heard a sudden racket. Glancing toward it, she made out man-shapes dim in the rain and mist. They shifted about. Somebody yelled. A thud followed, and a roar that stopped the jabber. It seemed to be a scuffle among fewer than ten men, maybe a fight between two workers that somebody of higher rank called a halt to—nothing worth lingering for.

Striding onward, she felt the aches dwindle and a new strength rise. Whether she had gained anything for Sigurd, for any of her children, was unknowable. But that she had taken her stand and tried lifted her heart.

Warmth, firelight, richness of carvings and hangings, slight sweet smoke-smell, were very welcome. A maid took her cloak; another had a cup of mulled ale ready. Gunnhild sank into a chair.

A knock boomed on the door. What now? "Let him in," she sighed. The manservant who was on hand opened it. Dank chill seeped through.

Arinbjörn Thorisson atood there. Harald Grayfell had called him down from Sygnafylki, to meet with him and other trustworthy chieftains. They would talk about what to do next; then those men would go home and work to keep the unrest from spreading beyond Hördaland and to calm it within the shire.

Beneath the gray mane, Arinbjörn's face was a rugged mask of wrath. In front of him shivered Kisping—Ögmund. Arinbjörn clutched him by the forearms, as hard as a blacksmith's tongs would have. He whimpered with the pain. The snaggle teeth chattered. A bruise was flowering on a cheekbone, blood trickling at his temple.

Gunnhild tautened. "What's this?"

"For your ears alone, Queen," rumbled Arinbjörn. "Everybody else, out."

The housefolk cast her frightened glances. She nodded. They left. Arinbjörn's knee to Kisping's butt, as he let go, sent the footling asprawl on the floor. Arinbjörn stepped through, shut the door, slammed down the latch, and booted him in the ribs. "Up, wretch," he said.

"Hold," said Gunnhild quietly. "This is my man, you know."

"Yes, Queen, yes," stammered Kisping. He lurched to his feet, hugged himself, and shuddered before her. "Al-

always yours, great lady. This, this—this lord—he mistook me, when I, I spoke in your praise—"

"Be still," said Gunnhild.

"But, Queen—"

"Be still, I bade you." Kisping cowered. Gunnhild looked into Arinbjörn's eyes. "Tell me."

His scowl deepened. His words fell heavy and harsh. "Queen, I was on the way to the hall from the backhouse when I came by a knot of lowborn hirelings. They didn't mark me, for they were listening and laughing while this dog made mock of you. I knocked him down, got the names of the rest, warned them how much worse they'd fare than they were going to if they let slip one word of it, and brought the little sneak here."

"What was it?"

He flushed red. "Queen, I'd liefest not befoul my lips. Make him tell."

Kisping had gathered his wits. The scrawny form trembled yet, but he spread his hands, smiled shakily, and cast her a fluttering look. "Great Queen," rattled from him, "ever were you good to me, like a goddess, a—an angel. And ever have I striven to be worthy of it in my small way. Never have I hung back from doing your will, however dangerous the doing might be to my life or—" The voice sank. "—my very soul." He spoke louder, half boldly. "Always have I honored you, Queen, and your kingly sons, and always have I upheld that honor before everybody, for is it not best that folk know of these wonders?"

"I know what a smooth tongue is yours," said Gunnhild. "What were you using it for today?"

"Well, Queen, I got into talk with those fellows, and they asked what happened on the visit to yonder hall that the queen and King Harald have lately come back from. Amidst the flurry and mourning at the dreadful news of beloved King Sigurd's passing away—may the gates of Heaven swing wide for him—surely they will—anyhow, some hints, some snippets of loose chatter went about among their kind. I won't hide from the queen, I was shocked when I heard. Useemly falsehoods! Whoever first

gave them out must have been dead drunk at the time, if
indeed he witnessed it himself. My clear duty was to set
this right at once. So I told how the business really went."
Kisping's neck craned forward like a bird's. His grin beckoned. "And now, Queen, if it be your will, I'll seek to track
down him who blabbered first. The queen will then quickly
learn whether he did it in doltishness or ill will, and mete
out to him whatever he's earned."

Arinbjörn knotted his fists. He growled in his beard.
Gunnhild waved him to hush. Her gaze speared Kisping.
"Go on," she bade starkly. "Give me the whole of it."

Sickness rose in her throat. She had told herself that the
shame and the hurt lay behind her, to die away—to sink
down into forgottenness, like Aalof's ring into the bog. But
no, they followed at her heels, while they also spread
abroad on the wind.

Kisping talked fast: "I told those drudges the eyewitness
truth, Queen, for them to tell others. I told them how you
and the king saw an Icelander, Thorgils, who was already
a guest, and asked who such a good-looking man might be.
When they heard what the inheritance was that Thorgils
claimed, the king said it was now held by the queen mother,
and counseled him to win her goodwill; then he should do
well. The queen mother spoke to him kindly, I said. She
told him that, as usage has been—hasn't it?—he should
join the king's guard and show himself worthy. She would
gladly give him redes about best to further his cause. They
could speak together at length. How openhanded of her!
But Thorgils, dullard, lout, said this did not fit in with what
he had in mind. Thereupon the queen cast him from her,
and cold was his seat while the queen and her kingly son
stayed there. As was right for such a boor." He wrung his
hands. "Queen, if I've somehow gotten this wrong and mis-
told it, I can but beg forgiveness and plead that I meant
nothing but to uphold the queen's honor. And this is the
whole of it, Queen."

"He lies!" cried Arinbjörn. "I heard what he hissed, how
he cackled."

Kisping slipped closer to Gunnhild. "Queen," rushed

from him, "I say nothing against this mighty lord. He's
faithful, he's true, of course. But it's known he's gotten
hard of hearing. He overheard no more than a snatch. He
misunderstood altogether. The queen knows well how often
the most honest eyewitnesses and earwitnesses are mistaken. Queen, if you will, bethink how long I've been, may
I dare say, your right hand, how much I've done for you
and found out for you. Would you set that aside merely
because a man newly come here—oh, a righteous man,
everybody knows, and mostly wise, but maybe today not
hearing so well, and catching only a few words, a laugh or
two—for, yes, Queen, I did make fun of the foolishness
itself—"

"My ears are still good enough that I heard full well,"
Arinbjörn broke in. "I stood there listening, for it was hard
to believe at first that anybody would say such things, till
I could stand it no longer. Queen, if you want, I'll go fetch
those carls, take them aside one by one, and squeeze what
they know from them. One by one, so they can't raise a
shield-wall of lies. You, Queen, or some man you name,
can stand by. Then deem for yourself, Queen." He shook
with outrage.

"That should not be needful," Gunnhild answered. "Ögmund, who was Kisping, say frankly what went on."

"No more than I've told!" he screamed. He jittered on
his feet; his hands flapped; his eyes darted to and fro; sweat
studded his face and wet his shirt under the arms.

"Then do you tell me, Arinbjörn," Gunnhild said.

"That's a foul task, Queen," the hersir grated. "I'd sooner
muck out a stoolhouse."

"It wasn't that bad!" wailed Kisping. "It was—it was—"

"Hold your jaw, or I'll knock you flat again," Arinbjörn
said. Kisping huddled into stillness. Arinbjörn's voice
trudged, while his gaze stayed on the uneasy shadows: "If
the queen wants. Before God I swear I'll never let out this
nastiness, not to the priest at my deathbed or anybody, unless you yourself—" He caught his breath. "Your footling,
he told how—he said you rolled your eyes at that Thorgils,
and—and lickerishness dripped from your words to him,

but he—" Arinbjörn gagged. "Bear with me, Queen. Ögmund went on about how—when Thorgils told you no, thanks—everybody saw he wanted no such doings with—with the old crone, Ögmund said—and as Thorgils stood there before you at the high seat and said no, you—flew into a rage and kicked him so he stumbled back off the dais—The old mare in heat kicked the unwilling stallion, Ögmund said. And they laughed with him, those hogswillers, barn-shovelers, sheep-swivers. Aaargh!"

"No, no, no!" Kisping fell to his knees. He threw his arms around her ankles. "It wasn't—Only a little spoof, Queen, only to—to make them know how, how laughable the lie was—"

She wanted to kick *him* and splinter his teeth. But that would be unbecoming. "Shut him up, Arinbjörn," she said.

The hersir's boot slammed anew into the ribs. Did she hear something break? Kisping rolled from her. He twitched on the floor. He moaned. The hearthfire danced and chuckled.

"Drag him out, Arinbjörn," said Gunnhild. "Take him off. Hang him."

The hersir steadied. She knew what lay behind the long look he gave her. Oh, he understood. Or did he? Could any man understand a rush of love and longing—for a last short, stolen springtime—or how the sudden loathing the beautiful young man could not quite hide stabbed her?

Yes, she should have taken it calmly and coolly. She should already have known in her marrow how time had overtaken her. A Christian should have; a Finn would have. But caught off guard, the daughter of Özur Dapplebeard and granddaughter of Rögnvald Jarl, wounded, struck back. Now she must live it down.

Kisping reeled to his feet. Beneath the gasping, the trapped weasel snarled. "I've kept your secrets, Queen, I don't want to tell about the witch-arrow or the dead man or anything, but—"

"Still him," Gunnhild bade.

Arinbjörn's fist jumped. The skinny form staggered back

and fell in a heap. Did she see the jaw askew? Blood ran
from the mouth.

"Do as I told you," she said. "Then come back here. You
shall be well rewarded."

"That's not needful, Queen," he mumbled. "I'll come,
yes, if you want, but this is—no more than my task."

She heard how he hated the whole business. He had
given his oath to Eirik Blood-ax and afterward to Harald
Grayfell, through them to her, and that was all.

"Where shall we bury him?" he asked.

"Wherever they bury ill-doers hereabouts. Now I want
to be alone for a while."

Gunnhild sat long by herself. They had taken their big
meal at the hall before she went to the church. She had
made known that she was fasting. Though now dusk crept
inward, she felt no hunger.

So Kisping had turned in her hand and cut her. She might
have foreseen. She picked him out because she found him
slippery. Then she gave him little more thought, between
uses, than she would give any other tool. A mistake, maybe.
When she forbade him to confess, had that kindled his hatred, or only made long-smoldering feelings flame up? How
lucky that Arinbjörn caught him early at his undermining
of her. Nonetheless, she would miss his readiness, cunning,
and, yes, fleering mirth.

Well, if she could not trust him, she must do away with
him. She would tell off a man on whom she had a firmer
hold to find Kisping's hoard and bring it to her.

Meanwhile and beyond loomed Haakon Jarl. During this
fall and winter, together with the sons who were left to her,
Harald, Ragnfröd, Erling, Gudröd, she would work out how
to get rid of him forever.

XII

Early in summer, the kings went to war. Erling stayed
behind in Vikin, as Ragnfröd did at Hardanger. Hördaland had quieted somewhat, but they needed the West

and the South kept safe. Harald Grayfell and Gudröd raised a host in the eastern shires and moved north on the Thraandlaw.

When Haakon Jarl learned what overwhelming strength was once more bound against him, he did otherwise than at the last time. If he levied the yeomen, he was law-bound to let them go home before harvest; and he thought his foes would keep the field longer than that, laying the land waste. The ships and warriors he gathered were not few, but those men could and would stay abroad with him until he had, somehow, made himself a way of return.

They steered along the coast to South Moerr, where they harried. That was not wantonly. Haakon's uncle Grjotgard, who had taken part in the burning of his own brother Sigurd, Haakon's father, had been set here by the Gunnhildssons to ward the shire. Now Grjotgard must meet him.

It became a bloody fight. Besides his own troops, Grjotgard brought two other jarls and theirs. All three fell, with a flock of their men, before their ranks broke and fled.

"Long have you waited for this, Father," said Haakon amidst the groans of the wounded and the croaking of the ravens. "I too, I too. And I am not done yet."

When he had taken care of his wounded followers, buried his dead, and let the hale rest for a day or two, he started off again. While the clash had taken toll of his crews, they were a band to reckon with. However, Haakon stood far out to sea and bore south unseen by any but whale and fulmar.

Thus the Thraandlaw lay open to Harald and Gudröd. Their brothers now felt free to join them, for this easy victory must have made a deep mark on the whole kingdom. They rode around unchallenged. At every Thing-meeting they called, the yeomen made sullen submission. The kings took scot and duties; they laid heavy gilds for frowardness and arrears of payment. Thrice hurtful was that in these lean times. "It should tame them," said Erling, "and make Norsemen everywhere take heed."

He stayed there when his brothers turned south in fall. His warriors seemed to be enough to keep the Thraands in their place. Sternly did King Erling rule. He burned Haakon Jarl's shrine at Hladi and other halidoms wherever he found them. He took as much from the meager stocks of the folk as he wanted to keep his household and troops well fed. When he heard cases, his judgments were harsh. Any word or deed that he thought was against him could spell death.

The Thraands took it ill. Among themselves they bared teeth. Men began to meet in secret.

Meanwhile Harald Grayfell came gladly home. The feast he gave went on for days. Among the highborn, Queen Gunnhild alone was withdrawn, brooding.

They had not won what she most hoped for. Haakon Jarl was still alive.

XIII

Tidings of him reached her over the months, along with the other news that wayfarers and seamen brought. As erstwhile, he had touched at Denmark, then gone on to plunder the Eastlands. In fall he went back to Denmark. Harald Bluetooth was then at Roskilde in Sjaelland. Haakon entered the hall with costly gifts—gold, amber, furs, captives—and blandishing words.

"Be welcome," said the king. "I will do better by you than the sons of Gunnhild have."

"Or have done by you, lord," answered Haakon, slightly smiling.

Harald's cheeks mottled red. He was now gray-haired, paunchier than before, fewer teeth in his mouth, though the great fang still overhung his lip. "We'll not speak of that today," he snapped. Regaining smoothness, he went on: "No, we'll feast. You and your men shall lodge with me as long as you wish. Everyone says you are a man of wisdom and shrewdness, as well as a doughty fighter. Here is another guest. You two haven't met, but each of you has much to tell."

This was a big man of some thirty winters. His face was cleanly molded, as if in bronze, his hair and beard tawny.

He wore fine garments with an ease that showed he was used to them. His smile charmed. He was the king's nephew, and also named Harald.

King Gorm the Old had had two sons who lived, Knut and Harald. Knut, the elder, was handsome, lively, well-liked, their father's choice to rule after him; folk called him Knut the Dane-jewel. But while he and his brother were raiding in Ireland, an arrow killed him. It was believed that Gorm died of grief on hearing that. Hence dour Harald Bluetooth became king of Denmark. He raised great mounds and had a great runestone carved, memorials to his father and mother; after taking baptism, he founded churches; but he was never beloved.

Knut had left this son, Harald, who grew up to be a mighty viking. He won so much booty and did so well in trading it that his nickname was Gold-Harald. Now he wanted to settle down. His uncle had received him rather coolly. A strong and high-reaching man with kingly blood in him might spell trouble. However, Gold-Harald and Haakon hit it off at once. The jarl's sharp wit delighted the wanderer, while making him thoughtful too.

Shortly afterward, the king, with household and guests, moved over to Randers in Jutland, where he meant to spend the winter. The town lay at the end of a narrow, low-banked fjord which opened on the Kattegat and thus on the outside world. Haakon got a house and servants to himself near the hall. His friendship with Gold Harald ripened, while he—openly heathen in a now Christian land—also stayed on a good footing with Harald Bluetooth.

Soon, though, he spent most of his time in bed, eating and drinking no more than he must to keep his strength up. He said he was not sick. Rather, he needed to think, think broadly and deeply, often lying wakeful through the lengthening nights, unvexed by lesser doings, even lustfulness. He did allow some visitors, Gold-Harald among them. They came in wonderingly and went out awed. This was unheard-of. Whatever their faith, they harked back to Mimir, from whose head Odin himself took counsel.

That much could Gunnhild follow; it was news. Beyond

rose a wall, with every door barred. The swallow could not see or hear what went on beneath roofs. The shadow could not steal past whatever powers stood watch yonder, be they Harald Bluetooth's witchcraft-hating saints or Haakon Jarl's hawk-valkyrie. She learned this by a dream she drummed and sang forth from the darkness. When she cast runes, they showed nothing meaningful. That alone boded ill.

Only afterward, too late, did she hear.

Ships still plied the waters between the kingdoms. Haakon sent one of his back to Thraandheim with a crew of men handfasted to him, their leaders from outstanding families. The ship ran secretly into a small bight and lay tucked away. The spokesmen bought horses from nearby dwellers, who were very willing to help, and rode off around the shires. At steading after steading they met with those yeomen whose word carried the most weight. They heard how unhappy the Thraands were with King Erling. They urged that the folk gather this winter and kill him. Before his brothers could avenge him, come summer, Haakon Jarl would return and set them free.

And so it fell out. Toward Yule, when Erling was at feast with an inland jarl sworn to him, a host from everywhere in the Thraandlaw overran his outposts and stormed the hall. The fight raged like surf upon rocks, yeomen died, but more of the guards did, and with them their king.

In these gaunt years there was little to spare for the gods. The foes whom the yeomen bore off alive, they hanged while balefires blazed high, an offering in hope of a better morrow.

Those tidings flew south to Gunnhild faster than hoofs or keels could bring them. She woke in a thick midnight choking on a scream. Then she lay sleepless. But she would not weep. Not yet. Maybe never. Maybe all tears were dried out of her.

In the morning she asked Harald Grayfell to come to her by himself. "Erling is dead," she told him when he had shut the door on them.

He stared. "What? How do you know?"

"From a dream."

He frowned. "A nightmare."

"Yes, but this bore truth."

He crossed himself. "Mother, you know things that—" He broke off. "What did the dream show you?"

"A pack of murderous landsmen, too big to stave off. He died like your father, overcome but unbending. They were yelling about Haakon Jarl. And who else could have lured them to this?"

Harald narrowed his eyes. "We must wait for real word," he said slowly. "We won't get it in one speech, either. Meanwhile, we may hope your dream was wrong."

"It wasn't," said Gunnhild. "I tell you today lest the tale hit you like a broadside wave. We should begin *now* thinking on what to do."

"Well, masses—" Harald drew a ragged breath. "Along with the masses for Sigurd."

Yes, Gunnhild thought, Erling had gone the selfsame way, like Guthorm before him, and Gamli before him, and young Rögnvald so long ago. Erling was the coldest, most unforgiving among them, the least open to her or to anyone else. Yet once he too lay small and warm and, yes, wet and noisy in her arms; once he too toddled about, then ran and leaped about, rode at breakneck speed, sailed into stiff winds and white-maned seas, as he grew to manhood under her eyes. He became the most earnest Christian of them, and sometimes she had wondered whether it would be he who at last got the most queenly wife, Danish or Swedish or German or English, and fathered the king who was to weld Norway together.

Best she not pray for him as she did for Sigurd. Nor could she spend much time in mourning them. God rest their souls. Three sons were left her.

"We must make ready for whatever Haakon does next," she said.

But what might that be?

XIV

Snowfall was scant in most Danish winters, but rain and gloom fell heavily. Haakon's talk lightened Gold-Harald's heart. He called on the jarl ever oftener, until they were the best of friends. At last one day, sitting at the bedside, where lamplight and candlelight struggled against murk and a peat fire against chill, he asked about something Haakon had already, quietly, become aware of in him. Everybody knew he wanted to end his roving. But he had no wish to live as an underling. What did the Norseman believe King Harald would say if Gold-Harald craved his share of the kingship?

"I shouldn't think the Dane-king would refuse you your birthright," answered Haakon. "But you'll know more if you speak to the king himself. You can't get kingship if you don't claim it."

Gold-Harald went away full of eagerness. Haakon leaned back on his pillows and grinned.

Shortly afterward, Gold-Harald did bring the question up before King Harald. Many great men were on hand. Gold-Harald said boldly that the king ought to give him half the kingdom, as befitted his birth to a father who would have had all of it.

At this King Harald burst out in wrath. He cried that nobody would have dared bid his father King Gorm make himself half-king of Denmark, or his grandfather Hörda-Knut, or his forebears Sigurd Snake-in-Eye or Ragnar Hairybreeks! So raging was Harald Bluetooth that no man could speak with him for the rest of the evening. Gold-Harald went quickly out, though with head high.

It looked worse for him than ever; he had no more kingdom than before, but more kingly anger. Next day he sought back to his friend Haakon Jarl and asked for a good rede, if there was any. He was bound he would have the kingship, even if he must take it with weapons.

Haakon warned him not to say this to others, who might

spread it farther. "This is a thing of life and death, and you must carefully weigh what you're able to do. Such a mighty work calls for men who're both daring and steadfast, who're chary of neither good nor evil when it comes to forwarding their plans. But he reaps only shame, who sets up a high purpose and then lets it slip from his hands."

"I won't spare my own hands from killing the king himself, can I but get at him, if he withholds what's mine by right," snarled Gold-Harald. He rose and stalked away.

Not long afterward, it was King Harald who visited in search of counsel. He told the jarl what Gold-Harald wanted of him and how he felt about it. For no price whatsoever would he lessen his kingdom, "and"—His voice lowered— "if Gold-Harald keeps up this demand, it'll be easy enough for me to have him killed; for I don't trust him while he goes around with such thoughts in his head."

Haakon met the slitted gaze and spoke calmly, with every seeming of frankness: "I do think Gold-Harald's put so much into this cause that he won't drop it. And if he raises unrest in your land, we can look for his getting a lot of help, the more so because his father is fondly remembered. To kill him would bring dishonor on you; for he's the son of your brother, and men will deem him guiltless." The king stiffened in his chair. Haakon lifted a hand. "Yet I don't urge you to become less than your father Gorm, who always widened his kingdom but never narrowed it."

"What, then, is your rede, Haakon, if I'm neither to split my kingdom nor rid myself of this troublemaker?"

"Let us sleep on it," said the jarl, "and meet again in a few days. I have to think my way through the tangle."

Thereupon the king left, followed by his men who had been waiting outside the door of the bedroom.

Haakon sent off most of his own household and ordered those few who stayed not to let anybody in. He must be alone with his thoughts.

Fog swirled and dripped, a gray-white blindness, when the king returned. Flamelight flickered dull. Harald shivered where he sat and hugged his furs to him. Haakon, in a woolen nightshirt and a blanket over his legs, showed no sign of being cold. "Well," rasped Harald, "have you gotten to the bottom of what we were speaking of?" His fang glistened wet.

The jarl nodded his dark head. "I have been wakeful day and night," said he, "and I see nothing better than that you keep the power over the whole kingdom that your father wielded, while you give your nephew Harald another kingdom in which he'll have honor."

Harald Bluetooth squinted. "What kingdom might that be," he asked slowly, "which I can allow Harald lawful title to, and still leave Denmark unsundered?"

"It's a land called Norway. The kings who now rule over it ill-use the folk. Every Norseman wishes harm on them."

Harald Bluetooth frowned, tugged his beard, and sat still for a while before he said: "Norway's a big land, and the folk there are a quarrelsome lot, not easy for an outland host to come to grips with. We learned this when Haakon Aethelstan's-foster warded the land; it cost us many men, but victory had we never. Besides, the real king today, Harald Eiriksson, I gave him the name of foster son."

"This have I always known," said Haakon sharply, "that over and over have you helped the Gunnhildssons, and they've repaid you with nothing but thanklessness." He leaned on his left hand, forward toward the other. His words flowed like a mountain stream. "We'll win Norway much more easily than by fighting for it with the whole Danish host. Send to that fosterling of yours and offer him the fief of those holdings they had while they were here in Denmark. Set a meeting ground. Then Gold-Harald can make a short end to the business and wrest the kingship from Harald Grayfell."

Harald Bluetooth gaped. He swallowed. "That would be reckoned a low deed, to betray a foster son," he said, though not very strongly.

"I believe," thrust from Haakon, "the Danes will call it better to slay a Norse viking than your Danish brotherson."

They talked for a long time, the jarl smoothly but unswervingly, the king more and more haltingly. The upshot was that they agreed on it.

Gold-Harald had known that they met, and fretted. When next he came to the house, the door swung wide for him. He found Haakon out of bed, fully clad. Hardly had he begun to ask what it meant than Haakon clasped his shoulder and told how he had worked on his friend's behalf until a readily seizable kingdom lay waiting for him in Norway. "And afterward," he went on, "we two shall hold fast to our fellowship. I can be of the greatest help to you in Norway. Take that kingship first. It need not be all. Your uncle King Harald grows old, and has only one living son, by a leman at that, whom he doesn't like." Of course, this was not to be said to his face. Haakon soon talked Gold-Harald into going along.

Thereafter the three of them were often together, with none else to hear, hammering out their plot.

XV

Three big ships left Jutland, crossed the Skagerrak, and bore north along Norway. It was late winter, hardly anyone else at sea, but the leader, Fridleif Ivarsson, was a bold sailor as well as quick of wits and tongue.

Foul winds made the going slow and hard. More than once a storm drove the crews to anchorage. At such times, and when they camped ashore each night, they got a closer look at the land. Even this far south they saw hunger. Livestock were scant on the farms, most long since eaten, the rest scrawny. Folk stood haggard in garb often threadbare. The very young and the very old were few; the hard years had taken them off.

The dwellers in Leirvik town on Stord at Hardanger were no happier. When Fridleif and his men came to the great hall, the benches were half empty, the noise and bustle of a king's house sunken to hardly more than they might have been at a hersir's. Still, the guards and staff were full-fleshed. King Harald Grayfell and his mother sat in the high seat, richly clad and haughty of bearing.

Having named himself and his errand at the door and

been let in, Fridleif went to stand before them, a stout, curly-haired man with a broad smile. After the greetings he said: "My lord the Dane-king Harald Gormsson hails his well-beloved kinsmen, the sons of King Eirik, kings in Norway, and—" His glance flitted to her. "—their mother Queen Gunnhild. From him I bring these gifts of goodwill."

A murmur went around the long room when they were set forth: a Frankish sword, two golden arm-rings, a gilt helmet with a facepiece like a boar's head, a silver bowl finely wrought and set with garnets, a cloak of heavy silk trimmed with ermine, and more. Harald and Gunnhild hardly stirred.

"Openhanded is my namesake King Harald," said Grayfell, his voice without warmth. "You shall take back my thanks—in kind." The last words jerked the least bit. Honor called for them, but it would be heavy enough feeding so many guests.

"This is not something we awaited," added Gunnhild. "Little have we heard from King Harald—" Bluetooth, said her scornful thought. "—for years, and that not always the friendliest."

"My lord bade me acknowledge there have been some misunderstandings," answered Fridleif smoothly. "He wishes they had never arisen, and wants to set them right."

"Yet he gives house and help to our foe Haakon Sigurdarson." Although Gunnhild spoke quietly, a kind of sigh passed through the hall and men tautened.

"King, Queen," ran the soft words, "this is among the things my lord hopes I can make clear to you. When a highborn and famous man seeks to him, he must tender hospitality, must he not?" Gunnhild harked back to Egil with Arinbjörn. But those had been close friends. "Thereafter, of course, Jarl Haakon was guest-holy. But, King, I think that's behind us. When I started off, Haakon lay deathly ill, raving in fever. By now he's likely dead."

Startlement gusted over the benches. Gunnhild scanned the Danes. Most were bluff sailors and warriors, who could not hide a lie from her search. They stood at ease. Some nodded.

"That's welcome news to us," Harald said, still rather warily. "Take the honor seat, Fridleif, since you speak for your king. Let your men be seated among mine. Let drink be brought. Soon we'll dine. Meanwhile the steward shall see to your lodgings."

"I have much to speak of, King."

"We'll hear you tomorrow, after you've rested from your voyage." Harald did not want to seem worried, Gunnhild knew. However, he was unable to seem cheerful. She withdrew early, to lie wakeful for much of the night, wondering, thinking, rallying herself to fight with what weapons were hers.

She was there in the morning, when Fridleif gave out his message. Otherwise Harald had no more than a few guards, his most steadfast, so talk could be straightforward.

King Harald Gormsson remembered the love that was between him and the Eirikssons in Denmark, Fridleif said. It grieved him that this later dwindled. Then as he heard what bad seasons and other woes they suffered in Norway, he got understanding of how such unhappy turns as the withholding of scot had come about. At last he felt he should help. Good faith and good wishes could mend every rift.

Moreover, Fridleif said to the doubts he saw, frankly, his lord would be glad of a staunch ally. It was strained between him and the Empire. Claims to land clashed in the marches. Raids had gone back and forth. The sons of Eirik were peerless fighting men who could call up great strength.

"Hm," said Harald Grayfell. "What has the Dane-king in mind?"

"King, he offers you, in fief, those lands you and your brothers had the use of in Denmark, with a light scot to pay him and otherwise everything you take from them yours. So shall you and he stand together as one."

"This is—astounding," said Harald Grayfell slowly.

"It must be thought on," said Gunnhild. "My son, send for wise and trusty men; take counsel with them."

"Indeed. Fridleif, you and your following will bide here

till we have a word for you to take back." Harald smiled. "By then the sailing ought to be better."

Gunnhild smiled too, sweetly. "We'll make it a merry time," she promised.

Yes, drinking and eating well, however low the stores had gotten. Sports, hunting and hawking, women—Keep up the show. Keep them from seeing all the leanness underneath.

XVI

They met in her house when the last had arrived, the lendmen, yeomanly chieftains, and a jarl, who were tried and true and could get here fairly quickly. Arinbjörn of Sygnafylki bulked among them.

"Well," said Harald, "you have the tale. Give me your redes."

"What does the king think?" asked Orm Jarl.

Arinbjörn laughed. "If he were sure of that, we wouldn't be drinking this ale."

Orm scowled at such freeness from one of lower rank and opened his mouth. Harald waved him to silence, then said with a frown of his own, "I'll mislike having the Daneking above me, be it only in those holdings he offers."

"But they are rich, King," said the lawman Bui Gizurason. "Denmark hasn't been stricken like Norway. They'll yield food, cloth, and other things we sorely need, to ship to us."

Gunnhild had already spoken against it when alone with her son, though she hadn't risked pressing him too hard. Now she said before the gathering, "You meant to avenge your brother Erling this year, and bring the Thraands back under our house."

"That can wait," said the battle-scarred lendman Ranulf Kaarason bluntly. "Hungry men don't fight well. Let's first get ours better fed than them."

"Going to Denmark may not be wholly safe," warned Arinbjörn.

"Neither is starving," said his fellow hersir Ketil the Red.

"I have a bad feeling about Haakon Sigurdarson," Gunnhild told them. "That he should waste away seems too lucky for us."

"We did hear, months ago, how he was keeping to his bed, Queen," Bui reminded.

"We also heard he said he was not sick."

"What else would he say, Queen?" Ranulf wondered. "He could ill afford to show weakness."

Ketil nodded. "Not often do men rise again from weeks in bed. When they do, it's seldom for long."

"A fox like that can easily sham his dying," Gunnhild said.

"Why would he want to, Queen?"

"To lure the hares within reach."

At once she saw she had made a mistake. Harald Grayfell did not take kindly to being likened to a hare. "Shall we fear him, either way?" spat the king. "By every saint, if he is dead I'll be almost sorry. I want to kill him myself." The tide of that bore him along. "I could. *I've* given him no roof."

"I'd be leerier of your namesake Harald Bluetooth," said Arinbjörn weightily. "We've known him and known of him. They have mires in Denmark that, if a man tries to cross them, suck him down to his death."

Gunnhild had felt the fire smoldering in her Harald. She had hoped she could douse it or that it would die of itself. Instead, today it flared. "Stay watchful, yes." His voice picked up speed. "However, we did do well with him formerly, and he does have use for us. Also—I'd often be down there. Near to whatever happens. He waxes old. He's at odds with his son. There may be a kingdom to gain."

"Or to lose," said Gunnhild.

"Lord, you could lose yours here at home if these bad years go on and nothing is done," blurted Ranulf. A yea rumbled in several throats.

Orm crossed himself. "Maybe God has touched the heart of the Dane-king."

"I'd call that the unlikeliest of everything," sneered Gunnhild. She turned to Harald. "Rash is this faring, my son." She heard her own forlornness.

He bridled. "None shall say I hung back out of fear."

The talk went on. Gunnhild kept still. She knew she had lost.

"Well, King," said Arinbjörn at the end of endlessness, "since you're bound on going, I'll come along."

Harald mildened a little. "That's good of you, but not needful. We can't take a war-fleet when our aim is peace."

"We can take as much as befits you." Gunnhild felt the misgivings beneath Arinbjörn's bluntness. "Besides being my king, you're my foster brother. Let me hold by my oaths."

So it was settled. Harald would tell his brothers and have them ward the kingdom while he was gone. He himself would sail in early summer, at a given time to a given spot in Jutland, where Harald Bluetooth was to meet him. "That will be a happy day for my lord," said Fridleif before he went from them.

XVII

The wanderfowl began to come home. Starling, lapwing, and suchlike reached Denmark when cold still whistled over a sodden earth where ice puddles often crackled underfoot in the morning. Warming went onward; days lengthened; geese bore the spearheads of their flocks between clouds gone tall and white; their honking drifted lonesome over new grass and blossoms on boughs. Kine were let out to graze, ragged till they shed their winter coats. Leaf buds opened. Songbirds flitted and twittered among them. And then one bright day the storks were there, winging mightily back to their treetop and rooftop nests, bearers of rebirth. Folk welcomed them with balefires and dancing after dark; no few children were begotten.

Ever shorter and lighter grew the nights. Springtime swelled into summer. Already it was a good year, fields rippling in their fullness, shoals of fish agleam offshore.

For months, seafaring men had gotten more and more restless. They went over their ships and boats, caulking, tarring, making sure of tackle, talking with each other oftener than with their women. Fishers and sealers were the first to set forth. Soon thereafter the earliest traders stowed their wares, stocked their craft, and were off to Hedeby or Gotland or wherever markets were again astir. Some others sharpened weapons, oiled mail if they had any, and squinted into the sun-blink on the seas. Among them were Gold-Harald and his vikings.

It was hard for Haakon Sigurdarson to stay indoors as much as he did. Now that the lanes were opening, chapmen to Norway must not carry along talk about him being, after all, on his feet. If they did hear yonder that he lived, let them believe it was barely. Sometimes he went abroad after sunset in a hooded cloak, to walk or to ride at a gallop. This became easy to do in the light nights. Sometimes he met with the two Haralds at a well-guarded house. Sometimes he received visitors whom he could trust at his own dwelling; his servants there were handpicked, well paid, and deathly afraid of him. Then he could let his tongue and mind ramble, or his wit strike with its adder's teeth. "Too long has the weight of dear Queen Gunnhild been laid on Norway. And laid and laid—" When alone, he spent hours on end working to rebuild the strength he had lost during his weeks abed; weapons flashed in a narrow room, he leaped to and fro between the walls. And he did his thinking.

Now and then the thoughts were wistful, about the books he had seen and the many more Gunnhild once told him of. If only he had them, if only he could read them. Defiant, he would empty a horn in honor of the gods and the Shrine-bride.

When he deemed it was safe, he called in the skippers of those crews who followed him from Norway. He had regained health, he told them and showed them. Shortly he would make a viking cruise, for he and they had spent what they brought here and ought not turn into mere hangers-on of the Dane-king. Themselves chafing, they swiftly made ready.

Harald Bluetooth heard, and went to the jarl to find out more. "No threat to you, King." Friendliness throbbed in Haakon's voice. "How could it be, and why should it, when you've been so kind to me? True, there is more behind this than I've given out. I've learned of things that must be dealt with. If I tell you now, it's bound to get loose, and our plans will go aground. May I ask you, King, to wait a few days? Then we'll put our heads together, for this is a pressing business."

Harald let himself be talked over, though he ordered his guards to stand by. Haakon had awaited that.

A scout rode into Randers. He had worn out relays of horses posted beforehand. Harald Grayfell had come. He lay with three ships at Haals, a hamlet by the eastern mouth of the Limfjord. It had been agreed through Fridleif that this was where the Dane-king would meet him at about this time.

Gold-Harald embarked his men and set north up the Skagerrak with nine ships.

No sooner had he left than Haakon went to Harald Bluetooth. They shut themselves away in a loftroom. "Now," said the jarl, "I'm not sure but what we'll row off to war and nevertheless have war-gild to pay. Gold-Harald's on his way to kill Harald Grayfell and then take kingship in Norway. But do you really believe he'll keep the promises he's made you, when you've given him that much power? He told me this winter he'd kill you if he could."

Harald Bluetooth sat not altogether shocked. From the first, he had been doubtful of his nephew. Gold-Harald's later demands made it worse. In truth, it was mostly Haakon's counsel that had stayed his hand.

The other man leaned forward, smile white in the dark beard, talking fast. "But if you, lord, promise me I'll have to pay you only a light wergild, I'll undertake to do away with Gold-Harald. Then I'll be your jarl, plight my troth to you, and with your help keep a hold on the Norse and send you their scot. Then shall you rule over two kingdoms, and be a still greater king than your father."

They did not speak together very long.

Gold-Harald had taken nine ships. Haakon came after him with twelve.

XVIII

Also to Norway, at last, springtime brought warmth, sunshine, quickening, and hope. If crops were still small, it was only because too much seed grain had been eaten. Those fields that were sown bore lushly; there would be seed enough next year. Meanwhile kine, with no dearth of grazing even in the mountain meadows, bore young that would live. Swine fattened in the woods. The fish in the seas bade fair soon to teem as of yore. Folk looked at the world and each other in wonderment, like children.

Harald Grayfell had meant to go first down to Vikin. If he started thence for Jutland in good weather, it should hold through the short crossing over to the Kattegat. The day before he and Arinbjörn left Hardanger, Gunnhild had asked him to walk around for a while with her. "At best, the time will be long before we meet anew." She was not one to speak wistfully; nor did this quite sound like that. He had much to do. Nevertheless he shrugged, half grinned, and nodded. "Since you wish it, Mother."

Four guardsmen behind them, they went from the hall, away from the town and the water, on a road winding through farmland. The sun had baked its ruts dry; they could hear their footfalls under a hush that else was broken by birdcalls and a lark high overhead. A few clouds floated in a boundless blue. On their right, a thin mist floated above an oatfield. Behind a rail fence on the left, grass mingled with clover, a hundred shades of green, starred with wildflowers, the cows that cropped it rusty red. Here and there rose trees not cut down when the south half of Stord was cleared, gnarled and wide-spreading oak, pillarlike beech, soaring elm. Light and shadow dappled their crowns.

Smoke from a farmstead in the offing lost itself aloft. The men at work yonder seemed ant-small. Thyme lent a slight sharpness to sweet earth-smells.

Neither Harald nor Gunnhild had anything to say at once. The walk began to pain her left hip, as had been happening of late. She gave no sign and did not let it show that she limped. In this, at least, she thought wryly, skirts were more helpful than breeks.

At length the king, gazing straight ahead, spoke, somewhat awkwardly. "I think we can look for trouble-free sailing."

"That's tomorrow," said Gunnhild low. "Today take gladness in the sun."

"It bodes well. Everything seems to."

"For whom?" she murmured.

"For my faring. For us. For everything." He crossed himself, which she did not often see him do. "Let God not take that amiss. I'm not as pious as the priests hold I should be—" His voice stumbled.

That was a guess, Gunnhild thought. None of them other than, maybe, Aelfgar would risk saying it aloud.

"But before we go, we'll hear mass and give thanks for these blessings," Harald ended.

Only in her mind could Gunnhild wonder why the Christians had not blamed their God, in those long years when he never heeded their prayers, but Sigurd and Erling were slain while the land suffered and seethed. "The heathen also are offering to their gods," she said.

Harald scowled. "Sira Aelfgar believes the true God's been angry with them, that they will not hear the word of Christ." Harshly: "We may yet see about that."

"Why has Svithjod fared so well?" she flung forth.

The heathen bargained, the Christians beseeched, she thought. But was mankind really altogether strengthless against Heaven?

Harald's stride faltered. His look at her was almost shocked. "Mother, that's a wicked question."

Her thoughts ran on, an underground river. Could it be merely that more Finns lived nearer to the Swedes, and when they helped their own land the spells reached out to their neighbors?

But how then could the Swedes and Norse make booty of them, while the Kvaens felled their woods, drained their marshes, and pushed them from their olden ranges and the graves of their forebears into far northern wilderness?

"I won't press it if it frightens you," she said.

Her coldness covered an inward shudder. Might the ill luck that had hounded her and hers be vengeance for Aimo and Vuokko?

No, unlikely. The Finns were not a vengeful folk.

And yet—if a great wrong had been done, could it of itself so upset the world that harm must follow, like a fisherman's boat capsizing when he sailed too recklessly? Could she, her man, her sons have been clinging to a keel throughout the years, till the storm-waves plucked them off and hauled them down, one by one?

A sudden, astonishing tenderness drew her back to the sun. Harald had stopped. She did too. He turned to her. It was as if beneath the strong-boned, golden-bearded man-face there fleeted a glimpse of the little boy she met on her all too short visits to his foster home. "Mother," he burst out, softly, shakenly, "I meant no cut at you. Always you've striven for us. Your findings, redes, wisdom have been a, a torch in the dark. And—and—I've wondered about some things. Many men have. But I didn't ask, did I? Nor did I ever let anyone ask. Oh, sometimes I've wished—" He swallowed. "But that shall stay between you and Christ."

The words hardened and clanged: "I'll never forsake you."

Love rushed like a tide-race at her girlhood home.

She came near crying, "You're about to, Harald. After all my warnings, forebodings, bad dreams, and, yes, rune-casts, you're bound away. I beg you, don't break my heart."

No. She reined herself in. It was his pride as much as his troth that had uttered the vow. Hers could be no less. She was the mother of kings.

And she might, she might be mistaken.

"I was going to ask you this one last time to think again about your faring," she said.

He had regained steadiness. "I knew that." He sighed and smiled. "Well, I'll bear with you."

She shook her head. "No. It would be useless." She took his arm. "Come, let's walk together through this lovely day, for as long a while as you can spare."

That was an hour or two. Mostly she kept them talking about such quiet, happy times as they had had together. Now and then she made him laugh.

Afterward the short night fell. A few stars glimmered through its half-dusk.

In the morning, two longships left on the outgoing tide. Harald skippered one, Arinbjörn the other. A third would join them in Vikin. The water glittered; the lean hulls danced. Strong young men crowded the bulwarks, to wave and shout farewell. The racket startled gulls, cormorants, puffins, auks, every kind of seabird into a storm of wings and shrieks. Because the ships went in peace, their haughty figureheads were down; but Harald stood at the prow of his, a flame-red cloak fluttering from his shoulders.

Yardarms rattled up masts. Bright-striped sails, the blackness of a raven across Harald's, caught the wind. The ships canted and took bones in their teeth.

"Farewell, farewell," called the men, women, boys, maidens on the wharf. "Thor help you; Njörd be kind to you," wished some, and fewer: "Christ and his saints be with you."

Gunnhild stood unspeaking, her guards walling her off. She must not make any heathen offering. Her spells had failed. She could not tell how Christ would take it if she in her sins prayed for her son. Therefore she dared not.

XIX

A horn blew, wild as the bellow of the aurochs which had borne it. Gulls, wheeling white, gave answer. Men peered seaward. Their gleeful yells rang across the water.

Before them lay the long Limfjord, about half a mile wide where it opened on the Kattegat. A salt breeze ruffled it; a midmorning sun struck gleams and flashes. Land stretched low and green from sandy strands, wooded on the south. On the north were also woods, oak and beech, looming behind paddocks and sown fields. Folk here were more fishers than farmers, swineherds, charcoal burners, or hunters. They lived together in Haals. That hamlet stood at the mouth of the bight, a huddle of dock, boathouses, homes, and workshops. In back of their row, two newer works, ordered by King Harald Bluetooth, reared above thatch and turf roofs, a chapel and a gallows. Black against the sky, something swayed at the end of a rope, the lich of a thief or robber. The fowl had taken eyes and flesh but, dried by the wind and this warm summer, enough sinew was left to hold some bones in the rags.

Hardly any boats lay moored. Having learned that the Norse meant no harm when they got here three days ago, the fishers went back to their work. Not to risk a brawl—over a woman, say—Harald Grayfell had gone on inland a mile. Nor did he want to risk suddenly having to launch grounded ships at low tide. He stayed anchored, allowing only a few at a time to go ashore. The crews grumbled, though not in his hearing or Arinbjörn's.

Now cheer leaped in them. "The king!" they whooped. "Bluetooth is here," and lifted arms in greeting. "We'll feast, lads!"

The Danish ships strode on oars, past a holm and past the hamlet. Harald scowled. They were nine, all dragons. Shields were not hanging on the sides but inboard, ready to snatch up. Sunlight flared off helmets, byrnies, spears. Harald glanced across to Arinbjörn, who stood in the bow of his own craft. He saw that the hersir did not like the look of this either.

"Break out the war-gear," said Harald quietly. "Blow the same order to the rest. Make no move, though, till we know what these men have in mind." A snarl went the length of the hull, a stamping and growling as warriors crowded around the sea chests.

The lead Dane drew hailing-near. Harald himself cupped hands around mouth and called from the depths of his broad breast, "Ahoy, there! Are you from King Harald Gormsson? Here is King Harald Eiriksson of Norway, come to deal with him as he asked."

A tall man in the other prow gave back, "Here is Harald, son of King Knut Gormsson. I bid you to battle, Harald Gunnhildsson, for your evildoing, bad faith, and the kingship you wrongfully hold."

"The Dane-king will have your head."

"The Dane-king sent me."

Harald stood silent for the span of a bowshot, hardly hearing the outrage aft of him. He scanned to and fro. The nine ships were in a line across the fjord. Wind and tide were against him. He spied no way to slip between. Two or three could lay alongside each of his. Whatever hope was left him flickered on the land.

"I'll meet you ashore," he roared, "and take your head myself. God send the right!"

He swung about and rapped his bidding. The anchor came up; the oars came out, driving the ship till her keel grated in the northside shallows. His other crews did likewise. Overboard they sprang and waded up onto the sands. The last men off dropped anchors again. This fight would likely end before the tide turned.

One helped the king don his mail. While the rest were noisily making ready, he got a few words with Arinbjörn.

Wrath glared ice-blue. Nevertheless he spoke evenly. "With lies were we lured here. Men should forever after spit at the name of Harald Bluetooth. I had no thought he'd turn like this on one he used to called his foster son."

"From what I've heard, lord, he's not that cunning."

"I've an inkling—too late—that Haakon Sigurdarson's behind it. The queen mother tried to warn me." Harald bared his teeth. "Well, now there's nothing to do but break this tool of his."

"The odds are heavy," said Arinbjörn in his slow way. "However, once in a while men have won against worse. It's not for me to tell you your trade, King. Still, I think we can only win through this by sheer will. Let me rede you, lord, to hearten the boys and rouse rage in them, till they don't care whether they live or die if they can but kill."

Harald nodded. "Well thought. I will." His gaze and his voice softened. He laid a hand on Arinbjörn's shoulder. "Old friend, we've fared long and far, the two of us. Never were you anything other than faithful. Even when troths clashed in you—I forgave that years ago, Arinbjörn. Today I believe I understand it."

"Thank you, King," said Arinbjörn. "It behooves a man to stand by his friends and his lord. I—I'm glad I can." He turned his craggy face aside and knuckled an eye. "Best we get to our business, I think."

Harald's crews had armed themselves. Their headmen had gotten them into ranks. Banners waved in the sea-wind. Half a mile toward Haals, the foe had also landed and were mustering. With their greater number, it went more slowly. Harald had time to tread before his following, raise his hand, and say to them:

"Men of Norway, sprung from heroes, hear me, your king to whom you gave your oaths! You know we came here in peace and honestly. Murderous falsehood lay in wait for us. No man foresees his weird, nor may he flee it. His freedom is in meeting it undaunted, so mightily that his name lives on ever afterward, even to the end of the world. Scant is the honor to be won on a sickbed. Happiest is he who falls in the fight after reaping a harvest that grieves his foes, for never will men forget him and what he did.

"Yet on this day we can overcome. Cowards they are, who lurked behind lies, afraid to say what they wanted of us. True, they are thrice as many." He grinned. "Every one of you must kill three." That drew scattered laughs. "A wolf set upon by three mangy curs will slash the throat of the first, break the neck of the second, and fling the third aside with its guts ripped out. We shall not stand and let them snap at us. We'll take the swine-array and go on the attack. I myself will be first.—"

Thus he harangued. Soon cheers and howls gave answer.

His chief skald, Glum Geirason, had not gone along. Afterward, though, off in Orkney, Glum made a memorial poem, which he gave before the last two sons of Eirik and Gunnhild. It began:

"The Odin of the iron,
who often reddened fields,
Harald, bade men lay hands
on hilt and shaft of weapons
and bare their swords for battle,
boldly, eyes unblinking.
The warriors deemed his words
worthy of a king."

The Norse went forward. Spears sleeted. Then they were in among the Danes. The snout of their ranking plowed, their tusks gored right and left. Blades rose and fell; axes thundered; red drops flew on the wind. Shields splintered. Men sank, writhed, yammered, and were trampled. The stink of death overwhelmed every other smell.

Gold-Harald led no levy of yeomen. His were vikings, who had raided from Wendland through Friesland to Ireland and on into France. Skillful, they let the Norse break in, then swirled back around on every side. Banners swayed. They toppled. The Danes waged war.

At the end, some of the Norse found themselves on the rim of the maelstrom and got away into the woods. A few among these later talked themselves aboard boats going across the Kattegat and came home. Glum Geirason drew much of his tale from them.

"He, who rode high-hearted
the horses of the sea,
now made his longships lie
at Limfjord strand by Haals.
He fell, his brave blood flowing
forth into the sands.
With wily words his foes
had worked to get him slain."

But when the news reached him out in Iceland that Arinbjörn was dead, Egil Skallagrimsson mourned:

> "Fewer become my friends,
>   the fearless, the openhanded,
>   steadfast in every strife
>   and stinting never their gold.
>   Where now may I look for their like,
>   who in lands across the sea
>   hailed silver upon the skald
>   for saying the truth about them?"

XX

The slow sun of summer wheeled past noon. Rising tide lapped on those who had fallen at the water's edge. Blood swirled wan, but made dark blots in the sand. The dead sprawled ungainly, unclean, emptily gaping. Flies buzzed through the stench and settled on dry tongues. Overhead, gulls mewed, crows cawed, ravens croaked, kites dipped and soared, waiting for the living to go away. Danes went around to make an end of wounded Norse, carry off their own hurt friends and care for them, strip the bodies. Gold-Harald said naught about returning Danish arms and mail to families—few of his men had one—other than to chuckle, "After all, it's unchristian to bury folk with worldly goods."

His mood was high. Though he had fought as sternly as any, he took no more than shallow cuts and a bruise where an ax hit his shoulder without breaking the ring-mail. Having seen Harald Grayfell alive during the struggle, he had now looked upon him dead, hacked and stabbed but his face still a mask of rage.

"They're too many for us to bury," said a skipper who heard. "We're tired, thirsty, hungry."

"When the fishers get back at evening, we'll put them to it," said Gold-Harald. "Meanwhile, watchmen shall keep those birds off. Our men should rest fittingly, in hallowed ground—yes, and the Norse too, for honor's sake."

The skipper glanced toward Haals. "The graveyard here can't be nearly big enough."

"No, but I daresay the priest can hallow ours."

"If he's on hand. It's lonely, this far end of Jutland. I shouldn't wonder but what he serves half the shire."

"We'll find out, and leave word if need be. For now, let some men go there and see whether yon households have food and ale better than what we brought. Our crews have earned it—" Gold-Harald broke off. "Hoy! What's that?"

A longship slipped into sight around the southern lip of the fjord. Every man aboard, rowing or not, was clad for battle. Sunlight shone off steel almost as brightly as off the water. The ship rounded the point and surged west. Another followed, another, another. "Sound the horns!" cried Gold-Harald. "Form up the ranks!"

A full dozen warcraft lay to between him and the town. They fenced in his nine and the three hollow hulls he had seized. The lead ship drew closer, to rock a few yards off. Gold-Harald heard stifled groans and foul words at his back as he walked to the water. Maybe there were a few muttered prayers too, though these were not a prayerful lot. A shield-bearer went on either side of him, lest someone loose an arrow.

When he made out who stood on the foredeck, the lithe shape and neatly trimmed black beard, he knew starkly what it meant. Yet he must ask, "Why are you here, Haakon Sigurdarson?"

He felt no astonishment at the jarl's answer. "To halt your misdeeds, Harald Knutsson. We'll fight you here and now, unless you flee for us to hunt down."

"The Dane-king will have your head for this."

Haakon grinned. "I think not. Anyhow, it's nothing you need worry about. Shall we begin?"

"Yes, and Christ cast you down into Hell, you double-tongued, heathen dog!" Gold-Harald turned on his heel and stalked back to his men.

He gave them no speech. Few vikings died old. It did seem unfair, an onslaught before they had rested and re-

gained strength. However, they themselves had never
spared the weak, had indeed always sought the easiest prey.

The Norse and the Danes with them grounded and dis-
embarked. Gold-Harald wished he could make a rush and
fall on them before they were arrayed. But his weary crews
must stand where they were. "String bows," he bade. "Keep
spears and slings to hand. Slay them as they come." The
words rang dull in his own ears. At best, a half-score or so
of the jarl's men would fall, mostly not killed, and then the
rest would close. At best.

He had hoped to be a king. Well, he could die like one.

Now the Norse were headed for him. God give that Haakon the Wicked also meet death. But it seemed unlikely
that Gold-Harald would ever know, this side of the Otherworld.

The shafts and stones flew.

The shields crashed together.

The battle was short, however long it felt. Haakon's warriors flanked Gold-Harald's and took them front and rear.
With sword and ax they worked their way inward. Driven
back into the ruck, Gold-Harald tried to cut room for himself. He was too crowded to swing his blade freely. It
banged on rims and slid off helms. Then two shields
pressed in like the upper and lower shells of an oyster. They
jammed his arm to his side. Blows thudded. Dazed, he sank
to his knees.

While he crawled back to awareness and stumbled up
with his hands tied behind him, the fight ended. The aftermath went quickly.

His head throbbed. Every bone hurt. He saw Haakon
blurrily. "How—could the king—let this happen?" he
mumbled.

"The king doesn't trust you," said Haakon, "as well he
might not."

"Foolish was I to trust *you*. Who will you next betray?"

"You're hardly one to say what's betrayal. The world
will be well rid of you. I see a gallows yonder."

Horror smote. "Hanged? Like a thief? No!"

Haakon smiled. "Oh, honorable enough. Kings have gone thus to Odin. The god himself did." He nodded at the men who gripped the captive. "Take him away."

XXI

Back in Randers, the jarl went before Harald Bluetooth, made known what he had done, and gave the king self-judgment in the case. Harald set the wergild of his nephew at three hundred in silver. It was easily paid, for, like Egil Skallagrimsson, Gold-Harald had been wont to take much of his treasure along with him when he traveled.

At the same time arrived Harald Grenska, son of that King Gudröd in Vestfold whom Harald Grayfell slew, hence a great-grandson of Harald Fairhair. Upon his father's death this Harald, then a mere lad, fled to Svithjod, where he struck up friendship with the warlike Skögul-Tosti. They often went in viking together, and Harald Grenska won a name for himself early on. He was now a young man of some eighteen winters with a following of his own. At Haakon's counsel, the Dane-king had sent to him, offering alliance against the last Eirikssons.

Gold-Harald had been in on this. Himself lacking all blood of Harald Fairhair, he could not hold kingship in Norway without the backing of somebody who had it. Otherwise the only ones left were aging Haalfdan Sigurdarson and his son Sigurd, offside in Hringariki. To this day they were looked at askance because they stemmed from Snaefrid, the witch who had been leman to Harald Fairhair and worked balefully on him. They found it best, as well as most to their liking, to stay peacefully home, take their scot, pay whatever they owed of it to whoever was high king, and care for their land. Someday the old wild strain in them might break forth, but it could not be awaited that either of these two would do anything one way or the other.

Let them keep the name of king. They were hardly more

than jarls, and would become less. Harald Bluetooth promised Harald Grenska lordship over Vestfold, Vingulmörk,
Grenland, and Agdir as far as the southern tip of Norway—
that is, the shires at the head of the Oslofjord and down
the western shore of the Skagerrak. It would be with the
same rights and duties as Harald Fairhair gave his sons
when he set them up as kings under himself.

This drew other Norse chieftains, whom the Eirikssons
had driven from their holdings, into the fellowship. Between them, they and Harald Grenska had at their beck no
few keels and warriors.

And the Dane-king ordered a great levy of seven hundred
and twenty fully manned ships.

All this he set under the leadership of his good, wise
friend Haakon Jarl. Who could use it better, or raise more
of the Norse at home to rally around it?

Besides Thraandheim, the Dane-king gave into Haakon's
hands Rogaland and Hördaland, Sogn and Sygnafylki, both
the Moerrs, and Raumsdalr. Haalogaland in the north went
without saying. It meant the whole west of Norway, likewise with the same rights and duties as the sons of Harald
Fairhair, though none of them had held this broad a sway
until Eirik Blood-ax in his father's old age.

In return, Haakon would come to help Denmark when
called. As long as there was a threat from the Gunnhildssons, he would stave it off, and while this lasted be free
from paying scot.

A shrewd move, the Dane-king believed. The Norsemen
would think of Harald Grenska as their king by right, and
rise for his sake; but he would in truth hold little more than
a part of Vikin. Haakon would be the real overlord. Yet,
lacking heirship on the spear side from Harald Fairhair, he
could never take any rank higher than jarl, and must needs
stay Harald Bluetooth's man.

Haakon, who had planted and tilled these thoughts, did
nothing as yet to wither them.

The fleet started forth.

XXII

A bitter wind dashed rain against roofs. Walls barely muffled its booming and whistling. Noontide lamps and candles held darkness somewhat at bay in Gunnhild's house. The hearthfire tried to stave off chill. Smoke eddied blue-gray and sharp.

Maids had brought drink and withdrawn from the room. She sat straight in her chair, though her flesh wanted to creep into bed, and looked steadily at her sons in theirs. The cloaks and hats they had worn on the short walk from the hall hung dripping. Sheathed swords leaned nearby. A few guards waited outside, men who would never openly say anything that sounded weak but who were surely unhappy.

"You know why I've asked you to come here," she said.

Gudröd nodded. A flame-flicker touched the wetness still in his beard. "So we can speak among ourselves, as we've often done."

But then they were more, she thought. And now Harald too was gone, Grayfell, best and dearest of them all. After that news reached her she had walked off alone in the night, unseen, until she could scream her wrath and grief aloud to the moon. She would not let sorrow sap what was left of her strength. In the iron days and haunted nights since then, she had mastered it. But she knew the ghost would not leave her while she lived.

"And say between us what we dare not say before our men," she filled out.

Ragnfröd's red head went back, like the head of a bridling stallion. "Dare not?"

"You understand what our mother means," Gudröd said to him. "Or you should."

Ragnfröd glared. A hand dropped to the knife at his belt. Gudröd glowered. Both were wayworn, their forbearingness drawn close to breaking.

Gunnhild spoke quickly. "It would be most unwise to throw yea and nay to and fro in their hearing, as daunted and jumpy as they are. Once we've crafted the right words, yes, then of course you shall give them your bidding."

"And what will that be?" asked Ragnfröd harshly.

"That they follow us to Orkney, those who're still faithful."

How few, how few. Her sons had been riding and rowing everywhere that time allowed, sending war-arrows, calling on men to take weapons, fall on the invaders, avenge King Harald Grayfell, uphold his brothers. It did not happen. Instead, they heard how down south folk streamed to welcome Harald Grenska and join his host, how the North had risen on behalf of its Jarl Haakon, how the Uplands and the great Dale boiled. A few score ships lay at the Hardangerfjord. Their crews huddled with some guards in the hall and its outbuildings, eating meagerly.

"What else can we do?" Gunnhild ended.

"Stand fast," snarled Ragnfröd. "Fight."

"And fall." Gudröd sighed. "No."

"To what use?" Gunnhild said. "Better to bide our time in Orkney."

Ragnfröd gagged. "Again?"

"Your father did," said the queen stiffly, "and no man ever called him coward. He never gave up. Nor shall we. To die here and now would be to yield."

How much easier, whispered an outlaw thought. To slip from the weight and pain of the bones, lie down, and have done.

No.

Ragnfröd scowled. "Well—"

"We'll gather new might," Gunnhild said. "We'll come home and take the kingdom back."

She heard how the heart lifted in him. "Next year!"

"Hardly so soon," Gudröd warned.

"Yes." Fire kindled. "I've been in Orkney oftener than you, remember, bound for west-viking. I've given gifts, made friends. There's no dearth of men and ships. Land-hungry men, who'll fight still more gladly for homes in

Norway than for fame or loot. Ships better fitted for war than most you see hereabouts. We'll crush the foe. With any luck, Haakon won't be slain, but we'll grab him alive for the gallows. Or we'll burn him in his house, as our father did his."

"In time, in time. Heed our mother's wisdom."

"What would *you* have us do?"

"Hlödvir Jarl in Orkney will give us a holding. From it, we'll raid for a few years in Ireland, Scotland, England, Denmark, Friesland, France, maybe as far south as Córdoba. We'll gain wealth. Then we can build up a big fleet and troops for it."

"How big do you need it?" A sneer showed Ragnfröd's teeth. "Are you that afraid of Haakon?"

Gudröd reddened. "Are your wits that much less than his?"

Ragnfröd half rose. Gudröd did too. They seemed almost ready to come to blows, or even swords.

Gunnhild sprang to her feet. She spread out her arms. "My sons, my sons," she cried, "hold together! We have nobody but each other. You bear the last blood of your father."

Oh, it ran in many a by-blow, she thought, but it ran cold and thin. Not one foster father or foster brother of an acknowledged child was here today. Not one leman had borne her a grandson who might someday want the kingship; none was being raised to have such a wish. She had believed that was best, for then the sons of queens who stemmed from mighty houses would not be troubled by them. But she had not foreseen that all those houses would hang back from giving a daughter, nor that the same wariness and, yes, growing hatred would eat away the bonds of fostership.

Ragnfröd and Gudröd sank into their chairs. Gunnhild lowered her arms, squared her shoulders, and spurred her soul. "We'll lay our plans, whatever they turn out to be, in Orkney," she said. "And after a while we'll get you the right wives, as we should have done long ago."

Gudröd gazed at her and murmured, "It's hard to find one like you, Mother."

Ragnfröd had also calmed a little. "We'll see about that. Meanwhile, though, let's indeed think on how best to break the news to our men and busk ourselves for the crossing."

Gunnhild sat down. She guided the talk as quietly as she could, not to flick the wounded pride of either man. It went fairly well. The rift seemed to have healed. Yet she could not shake off a feeling that it had boded ill.

And again she must fare on a ship. Already she ached with the weariness of it.

The wind howled louder. Rain roared. A burst of hail rattled over shingles and timber. This was the first bad weather in a mild and bountiful summer. It was as if the land were casting them out.

XXIII

They passed down the strait called the String, between the ruddy cliffs of Shapinsay and Mainland, then swung south down Wide Firth into the bay and on toward the haven nestled there. It had grown—more houses and sheds, more boats lying at longer docks or out on the water. The sound of horns blew faint across two or three miles. Sparks and flashes glinted along the wharves, sunshine glancing off mail.

When summer waned over Orkney, it was apt to become the loveliest time of year. Light spilled past a few fleece-white clouds, to play on wavelets that rippled and chuckled in bewilderingly changeable blues and greens. Green also were the islands above their steeps, with foam at their feet and around the strewn holms, skerries, and stacks. Seafowl in hundreds wove a web of cries through the soft breeze.

Ragnfröd must have given an order, for his rowers bent their backs and the ship leaped ahead of the rest. The sail was down but the mast still up, a white shield at the top. Other shields hung along the sides, colorful, peaceful. Squinting against the glitter, Gunnhild, aboard Gudröd's, thought she could make out how the ranks ashore eased. Though it was getting hard to see things close to her clearly, her sight across long reaches had sharpened. Sometimes she wondered whether this meant she was beginning to drift from the earth, on into whatever waited beyond.

Oars backed water. Ragnfröd's longship lay broadside to the land, a few yards off. Tall on the foredeck, he bared his red head, waved, and shouted. Halloos rang in answer. A man at the forefront stepped from the banner to call and beckon. They knew this son of Gunnhild.

Home again, she thought bleakly.

The ship moved on to an empty berth. Mooring lines were flung; willing hands made them fast; a gangplank shot forth. Ragnfröd bounded up it onto the wharf. The leader went to meet him. They clasped hands and broke into swift, hard-edged talk.

Gudröd's craft followed, likewise docking. He pushed his way down the crowded hull to her. "You shall walk beside me, Mother," he said.

She felt it as a breath of warmth after the cold winds, colder waters, and flung spindrift of the sea. Yes, they had made the crossing quickly, but that was because they took no slower ship. Aboard a knarr she had had at least some damp, cramped shelter. Here they could only rig a ring of homespun for her to try to sleep, or do what else she must. A sailor dumped her pot overside; he took care not to say anything or look at her.

Well, she would have suffered more than that, not to be left behind for Haakon. He might have had her killed. He might have kept her always under guard, which would be much worse.

"This is good of you, Gudröd," she said.

"No, it's merely your rightful honor. The jarl shall know from the outset that you're his queen."

Her clothes hung clammy, grubby, smelly. Her headcloth was no better. She opened a chest and took a cloak of scarlet silk, marten fur around the hood, as well as a silver brooch in the shape of a dragon, to drape over herself and pin at the throat. Gudröd waited, smiling. He lent her a hand up the gangplank and, on the wharf, his arm.

The ground swayed underfoot. It would take a while to

get her land legs back—longer than when she was young. Leaning on him, she could walk steadily at his side, queen with king.

The Orkney troopers had loosened their array and stood listening if they were nearby, chatting if they were not. Townsfolk crowded and gabbled behind them. Ragnfröd and the leader stopped their own talk and turned. "King Gudröd my brother, Queen Gunnhild my mother, here stands Hlödvir Thorfinnsson, jarl of Orkney and Caithness. True to the olden oaths, he makes us welcome."

The other was strongly built, rugged of face, dark amber of hair and beard, better-looking than his father. Helm and byrnie, sword slung at shoulder, shield in the hands of a youth at his side, told what a fight he would have given if he must.

A bit jerkily, he lifted hand to brow and nodded his head. "My lord, my lady," he greeted. "I know you, of course, King Gudröd, though you haven't visited us very often." His voice went flat. "And I remember you well, Queen, though I was but a stripling when you last dwelt among us."

Twenty years ago, she recalled. Already?

She felt how his gaze ransacked wrinkles, sallow skin, flesh thin over skull, stray wisps of gray hair, and he still in the fullness of manhood. She hardened her backbone and gave him stare for stare.

"Bad are your tidings. We'll do what we can to help you toward a better day," he said. "If you wish, Queen, I'll have some guardsmen take you straight to the bower, where you can refresh yourself before you come to the hall—unless you'd rather have food brought to you and then go to bed."

"My thanks, Jarl," she said, unsmiling the same as he. "My own men will carry my chests. First I want to bathe."

Gudröd laughed. "We could all use that."

"Yes, yes, the bathhouse fires shall be lighted and stoked at once," Hlödvir promised. "But would the queen like to rest tonight in the bower? Tomorrow I'll find you a worthier abode, and handmaidens to tend you."

Handmaidens—and others—to keep watch on her, Gunnhild knew. "You are kind, Jarl," she said. "It will need a room that can be shut off when I sit in council with my sons."

Hlödvir could not hide his dislike of that. "I hope this doesn't have to happen, Queen. King Ragnfröd tells me he means to return to Norway next year. We hope King Gudröd will too, but he'll decide for himself. Whatever he chooses, King Ragnfröd and I will be busy planning and readymaking—man-work, the queen understands."

Gudröd opened his mouth. Gunnhild nudged him to stay silent. She made a smile. "Jarl, I've learned when I can be helpful and when I'd only be in the way. I ask merely that I be able to give a rede within four walls if somebody would like one. He need not follow it."

Hlödvir flushed. "The queen is wise. It shall be as she wishes."

Her heart stumbled, though she spoke evenly. "Now tell me, how fares my daughter Ragnhild, sister of kings?"

"The last I heard, she was doing well enough." It was clear that Hlödvir didn't care to say more.

From Denmark and later from Norway, Gunnhild had tried to keep up with what happened. That was through seamen, for Ragnhild herself sent never a word. After the death of her third husband, Ljot, the new jarl, Hlödvir, had given her a steading at Rackwick on the island Hoy. North, south, and east of that cleft in its cliffs reared the highest uplands in the Orkneys. The dwellers there were few, visitors from outside fewer yet.

"She must be lonely," Gunnhild said.

Hlödvir's answer went like shears cutting a thread. "I told you, Queen, she's well enough off. I had nothing better for her."

Gunnhild knew why. It was half hatred, half fear.

He was the last of the Thorfinnssons. There had been no hiding Ragnhild's unwillingness to wed his brother Arnfinn, and much pointed to her having brought about the murder. There was no question but what she had wrought the death of her second husband, his brother Haavard. Nevertheless she snared a third brother, Ljot. They two got along. However, folk believed she had much to do with egging on the strife for the jarlship that led to the slaying of the fourth brother, Skuli. This in turn launched war with the Scots, in which Ljot got his death-wound. Belike Ragnhild had not wanted that. By then, though, men shuddered. It was as if she, otherwise barren, bore death after death.

Hlödvir could have done worse by her than he did. But she was, after all, sister to his overlords, the kings of Norway.

And daughter to Gunnhild, who herself had bred far more slayings and, folk muttered, was an outright witch, no mere house-witch but one with night at her beck.

In high cheekbones and eyes of a gray-green never twice quite the same, they two even looked somewhat alike.

"We'll call on her, Mother," said Gudröd. "I'll take you there."

"Why stand we here?" cried Ragnfröd in a gust of raw merriment. "Let's be off to the hall and the ale!"

XXIV

From Scapa Bay on the southern side of the neck of Mainland, out into Scapa Flow, then westward past Graemsay to Hoy Sound, rounding Hoy, and southward to Rora Head, was no great ways. Lustily rowed by a dozen men at a time, the skuta that Gudröd used made it in less than half of a late-summer day. Yet to Gunnhild it felt like a crossing between worlds.

When the prow turned east, the headland on her left, stretching some two miles out into the sea, and the shoreline on her right sheered up in cliffs at whose feet surf raged over rocks and reefs. The one break in them lay before her, a narrow dale slanting down from the inland heights. While it was green—a green all the deeper and brighter against that stark shoreline—she spied only a few buildings here and there. Wind tattered the smoke from them.

Clouds scudded low, so that light flashed off the water and then it went gray again. The wind whistled and bit.

Spindrift flew salty. Waves rushed white-maned to crash
against the land. The cormorants were many. She remembered how the Norse fisherfolk around Ulfgard and the
Finns believed that sea-wights could take the shape of those
black fowl.

Aft was nothing but sea, to worldrim and beyond. Scattered in it lay the Hebrides, the Shetlands, the Faeroes, and
Iceland. She had heard of a sighting farther on, from a ship
blown off course, maybe fifty years ago, lucky enough to
win back. But if sailors bore straight west from here it
would be into the utter unknown.

Here dwelt her daughter.

Stones had been piled out from the strand to make a
small mole and breakwater. Planks had been fastened on
top to give mooring and footing. Gunnhild wondered how
long the tides would take to break it asunder if men stopped
tending it. A lifespan, she guessed. The skuta was coming
in at low ebb, stiffer rowing but safer than at another time.

No warriors kept watch. A shepherd or someone like that
must have seen the craft from above, for a handful of men
had gathered. They owned no mail, only spears or axes and
one rusty kettle helm. They looked readier to flee than fight.
Gudröd signed peace. The three boldest came slowly down
to help him dock. Then the rest hurried after them, big-
eyed and stammering.

Gudröd picked a guide from among them, left his crew
to talk and chaffer with the rest, and took his mother up a
path near a stream. Both wore goodly cloaks. Gunnhild's
hip was hurting. She helped her gait with a staff. Gold
bands ringed its upper end, which was topped with a little
silver man's head.

They soon came to the house they sought. Its roof and
thick walls were of turf but not of mean size. Lesser buildings lay behind it, barn, byre, shed, and the like, with a
half-underground hut where the lowly slept crammed
together. Haystacks were for a few milch cows, maybe a
horse or two, now at graze in a haugh fenced by driftwood
rails. But this was not really a farm. It and most of the land
around belonged to the jarl. Whoever lived here was his

overseer, getting foodstuffs, wool, and so forth from the tenant crofters. Hlödvir had not been too niggardly when he turned it over to Ragnhild.

That was a shrewd move, Gunnhild thought. He did not want one whom he looked on as a troublemaker and bearer of woe anywhere near him. To have her stealthily killed would have been risky, and a nithing's work—her kind of deed, he must have sneered to himself. And, in a way, he did owe his jarlship to her. At Rackwick she was not poor, but she was cut off from him and his. In his place, Gunnhild thought, she might have done the same. That did not mean she must meekly abide by it.

An awed thrall met her and her son at the door. They passed through an entry to the main room. There sat her daughter.

Greetings and other seemly speech went stiffly back and forth. Then Gudröd said he had better go see to his men. They would take their big meal here every day, of course, as Ragnhild's honor called for, during their short visit. But the house was no hall. He did not want to clutter it with a score of snorers. Nearby farmers would gladly give them shelter—new faces, new tales, from as far away as Norway! He would return at eventide with none but the Orkneyman pilot, bearing gifts.

Gunnhild had asked him to do so, after she had found out more or less how things were here. Now Ragnhild told her housefolk to bring mead and begone. The two women sat alone, side by side in the high seat.

It had no carven pillars or the like, it was only raised slightly above the benches along the walls; but embroidered cushions rather than sheepskins lay on it. Doors and the shutters of the two windows stood open to let in the restless daylight, also a chill that a low-burning peat fire did not do much to hold off. A stone-weighted loom stood near the entryroom door, the best-lighted spot, with a big half-woven cloth in the frame. Rushes covered an earthen floor. The benches could seat about two dozen. There would seldom be that many, only such freemen as worked on the grounds. While this visit lasted, most of them would have to eat elsewhere.

Yet Gunnhild had never seen tapestries more craftily made than the ones hung on these walls. Worthy of a king's hall, they were—though what they showed was unlike anything else she had ever met, uncanny—She heard a mewing. Four cats were curled near the hearth or draped on a bench. One had come over to the high seat. Ragnhild made a kissing sound. The cat sprang up onto her lap. She stroked it lovingly. Did she love anything else anymore?

"So we meet again," Gunnhild said, to make a beginning.

"When we bade farewell, you told me you had a feeling we would." Ragnhild's words were low and slow. Her gaze dwelt on a hanging across the room, in which were shapes that might be trolls.

Gunnhild turned her head to look more closely at her daughter. Ragnhild sat in a finely made gown. The panels over it and the cloth over her ruddy braids were cunningly embroidered. But she herself was thin, the hand bony that played with the cat, the face haggard.

"I hoped then it would be sooner and happier than this," murmured Gunnhild. Ragnhild's wan mouth stayed shut. "Tell me in truth, how do you fare?"

"I'm the lady of the household, the tenants, and the land." Still Ragnhild stared at the trolls. "Callers are far between, hardly ever anyone but smallholders on small business. They don't linger."

"Hard must it for you to live alone, who was wife to the jarl of Orkney and Caithness."

At that Ragnhild gave her mother a glance, eyes as green as the cat's. "You too have fallen." A smile barely flickered. Did it gloat?

Gunnhild sat straight. "I—Gudröd, Ragnfröd, and I—we'll take back what is ours."

"I don't know whether to wish for that or not."

It hit like a knife. "What?" Gunnhild whispered. "How can you say such a thing?"

Ragnhild's free arm waved about the room. "You brought me to this, you know." Gunnhild caught her breath.

Ragnhild's fingers crooked. The cat jumped off her lap. "When you gave me to the Arnfinn swine," Ragnhild hissed. "And needless that was. Hardly had it been done but you were off to the Dane-king."

"That, that was not foreseeable."

"Why not? They call you a witch. Aren't you even a spaewife?"

Gunnhild braced her soul. "No man escapes his weird, nor any woman either," she said. "Don't feel sorry for yourself. You won at last to happiness, didn't you?"

Ragnhild spoke more evenly, though no more warmly. "With Ljot? Well, it wasn't bad. It might have become better, had he lived. His other two wives and I didn't like each other, but I was getting them in hand."

"Had you borne him a son—" Gunnhild bit it off when she saw the sudden pain behind the mask.

Ragnhild looked away again. "That did not happen," she said.

After she shut her womb against her first two men, if that was what she did, why had she not gotten children when she wanted them? Did Christ punish her sins? Did Freyja disown a woman who had kept herself barren? Had her doings by themselves dried her wellspring of life?

"And then Ljot died," she ended.

Gunnhild nodded. "Grief falls on everyone. In England, I lost your father." Eirik, Eirik! She could still wake in the middle of the night from dreams of him. She could still feel him in the wind or see him when a hawk stooped on its prey. Her words went soft. "Oh, Ragnhild, my road has been as stony as yours, longer, darker, and too much of the blood spilled on it was dear to me."

The other grinned. "It's led you back to Orkney."

Pride lifted. "I told you we shall win home anew." Tenderness returned. "And then, Ragnhild, we'll send for you."

"Is this the first time you've thought of that?"

"We didn't hear in Norway how you lived. You could have let us know. One of your brothers would have come for you."

"What tales *I* heard were of such unrest that I saw scant

gain to be had." A laugh rattled. "I was right."

They sat unspeaking for a span. The flames shivered, the light from outside sickled between sun and shadow. Yet it seemed to Gunnhild that her daughter eased somewhat beside her, that the scorn left her lips—as if, having spat forth a bitterness long locked away, she was not unwilling to talk with her mother.

"Then you aren't altogether wretched here," said Gunnhild carefully.

Ragnhild shrugged. "I've grown used to it."

"How do you pass your days? I can't believe you do nothing but oversee a house and a few crofts."

"I weave, sew, and embroider. That's my work you see."

"It's wonderful. I've never known anything quite like it."

"Yes, my own insights. Come." Ragnhild stepped lithely to the floor. Gunnhild limped after, not wincing when it stabbed in her hip. Ragnhild led her around the room, pointing at the eerie figures, talking fast. "See, here's Ragnar Hairybreeks dying in the pit of adders. Here's Sigurd Faafnir's-bane, murdered in his bed but killing his killer. Here are Odin and the Fenris wolf, Thor and the Midgard snake, Frey and Surt, Heimdall and Loki, in their death-fights at the Wreck of the Gods."

Here was hatred writing with skillful fingers, Gunnhild thought. Nevertheless, "Work such as this would make lordly gifts," she said.

"Now and then I send things to Hlödvir and his wife—though the kind they like is dull to do—and he sends me stuff I can use or trade off."

"But you never meet with him?" Gunnhild reached toward the slight openness she believed she felt, longing to do so with her arms. "Are you always lonely?"

"Why, no. I have my cats. More of them are outdoors right now. I have my thoughts. I have my loom and needles."

"It must be hard to ply them as—neatly—as you do in winter." Huge nights, short gloomy days, dim flamelight.

"Oh, in many ways I like winter better than summer. The summer days are too long. The dwellers and their work make too many calls on my heed. The sea-blink is too bright. In winter I can sleep and sleep, or lie awake in the dark, by myself. I don't let the cats into my shut-bed. I'm learning beforehand how to be dead."

The big eyes gleamed; the mouth drew back from the teeth in a bone-stiff smile. Ragnhild was a little mad, Gunnhild thought. Maybe more than a little.

She quelled the inward shudder. She had known enough otherness that she could deal with this. "Well, let's lay heavy things aside and take what cheer we can while Gudröd and I are here. I do hope we aren't unwelcome guests."

"No," said Ragnhild. "I've naught against it." She might have been answering a field hand's question about some everyday task.

"I'll come back. Once things are better settled for us, when we understand more clearly what we should do in our war, I can stay longer."

"As you wish." Ragnhild tautened, struck by a thought. When she spoke again, it was slyly. "There's a room in the house that you can have to yourself. It's small, but you can do whatever you want in it."

Do witchcraft, Gunnhild knew.

She had seen no cross on the wall, no sign of Christ. Ragnhild must have forsaken him. That was easy, in this heathen land where she could not have met a priest for years. But she had not offered to the old gods either. Instead, she found an icy gladness in weaving their doom.

Gunnhild smiled grimly. "It's true, my doings are sometimes a bit strange."

Ragnhild bent toward her. "They watch you on Mainland, don't they?" she breathed. "They won't let you work. That's why I never go elsewhere. Here I'm away from all the eyes." Again she grinned. "Yes, Mother, I think you may find much that's to your liking, here with me."

XXV

Hlödvir Jarl gave Gunnhild a house on Scapa Bay, about two miles from his hall and the town around it on the north shore. A fisher hamlet lay near, otherwise only wharves and sheds. Still, it was a house not unworthy of her, fairly big, with as much timber as turf gone into its making, well furnished, with hangings—not like Ragnhild's—to brighten its main room and help keep it warm. As at Rackwick, there were cows for fresh milk and butter, chickens for fresh eggs and meat, fields to feed them. All this took a staff of men and women to do the work, and some of them had children. They were always on hand for the queen.

Always watchful. Gunnhild understood.

Hlödvir guested her sons well. That he hardly ever asked her to visit could not be taken as a slight. She was a widow, and old. The jarl's father, Thorfinn Skull-splitter, would nonetheless often have met with her; but Thorfinn was long dead. Hlödvir kept faith with her kin as best he could bring himself to do. For that she forgave him all else, or at least let it go by.

Even in the dark months, he was much on the move between his holdings throughout the islands. Ragnfröd and Gudröd went too, looking for brothers-in-arms, unless they were off on their own doing the same thing. Thus she seldom saw them either, and then only for short whiles.

At one such time, early on, when they happened to call on her together, she won a kind of victory. Ragnfröd was set on seeking out Haakon Jarl in Norway come summer. Strike before the heathen dog got the land bulwarked against them, as his namesake Haakon Aethelstan's-foster had done. Naught but a miracle brought that unrightful king down at last, after he had won the battle at Fitjar—God's mercy, cried Ragnfröd, whereupon he and Gudröd glanced sideways at their mother, lowered their eyes, and said no more about that. She kept her face locked.

No, answered Gudröd, it was too soon. They might throw Haakon back at first, but unless they had the high good luck to fell him, he would raise the folk as he well knew how, he and his slippery tongue. Thrice had the sons of Eirik Blood-ax and Gunnhild surged at Aethelstan's-foster and shattered, like surf; and that was with the might of Denmark behind them. These days they had merely whatever they could find in the Western Islands. Wisest was to hold off and gather strength until it was overwhelming.

Yes, Gunnhild quietly put in, the friendship between Haakon Jarl and King Harald Bluetooth would likely wear thin. Meanwhile they should send feelers to Harald's son Sveinn. There was no love to speak of between him and his father. Should the two fall out—which could maybe be helped along—and Sveinn gain Denmark, something might well be done.

"Do you want to die here, Mother?" burst from Ragnfröd. "And you, Gudröd, I tell you you'll do better as a man than a spider!"

"A man, yes," roared the other, "but not a blind berserker!"

They sprang from their seats. Gunnhild did likewise. She put her small body between them, calmed them like a horseman calming two stallions, and got them to drink from the same horn of mead.

By now, so much had been said in the hearing of so many men that neither could back down, whatever his second thoughts might be. But she brought them to agreement. Gudröd would keep a half-score ships, to fare in viking. The brothers would share his booty. The rest of the warriors from Norway would follow Ragnfröd, together with such allies as he had gotten in the Orkneys, Hebrides, and Shetlands. If he won his war, he would be the foremost king in Norway; Gudröd would have Harald Grenska's shires. If Ragnfröd lost, but later the Gunnhildssons won, Gudröd would be overlord.

They clasped hands on that. The heat cooled, the coldness thawed—not altogether, but enough.

Well, Gunnhild thought, hiding a lopsided smile, a she-wolf must keep her young from each other's throats.

They went their ways. The black months drew in.

She was not left alone. If only she could be, once in a while. There was nowhere to send the servants and the few guards for a night. Were she to do so anyhow, the jarl would soon hear. He had as good as told her he would not stand for anything like seid anywhere near him. She was not now the queen mother of Norway, nor were her sons its kings, who never questioned her and to whom nobody dared drop a hint. They could not afford to upset Hlödvir. In a tiny offside room she kept such costly things as she had been able to take along with her, and the chest that only she ever opened. But somebody would know when she closed that door behind her. It was not thick. They would listen.

She doused anger and gave the staff no more heed than was needful. At least she was free to think. However gloomy, the Orkney winter was fairly mild. She walked along strand and cliffs, or inland for miles, beyond sight of men other than the guards, who had learned to stay well behind and not speak. When walking hurt too much she had a horse saddled and rode. If she lingered for a span at a barrow or standing stone raised by folk of old—or by elves or gods or giants; who really knew?—that was her own business. They saw her brooding. For all they could tell, she was silently praying.

And when she slid shut the panel of her bed, then she was by herself for as long as she wanted.

Like Ragnhild. But no, she would not spend its darkness on getting used to the grave. Too much was left to do. She lay thinking, until she slipped off into meaningless dreams.

Besides, she did not know what awaited her after death, a sleep or an unrestful prowling or the fires of Hell or a rebirth or a oneness with the world or what. She would neither cower nor hope; she would work for the blood of Eirik.

Nor were these days wholly cheerless. Of course she was at the Yuletide feasting. There—as well as a time or two earlier, a time or two later—she got into talk with men of standing, whose ken reached well beyond the islands, from Iceland to Gardariki, from here to Miklagard and Serkland. When she liked them, or it seemed they might be useful to her sons, she set about charming them. That was harder than when she was young and fair to behold. Still, the crone had a whetted wit; her knowledge went both widely and deeply; they had never before met anybody like her. So when she now and then sent a footling to invite this or that one to visit, oftenest he did.

It had become toilsome for her to make those times merry. However, she had not lost the gift of words. If her smile was creased, it showed white teeth, and she had not forgotten how to aim shining eyes. Some of the men were handsome, which helped. She led them on to talk about themselves, thence about loftier things, such as what was going on in Scotland or England and what should be done about it. Her words got as sharp as any man's, more so than most. Her guests went home thoughtful, not unwilling to call again. Meanwhile, they would pass on to her whatever news came their way.

Thus Gunnhild began to weave her web anew.

The sun sank to its lowest and swung back northward. Ragnfröd sought her. Eagerness flowed out of the hard, weathered face, the whole hard body: "Mother, great tidings for us! I stumbled on it, unless Heaven guided me. I found that an Irish thrall of Hlödvir's is a priest. Snatched by vikings, passed from hand to hand, set to drudge work, but a hallowed Christian priest. I've bought and freed him. Cael, his name is. He'll hear our confessions, cleanse us of our sins, and call on Christ to give us victory over heathen Haakon!"

"Well, good," said Gunnhild. Remembering York better than Ragnfröd did, remembering Denmark and Britnoth, she wondered how much this could be worth. Where was the altar, where the holy water, where the Church itself?

But she would say nothing to dishearten her son. She didn't like the look of a little, round, grayish growth lately showing on his right cheek. The skin of redheads was less tough than that of others. She kept silence about it, because

he would not have taken her elsewhere to try a healing
spell. If she went along with this priest, maybe Christ or a
saint would remove it.

Cael was young and sturdy, but broken. He no longer
knew quite how to say mass—not that he could well have
held one here. He did his poor best, though. When Ragnfröd brought him around, Gunnhild knelt at his feet in the
offside room and told him she had sinned. By now, she
said, she could not recall each misdeed, but she knew she
had been prideful, envious, and angry. Cael gave her a few
Aves and Paternosters for penance and signed the Cross on
her brow.

She said them. It did not stop the wonderings that tumbled in her head.

Men of the islands were making agreements with Ragnfröd. Gudröd meant to take his few ships in viking to Ireland, Wales, maybe Friesland or Brittany; these days, the
Normans in France warded their own shores too fiercely.
Gunnhild feared for them both.

One night in late winter was cold and utterly clear. She
could not sleep. At last she got up, pulled shoes on her feet,
threw a cloak around her gown, and stepped outside. Two
men on watch drowsily followed. To her they were no more
than shadows.

The air lay still and keen. She heard only a mumble that
was the tide washing onto the land. Her breath smoked as
white as the rime underfoot. Overhead loomed hugeness,
stars crowding the black, the Winterway a frozen stream
out of she knew not where.

Gods, Powers, Earth, Sky, hearken, she whispered to
them. Here I stand, not to beg but to offer. Give my sons
victory. Give me a sign, any kind of sign, a sight, a bird-
flight, a dream, anything. Then if it was you, Christ, I will
be yours. I will forswear all others and all that you say is
wicked, I will pray and weep, strive for the Faith and put
down the heathen, go on pilgrimage, take vows as a nun,
whatever you let me know you want of me.

Or if it was you, Odin, I will make great offerings.
Flocks and herds shall bleed in your halidoms, yes, men

shall swing hanged, and churches shall burn. Oh, first I
must win my sons over, but I can. Odin, All-Father, Lord
of War; Thor, Warder, Stormbringer; Frey, Freyja, Njörd,
who make life quicken and the sea yield its riches: give us
victory and give me a sign.

Meanwhile—Earth, Sky, Waters, Fire, and every hidden
Power—I shall go to the house of my daughter, Eirik's
daughter, where I am free to call upon you. Do you give
us victory, and I—I know not what, other than that we shall
be kinder to your Finns than erstwhile. With you I cannot
bargain. I must seek.

Whoever or whatever you are, only give us victory. Only
let me know.

The stars gleamed wordless. Gunnhild went back inside.
In the morning she took up everydayness again.

The year wheeled onward, the sun into spring. The earliest ships with the boldest crews plied the North Sea.

Thus to Orkney came news from Norway. Weather
stayed sweet. Fields and fisheries promised good harvests.
Folk were happy. Heathendom waxed; Christendom waned.
Haakon Jarl had wedded Thora, a daughter of the mighty
chieftain Skaga Skoptason. She was very fair and he loved
her, although—snickered the man who told of this—it did
not keep him from bedding women elsewhere.

Haakon was good enough for such a house, Gunnhild
thought bitterly. Her sons had not been.

They would see about that.

Gudröd gathered his vikings, Ragnfröd his fleet.

Gunnhild made ready to return to Rackwick.

XXVI

Wind blew hard and cold from the west. Clouds fled
smoky before it. They dimmed the sun as it rose
above the heights of Hoy. Seafowl huddled on their stacks
and skerries. Froth flew off waves. They ran iron-gray,
green when light broke across them. They hit northern
headland and southern cliffs, smashed, burst, thundered,

churned back with their undertow gulping and sucking; then the next smote and the next. Even between Ragnhild's thick walls, Gunnhild heard the air skirl and thought that in the bones of her feet she felt an underground shudder.

She had left her bed to find Ragnhild up. With doors shut and windows shuttered against the weather, the room was as murky as in winter. A hearthfire sputtered and reeked, giving scant warmth. It made the eyes of a crouching cat glow like marshlights. The younger woman was dressed for this, while the older wore merely a woolen nightgown, but the face inside the headcloth was pinched and bloodless.

"You've slept late, Mother," she said low.

"My dreams kept me," Gunnhild answered.

"What did they tell you?"

"If I am to watch over King Ragnfröd, my son, your brother, today is the day to begin."

"Can you trust them?" Ragnhild's voice thinned. "Mine are so often baneful. Drows walk from their barrows and ride the roof. It groans under their weight. They drum on it with their heels. Or I'm out alone on the heath and dead men come after me. Their wounds gape like mouths."

Were Arnfinn and Haavard among them? And how many more? Gunnhild wanted to hold her daughter close, stroke the ruddy hair, sing her to rest. No, she saw, that could not be. Maybe later, back in Norway, after years of being a queen and beloved, the child buried in Ragnhild would awaken and laugh again. But until then, the wind would snatch any lullabies away. Nor dared Gunnhild linger. Her spellcraft was upon her.

She had nothing to say but "The daughter of Eirik Blood-ax should have no need to fear barrow-wights or ghosts. I never have." That was not wholly true. She drove off memory of some things. "And, yes, my dreams were what I called for. You heard me sing by myself yestereven. I know what I was doing. Now I must go on, or lose the power."

"Will you—eat first?"

"No, this is best worked while fasting. Only see to it that I'm left alone. Let there be no noises either to trouble me."

Ragnhild hardened. "There won't be." She glanced at the two thralls, man and woman, who had crept into a corner, and pointed. They slunk out. No tales would slip loose from this garth.

Gunnhild lighted a candle at the fire, took it into the offside room, and closed the door. Windowless, about ten feet wide beneath gnarled driftwood beams and the blackness under the rafters, the room was a night around her tiny, guttering flame. Rushes rustled dryly underfoot. She had had a tall three-legged stool made, on which she now put the candlestick. Bending over, she tipped her locked chest and took the key it had been hiding. The weight seemed to shoot a barbed arrowhead into her hip.

She unpacked drum, necklace, bones. She flung her nightgown aside. The chill and the damp gnawed. She undid her braids and shook the frosty tresses down over limply hanging breasts to the belly that sagged—oh, not so much yet—from her hips. It was as white as the belly of a fish. But her hands, her hands at their work were only a little wrinkled at knuckles and finger joints; she kept the nails trimmed; Eirik would have known those hands.

She took the hallowed mushrooms from the bowl where they had soaked overnight and ate them.

She danced, sang, drummed, swayed, gave herself utterly to it.

Sooner than she had hoped, the great bees hummed, the quern milled, she laid her flesh down on a straw tick and went forth into the wind.

Mist scudded. She drew it to her, around her, a thin cloak against the sun. The shadow flew eastward with the cloud shadows.

Orkney, strewn green and brown on a wrinkled, white-flecked sea, fell behind her. The sun lifted in her sight. The sky cleared; water gleamed. Surf made a webwork along the islands and strands of Norway.

She did not cast about in search. The spell led her. A fleet was bound north past fjord-cliffs. From this height the ships were slivers, but she knew them.

She had not feared for them, not so far. Her flight was

to spy things out, things of earth and things beyond. If danger waited for her son, she would think on how to warn him, or seek through dream and drumbeat how to help him.

The shadow was too flimsy, too dim. She swooped down to the waves. From their salt and from torn-off kelp afloat on them, she breathed wholeness. Eyes keen, hearing sharp, aware through every feather, a swallow skimmed toward the ship at the fore.

The figurehead was up, a wolf's head on a snake's neck. So was the mast. Sail poled out and straining, stays a-thrum, the hull ran heeled over on a long tack. Water hissed by the strakes. Warriors clustered and clung within. Ragnfröd had the steering oar. A smile on his lips, he handled the tiller as deftly and happily as he would the reins of a horse, belike more than he would a woman. He wore no hat or hood, and his hair fluttered like fire.

The swallow swung high and scanned. She saw nothing else at sea but a few fisher boats, fleeing from the warcraft, and a pod of whales, huge, barnacle-studded, on their own course—nothing of warlocks or trolls or angry gods. Best she withdraw.

She let go of the bird, let the wind break and scatter what it had been. Wrapped again in mist, the shadow hastened west from a sun with too few clouds around.

That was into the wind. It stiffened as she went, yelled, tore. She must fight to keep her cloak whole. The flight home became one long struggle.

She won back to her body. For a span she groped through bewildered half-wakefulness. Thereafter she lay while the candle burned low, staring into the dark beneath the roof. Every bone and thew ached. She was too wrung out even to shiver much in the cold.

A sending always left her weary, but never before like this. Well, she had grown old.

At last she gathered the will to rise, put her gown on, squat to stow the shaman things, lock the chest, and hide the key. When she hobbled to the door and opened it, a gust blew out the candle.

Ragnhild hurried to her. "Mother," she cried, as she had

not cried since she was small, "are you well? You look ghastly. What can I do?"

"I'm very tired," Gunnhild whispered. "What I found was good. Bring me some broth in my bed. Then leave me to sleep."

And sleep and sleep.

Afterward she must fly anew, over and over. Not daily, though. She must spare most of her strength against dire need. She could not sit back as formerly and wait to hear how the battles afar had gone. Too much hung on this, when only two sons of Eirik and her were left alive.

XXVII

Having learned that Haakon Jarl was in the Thraandlaw, Ragnfröd steered north past Stad and harried in South Moerr. No few men of that shire joined him. Thus it is when invaders go through a land; those who bear the brunt seek whatever help for their homes and themselves is nearest.

When Haakon heard, he called out his ships, had war-arrows cut and sent, and readied as fast as he was able. It was not hard for him to raise a following. Soon he was outbound down the fjord.

He and Ragnfröd met in the fairway along northern South Moerr and at once fought. The jarl had the most men, but smaller ships. The strife grew furious. They struck at each other from the bows, as was wonted in a clash at sea; but Ragnfröd's crews did so out of their higher freeboards, and Haakon's began to give way. A current in the sound started all drifting shoreward. Thereupon the jarl, with horns and shouts, had his ships back water to a spot which he saw offered the easiest landing.

As they grounded, he and his men sprang overside and dragged the hulls up after them, lest the foe haul them off. He formed his array where the footing was good and egged Ragnfröd to do battle there. But Ragnfröd did not take the challenge. He lay to farther out. The air thickened with arrows. Little came of it. At length Ragnfröd led his fleet away. He feared that Haakon would get fresh warriors from inland.

However, Haakon did not give chase. It seemed to him the ships were too unlike. He returned to Thraandheim.

Hence King Ragnfröd was free to bring the lands south of Stad under himself: Sogn, Sygnafylki, Hördaland, and Rogaland. Here he kept a big troop.

Throughout the winter, both lords would be busking for war. Meanwhile Norway lay unhappy but quiet.

That was well for Gunnhild. The flights she made, to watch how her son was doing, had drained her. She too needed rest, renewing herself if she could, against this coming spring.

Then let there at last be an end, and she at peace.

XXVIII

It was seldom warm here. Though the sea glittered green beneath a blue empty of all but screaming, wheeling fowl, wind whistled from the west, sharp and salt. Scud blew off the manes of the waves. Even at low tide, surf growled loud at rocks and cliffs.

A skuta bucked its way around the headland and inward to the mole. As oars were drawn from their ports to clatter across benches, men ashore caught the mooring lines tossed them and made fast. They kenned this crew from before, and mingled eagerly. Gudröd went up the path with two others. When he reached the house, his face brightened beneath the hat-brim. Gunnhild and Ragnhild were waiting at the door.

He halted before his mother and grabbed both her hands in his own horn-hard paws. "Welcome; welcome," she said, not quite evenly.

Ragnhild stayed aside. No smile crinkled her hollow cheeks. Her voice was flat. "How went your faring?"

"Well enough," answered Gudröd, mostly toward Gunnhild. "Back again, I heard you were still here."

"Someone was to come for me about the first of fall," she reminded him.

"Is this too soon, then?"

"Oh, no!" Her body longed for the snug house on Mainland. "How good of you to come yourself." It kindled a glow in her that grew. But she could not say so aloud, she a queen, he a king, and two vikings listening.

Glee sprang from Gudröd's lips. "If nothing else, I wanted to be the one to bring you the news. Ragnfröd beat Haakon. He's taken the southwestern shires."

"Yes, we know," said Ragnhild.

Gudröd stared. "What? How? Surely no fisherman—"

Gunnhild cast a slight frown and head-shaking at her daughter, to bid silence. "I dreamed about it," she said. "My dreams are often true."

The warriors looked a bit uneasy. Gudröd was slow to speak. "Are the saints that kind to you?"

Gunnhild's mind grinned, while the little hearthfire in her died down. "Who am I to question Heaven?" She heard how that sounded almost like mockery, and went on in haste, "But come inside, do, you, Folkvid, Thorgeir." The men smiled when she remembered their names. It was a skill she had always found useful. "Sit down by the hearth and wash the spindrift from your mouths with a stoup or three."

Ragnhild pinched her lips together, irked. "Yes, of course." As the lady of the house, she should have made the offer, But she hadn't thought of it. How much else had she lost in her years alone?

They entered, settled themselves, took brimful ale horns from a maid. Gudröd told at length how first a ship sent by his brother, then later chapmen from Norway, had brought the tidings.

"Good thus far," said Gunnhild. Flamelight in the dim, shut room showed grimness come upon her. "But Haakon lives. He'll be back next year, with more behind him than formerly."

"Ragnfröd will have more too," said Gudröd. "I know him."

"Will you be among them?"

Gudröd sighed. "I've thought on that. But—" Wrathfully: "Believe me, my first wish is to meet Haakon shield to shield and kill him myself." He calmed somewhat. "Ragnfröd, though, he already has nearly everything and everyone we could get in the West. As I said, he'll have raised more in Norway. What could the few ships left me add to that? Better I stand by with them."

Gunnhild nodded. "Lest the war-tide turn against him."

"We pray not. But no man foreknows." Now Gudröd dragged his words out. "I won't go in viking again, however much my crews chafe, before we've heard that it went well yonder." The voice softened. "Come the worst, I'll be here for you."

The last was only to Gunnhild. Ragnhild marked that. Gunnhild saw her inwardly withdraw further yet. It hurt to understand that she did so neither in sorrow nor in anger. "For us," said Gunnhild. "Your father's house."

"Yes, it's what I meant," said Gudröd, having had it called to his heed.

"This can't be easy for you," Gunnhild gave him. "We know you're neither afraid nor unwise. Thank you, my son."

He tried for heartiness. "Well, it lies months hence. No use in fretting, is there? We'll live merrily on Mainland while we wait."

Gunnhild turned to her daughter. "Won't you come too?" she asked. "We'll share my home."

"No," Ragnhild said.

Gudröd looked around him, through the shadows, at the cats, the eerily woven hangings, and furniture otherwise not much better than a farmer's. "This is no life for a sister of mine," he grumbled.

Ragnhild shrugged. "It's what the jarl gave me. If I don't keep it, he'll take it back. Then what will I have?"

"No, he won't. I'll see to that."

"Nonetheless, I'll stay. I'm wont to it. Being among the highborn, being like them, isn't worth the work."

He and his man sat shocked.

"We don't see many where I dwell," Gunnhild told her.

Gudröd scowled. "High time something was done about that too, Mother."

"No need. I've household enough, for Orkney." More than she wanted, Gunnhild thought. "Once we have Norway, it'll be otherwise." Her glance and heart reached for her daughter. "But would you truly liefest stay behind?"

"I will," said Ragnhild.

Gunnhild could not but feel a kind of easing. Here at Rackwick, where they need reckon with nobody else, they had found how to live together, the older woman's witchcraft, the younger woman's moodiness, sometimes day after day with hardly a word between them, then times by themselves when they harked back—warily, neither of them opening her soul, but with a rich hoard of memories from the old years to draw on. Her house on Mainland was not so offside that this wouldn't raise awkward questions.

Still, "If you change your mind before we go, we'll not think the worse of you," Gunnhild said.

"I won't," answered Ragnhild.

"Well, you'll not be alone forever," with the ghosts. "I'll return early in spring."

"Why on earth?" barked Gudröd.

"To be with my daughter," Gunnhild told him and the world. "And to keep—vigil unbroken—for Ragnfröd's sake."

To send the shadow and the swallow as often as she was able, watching over him. To spend everything that was in her if she must, on a spell for him and all their hopes.

Gudröd gulped. "As you wish, Mother, if, if you think it's right." He shivered and beckoned the maid to refill his ale horn.

XXIX

Men flocked to Hladi from far and wide that Yule, not only to feast and do worship. Haakon made great offerings. Blood streamed; flesh seethed; hlaut-staves reddened halidom and throng. Ale went down in rivers. When the gathering drank Odin's beaker, they shouted that this was for victory not to the king but to the jarl. To Njörd they said that the gods ought to keep on giving them good harvests, for then they would have the strength to fight. The Bragi draught plighted that they would die where they stood, free, before yielding their foe one more foot of Norse earth.

Later Haakon got their leaders, jarls, reeves, hersirs, great yeomen, aside for workmanlike talk. Before the last guest had started home, the first messengers were bound off. From house to house would the word go, north to Naumdoelafylki and Haalogaland, south over the Uplands, through the Dale, along the shores to the marches of the shires held by Ragnfröd, on into Vikin. Let men everywhere take weapons and whatever else they needed. On foot, on horseback, on ship or boat, let them set forth as day-length drew close to night-length, to meet with him and his Thraands and then with the son of Witch-Gunnhild, a springtide storm that would cleanse the land.

For a while afterward Hladi seemed almost forsaken. When Haakon went outside, he found a still deeper hush. Some snow had newly fallen, a thin whiteness over trampled soil. The air lay barely cold under a leaden sky, with no whisper of wind. The fjord glimmered steely. A few gulls mewed above it. Now and then a crow cawed, a lonesome noise quickly lost.

Haakon waved guards aside. "I go by myself today," he said. They nodded. He would not need the spear he carried. Soon after his return he had hunted down whatever outlaws had skulked in the neighborhood while he was away, he happy to chase game as risky as boar or aurochs.

Snow and the duff beneath muffled his footsteps on a path into the woods. Nobody else took it without his leave. It ended at a clearing wherein stood a cote, small but well-made. Haakon leaned his spear by the carven sign of the blood-knot, unbarred the door, and trod through.

Wintry light followed him. To right and left, tapestries decked the walls of the one room. At the far end, the man-high graven image of a woman stood on a dais behind a stone block. Brightly painted, a helmet on her head, she wore a byrnie over a gown of the finest linen; a scarlet cloak lined with ermine hung from her shoulders; a golden ring coiled on either arm, a silver ring around a finger. Everything was new. The Gunnhildssons had burned the former shrine and chopped that idol up for firewood.

Haakon lifted his sword-hand. "Greeting and honor to you, Thorgerd Shrine-bride, you who watch over me, speak for me to the gods, and at the end will bring me to the afterworld," he said. "True to my oath, I have brought your offering."

He undid the purse at his belt and laid it on the block. Coins chinked, English, German, French, Roman, Moorish, Arabian, enough to ransom three men's lives. He would take it back with him to the coffer he kept for her.

She did not stir, nor were there any shadows today to play across her face.

"Well do you know of the battle awaiting us," Haakon said. "Help us win. This is not merely for ourselves. It's for the gods. Remember what my foes did. It will go like that in all of Norway, unless I overcome them. Who then will give the gods their honor?"

Maybe that was too haughty. Haakon went on his knees. "Thorgerd," he said, "I ask for victory; I ask for the might to hold this land against the wolves that want it. Give me that, and I will build you a halidom like none ever seen before. It shall be as big as a church, in its own staked-off grounds. There shall be glass windows, so that nowhere during the day is your house dark. There shall be wonderful carvings, inlaid with gold and silver. The images of the high gods shall stand with yours. And always will I call on you and give to you."

He lay down full length. He had seen Christians do that in Denmark and the Westlands; and Christendom held sway from Ireland to Armenia.

Through the open door and the cold silence rang the croak of a raven.

Haakon rose. He bowed, went out, shut the door, took his spear, and turned homeward. He had done what he could. The norns foredoomed the world long ago. But a man kept the freedom to meet his weird undaunted.

XXX

Spring drew near. In Norway, jarl and king gathered men and ships. In Orkney, a storm roared out of the west. Next day, the waves that crashed on the cliffs of Hoy were still overrunning the mole at Rackwick. As they lessened, folk who went down to see how things were found a dead man on its rocks. He must have been washed off some craft, unless it foundered altogether, and borne here. The gulls were already at him. Torn and sodden, his clothes told nothing about who he had been, and his face was battered beyond any knowing. It did seem he had been young.

As they were bringing him up the path, Gunnhild came from her daughter's house. The fishers halted for her. She stood awhile in the salt wind and thunder of surf before she asked, "What will you do with him?"

"What we do with all such, lady," said one. "Dig him a grave. We've a spot nearby for 'im."

"No," she answered. "This man shall have better than that."

She made them lay him out in good garb, which she paid for, and bury him on Rora Head to overlook the sea that had been his life. Before they covered him she put a gold ring on his breast. "Whoever steals this will soon die a bad death," she warned. They heaped a cairn above and slaughtered a cock, which she had also bought. A bigger offering would have made them wonder too much. Besides, a golden cock in Aasgard and a black cock in Helheim would one day waken the dead to fight at the ending of the world.

By the time it was done, the sun had sunk low above a broken bridge of light and shadows were long. "Go home," she told the men. They went, stiff with an unacknowledged fear.

Alone with him, she said, slowly and evenly, "Now be you my witness before the gods. I have given you back to them, and, through you in your namelessness, all men who were ever lost at sea—yes, and women and children—for the sake of my seafaring sons and for the sake of the gods themselves." She looked aloft, beyond wings and clouds into the deeps of heaven. "Do you hear me, Odin, Thor, Frey, Njörd, your brethren, goddesses, elves, every olden Being throughout the North? By this man who is dead, by the strength of death itself, I bind your weird to mine and to the house of kings that you founded. Hark well, you gods, for your strength shall be mine."

She turned and made her way back. Each step hurt. Weariness weighted her bones. Her sendings since she returned had worn her down. The greatest was yet before her, for when last the swallow flew it saw fleets bound off to their meeting.

The sun was set and dusk had begun to fall when she passed the door. Firelight wavered over Ragnhild's weavings. She went to greet her mother. A cat bristled, arched its back, spat, and slipped off into a corner.

"You're late," said Ragnhild uneasily. "Will you eat? I've had the stew kettle kept hot for you."

"No, I'm not hungry," said Gunnhild.

"You've taken hardly a bite for days. You're gaunt as the wind."

"I've other things to do. I am thirsty, though."

"Bring ale," Ragnhild bade her maid. "And mead. You can at least drink the soul of honey."

Gunnhild gazed into the thin face, the big eyes. "You've never been unkind to me," she said, "but neither have I erenow heard such care from you."

Ragnhild shivered. "You've been dealing so much with the unknown."

"Because I must."

"What did you really do today? Why?"

"It was nothing to harm you. Rather, it was for those I once bore under my heart; and you're the third who's left. I want to give you back your hope."

"That's what makes me afraid," whispered Ragnhild.

The maid brought the vessels. Gunnhild drained the ale fast. Thereafter she sipped the mead. The fire hissed, mumbled, and dimmed the flames with its stinging smoke. "I don't understand," she said.

Ragnhild stared into the shadows. "You couldn't. It's not in you to yield and have done."

Gunnhild's free hand reached for the other's. How small it was in her clasp, how cold. "I've had my man and his blood to fight for."

"Yes. You've had them." Ragnhild wrenched loose. "What will you do now?"

"Tomorrow many men will die," Gunnhild said. "May Haakon Jarl be among them. Whatever happens, your brother shall not be."

"You'll try—" Ragnhild lifted her arms a little, almost as if begging. Her voice cracked. "You're killing yourself. There are too many ghosts here already."

"Is this the daughter of Eirik Blood-ax who speaks?"

The arms dropped. "As you will, Mother," Ragnhild sighed. "What do you want of me?"

"Keep the wretched household off my back," Gunnhild snapped.

"As I've done before. Well, best I seek my bed."

Her narrow bed, Gunnhild thought. "Goodnight," she said, knowing it would not be.

A carl stole in to do such tasks as banking the fire. Gunnhild put the emptied mead cup down, took a lighted candle in a holder, and limped to her chosen room. The bees of lost summers had begun buzzing ever so slightly in her head. She needed what warmth they brought with them, but had better drink no more. Soon she would again be going beyond herself.

Fireless, the room was chill, a hollow of night. After she shut the door, she could not but think of the man she had had laid to rest beneath the stones—if rest it was. Often she had kept from telling Ragnhild that she, witch, spaewife, wisewoman, had learned mostly that she did not know what waited yonder, or what the God or gods were whom Ragnhild had forsaken.

Let her brothers be victorious, kings once more, and they would take her home. They would find her a man as good as—no, Eirik would never have brooked her moods or tried to heal her—as Arinbjörn. Then maybe someday she would win her own victory, over the men she had murdered.

That lay now with Ragnfröd, and with his mother.

Gunnhild set the candle on the witching-stool, in front of a crucifix. The image was carved from wood, about a foot high, with a stand at the bottom. Most of the paint and gilt had worn off in the unrestful years, albeit Gudröd seldom took it out of the chest in which he kept things he had brought with him from York. Somehow this made the outspread shape the more taut, the gaze the more stern. He had been glad to lend it to her when she asked, thinking that showed she would not be doing what he had feared.

A kind of smile twisted her mouth before she knelt, folded her hands, and spoke into the stillness.

"Lord Christ, Son of Mary, one with the Father and the Holy Ghost, who walked on earth that we might know the truth, died to redeem us from our sins, and rose from the tomb that we might live forever in your nearness—" So had Brihtnoth prayed, and wanted her to pray. He flitted wistful across her awareness. "—hear me. Tomorrow a king goes to war for your Faith." More for himself, but leave that aside. "I call on you to keep faith with him. So shall men see that you are indeed the Lord on high, and plight their troth to you." Anyhow, some would, and the sons and grandsons of the rest. "Otherwise they will abide by the gods who stood by the foe of the kingly house. Whatever you may do with me, know that I will work to keep this unrightfulness from throwing the world awry.

"Enough. Amen."

Stiff and in pain, she climbed back to her feet. If Christ was as the Christians believed he was, he had foreknown. But to say something aloud gave it power, the spellcraft of words and runes.

If by calling on him as well as on the heathen gods she

had angered them all, let their wrath fall wholly on her. Ragnfröd knew nothing of this. Gunnhild's thought had been to challenge them, and even lay her will on them, as the Finnish wizards sought to do.

She would go that way too, the third and oldest way, on the road of spells and dreams, for then she would not be waiting altogether helpless while her son fought.

A cough racked her. It burned her lungs. Her cheeks and brow felt hot. She went to her bed. There was no need for haste. At this time of year the night was about as long as the day. She lay remembering.

When she got up and ate the mushrooms she had left in a bowl of water, they quickly told hold. Weariness dropped away. Almost lithely, she made ready for her faring.

Unclad but for the feathers, claws, and teeth, hair unbound, she danced around the stool, drummed, sang, shook the witchy bones, sat down and swayed, heard ever louder the grinding of the world-quern. Blackness whirled. Her body sank. Her soul soared from it, out through the candleflame.

Dawn barely lightened a sky of ragged clouds, raw wind, and spatters of rain. Manes tossed white on the horses of the sea. The shadow winged eastward.

XXXI

The clouds over Norway were a wild gray flock in flight from the north wind. A darkness lifting behind them threatened storm. Low above mountains, the morning sun cast shafts that shattered on roaring, rushing waters. The steeps along the Sognefjord and the islands that sheered upward at its mouth somewhat checked the wind, though it whistled bitter and waves chopped. Few fowl were aloft. Nonetheless, nobody marked a lone swallow. Here was where men would fight.

Southbound past Stad, Haakon had learned that Ragnfröd's fleet was at the fjord. The jarl's ships put into the sheltered narrows. They swarmed, dragons, knarrs, karfis, skutas, fisher boats, hulls and oars across a mile or more, men come from end to end of the kingdom. Sunbeams flitted to flash off iron. While most of Ragnfröd's craft were bigger, they numbered only a third as many.

Haakon left them where they rode and went on by. Hornblasts and yells rang between. He made for the southern shore of the mainland, a spur called Dinganess. Seen against the heights everywhere around, it was nearly flat, bedecked with new grass whose green seemed astoundingly bright in this weather. A few stands of woodlot trees tossed their boughs. A few buildings clustered offside, a hamlet, its dwellers fled with their livestock when the king's ships hove in sight.

Haakon's keels grounded. He was among the first ashore, staking off a battlefield, As his crews landed, their leaders shouted and beckoned to muster them. Banners snapped in the wind.

Ragnfröd could ill withdraw south. Half Haakon's ships waited manned, to waylay his if he tried. Should he get through, the jarl would come after, sooner or later catching him; and by then much of his following would be gone. The wolf bared fangs and stalked forward. He made land not far north of his foe. His pack splashed through the shallows to the strand and gathered itself. Haakon, busy disembarking the rest of his crews now that they were not wanted afloat, let him.

Soaring above, Gunnhild watched. She could do nothing else, not yet; she must keep her strength against the sorest need.

Haakon stayed where he was. Ragnfröd moved toward him. Gunnhild understood. The king had drawn his ranks into the wedgelike swine-array that Odin long ago taught Harald Battle-tooth. He would make straight for the jarl. Lesser hosts had beaten greater in the past. How well her son must remember what Haakon Aethelstan's-foster did. If he could cleave through to this Haakon and fell him, the jarl's troops would soon break.

Horns brayed. Ragnfröd's guardsmen burst into a run. Well drilled, they kept shield near shield. The levies trotted after. The swallow beheld their awkwardness, worse than might have been awaited.

Arrows whirred. Spears and stones leaped. Only she heard the shriek, felt the cold, and staggered in the sky, flung aside by a newly torn-off soul. Warriors below might or might not have spied the youth who sagged down, a shaft in his eye. They were likeliest too caught up in their onslaught. Feet trampled the body to shapelessness.

Man shocked against man. Swords flared; axes thudded. Bone split; flesh spurted blood. Step by red step, Ragnfröd hewed his way onward and inward.

Haakon stood firm. As men fell, the dead and the groaning, writhing wounded became a heap in front of him. The attackers slipped and stumbled. The defenders caught them unready and cut them down. Suddenly Ragnfröd fought stalled. The stream of the angry dead swept Gunnhild off over the ships.

From there she saw with horror—the faraway feeling of a soul unclad and alone—how Haakon's right and left wings swung around to close in from the sides. He must have planned this, told his headmen, given them the horncalls that would say when he wanted it done.

Could she but have foreseen; could she but have forewarned!

How? And to what use?

Ragnfröd's flanks crumpled. Those yeomen, farmhands, fishers, sealers, herders, trappers, hunters, folk lowlier still, had no wish for strife with their fellows. Some fought forlornly until they died. More dropped their weapons and ran. Many did not get free.

Murk from the north was overflowing heaven. What sunlight struck through had gone brass-yellow. Ever stronger, the wind boomed and shrilled.

Ragnfröd and his seasoned warriors held fast, shields a bulwark around their king. Haakon's tides surged against it, fell back, surged forward anew. Warded by him and his nearest men, Ragnfröd's standard bearer struggled ahead. Horns defied the wind. The king began beating a way back to his ships.

But as they ended their slaughterer's work, Haakon's wings turned about and bore in. So thick was the press that some slain men did not fall straightaway to earth. They flopped and gaped between others; they hindered their friends as if they had become foes. Howls, screams, clattering, banging tore through the weather.

Now if ever it was Gunnhild's time. For this she would spend all that she was.

The swallow scattered apart. The shadow swept earthward, unseen beneath the flying gloom or above torn, blood-muddied soil. Akin to the dead, it wove between their flights. Their shrieks keened at it more sharply than the wind. Gunnhild went on through.

She would come at Haakon's men from behind. None in the outermost of the throng were dying. They were not close enough for the iron to reap them. Instead, they gave weight to the attack; they were a wall that held the fight where it was.

She would slide through byrnies, slip past ribs, bring night and ice into heart after heart. She would be fear. The battle was a maelstrom where men churned blindly, unwitting of what went on beyond themselves. Once dread had taken some, they knew not why, it would go from one to the next until it overwhelmed everybody but the guardsmen whose life was war. If those did not bolt, they would at least mill back, for Ragnfröd to cast aside and fend off.

Out of the northern darkness, black and huge, eyes like fire and mane like storm-billows, a stallion galloped. He bore a woman as mighty, mail-clad, who gripped a dripping spear. Only the shadow saw, only the shadow heard those hoofs and the wolf-cry of the rider. Gunnhild knew her from aforetime. Then she had fled. Today she must not.

The shadow rose to meet Thorgerd Shrine-bride.

The spear stabbed. The shadow flowed on around the wound. It took hold of the rider's neck. Thorgerd clawed at it. Her nails ripped. Gunnhild clung and tightened. The horse reared, neighed, himself afright. Thorgerd let go of the shadow to grab the reins. Gunnhild afar snarled in her sleep. The shadow reached a smoke-arm down the rider's open mouth, through the strangled gasps, into the throat, and on toward the heart.

Even as it did, Gunnhild felt her strength wane. Be this a war of gods or a fight between a witch and one Being, she was an old woman who could merely do her utmost to save her son and the blood of her son.

Thorgerd hauled the horse to a shivery halt on the wind. She tore the shadow loose and flung it from her. The spear lunged after it and pierced. Shredded, the shadow gave way.

Yet Thorgerd had also suffered, had lost her grip on the victory she brought.

And meanwhile men felt the strangeness of it. Something, they knew not what, was going on, and awful. The unease spread. Haakon's levies wavered. Undaunted, Ragnfröd's guards thrust ahead.

Thus did he win to his ships with the last of his followers, launched those few he could man, and stood out to sea. Folk reckoned that behind him lay some three hundred and sixty of his own. Haakon's losses were much less. A skald of his boasted afterward in a poem that the jarl could walk from the field to the strand on the heads of the slain.

Thorgerd Shrine-bride left him there. The shadow of a shadow flew slowly back to Orkney.

XXXII

Gunnhild needed no witchcraft to know she was dying. What she had shed in the sky above the Sognefjord was not blood; it was life. The fever in her flesh, the noises in her lungs, brought Harald Fairhair to memory. Yes, they were like a low surf on the shore that was herself.

She lay in a guest-bed in the same room as Ragnhild's. It was fairly bright by day, and a lamp burned there at night. Her locked box stood in the offside room with the witching-stool and the crucifix. She had ordered that when she was gone, it be taken out to sea and cast overboard.

Ragnhild tended her mother with broth and bathings. She

still said little, but never since that first bitter farewell had Gunnhild seen tears on her lashes. Maybe the winter within her was thawing toward a springtide.

As the illness worsened, she sent a boat to Gudröd on Mainland. The next afternoon his bulk blocked the doorway. He strode to the bedside and took both Gunnhild's hands in his. "How fare you, Mother?" he asked hoarsely.

She looked up into the rugged face and half smiled. "Away from the world," she answered in the near-whisper that was now her loudest speech.

"I hoped otherwise." She could see that any such hope had gone from him. He let go and stiffened his shoulders.

"Late or soon, it happens to each of us," Gunnhild said. "I've lived longer than most. What is your news?"

She had foreseen his grimness. "Bad. As I was starting off, Ragnfröd made haven with a handful of ships and men. Haakon won."

"I know."

He stared, a bit shaken. "What?"

"At least Ragnfröd lives." That was her doing, but she could say nothing about it to this man. Not that she cared to.

"He couldn't come with me," Gudröd said, as if to sweep shame aside. "He's worn out. They were storm-bound; then when they could sail it went hard. And he has wounded to tend to."

"I understand."

"He sends—greetings."

"Bring him mine, with my blessing." For whatever that was worth, Gunnhild thought wryly. "It was good of you to come."

His voice stumbled. "How could I not?"

This much love lived yet. The thought held a sweetness she had nearly forgotten. "And fare you likewise well, my son."

Gudröd lifted a fist. "We'll go back to Norway," he growled. "Oh, we may want years to gather new strength, but one day we'll take what is ours—and was yours, Mother."

"Luck be with you," Gunnhild said.

She knew it would not. Was that a sight into time that the shadow had had, or only the hard wisdom that oftener belonged to women than to men? Her sons would never again be other than sea-kings, highborn but holding scant land, vikings because nowise else could they wrest a living. Yes, they might try once or twice, but it would be doomed. Their own leman-born sons, her grandsons, were already lost in the ruck of rovers. Her work had gone for naught.

"God be with us," Gudröd said.

"As you wish."

Shocked again, he promised: "When I'm where I can get it done right, I'll buy masses for your soul's peace."

"Ever were you the kindest of us." To say more than that would be a mockery, which his God might avenge on him.

Her eyelids drooped.

"I'll leave you to rest," he mumbled. "Sleep well."

She nodded. She heard his heavy tread go out. He closed the door behind him.

The murmur in her breast lulled. She dozed off.

When she woke, the lamp guttered low in an unrestful gloom. Air hung thick. Not a sound trickled through. Ragnhild's bed was shut. It must be nighttime. Her slumber had become fitful.

But seldom was she this awake. She wanted to rise and move about. No, getting up for the pot was as much as she could do anymore. Nonetheless she longed. Had the world really shrunken to one small room?

How boundless that world had been. She found herself harking back over her whole life, back to childhood and maidenhood and olden dreams. A song came to her lips, as if singing itself under the rustling breath.

Why, it was Finnish; it was a spell-song.

None of those she had wielded against men. It was a song to call the sun home to summer and welcome the life that quickened on earth. It called to her.

She would not die in this stifling dark. She *would* not.

It was astonishingly easy to throw off the blankets and rise. The rushes rustled under her bare feet. Quietly, go quietly, or someone well-meaning would hear and take her back.

Coals lay dull red on the hearth. They gave barely enough glow for her to pass. The snores and the smells of men stretched on benches stuffed the main room. She crooned a sleep-song while she went by.

A full moon stood high in the west. Its brightness flooded most stars out of heaven and scattered them onto the hoar-frosty grass along the path. Nothing broke the hush other than the gurgle of the brook and the sound of the surf ahead, strong and deep, calling to the tide in her. A breeze flowed cold, but although she wore only a bed-gown, the heat in her blood kept any chill from her. Nor did the clay and pebbles below seem to bite.

Her head felt as light and far off as the moon. She was bound she knew not where, to a meeting with she knew not what.

Folk believed they did. But why then were their beliefs not the same?

She neared the water. On her right loomed the headland. Suddenly she spied three shapes atop it, black athwart the lower stars. Two reared as high as ever eagles flew, like skeletons, and men hung there. The third, between them, was dancing.

The Man on the Gallows, the Man on the Cross, the Man with the Drum. All had she known, but never altogether. Had any of them ever truly known her?

The seeing lost itself again in the moonlight.

Waves ran dark, backs ashimmer, crests fleetingly agleam. Where they broke moon-white under the cliffs, their rushing rose to a roar. That song would go on till the ending of the world.

Gunnhild halted. Her gaze went left, southward, toward unseen England and Eirik's bones, before she looked west, out to sea. If his soul was anywhere tonight, it might well be roaming yonder. Did she see something beckon?

Her awareness flickered to and fro, as in dream. She had lost everything, she thought; yet in a way she had won everything, she who wrought mightily and never yielded. Men would remember her and her man.

Her strength ebbed into the wind. She sat down, then lay down, her face turned seaward. It felt as if the moonlight streamed through her.

XXXIII

The news reached Egil in Iceland on his farmstead at Borg. Although he was still one whom everybody must reckon with, he knew himself for an elder.

He sat on a bench outdoors, leaned back against the wall of the house, drinking summer's warmth while he drank from a horn in his hand. Meadows sloped to the fjord. He could no longer quite make out the glimmer off it. A thin haze brooded over their green.

After a while he nodded a head that was getting heavy. "Well," he said, "wicked she was, but who had ever a worthier foe? Should we somehow, sometime, in the elsewhere and elsewhen, find one another, I wonder if we might not become friends."

AFTERWORD

Vikingetidens Fylgje—the embodied female spirit of the Viking Age. So did the Danish writer Johannes V. Jensen title Gunnhild, Mother of Kings, in his book on the women of that time.

She really lived. Likewise did most of the persons in this novel, and their lives went very much as it tells. Among them she loomed so large that she became a figure of legend, even of myth.

In all probability, the historical Gunnhild was a Danish princess, sister or half-sister of Harald Bluetooth, married to Eirik Blood-ax for the usual political reasons. There is no good evidence that husband and wife were more ruthless than was common then, among both Christians and pagans, or that she practiced witchcraft. Indeed, their affection and close partnership, and the way she raised their sons after his death, speak rather well for them.

However, inevitably they made enemies. Among these was Egil Skallagrimsson, greatest of the skaldic poets. His influence doubtless had much to do with the Icelanders coming to imagine her as the daughter of a chieftain in northern Norway, the pupil of two Finnish magicians, and a sinister enchantress.

By "Finns" they meant the people we know today as Lapps or, better, Saami. Besides oppressing and exploiting these nomads, the Scandinavians laid on them, quite unjustly, a reputation for sorcery, which in some areas persisted into the nineteenth century. We have little information about their lives and religion a thousand years ago. My conjectures deal less with that than with what Gunnhild's folk supposed she had experienced among them.

It is, after all, this tale of her, which later generations believed, that I have tried to bring together, flesh out where the original accounts are sparse, and tell from her viewpoint. Although I would not otherwise compare myself to Shakespeare, his treatment of Macbeth is analogous.

Apart from the mythic element, I have stayed as close to history as was possible. The principal literary source is Snorri Sturluson's thirteenth-century *Heimskringla*. Egil's saga, one of the finest biographical novels ever written, is hardly less important. Sidelights occur in others, notably those of Burnt Njaal, the Orkney jarls, and the Faeroe dwellers. The *Anglo-Saxon Chronicle* is especially valuable in providing tenth-century dates. Of course, we also have such modern authorities as Brøndsted, Foote and Wilson, and Gwyn Jones, together with a wealth of archeological material. But a bibliography would be out of place in a book like this.

So would a historiographical essay be. Much detail is lacking in the sources and must be guessed at. Sometimes they contradict each other or even, when closely read, themselves. To give a single example, Egil's saga has King Aethelstan of England living considerably longer than he actually did. I made this emendation with fewer qualms than elsewhere. If I've nevertheless gotten the chronology wrong now and then, that hasn't been for lack of trying.

As said, the principal characters here are historical. Fictitious ones generally stand in for real persons who must have done more or less the same things but are not recorded. (The main exception is Brihtnoth, but King Haakon may well have had such a friend.) Dag the skald is imaginary, and the first two poems of his that we see in part are my own, meant to give an idea of the role and the art in viking society. The memorial poem for Eirik is attributed to Dag because its authorship is unknown; but somebody back then did compose it. This English version is mine, as are the translations of all other verse.

They're pretty free. Not only is Old Norse a highly inflected language, but the skalds went in for intricate tropes, "kennings," with layer upon layer or reference. For example, one phrase for "battle" is "the storm of the moons of the ships." That is, a battle was the storm of shields, which were usually round in shape and hung like moons along the sides of a warship when show was desired. Egil makes Odin "the speech-friend of the Goths," "the lord of the spear," "the brother of Vili," "the foe of the wolf" (i.e. the Fenris wolf), and more. Snorri's *Younger Edda* is devoted mainly to explication of many kennings. The prosody can get nearly as complex. Most translators have taken different approaches to the problem from mine, which is frankly impressionistic.

The Old Norse alphabet includes letters not in ours, as well as diacritical marks. I have often done violence to spelling and occasionally to grammar in the interest of clarity for the general reader, and hope that scholars will bear with this and other liberties. As for pronuciations, stress is on the first syllable. A double consonant indicates that the preceding vowel is short. The renditions *aa* and *ae* are sounded, respectively and approximately, as about midway between *aw* and *oh* and as *eh*; *ei* is as in *rein*; *j* equals *y* in English *yet*; *y* itself is like German *ü*. The umlauted *ö* represents two different non-English letters, one equivalent to the German, the other sometimes given as *au,* sometimes as a simple *o,* sometimes as it is here. The letter *d* does not always indicate the sound of ours, but may stand for *edh,* pronounced like *th* in *that*: for example, in *Odin* and *Sigurd.* Readers need not worry about all of this any more than they care to.

While regretting that so many names are similar or identical, I could do nothing about it other than work to keep clear who's who. Toward this end of minimizing confusion, the nominative ending *-r,* otherwise omitted, is retained in "Thori," which thus appears as "Thorir." Likewise, "Egil" properly has two *l*'s, but that would suggest an incorrect placement of stress. The meanings of some nicknames, such as "Toti" and "Sleva," are uncertain; I have had to choose among suggestions made by scholars (in these cases, "Dapplebeard" and "Loudmouth").

Names of people are, more or less, in their Old Norse and Old English forms. Names of the gods are in their modern English forms.

Place names outside of Norway are, as much as possible, also modern English. So are geographical names in general, the chief exception being "Thraandheimsfjord" because of the importance of the stem. (It's "Trondheimsfjord" now, but the city did not then exist.) Political names within Norway, usually those of districts, are mostly—and approximately—Old Norse. After all, much of the story turns on them and their relationships. Even those whose names and boundaries today are somewhat the same were in the tenth century not mere counties. Most of them had, not so long ago, been independent, and had not forgotten it. I have, though, avoided the intricacies and, in general, simplified by lumping some terms with distinct meanings together in such words as "shire"—admittedly a loose usage of the English too.

Likewise for most societal words, such as those for rank and role. But it seemed especially necessary to keep "jarl." While it is cognate with English "earl," in those days it meant a man of far higher standing, second only to a king.

Aftermath: The thoroughly unreliable saga of the Jom vikings has King Harald Bluetooth lure Gunnhild to her death in Denmark. This assumes, among other things, that she had lost her mind. We had better stay with Snorri, who says that she and her last two sons withdrew to Orkney.

When the Emperor Otto invaded Denmark, Haakon Jarl went to the aid of Harald Bluetooth as promised. They were defeated. The peace terms included the baptism of Haakon and his men and their conveyance of Christian missionaries back with them. As soon as he was safely away, Haakon set those priests ashore. Once home, he went on encouraging paganism and no longer acknowledged Harald's suzerainty. The Dane sent an expedition against him, but Haakon won that fight and remained king of Norway in all but name.

Meanwhile Olaf Tryggvason had been bought as a slave in Estonia, by a family who treated him kindly. Eventually his mother's brother happened by, learned who he was, redeemed him, and took him to Russia, where he avenged his foster father and rose to high esteem at the court in Novgorod. There followed a career as a viking, with an impact on England that is in the chronicles. Converted to

Christianity, at last he looked toward the heritage in his motherland.

Popular at first, in the course of years Haakon Jarl had antagonized many by his ever-increasing harshness and lust, which led him to disgrace men's wives and daughters. When Olaf landed, he was welcomed. Haakon must flee from his own folk, to suffer an ignominious death. This was in 995.

Ragnfröd presumably died about then or earlier, because we find no reference to him after the battle at the Sogne-fjord. In 999 Gudröd made another attempt on Norway, but was killed. "Now they were all dead, the sons of Eirik and Gunnhild," wrote Snorri.

Fanatical as King Haakon Aethelstan's-foster had not been, nor yet those brothers, King Olaf set about destroying paganism and establishing the Church. The work was completed by his successor—after an interregnum—and namesake Olaf the Saint, a son of Harald Grenska. Where persuasion failed, they did it by the sword.

The line of Harald Fairhair and Snaefrid—or whoever she was in reality—did not continue sitting quietly on its estates. Their great-great-grandson was Harald Sigurdarson, nicknamed Hardrede (1015–1066), whose wildly adventurous career took him through Russia to Constantinople and then back home to become sole king of Norway. After warring for long years in an unsuccessful effort to win the crown of Denmark too, he fell in battle while invading England, three days before his distant kinsman William of Normandy landed at Pevensey.

For good advice and encouragement in what proved to be a big undertaking I am indebted to Karen Anderson, Ted Chichak, Randi Eldevik, and Robert Gleason. They are not in any way responsible for my errors, omissions, and other blunders. As Sherlock Holmes said, "We can but try."

Dramatis Personae

Aaki: A Danish viking, friend of Egil.

Aalf Özurason the Shipman: A brother of Gunnhild.

Aalof Aasbjarnardottir: Wife of Klypp Thordarson.

Aasbjörn of Medalhus: A Thraandish chieftain.

Aasgerd Bjarnardottir: Daughter of Björn Brynjolfsson and Thora Orfrey-sleeve; wife of Thorolf Skallagrimsson, later of Egil.

Aastrid Eiriksdottir: Wife of King Tryggvi Olafsson.

Aegir: A sea god.

Aelfgar: An English priest in Norway.

Aesir: The gods of sky and war: Odin, Thor, et al., and their wives.

Aethelstan: King in England, 924–940.

Aimo: A Finnish shaman.

Arinbjörn Thorisson: Son of Thorir the hersir, friend of Egil, guardsman of Eirik Blood-ax, and foster father of Eirik's son Harald.

Arnfinn Thorfinnsson: A son of Thorfinn Skull-splitter, lord of Caithness, first husband of Ragnhild Eiriksdottir.

Arni: A skipper and a guardsman of Harald Grayfell.

Arnkel Einarsson: Brother of Thorfinn Skull-splitter.

Arnvid: Norse jarl in Värmland.

Atli Thorgeirsson the Short: Brother of Berg-Önund.

Baldr: Son of Odin and Frigg, murdered by Loki's trickery but apparently still having a cult.

Bard: Eirik's tenant on Atley.

Bera: Skallagrim's wife, mother of Thorolf and Egil.

Bera Egilsdottir: A daughter of Egil and Aasgerd.

Bergljot: Wife of Sigurd Haakonarson Jarl.

Berg-Önund: A landholder on Askey, son-in-law of Björn Brynjolfsson.

Björn Brynjolfsson: Father of Aasgerd.

Björn Haraldsson the Chapman (or Skipper): A son of Harald Fairhair; shire-king of Vestfold.

Bödvar Egilsson: Oldest son of Egil and Aasgerd.

Bragi: God of poetry and vows.

Brihtnoth: An English priest, friend of King Haakon Haraldsson.

Dag Audunarson: A skald of Eirik Blood-ax.

Dale-Gudbrand: A powerful Norse chieftain.

Eadmund: King in England, 940–946.

Eadred: King in England, 946–955.

Eadwin: An English priest brought to Norway.

Egil Skallagrimsson: An Icelandic viking, skald, and chieftain.

Egil Woolsark: An old Norse warrior.

Einar Bread-and-Butter: A chieftain in Orkney, a nephew of Haavard Thorfinnsson.

Einar Hardmouth: A chieftain in Orkney, a nephew of Haavard Thorfinnsson.

Einar Rögnvaldsson: A jarl of Orkney, an uncle of Gunnhild.

Eirik Haraldsson Blood-ax: A son and the successor of Harald Fairhair.

Elli: The embodiment of old age.

Erlend Einarsson: Brother of Thorfinn Jarl.

Erling Eiriksson: Sixth son (seventh child) of Eirik and Gunnhild.

Eyvind Finnsson Skald-cribber: A skald in Norway, who served Harald Fairhair, Haakon Aethelstan's-foster, and eventually Eirik Blood-ax.

Eyvind Özurarson the Braggart: A brother of Gunnhild.

Frey: The fertility god, one of the Vanir.

Freyja: The goddess of love and fertility, one of the Vanir.

Fridgeir: A Norse hersir whose daughter Egil saved from Ljot the Sallow.

Fridleif Ivarsson: A man of Harald Bluetooth's.

Frigg: Wife of Odin.

Gamli Eiriksson: First son of Eirik and Gunnhild.

Geir Ketilsson: Icelander, married Thorunn Skallagrimsdottir.

Geira: A witch.

Glum Geirason: Foremost of Harald Grayfell's skalds.

Gold-Harald Knutsson: Nephew of Harald Bluetooth.

Gorm the Old: The king who united Demnark.

Grim Kveldulfsson: See Skallagrim.

Grjotgard Haakonarson: Brother of Sigurd Jarl.

Gudröd Bjarnarson: Son of King Björn of Vestfold.

Gudröd Eiriksson: Seventh son (eighth child) of Eirik and
Gunnhild.

Gudröd Haraldsson Gleam: A son of Harald Fairhair and
Snaefrid.

Gunnar Egilsson: Second son of Egil Skallagrimsson; died
young.

Gunnhild Özurardottir: Wife of Eirik Blood-ax.

Guthorm Eiriksson: Third son of Eirik and Gunnhild.

Guthorm Sindri: A skald of Haakon Aethelstan's-foster.

Gyda Aaslaugsdottir: Wife of Haakon Aethelstan's-foster.

Haakon (no other name given): A man of Gunnhild's.

Haakon Haraldsson Aethelstan's-foster: Son of Harald Fairhair and Thora Mostr-staff; became king of Norway.

Haakon Sigurdarson Jarl: Son of Sigurd Haakonarson and
his successor as jarl of Hladi.

Haakon the Old: A Swedish chieftain, who gave shelter to
Aastrid.

Haalfdan Haraldsson Longleg: A son of Harald Fairhair and
Snaefrid, killed by Turf-Einar.

Haalfdan Haraldsson the Black: A son of Harald Fairhair,
shire-king with his brother Sigröd in Thraandheim.

Haalfdan Haraldsson the White: A son of Harald Fairhair,
killed while in viking.

Haavard Thorfinnsson the Fruitful: A son of Thorfinn
Skull-splitter, second husband of Ragnhild Eiriksdottir.

Hadd: Brother of Berg-Önund.

Harald Eiriksson Grayfell: Fourth son of Eirik and Gunnhild; became the chief of the kings in Norway.

Harald Gormsson Bluetooth: King of Denmark.

Harald Gudrödarson Grenska: Son of King Gudröd Bjarnarson.

Harald Haalfdanarson Fairhair: First king of a united Norway.

Harald Knutsson: See Gold-Harald.

Heimdall: Watchman of the gods, ancestor of the different classes of humans.

Hel: Goddess of the dead.

Helga Geirmundardottir: Second wife of Özur Dapplebeard.

Hermod: Messenger of the gods.

Heth: A thrall of Arnfinn's.

Hlödvir Thorfinnsson Jarl: A brother of Ljot; his successor as jarl of Orkney.

Höskuld Dale-Kolsson: Icelandic chieftain, father of Olaf the Peacock.

Hrolf Rögnvaldsson the Walker: Conqueror of Normandy, known to later history as Rollo.

Hrut Herjolfsson: A young, wellborn Icelander.

Jörd: Earth, on whom Odin begot Thor.

Kaari of Gryting: A Thraandish chieftain.

Kisping: Gunnhild's Danish footling, later known as Ögmund.

Klerkon: An Estonian viking.

Klypp Thordarson: A hersir in Hördaland.

Knut Gormsson: Older brother of Harald Bluetooth, killed in viking.

Kol: An outlaw.

Kraka Rögnvaldsdottir: Wife of Özur Dapplebeard, mother of Gunnhild.

Kveldulf: Father of Skallagrim and the older Thorolf.

Ljot the Sallow: A Swedish berserker slain by Egil.

Ljot Thorfinnsson: A son of Thorfinn Skull-splitter; third husband of Ragnhild Eiriksdottir.

Loki: An ambiguous figure, blood brother of Odin, friend of Thor, but a trickster and at last the foremost enemy of the gods.

Melkorka: Irish mother of Olaf the Peacock.

Mimir: A giant, or possibly one of the Vanir, whose severed head Odin often consulted.

Mörd: An outlaw.

Mörd Fiddle: An Icelandic chieftain, father-in-law of Hrut.

Myrkjartan: An Irish petty king, father of Melkorka.

Njörd: A sea god, one of the Vanir.

Norn: A female being who set the fates of humans and gods. There were three great ones, dwelling under the world-tree Yggdrasil, and many lesser.

Odin: King of the gods, who received the souls of fallen warriors in Valhall, but was also closely associated with magic, runes, and poetry.

Ögmund: Name taken by Kisping in Norway.

Olaf Haraldsson: A son of Harald Fairhair, shire-king of Vingulmörk and later also of Vestfold.

Olaf Höskuldarson the Peacock: A young Icelander, son of Höskuld and Melkorka.

Olaf Sigtryggsson Sandal: Norse chieftain in England and Ireland, briefly king in York, later high reeve in Cumbria.

Olaf Tryggvason: Posthumous son of King Tryggvi Olafsson by Aastrid.

Ölvir: Steward of Thorir the hersir.

Önund Thorgeirsson: See Berg-Önund.

Oswulf: King Eadred's high reeve at Bamburh in North Northumbria, later earl of York.

Otto II: Son and successor of Otto the Great.

Otto the Great: German king; Holy Roman Emperor, 962–973.

Özur: Icelandic trader, uncle of Hrut Herjolfsson.

Özur Thorsteinsson Dapplebeard: A chieftain in Haalogaland, father of Gunnhild.

Poppo: A German bishop and missionary.

Ragnfröd Eiriksson: Fifth son of Eirik and Gunnhild.

Ragnhild Eiriksdottir: Daughter of Eirik and Gunnhild.

Ragnhild Eiriksdottir the Mighty: A Danish princess, a wife of Harald Fairhair, mother of Eirik Blood-ax.

Ran: A sea goddess, wife of Aegir.

Reginhard: Bishop at Aarhus in Denmark.

Rögnvald Eiriksson: Second son of Eirik and Gunnhild; killed by Egil.

Rögnvald Eysteinsson Jarl: Father of Kraka.

Rögnvald Haraldsson Highbone: A son of Harald Fairhair and Snaefrid; a warlock.

Saeunn Skallagrimsdottir: Sister of Thorolf and Egil.

Seija: A Finnish woman.

Sigröd Haraldsson: A son of Harald Fairhair; shire-king with his brother Haalfdan the Black in Thraandheim.

Sigurd Eiriksson Loudmouth: Youngest son and ninth child of Eirik and Gunnhild.

Sigurd Haakonarson Jarl: Son of Haakon Grjotgardson; his successor as jarl at Hladi.

Sigurd Haraldsson the Huge or the Giant: A son of Harald Fairhair and Snaefrid; shire-king in Hringariki.

Skallagrim: A son of Kveldulf, father of Thorolf and Egil.

Skuli Thorfinnsson: A son of Thorfinn Skull-splitter.

Snaefrid: A witch who bore sons to Harald Fairhair.

Soti: Claimant to Hrut Herjolfsson's inheritance in Norway.

Surt: The fire-giant who shall kill Frey at Ragnarök.

Suttung: A giant from whom Odin stole the mead of poetry.

Thor: The storm god, chief defender of earth and heaven against their enemies.

Thora Haakonardottir: Daughter of Haakon Aethelstan's-foster and Gyda.

Thora Hroaldsdottir Orfrey-sleeve: Sister of Thorir Hroaldsson.

Thora Mostr-staff: Mother of Haakon Aethelstan's-foster by Harald Fairhair.

Thoraalf Skaalmsson the Mighty: A young Norse warrior.

Thordis: Daughter of Thorolf Skallagrimsson and Aasgerd.

Thorfinn Einarsson Skull-splitter: Jarl of Orkney and Caithness.

Thorfinn the Stern: A friend of Thorolf Skallagrimsson.

Thorgeir Thornfoot: Father of Berg-Önund.

Thorgerd Brak: An Icelandic serving woman, foster mother of Egil, killed by Skallagrim.

Thorgerd Egilsdottir: Daughter of Egil Skallagrimsson and Aasgerd, wife of Olaf the Peacock.

Thorgerd Shrine-bride: A goddess or valkyrie, not told of in the *Edda* but one to whom Haakon Jarl had a special devotion.

Thorir Hroaldsson: Hersir in Sygnafylki, foster son of Skal-lagrim, foster father of Eirik Blood-ax.

Thorir Rögnvaldsson: Brother of Kraka.

Thorleif the Wise: A Thraandish chieftain, counselor to King Haakon Aethelstan's-foster.

Thorolf Kveldulfsson: A son of Kveldulf, slain by King Harald Fairhair.

Thorolf Louse-beard: Foster father and faithful companion of Aastrid.

Thorolf Skallagrimsson: Icelander, older brother of Egil.

Thorstein (no other name given): A Norseman who became a friend of Egil in Norway.

Thorstein Egilsson: Third son of Egil and Aasgerd.

Thorstein Özurarson: Son of Özur Dapplebeard and Helga.

Thorunn Skallagrimsdottir: Sister of Thorolf and Egil.

Thorvald the Hothead: A friend of Thorolf Skallagrimsson.

Tryggvi Olafsson: Son of King Olaf of Vingulmörk.

Turf-Einar: See Einar Rögnvaldsson.

Ulf Bjalfason: See Kveldulf.

Unn Mördardottir: Hrut Herjolfsson's betrothed in Iceland, then for a while his wife.

Vanir: The gods of the sea and of fertility, notably Njörd, Frey, and Freyja.

Vemund: Leader of a revolt against Sigurd Loudmouth.

Vuokko: A Finnish shaman, brother of Seija.

Wulfstan: Archbishop of York.

Yngvar: A man of Özur Dapplebeard's.

Geographical Glossary

Aalrekstad: A royal estate, near present-day Bergen.

Agdir: Southwestern coastland of Norway.

Aldeigjuborg: Norse town on Lake Ladoga; Staraya Ladoga.

Bjarmaland: Region south of the White Sea and along the Dvina.

Bleking: Danish shire east of Skaaney, now Swedish.

Boknafjord: In southwest Norway; present-day Stavanger is on its south side.

Borg: Icelandic home of Skallagrim and, later, Egil.

Borgarfjord: In western Iceland, north of Reykjavik.

Brunanburh: Battlefield in England, 937; perhaps in Dumfriesshire.

Byfjord: The inlet at the head of which now stands Bergen.

Caithness: The extreme northeast of the Scottish mainland.

Cumbria: English earldom occupying, approximately, present-day Cumberland, Westmorland, and Lancashire.

Danelaw: Region of eastern England occupied by Danes but eventually brought under English rule.

Eidskog: A wilderness along the southern border of Norway and Svithjod.

Eidsvold: Thingstead about forty miles north of modern Oslo.

Finnmörk: Approximately, Lapland, but more vaguely defined.

Fitjar: A royal estate on Stord.

Frosta: Thingstead on the Thraandheimsfjord.

Fyn: Second largest of the Danish islands.

Gardariki: Norse name for western Russia.

Gaula: A Thingstead in Sygnafylki.

Gothland: Tributary shires in southern Svithjod.

Gula: Thingstead near the mouth of the Sognefjord.

Haalogaland: Northernmost shire of Norway.

Haals: A hamlet on the Limfjord, east coast of Jutland.

Hadaland: A shire north of Hringariki.

Haddingjadalar: A shire in south central Norway.

Hafrsfjord: In southern Norway just south of the Boknafjord; battlefield, date uncertain.

Halland: A Danish shire in what is now southern Sweden,
on the Kattegat just south of Hising.

Haugar: A royal estate across the strait from Körmt.

Hedeby: A market town in Schleswig, then Danish.

Heidmörk: An Upland shire.

Hising: The southernmost Norse shire along the east side
of the Kattegat, just south of Ranriki; now Swedish.

Hladi: On the Thraandheimsfjord, the main seat of the
Thraandish jarls; today Lade, a district of Trondheim.

Holmgard: Novgorod.

Hördafylki: A shire in southwestern Norway.

Hringariki: A shire north of the Oslofjord.

Jämtland: A Swedish district on the Norwegian border op-
posite the Thraandlaw.

Karelia: Region between modern Finland and the White
Sea.

Keel: The mountain range between much of Norway and
Sweden.

King's Crag: Konungahelle, a town at the southern end of
Ranriki.

Körmt: An island off the Boknafjord, site of a royal estate.

Leirvik: A town on Stord (modern name; its tenth-century
existence is conjectural).

Lidandisness: The southernmost tip of Norway on the west
side of the Kattegat bight.

Mainland: Largest of the Orkney Islands.

Miklagard: Norse name of Constantinople ("great town" or "great estate").

Mostr: An island on the west coast of Norway.

Murkle: A farmstead in Caithness.

Naumdoelafylki: Shire between the Thraandlaw and Haalogaland.

Nid: A river emptying into the Thraandheimsfjord. Present-day Trondheim is at its mouth.

North Moerr: Shire along coast on either side of the Thraandheimsfjord; often spoken of as one with South Moerr.

North Northumbria: English earldom occupying approximately modern Northumberland and Durham.

Öglo: A farmstead in the Stjordoelafylki.

Oprostadir: Home of Aastrid's father, probably in Hördafylki.

Ranriki: Norse shire along eastern side of the Kattegat, south of Vingulmörk; it is now Swedish.

Rastarkaalf: Battlefield on the coast of North Moerr.

Raumsdalr: Shire between North and South Moerr.

Rogaland: Shire in southwestern Norway.

Romaborg: Norse name of Rome.

Saeheim: 1. A settlement and royal estate on the west coast, north of present-day Bergen.
2. A hamlet a short way north of Tunsberg.

Saltfjord: In the area of modern Bodø. Site of Ulfgard.

Saxland: Norse name of northern Germany.

Serkland: Norse name for eastern North Africa and part of Asia Minor.

Sjaelland: Largest of the Danish islands.

Skaaney: Modern English Scania, a Danish shire at the southern end of what is now Sweden.

Shapinsay: Island north of Mainland in Orkney.

Sogn: Area along the northern shore of the Sognefjord, forming one shire with Sygnafylki.

Sognefjord: Great fjord on the central Norwegian coast.

Sölvi: A royal homestead near the mouth of the Thraandheimsfjord.

South Moerr: Shire between Raumsdalr and Sogn; often spoken of as one with North Moerr.

South Northumbria: See York.

Stad: A point of land at the southern end of South Moerr, a little north of the Nordfjord.

Stainmore: Hamlet near the eastern border of Cumbria; battlefield, 954.

Stjordoelafylki: A shire of the Thraandlaw, reaching east from the southern side of the Thraandheimsfjord.

Stord: A large island at the mouth of the Hardangerfjord.

Streamfjord: In the area of modern Tromsø.

Svithjod: The kingdom of the Swedes, extending north from the Norse and Danish shires, with the Goths along those borders being tributary to the Swedish king.

Sygnafylki: Area along the southern shore of the Sognefjord, forming one shire with Sogn.

Thraandheim: The shires around the Thraandheimsfjord, extending east to Jämtland.

Thraandheimsfjord: Now called Trondheimsfjord.

Thraandlaw: The Thraandheim shires, whose dwellers had their own law and thought of themselves as a distinct people.

Tunsberg: A town on the west side of the Oslofjord.

Ulfgard: Home of Özur Dapplebeard, in Haalogaland on the Saltfjord.

Uplands: The mountainous central part of Norway, encompassing several shires.

Värmland: Same as present district in Sweden.

Västergötland: Same as present district in Sweden.

Vestfold: Shire on the west side of the Oslofjord.

Vikin: The area around the Oslofjord and the shires facing Denmark.

Vingulmörk: Shire on the east side of the Oslofjord.
Vörs: A Thingstead in Hördafylki.

Wendland: Norse name for the Baltic shorelands of present-day Prussia, Poland, Lithuania, and Latvia.
Wide Firth: Between Mainland and Shapinsay.

York: City in England; also the Danish kingdom occupying approximately modern North Yorkshire, later made an English earldom; sometimes called South Northumbria.

New York Times bestselling and
multiple award–winning author
Poul Anderson's journey into a world of
mystery, discovery, and wonder
on a cosmic scale . . .

FOR LOVE
AND GLORY

Another classic from one of the legends
and luminaries of SF and Fantasy

Turn the page for a preview!

1

At first sight Lissa thought it was an island—a strange one, yes, but this whole world was strange to her. Then as she and Karl came out of the woodland and went on toward the river, she knew it could not be. It lay in midstream, dully iridescent, about twenty meters long, perhaps a fourth as wide, curving up to a gently rounded top one meter or so above the water. Someone or something had made it.

But there were no native sophonts anywhere around this star. Scant though exploration had been in the seven Terran years since the system was first visited, that much was certain.

So who, and when, and why?

She halted. "What the chaos? Have you any idea what that might be?"

Karl stopped too. "None," he said. "I do not recall any such artifact from my experience or other sources of information. A slight resemblance to some dwellings of the Orcelin civilization." The tip of his tail gestured at the camp near the shore. "Obviously it is not the work of yonder persons. I presume they are studying it. They may have learned something."

The translator clinging to Lissa's backpack rendered his answer into flat-voiced Anglay. He could follow her words readily enough. If he had tried to utter them the result would be grotesque. For her part, she could not hear most of his language, let alone pronounce those trills, whistles, and supersonic melodies. Once it had struck her funny that such a huge creature should have so thin a voice. But that was in her silly girlhood. She had since met beings much more paradoxical and less comprehensible, and learned that to them humans were likewise.

She did still sometimes wonder whether Karl—her name for him, honoring a friend at home—really spoke as academically as the device rendered it. He was a scientist, but also a top-class waymate. Yet she would never understand the nuances of his personality, nor he hers. They could never be more than comrades.

"Let's have a better look." She unsheathed her optic, raised it to her eyes, and activated it. His keener vision had already made out what she now did. The surface was not actually smooth, it was subtly, bewilderingly complex. Increasing the magnification gave small help. Noontide shadows were too short to bring out enough relief.

The idea struck her like a fist. Her hands dropped. "Forerunner work?" she cried.

Amidst the tumult in her head she felt that the translator's level tone was, for once, conveying an emotion. Calm. "I immediately suspected so." Somebody with Karl's size and strength might not be very excitable. Interested, yes; delighted, maybe; but free of the chills that ran up her spine, out to the ends of her fingers.

Steadiness returned. She lifted the optic again.

Two beings poised on the thing, with a variety of instruments set forth. One was a male human, the other an anthropard from Rikha or a Rikhan colony. She watched them come to full alertness, peer her way, and hasten down the whaleback curve. Their boat lay alongside, tethered by a geckofoot grapnel. They got in, cast off, and motored toward the land.

Lissa swung her gaze about and found their camp, which from here was half screened by brush. She put her optic back.

"Do you recognize either of them?" asked Karl.

"No," she said, "nor why they haven't been in touch." She scowled as she started off again. "We'll find out. We'd better."

The camp amounted to three dome shelters. But the vehicle standing by was no ordinary flyer adapted for this planet. Twice the size, it was clearly capable not simply of flitting through atmosphere, hovering, vertical landings and takeoffs, but of making orbit. Indeed, when last she and Karl heard from headquarters, personnel had detected a small spaceship circling farther out than theirs in a sharply canted plane. Apparently those who had been aboard would rather not be noticed.

Otherwise the landscape lay primeval, hills rolling low in the east and on either side of the valley, thickly wooded. The vegetation was unlike any she knew of anywhere else, curiously shaped boles and boughs, foliage in shades of dark yellow and brown, eerie blossoms—another world, after all. Animal life was as alien and as abundant; the sky was full of wings and clamor. The fundamental biochemistry resembled hers in a number of ways, and the basis of life itself was microbial here too. But that was due to the working of the same natural laws on more or less Earthlike planets. How many centuries until the biology of even this single continent would be even sketchily charted?

Depends partly on how much of an effort scientifically oriented sophonts feel is worth making, passed banally through her mind. The galaxy's so huge, so various, and always so mysterious.

Odd, how high and steep the riverbanks were. In fact, it flowed at the bottom of a rocky canyon. Farther inland, its sides were low, begrown to the very edge of the water. Only as she neared did she see that here the stream had broadened to almost a kilometer.

She reviewed the local geography as scanned by a satellite. Flowing westward, the river became wider still. Fifty kilometers hence its estuary was salt marshland. There it emptied into a channel that in turn led to an ocean.

Evidently local topography had made it cut this gorge. Hadn't that taken time on a geological scale? But the rock wasn't wind-sculpted, merely littered with boulders where ledges and cracks offered resting places.

Nor was the ground above richly forested, like upstream. A strip of thin, poor, rocky soil reached back some fifty meters from either verge. Tough-looking, deep-rooted little bushes stood sparsely, interspersed with lesser plants that she guessed were evanescent opportunists. She saw just a few tiny animals scuttering between, though winged creatures continued plentiful. The camp was at the edge of the semi-desert, half surrounded by fairly large shrubs, trees behind it.

One of countless puzzles. . . . At the moment, she had too much else to think about. Surely in due course somebody would reason this out.

She eased her pace. In spite of a noticeably denser atmosphere and higher partial pressure of oxygen, in spite of her being in athletic condition and having trained beforehand, a surface gravity fifteen percent above Earth normal added nine kilos to her weight.

Karl slowed to match her. By his standards, he was taking baby steps. Carrying nearly all their field equipment on his back, as well as his own mass, he seemed to move effortlessly.

With him at her side she'd scarcely need the pistol at her hip. Not that she supposed the pair ahead of her had violent intentions. Still, however mild-mannered, Karl was bound to be a trifle overawing. Looming a meter above her, he was not wholly unlike a, well, a tyrannosaur. Longer arms, yes, and four-fingered hands; short muzzle, big green eyes, tall ears, gray skin; the taloned feet bare rather than booted. His many-pocketed coverall resembled hers, though open in back for a formidable tail.

The air had cooled, while keeping a medley of odors, sweet, pungent, acid, sulfury. Wind boomed from the west, where clouds lifted massive. Their hollows were dark blue, their heights amber, against a sky almost purple. The sun brooded overhead, two and a fourth times the size of Sol seen from Earth. To the human eye, an MO dwarf is pale yellow, and you can look straight at it for a moment without being blinded. To Lissa, the summer light recalled autumn at home.

And the noontide would last and last. This planet orbited close in, with a two-thirds rotational lock. A hundred and twenty-three of Earth's days would pass before noon came back.

She thrust her stray thoughts aside. The man and his partner had reached a wooden dock that a robot—they must have one or two along—had doubtless constructed, and were debarking. In a few minutes she'd meet them.

11

The spot was about halfway between. All four halted. For an instant only the wind spoke.

After an appraising look, the man apparently decided that Anglay was their likeliest common language. "Greeting, my lady, sir." She didn't recognize his accent. The voice was resonant, though she guessed from it that he couldn't carry a tune if it had handles. "Welcome. Maybe." He added the last word with a grin. She suspected it was not entirely in jest.

"Thank you," she replied. Her glance searched him. He stood tall in his rough garb, thick-shouldered, slender-hipped. The head was round, the face blunt, blue-eyed, weatherbeaten; a stubble of beard showed he hadn't bothered lately with depilatory. The light-brown hair grew a bit thin on top but peeked abundantly from under collar and sleeves. By no means unattractive, she thought. "I'm Lissa Davysdaughter Windholm of Asborg—Sunniva III. My companion's name for human purposes is Karl."

"What language does he prefer? I know a few."

"His own. The dominant one on Gargantua," as humans called the mother planet of that race, a back formation from their name for the race itself. "He understands us quite well."

"We'd like to understand him, though, wouldn't we?"